KU-284-596

Tales from 1,001 Nights

Tales from 1,001 Nights

Aladdin, Ali Baba and Other Favourite Tales

Translated by MALCOLM C. LYONS,
with URSULA LYONS
Introduced and Annotated by ROBERT IRWIN

PENGUIN CLASSICS
an imprint of
PENGUIN BOOKS

PENGUIN CLASSICS

Published by the Penguin Group

Penguin Books Ltd, 80 Strand, London WC2R ORL, England
Penguin Group (USA) Inc., 375 Hudson Street, New York, New York 10014, USA
Penguin Group (Canada), 90 Eglinton Avenue East, Suite 700, Toronto, Ontario, Canada M4P 2Y3
(a division of Pearson Penguin Canada Inc.)
Penguin Ireland, 25 St Stephen's Green, Dublin 2, Ireland (a division of Penguin Books Ltd)
Penguin Group (Australia), 250 Camberwell Road, Camberwell, Victoria 3124, Australia
(a division of Pearson Australia Group Pty Ltd)
Penguin Books India Pvt Ltd, 11 Community Centre, Panchsheel Park, New Delhi – 110 017, India
Penguin Group (NZ), 67 Apollo Drive, Rosedale, North Shore 0632, New Zealand
(a division of Pearson New Zealand Ltd)
Penguin Books (South Africa) (Pty) Ltd, 24 Sturdee Avenue, Rosebank, Johannesburg 2196, South Africa

Penguin Books Ltd, Registered Offices: 80 Strand, London WC2R ORL, England

www.penguin.com

First published in three volumes by Penguin Classics 2008
This abridged edition published 2010
1

All stories translation copyright © Malcolm C. Lyons, 2008
except the translation of 'Ali Baba and the Forty Thieves Killed by a Slave Girl' and 'The Story of Aladdin'
copyright © Ursula Lyons, 2008
Introduction, Glossary and Further Reading copyright © Robert Irwin, 2010

The moral right of the translators and introducer has been asserted

Cover images © The Art Archive
Cover design Coralie Bickford-Smith

All rights reserved
Without limiting the rights under copyright
reserved above, no part of this publication may be
reproduced, stored in or introduced into a retrieval system,
or transmitted, in any form or by any means (electronic,mechanical,
photocopying, recording or otherwise), without the prior
written permission of both the copyright owner and
the above publisher of this book

Set in 10.5/14 pt Postscript Adobe Sabon
Typeset by Ellipsis Books Limited, Glasgow
Printed in Great Britain by Clays Ltd, St Ives plc

A CIP catalogue record for this book is available from the British Library

ISBN: 978-0-141-19165-2

www.greenpenguin.co.uk

Mixed Sources
Product group from well-managed forests and other controlled sources
www.fsc.org Cert no. SA-COC-1592
© 1996 Forest Stewardship Council
FSC

Penguin Books is committed to a sustainable future
for our business, our readers and our planet.
The book in your hands is made from paper
certified by the Forest Stewardship Council.

Contents

Editorial Note

This selection of stories from *The Arabian Nights* (also known as *The Thousand and One Nights*) is taken from the three-volume Penguin Classics edition (2008), the first complete translation of the Arabic text known as the Macnaghten edition or Calcutta II since Richard Burton's famous translation of it in 1885–8.

In addition to Malcolm Lyons's translations from the Arabic text of Calcutta II, this selection includes Ursula Lyons's translations of the tales of Aladdin and Ali Baba from Antoine Galland's eighteenth-century French. (For these stories no original Arabic text has survived and consequently they are classed as 'orphan stories'.)

For this selected edition, the 'nights' format has been removed, but the 'nights' covered by each story cycle are indicated in a note at the end of each chapter. As the two 'orphan stories' are not included within the 'nights' structure (and neither are the opening and concluding chapters, which 'frame' the stories told by Shahrazad), no notes are given for these.

As often happens in popular narrative, inconsistencies and contradictions abound in the text of the *Nights*. It would be easy to emend these, and where names have been misplaced this has been done, to avoid confusion. Elsewhere, however, emendations for which there is no textual authority would run counter to the fluid and uncritical spirit of the Arabic narrative. In such circumstances no changes have been made.

Introduction

In the caliph's palace, a girl is frying multi-coloured fish when a woman with a wand bursts through the wall and demands to know of the fish if they are true to their covenant . . . A young man mounts a flying horse; the horse strikes out one of his eyes with a lash of its tail and lands him on a building where he will encounter ten more one-eyed men . . . A travelling merchant is entombed alive with his deceased wife . . . It was the strangeness of the plotting and imagery, as well as the freedom from classical constraints derived from such authors as Homer, Ovid and Virgil, that appealed to the earliest Western readers of *The Thousand and One Nights* (best known in English as *The Arabian Nights*). 'Read Sinbad and you will be sick of Aeneas', as the eighteenth-century gothic novelist Horace Walpole declared. Yet behind the apparent wildness of the stories, there are patterns and correspondences and the playing off of themes and images against one another by the tales' anonymous authors.

'*One Thousand and One Nights* is a marvel of Eastern literature', according to the Nobel Prize-winning Turkish novelist Orhan Pamuk in his essay 'Love, Death and Storytelling' (*New Statesman*, 26 December 2006). It was a book that was familiar to Pamuk since childhood, but he has recently described how he decided to reread it in order to understand what fascinated Western authors like Stendhal, Coleridge, De Quincey and Poe in these stories and made the book a classic: 'I saw it now as a great sea of stories – a sea with no end – and what astounded me was its ambition, its secret internal geometry . . . I was able finally to appreciate *One Thousand and One Nights* as a work of art, to enjoy its timeless games of logic, of disguises, of hide-and-seek, and its many tales of imposture.'

It seems most probable that the core of the Arabic story collection, *Alf Layla wa-Layla* ('The Thousand and One Nights'), originated in a fairly brief and simple form in ancient India. Then, some time before the ninth century AD, these Sanskrit tales were translated into Persian under the title *Hazar Afsaneh* ('The Thousand Tales') and doubtless some Persian stories were added to this collection. By the ninth century at the latest, an Arabic version known as *Kitab Hadith Alf Layla* ('The Book of the Tale of One Thousand Nights') was in circulation. But *The Thousand and One Nights* in the form we have it today, with its elaborate frame story about King Shahriyar and the storyteller Shahrazad, was compiled much later. The oldest substantially surviving manuscript of the *Nights* seems to date from the late fifteenth century. In the opening frame story, which is included in this edition, Shahrazad tells Shahriyar stories night after night in order to postpone her execution. The 'nights' function as story breaks; there are not actually a thousand and one stories. Some stories are very short, others very long, told over many nights. Some are about criminals, some about saints. Some feature magic and monsters, while others centre on commercial transactions or romantic assignations. It is the sheer variety of stories that gives the *Nights* its unique quality.

In bookshops and libraries it is common to find the *Nights* shelved with fairytales, even though fairies feature very rarely in the Arab stories. But a fairytale is not defined by the presence of fairies within it. Such Western stories as 'Puss in Boots' or 'Bluebeard' have no fairies in them, but they are still universally regarded as fairytales. A fairytale, rather, is a story that relies on the fantastic to induce wonder. In this sense, a very high proportion of the stories in the *Nights* can be regarded as fairytales. Even so, there are also plenty of stories in which the fantastic and the supernatural do not feature – stories about cunning adulterers, learned slave girls, pious hermits, master criminals, benevolent or despotic rulers and so on. Jorge Luis Borges once remarked that all great literature becomes children's literature. (Doubtless he was thinking of such works as *Robinson Crusoe* and *Gulliver's Travels*.) In recent times, *The Thousand and One Nights*, together with other fairytale collections, has been carelessly classified as children's literature. But in the seventeenth century, by contrast, Charles Perrault and the Comtesse d'Aulnoy aimed their famous collections of fairytales at sophisticated adult audiences and, as we shall see, Antoine Galland presented his translation to the same audience in the opening decades of the eighteenth century. There is certainly a great deal in the *Nights* that is not suitable for children.

Although some scholars have discussed the stories of the *Nights* as if they were in origin oral folktales that eventually happened to get collected and written down, this is only occasionally and partially true, for it is clear that some stories were originally told at the courts of the caliphs, others were artfully composed by skilled, if anonymous, authors, and even those which do seem to have had a folk origin have had their prose polished by later scribes and editors. Taken as whole, *The Thousand and One Nights* is close to pulp fiction, albeit pulp fiction with decidedly literary pretensions.

The insertion of passages of poetry in classical Arabic into the stories, including some verses by well-known poets, is one of the signs that the *Nights* is not just a collection of folktales. The poetry quoted in the stories does not serve to carry the narrative along, but, in general, it is used in order to express moments of high emotion. On occasions when the tales were narrated by professional storytellers, it is likely that the recitation of the poems was accompanied by music. Melancholy resignation seems to be one of the commonest themes of the poetry. The structure of Arabic vocabulary makes rhyming easy and, besides rhymed metrical poetry, passages of rhymed prose (*saj*ʿ) also feature. Rhymed prose, often used to evoke love, despair or violent conflict, also had the effect of slowing the narrative down. (The effect of rhymed prose has not been reproduced in this translation; read out aloud in Arabic, it sounds fine, but printed in an English translation it looks grotesque.)

Until quite recently, the stories of the *Nights* were not particularly esteemed in the Arab world. A French antiquarian and Orientalist, Antoine Galland (1646–1715), was chiefly responsible for their rediscovery and subsequent fame. In the years 1704–17, he translated the stories in the oldest substantially surviving manuscript and to this translation he added some stories from other sources. The earnest purpose of his translation was to instruct his readers in the manners and customs of the contemporary Orient and to use the tales to provide improving lessons in morality. Since ladies at the court of Versailles were his target readership and since the Arabic he was translating seemed to him somewhat crude, he took pains to remove what he saw as medieval barbarisms and improve the tales by rendering them into a polished and courtly French. In order for his translation to find favour, Galland had to take liberties with it. Translators translate not just into a language but also into a time and it is for this reason that Homer, Dostoevsky and Proust have had to be regularly retranslated. As it was, for over two centuries Galland's translation would inspire countless other versions and imitations.

The stories of the *Nights* were an immediate success with French courtiers and intellectuals. The French literary historian Paul Hazard in *La Crise de la conscience européene* (published in 1935 and translated into English in 1953) has described how the craze for Shahrazad's storytelling replaced the slightly earlier craze for the traditional French fairytales as rewritten by Charles Perrault: 'Then did the fairies Carabosse and Aurora make way for the throng of Sultanas, Viziers, Dervishes, Greek doctors, Negro slaves. Light fairylike edifices, fountains, pools guarded by lions of massy gold, spacious chambers hung with silks and tapestries from Mecca – all these replaced the palace where the Beast had waited for Beauty to open her loving eyes.'

Galland had first published a translation of 'Sindbad', around 1698, and this had been well received. Someone then misled him into believing that 'Sindbad' was part of a larger collection known as *The Thousand and One Nights*. More by luck than judgement, Galland went on to translate the oldest substantially surviving Arabic version of the *Nights*. This probably dates from the late fifteenth century, but it is clear from literary references that there were earlier, less elaborate versions of the story collection in Arabic. There is also at least one Turkish manuscript that is older than the Arabic one which Galland translated. Though some of the stories in the *Nights* derive from much earlier Indian and Persian versions, the stories as we have them are thoroughly Arabized and Islamized. Galland's French translation, *Les Mille et une nuits*, was swiftly translated into English and other languages. In the three centuries that followed there were also several English translations of the *Nights* directly from the Arabic.

In the course of the early nineteenth century, a series of printed editions in Arabic were published in Cairo, Breslau and Calcutta. Of these, the most compendious is known as Calcutta II, or the Macnaghten edition. Like the Cairo and Breslau editions, Calcutta II contains far more stories than are found in the Galland manuscript (and it is the Calcutta II text that is the basis of the Penguin translation by Malcolm Lyons). Because of the way some stories lead into other stories, and some frame others, which in turn contain yet more stories within them, it is difficult to say exactly how many stories are in Calcutta II, but certainly over 640. However, in the eighteenth century, English readers made do with what is known as the Grub Street translation of Galland's French text. (According to Samuel Johnson in his *Dictionary*, Grub Street in London was 'much inhabited by writers of small histories, dictionaries and temporary poems, whence any mean production is called grubstreet'.) It was the

Grub Street version that inspired and delighted Addison, Walpole, Wordsworth, Coleridge and many others. Then, in the course of the nineteenth century, English translations were made from one or other of the printed Arabic editions. The history of those translations, however, is one of pedantry, pretension and plagiarism.

In 1838–41, Edward William Lane (1801–76) published a translation of some of the Cairo edition. Previously he had written a survey of everyday life in Egypt entitled *Manners and Customs of the Modern Egyptians* (1836). In the course of that book he had referred to *Nights* as 'being a faithful picture of Arab life'. Apparently forgetting about the *jinn*, flying horses, cannibalistic *ghuls*, giant *rukhs*, Amazon warrior women, men turned into animals by magic, and improbably opulent palaces, he saw the stories as primarily having documentary value. But since he was both pious and prudish, when he came to translate an Egyptian printed text of the *Nights* known as the Bulaq edition, he cut out sexual scenes and omitted many stories as unfit for gentlefolk. In the opening frame story, for instance, Lane's Shahriyar and Shah Zaman do not have sex with the lady carried in a chest. They merely engage in 'conversation' with her. As well as cutting out the sex, Lane was not so fond of fantasy and he omitted some stories for this reason. He was also under pressure from his publisher to bring the unprofitable publication to a speedy end. Lane was hostile to Galland's polishing the text up and giving the dialogue a courtly feel. Piety also led him to try to model his prose on that of the King James Bible, but he succeeded only in reproducing the archaism of his model without matching its eloquence. There may also be another reason why he did this: because it was one of the very few books in English that he had read in his life. (He had become so accustomed to reading Arabic manuscripts that he used to complain that reading English print hurt his eyes.) Since he earnestly intended his translation to offer a guide to the manners and customs of the contemporary Egyptians, his text also served as a pretext for hundreds of pages of ethnographic notes.

In 1882–4, John Payne published a much more literary translation, of the Calcutta II text, in which the sexual episodes were kept in, but played down. Payne (1842–1917) was a self-taught polyglot and he published translations from Latin, French and Portuguese. He did his translation of the *Nights* riding around London on the top deck of a horse-drawn omnibus. Unfortunately, his translation, which deploys a wide range of archaic English, is abominably affected and almost unreadable. Although very few read Payne's expensive translation, which was published in a limited subscribers' edition, it was influential in two important respects. First, it enthused the fastidious poet and translator Stephan Mallarmé, who was a friend of Payne's, and it was Mallarmé who urged Joseph Charles Mardrus (1868–1949) to produce a translation into French that was intended to rival what were seen as the literary qualities of Payne's work. Secondly, that bold traveller and scoundrel Sir Richard Burton (1821–90), who was also a friend of Payne, having noted how the latter's translation had rapidly sold out, calculated that if he also produced a translation, this might make him a lot of money. (Burton was usually strapped for cash.)

Burton's version appeared in 1885–8 and it plagiarized both Lane and Payne (while relentlessly disparaging Lane's work). Burton's deployment of weird and archaic vocabulary makes him even more unreadable than Payne. Burton also exaggerated the eroticism and violence of the stories and he added a mass of unnecessary footnotes, many of them dealing with race or sex or both together. However, the Burton translation remained the most complete English version of the *Nights* until the translation for Penguin by Malcolm Lyons in 2008. Lane's translation had not sold well. Burton's and Payne's editions were for private subscribers only. Therefore in the nineteenth century most English readers stuck with the Grub Street *Nights*.

In 1899–1904, Mardrus, egged on by his friend and patron Mallarmé, produced what purported to be a new French translation of an Arabic manuscript, but his translation was really a fraud. Where he was translating stories from the *Nights*, his renderings were deformed by obvious errors and eccentric translation strategies. In addition, he brought in stories from other collections and cultures and he seems to have made up some stories himself. Although his 'translation' has no scholarly merit, it has some literary value and his version inspired Yeats, Proust, Gide, Cocteau and James Elroy Flecker, as well as the *Schéhérazade* of the Ballets Russes.

This fresh translation of *The Arabian Nights: Tales of 1001 Nights*, made from Calcutta II by Malcolm Lyons (together with translations from Galland by Ursula Lyons), aims to reinstate the work as literature, to present it once again to an adult readership and to make it once more a pleasure to read its marvellous stories. The complete translation by Lyons has been published by Penguin in three volumes. This selected edition includes stories chosen from all three of these volumes.

Galland's translation of the *Nights* and the various translations from Galland's French into other European languages constituted a major event in Western literature. Imitations, pastiches, parodies and moralistic rewritings followed, as well as major works of literature that were influenced by the *Nights* in subtler ways. A full survey of the influence of the *Nights* on Western literature would have to discuss works by Addison, Johnson, Byron, Southey, Coleridge, the Brontë sisters, George Eliot, Tennyson, Thackeray, Stevenson, Rushdie, Diderot, Voltaire, Proust, Perec, Yeats, Joyce, Poe, Washington Irving, Roth, Twain, Barth, Cocteau, Hans Christian Andersen, Goethe, Hofmannstahl, Jünger and many others.

Here examples will be confined to three writers, each very different. First is William Beckford (1760–1844), whose *Vathek* (1782) was the finest of the numerous pastiches of the *Nights* produced in Britain and France during the eighteenth century. Beckford, an eccentric millionaire who knew some Arabic, made a particular study of the *Nights*. *Vathek* is the tale of a hedonistic caliph who is lured by an emissary of Eblis, the Devil, and his promises of knowledge of infernal secrets, into the depths of Hell. The narrative mingles Oriental lore, much of it concerning the supernatural, taken from the *Nights* and from Barthélemy d'Herbelot's encyclopedia of Islamic culture, the *Bibliothèque orientale* (completed in 1697 by Galland), together with elements of lightly disguised autobiography. Although Beckford affected a tone of civilized irony, the book has since been acclaimed as a masterpiece of gothic horror.

Second is Dickens, about whom the nineteenth-century novelist and essayist George Gissing wrote in *Charles Dickens: A Critical Study* (1898):

> Oddly enough, Dickens seems to make more allusions to the *Arabian Nights* than to any other book or author . . . Where the ordinary man sees nothing but everyday habit, Dickens is filled with the perception of marvellous possibilities. Again and again he has put the spirit of the *Arabian Nights* into his pictures of life by the river Thames . . . He sought for wonders amid the dreary life of common streets; and perhaps in this direction was also encouraged when he made acquaintance with the dazzling Eastern fables, and took them alternately with that more solid nutriment of the eighteenth-century novel.

Dickens, who had read the *Nights* as a boy, was delighted by the stories and, as his writing shows, strongly affected by them. At one point in the *The Old Curiosity Shop* (1841), for instance, Dick Swiveller wakes up in a strange bed: 'If this is not a dream, I have woke up, by mistake, in a dream in an Arabian Night, instead of a London one.' Then again David Copperfield, who as a schoolboy is compelled by the domineering Steerforth to tell stories late at night, compares his fate to that of Shahrazad. (And, of course, since Dickens both published many of his novels in serial sections and gave readings from them, it would be natural for him to think of himself as a latter-day male version of Shahrazad.) It would be very easy to go on listing overt and covert references to the *Nights* elsewhere in Dickens's works. What is more important is the feel of the *Nights* stories and their impalpable but pervasive influence over Dickens's fantastical plots with their moralizing outcomes. Enigmatic philanthropists cloaked in disguise walk the streets at night following in the footsteps of Harun al-Rashid. Baghdad is reconfigured as London, and the Dickensian city of mysteries and marvellous possibilities teems with grotesque characters who are distant descendants of the princes, sorceresses, porters and dervishes of the *Nights*.

Third is the French novelist Stendhal (1783–1842), who wrote of the *Nights* in his *Souvenirs d'égotisme* (1832): 'I would wear a mask with pleasure. I would love to change my name. *The Arabian Nights* which I adore occupies more than a quarter of my head.' It would probably be fruitless to search *Le Rouge et le noir* (1830) or *La Chartreuse de Parme* (1839) for plots or borrowed props. Nevertheless the *Nights*, and in particular its stress on magical powers, did help shape Stendhal's image of himself as a novelist. Late in life he awarded himself magical powers, including becoming another person (as all good novelists should strive to do). He wanted to live like Harun in disguise. (He also wished for the ring of Angelica which conferred invisibility in Ariosto's *Orlando Furioso*.) The power to become invisible, to assume another's identity, to read another's mind – all these staples of Islamic occultism and storytelling gave Stendhal metaphors for himself as an observer of humanity and a writer.

The influence of the *Nights* was not confined to Europe and America. Yukio Mishima is probably the best-known Japanese writer to have found inspiration in the stories and, though the *Nights* was for a long time despised in the Arab world for its poor style and what was deemed to be implausible plotting, from the twentieth century onwards leading Arab novelists, playwrights and poets have acclaimed the stories – among them such well-known writers as Tawfiq al-Hakim, Taha Husayn, 'Abbas Mahmud al-'Aqqad, Jabra Ibrahim Jabra, Adonis, Salah 'Abd al-Sabbur,

Nawal al-Sadawi, Tayeb Salih, Gamal al-Ghitani and Edwar al-Kharrat.

The stories in this Penguin selection have been chosen to suggest the range of themes and treatments in the *Nights*. The opening frame story, the tale of King Shahriyar, his brother Shah Zaman and Shahrazad the storyteller, can be and has been read as a profound fable about storytelling and its relationship to sex and death. Shahriyar, who has been sexually betrayed by his wife, executes her and thereafter resolves to avoid ever being betrayed in such a way again by taking only virgins to his bed every night and having them executed on the following morning. The vizier's elder daughter, Shahrazad, decides to offer herself as a hostage for the virgins of Shahriyar's kingdom. Her father tries to dissuade her by telling her 'The Story of the Donkey and the Bull'. This tale about a man who understands the language of animals is amusing, yet there is nothing in it that should dissuade Shahrazad from her decision to offer herself to Shahriyar. She does so, but after they have had sex she starts a story, then breaks off at dawn with the story still unfinished. So Shahriyar postpones her execution in order to hear the end of the story. But when Shahrazad finishes a story she starts another, and so from then on, night after night, she is talking for her life for one thousand and one nights.

The tales she tells for so many nights carry no single message, but instead demonstrate the immense richness and diversity of existence. However, life and death alternatives dominate the opening tales and several of them are about telling stories in order to save one's life. This is the case in 'The Fisherman and the *'Ifrit*'. (An *'ifrit* is a powerful kind of *jinni*.) In this story, the fisherman pleading with the murderous *'ifrit* is like Shahrazad and his story frames yet other stories. 'Spare me and God will spare you' is his theme. 'The Story of King Yunan and Duban the Sage', again about somebody seeking to avoid arbitrary execution, is one of the most remarkable in the *Nights*.

Later on in the *Nights*, the encounter of the porter with the three ladies of Baghdad inaugurates a new cycle of stories in which characters find themselves telling stories in order to save their lives. (It is noteworthy, by the way, that a porter features prominently in this adventure. Arabic high literature in the Middle Ages tended to be about princes, princesses and mighty warriors. The *Nights* has it share of these, but it also includes stories which have as their protagonists humbler folk such as shopkeepers, craftsmen or woodcutters.) The porter, who is well entertained by the three ladies, receives a warning: 'ask no questions about what does not concern you'. Although the porter heeds the warning, three one-eyed dervishes who have sought hospitality in the same house and who have witnessed the mysterious whipping of the dogs, are less discreet. Under threat of death for their importunity, they find themselves telling tales as ransom for their lives. The stories they tell, of the workings of fate, subterranean and illicit sex, magical transformation, indiscreet curiosity and regret, are indeed remarkable. The tale of the third dervish, in particular, is in part a story about ill-fated curiosity. Left alone by the maidens in a palace with forty doors, he is told that he may open any door except the fortieth . . . It is the first of several ill-omened and forbidden doors in the stories of the *Nights*.

Just as life-or-death stories echo the opening frame of the *Nights*, so too do tales of sexual betrayal and revenge echo the story of Shahriyar, including 'The Story of the Semi-petrified Prince', as well as 'The Story of the Lady of the House' and 'The Story of the Doorkeeper' which cap the tales of the three dervishes. The prevailing tone of the latter two stories is tragic, for in one way or another love or trust has been abused and betrayed. 'The Story of 'Aziz and 'Aziza', another tragic tale, is particularly noteworthy for its exposition of the demanding etiquette of love. Also, as so often in *Nights* stories, the man is weedy and useless, while the woman is clever and resourceful. But love stories in which true love eventually wins through also feature prominently in the *Nights*. Among such stories included in this selection are 'The Story of Nur Al-Din and Shams Al-Din', 'The Story of Taj Al-Muluk and Princess Dunya' and 'The Ebony Horse'.

In the *Nights* and in several other well-known story collections, most notably the medieval Arab version of *Kalila wa-Dimna*, the rhetoric of animals was deployed in the service of teaching wisdom, resignation to the will of God, warning against misplaced trustfulness and urging the need for useful friendships. Sometimes the animals, like Shahrazad, find themselves talking for their lives, as they tell stories to persuade their predatory listeners that they should not be killed. Such simple fables were probably among the stories to feature in the very earliest compilations of the *Nights*. Several such stories feature in this selection, beginning with 'The Weasel and the Mouse' and 'The Crow and the Cat'. There is a pietistic feel to some of these animal fables and this is echoed in other similarly short tales of religious admonition, such as 'The Angel of Death and the Rich King' and 'The Angel of Death and the King of the Israelites', while 'Alexander the Great and the Poor King' is a story in praise of poverty. In medieval Arabic literature all sorts of improving stories were attached to Alexander the Great, who was thereby transformed from a historical figure into a legendary one. Harun al-Rashid features in the cycle of stories associated with the three ladies of Baghdad. As was the case with Alexander, the historical eighth-century caliph has been transformed into a figure who in quite a number of stories in the *Nights* has fantastic adventures or on occasion listens to applaud the adventures of others. Furthermore, all sorts of wisdom was retrospectively attached to historical figures, especially the pre-Islamic Persian kings, and the *Nights* story 'King Anushirwan the Just' exemplifies this.

Of course, not all the stories in the *Nights* were so improving. Quite a few start with idle and feckless protagonists who, more by luck and the good offices of the *jinn* than real effort and merit, blunder into fortune. This was a theme that must have been popular with the idle people who sat listening to these stories in market squares or cafés. 'Abu Muhammad the Sluggard' and ' 'Ali, the Cairene Merchant' are among such tales.

While some stories make heroes of idle youths who at the beginning of their adventures have squandered their inheritance, a number of other tales celebrate outright criminals and their cunning. 'The Adventures of 'Ali Al-Zaibaq' is an example of this kind of tale. The stories in the *Nights* featuring thieves reflect a historical reality, as there is evidence in the medieval chronicles that some of the most successful crooks became cult figures among the common people, just as in Western culture the exploits of Robin Hood, Dick Turpin and the dandy criminal Pierre François Larcenaire were told and retold. More generally, there are a large number of stories in the *Nights* in praise of cunning, whether the cunning is that of a determined thief, a smooth-talking animal or an adulterous woman bent on deceiving her husband.

'The Ebony Horse' is a tale of magic. It almost certainly derives from an ancient Sanskrit original in which the hero travels not on a mechanical horse, but on an artificial image of the Hindu bird god Garuda. Like many stories in the *Nights*, the reach of this story was international, as in variant forms it features in various Oriental and medieval Western versions, including Chaucer's unfinished 'The Squire's Tale'. (There is also a flying horse in 'The Story of the Third Dervish', although there the creature proves to be malign.)

'Sindbad the Sailor', the tale of his seven voyages on strange seas, is one of the most famous stories associated with the *Nights*, yet its status within that collection is anomalous. Galland found an independent manuscript of the Sindbad stories and published a translation of it which had some success with the reading public. Then, as has been noted above, someone told him that these stories were part of a greater story collection. Though untrue, this information led Galland on to seek out and translate a manuscript of the *Nights* and, when he published that translation, he added the Sindbad stories to it. Subsequent printed Arabic editions of the *Nights* also included these stories in the *Nights* corpus. Sindbad's fictional adventures find some parallels in earlier non-fiction in Arabic written to guide sailors and merchants trading in the Indian Ocean and points further east; mistaking a whale for an island, for example, features both in the adventures of Sindbad and in the earlier literature of mariners and merchants. The marvels are certainly to the fore in the adventures of Sindbad. What is less obvious is the occasional inclusion of serious details about trading commodities. What is even more important is the intense piety of these stories. Invocation of God comes as naturally to Sindbad as breathing. The marvels he encounters are signs of the creative powers of the Almighty. Sindbad survives many perils because he puts his trust in God.

The status of 'The Story of Aladdin, or the Magic Lamp' and 'The Story of Ali Baba and the Forty Thieves Killed by a Slave Girl' within the *Nights* is also anomalous. Though they are among the best-known stories, they really belong to the *Nights* apocrypha, as no Arabic original has been found for them (and consequently they have been translated from Galland's French for this edition). Rather these 'orphan stories' seem to have been told to Galland by a Syrian Christian called Hanna Diyab who was visiting Paris. Galland wrote down the skeletons of these two stories and a handful of others and then fleshed them out into much fuller versions, more French in feeling and with more stress on psychological motivation and moral messages than are commonly found in the main corpus of Arabic stories. Though 'The Story of Aladdin', featuring yet another of those initially feckless youths, is set in China, it is clear that whoever first put this tale together had no idea what China was really like. His 'China' was merely a distant land where fantastic things could happen. As for 'Ali Baba', perhaps this should really be called 'Marjana', as it is the slave girl rather than her master who proves to be bold and resourceful. Although some people have suspected that Galland might have made up the 'orphan stories', this does not seem to be the case and variant versions of 'Ali Baba' seem to have circulated in the Middle East and the Balkans, while a version has been found in an early Turkish manuscript.

Finally, this selected translation includes the ending of the *Nights* as given in Calcutta II, in which Shahriyar forgives Shahrazad after she has shown him the children she has borne him. She has survived a perilous thousand and one nights through complete submission to her husband, both entertaining him and proving her fertility. Her sisters in the twenty-first century might not be so pleased with her. Yet the stories she has told are marvellous. As the well-known Austrian writer Hugo von Hofmannsthal (1874–1929) has written in the introduction to a German translation of the *Nights* by Felix Paul Greve, published in 1907:

> Here is a poem on which more than one person has worked, but it seems that it originated from one soul. It is a whole, it is a complete world. And what a world! Compared to this Homer appears pale and artificial. Here one finds bright colours and profundity, a stunning fantasy and a sharp practical wisdom. Here one finds endless adventures, dreams, aphorisms, jokes, indecencies, mysteries. Here the bawdiest spirituality and the most perfect sensuality are woven together. There is not one of our senses that is not aroused, from the outside and the inside. Everything in us is revitalised and encouraged to enjoy.

Or, as storytellers within the *Nights* put it more solemnly, it is 'a story that, were it written with needles on the inner corners of the eye, would serve as a warning to those who take heed'.

Robert Irwin
London

Tales from 1,001 Nights

King Shahriyar, Shah Zaman and Shahrazad

Among the histories of past peoples a story is told that in the old days in the islands of India and China there was a Sasanian king, a master of armies, guards, servants and retainers, who had two sons, an elder and a younger. Although both of them were champion horsemen, the elder was better than his brother; he ruled over the lands, treating his subjects with justice and enjoying the affection of them all. His name was King Shahriyar, while his younger brother, who ruled Persian Samarkand, was called Shah Zaman. For ten years both of them continued to reign justly, enjoying pleasant and untroubled lives, until Shahriyar felt a longing to see Shah Zaman and sent off his vizier to fetch him. 'To hear is to obey,' said the vizier, and after he had travelled safely to Shah Zaman, he brought him greetings and told him that his brother wanted a visit from him.

Shah Zaman agreed to come and made his preparations for the journey. He had his tents put up outside his city, together with his camels, mules, servants and guards, while his own vizier was left in charge of his lands. He then came out himself, intending to leave for his brother's country, but at midnight he thought of something that he had forgotten and went back to the palace. When he entered his room, it was to discover his wife in bed with a black slave. The world turned dark for him and he said to himself: 'If this is what happens before I have even left the city, what will this damned woman do if I spend time away with my brother?' So he drew his sword and struck, killing both his wife and her lover as they lay together, before going back and ordering his escort to move off.

When he got near to Shahriyar's city, he sent off messengers to give the good news of his arrival, and Shahriyar came out to meet him and greeted him delightedly. The city was adorned with decorations and Shahriyar sat talking happily with him, but Shah Zaman remembered what his wife had done and, overcome by sorrow, he turned pale and showed signs of illness. His brother thought that this must be because he had had to leave his kingdom and so he put no questions to him until, some days later, he mentioned these symptoms to Shah Zaman, who told him: 'My feelings are wounded,' but did not explain what had happened with his wife. In order to cheer him up, Shahriyar invited him to come with him on a hunt, but he refused and Shahriyar set off by himself.

In the royal palace there were windows that overlooked Shahriyar's garden, and as Shah Zaman was looking, a door opened and out came twenty slave girls and twenty slaves, in the middle of whom was Shahriyar's very beautiful wife. They came to a fountain where they took off their clothes and the women sat with the men. 'Mas'ud,' the queen called, at which a black slave came up to her and, after they had embraced each other, he lay with her, while the other slaves lay with the slave girls and they spent their time kissing, embracing, fornicating and drinking wine until the end of the day.

When Shah Zaman saw this, he told himself that what he had suffered was less serious. His jealous distress ended and, after convincing himself that his own misfortune was not as grave as this, he went on eating and drinking, so that when Shahriyar returned and the brothers greeted one another, Shahriyar saw that Shah Zaman's colour had come back; his face was rosy and, following his earlier loss of appetite, he was eating normally. 'You were pale, brother,' Shahriyar said, 'but now you have got your colour back, so tell me about this.' 'I'll tell you why I lost colour,' his brother replied, 'but don't press me to tell you how I got it back.' 'Let me know first how you lost it and became so weak,' Shahriyar asked him, and his brother explained: 'When you sent your vizier to invite me to visit you, I got ready and had gone out of the city when I remembered a jewel that was intended as a present for you, which I had left in my palace. I went back there to find a black slave sleeping in my bed with my wife, and it was after I had killed them both that I came on to you. I was full of concern about the affair and this was why I became pale and sickly, but don't make me say how I recovered.' Shahriyar, however, pressed him to do this, and so Shah Zaman finally told him all that he had seen.

'I want to see this with my own eyes,' said Shahriyar, at which Shah Zaman suggested that he pretend to be going out hunting again and then hide with him so that he could test the truth by seeing it for himself. Shahriyar immediately announced that he was leaving to hunt; the tents were taken outside the city and the king himself went out and took his seat in one of them, telling his servants that nobody was to be allowed in to visit him. Then secretly he made his way back to the palace where his brother was and sat down by the window overlooking the garden. After a while the slave girls and their mistress came there with the slaves and they went on acting as Shah Zaman had described until the call for the afternoon prayer.

Shahriyar was beside himself and told his brother: 'Come, let us leave at once. Until we can find someone else to whom the same kind of thing happens, we have no need of a kingdom, and otherwise we would be better dead.' They left by the postern gate and went on for some days and nights until they got to a tall tree in the middle of a meadow, where there was a spring of water by the seashore. They drank from the spring and sat down to rest, but after a time the sea became disturbed and from it emerged a black pillar, towering up into the sky and moving towards the meadow. This sight filled the brothers with alarm and they climbed up to the top of the tree to see what was going to happen. What then appeared was a tall *jinni*, with a large skull and a broad breast, carrying a chest on his head. He came ashore and went up to sit under the tree on top of which the brothers were hiding. The *jinni* then opened the chest, taking from it a box, and when he had opened this too, out came a slender girl, as radiant as the sun, who fitted the excellent description given by the poet 'Atiya:

She shone in the darkness, and day appeared
As the trees shed brightness over her.
Her radiance makes suns rise and shine,
While, as for moons, she covers them in shame.
When veils are rent and she appears,
All things bow down before her.
As lightning flashes from her sanctuary,
A rain of tears floods down.

The *jinni* looked at her and said: 'Mistress of the nobly born, whom I snatched away on your wedding night, I want to sleep for a while.' He placed his head on her knee and fell asleep, while she, for her part, looked up at the tree, on top of which were the two kings. She lifted the *jinni*'s head from her knee and put it on the ground, before gesturing to them to come down and not to fear him. 'For God's sake, don't make us do this,' they told her, but she replied: 'Unless you come, I'll rouse him against you and he will put you to the cruellest of deaths.' This so alarmed them that they did what they were told and she then said: 'Take me as hard as you can or else I'll wake him up.' Shahriyar said fearfully to his brother: 'Do as she says.' But Shah Zaman refused, saying: 'You do it first.'

They started gesturing to each other about this and the girl asked why, repeating: 'If you don't come up and do it, I'll rouse the *jinni* against you.' Because they were afraid, they took turns to lie with her, and when they had finished, she told them to get up. From her pocket she then produced a purse from which she brought out a string on which were hung five hundred and seventy signet rings. She asked them if they knew what these were and when they said no, she told them: 'All these belonged to lovers of mine who cuckolded this *jinni*, so give me your own rings.' When they had handed them over, she went on: 'This *jinni* snatched me away on my wedding night and put me inside a box, which he placed inside this chest, with its seven heavy locks, and this, in turn, he put at the bottom of the tumultuous sea with its clashing waves. What he did not know was that, when a woman wants something, nothing can get the better of her, as a poet has said:

Do not put your trust in women
Or believe their covenants.
Their satisfaction and their anger
Both depend on their private parts.
They make a false display of love,
But their clothes are stuffed with treachery.
Take a lesson from the tale of Joseph,
And you will find some of their tricks.
Do you not see that your father, Adam,
Was driven out from Eden thanks to them?

Another poet has said:

Blame must be matched to what is blamed;
I have grown big, but my offence has not.
I am a lover, but what I have done
Is only what men did before me in old days.
What is a cause for wonder is a man
Whom women have not trapped by their allure.'

When the two kings heard this, they were filled with astonishment and said to each other: '*Jinni* though he may be, what has happened to him is worse than what happened to us and it is not something that anyone else has experienced.' They left the girl straight away and went back to

Shahriyar's city, where they entered the palace and cut off the heads of the queen, the slave girls and the slaves.

Every night for the next three years, Shahriyar would take a virgin, deflower her and then kill her. This led to unrest among the citizens; they fled away with their daughters until there were no nubile girls left in the city. Then, when the vizier was ordered to bring the king a girl as usual, he searched but could not find a single one, and had to go home empty-handed, dejected and afraid of what the king might do to him.

This man had two daughters, of whom the elder was called Shahrazad and the younger Dunyazad. Shahrazad had read books and histories, accounts of past kings and stories of earlier peoples, having collected, it was said, a thousand volumes of these, covering peoples, kings and poets. She asked her father what had happened to make him so careworn and sad, quoting the lines of a poet:

Say to the careworn man: 'Care does not last,
And as joy passes, so does care.'

When her father heard this, he told her all that had happened between him and the king from beginning to end, at which she said: 'Father, marry me to this man. Either I shall live or else I shall be a ransom for the children of the Muslims and save them from him.' 'By God,' he exclaimed, 'you are not to risk your life!' She insisted that it had to be done, but he objected: 'I'm afraid that you may experience what happened to the donkey and the bull with the merchant.' 'What was that,' she asked, 'and what happened to the two of them?' HER FATHER TOLD HER:

The Story of the Donkey and the Bull

You must know, my daughter, that a certain merchant had both wealth and animals and had been given by Almighty God a knowledge of the languages of beasts and birds. He lived in the country and had at home a donkey and a bull. One day the bull went to the donkey's quarters and found them swept out and sprinkled with water; there was sieved barley and straw in his trough, while the donkey was lying there at his ease. At times his master would ride him out on some errand, but he would then be taken back.

One day the merchant heard the bull say to the donkey: 'I congratulate you. Here am I, tired out, while you are at your ease, eating sieved barley. On occasion the master puts you to use, riding on you but then bringing you back again, whereas I am always ploughing and grinding corn.' The donkey replied: 'When they put the yoke on your neck and want to take you out to the fields, don't get up, even if they beat you, or else get up and then lie down again. When they bring you back and put beans down for you, pretend to be sick and don't eat them; for one, two or three days neither eat nor drink and you will have a rest from your hard labour.'

The next day, when the herdsman brought the bull his supper, the creature only ate a little and next morning, when the man came to take the bull out to do the ploughing, he found him sick and said sadly: 'This was why he could not work properly yesterday.' He went to the merchant and told him: 'Master, the bull is unwell and didn't eat any of his food yesterday evening.' The merchant realized what had happened and said: 'Go and take the donkey to do the ploughing all day in his place.'

When the donkey came back in the evening after having been used for ploughing all day, the bull thanked him for his kindness in having given him a day's rest, to which the donkey, filled with the bitterest regret, made no reply. The next morning, the herdsman came and took him out to plough until evening, and when the donkey got back, his neck had been rubbed raw and he was half-dead with tiredness. When the bull saw him, he thanked and praised him, but the donkey said: 'I was sitting at my ease, but was unable to mind my own business.' Then he went on: 'I have some advice to give you. I heard our master say that, if you don't get up, you are to be given to the butcher to be slaughtered, and your hide is to be cut into pieces. I am afraid for you and so I have given you this advice.'

When the bull heard what the donkey had to say, he thanked him and said: 'Tomorrow I'll go out with the men.' He then finished off all his food, using his tongue to lick the manger. While all this was going on, the merchant was listening to what the animals were saying. The next morning, he and his wife went out and sat by the byre as the herdsman arrived and took the bull out. When the bull saw his master, he flourished his tail, farted and galloped off, leaving the man laughing so much that he collapsed on the ground. His wife asked why, and he told her: 'I was laughing because of something secret that I saw and heard, but I can't tell you or else I shall die.' 'Even if you do die,' she insisted, 'you must tell me the reason for this.' He repeated that he could not do it for fear of death, but she said: 'You were laughing at me,' and she went on insisting obstinately until she got the better of him. In distress, he summoned his children and sent for the *qadi* and the notaries with the intention of leaving his final instructions before telling his wife the secret and then dying. He had a deep love for her, she being his cousin and the mother of his children, while he himself was a hundred and twenty years old.

When all his family and his neighbours were gathered together, he explained that he had something to say to them, but that if he told the secret to anyone, he would die. Everyone there urged his wife not to press him and so bring about the death of her husband and the father of her children, but she said: 'I am not going to stop until he tells me, and I shall let him die.' At that, the others stayed silent while the merchant got up and went to the byre to perform the ritual ablution, after which he would return to them and die.

The merchant had a cock and fifty hens, together with a dog, and he heard the dog abusing the cock and saying: 'You may be cheerful, but here is our master about to die.' When the cock asked why this was, the dog told him the whole story. 'By God,' exclaimed the cock, 'he must be weak in the head. I have fifty wives and I keep them contented and at peace while he has only one but still can't keep her in order. Why doesn't he get some mulberry twigs, take her into a room and beat her until she either dies or repents and doesn't ask him again?'

The vizier now said to his daughter Shahrazad: 'I shall treat you as that man treated his wife.' 'What did he do?' she asked, AND HE WENT ON:

When he heard what the cock had to say to the dog, he cut some mulberry twigs and hid them in a room, where he took his wife. 'Come,' he said, 'so that I can speak to you in here and then die with no one looking on.' She went in with him and he locked the door on her and started beating her until she fainted. 'I take it all back,' she then said, and she kissed his hands and feet, and after she had repented, she and her husband went out to the delight of their family and the others there. They lived in the happiest of circumstances until their deaths.

Shahrazad listened to what her father had to say, but she still insisted on her plan and so he decked her out and took her to King Shahriyar. She had given instructions to her younger sister, Dunyazad, explaining: 'When I go to the king, I shall send for you. You must come, and when you see that the king has done what he wants with me, you are to say: "Tell me a story, sister, so as to pass the waking part of the night." I shall then tell you a tale that, God willing, will save us.'

Shahrazad was now taken by her father to the king, who was pleased to see him and said: 'Have you brought what I want?' When the vizier said yes, the king was about to lie with Shahrazad but she shed tears and when he asked her what was wrong, she told him: 'I have a young sister and I want to say goodbye to her.' At that, the king sent for Dunyazad, and when she had embraced Shahrazad, she took her seat beneath the bed, while the king got up and deflowered her sister. They then sat talking and Dunyazad asked Shahrazad to tell a story to pass the waking hours of the night. 'With the greatest pleasure,' replied Shahrazad, 'if our cultured king gives me permission.' The king was restless and when he heard what the sisters had to say, he was glad at the thought of listening to a story and so he gave his permission to Shahrazad. SHE BEGAN:

The Fisherman and the 'Ifrit

I have heard, O fortunate king, that there once was a poor, elderly fisherman with a wife and three children, who was in the habit of casting his net exactly four times each day. He went out to the shore at noon one day, put down his basket, tucked up his shirt, waded into the sea and cast his net. He waited until it had sunk down before pulling its cords together and then, finding it heavy, he tried unsuccessfully to drag it in. He took one end of it to the shore and fixed it to a peg that he drove in there, after which he stripped and dived into the sea beside it, where he continued tugging until he managed to get it up. He climbed out delightedly, put his clothes back on and went up to the net, only to find that what was in it was a dead donkey, and that the donkey had made a hole in the net. The fisherman was saddened by this and recited the formula: 'There is no might and no power except with God, the Exalted, the Omnipotent,' before saying: 'This is a strange thing that God has given me by way of food!' and then reciting:

You who court danger, diving in the dark of night,
Give up; your efforts do not win your daily bread from God.
The fisherman rises to earn his keep;
There is the sea, with stars woven in the sky.
He plunges in, buffeted by waves,
His eyes fixed on his billowing net.
Happy with his night's work, he takes back home
A fish, its jaw caught up on his pronged hook.
This fish is bought from him by one who spent his night
Out of the cold, enjoying his comforts.
Praise be to God, Who gives and Who deprives;
For one man eats the fish; another catches it.

He encouraged himself, saying that Almighty God would show favour and reciting:

When you are faced with hardship, clothe yourself
In noble patience; that is more resolute.
Do not complain, then, to God's servants; you complain
To those who have no mercy of the Merciful.

He freed the donkey from the net, which he then wrung out before spreading it out again and going back into the sea. Invoking the Name of God, he made another cast, waited until the net had settled, and found it heavier and more difficult to move than before. Thinking that it must be full of fish, he fastened it to his peg, stripped off his clothes and dived in to free it. After tugging at it he got it up on shore, only to discover that what was in it was a large jar full of sand and mud. Saddened by this sight, he recited:

Troubles of Time, give up!
Stop, even if you have not had enough.
I came out looking for my daily bread,
But I have found there is no more of this.
How many a fool reaches the Pleiades!
How many wise men lie hidden in the earth!

The fisherman threw away the jar, wrung out his net, cleaned it and went back a third time to the sea, asking God to forgive him. He made his cast and waited for the net to settle before drawing it in, and this time what he found in it were bits of pots, bottles and bones. He was furious and, shedding bitter tears, he recited:

You have no power at all over your daily bread;
Neither learning nor letters will fetch it for you.
Fortune and sustenance are divided up;
One land is fertile while another suffers drought.
Time's changes bring down cultured men,
While fortune lifts the undeserving up.
Come, Death, and visit me, for life is vile;
Falcons are brought down low while ducks are raised on high.
Feel no surprise if you should see a man of excellence
In poverty, while an inferior holds sway.

One bird circles the earth from east to west;
Another gets its food but does not have to move.

He then looked up to heaven and said: 'O my God, You know that I only cast my net four times a day. I have done this thrice and got nothing, so this time grant me something on which to live.' He pronounced the Name of God and cast his net into the sea. He waited until it had settled and then he tried to pull it in, but found that it had snagged on the bottom. He recited the formula: 'There is no power and no might except with God,' and went on:

How wretched is this kind of world
That leaves us in such trouble and distress!
In the morning it may be that things go well,
But I must drink destruction's cup when evening comes.
Yet when it is asked who leads the easiest life,
Men would reply that this was I.

The fisherman stripped off his clothes and, after diving in, he worked his hardest to drag the net to shore. Then, when he opened it up, he found in it a brass bottle with a lead seal, imprinted with the inscription of our master Solomon, the son of David, on both of whom be peace. The fisherman was delighted to see this, telling himself that it would fetch ten gold dinars if he sold it in the brass market. He shook it and, discovering that it was heavy as well as sealed, he said to himself: 'I wonder what is in it? I'll open it up and have a look before selling it.' He took out a knife and worked on the lead until he had removed it from the bottle, which he then put down on the ground, shaking it in order to pour out its contents. To his astonishment, at first nothing came out, but then there emerged smoke which towered up into the sky and spread over the surface of the ground. When it had all come out, it collected and solidified; a tremor ran through it and it became an *'ifrit* with his head in the clouds and his feet on the earth. His head was like a dome, his hands were like winnowing forks and his feet like ships' masts. He had a mouth like a cave with teeth like rocks, while his nostrils were like jugs and his eyes like lamps. He was dark and scowling.

When he saw this *'ifrit* the fisherman shuddered; his teeth chattered; his mouth dried up and he could not see where he was going. At the sight of him the *'ifrit* exclaimed: 'There is no god but the God of Solomon, His prophet. Prophet of God, do not kill me, for I shall never disobey you again in word or in deed.' '*'Ifrit*,' the fisherman said, 'you talk of Solomon, the prophet of God, but Solomon died eighteen hundred years ago and we are living in the last age of the world. What is your story and how did you come to be in this bottle?' To which the *'ifrit* replied: 'There is no god but God. I have good news for you, fisherman.' 'What is that?' the fisherman asked, and the *'ifrit* said: 'I am now going to put you to the worst of deaths.' 'For this good news, leader of the *'ifrits*,' exclaimed the fisherman, 'you deserve that God's protection be removed from you, you damned creature. Why should you kill me and what have I done to deserve this? It was I who saved you from the bottom of the sea and brought you ashore.'

But the *'ifrit* said: 'Choose what death you want and how you want me to kill you.' 'What have I done wrong,' asked the fisherman, 'and why are you punishing me?' The *'ifrit* replied: 'Listen to my story,' and the fisherman said: 'Tell it, but keep it short as I am at my last gasp.' 'Know, fisherman,' the *'ifrit* told him, 'that I was one of the apostate *jinn*, and that together with Sakhr, the *jinni*, I rebelled against Solomon, the son of David, on both of whom be peace. Solomon sent his vizier, Asaf, to fetch me to him under duress, and I was forced to go with him in a state of humiliation to stand before Solomon. "I take refuge with God!" exclaimed Solomon when he saw me, and he then offered me conversion to the Faith and proposed that I enter his service. When I refused, he called for this bottle, in which he imprisoned me, sealing it with lead and imprinting on it the Greatest Name of God. Then, at his command, the *jinn* carried me off and threw me into the middle of the sea.

'For a hundred years I stayed there, promising myself that I would give whoever freed me enough wealth to last him for ever, but the years passed and no one rescued me. For the next hundred years I told myself that I would open up all the treasures of the earth for my rescuer, but still no one rescued me. Four hundred years later, I promised that I would grant three wishes, but when I still remained imprisoned, I became furiously angry and said to myself that I would kill whoever saved me, giving him a choice of how he wanted to die. It is you who are my rescuer, and so I allow you this choice.'

When the fisherman heard this, he exclaimed in wonder at his bad luck in freeing the *'ifrit* now, and he went on: 'Spare me, may God spare you, and do not kill me lest God place you in the power of one who will kill you.' 'I must kill you,' insisted the *'ifrit*, 'and so choose how you want to die.' Ignoring this, the fisherman made another appeal, calling on the *'ifrit* to show gratitude for his release. 'It is only because you freed me that I am going to kill you,' repeated the *'ifrit*, at which the fisherman said: 'Lord of the *'ifrits*, I have done you good and you are repaying me with evil. The proverbial lines are right where they say:

We did them good; they did its opposite,
And this, by God, is how the shameless act.
Whoever helps those who deserve no help,
Will be like one who rescues a hyena.'

'Don't go on so long,' said the *'ifrit* when he heard this, 'for death is coming to you.' The fisherman said to himself: 'This is a *jinni* and I am a human. God has given me sound intelligence which I can use to find a way of destroying him, whereas he can only use vicious cunning.' So he asked: 'Are you definitely going to kill me?' and when the *'ifrit* confirmed this, he said: 'I conjure you by the Greatest Name inscribed on the seal of Solomon and ask you to give me a truthful answer to a question that I have.' 'I shall,' replied the *'ifrit*, who had been shaken and disturbed by the mention of the Greatest Name, and he went on: 'Ask your question but be brief.' The fisherman went on: 'You say you were in this bottle, but there is not room in it for your hand or your foot, much less all the rest of you.' 'You don't believe that I was in it?' asked the *'ifrit*, to which the fisherman replied: 'I shall never believe it until I see it with my own eyes.'

A shudder ran through the *'ifrit* and he became a cloud of smoke hovering over the sea. Then the smoke coalesced and entered the jar bit by bit until it was all there. Quickly the fisherman picked up the brass stopper with its inscription and put it over the mouth of the bottle. He called out to the *'ifrit*: 'Ask me how you want to die. By God, I am going to throw you into the sea and then build myself a house in this place so that I can stop anyone who comes fishing by telling them that there is an *'ifrit* here who gives anyone who brings him up a choice of how he wants to be killed.'

When the *'ifrit* heard this and found himself imprisoned in the bottle, he tried to get out but could not, as he was prevented by Solomon's seal, and he realized that the fisherman had tricked him. 'I was only joking,' he told the fisherman, who replied: 'You are lying, you most despicable, foulest and most insignificant of *'ifrits*,' and he took up the bottle. 'No, no,' called the *'ifrit*, but the fisherman said: 'Yes, yes,' at which the *'ifrit* asked him mildly and humbly what he intended to do with him. 'I am going to throw you into the sea,' the fisherman told him. 'You may have been there for eighteen hundred years, but I shall see to it that you stay there until the Last Trump. Didn't I say: "Spare me, may God spare you, and do not kill me lest God place you in the power of one who will kill you"? But you refused and acted treacherously towards me. Now God has put you in my power and I shall do the same to you.' 'Open the bottle,' implored the *'ifrit*, 'so that I can do you good.' 'Damned liar,' said the fisherman. 'You and I are like the vizier of King Yunan and Duban the sage.' 'What is their story?' asked the *'ifrit*, AND THE FISHERMAN REPLIED:

The Story of King Yunan and Duban the Sage

You must know, *'ifrit*, that once upon a time in the old days in the land of Ruman there was a king called Yunan in the city of Fars. He was a wealthy and dignified man with troops and guards of all races, but he was also a leper, who had taken medicines of various kinds and used ointments, but whose illness doctors and men of learning had been unable to cure.

There was an elderly physician known as Duban the sage, who had studied the books of the Greeks, the Persians, the Arabs and the Syrians. He was a master of medicine and of astronomy and was conversant with the fundamental principles of his subject, with a knowledge of what was useful and what was harmful. He knew the herbs and plants that were hurtful and those that were helpful, as well as having a mastery of philosophy, together with all branches of medicine and other sciences. When this man arrived at the city, within a few days he had heard that the king was suffering from leprosy and that no doctor or man of learning had been able to cure him. He spent the night thinking over the problem, and when dawn broke he put on his most splendid clothes and went to the king, kissing the ground before him and calling eloquently for the continuance of his glory and good fortune. After introducing himself, he went on: 'I have heard, your majesty, of the disease that has afflicted you and that, although you have been treated by many doctors, they have been unable to remove it. I shall cure you without giving you any medicine to drink or applying any ointments.'

Yunan was amazed to hear what he had to say and asked how he was going to do that, promising to enrich him and his children's children. 'I shall shower favours on you,' he said, 'and grant you all your wishes, taking you as a boon companion and a dear friend.' He then presented Duban with a robe of honour and treated him with favour, before asking: 'Are you really going to cure my leprosy without medicines or ointment?' Duban repeated that he would and the astonished king asked when this would be, urging him to be quick. 'To hear is to obey,' replied Duban, promising to do this the very next day.

Duban now went to the city, where he rented a house in which he deposited his books, his medicines and his drugs. He took some of the latter and placed them in a polo stick, for which he made a handle, and he used his skill to design a ball. The next day, after he had finished, he went into the presence of the king, kissed the ground before him, and told him to ride out to the polo ground and play a game. The king was accompanied by the emirs, chamberlains, viziers and officers of state, and before he had taken his seat on the ground, Duban came up to him and handed him the stick. 'Take this,' he said. 'Hold it like this and when you ride on to the field, hit the ball with a full swing until the palm of your hand begins to sweat, together with the rest of your body. The drug will then enter through your palm and spread through the rest of you. When you have finished and the drug has penetrated, go back to your palace, wash in the baths and then go to sleep, for you will have been cured. That is all.'

At that, the king took the stick from him and mounted, holding it in his hand. He threw the ball ahead of him and rode after it, hitting it as hard as he could when he caught up with it, and then following it up and hitting it again until the palm of his hand and the rest of his body became sweaty because of his grip on the stick. When Duban saw that the drug had penetrated into the king's body, he told him to go back to his palace and bathe immediately. The king went back straight away and ordered that the baths be cleared for him. This was done, and house boys and mamluks hurried up to him and prepared clothes for him to wear. He then entered the baths, washed himself thoroughly and dressed before coming out, after which he rode back to his palace and fell asleep.

So much for him, but as for Duban the sage, he returned to spend the night in his house, and in the morning he went to ask permission to see the king. On being allowed to enter, he went in, kissed the ground before him and addressed him with these lines which he chanted:

Virtues are exalted when you are called their father,
A title that none other may accept.
The brightness shining from your face removes
The gloom that shrouds each grave affair.
This face of yours will never cease to gleam,
Although the face of Time may frown.
Your liberality has granted me the gifts
That rain clouds shower down on the hills.
Your generosity has destroyed your wealth,
Until you reached the heights at which you aimed.

When Duban had finished these lines, the king stood up and embraced him, before seating him by his side and presenting him with splendid robes of honour. This was because when he had left the baths he had looked at his body and found it, to his great delight and relief, pure and silver white, showing no trace of leprosy. In the morning, he had gone to his court and taken his seat on his royal throne, the chamberlains and officers of state all standing up for him, and it was then that Duban had come in. The king had risen quickly for him, and after the sage had been seated by his side, splendid tables of food were set out and he ate with the king and kept him company for the rest of the day. The king then made him a present of two thousand dinars, in addition to the robes of honour and other gifts, after which he mounted him on his own horse.

Duban went back to his house, leaving the king filled with admiration for what he had done and saying: 'This man treated me externally without using any ointment. By God, that is skill of a high order! He deserves gifts and favours and I shall always treat him as a friend and companion.' The king passed a happy night, gladdened by the soundness of his body and his freedom from disease. The next day, he went out and sat on his throne, while his state officials stood and the emirs and viziers took their seats on his right and his left. He asked for Duban, who entered and kissed the ground before him, at which the king got up, greeted him, seated him by his side and ate with him. He then presented him with more robes of honour as well as gifts, and talked with him until nightfall, when he gave him another five robes of honour together with a thousand dinars, after which Duban went gratefully home.

The next morning, the king came to his court, where he was surrounded by his emirs, viziers and chamberlains. Among the viziers was an ugly and ill-omened man, base, miserly and so envious that he was in love with envy. When this man saw that the king had taken Duban as an intimate and had rewarded him with favours, he was jealous and planned to do him an injury. For, as the sayings have it: 'No one is free of envy' and 'Injustice lurks in the soul; strength shows it and weakness hides it.'

This vizier came up to King Yunan, kissed the ground before him and said: 'King of the age, I have grown up surrounded by your bounty and I have some serious advice for you. Were I to conceal it from you, I would show myself to be a bastard, but if you tell me to give it to you, I shall do so.' Yunan was disturbed by this and said: 'What is this advice of yours?' The vizier replied: 'Great king, it was a saying of the ancients that Time was no friend to those who did not look at the consequences of their actions. I have observed that your majesty has wrongly shown favour to an enemy who is looking to destroy your kingdom. You have treated this man with generosity and done him the greatest honour, taking him as an intimate, something that fills me with apprehension.'

Yunan was uneasy; his colour changed and he asked the vizier who he was talking about. 'If you are asleep, wake up,' the vizier told him, and went on: 'I am talking about the sage Duban.' 'Damn you!' exclaimed Yunan. 'This is my friend and the dearest of people to me, for he cured me through something that I held in my hand from a disease that no other doctor could treat. His like is not to be found in this age or in this world, from west to east. You may accuse him, but today I am going to assign him pay and allowances, with a monthly income of a thousand dinars, while even if I divided my kingdom with him, this would be too little. I think that it is envy that has made you say this, reminding me of the story of King Sindbad.'

The Story of King Sindbad and the Falcon

You must know that there was a Persian king with a passion for enjoyment and amusement, who had a fondness for hunting. He had reared a falcon which was his constant companion by night and by day, and which would spend the night perched on his wrist. He would take it hunting with him and he had a golden bowl made for it which he hung round its neck and from which it could drink. One day the chief falconer came to where he was sitting and told him that it was time to go out hunting. The king gave the orders and went off with the falcon on his wrist until he and his party reached a wadi, where they spread out their hunting cordon. Trapped in this was a gazelle and the king threatened that anyone who allowed it to leap over his head would be put to death. When the cordon was narrowed, the gazelle came to where the king was posted, supported itself on its hindlegs and placed its forelegs on its chest as though it was kissing the ground before him. He bent his head towards it and it then jumped over him, making for the open country. He noticed that his men were looking at him and winking at each other and when he asked his vizier what this meant, the man explained: 'They are pointing out that you said that if anyone let the gazelle jump over his head, he would be killed.'

The king then swore that he would hunt it down and he rode off in pursuit, following the gazelle until he came to a mountain. There it was about to pass through a cleft when the king loosed his falcon at it and the bird clawed at its eyes, blinding and dazing it, so that the king could draw his mace and knock it over with a single blow. He then dismounted and cut its throat, after which he skinned it and tied it to his saddlebow. As this was in the noonday heat and the region was desolate and waterless, both the king and his horse were thirsty by now. The king scouted round and discovered a tree from which what looked like liquid butter was dripping. Wearing a pair of kid gloves, he took the bowl from the falcon's neck, filled it with this liquid and set it in front of the bird, but it knocked the bowl and overturned it. The king took it and filled it again, thinking that the falcon must be thirsty, but the same thing happened when he put it down a second time. This annoyed him and he went a third time to fill the bowl and take it to his horse, but this time the falcon upset it with its wing. The king cursed it, exclaiming: 'You unluckiest of birds, you have stopped me drinking, and have stopped yourself and the horse.' He then struck off its wing with a blow from his sword, but the bird raised its head as though to say by its gesture: 'Look at the top of the tree.' The king raised his eyes and what he saw there was a brood of vipers whose poison was dripping down. Immediately regretting what he had done, he mounted his horse and rode back to his pavilion, bringing with him the gazelle, which he handed to the cook, telling him to take it and roast it. As he sat on his chair with the falcon on his wrist, it drew its last breath and died, leaving its master to exclaim with sorrow for having killed it, when it had saved his life. So ends the story of King Sindbad.

'Great king,' the vizier said, 'Sindbad acted out of necessity and I can see nothing wrong in that. I myself am acting out of sympathy for you, so that you may realize that I am right, for otherwise you may meet the same fate as the vizier who schemed against the prince.' 'How was that?' the king asked, AND THE VIZIER SAID:

The Story of the Treacherous Vizier

You must know, your majesty, that there was a vizier in the service of a certain king with a son who was passionately fond of hunting. This vizier had been ordered to accompany the prince wherever he went, and so, when he went off to hunt one day, the vizier rode with him. While they were riding they caught sight of a huge beast and the vizier encouraged the prince to pursue it. The prince rode after it until he was out of sight and the beast then vanished into the desert, leaving the prince with no idea of where to go. Just then, ahead of him he saw a weeping girl and when he asked her who she was, she told him: 'I am the daughter of one of the kings of India and while I was in this desert I became drowsy. Then, before I knew what was happening, I had fallen off my beast and was left alone, not knowing what to do.'

When the prince heard this, he felt sorry for the girl and took her up behind him on the back of his horse. On his way, he passed a ruined building and the girl said she wanted to relieve herself. He set her down, but she was taking so long that he followed her, only to discover that, although he had not realized it, she was a female *ghul* and was telling her children: 'I have brought you a fat young man today.' 'Fetch him to us, mother,' they said, 'so that we can swallow him down.' On hearing this, the prince shuddered, fearing for his life and certain that he was going to die. He went back and the *ghula* came out and, seeing him panic-stricken and shivering, she asked why he was afraid. 'I have an enemy whom I fear,' he told her. 'You call yourself a prince?' she asked, and when he said yes, she went on: 'Why don't you buy him off with money?' 'He won't accept money but wants my life,' he told her, adding: 'I am afraid of him and I have been wronged.' 'In that case, if what you say is true, then ask help from God,' she said, 'for He will protect you against your enemy's evil and the evil that you fear from him.' At that the prince lifted his head towards heaven and said: 'God, Who answers the prayers of those in distress when they call on You, and Who clears away evil, may You help me against my enemy and remove him from me, for You have power to do what You wish.'

After hearing the prince's prayer, the *ghula* left him. He went back to his father and when he told him about the vizier's advice, his father summoned the man and had him killed. As for you, your majesty, if you put your trust in this sage, he will see to it that you die the worst of deaths, and it will be the man whom you have well treated and taken as a friend who will destroy you. Don't you see that he cured your disease externally through something you held in your hand, so how can you be sure that he won't kill you by something else you hold?

'What you say is right, vizier, my sound advisor,' agreed the king, 'for this man has come as a spy to destroy me and if he could cure me with something I held, it may be that he can kill me with something that I smell.'

Then he asked the vizier what was to be done about Duban. The vizier said: 'Send for him immediately, telling him to come here, and when he does, cut off his head and then you will be safe from any harm he may intend to do you. Betray him before he betrays you.' The king agreed with the vizier, and sent for Duban, who came gladly, not knowing what God the Merciful had ordained. This was as the poet said:

You who fear your fate, be at your ease;
Entrust your affairs to Him Who has stretched out the earth.
What is decreed by fate will come about,
And you are safe from what is not decreed.

Duban the wise came into the presence of the king and recited:

If I do not show gratitude
In accordance with part, at least, of your deserts,
Tell me for whom I should compose my poetry and my prose.
Before I asked, you granted me
Favours that came with no delay and no excuse.
Why then do I not give you your due of praise,
Lauding your generosity in secret and in public?
I shall record the benefits you heaped on me,
Lightening my cares, but burdening my back.

He followed this with another poem:

Turn aside from cares, entrusting your affairs to fate;
Rejoice in the good that will come speedily to you,
So that you may forget all that is past.

There is many a troublesome affair
Whose aftermath will leave you in content.
God acts according to His will;
Do not oppose your God.

He also recited:

Leave your affairs to God, the Gentle, the Omniscient,
And let your heart rest from all worldly care.
Know that things do not go as you wish;
They follow the decree of God, the King.

He then recited:

Be of good cheer, relax; forget your cares;
Cares eat away the resolute man's heart.
Planning is no help to a slave who has no power.
Abandon this and live in happiness.

The king asked him: 'Do you know why I have sent for you?' 'No one knows what is hidden except for God,' Duban replied. 'I have sent for you,' said the king, 'in order to kill you and take your life.' This astonished Duban, who said: 'Why should you kill me, your majesty, and what is my crime?' 'I have been told that you are a spy,' answered the king, 'and that you have come to murder me. I am going to kill you before you can do the same to me.' The king then called for the executioner and said: 'Cut off this traitor's head, so that we may be freed from his evil-doing.' 'Spare me,' said Duban, 'and God will spare you; do not kill me, lest He kill you.'

He then repeated what I repeated to you, *'ifrit*, but you would not give up your intention to kill me. Similarly, the king insisted: 'I shall not be safe unless I put you to death. You cured me with something that I held in my hand, and I cannot be sure that you will not kill me with something that I smell or in some other way.' Duban said: 'My reward from you, O king, is the reward of good by evil,' but the king insisted: 'You must be killed without delay.'

When Duban was certain that the king was going to have him killed, he wept in sorrow for the good that he had done to the undeserving, as the poet has said:

You can be sure that Maimuna has no sense,
Though this is what her father has.

Whoever walks on dry or slippery ground,
And takes no thought, must fall.

The executioner then came up, blindfolded him and unsheathed his sword, asking the king's permission to proceed. Duban was weeping and imploring the king: 'Spare me and God will spare you; do not slay me lest God slay you.' He recited:

I gave my good advice and yet had no success,
While they succeeded, but through treachery.
What I advised humiliated me.
If I live, never shall I give advice again;
If not, after my death let all advisors be accursed.

Then he said to the king: 'If this is how you reward me, it is the crocodile's reward.' The king asked for the story of the crocodile, but Duban replied: 'I cannot tell it to you while I am in this state. I conjure you by God to spare me so that God may spare you.' At that one of the king's courtiers got up and asked the king for Duban's life, pointing out: 'We have not seen that he has done you any wrong, but only that he cured you of a disease that no wise doctor was able to treat.' The king said: 'You do not know why I have ordered his death, but this is because, if I spare him, I shall certainly die. A man who cured me of my illness by something that I held in my hand is able to kill me by something that I smell. I am afraid that he has been bribed to murder me, as he is a spy and this is why he has come here. He must be executed, and after that I shall be safe.'

Duban repeated his plea for mercy, but on realizing that he could not escape execution, he said to the king: 'If I must be killed, allow me a delay so that I may return to my house, give instructions to my family and my neighbours about my funeral, settle my debts and give away my books of medicine. I have a very special book which I shall present to you to be kept in your treasury.' 'What is in the book?' asked the king. 'Innumerable secrets,' Duban replied, 'the least of which is that, if you cut off my head and then open three pages and read three lines from the left-hand page, my head will speak to you and answer all your questions.' The astonished king trembled with joy. 'When I cut off your head, will you really talk to me?' he asked. 'Yes,' said Duban. 'This is an amazing thing!' exclaimed the king, and he sent him off under escort.

Duban returned to his house and settled all his affairs, and then the next day he came back to the court, where all the viziers, chamberlains, deputies and officers of state assembled, until the place looked like a garden in flower. He entered and was brought before the king, carrying with him an old book together with a collyrium case containing powder. He sat down and asked for a plate, which was brought. He then poured the powder on it and spread it out, after which he said: 'King, take this book, but don't open it until you cut off my head. When you have done that, set the head on the plate and have it pressed into the powder. At that, the flow of blood will halt and you can then open the book.'

The king took the book from him and gave orders for his execution. The executioner cut off his head, which fell on the plate, where it was pressed down into the powder. The blood ceased to flow and Duban the wise opened his eyes and said: 'O king, open the book.' The king did this, but he found the pages stuck together, so he put his finger into his mouth, wet it with his spittle, and with difficulty he opened the first, the second and the third pages. He opened six pages in all, but when he looked at them, he could find nothing written there. 'Wise man,' he said, 'there is no writing here.' 'Open more pages,' said Duban. The king opened three more, but soon afterwards he felt the poison with which the book had been impregnated spreading through him. He was wracked by convulsions and cried out that he had been poisoned, while Duban recited:

They wielded power with arrogance,
But soon it was as though their power had never been.
If they had acted justly, they would have met with justice,
But they were tyrants and Time played the tyrant in return,
Afflicting them with grievous trials.
It was as though here fate was telling them:
'This is a return for that, and Time cannot be blamed.'

As soon as Duban's head had finished speaking, the king fell dead.

'Know then, *'ifrit*,' said the fisherman, 'that had he spared Duban, God would have spared him, but as he refused and looked to have him killed, God destroyed him. Had you spared me, I would have spared you, but you wanted nothing but my death and so now I am going to destroy you by throwing you into the sea here, imprisoned in this bottle.' The *'ifrit* cried out: 'I implore you, in God's Name, fisherman, don't do this! Spare me and don't punish me for what I did. If I treated you badly, do you for your part treat me well, as the proverb says: "You who do good to the evil-doer, know that what he has done is punishment enough for him." Do not do what 'Umama did to 'Atika!' 'What was that?' asked the fisherman, but the *'ifrit* said: 'I cannot talk while I am imprisoned, but if you let me out, I shall tell you the story.' The fisherman said: 'Stop talking like this, for I shall certainly throw you into the sea and I am never going to release you. I pleaded with you and begged you, but all you wanted to do was to kill me, although I had done nothing at all to deserve this and, far from doing you any harm, I had helped you by freeing you from your prison. When you did that to me, I realized that you were an evil-doer. Be sure that, when I throw you into the sea, if anyone brings you out, I will tell him what you did to me and warn him, so that he may throw you back again and there you will stay until the end of time or until you perish.' 'Free me,' pleaded the *'ifrit*. 'This is a time for generosity and I promise you that I shall never act against you again but will help you by making you rich.'

At this, the fisherman made the *'ifrit* promise that were he freed, far from hurting his rescuer, he would help him. When the fisherman was sure of this and had made the *'ifrit* swear by the Greatest Name of God, he opened the bottle and the smoke rose up, until it had all come out and had formed into a hideous shape. The *'ifrit* then picked the bottle up and hurled it into the sea, convincing the watching fisherman that he was going to be killed. The man soiled his trousers, crying: 'This is not a good sign!' but then his courage came back and he said: 'God Almighty has said: "Fulfil your promise, for your promise will be questioned."* You gave me your word, swearing that you would not act treacherously to me, as otherwise God will do the same to you, for He is a jealous God, Who bides His time but does not forget. I say to you what Duban the wise said to King Yunan: "Spare me and God will spare you."'

The *'ifrit* laughed and told the fisherman to follow him as he walked ahead. This the fisherman did, scarcely believing that he was safe. The pair of them left the city, climbed a mountain and then went down into a wide plain. There they saw a pool, and after the *'ifrit* had waded into the middle of it, he asked the fisherman to follow him, which he did. When the *'ifrit* stopped, he told the fisherman to cast his net, and the man was astonished to see that the pond contained coloured fish – white, red, blue and yellow. He took out his net, cast it and when he drew it in he found four fish, each a different colour. He was delighted by this, and the *'ifrit* said: 'Present these to the sultan and he will enrich you. Then I ask you in God's Name to excuse me, since at this time I know no other way

* Quran 17.36.

to help you. I have been in the sea for eighteen hundred years and this is the first time that I have seen the face of the land.' After advising the fisherman not to fish the pool more than once a day, he took his leave, speaking words of farewell. Then he stamped his foot on the earth and a crack appeared into which he was swallowed.

The fisherman returned to the city, full of wonder at his encounter. He took the fish to his house, where he brought out an earthenware bowl, filled it with water and put them in it. As they wriggled about in the water, he placed the bowl on his head and went to the palace as the *'ifrit* had told him. When he came to the king and presented him with the fish, the king was astonished, for never in his life had he seen anything like them. He gave orders that they were to be handed over to a slave girl who was acting as cook but whose skill had not yet been tested, as she had been given him three days earlier by the king of Rum. The vizier told her to fry the fish, adding that the king had said that he was testing her only in the hour of need, and that he was putting his hopes in her artistry and cooking skills, for the fish had been given him as a present.

After issuing these instructions, the vizier went back to the king, who told him to hand the fisherman four hundred dinars. After he had passed over the money, the man stowed it inside his clothes and set off back home at a run, falling, getting up and then stumbling again, thinking that this was all a dream. He bought what was needed for his family and then returned to his wife in joy and delight.

So much for him, but as for the slave girl, she took the fish and cleaned them. Then, after setting the frying pan on the fire, she put the fish in it and when one side was properly cooked, she turned them on to the other. All of a sudden, the kitchen wall split open and out came a girl, with a beautiful figure and smooth cheeks, perfect in all her attributes. Her eyes were darkened with kohl and she had on a silken *kaffiyeh* with a blue fringe. She was wearing earrings; on her wrists were a pair of bracelets, while her fingers were adorned with rings set with precious gems, and in her hand she held a bamboo staff. Thrusting this into the pan, she asked: 'Fish, are you still faithful to your covenant?' at which the cook fainted. The girl repeated her question a second and a third time and the fish raised their heads from the pan and said: 'Yes, yes,' in clear voices, and then they recited:

If you return, we return;
If you keep faith, then so do we,
But if you go off, we are quits.

At that, the girl turned the pan upside down with her staff and left through the hole from which she had come, after which the wall closed up behind her. The cook recovered from her faint and saw the four fish burned like black charcoal. She exclaimed: 'His spear was broken on his very first raid!' and fell unconscious again on the floor. While she was in this confused state, the vizier came and saw that something had gone badly wrong with her, so much so that she could not even tell what day of the week it was. He nudged her with his foot, and when she had recovered her senses, she explained to him, in tears, what had happened. He was astonished, and exclaimed: 'This is something wonderful!' He then sent for the fisherman and, when he was brought in, the vizier told him to fetch another four fish like the first ones.

The fisherman went to the pool, cast his net and when he drew it in, there were four fish like the first. He took them to the vizier, who brought them to the cook and said: 'Fry these in front of me so that I can see what happens.' The cook got up, prepared the fish, put the pan over the fire and threw them into it. As soon as she did, the wall split open and out came the girl, looking as she had done before, with a staff in her hand. She prodded the pan and asked: 'Fish, fish, are you true to your old covenant?' At this, all the fish raised their heads and repeated the lines:

If you return, we return;
If you keep faith, then so do we,
But if you go off, we are quits.

When the fish spoke, the girl overturned the pan with her staff and then left by the way she had come, with the wall closing behind her. At that, the vizier got up and said: 'This is something which must not be kept from the king.' So he went to the king and told him the story, explaining what he had seen for himself. 'I must see this with my own eyes,' said the king, and at that the fisherman was sent for and told to bring another four fish like the others. He went down to the pool with three guards as an escort and brought the fish immediately. The king ordered him to be given four hundred dinars, after which he turned to the vizier and told him: 'Come and cook these fish in my presence.' The vizier did as he was told, brought the pan and, after preparing the fish, he put the pan over the fire and threw them into it. As soon as he did so, the wall split open and out came a black slave, tall as a mountain or like a survivor of the race of 'Ad. In his hand was a green bough and he asked in a hectoring voice: 'Fish, fish, are you true to your old covenant?' The fish raised their heads from the pan and replied: 'Yes, yes, we keep to our covenant.

If you return, we return;
If you keep faith, then so do we,
But if you go off, we are quits.'

The slave came up to the pan, overturned it with the branch that he was holding, and left by the way that he had come. The vizier and the king looked at the fish and saw that they were now like charcoal. The king was amazed and said: 'This is something that cannot be kept quiet and there must be some secret attached to them.' So he gave orders for the fisherman to be summoned and when the man came, the king asked him where the fish came from. 'From a pool surrounded by four mountains,' replied the fisherman, 'and it is under the mountain outside the city.' The king turned and asked: 'How many days' journey is it?' and the fisherman told him that it was half an hour away.

This astonished the king and he ordered his troops to mount and ride immediately, with the fisherman at their head, while the fisherman, in his turn, as he accompanied the king, spent his time cursing the *'ifrit*. The riders climbed up the mountain and then went down into a broad plain that they had never seen before in their lives. Everyone, including the king, was filled with wonder when they looked at it and at the pool in its centre, set as it was between four mountains, with its fish of four colours – red, white, yellow and blue. The king halted in astonishment and asked his soldiers and the others there whether they had ever seen the pool before. 'King of the age,' they replied, 'never in all our lives have we set eyes on it.' The elderly were asked about it, but they too said that they had never before seen the pool there.

The king then swore by God: 'I shall not enter my city or sit on my throne again until I find out the secret of this pool and of these fish.' He gave orders for his men to camp around the mountains, and then summoned his vizier, a learned, wise and sensible man, with a knowledge of affairs. When he came into the king's presence, the king said to him: 'I am going to tell you what I want to do. It has struck me that I should go out alone tonight and investigate the secret of this pool and of these fish. I want you to sit at the entrance of my tent and to tell the emirs, viziers, chamberlains and deputies, as well as everyone who asks about me, that I am unwell and that you have my instructions not to allow anyone to come in to see me. Don't tell anyone what I am planning to do.'

The vizier was in no position to disobey and so the king changed his clothes and strapped on his sword. He climbed down from one of the mountains and walked on for the rest of the night until morning. He spent all the next day walking in the intense heat, and carried on for a second night until morning. At that point, he was pleased to see something black in the distance, and he said to himself: 'Perhaps I shall find someone to tell me about the pool and the fish.' When he went nearer he found a palace made of black stones plated with iron, one leaf of whose gate was open and the other shut. Joyfully he stood by the door and knocked lightly; on hearing no reply, he knocked a second and a third time, and when there was still no answer, he knocked more loudly. When no one answered, he was sure that the palace must be empty and so, plucking up his courage, he went through the gate to the passage that led from it, and called out: 'People of the palace, here is a passing stranger. Have you any food?'

He repeated this a second and a third time, and when there was still no reply, emboldened and heartened, he went through the passage to the centre of the palace. This was furnished with silks, starry tapestries and other hangings, but there was no one there. In the centre was an open space, leading to four halls. There was a stone bench, and one hall next to another, then an ornate fountain and four lions of red gold, from whose mouths water poured, glittering like pearls or gems. Round and about were birds and over the top of the palace there was a net of gold that kept them from flying away, but the king was astonished and saddened that he had not seen anyone whom he could ask about the plain, the pool, the fish, the mountains and the palace.

He was sitting between the doors, sunk in thought, when suddenly he heard a plaintive sound coming from a sorrowful heart, with a voice chanting these lines:

I try to hide what I suffer at your hands, but this is clear,
With my eyes exchanging sleep for sleeplessness.
Time, you neither spare me nor cease your work,
And it is between hardship and danger that my heart lies.
Have you no mercy on one whom love's law has abased,
Or on the wealthy who is now made poor?
I was jealous of the breeze as it blows over you,
But when fate pounces, then men's eyes are blind.
What can the archer do if, as he meets the foe,

His bow-string snaps just when he wants to shoot?
When cares mass to assault a man,
Where can he flee from destiny and fate?

When the king heard this lament, he got up and, following the sound, he found a curtain lowered over the door of a room. He lifted it and behind it he found a handsome young man, well made, eloquent, with a bright face, ruddy cheeks and a mole on his cheek like a disc of amber. He was seated on a couch raised one cubit from the ground and he fitted the poet's description:

There is many a slender one whose dark hair and bright forehead
Have made mankind to walk in dark and light.
Do not find fault with the mole upon his cheek:
I would sell my brother in exchange for such a speck.

The king was glad to see him and greeted him. He, for his part, was sitting there wearing a silk gown embroidered with Egyptian gold, and on his head was a crown studded with gems. He was showing signs of grief, but when the king greeted him, he replied with the utmost courtesy: 'Your dignity deserves that I should rise for you, but I have an excuse for not doing so.' 'I excuse you, young man,' said the king. 'I am your guest and I am also here on an important errand. I want you to tell me about the pool, the fish, this palace, the reason why you are here alone and why you are weeping.'

When the young man heard this, tears coursed down his cheeks and he wept bitterly until his breast was drenched. He then recited:

Say to the one to whom Time grants sleep,
How often misfortunes subside only to rise up!
While you may sleep, God's eye remains sleepless.
For whom is Time unclouded and for whom do worldly things
endure?

He sighed deeply and continued to recite:

Entrust your affair to the Lord of all mankind;
Abandon care and leave aside anxious thoughts.
Do not ask how what happened has occurred,
For all things come about through the decree of fate.

The king, filled with wonder, asked the youth why he was weeping.

'How can I not shed tears,' he replied, 'when I am in this state?' and he reached down to the skirts of his robe and raised it. It could then be seen that the lower half of his body, down to his feet, was of stone, while from his navel to the hair of his head he was human. When he saw this condition of his, the king was filled with grief and regret. He exclaimed in sorrow: 'Young man, you have added another care to my cares! I was looking for information about the fish, but now I see I must ask both about them and about you.' He went on to recite the formula: 'There is no power and no strength except with God, the Exalted, the Omnipotent,' and added: 'Tell me at once what your story is.'

'Listen and look,' said the young man. 'My ears and eyes are ready,' replied the king, and the young man continued: 'There is a marvellous tale attached to the fish and to me, which, were it written with needles on the corners of the eyes, would be a lesson for all who can learn.' 'How is that?' asked the king, AND THE YOUNG MAN REPLIED:

The Story of the Semi-petrified Prince

You must know that my father was the ruler of this city. His name was Mahmud and he was the king of the Black Islands and of these four mountains. He died after a reign of seventy years and I succeeded him on the throne. I married my cousin, who loved me so deeply that, if I left her, she would neither eat nor drink until my return. She stayed with me for five years but then one day she went in the evening to the baths. I told the cook to prepare a quick supper for me and then I came to these apartments and lay down to sleep in our usual place, telling the slave girls to sit, one at my head and one at my feet. I was disturbed because of my wife's absence, and although my eyes were shut, I could not sleep and I was still alert.

It was then that I heard the slave girl who was sitting at my head saying to her companion: 'Mas'uda, how unfortunate our master is and how miserable are the days of his youth! What damage he suffers at the hands of that damned harlot, our mistress!' 'Yes,' answered the other, 'may God curse treacherous adulteresses. A man like our master is too young to satisfy this whore, who every night sleeps outside the palace.' The girl at my head said: 'Our master is dumb and deluded in that he never asks questions about her.' 'Do you think that he knows about her and that she does this with his consent?' exclaimed the other, adding: 'She prepares him a drink that he takes every night before he goes to sleep and in it she puts a sleeping drug. He knows nothing about what happens or where she goes. After she has given him the drink, she puts on her clothes, perfumes herself and goes out, leaving him till dawn. Then she comes back to him and burns something under his nose so that he wakes from his sleep.'

When I heard what the girls were saying, the light became darkness in my eyes, although I could not believe that night had come. Then my wife returned from the baths; our table was spread and we ate, after which we sat for a time talking, as usual. Then she called for my evening drink and when she had given me the cup which she had poured out, I tipped the contents into my pocket, while pretending to be drinking it as usual. I lay down immediately and, pretending to be asleep, I heard her saying: 'Sleep through the night and never get up. By God, I loathe you and I loathe your appearance. I am tired of living with you and I don't know when God is going to take your life.' She then got up, put on her most splendid clothes, perfumed herself and, taking my sword, she strapped it on and went out through the palace gates, while for my part I got up and followed her out. She made her way through the markets until she reached the city gate. She spoke some words that I could not understand, at which the bolts fell and the gate opened.

My wife went out, without realizing that I was following her, and passed between the mounds until she came to a hut with a brick dome. As she went in through its door, I climbed on to the roof and looked down to see her enter and go up to a black slave. One of his lips looked like a pot lid and the other like the sole of a shoe – a lip that could pick up sand from the top of a pebble. The slave was lying on cane stalks; he was leprous and covered in rags and tatters. As my wife kissed the ground before him, he raised his head and said: 'Damn you, why have you been so slow? My black cousins were here drinking, and each left with a girl, but because of you I didn't want to drink.' She said: 'My master, my darling, delight of my eyes, don't you know that I am married to my cousin, whose appearance I hate and whose company I loathe? Were it not that I am afraid for you, I would not let the sun rise before the city had been left desolate, echoing to the screeches of owls and the cawing of crows, the haunt of foxes and wolves, and I would move its stones to behind Mount Qaf.' 'You are lying, damn you,' said the black man. 'I swear by the chivalry of the blacks – and don't think that our chivalry is like that of the whites – that if you are as late as this once more, I will never again keep company with you or join my body to yours. You are playing fast and loose with me. Am I here just to serve your lust, you stinking bitch, vilest of the whites?'

As I looked on and listened to what they were saying, the world turned black for me and I didn't know where I was. My wife was standing weeping, humbling herself before the slave and saying: 'My darling, fruit of my heart, if you are angry with me, who will save me, and if you throw me out, who will shelter me, my darling and light of my eyes?' She went on weeping and imploring him until, to her delight, she managed to conciliate him. She then got up and took off all her clothes. 'My master,' she said, 'is there anything for your servant to eat?' 'Lift the pan cover,' he said. 'There are some cooked rat bones beneath it that you can eat, and you can then go to this jar and drink the remains of the beer there.'

After my wife had eaten and drunk, she washed her hands and her mouth before lying down naked on the cane stalks with the slave, and getting in with him beneath the rags and tatters. When I saw what she had done, I lost control of myself and, climbing down from the top of the roof, I drew the sword that I had brought with me, intending to kill them both. I struck the slave with the intention of cutting off his head but I had failed to sever his jugular and only cut his gullet, skin and flesh. He let out a loud snort and, as my wife stirred, I stepped back, returned the sword to its sheath and went back to the city, where I entered the palace and lay down on my bed until morning. There was my wife coming to wake me, with her hair shorn, wearing mourning. She said: 'Cousin, don't object to what I am doing, as I have had news that my mother has died and that my father has been killed fighting the infidels, while one of my brothers has died of a fatal sting and the other of a fall. It is right for me to weep and grieve.'

When I heard this, I did not tell her what I knew but said: 'Do what you think proper and I shall not oppose you.' From the beginning to the end of a whole year she remained miserable and in mourning, and then she said to me: 'I want you to build me a tomb shaped like a dome beside your palace, which I shall set aside for grief and call the House of Sorrows.' 'Do as you please,' I said, and she built her House of Sorrows, over which was a dome, covering what looked like a tomb. She brought the slave there and installed him in it, but he could no longer be of any service to her. He went on drinking wine, but since the day that I had wounded him he could no longer speak, and he was alive only because his allotted span had not yet come to an end. Every day, morning and evening, my wife would go to the tomb weeping and lamenting for him, and she would give him wine and broth.

Things went on like this until it came to the second year. I had been long-suffering and had paid no attention to her, until one day, when I came to her room unexpectedly, I found her exclaiming tearfully: 'Why are you absent from my sight, my heart's delight? Talk to me, O my soul; speak to me, my darling.' She recited:

If you have found consolation, love has left me no endurance.
My heart loves none but you.
Take my bones and my soul with you wherever you may go,
And where you halt, bury me opposite you.
Call out my name over my grave and my bones will moan in answer,
Hearing the echo of your voice.

Then she went on:

My wishes are fulfilled on the day I am near you,
While the day of my doom is when you turn from me.
I may pass the night in fear, threatened with destruction,
But union with you is sweeter to me than safety.

Next she recited:

If every blessing and all this world were mine,
Together with the empire of the Persian kings,
To me this would not be worth a gnat's wing,
If my eyes could not look on you.

When she had finished speaking and weeping, I said to her: 'Cousin, that is enough of sorrow, and more weeping will do you no good.' 'Do not try to stop me doing what I must do,' she said, 'for in that case, I shall kill myself.' I said no more and left her to do what she wanted, and she went on grieving, weeping and mourning for a second year and then a third. One day, I went to her when something had put me out of temper and I was tired of the violence of her distress. I found her going towards the tomb beneath the dome, saying: 'Master, I hear no word from you. Master, why don't you answer me?' Then she recited:

Grave, grave, have the beloved's beauties faded?
And has the brightness and the radiance gone?
Grave, you are neither earth nor heaven for me,
So how is it you hold both sun and moon?

When I heard what she said and the lines she recited, I became even angrier than before and I exclaimed: 'How long will this sorrow last?' Then I recited myself:

Grave, grave, has his blackness faded?
And has the brightness and the foulness failed?
Grave, you are neither basin nor a pot,
So how is it you hold charcoal and slime?

When she heard this, she jumped up and said: 'Damn you, you dog. It was you who did this to me and wounded my heart's darling. You have caused me pain and robbed him of his youth, so that for three years he has been neither dead nor alive.' To which I replied: 'Dirty whore, filthiest of the fornicators and the prostitutes of black slaves, yes, it was I who did that.' Then I drew my sword and aimed a deadly blow at her, but when she heard what I said and saw that I was intending to kill her, she burst out laughing and said: 'Off, you dog! What is past cannot return and the dead cannot rise again, but God has given the man who did this to me into my power. Because of him there has been an unquenchable fire in my heart and a flame that cannot be hidden.'

Then, as she stood there, she spoke some unintelligible words and added: 'Through my magic become half stone and half man.' It was then that I became as you see me now, unable to stand or to sit, neither dead nor alive. After this, she cast a spell over the whole city, together with its markets and its gardens. It had contained four different groups, Muslims, Christians, Jews and Magians, and these she transformed into fish – the white fish being the Muslims, the red the Magians, the blue the Christians and the yellow the Jews – and she transformed the four islands into four mountains that surround the pool. Every day she tortures me by giving me a hundred lashes with her whip until the blood flows down over my shoulders. Then she dresses me in a hair shirt of the kind that I am wearing on my upper half, over which she places this splendid gown.

The young man then wept and recited:

O my God, I must endure Your judgement and decree,
And if that pleases You, I shall do this.
Tyrants have wronged me and oppressed me here,
But Paradise may be my recompense.

My sufferings have left me in sad straits,
But God's choice as His favoured Prophet intercedes for me.

The king then turned to the youth and said: 'Although you have freed me from one worry, you have added another to my cares. Where is the woman and where is the tomb with the wounded slave?' 'He is lying in his tomb beneath the dome,' said the young man, 'and she is in that chamber opposite the door. She comes out once each day at sunrise, and the first thing she does is to strip me and give me a hundred lashes. I weep and call out but I cannot move to defend myself, and after she has tortured me, she takes wine and broth to the slave. She will come early tomorrow.' 'By God, young man,' said the king, 'I shall do you a service for which I shall be remembered and which will be recorded until the end of time.' He then sat talking to him until nightfall, when they both slept.

Close to dawn the king rose, stripped off his clothes, drew his sword and went to where the slave lay, surrounded by candles, lamps, perfumes and unguents. He came up to the slave and killed him with one blow, before lifting him on to his back and throwing him down a well in the palace. After that, he wrapped himself in the slave's clothes and lay down in the tomb with the naked sword by his side. After an hour, the damned sorceress arrived, but before she entered the tomb, she first stripped her cousin of his clothes, took a whip and beat him. He cried out in pain: 'The state that I am in is punishment enough for me, cousin; have pity on me.' 'Did you have pity on me,' she asked, 'and did you leave me, my beloved?' She beat him until she was tired and the blood flowed down his sides; then she dressed him in a hair shirt under his robe, and went off to carry the slave a cup of wine and a bowl of broth.

At the tomb she wept and wailed, saying: 'Master, speak to me; master, talk to me.' She then recited:

How long will you turn away, treating me roughly?
Have I not shed tears enough for you?
How do you intend abandoning me?
If your object is the envious, their envy has been cured.

Shedding tears, she repeated: 'Master, talk to me.' The king lowered his voice, twisted his tongue, and speaking in the accent of the blacks, he said: 'Oh, oh, there is no might and no power except with God, the Exalted, the Omnipotent!' When she heard this, she cried out with joy and then fainted. When she had recovered, she said: 'Master, is this true?'

The king, in a weak voice, said: 'You damned woman, do you deserve that anyone should talk to you or speak with you?' 'Why is that?' she asked. 'Because all day long you torture your husband, although he cries for help, and from dusk to dawn he stops me from sleeping as he calls out his entreaties, cursing both me and you. He disturbs me and harms me, and but for this I would have been cured. It is this that keeps me from answering you.' 'With your permission,' she replied, 'I shall release him.' 'Do that,' said the king, 'and allow me to rest.' 'I hear and obey,' she replied and, after going from the tomb to the palace, she took a bowl, filled it with water and spoke some words over it. As the water boiled and bubbled, like a pot boiling on the fire, she sprinkled her husband with it and said: 'I conjure you by the words that I have recited, if you are in this state because of my magic, revert from this shape to what you were before.'

A sudden shudder ran through the young man and he rose to his feet, overjoyed at his release, calling out: 'I bear witness that there is no god but God and that Muhammad is the Apostle of God – may God bless him and give him peace.' His wife shouted at him, saying: 'Go, and don't come back, or else I shall kill you!' He left her and she went back to the tomb, where she said: 'Master, come out to me, so that I may see your beautiful form.' In a weak voice the king replied: 'What have you done? You have brought me relief from the branch but not from the root.' 'My beloved, my black darling,' she said, 'what is the root?' 'Curse you, you damned woman!' he replied. 'It is the people of the city and of the four islands. Every night at midnight the fish raise their heads asking for help and cursing me and you. It is this that stops my recovery. Go and free them quickly and then come back, take my hand and help me to get up, for I am on the road to recovery.'

On hearing these words and thinking that he was the slave, the sorceress was delighted and promised in God's Name willingly to obey his command. She got up and ran joyfully to the pool, from which she took a little water and spoke some unintelligible words over it. At this the fish danced, lifted their heads and immediately rose up, as the magic spell was removed from the city. It became inhabited again, the merchants buying and selling and each man practising his craft, while the islands were restored to their former state. The sorceress went straight away to the tomb and said to the king: 'Give me your noble hand, my darling, and get up.' In a low voice, the king replied: 'Come to me.' When she did this he, with the drawn sword in his hand, struck her in the breast as she clung on to him, so that it emerged gleaming from her back. With another blow he cut her in two, and threw the two halves on the ground.

When he came out he found the young man whom she had enchanted standing waiting for him, congratulating him on his escape, kissing his hand and thanking him. The king asked him whether he would prefer to stay in his own city, or to go with him to his. 'King of the age,' said the young man, 'do you know how long a journey it is to your city?' 'Two and a half days,' replied the king. 'If you have been sleeping,' said the young man, 'wake up. Between you and your city is a full year's worth of hard travelling. You only got here in two and a half days because this place was under a spell. But I shall not part from you for the blink of an eye.' The king was glad and said: 'Praise be to God, Who has given you to me. You shall be my son, for all my life I have been granted no other.'

They embraced with great joy and then walked to the palace. Here the young man told his courtiers to make ready for a journey and to collect supplies and whatever was needed. This took ten days, after which the young man and the king set off, the latter being in a fever of anxiety to get back his own city. They travelled with fifty mamluks and magnificent gifts, and their journey continued day and night for a whole year until, as God had decreed their safety, they eventually reached their goal. Word was sent to the vizier that the king had arrived safe and sound, and he, together with his soldiers, who had despaired of him, came to greet him, kissing the ground before him and congratulating him on his safe arrival.

The king then entered the city to take his seat on his throne, and the vizier, on presenting himself and hearing of all that had happened to the young man, added his own congratulations. Then, when things were settled, the king presented gifts to many people and he told the vizier to fetch the man who had brought him the fish and who had been responsible for saving the people of the enchanted city. A messenger was sent to him and when he was brought to the palace, the king presented him with robes of honour and asked him about his circumstances, and whether he had any children. The fisherman replied that he had two daughters and one son. The king sent for them and married one of the girls himself, giving the other to the young man. The fisherman's son was made treasurer, while the vizier was invested and sent off as ruler of the capital of the Black Islands, the young man's city. With him were sent the fifty mamluks who had come with the king, and he was given robes of honour to take to the emirs of the city. He kissed the king's hands and started out immediately, while the king remained with the young man. The fisherman, meanwhile, had become the richest man of his age, while his daughters remained as wives of kings until they died.

[Nights 3–9]

The Porter and the Three Ladies

There was an unmarried porter who lived in the city of Baghdad. One day, while he was standing in the market, leaning on his basket, a woman came up to him wrapped in a silken Mosuli shawl with a floating ribbon and wearing embroidered shoes fringed with gold thread. When she raised her veil, beneath it could be seen dark eyes which, with their eyelashes and eyelids, shot soft glances, perfect in their quality. She turned to the porter and said in a sweet, clear voice: 'Take your basket and follow me.' Almost before he was sure of what she had said, he rushed to pick up the basket. 'What a lucky day, a day of good fortune!' he exclaimed, following her until she stopped by the door of a house. She knocked at it and a Christian came down to whom she gave a dinar, taking in exchange an olive-coloured jar of strained wine. She put this in the basket and said to the porter: 'Pick this up and follow me.' 'By God,' repeated the porter, 'this is a blessed and a fortunate day!' and he did what she told him.

She then stopped at a fruiterer's shop, where she bought Syrian apples, Uthmani quinces, Omani peaches, jasmine and water lilies from Syria, autumn cucumbers, lemons, *sultani* oranges, scented myrtle, privet flowers, camomile blossoms, red anemones, violets, pomegranate blooms and eglantine. All these she put into the porter's basket, telling him to pick it up. This he did and he followed her until she stopped at the butcher's, where she got the man to cut her ten *ratls*' weight of meat. He did this, and after paying him, she wrapped the meat in banana leaves and put it in the basket, giving the porter his instructions. He picked up the basket and followed her to the grocer, from whom she bought pistachio kernels for making a dessert, Tihama raisins and shelled almonds. The porter was told to pick them up and to follow her. Next she stopped at the sweetmeat seller's shop. This time she bought a bowl and filled it with all that he had – sugar cakes, doughnuts stuffed with musk, 'soap' cakes, lemon tarts, Maimuni tarts, 'Zainab's combs', sugar fingers and '*qadis*' snacks'.

Every type of pastry was piled on to a plate and put into the basket, at which the porter exclaimed: 'If you had told me, I'd have brought a donkey with me to carry all this stuff.' The girl smiled and gave him a cuff on the back of the neck. 'Hurry up,' she said. 'Don't talk so much and you will get your reward, if God Almighty wills it.' Then she stopped at the perfume seller's where she bought ten types of scented water – including rosewater, orange-flower water, waters scented with water lilies and with willow flowers – two sugar loaves, a bottle of musk-scented rosewater, a quantity of frankincense, aloes, ambergris, musk and Alexandrian candles. All of these she put in the basket, telling the porter to pick it up and follow her.

He carried his basket and followed her to a handsome house, overlooking a spacious courtyard. It was a tall, pillared building, whose door had two ebony leaves, plated with red gold. The girl halted by the door, raised the veil from her face and knocked lightly, while the porter remained standing behind her, his thoughts occupied with her beauty. The door opened and, as its leaves parted, the porter looked at the person who had opened it. He saw a lady of medium height, with jutting breasts, beautiful, comely, resplendent, with a perfect and well-proportioned figure, a radiant brow, red cheeks and eyes rivalling those of a wild cow or a gazelle. Her eyebrows were like the crescent moon of the month of Sha'ban; she had cheeks like red anemones, a mouth like the seal of Solomon, coral red lips, teeth like camomile blossoms or pearls on a string, and a gazelle-like neck. Her bosom was like an ornate fountain, with breasts like twin pomegranates; she had an elegant belly and a navel that could contain an ounce of unguent. She was as the poet described:

Look at the sun and the moon of the palaces,
At the jewel in her nose and at her flowery splendour.
Your eye has not seen white on black
United in beauty as in her face and in her hair.
She is rosy-cheeked; beauty proclaims her name,
Even if you are not fortunate enough to know of her.
She swayed and I laughed in wonder at her haunches,
But her waist prompted my tears.

As the porter stared at her, he lost his wits and the basket almost fell from his head. 'Never in my life,' he repeated, 'have I known a more blessed day than this!' The girl who had answered the door said to the other, who had brought the provisions: 'Come in and take the basket from this poor porter.' So the two girls went in, followed by the porter, and they went on until they reached a spacious, well-designed and beautiful courtyard, with additional carvings, vaulted chambers and alcoves, and furnished with sofas, wardrobes, cupboards and curtains. In the middle of it was a large pool filled with water on which floated a skiff, and at its upper end was a couch of juniper wood studded with gems over which was suspended a mosquito net of red satin, the buttons of whose fastenings were pearls as big as or bigger than hazelnuts.

From within this emerged a resplendent girl of pleasing beauty, glorious as the moon, with the character of a philosopher. Her eyes were bewitching, with eyebrows like bent bows; her figure was slender and straight as the letter *alif*; her breath had the scent of ambergris; her lips were carnelian red, sweet as sugar; and her face would shame the light of the radiant sun. She was like one of the stars of heaven, a golden dome, an unveiled bride or a noble Bedouin lady, as described by the poet:

It is as though she smiles to show stringed pearls,
Hailstones or flowers of camomile.
The locks of her hair hang black as night,
While her beauty shames the light of dawn.

This third girl rose from the couch and walked slowly to join her sisters in the centre of the hall. 'Why are you standing here?' she said. 'Take the basket from the head of this poor porter.' The provision buyer or housekeeper came first, followed by the doorkeeper, and the third girl helped them to lower the basket, after which they emptied out its contents and put everything in its place. Then they gave the porter two dinars and told him to be off. For his part, he looked at the lovely girls, the most beautiful he had ever seen, with their equally delightful natures. There were no men with them and, as he stared in astonishment at the wine, the fruits, the scented blossoms and all the rest, he was reluctant to leave. 'Why don't you go?' asked the girl. 'Do you think that we didn't pay you enough?' and with that, she turned to her sister and said: 'Give him another dinar.' 'By God, lady,' said the porter, 'it was not that I thought that the payment was too little, for my fee would not come to two dirhams, but you have taken over my heart and soul. How is it that you are alone with no men here and no pleasant companion? You know that there must be four to share a proper feast and women cannot enjoy themselves except with men. As the poet says:

Do you not see that four things join for entertainment –
Harp, lute, zither and pipe,
Matched by four scented flowers –
Rose, myrtle, gillyflower, anemone.
These only become pleasant with another four –
Wine, gardens, a beloved and some gold.

There are three of you and so you need a fourth, who must be a man of intelligence, sensible, clever and one who can keep a secret.'

The three girls were surprised by what the porter said, and they laughed at him and asked: 'Who can produce us a man like that? We are girls and are afraid of entrusting our secrets to someone who would not keep them. We have read in an account what the poet Ibn al-Thumam once said:

Guard your secret as you can, entrusting it to nonc,
For if you do, you will have let it go.
If your own breast cannot contain your secret,
How is it to be held by someone else?

And Abu Nuwas has said:

Whoever lets the people know his secret
Deserves a brand imprinted on his forehead.'

When the porter heard what they said, he exclaimed: 'By God, I am an intelligent and a trustworthy man; I have read books and studied histories; I make public what is good and conceal what is bad. As the poet says:

Only the trustworthy can keep a secret,
And it is with the good that secrets are concealed.
With me they are kept locked inside a room
Whose keys are lost and whose door has been sealed.'

When the girls heard this quotation, they said: 'You know that we have spent a great deal of money on this place. Do you have anything with you which you can use to pay us back? We shall not let you sit with us as our companion and to look on our comely and beautiful faces until you pay down some money. Have you not heard what the author of the proverb said: "Love without cash is worthless"?' The doorkeeper said: 'My dear, if you have something, you are someone, but if you have nothing, then go without anything.' At that point, however, the housekeeper said: 'Sisters, let him be. For, by God, he has not failed us today, whereas someone else might not have put up with us, and whatever debt he may run up, I will settle for him.' The porter was delighted and thanked her, kissing the ground, but the girl who had been on the couch said: 'By God, we shall only let you sit with us on one condition, which is that you ask no questions about what does not concern you, and if you are inquisitive you will be beaten.' 'I agree, lady,' said the porter. 'I swear by my head and my eye, and here I am, a man with no tongue.'

The housekeeper then got up, tucked up her skirts, set out the wine bottles and strained the wine. She set green herbs beside the wine-jar and brought everything that might be needed. She then brought out the wine-jar and sat down with her two sisters, while the porter, sitting between the three of them, thought he must be dreaming. From the wine-jar that she had fetched she filled a cup, drank it, and followed it with a second and a third. Then she filled the cup and passed it to her sister and finally to the porter. She recited:

Drink with pleasure and the enjoyment of good health,
For this wine is a cure for all disease.

The porter took the cup in his hand, bowed, thanked her and recited:

Wine should be drunk beside a trusted friend,
One of pure birth from the line of old heroes.
For wine is like the wind, sweet if it passes scented flowers,
But stinking if it blows over a corpse.

Then he added:

Take wine only from a fawn,
Subtle in meaning when she speaks to you,
Resembling the wine itself.

After he had recited these lines, he kissed the hand of each of the girls. Then he drank until he became tipsy, after which he swayed and recited:

The only blood we are allowed to drink
Is blood that comes from grapes.
So pour this out for me, and may my life
And all I have, both new and old,
Serve to ransom your gazelle-like eyes.

Then the housekeeper took the cup, filled it and gave it to the door-keeper, who took it from him with thanks and drank it. She then filled it for the lady of the house, before pouring another cup and passing it to the porter, who kissed the ground in front of her, thanked her and recited:

> Fetch wine, by God; bring me the brimming glass.
> Pour it for me; this is the water of life.

He then went up to the mistress of the house and said: 'Lady, I am your slave, your mamluk and your servant.' He recited:

> By the door there stands a slave of yours,
> Acknowledging your kindly charity.
> May he come in, fair one, to see your loveliness?
> I swear by love itself I cannot leave.

She replied: 'Enjoy yourself, drink with pleasure and the well-being that follows the path of health.' He took the cup, kissed her hand and chanted:

> I gave her old wine, coloured like her cheeks,
> Unmixed and gleaming like a fiery brand.
> She kissed it and said, laughingly:
> 'How can you pour us people's cheeks?'
> I said: 'Drink: this comes from my tears;
> Its redness is my blood;
> My breath has heated it within the glass.'

She replied with the lines:

> Companion, if you have wept blood for me,
> Pour it obediently for me to drink.

She then took the cup, drank it and sat down with her sister. They continued to drink, with the porter seated between them, and as they drank, they danced, laughed and sang, reciting poems and lyrics. The porter began to play with them, kissing, biting, rubbing, feeling, touching and taking liberties. One of them would give him morsels to eat, another would cuff him and slap him, and the third would bring him scented flowers. With them he was enjoying the pleasantest of times, as though he was seated among the houris of Paradise.

They went on in this way until the wine had taken its effect on their heads and their brains. When it had got the upper hand of them, the doorkeeper stood up, stripped off her clothes until she was naked, and letting down her hair as a veil, she jumped into the pool. She sported in the water, ducking her head and then spitting out the water, after which she took some in her mouth and spat it over the porter. She washed her limbs and between her thighs, after which she came out from the water and threw herself down on his lap. 'My master, my darling, what is the name of this?' she said, pointing to her vagina. 'Your womb,' he replied. 'Oh!' she said. 'Have you no shame?' and she seized him by the neck and started to cuff him. 'Your vagina,' he said, and she cuffed him again on the back of his neck, saying: 'Oh! Oh! How disgusting! Aren't you ashamed?' 'Your vulva,' he replied. 'Do you feel no shame for your honour?' and she struck him a blow with her hand. 'Your hornet,' he said, at which the lady of the house pounced on him and beat him, saying: 'Don't speak like that.'

With every new name that he produced, the girls beat him more and more, until the back of his neck had almost dissolved under their slaps. They were laughing among themselves, until he asked: 'What do you call it, then?' 'The mint of the dykes,' replied the doorkeeper. 'Thank God, I am safe now,' said the porter. 'Good for you, mint of the dykes.' Then the wine was passed round again, and the housekeeper got up, took off her clothes and threw herself on to the porter's lap. 'What is this called, light of my eyes?' she asked, pointing at her private parts. 'Your vagina,' he said. 'Oh, how dirty of you!' she exclaimed, and she struck him a blow that resounded around the hall, adding: 'Oh! Oh! Have you no shame?' 'The mint of the dykes,' he said, but blows and slaps still rained on the back of his neck. He tried another four names, but the girls kept on saying: 'No, no!' 'The mint of the dykes,' he repeated, and they laughed so much that they fell over backwards. Then they fell to beating his neck, saying: 'No, that's not its name.' He said: 'O my sisters, what is it called?' 'Husked sesame,' they said. Then the housekeeper put her clothes back on and they sat, drinking together, with the porter groaning at the pain in his neck and shoulders.

After the wine had been passed round again, the lady of the house, the most beautiful of the three, stood up and stripped off her clothes. The porter grasped the back of his neck with his hand and massaged it, saying: 'My neck and my shoulders are common property.' When the girl was naked, she jumped into the pool, dived under water, played around and washed herself. To the porter in her nakedness she looked like a sliver of the moon, with a face like the full moon when it rises or the dawn when it breaks. He looked at her figure, her breasts and her heavy buttocks as they swayed, while she was naked as her Lord had created her. 'Oh! Oh!' he said, and he recited:

If I compare your figure to a sappy branch,
I load my heart with wrongs and with injustice.
Branches are most beautiful when concealed with leaves,
While you are loveliest when we meet you naked.

On hearing these lines, the girl came out of the pool and sat on the porter's lap. She pointed at her vulva and said: 'Little master, what is the name of this?' 'The mint of the dykes,' he replied, and when she exclaimed in disgust, he tried 'the husked sesame'. 'Bah!' she said. 'Your womb,' he suggested. 'Oh! Oh! Aren't you ashamed?' and she slapped the back of his neck. Whatever name he produced, she slapped him, saying: 'No, no,' until he asked: 'Sisters, what is it called?' 'The *khan* of Abu Mansur,' they replied. 'Praise God that I have reached safety at last,' he said. 'Ho for the *khan* of Abu Mansur!' The girl got up and put on her clothes and they all went back to what they had been doing.

For a time the wine circulated among them and the porter then got up, undressed and went into the pool. The girls looked at him swimming in the water and washing under his beard and beneath his armpits, as they had done. Then he came out and threw himself into the lap of the lady of the house, with his arms in the lap of the doorkeeper and his feet and legs in the lap of the girl who had bought the provisions. Then he pointed to his penis and said: 'Ladies, what is the name of this?' They all laughed at this until they fell over backwards. 'Your *zubb*,' one of them suggested. 'No,' he said, and he bit each of them. 'Your *air*,' they said, but he repeated 'No', and embraced each of them. They went on laughing until they said: 'What is its name, then, brother?' 'Don't you know?' 'No.' 'This is the mule that breaks barriers, browses on the mint of the dykes, eats the husked sesame and that passes the night in the *khan* of Abu Mansur.' The girls laughed until they fell over backwards and then they continued with their drinking party, carrying on until nightfall.

At this point, they told the porter that it was time for him to get up, put on his gaiters and go – 'Show us the width of your shoulders.' 'By God,' said the porter, 'if the breath of life were to leave me, it would be easier for me to bear than having to part from you. Let me link night with day, and in the morning we can all go our separate ways.' The girl who had bought the provisions pleaded with the others: 'Let him sleep here so that we can laugh at him. Who knows whether in all our lives we shall meet someone else like him, both wanton and witty?' They then said: 'You can only spend the night with us on condition that you accept our authority and that you don't ask about anything you see or the reason for it.' The porter agreed to this, and they then told him: 'Get up and read what is written over the door.' He went to the door and there he found written above it in gold leaf: 'Whoever talks about what does not concern him will hear what will not please him.' 'I call you to witness,' he said, 'that I shall not talk about what is no concern of mine.'

The housekeeper got up and prepared a meal for them, which they ate, and then they lit candles and lamps, dipping ambergris and aloes into the candles. They sat drinking and talking of past loves, after having reset the table with fresh fruits and more wine. They continued for a time, eating, drinking, carousing together over their dessert, laughing and teasing each other, when suddenly there was a knock on the door. This did not disrupt the party, however, and one of the girls went by herself to the door and returned to report: 'Our happiness is complete tonight.' 'How is that?' the others asked. She told them: 'At the door are three Persian dervishes, with shaven chins, heads and eyebrows. By a very remarkable coincidence, each of them has lost his left eye. They have only just arrived after a journey; they are showing the signs of travel and this is the first time that they have been to our city, Baghdad. They knocked on our door because they couldn't find a lodging for the night and they had said to themselves: "Perhaps the owner of this house would give us the key to a stable or to a hut in which we could pass the night." For they had been caught out by nightfall, and, being strangers, they had no acquaintance who might give them shelter – and, sisters, each of them is of a ludicrous appearance.'

She continued to persuade and cajole until the others agreed to let the Persians come in on condition that they would not talk about what did not concern them lest they hear what would not please them. The girl went off joyfully and came back with the three one-eyed men, with shaven beards and moustaches. They spoke words of greeting, bowed and hung back. The girls got up to welcome them and, after congratulating them on their safe arrival, told them to be seated.

What the visitors saw was a pleasant and clean room, furnished with greenery, where there were lighted candles, incense rising into the air, dessert, fruits and wine, together with three virgin girls. 'This is good, by God,' they all agreed. Then they turned to the porter and found him cheerfully tired out and drunk. They thought, on seeing him, that he must be one of their own kind and said: 'This is a dervish like us, either a foreigner or an Arab.' Hearing this, the porter glowered at them and said:

'Sit down and don't be inquisitive. Didn't you read what is written over the door? It is not for poor men who arrive like you to let loose your tongues at us.' The newcomers apologized submissively, and the girls laughed and made peace between them and the porter, after which food was produced for the new arrivals, which they ate.

They then sat drinking together, with the doorkeeper pouring the wine and the wine cup circulating among them. The porter then asked the visitors whether they had some story or anecdote to tell. Heated by wine, they, in their turn, asked for musical instruments and were brought a tambourine, a lute and a Persian harp by the doorkeeper. They then got up and tuned the instruments, after which each one took one of them, struck a note and began to sing. The girls added a shrill accompaniment and the noise rose. Then, while this was going on, there was a knock at the door and the doorkeeper got up to see what was going on.

The reason for this knocking was that the caliph Harun al-Rashid was in the habit of going around disguised as a merchant and he had come down from his palace that night on an excursion to listen to the latest news, accompanied by his vizier, Ja'far, and Masrur, his executioner. On his way through the city, he and his companions had happened to pass that house, where they heard music and singing. He had said to Ja'far: 'I want to go in here so that we may listen to these voices and see their owners.' Ja'far had replied: 'Commander of the Faithful, these people are drunk and I am afraid that they may do us some harm.' The caliph had then said: 'I must enter and I want you to think of some scheme to get us in.' 'To hear is to obey,' Ja'far had replied, before going up and knocking on the door. When it was opened by the doorkeeper, Ja'far advanced and kissed the ground. 'Lady,' he said, 'we are traders from Tiberias who have been in Baghdad for ten days. We have sold our goods and are staying at the merchants' *khan*, but this evening we were invited out by a colleague. We went to his house and, after he had given us a meal, we sat drinking with him for a time, but when he let us go night had fallen and, as we are strangers here, we could not find our way back to our hostel. Of your charity, and may God reward you, would you let us come in and spend the night with you?'

The girl looked at them and saw that they were dressed as merchants and appeared to be respectable people. So she went back to her sisters and passed on Ja'far's message. The others sympathized with the visitors' plight and told her: 'Let them in,' after which she went back and opened the door. The caliph, Ja'far and Masrur came in and when the girls saw them, they stood up, seated their visitors and ministered to their needs, saying: 'Welcome to our guests, but we lay a condition on you.' 'What is that?' they asked. 'That you do not speak of what does not concern you, lest you hear what will not please you.' 'We agree,' they replied, and they sat down to drink together.

Looking at the three dervishes, the caliph was surprised to find that each of them had lost his left eye. He was also thrown into confusion by the beauty and grace of the girls, which prompted his admiration. They began to drink together and to talk, but when the girls invited the caliph to drink, he said: 'I am proposing to go on the pilgrimage to Mecca.' The doorkeeper then got up and brought him an embroidered table cloth on which she set a china jar in which she poured willow-flower water, adding some snow and a sugar lump. The caliph thanked her and said to himself: 'By God, I shall reward her tomorrow for the good that she has done me.'

Then they all occupied themselves with drinking, and when the drink had gained the upper hand, the lady of the house got up, bowed to the company and then, taking the housekeeper by the hand, she said: 'Sisters, come, we must settle our debt.' 'Yes,' agreed the other two girls, and at that, the doorkeeper got up in front of them and first cleared the table, removed the debris, replaced the perfumes and cleared a space in the middle of the room. The dervishes were made to sit on a bench on one side of the room and the caliph, Ja'far and Masrur on a bench on the other side. Then the lady of the house called to the porter: 'Your friendship does not amount to much. You are not a stranger, but one of the household.' The porter got up, tightened his belt and asked: 'What do you want?' 'Stay where you are,' she said. Then the housekeeper stood up and set a chair in the middle of the room, opened a cupboard and said to the porter: 'Come and help me.'

In the cupboard he saw two black bitches, with chains around their necks. 'Take them,' said the girl, and he took them and brought them to the centre of the room. Then the lady of the house got up, rolled back her sleeves and took up a whip. 'Bring one of them,' she told the porter, and he did this, pulling the bitch by its chain, as it whimpered and shook its head at the girl. It howled as she struck it on the head, and she continued to beat it until her arms were tired. She then threw away the whip, pressed the bitch to her breast and wiped away its tears with her hand, kissing its head. Then she said to the porter: 'Take this one away and bring the other.' This he did and she treated the second bitch in the same way as the first.

The caliph was concerned and troubled by this. Unable to contain his curiosity about the story of the two bitches, he winked at Ja'far, but the latter turned to him and gestured to him to remain silent. Then the lady of the house turned to the doorkeeper and said: 'Get up and do your duty.' 'Yes,' she replied and, getting up, she went to the couch, which was made of juniper wood with panels of gold and silver. Then the lady of the house said to the other two girls: 'Bring out what you have.' The doorkeeper sat on a chair by her side, while the housekeeper went into a closet and came out with a satin bag with green fringes and two golden discs. She stood in front of the lady of the house, unfastened the bag and took from it a lute whose strings she tuned and whose pegs she tightened, until it was all in order. Then she recited:

You are the object of my whole desire;
Union with you, beloved, is unending bliss,
While absence from you is like fire.
You madden me, and throughout time
In you is centred the infatuation of my love.
It brings me no disgrace that I love you.
The veils that cover me are torn away by love,
And love continues shamefully to rend all veils.
I clothe myself in sickness; my excuse is clear.
For through my love, you lead my heart astray.
Flowing tears serve to bring my secret out and make it plain.
The tearful flood reveals it, and they try
To cure the violence of this sickness, but it is you
Who are for me both the disease and its cure.
For those whose cure you are, the pains last long.
I pine away through the light shed by your eyes,
And it is my own love whose sword kills me,
A sword that has destroyed many good men.
Love has no end for me nor can I turn to consolation.
Love is my medicine and my code of law;
Secretly and openly it serves to adorn me.
You bring good fortune to the eye that looks
Its fill on you, or manages a glance.
Yes, and its choice of love distracts my heart.

When the lady of the house heard these lines, she cried: 'Oh! Oh! Oh!', tore her clothes and fell to the ground in a faint. The caliph was astonished to see weals caused by the blows of a whip on her body, but then the doorkeeper got up, sprinkled water over her and clothed her in a splendid dress that she had fetched for her sister. When they saw that, all the men present were disturbed, as they had no idea what lay behind it. The caliph said to Ja'far: 'Don't you see this girl and the marks of a beating that she shows? I can't keep quiet without knowing the truth of the matter and without finding out about this girl and the two black bitches.' Ja'far replied: 'Master, they made it a condition that we should not talk about what did not concern us, lest we hear what we do not like.'

At this point, the doorkeeper said: 'Sister, keep your promise and come to me.' 'Willingly,' said the housekeeper, and she took the lute, cradled it to her breasts, touched it with her fingers and recited:

If I complain of the beloved's absence, what am I to say?
Where can I go to reach what I desire?
I might send messengers to explain my love,
But this complaint no messenger can carry.
I may endure, but after he has lost
His love, the lover's life is short.
Nothing remains but sorrow and then grief,
With tears that flood the cheeks.
You may be absent from my sight but you have still
A settled habitation in my heart.
I wonder, do you know our covenant?
Like flowing water, it does not stay long.
Have you forgotten that you loved a slave,
Who finds his cure in tears and wasted flesh?
Ah, if this love unites us once again,
I have a long complaint to make to you.

When the doorkeeper heard this second poem, she cried out and said: 'That is good, by God.' Then she put her hand to her clothes and tore them, as the first girl had done, and fell to the ground in a faint. The housekeeper got up and, after sprinkling her with water, clothed her in a new dress. The doorkeeper then rose and took her seat before saying: 'Give me more and pay off the debt you owe me.' So the housekeeper brought her lute and recited:

How long will you so roughly turn from me?
Have I not poured out tears enough?

How long do you plan to abandon me?
If this is thanks to those who envy me,
Their envy has been cured.
Were treacherous Time to treat a lover fairly,
He would not pass the night wakeful and wasted by your love.
Treat me with gentleness; your harshness injures me.
My sovereign, is it not time for mercy to be shown?
To whom shall I tell of my love, you who kill me?
How disappointed are the hopes of the one who complains,
When faithfulness is in such short supply!
My passion for you and my tears increase,
While the successive days you shun me are drawn out.
Muslims, revenge the lovesick, sleepless man,
The pasture of whose patience has scant grass.
Does love's code permit you, you who are my desire,
To keep me at a distance while another one
Is honoured by your union? What delight or ease
Can the lover find through nearness to his love,
Who tries to see that he is weighted down by care?

When the doorkeeper heard this poem, she put her hand on her dress and ripped it down to the bottom. She then fell fainting to the ground, showing marks of a beating. The dervishes said: 'It would have been better to have slept on a dunghill rather than to have come into this house, where our stay has been clouded by something that cuts at the heart.' 'Why is that?' asked the caliph, turning to them. 'This affair has distressed us,' they replied. 'Do you not belong to this household?' he asked. 'No,' they replied. 'We have never seen the place before.' The caliph was surprised and said, gesturing at the porter: 'This man with you may know about them.' When they asked him, however, he said: 'By Almighty God, love makes us all equal. I have grown up in Baghdad but this is the only time in my life that I ever entered this house and how I came to be here with these girls is a remarkable story.'

The others said: 'By God, we thought that you were one of them, but now we see that you are like us.' The caliph then pointed out: 'We are seven men and they are three women. There is no fourth. So ask them about themselves, and if they don't reply willingly, we will force them to do so.' Everyone agreed except for Ja'far, who said: 'Let them be; we are their guests and they made a condition which we accepted, as you know.

It would be best to let the matter rest, for there is only a little of the night left and we can then go on our ways.' He winked at the caliph and added: 'There is only an hour left and tomorrow we can summon them to your court and ask for their story.' The caliph raised his head and shouted angrily: 'I cannot bear to wait to hear about them; let the dervishes question them.' 'I don't agree,' said Ja'far, and the two of them discussed and argued about who should ask the questions until they both agreed that it should be the porter.

The lady of the house asked what the noise was about and the porter got up and said to her: 'My lady, these people would like you to tell them the story of the two bitches and how you come to beat them and then to weep and kiss them. They also want to know about your sister and why she has been beaten with rods like a man. These are their questions to you.' 'Is it true what he says about you?' the lady of the house asked the guests, and all of them said yes, except for Ja'far, who stayed silent. When the lady heard this, she told them: 'By God, you have done us a great wrong. We started by making it a condition that if any of you talked about what did not concern him, he would hear what would not please him. Wasn't it enough for you that we took you into our house and shared our food with you? But the fault is not so much yours as that of the one who brought you in to us.'

Then she rolled her sleeve back above the wrist and struck the floor three times, saying: 'Hurry.' At this, the door of a closet opened and out came seven black slaves, with drawn swords in their hands. 'Tie up these men who talk too much,' she said, 'and bind them one to the other.' This the slaves did, after which they said: 'Lady, give us the order to cut off their heads.' She replied: 'Let them have some time so that I may ask them about their circumstances before their heads are cut off.' 'God save me,' said the porter. 'Don't kill me, lady, for someone else's fault. All the rest have done wrong and have committed a fault except me. By God, it would have been a pleasant night had we been saved from these dervishes who entered a prosperous city and then ruined it.' He recited:

How good it is when a powerful man forgives,
Particularly when those forgiven have no helper.
By the sanctity of the love we share,
Do not spoil what came first by what then follows it.

When the porter had finished reciting these lines, the girl laughed in spite of her anger. She then went up to the men and said: 'Tell me about yourselves, for you have no more than one hour to live, and were you not people of rank, leaders or governors among your peoples, you would not have been so daring.' 'Damn you, Ja'far,' the caliph said. 'Tell her about us or else we shall be killed by mistake, and speak softly to her before we become victims of misfortune.' 'That is part of what you deserve,' replied Ja'far, but the caliph shouted at him: 'There is a time for joking, but now is when we must be serious.' The lady then went to the dervishes and asked them whether they were brothers. 'No, by God,' they said, 'we are only *faqirs* and foreigners.' She next asked one of them whether he had been born one-eyed. 'No, by God,' he said, 'but I have a strange and wonderful story about the loss of my eye, which, were it written with needles on the inner corners of the eyeballs, would serve as a warning to those who take heed.' The second and the third dervish, when asked, made the same reply, and they then said: 'By God, lady, each of us comes from a different country and each is the son of a king and is a ruler over lands and subjects.'

She turned to them and said: 'Each of you is to tell his story and explain why he came here and he can then touch his forelock and go on his way.' The first to come forward was the porter, who said: 'Lady, I am a porter and this girl, who bought you your provisions, told me to carry them from the wine seller to the fruiterer, from the fruiterer to the butcher, from the butcher to the grocer, from the grocer to the sweetmeat seller and the perfumer, and then here. You know what happened to me with you. This is my story, and that's all there is.' The girl laughed and said: 'Touch your forelock and go.' 'By God,' he said, 'I am not going to leave until I have heard the stories of my companions.' THE FIRST DERVISH THEN CAME FORWARD AND SAID:

The Story of the First Dervish

Lady, know that the reason why my chin is shaven and my eye has been plucked out is that my father was a king, who had a brother, also a king, who reigned in another city. His son and I were born on the same day. Years later, when we had grown up, I had got into the habit of visiting my uncle every so often, and I would stay with him for some months. My cousin treated me with the greatest generosity, and would kill sheep for me and pour out wine that he strained for me. Once, when we were sitting drinking and were both under the influence of the wine, he said to me:

'Cousin, there is something that I need from you. Please don't refuse to do what I want.' 'I shall obey you with pleasure,' I said. After binding me with the most solemn of oaths, he got up straight away and left for a short while. Back he came then with a lady, veiled, perfumed and wearing the most expensive of clothes, who stood behind him as he turned to me and said: 'Take this woman and go ahead of me to such-and-such a cemetery' – a place that I recognized from his description. 'Take her to the burial enclosure and wait for me there.'

Because of the oath that I had sworn, I could not disobey him or refuse his request and so I went off with the woman and we both went into the enclosure. While we were sitting there, my cousin arrived with a bowl of water, a bag containing plaster, and a carpenter's axe. Taking this axe, he went to a tomb in the middle of the enclosure and started to open it up, moving its stones to one side. Then he used the axe to prod about in the soil of the tomb until he uncovered an iron cover the size of a small door. He raised this, revealing beneath it a vaulted staircase. Turning to the woman, he said: 'Now you can do what you have chosen to do,' at which she went down the stairs. My cousin then looked at me and said: 'In order to complete the favour that you are doing me, when I go down there myself, I ask you to put back the cover and to replace the soil on top of it as it was before. Use the mortar that is in this bag and the water in the bowl to make a paste and coat the circle of the stones in the enclosure so that it looks as it did before, without anyone being able to say: "The inner part is old but there is a new opening here." I have been working on this for a full year and no one but God knows what I have been doing. This is what I need from you.' He then took his leave of me, wishing me well, and went down the stairs. When he was out of sight, I got up and replaced the cover and followed his instructions, so that the place looked just as it had before.

I then went back like a drunken man to the palace of my uncle, who was away hunting. In the morning, after a night's sleep, I thought of what had happened to my cousin the evening before and, when repentance was of no use, I repented of what I had done and of how I had obeyed him. Thinking that it might have been a dream, I started to ask after my cousin, but nobody could tell me where he was. I went out to the cemetery, looking for the enclosure, but I could not find it. I kept on going round enclosure after enclosure and grave after grave until nightfall, but I still failed in my search. I returned to the palace, but I could neither eat nor drink, for my thoughts were taken up with my cousin, as I did not know how he was, and I was intensely distressed. I passed a troubled night until morning came, when I went for a second time to the cemetery, thinking over what my cousin had done and regretting that I had listened to him. I went round all the enclosures but, to my regret, I still could not find the right one or recognize the grave.

For seven days I went on with my fruitless quest, and my misgivings increased until I was almost driven mad. The only relief I could find was to leave and go back to my father, but as soon as I reached the gate of his city, I was attacked by a group of men who tied me up. I was astonished, seeing that I was the son of the city's ruler and they were my father's servants, and in my alarm I said to myself: 'What can have happened to my father?' I asked my captors why they were doing this. At first they did not answer, but after a time one of them, who had been a servant of mine, said: 'Your father has fallen victim to the treachery of Time. The army conspired against him and he was killed by the vizier, who has taken his place. It was on his orders that we were watching out for you.'

I was stunned by what I heard about my father and fearful because I had a long-standing quarrel with the vizier, before whom my captors now brought me. I had been passionately fond of shooting with a pellet bow and the quarrel arose from this. One day when I was standing on the roof of my palace, a bird settled on the roof of the palace of the vizier. I intended to shoot it, but the pellet missed and, as had been decreed by fate, it struck out the eye of the vizier. This was like the proverb expressed in the old lines:

We walked with a pace that was decreed for us,
And this is how those under fate's control must walk.
A man destined to die in a certain land
Will not find death in any other.

When the vizier lost his eye, he could not say anything because my father was the king of the city, and this was why he was my enemy. When I now stood before him with my hands tied, he ordered my head to be cut off. 'For what crime do you kill me?' I asked. 'What crime is greater than this?' he replied, pointing to his missing eye [sic]. 'I did that by accident,' I protested. 'If you did it by accident,' he replied, 'I am doing this deliberately.' Then he said: 'Bring him forward.' The guards brought me up in front of him, and sticking his finger into my right eye, the vizier plucked it out, leaving me from that time on one-eyed, as you can see. Then he had me tied up and put in a box, telling the executioner: 'Take charge of him; draw your sword and when you have brought him outside the city, kill him and let the birds and beasts eat him.'

The executioner took me out of the city to the middle of the desert and then he removed me from the box, bound as I was, hand and foot. He was about to bandage my eyes before going on to kill me, but I wept so bitterly that I moved him to tears. Then, looking at him, I recited:

I thought of you as a strong coat of mail
To guard me from the arrows of my foes,
But you are now the arrow head.
I pinned my hopes on you in all calamities
When my right hand could no longer aid my left.
Leave aside what censurers say,
And let my enemies shoot their darts at me.
If you do not protect me from my foes,
At least your silence neither hurts me nor helps them.

There are also other lines:

I thought my brothers were a coat of mail;
They were, but this was for the enemy.
I thought of them as deadly shafts;
They were, but their points pierced my heart.

The executioner had been in my father's service and I had done him favours, so when he heard these lines, he said: 'Master, what can I do? I am a slave under command.' But then he added: 'Keep your life, but don't come back to this land or else you will be killed and you will destroy me, together with yourself. As one of the poets has said:

If you should meet injustice, save your life
And let the house lament its builder.
You can replace the country that you leave,
But there is no replacement for your life.
I wonder at those who live humiliated
When God's earth is so wide.
Send out no messenger on any grave affair,
For only you yourself will give you good advice.
The necks of lions would not be so thick
Were others present to look after them.'

I kissed his hands, scarcely believing that I had escaped death, in comparison with which I found the loss of my eye insignificant. So I travelled to my uncle's city and, after presenting myself to him, I told him what had happened to my father, as well as how I had come to lose my eye. He burst into tears and said: 'You have added to my cares and my sorrows. For your cousin disappeared days ago and I don't know what has happened to him, nor can anyone bring me news.' He continued to weep until he fainted and I was bitterly sorry for him. He then wanted to apply some medicaments to my eye, but when he saw that it was like an empty walnut shell, he said: 'Better to lose your eye, my boy, than to lose your life.'

At that, I could no longer stay silent about the affair of my cousin, his son, and so I told him all that had happened. When he heard my news, he was delighted and told me to come and show him the enclosure. 'By God, uncle,' I said, 'I don't know where it is. I went back a number of times after that and searched, but I couldn't find the place.' Then, however, he and I went to the cemetery and, after looking right and left, to our great joy I recognized the place. The two of us went into the enclosure and, after removing the earth, we lifted the cover. We climbed down fifty steps and when we had reached the bottom, we were met by blinding smoke. 'There is no might and no power except with God, the Exalted, the Omnipotent,' exclaimed my uncle – words that can never put to shame anyone who speaks them. We walked on and found ourselves in a hall filled with flour, grain, eatables and so on, and there in the middle of it we saw a curtain hanging down over a couch. My uncle looked and found his son and the woman who had gone down with him locked in an embrace, but they had become black charcoal, as though they had been thrown into a pit of fire.

On seeing this, my uncle spat in his son's face and said: 'You deserve this, you pig. This is your punishment in this world, but there remains the punishment of the next world, which will be harsher and stronger.' My uncle then struck his son with his shoe, as he lay there, burned black as charcoal. This astonished me and I was filled with grief for my cousin and at the fate that had overtaken him and the girl. 'By God, uncle,' I said, 'remove rancour from your heart. My heart and mind are filled with concern; I am saddened by what has happened to my cousin, and by the fact that he and this girl have been left like charcoal. Is their fate not enough for you that you strike your son with your shoe?' He said: 'Nephew, from his earliest days this son of mine was passionately in love with his sister. I used to keep him away from her and I would tell myself: "They are only children," but when they grew up they committed a foul sin. I heard of this and, although I did not believe it, I seized him and reproached him bitterly, saying: "Beware of doing what no one has done before you or will do after you and which will remain as a source of disgrace and disparagement among the kings until the end of time, as the news is carried by the caravans. Take care not to act like this or else I shall be angry with you and kill you."

'I kept him away from her and kept her from him, but the damned girl was deeply in love with him and Satan got the upper hand and made their actions seem good to them. When my son saw that I was keeping him from his sister, he constructed this underground chamber, set it in order and provisioned it, as you see. Then, taking me unawares when I had gone out hunting, he came here, but the Righteous God was jealous of them and consumed them both with fire, while their punishment in the next world will be harsher and stronger.'

He then wept and I wept with him, and he looked at me and said: 'You are my son in his place.' I thought for a time about this world and its happenings and of how my father had been killed by his vizier, who had then taken his place and who had plucked out my eye, and I thought of the strange fate of my cousin. I wept and my uncle wept with me. Then we climbed back up and replaced the cover and the earth and restored the tomb as it had been, after which we returned to the palace. Before we had sat down, however, we heard the noise of drums, kettle-drums and trumpets, the clatter of lances, the shouting of men, the clink of bridles and the neighing of horses. The sky was darkened by sand and dust kicked up by horses' hooves and we were bewildered, not knowing what had happened. When we asked, we were told that the vizier who had taken my father's kingdom had fitted out his troops, collected men, hired Bedouin, and come with an army like the sands that could not be numbered and which no one could withstand. They had made a surprise attack on the city, which had proved unable to resist and which had surrendered to them.

After this, my uncle was killed and I fled to the edge of the city, saying to myself: 'If I fall into this man's hands, he will kill me.' Fresh sorrows were piled on me; I remembered what had happened to my father and to my uncle and I wondered what to do, for if I showed myself, the townspeople and my father's men would recognize me and I would be killed. The only way of escape that I could find was to shave off my beard and my moustache, which I did, and after that I changed my clothes and went out of the city. I then came here, hoping that someone might take me to the Commander of the Faithful, the caliph of the Lord of creation, so that I might talk to him and tell him the story of what had happened to me. I got here tonight and was at a loss to know where to go when I came to where this dervish was standing. I greeted him and told him that I was a stranger, at which he said: 'I too am a stranger.' While we were talking, our third companion here came up to us and greeted us, introducing himself as a stranger, to which we made the same reply. We then walked on as darkness fell and fate led us to you. This is the story of why my beard and moustache have been shaved and of how I lost my eye.

The lady said: 'Touch your forelock and go.' 'Not before I hear someone else's tale,' the man replied. The others wondered at his story and the caliph said to Ja'far: 'By God, I have never seen or heard the like of what has happened to this dervish.' The second dervish then came forward and kissed the ground. HE SAID:

The Story of the Second Dervish

Lady, I was not born one-eyed and my story is a marvellous one which, were it written with needles on the inner corners of the eyes of men, would serve as a warning to those who take heed. I was a king, the son of a king. I studied the seven readings of the Quran; I read books and discussed them with men of learning; I studied astronomy, poetry and all other branches of knowledge until I surpassed all the people of my time, while my calligraphy was unrivalled. My fame spread through all lands and among all kings. So it was that the king of India heard of me and he sent a messenger to my father, together with gifts and presents suitable for royalty, to ask for me. My father equipped me with six ships and after a full month's voyage we came to land.

We unloaded the horses that we had taken on board with us and we loaded ten camels with presents, but we had only travelled a short way when suddenly we saw a dust cloud which rose and spread until it filled the sky. After a while, it cleared away to show beneath it fifty mail-clad horsemen like scowling lions, and on closer inspection we could see that they were Bedouin highwaymen. When they saw our small numbers, and that we had ten camels laden with gifts for the king of India, they rushed at us with levelled lances. We gestured to them with our fingers and said:

'We are envoys on our way to the great king of India, so do not harm us.' 'We don't live in his country,' they told us, 'and are no subjects of his.' Then they killed some of my servants, while the rest took flight. I was badly wounded and I too fled, but the Bedouin did not pursue me, being too busy sorting through the money and the gifts that we had brought with us.

Having been cast down from my position of power, I went off with no notion of where I was going, and I carried on until I reached the top of a mountain, where I took refuge in a cave until daybreak. I continued travelling like this until I came to a strong and secure city, from which cold winter had retreated, while spring had come with its roses. Flowers were blooming; there were gushing streams and the birds were singing. It fitted the description of the poet:

A place whose citizens are subject to no fear,
And safety is the master there.
For its people it is a decorated shield,
Its wonders being plain to see.

As I was tired out with walking and pale with care, I was glad to get there. With my changed circumstances, I had no idea where to go. Passing by a tailor in his shop, I greeted him and he returned my greeting and welcomed me with cheerful friendliness. When he asked me why I had left my own country, I told him what had happened to me from beginning to end. He was sorry for me and said: 'Young man, don't tell anyone about yourself, as I am afraid lest the king of this city might do you some harm as he is one of your father's greatest enemies and has a blood feud with him.' He then produced food and drink and he and I ate together. I chatted with him that night and he gave me a place to myself at the side of his shop and fetched me what I needed in the way of bedding and blankets.

I stayed with him for three days, and he then asked: 'Do you know any craft by which to make your living?' I told him: 'I am a lawyer, a scientist, a scribe, a mathematician and a calligrapher.' 'There is no market for that kind of thing here,' he replied. 'No one in this city has any knowledge of science or of writing and their only concern is making money.' 'By God,' I said, 'I know nothing apart from what I have told you.' He said: 'Tighten your belt, take an axe and a rope and bring in firewood from the countryside. This will give you a livelihood until God brings you relief, but don't let people know who you are or else you will be killed.' He then brought me an axe and a rope and handed me over to some woodcutters, telling them to look after me. I went out with them and collected wood for a whole day, after which I carried back a load on my head and sold it for half a dinar. With part of this I bought food and the rest I saved.

I went on like this for a year, and then when the year was up, I came out to the countryside one day, as usual, and as I was wandering there alone I found a tree-filled hollow where there was wood aplenty. Going down into the hollow, I came across a thick tree stump and dug round it, removing the soil. My axe then happened to strike against a copper ring and, on clearing away the earth, I discovered a wooden trapdoor, which I opened. Below it appeared a flight of steps, and when I reached the bottom of these, I saw a door, on entering which I saw a most beautiful palace set with pillars. In it I found a girl like a splendid pearl, one to banish from the heart all trace of care, sorrow and distress, while her words would dispel worries and would leave a man, however intelligent and sensible, robbed of his senses. She was of medium height, with rounded breasts and soft cheeks; she was radiant and beautifully formed, with a face shining in the black night of her hair, while the gleam of her mouth was reflected on her breast. She was as the poet said:

Dark-haired and slim-waisted,
Her buttocks were like sand dunes
And her figure like that of a *ban* tree.

There are other lines

There are four things never before united
Except to pierce my heart and shed my blood:
A radiant forehead, hair like night,
A rosy cheek, and a slim form.

When I looked at her, I praised the Creator for the beauty and loveliness that He had produced in her. She looked at me in turn and asked: 'What are you, a human or one of the *jinn*?' 'A human,' I told her, and she asked: 'Who brought you to this place where I have been for twenty-five years without ever seeing a fellow human?' I found her speech so sweet that it filled my heart, and I said, 'It was my lucky stars that brought me here, my lady, to drive away my cares and sorrows.' Then I told her from beginning to end what had happened to me and she found my plight hard to bear and wept. 'I, for my part,' she said, 'will now tell you my own story. You must know that I am the daughter of King Iftamus, lord of the

Ebony Islands. He had given me in marriage to my cousin, but on my wedding night I was snatched away by an *'ifrit* named Jirjis, son of Rajmus, the son of the maternal aunt of Iblis. He flew off with me and brought me down into this place, where he fetched everything that was needed – clothes, ornaments, fabrics, furniture, food, drink and everything else. He comes once every ten days, sleeps here for the night and then goes on his way, as he took me without the permission of his own people. He has promised me that if I need anything night or day, and if I touch with my hand these two lines inscribed on the inside of this dome, before I take my hand away he shall appear before me. Today is the fourth day since he was here, and so there are six left until he comes again. Would you like to stay with me for five days and you can then leave one day before he returns?' 'Yes,' I replied. 'How splendid it is when dreams come true!'

This made her glad and, rising to her feet, she took me by the hand and led me through an arched door to a fine, elegant bath. When I saw this, I took off my clothes and she took off hers. After bathing, she stepped out and sat on a bench with me by her side. Then she poured me out wine flavoured with musk and brought food. We ate and talked, until she said: 'Sleep, rest, for you are tired.' Forgetting all my troubles, I thanked her and fell asleep. When I woke, I found her massaging my feet. 'God bless you,' I said and we sat there talking for a time. 'By God,' she said, 'I was unhappy, living by myself under the ground, with no one to talk to me for twenty-five years. Praise be to God, Who has sent you to me.' Then she asked me whether I would like some wine, and when I said yes, she went to a cupboard and produced old wine in a sealed flask. She then set out some green branches, took the wine and recited:

Had I known you were coming, I would have spread
My heart's blood or the pupils of my eyes.
My cheeks would have been a carpet when we met
So that you could have walked over my eyelids.

When she had finished these lines, I thanked her; love of her had taken possession of my heart and my cares and sorrows were gone. We sat drinking together until nightfall, and I then passed with her a night the like of which I had never known in my life. When morning came we were still joining delights to delights, and this went on until midday. I was so drunk that I had lost my senses and I got up, swaying right and left, and I said: 'Get up, my beauty, and I will bring you out from under the earth and free you from this *'ifrit*.' She laughed and said: 'Be content with what you have and stay silent. Out of every ten days he will have one and nine will be for you.' But drunkenness had got the better of me and I said: 'I shall now smash the dome with the inscription; let him come, so that I may kill him, for I am accustomed to killing *'ifrits*.' On hearing this, she turned pale and exclaimed: 'By God, don't do it!' Then she recited:

> If there is something that will destroy you,
> Protect yourself from it.

She added more lines:

> You look for separation, but rein in
> The horse that seeks to head the field.
> Patience, for Time's nature is treacherous,
> And at the end companions part.

She finished her poem but, paying no attention to her words of warning, I aimed a violent kick at the dome. As soon as I had delivered my violent kick, it grew dark; there was thunder and lightning; the earth shook and everything went black. My head cleared immediately and I asked the girl: 'What has happened?' 'The *'ifrit* has come,' she said. 'Didn't I warn you? By God, you have brought harm on me, but save yourself and escape by the way that you came.' I was so terrified that I forgot my shoes and my axe. Then, when I had climbed up two steps, I turned to look back and I caught sight of a cleft appearing in the earth from which emerged a hideous *'ifrit*. 'Why did you disturb me?' he asked the girl. 'And what has happened to you?' 'Nothing has happened to me,' she said, 'but I was feeling depressed and I wanted to cheer myself by having a drink. So I drank a little, and then I was about to relieve myself, but my head was heavy and I fell against the dome.' 'Whore, you are lying,' said the *'ifrit*, and he looked through the palace, right and left, and caught sight of the shoes and the axe. 'These must belong to a man!' he exclaimed. 'Who was it who came to you?' 'I have only just seen these things,' she said. 'You must have brought them with you.' 'Nonsense; that doesn't deceive me, you harlot!' he cried.

Then he stripped her naked and stretched her out, fastening her to four pegs. He started to beat her to force her to confess, and as I could not bear to listen to her weeping, I climbed up the staircase, trembling with fear, and when I got to the top I put the trapdoor back in its place and covered it with earth. I bitterly repented what I had done, and I remembered how beautiful the girl was and how this damned *'ifrit* was torturing her, how she had been there for twenty-five years and what had happened to her because of me. I also thought about my father and his kingdom, and how I had become a woodcutter, and how my cloudless days had darkened. I then recited:

If one day Time afflicts you with disaster,
Ease and hardship come each in turn.

I walked away and returned to my friend the tailor, whom I found waiting for me in a fever of anxiety. 'My heart was with you all last night,' he said, 'and I was afraid lest you had fallen victim to a wild beast or something else, but praise be to God that you are safe.' I thanked him for his concern and entered my own quarters, where I started to think over what had happened to me, blaming myself for the impulsiveness that had led me to kick the dome. While I was thinking this over, the tailor came in to tell me that outside there was a Persian *shaikh* looking for me, who had with him my axe and my shoes. He had taken them to the woodcutters and had told them that, at the call of the muezzin, he had gone out to perform the dawn prayer and had found the shoes when he had got back. As he did not know whose they were, he asked about their owner. 'The woodcutters recognized your axe,' said the tailor, 'and so told him where you were. He is sitting in my shop and you should go to thank him and take back your axe and your shoes.'

On hearing these words, I turned pale and became distraught. While I was in this state, the floor of my room split open and from it emerged the 'Persian', who turned out to be none other than the *'ifrit*. In spite of the severest of tortures that he had inflicted on the girl, she had made no confession. He had then taken the axe and the shoes and had told her: 'As certainly as I am Jirjis of the seed of Iblis, I will fetch the owner of this axe and these shoes.' He then went with his story to the woodcutters, after which he came on to me. Without pausing, he snatched me up and flew off with me into the air, and before I knew what was happening he came down and plunged under the earth. He took me to the palace where I had been before and my eyes brimmed with tears as I saw the girl, staked out naked with the blood pouring from her sides.

The *'ifrit* took hold of her and said: 'Whore, is this your lover?' She looked at me and said: 'I don't recognize him and I have never seen him before.' 'In spite of this punishment, are you not going to confess?' he asked. She insisted: 'I have never seen this man in my life and God's law does not allow me to tell lies against him.' 'If you don't know him,' said the *'ifrit*, 'then take this sword and cut off his head.' She took the sword, came to me and stood by my head. I gestured to her with my eyebrows, while tears ran down my cheeks. She understood my gesture and replied with one of her own, as if to say: 'You have done all this to us.' I made a sign to say: 'Now is the time for forgiveness,' and inwardly I was reciting:

My glance expresses the words that are on my tongue,
And my love reveals what is concealed within.
We met as the tears were falling;
Though I was silent, my eyes spoke of you.
She gestured and I understood the meaning in her eyes;
I signed to her with my fingers and she understood.
Our eyebrows settled the affair between us,
And we kept silence, but love spoke.

When I had finished the poem, the girl threw down the sword and said: 'How can I cut off the head of someone whom I do not know and who has done me no harm? My religion does not allow this.' Then she stepped back, and the *'ifrit* said: 'It is not easy for you to kill your lover, and because he spent a night with you, you endure this punishment and do not admit what he did. Like feels pity for like.' Then he turned to me and said: 'Young man, I suppose that you too don't recognize her?' I said: 'Who is she? I have never seen her before.' 'Then take this sword,' he said, 'and cut off her head. By this, I shall be sure that you don't know her at all, and I shall then allow you to go free without doing you any harm.' 'Yes,' I said, and taking the sword, I advanced eagerly and raised my hand, but the girl gestured to me with her eyebrows: 'I did not fail you. Is this the way that you repay me?' I understood her meaning and signed to her with my eyes: 'I shall ransom you with my life,' and it was as though our inner tongues were reciting:

How many a lover has used his eyes to tell
His loved one of the secret that he kept,
With a glance that said: 'I know what happened.'
How beautiful is the glance! How elegant the expressive eye!
The one writes with his eyelids;
The other recites with the pupil of the eye.

My eyes filled with tears and I threw away the sword and said: 'O powerful *'ifrit*, great hero, if a woman, defective as she is in understanding and in religious faith, thinks that it is not lawful to cut off my head, how can it be lawful for me to cut off hers when I have not seen her before? I shall never do that even if I have to drain the cup of death.' The *'ifrit* said: 'The two of you know how to pay each other back for favours, but I shall show you the consequence of what you have done.' Then he took the sword and cut off one of the girl's hands, after which he cut off the other. With four blows he cut off her hands and her feet, as I watched, convinced that I was going to die, while she took farewell of me with her eyes. 'You are whoring with your eyes,' said the *'ifrit*, and he struck off her head.

Then he turned to me and said: 'Mortal, our code allows us to kill an unfaithful wife. I snatched away this girl on her wedding night when she was twelve years old and she has known no one but me. I used to visit her for one night in every ten in the shape of a Persian. When I was sure that she had betrayed me, I killed her. As for you, I am not certain that you have played me false, but I cannot let you go unscathed, so make a wish.' Lady, I was delighted and asked: 'What wish shall I make?' 'You can tell me what shape you want me to transform you into,' he said, 'that of a dog, an ass or an ape.' I was hoping that he would forgive me and so I said: 'By God, if you forgive me, God will forgive you, because you have spared a Muslim who has done you no harm.' I went on to implore him with the greatest humility, and, standing before him, I cried: 'I am wronged.' 'Don't talk so much,' he said. 'I am not far from killing you, but I will give you one chance.' 'Forgiveness befits you better, *'ifrit*,' I said, 'so forgive me as the envied forgive the envier.' 'How was that?' he asked, AND I REPLIED:

The Story of the Envious and the Envied

It is said, O *'ifrit*, that in a certain city there were two men living in two houses joined by a connecting wall. One of these two envied the other and because of this he used the evil eye against him and did all he could to injure him. So far did this envy increase that the envier lost appetite and no longer enjoyed the pleasure of sleep, while the man whom he envied grew more and more prosperous, and the more the envier tried to gain the upper hand, the more the other's prosperity increased and spread. On hearing of his neighbour's envy and of his attempts to injure him, he moved away from the district, leaving the country and saying: 'By God, I shall abandon worldly things for his sake.' He settled in another city and bought a piece of land there in which was a well with an old water wheel. On this land he endowed a small mosque for which he bought everything that was needed, and there he devoted himself with all sincerity to the worship of Almighty God. *Faqirs* and the poor flocked there from every quarter, and his fame spread in that city until eventually his envious neighbour heard how he had prospered and how the leading citizens would go to visit him. So he came to the mosque, where the object of his envy gave him a warm welcome and showed him the greatest honour.

The envier then said: 'I have something to tell you and this is why I have made the journey to see you. So get up and come with me.' The other did this and, taking the envier's hand, he walked to the farthest end of the mosque. 'Tell the *faqirs* to go to their rooms,' said the envier, 'for I can only speak to you in private where no one can hear us.' This the envied did, and the *faqirs* went to their rooms as they were told. The two then walked on a little until they came to the old well and there the envier pushed his victim into it without anyone knowing. He himself then left the mosque and went on his way, thinking that he had killed his former neighbour.

The well, however, was inhabited by *jinn*, who caught the falling man and lowered him gently on to the bedrock. They then asked each other whether any of them knew who he was. Most said no, but one of them said: 'This is the man who fled from his envier and who settled in this city where he founded this mosque. We have listened with delight to his invocations and to his reading of the Quran. The envier travelled to meet him and by a trick threw him down into our midst. But news of him has reached the king, who is intending to visit him tomorrow on the matter of his daughter.' 'What is wrong with his daughter?' asked one of the *jinn*. 'She is possessed by an evil spirit,' replied the other, 'for the *jinni* Marwan ibn Damdam is in love with her. If this man knew how to treat her, he could cure her, for the treatment is the easiest possible.' 'What is it?' asked the other. 'The black cat that he has with him in the mosque has a white spot as big as a dirham at the end of its tail. If he takes seven of its white hairs and uses them to fumigate the girl, the evil spirit will leave her head and never return and she will be cured there and then.'

The man was listening to all this, and so it was that the next morning, when dawn broke and the *faqirs* came, they found the *shaikh* rising out of the well, and as a result he became a figure of awe to them. Since he had no other medicines, he took seven hairs from the white spot at the end of the black cat's tail and carried them away with him. The sun had scarcely risen when the king arrived with his escort and his great officers of state. He told his men to wait and went in to visit the *shaikh*, who welcomed him warmly and said: 'Shall I tell you why you have come to me?' 'Please do,' replied the king. The man said: 'You have come to visit me in order to ask me about your daughter.' 'That is true, good *shaikh*,' the king agreed. 'Send someone to fetch her,' said the man, 'and I hope, if God Almighty wills it, that she will be cured immediately.' The king gladly sent for his daughter, who was brought tied up and manacled. The man sat her down and spread a curtain over her, after which he produced the seven cat hairs and used them to fumigate her. The evil spirit that was in her head cried out and left. She then recovered her senses, covered her face and said: 'What is all this? Who has brought me here?'

The joy that the king felt was not to be surpassed. He kissed his daughter's eyes and then the hands of the *shaikh*, after which he turned to his state officials and said: 'What do you say? What does the man who cured my daughter deserve?' 'He should marry her,' they said. 'You are right,' said the king, and he married the man to his daughter, making him his son-in-law. Shortly afterwards, the vizier died and when the king asked who should replace him, the courtiers said: 'Your son-in-law.' So he was appointed vizier and when, soon after that, the king himself died and people asked who should be made king, the answer was: 'The vizier.' Accordingly he was enthroned and ruled as king.

One day, as he was riding out, the envier happened to be passing by and saw the man he envied in his imperial state among his emirs, viziers and officers of state. The king's eye fell on him and, turning to one of his viziers, he said: 'Bring me that man, but do not alarm him.' When his envious neighbour was brought to him, he said: 'Give this man a thousand *mithqals* of gold from my treasury; load twenty camels for him with trade goods, and send a guard with him to escort him to his land.' Then he took his leave of the man who envied him, turned away from him and did not punish him for what he had done.

'See then, *'ifrit*, how the envied forgave the envious, who had started by envying him, then injured him, followed him, and eventually threw him into the well, intending to kill him. His victim did not pay him back for these injuries but forgave and pardoned him.' At this point, lady, I wept most bitterly before him and recited:

Forgive those who do wrong, for the wise man
Forgives wrongdoers for their evil deeds.
If every fault is mine,
Every forgiveness should be yours.
Who hopes that his superior will pardon him
Has to forgive inferiors their faults.

The *'ifrit* said: 'I shall not kill you, but neither shall I forgive you. Instead, I shall cast a spell on you.' Then he plucked me from the ground and flew up into the air with me until I could see the earth looking like a bowl set in the middle of water. He set me down on a mountain and, taking some earth, he muttered over it, cast a spell and scattered it over me, saying: 'Leave this shape of yours and become an ape.' Instantly, I became a hundred-year-old ape, and when I saw myself in this ugly form, I wept over my plight, but I had to endure Time's tyranny, knowing that no one is Time's master. After climbing down from the mountain top, I found a wide plain, across which I travelled for a month before ending at the shore of the salt sea. I stayed there for some time until suddenly I caught sight of a ship out at sea that was making for the shore with a fair breeze. I hid myself behind a rock and waited until it came by, when I jumped down into it. 'Remove this ill-omened beast,' cried one of the merchants on board. 'Let's kill it,' said the captain. 'I'll do that with this sword,' said another. I clung to the hem of the captain's clothes and wept copious tears.

The captain now felt pity for me and told the merchants: 'This ape has taken refuge with me and I have granted it to him. He is now under my protection, so let no one trouble or disturb him.' He then began to treat me with kindness, and as I could understand whatever he said, I did everything that he wanted and acted as his servant on the ship, so that he became fond of me. The ship had a fair wind for fifty days, after which we anchored by a large city, with a vast population. As soon as we had arrived and the ship had anchored, mamluks sent by the local king came on board. They congratulated the merchants on their safe voyage and passed on further congratulations from the king. Then they said: 'The king has sent you this scroll of paper, on which each one of you is to write one line. The king's vizier was a calligrapher and as he is now dead, the king has taken the most solemn of oaths that he will only appoint as his successor someone who can write as well as he did.'

The merchants were then handed a scroll which was ten cubits long and one cubit in breadth. Every last one of them who knew how to write, did so, and then I, in my ape's form, snatched the scroll from their hands. They were afraid that I was going to tear it and they tried to stop me, but I gestured to them to tell them I could write, and the captain signalled to them to leave me alone. 'If he makes a mess of it,' he said, 'we can drive him away, but if he can write well, I shall take him as a son, for I have never seen a more intelligent ape.' Then I took the pen, dipped it in the inkwell and wrote in the *ruka'i* script:

Time has recorded the excellence of the generous
But up till now your excellence has not been written down.
May God not orphan all mankind of you,
Who are the mother and father of every excellence.

Then I wrote in the *raihani* script:

He has a pen that serves every land;
Its benefits are shared by all mankind.
The Nile cannot rival the loveliness
That your five fingers extend to every part.

Then in the *thuluth* script I wrote:

The writer perishes but what he writes
Remains recorded for all time.
Write only what you will be pleased to see
When the Day of Resurrection comes.

I then wrote in *naskh*:

When we were told you were about to leave,
As Time's misfortunes had decreed,
We brought to the mouths of inkwells with the tongues of pens
What we complained of in the pain of parting.

Then I wrote in *tumar* script:

No one holds the caliphate for ever:
If you do not agree, where is the first caliph?
So plant the shoots of virtuous deeds,
And when you are deposed, no one will depose them.

Then I wrote in *muhaqqaq* script:

Open the inkwell of grandeur and of blessings;
Make generosity and liberality your ink.
When you are able, write down what is good;
This will be taken as your lineage and that of your pen.

I then handed over the scroll and, after everyone had written a line, it was taken and presented to the king. When he looked at it, mine was the only script of which he approved and he said to his courtiers: 'Go to the one who wrote this, mount him on a mule and let a band play as you bring him here. Then dress him in splendid clothes and bring him to me.' When they heard this, they smiled. The king was angry and exclaimed: 'Damn you, I give you an order and you laugh at me!' 'There is a reason for our laughter,' they said. 'What is it?' he asked. 'You order us to bring you the writer, but the fact is that this was written by an ape and not a man, and he is with the captain of the ship,' they told him. 'Is this true?' he asked. 'Yes, your majesty,' they said.

The king was both amazed and delighted. He said: 'I want to buy this ape from the captain,' and he sent a messenger to the ship, with a mule, a suit of clothes and the band. 'Dress him in these clothes,' he said, 'mount him on the mule and bring him here in a procession.' His men came to the ship, took me from the captain, dressed me and mounted me on the mule. The people were astonished and the city was turned upside down because of me, as the citizens flocked to look at me. When I was brought before the king, I thrice kissed the ground before him, and when he told me to sit, I squatted on my haunches. Those present were astonished at my good manners and the most astonished of all was the king. He then told the people to disperse, which they did, leaving me with him, his eunuch and a young mamluk.

At the king's command, a table was set for me on which was everything that frisks or flies or mates in nests, such as sandgrouse, quails, and all other species of birds. The king gestured to me that I should eat with him, so I got up, kissed the ground in front of him and joined him in the meal. Then, when the table cloth was removed, I washed my hands seven times, took the inkwell and the pen, and wrote these lines:

Turn aside with the chickens in the spring camp of the saucers
And weep for the loss of fritters and the partridges.
Mourn the daughters of the sandgrouse,
Whom I do not cease to lament,
Together with fried chickens and the stew.

Alas for the two sorts of fish served on a twisted loaf.
How splendid and how tasty was the roasted meat,
With fat that sank into the vinegar in the pots.
Whenever hunger shakes me, I spend the night
Applying myself to a pie, as bracelets glint.
I am reminded of this merry meal when I eat
On tables strewn with various brocades.
Endure, my soul; Time is the lord of wonders.
One day is straitened, but the next may bring relief.

I then got up and took my seat some way off. The king looked at what I had written and read it with astonishment. 'How marvellous!' he exclaimed. 'An ape with such eloquence and a master of calligraphy! By God, this is a wonder of wonders.' Then some special wine was brought in a glass, which he drank before passing it to me. I kissed the ground, drank and then wrote:

They burned me with fire to make me speak,
But found I could endure misfortune.
For this reason, hands have lifted me,
And I kiss the mouths of lovely girls.*

I added the lines:

Dawn has called out to the darkness, so pour me wine
That leaves the intelligent as a fool.
It is so delicate and pure that I cannot tell
Whether it is in the glass or the glass is in it.

When the king read the lines, he sighed and said: 'Were a man as cultured as this, he would surpass all the people of his age.' He then brought out a chessboard and asked whether I would play with him. I nodded yes and came forward to set out the pieces. I played two games with him and beat him, to his bewilderment. Then I took the inkwell and the pen and wrote these lines on the chessboard:

Two armies fight throughout the day,
The battle growing fiercer every hour,
But when night's darkness covers them,
Both sleep together in one bed.

* The speaker here is the wine.

On reading this, the king was moved to wonder, delight and astonishment and told a servant: 'Go to your mistress, Sitt al-Husn, and tell her that I want her to come here to see this wonderful ape.' The eunuch went off and came back with the lady. When she saw me, she covered her face and said: 'Father, how can you think it proper to send for me in order to show me to men?' 'Sitt al-Husn,' he said, 'there is no one here except for this little mamluk, the eunuch who brought you up, and I, your father. So from whom are you veiling your face?' She said: 'This ape is a young man, the son of a king, who has been put under a spell by the *'ifrit* Jirjis, of the stock of Iblis, who killed his own wife, the daughter of King Iftamus, the lord of the Ebony Islands. You think that he is an ape, but in fact he is a wise and intelligent man.'

The king was astonished by his daughter and he looked at me and said: 'Is what she says about you true?' I nodded yes and broke into tears. 'How did you know that he was under a spell?' the king asked his daughter. 'When I was young,' she replied, 'I had with me a cunning old woman who had a knowledge of magic, a craft she passed on to me. I remembered what she taught me and have become so skilled in magic that I know a hundred and seventy spells, the least of which could leave the stones of your city behind Mount Qaf and turn it into a deep sea, with its people swimming as fish in the middle of it.' 'By my life, daughter,' said the king, 'please free this young man so that I can make him my vizier, for he has wit and intelligence.' 'Willingly,' she replied, and taking a knife in her hand, she cut out a circle in the middle of the palace. Over this she wrote names, talismans and spells, and she recited words, some intelligible and some unintelligible.

After a time, everything grew dark and the *'ifrit* came down on us in his own shape. His arms were like winnowing forks, his legs like the masts of ships and his eyes like firebrands. We shrank from him in fear, and the princess said: 'There is no welcome for you,' at which he turned into a lion and said: 'Traitress, you have broken the covenant and the oath. Did we not swear that neither of us would oppose the other?' 'You accursed *'ifrit*,' she said, 'am I bound to one like you?' 'Take what comes to you,' said the *'ifrit*, and in his lion shape he opened its mouth and sprang at the girl. She quickly took one of her hairs, shook it in her hand and muttered a spell, so that the hair became a sharp sword. With this she struck a blow at the lion which cut it in two, but its head turned into a scorpion. For her part, the princess turned into a huge snake which attacked the damned *'ifrit* in his scorpion form. There was a fierce fight, and the scorpion turned into an eagle while the snake became a vulture. For some time the vulture pursued the eagle until it turned into a black cat. The princess then became a brindled wolf and for a time the two creatures fought together in the palace. Then the cat, finding itself beaten, became a large red pomegranate in the middle of the palace fountain. When the wolf came up to it, it rose in the air and fell on the palace floor where it burst, its seeds scattered, each in a different place, until they covered the floor. A shiver ran through the wolf and it became a cock, which started to pick the seeds so as not to leave a single one, but, as was fated, one of them was hidden by the side of the fountain.

The cock then started to crow and to flap its wings, gesturing to us with its beak. We could not understand what it meant and it crowed so loudly that we thought that the palace had fallen in on us. Then it went all around the floor until it saw the grain concealed beside the fountain. It pounced on this to peck it up, but the grain slipped into the middle of the water in the fountain and became a fish which dived down to the bottom. The cock turned into a bigger fish and went down after it. This second fish vanished from sight for some time and then suddenly we heard a loud cry and a scream, which made us shudder. Then out came the *'ifrit* like a firebrand, with fire coming from his open mouth and fire and smoke from his eyes and nose. He was followed by the princess in the form of a huge burning coal and the two fought for a time until both were covered by thick flames and the palace was choked with smoke. We were terrified and were about to plunge into the water, fearing we might be burned to death. The king recited the formula: 'There is no might and no power except with God, the Exalted, the Omnipotent. We belong to God and to Him do we return.' He added: 'I wish that I had not forced her to do this in order to rescue this ape, placing so huge a burden on her to confront this damned *'ifrit*, who cannot be matched by all the *'ifrits* to be found in the world. I wish that I had never known this ape – may God give him no blessing now or ever. I had wanted to do him a favour for God's sake and to free him from his spell, but my heart has been weighed down by misfortune.'

Meanwhile, I myself, lady, was tongue-tied and could not say anything to him. Then, before we knew what was happening, there was a shout from beneath the flames and the *'ifrit* was there in the hall with us, blowing fire into our faces. The princess caught up with him and blew back fire at him, while we were struck by sparks from both of them. Her sparks did us no harm, but one of his caught me in the eye while I was still in my ape form and blinded it. Another spark struck the king's face, half of which it burned, together with his beard and lower jaw, while all his lower teeth fell out. Yet another fell on the chest of the eunuch and he was immediately burned to death.

We were sure that we were about to die, but in the midst of our despair we heard a voice extolling God and adding: 'He has given victory and aid and has confounded those who disbelieve in the religion of Muhammad, the radiant moon.' This voice belonged to none other than the princess, who had burned the *'ifrit*, reducing him to a pile of ashes. She came up to us and said: 'Bring me a cup of water.' When this had been fetched, she spoke some incomprehensible words over it, sprinkled me with the water and said: 'I conjure you by the Truth, and by the Greatest Name of God, return freely to your original shape.' A shudder ran through me and suddenly I had gone back to being a man, although I had lost one eye.

The princess then cried out: 'The fire, father, the fire! I have not much longer to live. I have not been used to fighting with a *jinni*, although, had he been human, I would have killed him long ago. I was not in difficulty until the pomegranate burst and I picked up the seeds, but I forgot the one which contained the *'ifrit's* life. Had I picked it up in time, he would have died instantly, but I did not know what fate had ordained. Then he came back and we fought a hard battle under the earth, in the sky and in the water. Every time I tried a spell, he would reply with another, until he tried the spell of fire, and there are few who escape when this is used against them. Then destiny came to my aid and I burned him up before he could burn me, after I had summoned him to accept the religion of Islam. But now I am a dead woman – may God recompense you for my loss.' Then she cried for help against the fire and went on crying as a black spark leapt up to her breast and from there to her face. When it got there, she wept and recited: 'I bear witness that there is no god but God and that Muhammad is the Prophet of God.' We looked at her and all of a sudden she had become a pile of ashes lying beside those of the *'ifrit*. We grieved for her and I wished that I could have taken the place of my benefactress rather than see her beautiful face reduced to ashes, but God's decrees are not to be revoked.

On seeing what had happened to his daughter, the king plucked out what was left of his beard, struck his face and tore his clothes, as did I, and we both wept for her. The chamberlains and officers of state arrived to find the two piles of ashes and the king lying unconscious. For a time they stood around him in amazement and when he recovered and told what had happened to the princess in her encounter with the *'ifrit*, they were filled with distress and the women and the slave girls all screamed.

After seven days of mourning, the king gave orders for a huge dome to be built over his daughter's ashes, which was lit with candles and lamps, while the *'ifrit*'s ashes were scattered in the air, subject to God's wrath. The king then fell ill and was at the point of death, but he recovered after a month and his beard grew again. He sent for me and said: 'Young man, I passed my days living at ease, protected from the calamities of time, until you came here. How I wish that I had never set eyes on you or your ugly face, for it is you who have brought me to ruin! Firstly, I have lost my daughter, who was worth a hundred men. It was you whom my daughter rescued at the cost of her own life. Secondly, I was injured by fire; I lost my teeth, and my servant died. I recognize that none of this was your fault: all that happened to you and to me came from God – to Whom be praise. But now, my son, leave my land, for you have caused enough suffering, as was fated for me and for you. Go in peace, but if you come back and I see you again, I shall kill you.'

He shouted at me and I left his presence, scarcely believing that I had escaped and without knowing where to go. I thought over what had happened to me – how I had been abandoned on my journey, how I had escaped from my attackers, how I had walked for a month before entering the city as a stranger, how I had met the tailor and then the girl in the underground chamber, and how I had escaped from the *'ifrit* who had wanted to kill me. I relived all my emotions from the beginning to the end and I gave praise to God, saying: 'It has cost me my eye but not my life.' Before quitting the city, I went to the baths and shaved off my beard, after which I put on a black hair shirt and poured dust over my head. There is not a day on which I do not weep, thinking of the disasters that have struck me and of the loss of my eye. Every time I think of this, I shed tears and recite these lines:

By God, the Merciful, surely my affair bewilders me;
I do not know the source of sorrows that have surrounded me.
I shall endure until endurance itself cannot match mine,
Continuing until God closes my affairs.
I may be conquered, but I shall not show pain,
As a thirsty man endures in a hot valley.
I shall endure until endurance itself learns

I can endure what is more bitter than aloes,
Itself the bitterest of all,
But bitterer than all this would be for patience to betray me.
The secrets of my secret heart are its interpreter;
At the heart of the secret is my heart's secret love for you.
Were mountains to feel my sorrow, they would be crushed;
Fire would be quenched and winds would cease to blow.
Whoever claims that Time holds sweetness
Must sometime meet a day more bitter than aloes.

After that, I wandered through the world visiting cities and making for Baghdad, the House of Peace, in the hope of reaching the Commander of the Faithful and telling him what had happened to me. I arrived at the city tonight and there I found this first companion of mine standing in perplexity. I greeted him and talked to him and then our third companion arrived, greeted us and told us that he was a stranger. 'So are we,' the two of us said, 'and we have only just come on this blessed night.' The three of us then walked together without knowing each other's stories until fate brought us to this door and we came into your presence. This, then, is the reason why my beard and moustache have been shaven and my eye gouged out.

'Yours is a strange story,' said the lady of the house. 'You can touch your forelock and go on your way.' 'Not before I have heard my companions' stories,' he replied, at which THE THIRD DERVISH STEPPED FORWARD AND SAID:

The Story of the Third Dervish

Great lady, my tale is not like theirs but is more wonderful and more marvellous, and it explains the reason for the shaving of my beard and the plucking out of my eye. They both were victims of fate, but I brought this fate upon myself, burdening my own soul with sorrow. I was a king and the son of a king. After my father's death, I succeeded to the throne, ruled justly and treated my subjects well. I was fond of sailing and my city lay on the shore of a broad sea, in the middle of which many large islands were scattered, and I had fifty merchant ships, fifty smaller pleasure boats and a hundred and fifty warships. It so happened, that I decided to go on a pleasure trip to the islands and I set out with ten ships, taking provisions for a whole month. We had been sailing for twenty days when, one night, cross winds blew against us and the sea became very rough, with tumultuous waves, and we were plunged into thick darkness. Despairing of life, I said: 'A man who courts danger is not to be praised, even if he comes out safely.' We called on Almighty God and implored His help, but the wind continued to shift and the waves to clash together until daybreak. The wind then dropped; the sea became calm and the sun came out.

Looking out, we found ourselves by an island and so we landed on the shore, cooked and ate a meal and rested for two days. We then sailed on for another twenty days, when the currents turned against us and, as the captain of my ship did not recognize where we were, we told the lookout to climb to the crow's-nest to scan the sea. He went up the mast and shouted to the captain that to the right he could see fish on the surface, while at some distance away there was a dark shape, showing sometimes as black and sometimes as white. When the captain heard this, he dashed his turban on the deck, tore out hairs from his beard and said: 'Good news! We are all dead men; not one of us can escape.' He started to cry, and we all joined in, weeping for ourselves.

I then asked the captain what it was that the lookout had seen. 'Master,' he said, 'we went off course on the day of the gale when the wind did not die down until the following morning. That meant that we were off course for two days, and since that night we have been astray for eleven days, with no wind to blow us back on course. Tomorrow evening we shall come to an island of black stone that is called the Magnetic Mountain. The currents will force us under its lee and the ship will split apart, nails being drawn out to attach themselves to the rock. This is because God Almighty has set in it a secret power that attracts everything made of iron and God only knows how much of the metal is there, thanks to the many ships that have been wrecked on the rock over the course of time. By the shore there is a vaulted dome of brass set on ten columns and on top of this is a rider and his horse, both made of brass. In his hand the rider carries a brass lance and to his breast is fixed a lead tablet inscribed with names and talismans. It is this rider, O king,' he went on, 'who kills everyone who comes his way, and there is no escape unless the rider falls from his horse.'

At that, my lady, the captain wept bitterly and we were convinced that we were doomed. Each of us said farewell to his comrades and left his final instructions in case one should escape. We had no sleep that night and when morning came, we found ourselves close to the mountain. Then the force of the currents took us and when our ships were under the cliffs, they split apart, the nails and every iron object aboard being drawn towards the magnetic rock, to which they stuck. By the end of the day, we were drifting in the water around the mountain, and although some of us still lived, most were drowned, while the survivors could scarcely recognize each other, stunned as they were by the force of the waves and the gusts of wind. As for me, Almighty God preserved my life as it was His intention to distress, torture and afflict me further. I clung to a plank that was driven by the wind until it was blown ashore. There I found a beaten track, like a staircase carved in the mountain, leading to the summit. I pronounced the Name of Almighty God and called on Him with supplication. Then, gripping the cracks in the rock, I gradually managed to climb up. At that point, by God's permission, the wind died down and He helped me to make my way in safety until I reached the summit, where the only path that I could take led to the dome. I went in and then performed the ritual ablution as well as two *rak'as* in gratitude to God for bringing me to safety, after which I fell asleep under its shelter. In my sleep, I heard a voice saying: 'Ibn Khadib, when you wake, dig beneath your feet and you will find a bow of brass with three lead arrows, on which are inscribed talismans. Take the bow and the arrows and shoot the rider on top of the dome, for in this way you will rescue people from great distress. When you shoot him, he will fall into the sea and the bow will drop at your feet. Take it and bury it where you found it, and when you do this the sea will swell higher and higher, until it comes level with the mountain top. A little boat will then come up in which will be a man of brass – but not the one whom you shot. He will come to you with an oar in his hand and you must board his boat, but you are not to pronounce the Name of Almighty God. The man will row you for ten days and bring you to the Sea of Safety, where you will find someone to take you back to your own land, but all this will happen only if you do not mention the Name of God.'

When I awoke, I got up eagerly and did what the voice had told me. I shot the horseman and when he fell into the sea, the bow dropped at my feet and I took it and buried it. The sea then stirred and rose higher until it was level with me on the mountain, and before I had waited long, I saw a little boat making its way towards me, at which I called down praises on Almighty God. When it arrived, I found in it a man of brass with a lead tablet on his breast, inscribed with names and talismans. I boarded it silently, without speaking, and the brass sailor rowed day after day for the full ten days. Then, looking out, to my great joy, I saw the Islands of Safety. Because of the intensity of my joy, I invoked the Name of God, reciting the formula: 'There is no god but God,' and crying: '*Allahu akbar!*' As soon as I did this, the boat tipped me into the sea and then itself overturned.

I knew how to swim, however, and so I swam all that day until nightfall, by which time my arms could no longer support me and my shoulders were tired. Exhausted and in mortal danger, I recited the confession of faith, being sure that I was about to die. A violent wind stirred up the sea and I was carried on by a wave as big as a castle, which hurled me on to the land in accordance with God's will. I climbed up on the shore, where I squeezed out my wet clothes, spreading them out on the ground to dry overnight. The next morning, I put them on and went to see where I could walk. I came to a valley, only to discover, after walking round the edge of it, that I was on a small island surrounded by sea. 'Every time that I escape from one predicament,' I said to myself, 'I fall into another that is worse.'

While I was thinking over my plight and wishing that I was dead, at a distance I caught sight of a ship with people on it which was making for my island. I got up and sat in a tree, and from there I saw that the ship had come to land, and out of it emerged ten black slaves, each carrying a spade. They walked to the centre of the island where they dug until they had uncovered a trapdoor, which they raised up. They then went back to the ship and returned with bread, flour, butter, honey, sheep and utensils that someone living in the underground chamber would need. The slaves kept on going to and fro from the ship until they had moved all its cargo to the chamber. They then came back bringing the very finest of clothes and in the middle of them was a very old man, a skeletal figure, crushed by Time and worn away. He was wearing a tattered blue robe through which the winds blew west and east, as the poet has said:

What shudders are produced by Time,
And Time is strong and violent!
I used to walk without weakness,
But now I am weak and cannot walk.

The old man's hand was being held by a youth cast in the mould of splendour and perfection to the extent that his beauty deserved to be proverbial. He was like a tender branch, enchanting every heart with his grace and enslaving all minds with his coquetry. As the poet has said:

Beauty was brought to be measured against him,
But bowed its head in shame.
It was asked: 'Have you seen anything like this,
Beauty?' It answered: 'No.'

They walked on, lady, until they reached the underground chamber and went down into it. They stayed out of sight for an hour or more, and then the slaves and the old man came up, but the youth was not with them. They closed the door of the chamber as it had been before, after which they got into the boat and sailed out of sight. I climbed down from my tree and walked to the pile of earth, where I excavated the soil, removed it and worked patiently until I had cleared it all away. There was the trapdoor, made of wood and as big as a millstone. When I lifted it, I could see under it, to my astonishment, a vaulted stone staircase. Down this I went until I reached the bottom and there I found a clean chamber furnished with rugs and silks in which the youth was sitting on a raised dais, leaning back against a round cushion, holding a fan in his hand, with nosegays and scented herbs set before him. He was alone and when he saw me, he turned pale. I greeted him and said: 'Calm yourself; don't be alarmed. I mean you no harm. I am a mortal like you, and the son of a king, who has been brought to you by fate to cheer you in your loneliness. What is your story and how is it that you come to be living alone underground?'

When he was sure that I was a man like himself, his colour returned and he let me approach him. Then he said: 'My brother, my story is a strange one. My father is a merchant jeweller, who engages in trade, with slaves, black and white, acting for him, sailing to the furthest of lands with his goods, travelling with camels and carrying vast stores of wealth. He had never had a son, but then in a dream he saw that, although he would have one, this son would be short-lived. He woke in the morning after his dream, crying and weeping, and it was on the following night that my mother conceived me, a date that my father noted. When the period of her pregnancy ended, she gave birth to me, to his delight. He gave banquets and fed the mendicants and the poor because, so near the end of his life, he had been granted this gift. Then he summoned all the astrologers and astronomers, the sages and those who could cast a horoscope. They investigated my horoscope and told my father: "Your son will live for fifteen years, after which he will be faced by a danger, but if he escapes, his life will be a long one. The cause of his death will be as follows. In the Sea of Destruction is the Magnetic Mountain, on top of which stands a horse of brass with a rider on whose chest is a lead tablet. Fifty days after this rider falls from his horse, your son will die, killed by the man who shoots the rider, his name being 'Ajib ibn Khadib." This caused my father great distress, but he gave me the best of upbringings until I reached the age of fifteen. Then, ten days ago, he heard that the rider had fallen into the sea and that the name of the man who had shot him was 'Ajib, son of King Khadib. In his fear lest I be killed, my father brought me here. This is my story and this is why I am here all alone.'

When I heard this, I was astonished and I said to myself: 'I was the man who shot the rider, but by God I shall never kill this youth.' Speaking aloud, I said: 'Master, may you be preserved from disease and destruction, and if God Almighty wills it, you shall not see care, sorrow or confusion. I shall sit with you and serve you and then, having kept company with you throughout this period, I shall go on my way and you can take me to some of your mamluks, with whom I can travel back to my own lands.' I sat talking to him until nightfall, when I got up, set light to a large candle and lit the lamps. After having brought out some food, we sat down to a meal, and we then ate some sweetmeats which I had produced. We sat talking until most of the night had passed, when the youth went to sleep. I put a covering over him and settled down to sleep myself.

In the morning, I got up, heated some water and gently woke my companion. When he was awake, I brought him the hot water and he washed his face and thanked me. 'By God,' he said, 'when I am free from my present danger and safe from 'Ajib ibn Khadib, I shall ask my father to reward you, but if I die, may my blessing be on you even so.' I replied: 'May there never be a day on which evil strikes you and may God will it that the day of my death comes before yours.' I produced some food and we ate and I got him to perfume himself with incense. Then I made a draughts board for him and, after eating some sweetmeats, he and I started to play, going on until nightfall, when I got up, lit the lamps and brought out some more food. I sat talking to him until only a little was left of the night, when he fell asleep, after which I covered him up and slept myself. I went on doing this for a period of days and nights, becoming fond of him and forgetting my cares. 'The astrologers lied,' I said to myself, 'for by God I shall never kill this boy.'

I continued to serve him, to act as his companion and to talk with him for thirty-nine days until the night of the fortieth day. The youth was full of gladness and said to me: 'Thanks be to God, my brother, Who has saved me from death, and this is because of your blessing and the blessing brought by your arrival. I pray that God may restore you to your own land.' He then asked me to heat him water for a bath, which I willingly agreed to do. I warmed up a great quantity of water and brought it to him. He had a good bath, using lupin flour,* and I helped by rubbing him down and bringing him a change of clothes, after which I made up a high couch for him. He came and lay down to sleep there after his bath, saying: 'Brother, cut me up a melon and dissolve some sugar in its juice.' I went to the store cupboard and found a fine melon, which I put on a plate. 'Master,' I said to him, 'do you have a knife?' 'It is on this high shelf above my head,' he replied. So I got up quickly, took the knife and drew it from its sheath, but as I went back, I tripped. With the knife in my hand, I fell on top of the youth and, in accordance with the eternal decree, it quickly penetrated his heart and he died on the spot.

When this happened and I realized that I had killed him, I uttered a loud cry, beat my face and tore my clothes, saying: 'To God we belong and to Him do we return. O Muslims, this handsome youth had only a single night left of the dangerous period of forty days that the astrologers and sages had predicted for him, and his death came at my hands. How I wish I had not tried to cut this melon. This is an agonizing disaster, but it came about in order that God's decree might be fulfilled.' After this I got up, climbed the stairs and replaced the soil. Then I looked out to sea and caught sight of the ship making for the shore. I said fearfully: 'Now they will come and find the boy dead. They will know that it was I who killed him and they will be bound to kill me.' I made for a high tree, which I climbed, concealing myself among the leaves, and scarcely had I settled there than the black slaves and the youth's old father disembarked and went towards the hidden chamber. They cleared away the earth, found the trapdoor and went down. There they found the youth apparently asleep, his face glowing with the effect of his bath, dressed in clean clothes but with the knife plunged into his breast. They shrieked, wept, struck their faces, wailing and lamenting. The old man fainted for so long that the slaves thought that he would not survive his son. They wrapped the corpse of the youth in his clothes, covered him in a silken sheet and

* Used for soap.

returned to the boat. Behind them came the old man, but when he saw his son laid out, he fell to the ground, poured earth on his head, struck his face and plucked out his beard, while the thought that his son had been killed caused his tears to flow faster and he fainted again. One of the slaves got up and spread a piece of silk on a couch, upon which they laid the old man and then sat by his head.

While all this was going on, I was in the tree above them, watching what was happening. Because of the cares and sorrows that I had suffered, my heart turned grey before my hair and I recited:

How many hidden acts of grace does God perform
Whose secrets are too subtle to be grasped by clever men?
How often in the morning trouble comes,
While in the evening follows joy?
How many times does hardship turn to ease,
As pleasure follows the sad heart's distress?

The old man did not recover from his swoon until it was close to evening. Then, looking at the body of his son, he saw that what he had feared had come to pass. He slapped his face and his head and recited these lines:

The loved ones left me with a broken heart,
And floods of tears rain from my eyes.
My longing is for what lies distant, but, alas,
How can I reach this? What can I say or do?
I wish that I had not set eyes on them.
What can I do, my masters, in these narrow paths?
How can I find my solace in forgetfulness?
The blazing fire of love plays with my heart.
I wish we had been joined by death
In an inseparable link.
In God's Name, slanderer, go slow;
Join me with them while this can still be done.
How pleasantly we were sheltered by one roof,
Living a life of constant ease, until
Arrows of separation struck and parted us.
And who is there with power to endure them?
A blow struck us through the dearest of all men,
Perfect in beauty, unique in his age.

I called him – but the silent voice preceded me.
My son, would that your fate had not arrived.
How may I rush to ransom you, my son,
With my own life, were that acceptable?
I say: he is the sun, and the sun sets.
I say: he is the moon, and moons decline.
The days bring sorrow and distress for you.
I cannot do without you. None can take your place.
Your father longs for you, but you are dead,
And he is helpless. The envious look at us today
To see what they have done; how evil was their deed!

At that, with a deep sigh his soul parted from his body. 'O master,' cried the slaves, and, pouring dust on their heads, they wept more and more bitterly. Then they put his body on the ship beside that of his son and, unfurling the sail, they passed out of sight. I came down from the tree, went through the trapdoor and thought about the youth. Seeing some of his belongings, I recited:

I see their traces and so melt with longing,
Weeping in places where they used to dwell.
I ask God, Who decreed that they should leave,
That one day He may grant that they return?

I then went out and passed my time wandering around the island by day and going into the underground chamber by night. In this way a month went by and, as I looked out over the western tip of the island, I could see that with every day that passed the water was drying up. Eventually there was very little of it left to the west and there was no longer any current. By the end of the month, to my joy, the sea had dried up in that direction and, sure that I was now safe, I got up and waded through what water was left until I reached the mainland. There I encountered sand dunes in which camels would sink up to their hocks, but, steeling myself, I managed to cross them, and then far off I caught a glimpse of a fire burning brightly. I made for it, hoping to find relief. Meanwhile I recited:

It may perhaps be that Time will direct its reins
Towards some good – but Time is envious.
Were it to aid hopes and fulfil my needs,
It might bring pleasure after this distress.

When my course brought me nearer, I saw a palace with a door of brass which, when the sun shone on it, gleamed from a distance like fire. I was delighted at the sight and sat down opposite the door. Scarcely had I taken my seat when there came towards me ten young men, wearing splendid clothes, with a very old companion. All the young men had lost their right eyes, and I was astonished by their appearance and at this coincidence. When they saw me they greeted me and asked me about myself and about my story. They were amazed when I told them what had happened to me and of my misfortunes, and they then brought me into the palace. Ranged around the hall were ten couches, each spread with and covered in blue material. In the middle of these was a small couch whose coverings, like those of the others, was also blue.

When we entered the room, each of the young men went to his own couch and the old man went to the small one in the middle. He told me to sit down, but warned me not to ask questions about him and his companions or why they were one-eyed. He then brought food for each man in one container and drink in another and he did the same for me. After that, they sat asking me about my circumstances and my adventures, and their questions and my replies took up most of the night. Then they said: '*Shaikh*, bring us our due.' 'Willingly,' the old man replied, and after going away into a closet, he came back carrying on his head ten trays, each with a covering of blue, and gave one to each of the young men. Then he lit ten candles, fixing one to each tray, and removed the covers. There beneath the covers on the trays was nothing but ashes and grime from cooking pots. All the young men rolled up their sleeves and, with tears and sobs, they smeared and slapped their faces, tore their clothes and beat their breasts, saying: 'We were seated at our ease but our inquisitiveness did not leave us.' They went on doing this until it was nearly morning, when the old man got up and heated water for them with which they washed their faces before putting on fresh clothes.

When I saw this, I said: 'I am astonished, amazed and afire with curiosity.' I forgot what had happened to me and, unable to keep silent, I asked them: 'Why have you done this, after we had become pleasantly tired? You are men of sound minds – praise be to God – and it is only madmen who act like this. I implore you by what you hold dearest to tell me your story and why you have lost your eyes and why you smear your faces with ashes and grime.' They turned to me and said: 'Young man, do not be led astray by your youth and do not press your question.' Then they got up and so did I, after which the old man brought out food, and when we had eaten and the plates had been removed, they sat talking until nightfall. The old man then rose and lit candles and lamps, before bringing us food and drink.

We sat talking in a friendly way to one another until midnight. 'Bring us our due,' they then told the old man, 'as it is time for sleep.' He brought the trays with the black ashes and they did what they had done on the first night. The same thing went on for a whole month while I stayed with them, as every night they would smear their faces with ashes before washing them and then changing their clothes. I was astonished at this and became more and more uneasy, to the extent that I could neither eat nor drink. 'Young men,' I said, 'you must satisfy my concern and tell me why it is that you smear your faces.' They said: 'It is better to keep our secret hidden,' but as I was too perplexed to eat or drink, I insisted that they tell me. 'This will go hard with you,' they replied, 'as you will become like us.' 'There is no help for it,' I said, 'unless you allow me to leave you and go back to my family, so that I may no longer have to watch all this. As the proverb has it, it is better for me to be far away from you, for what the eye does not see the heart does not grieve over.' At this, they took a ram, slaughtered it and skinned it, then told me to take a knife, wrap the skin around me and sew it up. They went on: 'A bird called a *rukh* will swoop on you and lift you up, before setting you down on a mountain, where you should slit open the skin and come out. The bird will be scared away from you and will go off, leaving you alone. Walk on for half a day and you will find in front of you a strange-looking palace. Enter it and you will have achieved what you wanted, as it was because we went into it that we blacken our faces and each of us has lost an eye. It would take a long time to explain all this, as each of us has a tale to tell of how his right eye was plucked out.'

I was pleased when I heard this, and after I had done what they had instructed, the bird came and carried me off, leaving me on the mountain top. I got out of the skin and walked on until I reached the palace, where I found forty girls, beautiful as moons, at whom no one could tire of looking. On seeing me, they all greeted me warmly. 'We have been expecting you for a month,' they said, 'and praise be to God, Who has brought us one who deserves us and whom we deserve.' They seated me on a high dais and said: 'Today you are our lord and master and we are your slave girls, under your command, so give us your orders.' I was astonished by all this, but they brought me food and we ate together, after which they fetched drink. They clustered around me and five of them spread out a mat around which they set out quantities of scented flowers, together with fruits, fresh and dried. Then they brought wine and we sat down to drink as they sang to the music of the lute.

The wine circulated and such was my delight that I forgot all worldly cares. 'This is the life,' I said, and I stayed with them until it was time to sleep. 'Take whichever of us you choose to sleep with you,' they said. So I took one of them, with a beautiful face, dark eyes, black hair, well-spaced teeth, perfect in all aspects, with joining eyebrows, like a supple bough or a sprig of sweet basil, astonishing and amazing the mind. As the poet has said:

It shows ignorance to compare her to a tender branch,
And how far is she unlike a gazelle!
How can the dear gazelle have a form like hers
Or honeyed lips like hers – how sweet a drink –
Or her wide eyes, that act as murderers,
Capturing the desperate lover, tortured and then slain?
I yearn for her; mine is a heathen love;
No wonder that the lovesick is in love.

I recited to her:

My eyes see nothing but your loveliness;
Apart from you no thought enters my heart,
For every thought of mine is fixed on you;
In your love is my death and my rebirth.

I then got up and spent a night of unsurpassed pleasure sleeping with her. In the morning, the girls took me to the baths, washed me and gave me the most splendid of clothes to wear. Then they brought out food and drink and we ate and drank, the wine circulating until nightfall. This time I chose another lovely, pliant girl. As the poet describes:

I saw upon her breast two caskets sealed with musk,
Withheld from any lover's grasp,
Guarded with arrows she shoots from her eyes –
Arrows that strike down any who attack.

I passed the most delightful of nights, sleeping with her until dawn. In short, my lady, I spent a whole year with these girls, enjoying a carefree life, but as the next year began, they said: 'Would that we had never known you, but if you listen to us you can save yourself.' They then started to weep and when I asked them what the matter was, they explained: 'We are the daughters of kings, and we have been gathered together here for a period of years. We go away for forty days and then stay here for a year, eating, drinking, enjoying ourselves and taking our pleasure, after which we go off again. This is our custom and we are afraid that when we leave you, you will not do what we tell you. Here are the keys of the palace, which we are handing over to you. In the palace are forty rooms, thirty-nine of which you may enter, but you must take care not to open the door of the fortieth, or else you will be forced to leave us.' 'If that is so,' I said, 'then I shall certainly not open it.'

One of them then came to me, embraced me, wept and recited the lines:

If after separation we come close again,
The frown upon Time's face will turn into a smile.
If a sight of you serves as kohl for my eyes,
I shall forgive Time all its evil deeds.

Then I recited:

When she came close to say farewell, she and her heart
Were allies there to longing and to love.
She wept moist pearls, while my tears, as they flowed,
Were like carnelians, forming a necklace on her breast.

On seeing the girls' tears, I swore that I would never open the forbidden room, and after I had said goodbye, they went outside and flew away. So I sat in the palace by myself and when evening approached, I opened the door to the first chamber and went in. There I found a virtual paradise, a garden with green trees, ripe fruits, tuneful birds and gushing waters. I felt at rest as I walked among the trees, smelling sweet-scented flowers and listening to the song of the birds as they glorified the One God, the Omnipotent. I looked at apples whose colour was midway between red and yellow, as the poet has said:

An apple's nature has combined two shades –
The beloved's cheek and the complexion of the timorous lover.

Then I looked at quinces that put to shame the scent of musk and ambergris, as the poet has said:

Within the quince are all mankind's delights;
Its fame surpasses every other fruit.

Its taste is wine and its scent diffused musk,
Golden in colour, shaped like the full moon.

I then looked at apricots whose beauty delighted the eye like polished rubies, and after that I left the chamber and locked the door again. Next day I opened the door to the second chamber, went in and found a large space, with date palms and a flowing stream whose banks were carpeted with rose bushes, jasmine, marjoram, eglantine, narcissus and gillyflowers. Breezes passed over these scented flowers and the scent spread in all directions, filling me with perfect happiness. I left this chamber, locked the door behind me and opened the third. Here I found a hall, paved with coloured marble, valuable minerals and precious stones. In it were cages of sandalwood and aloes wood, with singing birds, such as the nightingale, the ringdove, blackbirds, turtledoves and the Nubian song thrush. I was delighted by this; my cares were dispelled and I slept there until morning. Then I opened the fourth door to discover a large chamber with forty closets whose doors were standing open. I went in and saw an indescribable quantity of pearls, sapphires, topazes, emeralds and other precious stones. In my astonishment I exclaimed: 'I do not think that there is a single king who has all this in his treasury.' Joy filled me, my cares leaving me, and I said: 'I am the supreme ruler of the age; my wealth is a gift granted me by God's grace; the forty girls are under my authority, and they have no other man besides me.' I went from place to place until thirty-nine days had passed, during which time I had opened all the rooms except for the one whose door I had been told not to open.

This one, which made the number up to forty, preoccupied me and, in order to bring me misery, Satan incited me to open it. I could not hold out against this, and so with only one day left before the girls were due to return, I went to the chamber, opened the door and went in. I found a fragrance the like of which I had never smelt before. It overcame my senses and I fell down in a faint, which lasted for an hour. Then I plucked up my courage and went further into the room, whose floor I found spread with saffron. Light was given by lamps of gold and candles from which was diffused the scent of musk and ambergris, and I saw two huge censers, each filled with aloes wood, ambergris and honeyed perfume whose scent filled the room. I saw a horse, black as darkest night, in front of which was a manger of clear crystal, filled with husked sesame, together with a similar manger filled with rosewater scented with musk. The horse was harnessed and bridled and its saddle was of red gold.

When I saw this, I was astonished and said to myself: 'There must be something of great importance here.' Satan led me further astray and so I took hold of the horse and mounted it. It didn't move and so I kicked it, and when it still refused to move, I took the whip and struck it. As soon as it felt the blow, it neighed with a sound like rumbling thunder and, opening up a pair of wings, it flew off with me, carrying me up into the sky way above the ground. After a time, it set me down on a flat roof and whisked its tail across my face, striking out my right eye and causing it to slide down my cheek. It then left me and I came down from the roof to find the ten one-eyed youths. 'No welcome to you,' they said. 'Here I am,' I replied. 'I have become like you, and I want you to give me a tray of grime with which to blacken my face and to let me sit with you.' 'No, by God,' they said, 'you may not do that. Get out!'

They drove me away, leaving me in dire straits, thinking over the misfortunes that had overtaken me. I was sad at heart and tearful when I parted from them, and I said to myself in a low voice: 'I was resting at my ease, but my inquisitiveness would not leave me.' So I shaved off my beard and whiskers and wandered from place to place. God decreed that I should remain safe and I reached Baghdad yesterday evening, where I found these two men standing in perplexity. I greeted them and introduced myself as a stranger. 'We too are strangers,' they said, so we agreed to go together, all of us being dervishes and all being blind in the right eye. This, lady, is why I am clean shaven and have lost my eye.

'You can touch your forelock and go,' she told him, but he replied: 'Not before I have heard what these other people have to say.'

The lady of the house then turned to the caliph, Ja'far and Masrur and said: 'Tell me your story.' Ja'far came forward and told her the story that he had told to the doorkeeper when they entered and when she heard this, she allowed them all to leave. In the lane outside, the caliph asked the dervishes where they were proposing to go as dawn had not yet broken. When they said that they did not know, he told them to come and spend the night with him. 'Take them,' he said to Ja'far, 'and bring them to me in the morning, so that we may write down what has happened.' Ja'far did as he was told and the caliph went up to his palace, but found himself unable to sleep that night.

In the morning, he took his seat on the imperial throne, and when his officials had assembled, he turned to Ja'far and told him to bring the three ladies, the two bitches and the three dervishes. Ja'far got up and brought them all, the ladies being veiled. Ja'far turned to them and said: 'You are forgiven because of your earlier kindness, although you did not know who we were. I can tell you now that you are standing before the fifth of the caliphs of the Banu 'Abbas, Harun al-Rashid, the brother of Musa al-Hadi and son of al-Mahdi Muhammad, the son of Abu Ja'far al-Mansur, the son of Muhammad, the brother of al-Saffah, son of Muhammad. You are to tell nothing but the truth.'

When the ladies heard what Ja'far had said as spokesman for the Commander of the Faithful, the eldest of them came forward and said to the caliph: 'Commander of the Faithful, mine is a story which, were it written with needles on the inner corners of the eyeballs of mankind, would serve as a warning to those who take heed and counsel to those who profit from counsel.' SHE WENT ON:

The Story of the Lady of the House

Mine is a strange story. The two black bitches are my sisters. Three of us were full sisters and these two, the doorkeeper and the housekeeper, were born of a different mother. When our father died, each of us took her share of the inheritance. Some days later, my mother died, leaving us three thousand dinars, and so each of us, I being the youngest, inherited a thousand dinars. My sisters were thus equipped with dowries and each married. Their husbands stayed for a time, but then they collected trade goods and, each of them taking a thousand dinars from his wife, they all went off on a voyage together, leaving me behind. They were away for five years, during which time the men lost their money and were ruined, abandoning their wives in foreign parts.

After five years, my eldest sister came to me in the most squalid of states, dressed as a beggar, with tattered clothes and a dirty old shawl. When I saw her, I didn't recognize her at first and took no notice of her. Then, realizing who she was, I asked her what had happened, but she said: 'It is no use talking, sister, the pen of fate has written God's decree.' So I sent her to the baths, gave her clothes to wear and said: 'Sister, you have been given to me in exchange for my father and mother. My share of what the three of us inherited has been blest by God and it has allowed me to thrive and become prosperous. You and I are equal partners.' I treated her with all kindness and she stayed with me for a whole year.

We were concerned about our other sister, but it was not long before she too arrived in an even worse plight than the eldest. I treated her even better than I had treated her sister and both of them shared in my wealth. Some time later, they told me that they wanted to marry again as they could not bear to remain without husbands. 'My dears,' I said, 'there is no longer any benefit to be got from marriage and good men are hard to find now. I don't see any advantage in your proposal and you have already had experience of marriage.' My sisters did not accept that and married without my approval, although I covered all their costs. They then left with their husbands, who very soon afterwards played them false, took all that they had and went off, abandoning them.

Once again they came back to me, covered in shame, apologized and said: 'Don't blame us. You may be younger than us but you are more intelligent; we shall never again mention marriage, so take us as your slave girls that we may have a bite to eat.' 'Welcome, sisters,' I said. 'No one is dearer to me than you.' And I kissed them and honoured them even more than before. This went on for a full year, after which I decided to fit out a ship to go to Basra. I chose a large one and loaded it with goods, merchandise and everything needed for the voyage. I asked my sisters whether they would prefer to sit at home until I returned from my voyage or whether they would like to come with me. 'We will go with you,' they said, 'as we cannot bear to be parted from you,' and so I took them along.

I had divided my wealth in two, taking half with me and leaving the other half behind, with the idea that, were the ship to be wrecked and we survived, there would be something to support us on our return. We sailed for some days and nights, but the ship then went astray as the captain had not kept to the right course, and without realizing it, we were sailing in the wrong direction. This went on for some time and over a period of ten days we had fair winds. After that, the lookout climbed up to investigate; he called out: 'Good news!' and came down full of joy and told us that he had seen what looked like a city resembling a dove. We were delighted and, within an hour, we could see the place in the distance. We asked the captain its name, but he said: 'By God, I don't know. I have never seen it before and never in my life have I sailed on this sea. But things have turned out safely and all we have to do is put in to harbour. Look out your merchandise and if you can sell, sell and then buy up whatever is there; if that does not work, we can rest here for two days, buy provisions and go on with our voyage.'

We put in and the captain went up to the city. He was away for a time and when he came back he told us: 'Come up and wonder at what God has done to those He created, and seek refuge from His anger.' We went to the city and when we came to the gate, we saw that it was guarded by men with sticks in their hands, but when we got nearer we found that they had been turned to stone, while in the city itself we found that everyone had been transformed to black stone and there was no trace of life. We were astonished, but as we threaded our way through the markets, we discovered that the traders' wares and the gold and silver had remained unchanged. This delighted us and, thinking that there must be some mystery here, we split up and walked through the city streets, each concerned to collect her own booty, money and fabrics.

I myself went to the castle, which turned out to be strongly fortified, and I then entered the royal apartments, where all the utensils were made of gold and silver. There I saw the king wearing robes of bewildering splendour, seated with his chamberlains, officers and viziers. When I approached, I found that he was sitting on a throne studded with pearls and gems, wearing cloth of gold, with every jewel gleaming like a star. Standing around him were fifty mamluks, dressed in silks of various kinds, with drawn swords in their stone hands – an astonishing sight. I then walked into the hall of the harem, whose walls were covered with hangings of silk with gold-embroidered branches. The queen was there asleep, wearing a robe ornamented with fresh pearls. On her head was a crown studded with gemstones of all kinds, while around her neck were necklaces of all sorts. Everything she was wearing, dress and ornaments, was unchanged, but she herself had been transformed to black stone.

I then found an open door and went up to it. There were seven steps and these led to a chamber whose marble floor was spread with gold-embroidered carpets. In it there was a couch made of juniper wood, inset with pearls and precious stones, together with two large emeralds, covered by a pearl-studded hanging. There was also a door from which I could see a light shining. I went to stand over it and there in the centre on a small chair I found a jewel the size of a duck's egg, burning like a candle and shedding light, while spread over the couch was an amazing array of silks. The sight filled me with astonishment. On looking further, I saw lighted candles. 'Someone must have lit these,' I said to myself, and I then went to another room and proceeded to search all through the building, forgetting myself in my astonishment at all this and plunged in thought.

I continued exploring until nightfall, but then, wishing to leave, I found I had lost my way and had no idea where the gate was. So I went back to the chamber with the lighted candles, sat down on the couch and, after reciting a portion of the Quran, wrapped myself in a coverlet, trying in vain to sleep but becoming uneasy. Then at midnight I heard a beautiful voice reciting the Quran. This filled me with joy and I followed the sound until I came to a small room whose door was shut. I opened it and looked inside, to find a chapel with a prayer niche in which hung lighted lamps together with two candles. In this chapel a prayer rug had been put down and on this sat a handsome young man with, before him, a copy of the holy Quran from which he was reading.

Wondering how he alone had been saved from out of all the inhabitants of the city, I entered and greeted him. He looked up and returned my greeting, at which I said: 'By the truth of what you have recited from the Book of God, I implore you to answer my question.' He looked at me, smiling, and replied: 'Servant of God, do you tell me why you came here and I will tell you what happened to me and the people of this city and how it was that I escaped.' So I told him my story, which filled him with wonder, and then I asked him about the townspeople. 'Wait, sister,' he said, and he then closed the Quran and put it into a bag of satin, before making me sit beside him. When I looked at him, I saw him to be the moon when it comes to the full, excellent in his attributes, supple and handsome; his appearance was like a sugar stick, with a well-proportioned frame. As the poet has said:

To the astrologer watching by night
Appeared a beautiful form dressed in twin robes.
Saturn had granted him black hair,
Colouring his temples with the shade of musk.
From Mars derived the redness of his cheek,
While Sagittarius shot arrows from his eyelids.
Mercury supplied keenness of mind
While the Bear forbade the slanderers to look at him.
The astrologer was bewildered by what he saw
And the ground before him was kissed by the full moon.

Almighty God had clothed him in the robe of perfection and embroidered it with the beauty and splendour of the down of his cheek, as the poet has said:

I swear by the intoxication of his eyelids,
By his waist and by the arrows that his magic shoots,
By the smoothness of his flanks, the sharpness of his glance,

His white complexion and the darkness of his hair,
His eyebrow that denies sleep to my eye,
Controlling me as he orders and forbids,
By his rosy cheek and the myrtle of its down,
By the carnelian of his mouth, his pearly teeth,
By his neck and by the beauty of his form,
With pomegranates showing on his chest,
By his haunches that quiver whether he moves or is still,
By his slender waist and by his silken touch,
The lightness of his spirit and all the beauty he encompasses.
I swear by his generous hand and by his truthful tongue,
His high birth and his lofty rank.
For those who know of musk, it is his scent,
And he it is who spreads the scent of ambergris.
Compared with him the radiant sun
Is nothing but the paring of a fingernail.

The glance that I gave him was followed by a thousand sighs and love for him was fixed in my heart. 'My master,' I said, 'answer my question.' 'Willingly,' he replied, and he went on: 'Know, servant of God, that this is my father's city and he is the king whom you saw sitting on the throne turned into black stone, while the queen whom you saw in the hall is my mother. All the people of the city were Magians, worshipping fire rather than Almighty God. They would swear by fire, light, shadows, the heat of the sun and the circling sphere. After my father had for long been without a son, late in his life I was born to him. He brought me up until I was a grown man, and good fortune always preceded me. With us there was an old Muslim woman who believed in God and His Apostle in secret, while in public she followed the practices of my people. My father had faith in her because he saw that she was trustworthy and chaste, and he showed her great respect, thinking that she was his co-religionary. When I grew older he entrusted me to her, saying: "Take him; give him a good upbringing; ground him in the tenets of our faith and look after him." When she had taken me, she taught me about the religion of Islam with the obligations of ritual purification and of prayer, and she made me learn the Quran by heart, telling me to worship none but Almighty God. When she had done all this, she told me to keep it hidden from my father and not to tell him lest he kill me. So I kept the secret for a few days, but then the old woman died and the people of the city sank ever further into unbelief and presumptuous error.

'While they were in this state, suddenly they heard a mighty voice like the rumbling of thunder, calling out in tones that could be heard far and near: "Citizens, turn away from the worship of fire and worship God, the Merciful King." The people were startled and they all came to my father, the king, and asked: "What is this alarming voice that we have heard, astounding and terrifying us?" "Do not be alarmed or frightened by it," he replied, "and do not let it turn you from your religion." Their hearts inclined to what he said; they persisted in their worship of fire and they acted even more wickedly until a year had passed from the first time that they had heard the voice. They then heard it for a second time and, after three years, for a third time – once each year – but they still clung to their beliefs. Then, at dawn one day, divine wrath descended and they, together with their animals and their flocks, were turned to black stone. I was the only one to escape and since that happened, I have been living like this – praying, fasting and reciting the Quran – but I can no longer endure being alone, with no one to keep me company.'

I had lost my heart to him, so I asked him whether he would go to Baghdad with me where he could meet the men of learning and the *faqihs*, and so add to his knowledge, understanding and grasp of religious law. 'Know,' I went on, 'that the slave who stands before you is the mistress of her people, with command over men, eunuchs and slaves. I have a ship laden with merchandise and it was fate that led us here in order that we should see these things, and it was ordained by destiny that you and I should meet.'

I continued to prompt him to leave with me, flattering him and using my wiles until he agreed to accept. I then spent the night at his feet, unable to believe what had happened to me because of my joy. In the morning, we got up and, going to the treasuries, we took what was both light to carry and valuable, after which we left the castle and went down to the city. There we met the slaves and the ship's captain, who were searching for me and who were filled with joy when they saw me. I told them, to their astonishment, what I had seen and explained to them the story of the young man and the reason for the curse that had struck the city, as well as what had happened to its people. When my sisters, now these two bitches, saw me with the young man, they became jealous of me and angry, and they secretly schemed against me. We boarded the ship gaily, overjoyed at the profit we had made, although I was more pleased because of the young man. We stayed waiting for a wind, and when it blew fair, we made sail and set off. My sisters sat with me and we started to talk. 'What are you going to do with this handsome young man?' they asked. 'I intend to take him as my husband,' I replied. Then, turning, I went up to him and said: 'Sir, I want to say something to you and I would ask you not to refuse me. When we reach Baghdad, our city, I shall propose myself to you in marriage; you shall be my husband and I shall be your wife.' He agreed to this, and I turned to my sisters and said: 'This young man is enough for me, so whatever profit others have made, they can keep.' 'That is well done of you,' they said, but secretly they continued to plot against me.

On we sailed with a fair wind until we left the Sea of Fear and reached safety. After a few more days of sailing, we came in sight of the walls of Basra. Evening fell and we settled down to sleep, but then my sisters got up, carried me on my mattress and threw me into the sea. They did the same thing with the young man, and as he could not swim well, he was drowned and God entered him in the roll of the martyrs. I wish that I had drowned with him, but God decreed that I should be saved, and so while I was floating in the sea, He provided me with a plank of wood on to which I climbed. The waves then swept me along until they threw me up on the shore of an island. There I walked for the rest of the night and, when morning came, I saw a track just broad enough for a human foot that connected the island to the mainland.

The sun had now risen and I dried my clothes in the sunlight, ate some of the island fruits and drank from its water. Then I set off on the track and went on walking until I was close to the mainland and only two hours away from the city. Suddenly, I saw a snake as thick as a palm tree darting towards me, and as it came I could see it swerving to right and to left until it reached me. Its tongue was trailing along the ground for the length of a span and it was sweeping aside the dust with the whole length of its body. It was being pursued by a dragon, thin and long as a lance. In its flight the snake turned to the right and the left, but the dragon seized its tail. The snake shed tears and its tongue lolled out because of its violent efforts to escape. Feeling sorry for it, I picked up a stone and threw it at the dragon's head, killing it instantly, after which the snake unfolded a pair of wings and flew up into the sky until it passed out of my sight.

I sat there in amazement, but I was tired and sleepy and so, for a time, I fell asleep where I was. When I awoke I found at my feet a girl with two bitches who was massaging my feet. I felt embarrassed by her presence and so I sat up and said: 'Sister, who are you?' 'How quickly you have forgotten me,' she replied. 'I am the one to whom you did a service, killing my foe and sowing the seed of gratitude. I am the snake whom you saved from the dragon. I am one of the *jinn*, as was the dragon. He was my enemy and it was only because of you that I escaped from him. After that, I flew on the wind to the ship from which your sisters threw you overboard, and after taking all its cargo to your house, I sank it. As for your sisters, I turned them into two black bitches, for I know the whole story of their dealings with you, but as for the young man, he had already drowned.' She then carried me off, together with the bitches, and set me down on the roof of my house, in the middle of which I could see all the goods that had been on the ship, not one thing being missing.

Then the snake girl said: 'By the inscription on the ring of our lord Solomon, on whom be peace, if you do not give each of these bitches three hundred lashes every day, I shall come and turn you into a bitch like them.' I told her that I would obey, and so, Commander of the Faithful, I have gone on beating them, although I feel pity for them and they realize that this is not my fault and accept my excuse. This is my story.

The caliph was filled with wonder, and he then asked the doorkeeper the reason for the whip scars on her body. 'Commander of the Faithful,' she replied, 'when my father died he left a great quantity of wealth, and soon afterwards I married the wealthiest man of his time.' SHE WENT ON:

The Story of the Doorkeeper

I stayed with him for a year, but he too then died and from him I inherited eighty thousand gold dinars, this being my portion in accordance with Islamic law. I was then exceedingly rich; my reputation spread, and I had ten costumes made, each worth a thousand dinars. As I was sitting one day, in came an old woman with pendulous cheeks, thinning eyebrows, popping eyes, broken teeth and a blotched face. She was bleary-eyed, with a head that looked as though it had been covered in plaster, grey hair and a bent body covered in scabs. Her skin was discoloured and she was dribbling mucus, as the poet has described:

An old woman of evil omen – may God have no mercy on her youth
Or pardon her sins the day she comes to die –

She could lead a thousand bolting mules
With a spider's web for reins, so domineering is she.

On entering, this woman greeted me and after she had kissed the ground before me, she said: 'I have a fatherless daughter and tonight is her wedding and the ceremony of her unveiling. We are strangers with no acquaintances in this city and our hearts are broken. Were you to come to the wedding, you would win reward and recompense from God, as the ladies of the city would hear that you were going and would come themselves. You would then mend my daughter's broken heart, for her only helper is God.' She then wept, kissed my feet and recited the lines:

Your presence there would honour us,
And that we would acknowledge.
While if you do not come,
We have no substitute and no replacement.

Moved by pity and compassion, I agreed, saying: 'I shall do something for her, if God wills, and she shall be married in my clothes with my jewellery and my finery.' The old woman was delighted: she bent down to kiss my feet and said: 'May God reward you and mend your heart as you have mended mine. But do not trouble yourself to do this service now. If you are ready in the evening, I will come and fetch you.' She then kissed my hand and left. I was ready when she came back and she said: 'My lady, the women of the town have come. I told them that you were going to be there and they were delighted and are waiting for you to arrive.' So I drew my veil and got up, taking my maids with me, and I went on until we came to a lane that had been swept and sprinkled with water, and where a cool breeze was blowing. There we arrived at an arched gate with a strongly built marble dome, leading to the door of a palace that soared from the ground to touch the clouds. Over the gate these lines were inscribed:

I am a house built for pleasure
And consecrated for all time to joy and relaxation.
In my centre is a fountain with gushing waters
That clear away all sorrows.
Flowers border it – anemones and the rose,
Myrtle, narcissus blooms and camomile.

When we got to the door, the old woman knocked, and when it was opened, we went in to find a hall spread with carpets, in which lighted lamps were hanging and candles were ranged, with gems and precious stones. We walked through the hall until we came to a room of unparalleled splendour, spread with silken rugs and lit by hanging lamps and two rows of candles. In the centre of it there was a couch of juniper wood studded with pearls and gems and covered with a buttoned canopy of satin. Before we knew what was happening, out came a girl. I looked at her, Commander of the Faithful, and saw that she was more perfect than the moon at its full, with a forehead brighter than daybreak, as the poet has said:

In the palaces of the Caesars she is a maiden
From among the bashful ones of the Chosroes' courts.
On her cheeks are rosy tokens;
How beautiful are those red cheeks.
A slender girl with a languid, sleepy glance,
She encompasses all beauty's graces.
The lock of hair that hangs above her forehead
Is the night of care set over joyful dawn.

She emerged from beneath the canopy and greeted me as her dear and revered sister, giving me a thousand welcomes and reciting:

Were the house to know who comes to visit it,
It would kiss in joyfulness the place where you have trod.
And call out with its silent voice:
'Welcome to the generous and noble one.'

She then sat down and said: 'Sister, I have a brother who has seen you at a number of weddings and festivals. He is a young man more handsome than I am, and he is deeply in love with you because of the richness of beauty and grace that you possess. He has heard that you are the mistress of your people, as he is the master of his. Because he wished to attach himself to you, he played this trick in order that I should meet you. He wants to marry you in accordance with the ordinance of God and of His Apostle, and there is no disgrace in what is lawful.' When I heard what she had to say and saw that I was now inside the house, I told her that I would agree. She was delighted and, after clapping her hands, she opened a door from which emerged a young man in the bloom of his youth, immaculately dressed, well built, handsome, graceful, splendid and perfect, with engaging manners. His eyebrows were like an archer's bow and his eyes could steal hearts with licit magic, as the poet's description has it:

His face is like a crescent moon,
Where marks of good fortune are like pearls.

How excellent also are the lines:

Blessed is his beauty and blessed is our God.
How great is He who formed and shaped this man!
Alone he has acquired all loveliness,
And in his beauty all mankind strays lost.
Upon his cheek beauty has written these words:
'I testify there is no handsome man but he.'

When I looked at him, my heart turned to him and I fell in love. He sat beside me and I talked to him for an hour, after which the girl clapped her hands for a second time. The door of a side room opened and from it emerged a *qadi* with four witnesses, who greeted us and then sat down. The marriage contract between me and the young man was drawn up, after which the others withdrew. 'May this be a blessed night,' said my bridegroom, turning to me. 'But, my lady,' he added, 'I impose one condition on you.' 'What is that?' I asked. He got up and fetched a copy of the Quran and said: 'Swear that you will not look at any other man but me, or incline to him.' I swore to that, to his great joy. He embraced me and my whole heart was filled with love for him. Servants then set out a table and we ate and drank our fill. Night fell and he took me to bed, where we continued to kiss and embrace until morning.

We continued in this state for a month, living in happiness and joy, and at the end of that time I asked my husband's leave to go to market to buy some material. After he had given me permission, I put on an outdoor mantle, and taking with me the old woman and a servant girl, I went down to the market. There I sat in the shop of a young merchant who was known to the old woman. She told me that he was a youth whose father had died, leaving him a huge amount of money. 'He has a great stock of goods,' she added. 'You will find whatever you want, and no trader in the market has finer fabrics.' Then she told the man to produce for me the most expensive stuff that he had and he replied: 'To hear is to obey.' The old woman then began to sing his praises, but I told her: 'There is no necessity for this. All we want is to get what we need and then to go back home.'

The man brought out what we were looking for and we produced the money for him, but he refused to take anything and said: 'This is a guest gift for you today from me.' I said to the old woman: 'If he refuses to accept the money, then give him back the stuff.' 'By God,' he said, 'I shall not accept anything from you, and all this is a gift from me in exchange for a single kiss, which is of more value to me than everything that is in my shop.' 'What good will a kiss do you?' asked the old woman, but then she told me: 'You heard what he said, daughter. What harm will a kiss do you, and you can then take what you want?' 'Don't you know that I have sworn an oath?' I asked, but she went on: 'Stay silent and let him kiss you. You will have done nothing wrong and you can take back this money.' She continued to inveigle me, until I fell into the trap and agreed. I then covered my eyes and hid myself from the passers-by with the edge of my veil. He put his mouth on my cheek beneath my veil and, after kissing me, he bit me hard, piercing the skin of my cheek so that I fainted.

The old woman held me to her breast and when I recovered my senses, I found the shop closed, with her grieving over me and saying: 'God has averted what could have been worse.' Then she said to me: 'Come back to the house with me and pull yourself together, lest you be shamed. When you get home, go to bed, pretend to be sick and cover yourself up. I will fetch you something with which to treat this bite and it will soon be better.' After a while, I got up, full of care and extremely fearful, and I walked very slowly home, where I acted as though I was sick. At nightfall, in came my husband. He asked: 'My lady, what happened to you while you were out?' 'I'm not well,' I said, 'and I have a headache.' He looked at me, lit a candle and came up to me. 'What is this wound on your tender cheek?' he asked. 'After receiving your permission to go out today to buy materials, I left the house but was pushed by a camel carrying firewood; my veil was torn and, as you can see, I got this wound on my cheek, for the streets are narrow here.' 'Tomorrow I will go to the governor,' he said, 'and tell him to hang everyone who sells firewood in the city.' I implored him not to burden himself with the guilt of wronging someone, adding: 'I was riding on a donkey which threw me and I fell on the ground where I struck a piece of wood which grazed my cheek and wounded me.' He said: 'Tomorrow I shall go to Ja'far the Barmecide and tell him what happened to you, so that he may put every donkey driver in this city to death.' 'Are you going to kill everyone because of me?' I asked. 'What happened was a matter of fate and destiny.' 'It must be done,' he said, and he kept on insisting on this until, when he got up, I turned around and spoke sharply to him.

At that, Commander of the Faithful, he realized what had happened to me. 'You have been false to your oath,' he said, letting out a great cry. The door opened and seven black slaves came in. On his orders, they dragged me from my bed and threw me down in the middle of the room. He told one of them to hold my shoulders and to sit on my head, while another was to sit on my knees and hold my feet. A third came with a sword in his hand and my husband ordered him to strike me with the sword and cut me in two and then said: 'Let each of you take a piece and throw it into the Tigris as food for the fish. This is the reward of those who betray their oaths and are false to their love.' He grew even more angry and recited these lines:

If I must have a partner in my love,
Even though passion slay me, I shall drive love from my soul.
I say to my soul: 'Die nobly,
For there is no good in a love that is opposed.'

Then he told the slave: 'Strike, Sa'd.' When the slave was sure that his master meant what he said, he sat over me and said: 'Lady, recite the confession of faith, and if there is anything that you want done, tell me, for this is the end of your life.' 'Wait a little, good slave,' I said, 'so that I can give you my last instructions.' Then I raised my head and saw the state that I was in and how I had fallen from greatness to degradation. My tears flowed and I wept bitterly, but my husband recited angrily:

Say to one who has tired of union and turned from me,
Being pleased to take another partner in love:
'I had enough of you before you had enough of me,
And what has passed between us is enough for me.'

When I heard that, Commander of the Faithful, I wept and, looking at him, I recited:

You have abandoned me in my love and have sat back;
You have left my swollen eyelids sleepless and have slept.
You made a pact between my eyes and sleeplessness.
My heart does not forget you, nor are my tears concealed.
You promised to be faithful in your love,
But played the traitor when you won my heart.

I loved you as a child who did not know of love,
So do not kill me now that I am learning it.
I ask you in God's Name that, if I die,
You write upon my tomb: 'Here lies a slave of love.'
It may be that a sad one who knows love's pangs
Will pass this lover's heart of mine and feel compassion.

On finishing these lines, I shed more tears, but when my husband heard them and saw my tears, he became even angrier and recited:

I left the darling of my heart not having tired of her,
But for a sin that she was guilty of.
She wanted a partner to share in our love,
But my heart's faith rejects a plural god.

When he had finished his lines, I pleaded with him tearfully, telling myself that if I could get round him with words, he might spare my life, even if he were to take everything that I had. So I complained to him of my sufferings and recited:

Treat me with justice and do not kill me;
The sentence of separation is unjust.
You loaded me with passion's heavy weight,
Although even one shirt is too much for my strength.
I am not surprised that my life should be lost;
My wonder is how, after your loss, my body can be recognized.

I finished the lines weeping, but he looked at me and rebuffed and reviled me, reciting:

You left me for another and made clear
You were forsaking me; this is not how we were.
I shall abandon you as you abandoned me,
Enduring without you as you endure my loss.
I cease to occupy myself with you,
For you have occupied yourself with someone else.
The severance of our love is set at your door, not at mine.

On finishing these lines, he shouted at the slave: 'Cut her in half and let us be rid of her, for there is no good to be got from her.' While we were sparring with each other in this exchange of lines and I had become certain I would die, despairing of life and commending my affair to Almighty

God, suddenly in came the old woman, who threw herself at my husband's feet, kissed them and said tearfully: 'My son, I have brought you up and served you. I conjure you by this to spare this girl, for she has not committed a crime that deserves death. You are very young and I am afraid lest she involve you in sin – as the saying goes, "Every killer is killed." What is this slut? Cast her off from you, from your mind and from your heart.' Then she wept and she kept on pressing him until he agreed and said: 'I shall spare her life, but I must mark her in a way that will stay with her for the rest of her life.' On his orders, the slaves then dragged me off, stripped me of my clothes and stretched me out. They sat on me while he fetched a rod from a quince tree and set about beating me. He went on striking my back and sides so severely that I lost consciousness, giving up hope of life. He then told the slaves that when night fell they should take the old woman with them as a guide, carry me off and throw me into my old house. They did as they were told and after throwing me into the house, they went off.

It was not until daybreak that I recovered from my faint and I then tried to soothe my wounds, treating my body with salves and medicines. As you can see, my ribs continued to look as though they had been struck with clubs, and for four months I remained weak and bedridden, tending to my own wounds until I recovered and was cured. I then went to the house that had been the scene of my downfall, only to find it ruined and reduced to a pile of rubble, with the lane in which it stood totally demolished. I could find no news of what had happened and so I came to my half-sister, with whom I found these two black bitches. After greeting her, I told her everything that had happened to me. 'My sister,' she said, 'who is unscathed by the misfortunes of Time? Praise be to God who brought a safe ending to this affair,' and she started to recite:

This is how Time acts, so show endurance
Whether you be stripped of wealth or parted from your love.

She then told me her own story, of what had happened to her with her sisters and how they had ended up. I stayed there with her and the word 'marriage' never crossed our lips. We were then joined by this girl who acts as our housekeeper, going out each day to buy what we need for the next twenty-four hours. Things went on like this until last night. Our sister had gone out as usual to buy our food when she returned with the porter, and the three dervishes arrived shortly afterwards. We talked with them, brought them in and treated them well. After only a little of the night had passed, we were joined by three respectable merchants from Mosul. They told us their story and we talked with them, but we had imposed a condition on all our visitors, which they broke. We paid them back for this breach and asked them all for their stories, which they recited. We then forgave them and they left. Today, before we knew what was happening, we were brought before you. This is our story.

The caliph was filled with amazement at this and had the account written down and placed in his archives. He then asked the first girl: 'Have you any news of the *jinn* lady who bewitched your sisters?' 'Commander of the Faithful,' she replied, 'she gave me a lock of her hair and told me that when I wanted her I should burn a single hair and she would come quickly, even if she were on the far side of Mount Qaf.' The caliph asked her to produce the lock of hair, which she did, and he then took a single strand and burned it. When the smell of the burning spread, the palace was rocked by a tremor; there was a sound like a peal of thunder and there stood the lady. As she was a Muslim, she greeted the caliph, who replied: 'Peace be on you and the mercy and blessings of God.' 'Know,' she went on, 'that this girl sowed the seed of gratitude for a good deed that she did me, for which I could not repay her, when she saved me from death and killed my enemy. I then saw what her sisters had done to her. At first I wanted to kill them but I was afraid that this might distress her, so then I thought that I should take revenge by turning them by magic into dogs. If you now want them to be set free, Commander of the Faithful, I shall release them as a favour to you and to her, for I am a Muslim.' 'Do so,' he said, 'and after that I shall begin to investigate the affair of the girl who was beaten. If it turns out that she was telling the truth, we shall avenge her on whoever wronged her.'

'Commander of the Faithful,' said the lady, 'I shall release the two and then tell you who it was who wronged this girl and seized her wealth – someone who is your closest relation.' She then took a bowl of water, cast a spell over it and recited some unintelligible words. She sprinkled water on the faces of the two bitches and said: 'Return to your former shapes as humans,' which they did. 'Commander of the Faithful,' she then said, 'the young man who beat the girl is your own son, al-Amin, the brother of al-Ma'mun. He had heard of her great beauty and set a trap for her. But he married her legally and was within his rights to beat her, as he had imposed a condition on her and got her to swear a solemn oath that she would do nothing to break it. Break it she did, however, and he was going to kill her, but for fear of God he beat her instead and sent her back to her own house. This is the story of the second girl, but God knows better.'

When the caliph heard what she had to say and learned how the girl had come to be beaten, he was filled with astonishment and said: 'Glory be to God, the Exalted, the Omnipotent, Who has granted me the favour of learning this girl's history and rescued these two others from sorcery and torture. By God, I shall do something that will be recorded after me.' Then he had his son al-Amin brought before him and he questioned him about the second girl, questions to which al-Amin returned a truthful answer. He then brought in *qadis* and notaries, as well as the three dervishes, together with the first girl and her two sisters who had been bewitched. He married the three of them to the three dervishes, who had told him that they were kings, and whom he now appointed as chamberlains at his court, giving them all they needed and assigning them allowances, as well as lodgings in the palace of Baghdad. He returned the girl who had been beaten to his son al-Amin, renewing their marriage contract, giving her a great store of wealth and ordering that their house should be rebuilt with the greatest splendour. He himself married the housekeeper and slept with her that night and in the morning he gave her a chamber of her own among his concubines, together with slave girls to serve her and regular allowances. The people were astonished at his magnanimity, generosity and wisdom. His orders were that all these stories should be written down.

[Nights 9–19]

The Story of Nur al-Din and Shams al-Din

It is said that in the old days there was in Egypt a just and upright sultan who loved the poor and would sit with men of learning. He had an intelligent and experienced vizier, with a knowledge of affairs and of administration. This vizier was a very old man and he had two sons, fair as moons, unequalled in comeliness and beauty. The name of the elder was Shams al-Din Muhammad, while the younger was Nur al-Din 'Ali. Nur al-Din was more conspicuously graceful and handsome than his brother, so much so that his fame had spread in other lands, and people came to Egypt to see his beauty.

It then happened that their father died. He was mourned by the sultan, who went to the sons, brought them close to him and gave them robes of honour. 'Do not be distressed,' he said, 'for you will take your father's place.' This delighted them and they kissed the ground in front of him. After a month of mourning for their father, they entered into office as joint viziers, sharing between themselves the power that had been in their father's hands, with one of them accompanying the sultan whenever he went on his travels.

It happened that the sultan was about to leave on a journey in the morning and it was the turn of the elder brother to go with him. On the night before, the two brothers were talking together and the elder said to the younger: 'Brother, it is my intention that you and I should marry on the same night.' 'Do what you want,' said his brother, 'for I agree to your suggestion.' When they had made this agreement, the elder said: 'If God so decrees, we shall marry two girls and consummate the marriage on one and the same night. Then they will give birth on the same day and, God willing, your wife will produce a boy and mine a girl. We shall then marry them to each other and they will be husband and wife.' 'What dowry will you ask from my son for your daughter?' asked Nur al-Din. 'I shall take from your son,' replied Shams al-Din, 'three thousand dinars, three orchards and three estates. On no other terms will the marriage contract be valid.'

When he heard this, Nur al-Din said: 'What is this dowry that you want to impose as a condition on my son? Don't you know that we two are brothers and that both of us, by God's grace, are joint viziers, equal in rank? You should give your daughter to my son without asking for any dowry at all, and if there must be one, then it should be fixed at something that will merely show people that a payment has been made. You know that the male is better than the female. My son is a male and it is through him and not through your daughter that we shall be remembered.' 'What about my daughter, then?' asked Shams al-Din. 'It will not be through her that we shall be remembered among the emirs,' his brother told him, and added: 'You want to deal with me like the man in the story who approached one of his friends to ask for something. "I swear by the Name of God," said his friend, "that I shall do what you ask, but tomorrow." In reply, the other recited:

If favours are put off until next day,
For those who know, that is rejection.'

Shams al-Din said: 'I see that you are selling me short and making out that your son is better than my daughter. It is clear that you lack intelligence and have no manners. You talk about our shared vizierate, but I only let you share out of pity for you, so that you might help me as an assistant and I might not cause you disappointment. Now, by God, after what you have said, I shall not marry my daughter to your son, even if you were to pay out her weight in gold.' Nur al-Din was angry when he heard this and said: 'I'm no longer willing to marry my son to your daughter.' 'And I'm not prepared to accept him as a husband for her,' repeated Shams al-Din, adding: 'Were I not going off on a journey I would make an example of you, but when I get back, I shall let you see what my honour requires.'

On hearing what his brother had to say, Nur al-Din was beside himself with anger, but he managed to conceal this. The two of them spent the night in separate quarters and in the morning the sultan set out on his journey, going by Giza and making for the Pyramids, accompanied by the vizier Shams al-Din. As for Shams al-Din's brother, Nur al-Din, after spending the night in a furious rage, he got up and performed the morning prayer. Then he went to his strongroom and, taking out a small pair of saddlebags, he filled them with gold. Remembering his brother's contemptuous remarks, he started to recite these lines:

Go, and you will replace the one you leave behind;
Work hard, for in this lies life's pleasure.
The stay-at-home is humble, arriving at no goal
Except distress, so leave your land and go.
I see that water left to stand goes bad;
If it flows, it is sweet, but if not, it is not.
Were the full moon not to wane,
The watcher would not always follow it.
Lions that do not leave their lair will find no prey;
Arrows not shot from bows can strike no target.
Gold dust when in the mine is worth no more than earth,
And aloes wood in its own land is merely used for fires.
When taken from the mine, gold is a precious object of demand,
While elsewhere in the world it is outranked by aloes wood.

When Nur al-Din had finished these lines, he told one of his servants to prepare the official mule with its quilted saddle. This beast, coloured like a starling, had a high, dome-like back; its saddle was of gold and its stirrups of Indian steel; its trappings were like those of the Chosroes; and it looked like a bride unveiled. Nur al-Din ordered that a silk carpet and a prayer rug should be put on it, with the saddlebags being placed under the rug. He then told his servants and slaves that he was going on a pleasure trip outside the city. 'I shall go towards Qalyub,' he said, 'and spend three nights away. None of you are to follow me, for I am feeling depressed.'

He quickly mounted the mule, taking with him only a few provisions, and he then left Cairo, making for open country. By noon he had reached Bilbais, where he dismounted, rested and allowed the mule to rest too. He took and ate some of his provisions, and in Bilbais he bought more food for himself and fodder for his mule. He then set out into the country, and when night fell, he had come to a place called al-Sa'diya. Here he spent the night, getting out some food, placing the saddlebags beneath his head and spreading out the carpet. He slept there in the desert, still consumed with anger, and after his night's sleep, he rode off in the morning, urging on his mule until he came to Aleppo. There he stayed for three days in one of the *khans*, looking around the place at his leisure until both he and the mule were rested. Then he decided to move on and, mounting his mule, he rode out of the city without knowing where he was heading. His journey continued until, without knowing where he was, he reached Basra. He stopped at a *khan*, unloaded the saddlebags from the mule and spread out the prayer mat. He then handed over the mule with all its gear to the gatekeeper of the *khan*, asking him to exercise it, which he did.

It happened that the vizier of Basra was sitting at the window of his palace. He looked at the mule with its costly trappings and thought that it might be a ceremonial beast, the mount of viziers or kings. Perplexed by this, he told one of his servants to bring him the gatekeeper of the city. The servant did as he was told, and the gatekeeper came to him and kissed the ground. The vizier, who was a very old man, asked him who the mule's owner might be and what he was like. 'Master,' said the gatekeeper, 'the owner of this mule is a very young man of the merchant class, impressive and dignified, with elegant manners, the son of a merchant.' On hearing this, the vizier got up and after riding to the *khan*, he approached Nur al-Din, who, seeing him coming, rose to meet him. He greeted the vizier, who, in turn, welcomed him, dismounted from his horse, and embraced him, making him sit beside him. 'My son,' he said, 'where have you come from and what do you want?' 'Master,' replied Nur al-Din, 'I have come from Cairo. I was the son of a vizier there, but my father moved from this world to the mercy of Almighty God.' He then told his story from beginning to end, adding: 'I have made up my mind that I shall never return until I have passed through every city and every land.' 'My son,' said the vizier when he heard this, 'do not obey the promptings of pride or you will destroy yourself. The lands are desolate and I am afraid lest Time bring misfortunes on you.'

He then had Nur al-Din's saddlebags placed on the mule and, taking the carpet and the prayer mat, he brought him to his house where he lodged him in elegant quarters and showed him honour, kindness and much affection. 'My boy,' he said to him, 'I am an old man and I have no son, but God has provided me with a daughter who is your match in beauty and whose hand I have refused to many suitors. I have conceived love for you in my heart and so I ask whether you would be willing to take her to serve you, while you become her husband. If you accept, I shall bring you to the sultan of Basra and tell him that you are the son of my brother, and I shall get him to appoint you as his vizier in my place. I shall then stay at home, for I am an old man.'

When Nur al-Din heard what he had to say, he bowed his head and said: 'To hear is to obey.' The vizier was delighted and he told his servants to set out food and to decorate the main reception hall where the weddings of the emirs were held. He collected his friends and invited the great officials of state together with the merchants of Basra. When they came, he told them: 'I had a brother, the vizier of Egypt. God provided him with two sons, while, as you know, He gave me a daughter. My brother had enjoined me to marry her to one of his sons. I agreed to this, and when the appropriate time for marriage came, he sent me one of his sons – this young man who is here with us. Now that he has arrived, I want to draw up the marriage contract between him and my daughter that the marriage may be consummated here, for he has a greater right to her hand than a stranger. After that, if he wants he can stay here, or if he prefers to leave, I shall send him and his wife off to his father.'

Everyone there approved of the plan and, looking at Nur al-Din, they admired what they saw. The vizier then brought in the *qadis* and the notaries, who drew up the contract. Incense was scattered, sugared drinks served and rosewater sprinkled, after which the guests left. The vizier then told his servants to take Nur al-Din to the baths. He gave him a special robe of his own and sent him towels, bowls and censers, together with everything else that he might need. When he left the baths wearing the robes, he was like the moon when it is full on the fourteenth night. He mounted his mule and rode on until he reached the vizier's palace, where he dismounted. Entering the vizier's presence, he kissed his hand and was welcomed. The vizier got up to greet him, saying: 'Go in to your wife tonight and tomorrow I will take you to the sultan. I hope that God will grant you every blessing.' Nur al-Din then did as the vizier had said.

So much for him, but as for Shams al-Din, his brother, when he came back from his journey with the sultan of Cairo and failed to find Nur al-Din, he asked the servants about him. They replied: 'The day that you left with the sultan, he mounted his mule with its ceremonial trappings and told us that he was going in the direction of Qalyub and would be away for a day or two. No one was to follow him, for he was depressed, and from that day to this we have heard no news of him.' Shams al-Din was disturbed by the departure of his brother and bitterly sorry to have lost him. 'This is because of my angry words to him that night,' he said to himself. 'He must have taken them to heart and gone off on his travels. I must send after him.' He went to the sultan and told him what had happened, and he then wrote notes and posted instructions to his agents throughout the lands. As it happened, however, in the twenty days that Shams al-Din had been away with the sultan, Nur al-Din had travelled to distant regions, and although Shams al-Din's agents searched, they had to come back with no news of him. Shams al-Din then despaired of his brother and said: 'I went too far in what I said to him about our children's marriage. I wish that I hadn't done this; it was due to my stupidity and mismanagement.'

Shortly after this, he proposed to the daughter of a Cairene merchant and after the contract had been drawn up, the marriage was consummated. As it happened, this coincided with the wedding of Nur al-Din to the daughter of the vizier of Basra, as God Almighty had willed it, in order that what He had decreed might be fulfilled among His creatures. What the brothers had said in their conversation came about, in that both their wives became pregnant. The wife of Shams al-Din, the Egyptian vizier, gave birth to the most beautiful girl who had ever been seen in Cairo, while the wife of Nur al-Din gave birth to a son as handsome as any of the people of his age. He was as the poet described:

A slender youth whose hair and whose forehead
Leave mankind to enjoy both dark and light.
Find no fault with the mole upon his cheek;
Every corn-poppy has its own black spot.

Another poet has produced these lines:

If beauty comes to be measured against him,
It must hang down its head in shame.
Asked: 'Have you ever seen a sight like this?'
It answers: 'No, I never have.'

Nur al-Din named his son Badr al-Din Hasan and his grandfather was overjoyed at his birth and gave banquets and feasts worthy of the sons of kings. He then took Nur al-Din and brought him to the sultan. When he appeared before the sultan, Nur al-Din kissed the ground and, being as eloquent as he was courageous, handsome and generous, he recited:

My lord, may your prosperity endure,
And may you live while dark and dawn remain.
When men talk of your high-mindedness,
Time itself dances as it claps its hands.

The sultan rose to greet his two visitors, thanked Nur al-Din for what he had said and asked the vizier who he was. The vizier told him Nur al-Din's story from beginning to end, adding that he was his own nephew. 'How can he be your brother's son,' asked the sultan, 'when we have never heard of him?' 'My lord, the sultan,' replied the vizier, 'I had a brother who was vizier of Egypt. On his death, he left two sons, the elder of whom has taken his father's place as vizier, while this, the younger son, has come to me. I swore that I would marry my daughter to no one else, and when he arrived, this is what I did. He is young and I am very old. I am hard of hearing and my control of affairs is weak, and so I would ask my master to appoint him in my place. He is my nephew, the husband of my daughter, someone well fitted to be vizier, as he is a man of judgement and a good manager.'

The sultan found what he saw of Nur al-Din to be to his taste and so he granted the vizier's request and promoted Nur al-Din to the vizierate. On his orders, the new vizier was given a robe of honour and one of the special mules, as well as pay and allowances. He kissed the sultan's hand and he and his father-in-law went back joyfully to their house, saying: 'This is due to the good luck brought by baby Hasan.' The next day, Nur al-Din went to the sultan, kissed the ground and recited:

Happiness is renewed on every day
Together with good fortune, confounding envious schemes.
May the whiteness of your days not cease,
While the days of your enemies are black.

The sultan ordered him to take the vizier's seat, which he did, and he then took in hand the duties of his office, investigating the affairs of the people and their lawsuits, as is the habit of viziers. Watching him, the sultan was astonished at what he was doing, his intelligence and powers of administration, all of which won him the sultan's affection and his intimate regard. When the court was dismissed, Nur al-Din went home and delighted his father-in-law by telling him what had happened. The young man continued to act as vizier until, both by night and by day, he became inseparable from the sultan. His pay and allowances were increased and he became rich; he owned shops that traded on his account, slaves, mamluks, and many flourishing estates with water wheels and gardens.

When Hasan was four years old, the old vizier, Nur al-Din's father-in-law, died and Nur al-Din gave him the most lavish of funerals. He then concerned himself with the upbringing of his son, and when the boy grew strong and had reached the age of seven, his father brought in a tutor to teach him at home, telling the man to give him the best instruction. The tutor taught Hasan to read and made him commit to heart many useful branches of learning, as well as getting him to memorize the Quran, over a period of years.

Hasan became ever more beautiful and well formed, as the poet puts it:

A moon reaches its full in the heavens of his beauty,
While the sun shines from his blooming cheeks.
All beauty is his and it is as though
All that is fair in men derives from him.

He was brought up in his father's palace, which throughout his early years he never left, until one day his father took him, clothed him in one of his most splendid robes, mounted him up on one of the best of his mules and brought him to the sultan. The sultan looked at the boy with admiration and felt affection for him. As for the townspeople, when he passed for the first time on his way to the sultan with his father, they were astonished at his beauty and they sat in the street waiting for him to come back so that they could have the pleasure of looking at his comely and well-shaped form. This was as the poet puts it:

One night as the astronomer watched, he saw
The form of a graceful youth wandering in his twin robes.
He observed how Gemini had spread for him
The graceful beauty that his flanks displayed.
Saturn had granted him black hair,
Colouring his temples with the shade of musk.
From Mars derived the redness of his cheeks,
While Sagittarius shot arrows from his eyelids.
Mercury supplied keenness of mind,
And the Bear forbade slanderers to look at him.
The astronomer was bewildered at what he saw
And then ran forward to kiss the earth before him.*

When the sultan saw Hasan, he conferred his favour and affection on him and told his father that he must always, and without fail, bring the boy with him to court. 'To hear is to obey,' replied Nur al-Din, after which he took him back home. Every day from then on he went with him to the sultan until the boy reached the age of fifteen. It was then that Nur al-Din fell ill and, sending for his son, he said: 'Know, my son, that this

*cf. p. 98.

world is transitory, while the next world is eternal. I wish to give you various injunctions, so try to understand what I have to say and take heed of it.' He then started to tell Hasan how to deal well with people and how to manage his affairs. Then he remembered his brother and his native land and he wept for the loss of loved ones. Wiping away his tears, he recited:

If I complain of distance, what am I to say,
And if I feel longing, what way of escape is there?
I might send messengers to speak for me,
But none of them can convey a lover's complaint.
I might show endurance, but after the beloved's loss
The life span of the lover is not long.
Nothing is left except yearning and grief,
Together with tears that stream down my cheeks.
Those whom I love are absent from my sight,
But they are found still settled in my heart.
Do you not see, though I have long been spurned,
My covenant is subject to no change?
Has her distance led you to forget your love?
Have tears and fasting given you a cure?
We are of the same clan, both you and I,
But you still try me with long-lasting censure.

When Nur al-Din, in tears, had finished reciting this, he turned to his son and said: 'Before I give you my injunctions, you must know that you have an uncle who is vizier of Egypt. I parted from him and left him without his leave. Take a scroll of paper and write down what I shall dictate.' Hasan took the paper and started to write, while his father dictated an account of what had happened to him from start to finish. He noted the date of the consummation of his marriage with the old vizier's daughter, explaining how he had arrived at Basra and met his father-in-law, adding: 'Many years have passed since the day of our quarrel. This is what I have written to him, and may God now be with him in my stead.'

He folded the letter, sealed it, and said: 'Hasan, my son, keep this testament, for in it is an account of your origin and your genealogy. If anything happens to you, go to Egypt, ask for your uncle and tell him that I have died in a foreign land, longing for him.' Hasan took the paper, folded it and sewed it up in a fold of material, before placing it in the wrapper of his turban, all the while shedding tears at the thought of being parted from his father while he himself was still young. Nur al-Din then said: 'I give you five injunctions. The first is: do not be on intimate terms with anyone, for in this way you will be safe from the evil they may do you. Safety lies in seclusion, so do not be too familiar with anyone. I have heard what the poet says:

There is no one in this age of yours for whose friendship you can
hope;
When Time is harsh to you, no friend will stay faithful.
Live alone and choose no one in whom to trust.
This, then, is my advice; it is enough.

The second injunction, my son, is to injure no man, lest Time injure you, for one day it will favour you and the next day it will harm you, and this world is a loan to be repaid. I have heard what the poet says:

Act slowly; do not rush to what you want.
Be merciful and be known for your mercy.
No power surpasses that of God,
And every wrongdoer will be oppressed.

The third injunction is to keep silent and to concern yourself with your own faults and not with those of others. The saying goes: "Whoever stays silent, escapes," and I have heard the poet say:

Silence is an adornment which affords you safety,
But if you speak, refrain from babble.
If you regret your silence once,
You will regret having spoken many times.

The fourth injunction, my son, is this: be on your guard against drinking wine, for wine is the root of all discord and it carries away men's wits, so I repeat, guard against it. I have heard the poet say:

I gave up drinking wine and have become
A source of guidance for its censurers.
Drink makes the drunken stray from the right path,
And opens the door to evil.

The fifth injunction is this: guard your wealth and it will guard you; protect it and it will protect you. Do not overspend or you will find yourself in need of help from the most insignificant people. Look after your money, for it will be a salve for your wounds. I have heard the poet say:

If I lack money, then I have no friends,
But all men are my friends when I have wealth.
How many friends have helped me spend,
But when the money went, they all deserted me.'

Nur al-Din went on delivering his injunctions to Hasan until his soul left his body, after which Hasan stayed at home mourning for him, with the sultan and all the emirs joining in his grief. His mourning extended for two months after the funeral, during which time he did not ride out, attend court or present himself before the sultan. This earned him the sultan's anger, as a result of which one of the chamberlains was appointed vizier in his place, with orders to set his seal on Nur al-Din's properties, wealth, buildings and possessions.

The new vizier set out to do this and to arrest Hasan and take him to the sultan to deal with the young man as he saw fit. Among his soldiers was one of the dead vizier's mamluks, and when he heard what was about to happen, he quickly rode to Hasan, and found him sitting by the door of his house, broken-hearted and with his head bowed in sorrow. The mamluk dismounted, kissed his hand and said: 'My master and son of my master, quick, quick, run away before you are doomed.' 'What is the matter?' asked Hasan, trembling. 'The sultan is angry with you and has ordered your arrest,' replied the mamluk. 'Misfortune is hot on my heels, so flee for your life.' 'Is there time for me to go inside to fetch some money to help me in exile?' Hasan asked. 'Get up now, master,' urged the mamluk, 'and leave at once.'

So Hasan got up, reciting these lines:

If you meet injustice, save your life
And let the house lament its builders.
You can replace the country that you lose,
But there is no replacement for your life.
Send out no messenger on any grave affair,
For only you yourself will give you good advice.
The lion's neck is only thick
Because it looks after all its own affairs.*

*cf. p. 59.

Then, heeding the mamluk's warning, he covered his head with the skirt of his robe and walked off until he got outside the city. He heard the people saying that the sultan had sent the new vizier to the old vizier's house, to set his seal on his wealth and his properties and to arrest his son, Hasan, in order to bring him for execution, and they were sorry for this because of the young man's beauty.

On hearing what they were saying, Hasan left the city immediately, without knowing where he was going, until fate led him to his father's grave. He entered the cemetery and made his way among the tombs until he reached that of his father. There he sat down, unwinding the skirt of his robe from his head. On the cloth were embroidered in gold the lines:

You whose face gleams
Like stars and dew,
May your fame last for ever
And your exalted glory stay eternally.

As he was sitting there, a Jew, who appeared to be a money-changer, came up to him, carrying saddlebags containing a great quantity of gold. After approaching him, this Jew said: 'Master, why is it that I see that you are drained of colour?' Hasan replied: 'I was sleeping just now, when in a dream I saw my father reproaching me for not having visited him. I got up in alarm, and I was afraid that if I did not pay him a visit before the end of the day, it might go hard with me.' 'Master,' said the Jew, 'your father sent out trading ships, some of which have just arrived and I want to buy the cargo of the first of them from you for this thousand dinars of gold.' He then brought out a purse filled with gold, from which he counted out a thousand dinars and gave them to Hasan in return for which he asked for a signed bill of sale. Hasan took a piece of paper, on which he wrote: 'The writer of this note, Hasan, son of Nur al-Din, has sold to Ishaq the Jew for a thousand dinars the cargo of the first of his father's ships to come to port, the sale price having been paid in advance.'

After Ishaq had taken the note, Hasan began to weep as he remembered the glory that had been his, and he recited:

The dwelling is no dwelling since you left,
And since you left, we have no neighbours there.
My old familiar friends are now no friends,
Nor are the moons still moons.
You left and this has made the world a wilderness,

And the wide lands are now all dark.
Would that the crow that croaked of your going
Were stripped of feathers and could find no nest.
I have scant store of patience. Now that you have gone,
My body is gaunt and many a veil is torn.
Do you think that those past nights will ever come again
As we once knew them, and the same home shelter us?

He wept bitterly, and as night drew in, he rested his head on his father's tomb and fell asleep. As he slept, the moon rose: his head slipped from the tombstone and he slept on his back, with his face gleaming in the moonlight. It so happened that the cemetery was frequented by *jinn* who believed in God. A *jinniya* came and looked at the sleeping Hasan and, struck by wonder at his beauty, she exclaimed: 'Glory to God, it is as though this youth is one of the children of Paradise.' She then flew off, making her customary circuit in the air. Seeing an *'ifrit* flying by, she greeted him and asked him where he had come from. 'From Cairo,' he said, and she asked: 'Would you like to go with me to see the beauty of this youth asleep in the cemetery?' The *'ifrit* agreed and they flew down to the tomb. 'Have you ever in your life seen anything to match this?' the *jinniya* asked. 'Glory be to the Matchless God!' the *'ifrit* exclaimed. 'But sister,' he added, 'would you like me to tell you what I have seen?' 'What was that?' she asked. 'I have seen someone who is like this youth in the land of Egypt. This is the daughter of Shams al-Din, a girl about twenty years old, beautiful, graceful, splendid, perfectly formed and proportioned. When she passed this age, the sultan of Egypt learned of her, sent for Shams al-Din, her father, and said: "Vizier, I hear that you have a daughter and I would like to ask you for her hand in marriage." "My master," said Shams al-Din, "accept my excuse and have pity on the tears that I must shed. You know that my brother Nur al-Din left us and went away we don't know where. He was my partner in the vizierate and the reason that he left in anger was that we had sat talking about marriage and children and this caused the quarrel. From the day that her mother gave birth to her, some eighteen years ago, I have sworn that I shall marry my daughter to none but my brother's son. A short time ago, I heard that my brother married the daughter of the vizier of Basra, who bore him a son, and out of respect for my brother I shall marry my daughter to no other man. I have noted the date of my own marriage, my wife's pregnancy and the birth of this girl. She is the destined bride of her cousin; while for the sultan there are girls aplenty."

'When he heard this, the sultan was furiously angry and said: "When someone like me asks for a girl's hand from a man like you, do you refuse to give her to me and put forward an empty excuse? I swear that I shall marry her off to the meanest of my servants to spite you." The sultan had a hunchbacked groom, with a hump on his chest and another on his back. He ordered this man to be brought to him and he has drawn up a contract of forced marriage between him and Shams al-Din's daughter, ordering him to consummate the marriage tonight. The sultan is providing the groom with a wedding procession and when I left him he was surrounded by the sultan's mamluks, who were lighting candles around him and making fun of him at the door of the baths. Shams al-Din's daughter, who bears the greatest resemblance to this young man, is sitting weeping among her nurses and maids, for her father has been ordered not to go to her. I have never seen anything more disgusting than the hunchback, while the girl is even more lovely than this youth.'

The *jinniya* replied: 'You are lying, for this young man is the most beautiful of all the people of his age.' The *'ifrit* contradicted her, saying: 'By God, sister, the girl is more lovely than he is, but he is the only fit mate for her, for they resemble one another like siblings or cousins. How sad will be her fate with the hunchback!' 'My brother,' said the *jinniya*, 'let us lift him from beneath and carry him to the girl you are talking about to see which of them is the more beautiful.' 'To hear is to obey,' replied the *'ifrit*. 'You are right, and there can be no better plan, so I shall carry him myself.' This he did, flying off into the air with Hasan, while the *jinniya* at his heels kept pace with him until he came to land in Cairo, where he set Hasan down on a bench and roused him.

When Hasan awoke and found that he was not by his father's grave in Basra, he looked right and left and discovered that he was in some other city. He was about to cry out when the *'ifrit* struck him. He had brought for him a splendid robe and made him put it on. Then he lit a candle for him, saying: 'Know that I have brought you here and am going to do you a favour for God's sake. Take this candle and go to these baths, where you are to mix with the people and walk along with them until you reach the bridal hall. Then go on ahead, entering the hall without fear, and once you are inside, stand to the right of the hunchbacked bridegroom. Whenever any of the maids, singing girls and attendants approaches you, put your hand in your pocket, which you will find filled with gold. Take a handful of the gold and throw it to them: you needn't fear that when you do this you will ever find your pocket empty, so you can scatter coins for everyone who comes up. Put your trust in your Creator, for this does not come about through any power of yours but at God's command.'

When Hasan heard what the *'ifrit* had to say, he wondered who the bride might be and why the *'ifrit* was doing him such a favour, but he lit the candle, went to the baths and found the hunchbacked bridegroom mounted on a horse. He joined the crowd in all the splendour of his beauty, wearing, as has been described, a tarboosh with a white covering and a mantle woven with gold. He continued to walk in the bridal procession and every time the singing girls stopped so that people might throw them money, he would put his hand in his pocket, find it filled with gold and, to the girls' astonishment, he would throw a handful into their tambourines, filling these up with dinars. His beauty moved the crowd, and they went on like this until they reached the house of Shams al-Din. Here the chamberlains turned back the crowd and would not let them enter, but the singing girls said: 'By God, we will not go in unless this young man comes too, for he has overwhelmed us with his generosity and we will not help display the bride unless he is there.'

At that, they entered the festal hall; Hasan was seated to the right of the hunchbacked bridegroom, while the wives of the emirs, viziers and chamberlains were drawn up in two lines, each carrying a large lighted candle and wearing a mouth-veil. The lines were drawn up to the right and left beneath the bridal throne, extending to the top of the hall beside the room from which the bride was to emerge. When the ladies saw Hasan's graceful beauty, with his face gleaming like the crescent moon, they were all drawn to him. The singing girls told them that the handsome young man had given them nothing but red gold: 'So be sure to serve him as best you can and do whatever he says.' The ladies crowded around him with their torches, looking at his beauty and envying him his gracefulness. There was not one of them who did not wish that they could enjoy his embrace for an hour or a year, and so far out of their senses were they that they let down their veils, exclaiming: 'Happy is she who has this young man as husband or master.' They then cursed the hunchback and the one who was responsible for his marriage to so beautiful a girl, while every blessing that they invoked upon Hasan was matched by a curse for the hunchback.

Then the singing girls beat their tambourines; the flutes shrilled and out came the maids with Shams al-Din's daughter in the middle of them.

They had covered her with perfume, dressed her hair beautifully and scented it, and robed her in clothes splendid enough for the kings of Persia. On top of these she wore a gown woven with red gold on which were embroidered pictures of beasts and birds, and round her throat was a Yemeni necklace worth thousands of dinars, comprising gemstones such as no king of Yemen or Byzantine emperor had ever possessed. She was like the moon when it is full on the fourteenth night, and when she came forward she was like a houri of Paradise – praise be to God, Who created her in beauty. The ladies surrounding her were like stars, while in their midst she was like the moon shining through clouds. Hasan was sitting there, the cynosure of all eyes, when she appeared and moved forward, swaying as she did so.

The hunchbacked bridegroom rose to greet her, but she turned from him and moved away until she stood before her cousin Hasan. The people laughed, and when they saw that she had turned towards Hasan, they shouted, while the singing girls raised a cry. Hasan put his hand in his pocket and, to their joy, he threw a handful of gold once more into their tambourines. 'Would that this was your bride,' they said. He laughed, and all those there pressed around him, while the bridegroom was left on his own, sitting hunched up like a monkey. Every time they tried to light a candle for him, he could not keep it alight, and as he could find nothing to say, he sat in the darkness looking down at the floor.

As for Hasan, he was confronted by people carrying candles, and when he looked at the bridegroom sitting alone in the shadows, he was filled with perplexity and astonishment, but this changed to joy and delight when he looked at his cousin. He saw her face shining radiantly in the candlelight, and he looked at the red satin dress that she was wearing, the first to be removed by her maids. As they unveiled her, this allowed Hasan to see her, swaying as she moved with artful coquetry, bewitching both men and women, and fitting the description of the poet:

A sun on a branch set in a sand hill,
Appearing in a dress of pomegranate blossom –
She let me drink the wine of her lips and with the gift
Of her cheeks she quenched the greatest fire.

The maids then changed her dress and clothed her in a blue gown, so that she looked like the gleaming full moon, with her black hair, smooth cheeks, smiling mouth, jutting breasts and beautiful hands and wrists.

When they showed her in this second dress, she was as the sublime poets have written:

She came forward in a gown of azure blue,
The colour of the sky.
I looked and saw within this gown
A summer moon set in a winter night.

They then changed that for another dress, using some of her hair as a veil and letting the remaining long, black locks hang loose. The length and blackness of this hair resembled the darkness of night and she shot at hearts with the magic arrows of her eyes. Of the third dress in which they showed her, the poet has written:

Veiled by hair draped over cheeks,
She was a temptation strong as burning fire.
I said: 'You have used night to veil the dawn.'
'No,' she replied, 'but I have veiled the moon in darkness.'

They then showed her in a fourth dress, and she came forward like the rising sun, swaying coquettishly and looking from side to side like a gazelle, while transfixing hearts with the arrows of her eyelids, as the poet has said:

The watchers saw a sun of loveliness,
Radiant in coquetry, adorned with bashfulness.
She turned her smiling face to the sun of day,
Since when the sun has veiled itself in cloud.

In her fifth dress, the adorable girl was like the branch of a *ban* tree or a thirsty gazelle. Her curls crept like scorpions and she showed the wonders of her beauty as she shook her hips and displayed the locks of hair covering her temples, as has been described in the lines:

She appeared as the full moon on a lucky night,
With tender hands and slender figure.
Her eye enslaves men with its loveliness;
The redness of her cheeks rivals the ruby.
Her black hair falls over her hips;
Beware the snakes that form those curling locks.
Her flanks are soft, but though they may be smooth,
Her heart is harder than the solid rock.

Her eyebrows shoot the arrows of her glance.
Even from far away, they strike unerringly.
If we embrace, I press against her belt,
But her breasts keep me from holding her too close.
Oh for her beauty which surpasses every grace!
Oh for her figure which shames the tender bough!

The sixth dress in which they showed her was green. Her upright posture put to shame the brown spear and her comeliness surpassed that of the beauties of every land. Her gleaming face outshone the shining moon; beauty yielded to her every wish; she captivated the boughs with her softness and suppleness, and she shattered hearts with her qualities, as has been described in the lines:

A girl trained in shrewdness –
You see that the sun is borrowed from her cheeks.
She came in a green dress,
Like pomegranate blossom veiled by leaves.
I asked her for its name and her reply
Was phrased with elegance:
'With it I cut men's hearts and so
The name I give it is "the bitter cut".'

The seventh dress in which they displayed her was part safflower red and part saffron. As the poet has said:

She sways in a dress part safflower, part saffron,
Scented with ambergris and musk and sandalwood –
A slender girl; youth urges her to rise;
Her buttocks tell her: 'Sit or move slowly.'
If I ask her for union, her beauty says:
'Be generous,' but coquetry says: 'Refuse.'

When the bride opened her eyes, she said: 'O God, make this my husband and free me from this hunchbacked groom.' So it was that she was shown in all her seven robes to Hasan of Basra, while the hunchbacked groom was left sitting by himself. When this had been done, the guests were allowed to leave, and all the women and children who had attended the wedding went out, leaving only Hasan and the hunchback. The maids took the bride to her room to change her ornaments and her clothes and make her ready for the bridegroom. At that, the hunchback approached

Hasan and said: 'Sir, you have been kind enough to favour us with your company this evening but it is time for you to get up and go.' 'In the Name of God,' said Hasan, and he got up and went out of the door. There, however, the *'ifrit* met him and told him to stop, saying: 'When the hunchback goes out to the latrine, enter at once and sit down in the alcove. When the bride comes, tell her: "I am your husband and the sultan only played this trick on you for fear that you might be hurt by the evil eye. The man whom you saw is one of our grooms." After this, go up to her and uncover her face. As far as we are concerned, this is a matter of honour.'

While Hasan was talking with the *'ifrit*, out came the hunchback and went to the latrine. As he sat down, the *'ifrit* in the form of a mouse emerged from the water bowl and said '*ziq*'. 'What is the matter with you?' said the hunchback. Then the mouse grew bigger until it became a cat, which said '*miya, miya*', after which it grew bigger still and turned into a dog, which said '*'awh, 'awh*'. At this, the hunchback became frightened and said: 'Go away, you ill-omened beast,' but the dog grew bigger and swelled up until it became an ass, which brayed and bellowed '*haq, haq*' in his face. The hunchback was even more frightened and called for help, but the donkey grew even larger until it was the size of a buffalo. Blocking the hunchback's retreat, it called to him in a human voice: 'You stinking fellow.' The hunchback could not control his bowels and sat down on the outlet of the latrine, still wearing his clothes, and with his teeth chattering. 'Do you find the world so narrow,' asked the *'ifrit*, 'that you can find no one to marry except my beloved? Answer me,' he went on, as the hunchback stayed silent, 'or else I shall put you in your grave.' 'By God,' said the hunchback, 'none of this is my fault. They forced me to marry the girl and I didn't know that she had a buffalo for a lover. I repent of the match to God and to you.' 'I swear to you,' said the *'ifrit*, 'that if you leave this place or speak a single word before the sun rises, I shall kill you. At sunrise you can go on your way, but never come back to this house.' Then he took hold of the hunchback and put him head first into the outlet of the latrine. 'I shall leave you here,' he said, 'but I shall be watching over you until sunrise.'

This is what happened to the hunchback, but as for Hasan, leaving the hunchback and the *'ifrit* quarrelling, he went into the house and took his seat in the middle of the alcove. At that moment, the bride appeared, accompanied by an old woman, who said: 'You well-made man, rise up and take what God has entrusted to you.' Then she turned back, while the bride, whose name was Sitt al-Husn, came into the alcove. She was heartbroken, saying: 'I shall never let him have me, even if he kills me.' But when she entered and saw Hasan, she exclaimed: 'Darling, are you still sitting here? I had told myself that you could share me with the hunchback.' 'How can the hunchback approach you?' said Hasan. 'And how could he share you with me?' 'But who is my husband,' she asked, 'you or he?' 'Sitt al-Husn,' said Hasan, 'we only did this as a joke to mock him. When the maids and the singing girls and your family saw your beauty being unveiled for me, they were afraid of the evil eye and your father hired this fellow for ten dinars to turn it away from us, and now he has gone.' When Sitt al-Husn heard this from Hasan, she smiled with joy and laughed gently. 'By God,' she said, 'you have quenched my fire, so I ask you to take me and crush me to your breast.'

She was without any outer clothing and when she now raised her shift up to her neck, her private parts and her buttocks were revealed. At this sight, Hasan's passion was aroused and, getting up, he stripped off his clothes. He took the purse of gold with the thousand dinars that he had got from the Jew and wrapped it in his trousers, placing it under the end of the mattress, and he took off his turban and set it on a chair, leaving him wearing only a fine shirt embroidered with gold. At that, Sitt al-Husn went up to him and drew him to her as he drew her to him. He embraced her and placed her legs around his waist. He then set the charge, fired the cannon and demolished the fortress. He found his bride an unbored pearl and a mare that no one else had ridden, so he took her maidenhead and enjoyed her youth. Then he withdrew from her and after a restorative pause, he returned fifteen times, as a result of which she conceived.

When he had finished, he put his hand beneath her head and she did the same to him, after which they embraced and fell asleep in each other's arms. This was as the poet has described:

Visit your love; pay no heed to the envious:
For such are of no help in love.
God in His mercy makes no finer sight
Than of two lovers on a single bed,
Embracing one another and clothed in content,
Pillowed on one another's wrists and arms.
When hearts are joined in love,
The iron is cold on which all others strike.
When your age has provided you a single friend,

How good a friend is this! Live for this one alone.
You who blame the lovers for their love,
Have you the power to cure the sick at heart?

This is what took place between Hasan and his cousin, Sitt al-Husn. As for the *'ifrit*, he said to the *jinniya*: 'Get up and go in beneath this young man so that we may take him back to where he came from lest morning overtakes us. It is almost dawn.' The *jinniya* did this as Hasan slept, still wearing his shirt and nothing else, and taking hold of him she flew off. She continued on her way, while the *'ifrit* kept pace with her, but midway through their journey they were overtaken by the dawn. The muezzin called to prayer and God permitted his angels to hurl a shooting star at the *'ifrit*, who was consumed by fire. The *jinniya* escaped, but she set Hasan down in the place where the *'ifrit* had been struck by the star, as she was too afraid for his safety to take him any further. As fate had decreed, they had reached Damascus and it was by one of the city gates that she left him, before flying away.

When the gates were opened in the morning, the people came out and there they found a handsome youth clothed only in a shirt and a woollen skullcap. Because of his wakeful night, he was sunk in sleep. When the people saw him, they said: 'How lucky was the one with whom this fellow spent the night, but he should have waited to put on his clothes.' Another said: 'They are poor fellows, these rich men's sons. This one must have just come out of the wine shop to relieve himself, when his drunkenness got the better of him, and as he couldn't find the place he was making for, he arrived instead at the city gate, only to find it locked. Then he must have fallen asleep here.'

As they were talking, a gust of wind blew over Hasan, lifting his shirt above his waist. Beneath it could be seen his stomach, a curved navel, and two legs and thighs like crystal. The people exclaimed in admiration and Hasan woke up to find himself by the city gate, surrounded by a crowd. 'Where am I, good people?' he said. 'Why have you gathered here and what have I to do with you?' 'When the muezzin gave the call to morning prayer,' they said, 'we saw you stretched out asleep, and that is all we know about the business. Where did you sleep last night?' 'By God,' replied Hasan, 'I slept last night in Cairo.' 'You've been eating hashish,' said one of them. 'You're clearly mad,' said another. 'You go to sleep in Cairo and in the morning here you are asleep in Damascus.' 'Good people,' he replied, 'I have not told you a lie. Last night I was in Egypt and yesterday I was in Basra.' 'Fine,' said one. 'He is mad,' said another, and they clapped their hands over him and talked among themselves, saying: 'What a shame for one so young, but he is undoubtedly mad.' Then they said to him: 'Pull yourself together and return to your senses.' 'Yesterday,' insisted Hasan, 'I was a bridegroom in Egypt.' 'Maybe you were dreaming,' they said, 'and it was in your dream that you saw this.' Hasan thought it over to himself and said: 'By God, that was no dream, nor did I see it in my sleep. I went there and they unveiled the bride before me, and there was a third person, a hunchback, sitting there. By God, brothers, this was not a dream, and had it been one, where is the purse of gold that I had with me and where is my turban and the rest of my clothes?'

He then got up and went into the city, with the people pressing around him and accompanying him as he made his way through the streets and markets. He then entered the shop of a cook, who had been an artful fellow, that is to say, a thief, but had been led to repent of his evil-doing by God, after which he had opened a cookshop. All the people of Damascus were afraid of him because of his former violence, and so when they saw that Hasan had gone into his shop, they dispersed in fear. The cook, looking at Hasan's grace and beauty, felt affection for him enter his heart. 'Where have you come from, young man?' he said. 'Tell me your story, for you have become dearer to me than my life.'

Hasan told him what had happened to him from beginning to end, and the cook exclaimed at how remarkable and strange it was. 'But, my son,' he added, 'keep this affair concealed until God relieves your distress. Stay with me here, and I shall take you as a son, for I have none of my own.' Hasan agreed to this and the cook went to the market and bought fine material for him, with which he clothed him. The two of them went off to the *qadi* and Hasan declared himself to be the cook's son. This is how he became known in Damascus, and he sat in the shop taking the customers' money, having settled down with the cook.

So much for him, but as for his cousin, Sitt al-Husn, when dawn broke and she awoke from her sleep, she did not find Hasan, and thinking that he must have gone to the latrine, she sat for a time waiting for him. Then in came Shams al-Din, her father, who was distressed at what the sultan had done to him and at how he had forced Sitt al-Husn to marry one of his servants, a mere groom and a hunchback. He said to himself that he would kill the girl if she had allowed that damned man to have her. So he walked to her room, stopped at the door and called out to her. 'Here I am, father,' she said, and she came out, swaying with joy. She kissed the ground and her face shone with ever more radiant beauty, thanks to the embrace of that gazelle-like youth.

When her father saw her in this state, he said: 'Are you so pleased with that groom, you damned girl?' When she heard this, she smiled and said: 'By God, what happened yesterday was enough, with people laughing at me and shunning me because of this groom who is not worth the paring of my husband's fingernail. I swear that never in my life have I spent a more delightful night than last night, so don't make fun of me or remind me of that hunchback.' When her father heard this, he glared at her in anger and said: 'What are you talking about? It was the hunchback who spent the night with you.' 'For God's sake, don't mention him, may God curse his father, and don't jest. The groom was hired for ten dinars and he took his fee and left. Then I arrived and when I went into the room I found my husband sitting there. This was after the singing girls had unveiled me for him and he had scattered enough red gold to enrich all the poor who were present. I passed the night in the embrace of my charming husband, with the dark eyes and the joining eyebrows.'

When her father heard this, the light before him turned to darkness. 'You harlot,' he said, 'what are you saying? Where are your wits?' 'Father,' she replied, 'you have broken my heart – enough of this ill humour. This is my husband who took my virginity. He has gone to the latrine, and he has made me pregnant.' Her father got up in astonishment and went to the latrine, where he found the hunchback with his head stuck in the hole and his legs sticking out on top. He was amazed and said: 'Surely this is the hunchback.' He called to the man, who mumbled in reply, thinking that it was the *'ifrit* who was speaking to him. Shams al-Din then shouted to him: 'Speak or else I shall cut your head off with this sword.' 'By God, *shaikh* of the *'ifrits*,' said the hunchback, 'since you put me here I have not raised my head, and I implore you by God to be kind to me.' 'What are you talking about?' said Shams al-Din when he heard this. 'I am the father of the bride and not an *'ifrit*.' 'Enough of that,' said the hunchback, 'for you are on the way to getting me killed, so go off before the *'ifrit* who did this to me comes back. What you have done is to marry me to the mistress of buffaloes and *'ifrits*. May God curse the man who married me to her and the one who was the cause of this.'

'Get up,' said Shams al-Din, 'and come out.' 'Do you think that I am mad,' said the hunchback, 'that I should go with you without the *'ifrit*'s permission? He told me to come out and leave at sunrise. So has the sun risen or not, for I can't come out of here until it has?' Shams al-Din then asked who had put him there. 'I came here last night to relieve myself,' the man replied, 'and suddenly a mouse came out of the water and squeaked, and then it went on growing bigger and bigger until it was as large as a buffalo. It spoke to me in tones that rang through my ears, after which it left me and went away. May God curse the bride and the man who married me to her!'

Shams al-Din went up and removed him from the latrine, after which he ran off, not believing that the sun had risen, and going to the sultan, he told him what had happened to him with the *'ifrit*. As for Shams al-Din, the bride's father, he went back in a state of perplexity, not understanding what had happened to his daughter, and he asked her to explain the matter again. She replied: 'The bridegroom, for whom I was unveiled yesterday, spent the night with me, took my virginity and has made me pregnant. If you don't believe me, here is his turban, in its folds, lying on the chair, and here are his other clothes underneath the bed, with something wrapped up in them, although I don't know what it is.' On hearing this, her father came into the alcove, where he found the turban of his nephew, Hasan. He took it in his hands, turned it over and said: 'This is a vizier's turban and it is of muslin.' He then looked and saw an amulet sewn into the tarboosh, which he took and opened, and he picked up the outer clothes, in which he found the purse containing the thousand dinars. Opening it, he found inside it a sheet of paper, which he read and which turned out to be the Jew's contract of sale, with the name of Badr al-Din Hasan, the son of Nur al-Din 'Ali, the Egyptian. He also found the thousand dinars.

On reading the paper, he uttered a loud cry and fell down in a faint. When he recovered and grasped what this all meant, he was filled with wonder and exclaimed: 'There is no god but God, Who has power over all things.' Then he said: 'Daughter, do you know who it was who deflowered you?' 'No,' she replied. 'It was my brother's son, your cousin,' he said, 'and these thousand dinars are your dowry. Glory be to God, but I wish I knew how this came about.' Then he reopened the amulet and in it he found a note in the handwriting of his brother Nur al-Din. After looking at his brother's handwriting, he recited:

I see the traces they have left and melt with longing,
And I pour down my tears over their former dwellings.
I ask the One who afflicted me with separation
That one day He might favour me with their return.

On finishing these lines, Shams al-Din read through what was in the amulet and there he found the date of Nur al-Din's marriage to the daughter of the vizier of Basra, its consummation, the date of Hasan's birth, and an account of Nur al-Din's life up until the time of his death. This astonished him; he trembled with joy and, on comparing what had happened to his brother with his own history, he found that they matched exactly, that the consummation of his marriage and that of his brother had happened on the same date, as had the birth of Hasan and that of his own daughter, Sitt al-Husn. Taking the paper, he brought it to the sultan and told him all that had happened from start to finish. The astonished sultan ordered that an account of this should be written down immediately.

Shams al-Din waited, expecting his nephew to come, but he did not come that day, or on the next, or on the third, and after seven days had passed, there was still no news of him. So Shams al-Din said: 'By God, I shall do something that no one has ever done before,' and taking an inkwell and a pen, he produced on a piece of paper a sketch plan of the whole house, with the alcove here, such-and-such a hanging there, and so on, including everything in the house. He then folded the paper and gave orders for all Hasan's things to be collected. He took the turban, the tarboosh, the mantle and the purse, which he locked up in his own room with a lock of iron, setting a seal on it to await his nephew's arrival.

As for his daughter, at the end of the months of her pregnancy, she gave birth to a boy, splendid as the moon, resembling his father in beauty, perfection, splendour and grace. The midwives cut the umbilical cord, spread kohl on his eyelids and then handed him over to the nurses, naming him 'Ajib. In one day he grew as much as other children grow in a month, and in a month as much as they do in a year. When he was seven years old, he was handed over to a teacher who was told to give him a good education and to teach him to read. He stayed at school for four years, but he began to fight with the other children and abuse them, saying: 'Which of you is my equal? I am the son of Shams al-Din of Egypt.' The other children went together to the monitor to complain of his rough behaviour. The monitor told them: 'When he arrives tomorrow, I'll teach you something to say to him that will make him give up coming to school. Tomorrow, when he arrives, sit around him in a circle and say to each other: "By God, no one may play this game with us unless he can tell us the names of his mother and father." Anyone who doesn't know these names is a bastard and won't be allowed to play.'

The next morning, they came to school and when ‘Ajib arrived, they surrounded him and said: ‘We are going to play a game but no one may join in with us unless he can tell us the names of his mother and father.’ They all agreed to this, and one of them said: ‘My name is Majid; my mother is ‘Alawiya and my father is ‘Izz al-Din.’ A second boy did the same and so did the others until it came to ‘Ajib’s turn. He then said: ‘My name is ‘Ajib; my mother is Sitt al-Husn and my father is Shams al-Din of Egypt.’ ‘By God,’ they said to him, ‘Shams al-Din isn’t your father.’ ‘Yes, he is,’ insisted ‘Ajib, and at that the boys laughed at him, clapped their hands, and said: ‘He doesn’t know who his father is; go away and leave us. We will only play with those who know their father’s name.’

At that, the children around him went off laughing and leaving him angry and choked with tears. The monitor told him: ‘We know that your grandfather, Shams al-Din, is not your father but the father of your mother, Sitt al-Husn; as for your own father, neither you nor we know who he is. The sultan married your mother to the hunchbacked groom, but a *jinni* came and slept with her and you have no father we know of. You won’t be able to compare yourself with the other boys in this school unless you find out who your father is, for otherwise they will take you for a bastard. You can see that the trader’s son knows his father, but although your grandfather is Shams al-Din of Egypt, as we don’t know who your father is, we say that you have no father. So act sensibly.’

When ‘Ajib heard what the monitor and the boys had to say and how they were insulting him, he went away immediately and came to his mother, Sitt al-Husn, to complain, but he was crying too hard to speak. When she heard his sobs, her heart burned and she said: ‘What has made you cry? Tell me.’ So he told her what he had heard from the children and from the monitor, and he asked her: ‘Who is my father?’ She said: ‘Your father is Shams al-Din of Egypt.’ But he said: ‘Don’t tell me lies. Shams al-Din is your father, not mine, so who is my father? If you don’t tell me the truth, I’ll kill myself with this dagger.’ When his mother heard him talk of his father, she burst into tears, remembering her cousin Hasan and how she had been unveiled for him and what he had done with her. She recited these lines:

They stirred up longing in my heart and left.
Those whom I love have now gone far away.
They left and with them has my patience gone.
After this loss, patience is hard to find.

They left, and were accompanied by my joy.
Nothing stays fixed; there is no fixity.
By leaving me, they brought tears to my eyes,
And thanks to this, my tears flow down in floods.
I yearn to see them, and for long
I have been yearning and awaiting them.
I call up pictures of them, and my inmost heart
Is home to passion, longing and to care.
Your memory has now become my cloak,
And under it I wear my love for you.
Beloved, for how long will this go on?
How long will you stay distant and shun me?

She wept and wailed, as did 'Ajib, and at that point suddenly in came Shams al-Din. When he saw their tears, his heart was burned and he asked what was the reason for all this grief. Sitt al-Husn told him what had happened to 'Ajib with the boys at his school, and Shams al-Din himself wept, remembering his brother and what had happened to the two of them, as well as what had happened to his daughter, the real truth of which he did not know. He then immediately got up and went to the court, where he came into the sultan's presence and told him his story, asking leave to travel to the east in order to make enquiries about his nephew in Basra. He also asked the sultan to give him written instructions addressed to all lands, allowing him to take his nephew with him wherever he might be found. He then burst into tears before the sultan, who was moved with pity for him and wrote him the orders for which he had asked. This delighted Shams al-Din, who called down blessings on his master, and then took his leave.

He immediately went home and made his preparations for the journey, taking with him all that he, his daughter and 'Ajib might need. They travelled day after day until they arrived at Damascus, which they found full of trees and watered by streams, as the poet has described it:

I passed a day and a night in Damascus, and Time swore
That with a city like this it could make no mistake.
I spent the night while night's wing paid no heed,
And dawn was smiling with grey hair.
On the branches there dew gleamed like pearls,
Touched gently by the zephyr and then falling.

The pool was like a page read by the birds,
Written by wind, with clouds as punctuation.

Shams al-Din halted in the Maidan al-Hasa, where he pitched his tents, telling his servants that they would rest there for two days. For their part, they then went into the city to do as they pleased, one selling, one buying, one going to the baths and another to the Umaiyad Mosque, whose like is to be found nowhere in the world. 'Ajib went out accompanied by a eunuch and they entered the city to look at the sights, with the eunuch walking behind holding a cudgel so heavy that were he to use it to strike a camel, the beast would never rise again. The people of Damascus looked at 'Ajib, his well-formed figure, his splendour and his beauty, for he was a remarkably handsome boy with soft manners, more delicate than the northern breeze, sweeter than cold water to the thirsty man and more delightful than the recovery of health to the sick. As a result, he was followed by a large crowd, some running behind him and others going on ahead and sitting in the road looking at him as he passed.

This went on until, as had been decreed by fate, the eunuch stopped at the shop of his father Hasan. In the twelve years that he had spent in Damascus, Hasan's beard had grown long and he had matured in intelligence. The cook had died and he had taken over his wealth and his shop, having been acknowledged before the judges and the notaries as his son. When 'Ajib and the eunuch halted by his shop that day, Hasan looked at 'Ajib, his son, and, taking note of how extremely handsome he was, his heart beat fast, blood sensed the pull of blood, and he felt linked to the boy by affection. He happened to have cooked a dish of sugared pomegranate seeds and as God had inspired him with love for his son, he called out to him: 'My master, who has taken possession of my heart and for whom I yearn, would you enter my shop, mend my broken heart and eat of my food?' Then, spontaneously, his eyes filled with tears and he thought of what he had been and what he now was.

As for 'Ajib, when he heard what his father had said, he felt drawn to him. He told this to the eunuch, adding: 'It is as though this cook is a man who has parted from his son. Let us go into his shop, so that we may comfort him and eat what he gives us as guests. It may be that, if I do this for him, God may unite me with my father.' 'A fine thing, by God!' exclaimed the eunuch when he heard this. 'Do viziers' sons stay eating in a cookshop? I use this stick to keep people away from you lest they even look at you, and I shall never feel safe in letting you go in here.' When

Hasan heard this, he was astonished and turned to the eunuch with tears running down his cheeks, while 'Ajib said: 'My heart is filled with love for this man.' 'Don't say that,' the eunuch replied, 'for you are never going in there.' Hasan himself then turned to the eunuch and said: 'Great one, why do you not mend my broken heart by entering my shop yourself, you who are like a chestnut, dark but with a white heart, you who fit the description of the poet?' 'What is this you say?' said the eunuch, laughing. 'Produce the description but keep it short.' So Hasan started to recite these lines:

Were he not educated and reliable,
He would hold no office in the royal palace
Or be given charge of the harem. Oh what a servant,
Who, for his beauty, heavenly angels serve!

The eunuch was filled with admiration when he heard this and, taking 'Ajib with him, he entered the shop. Hasan then ladled into a bowl an excellent mixture of pomegranate seeds, almonds and sugar and they both ate after Hasan had welcomed them, saying: 'You have done me a favour, so enjoy your meal.' 'Ajib then said to his father: 'Sit and eat with us, and it may be that God will bring us together with those whom we wish to meet.' 'My boy,' said Hasan, 'have you, young as you are, had to suffer the loss of dear ones?' 'Yes, uncle,' replied 'Ajib. 'This has caused me bitter distress, and the one whom I have lost is my father. My grandfather and I have come to search for him through all the lands, and I am filled with sad longing for him.' He then wept bitterly and his father wept because of his loss and because of the boy's tears, remembering the loss of his own loved ones and his separation from his father and his mother, while the eunuch shared his sorrow. They then ate their fill, after which the two got up, and when they left the shop, Hasan felt as though his soul had parted from his body and gone with them.

He could not endure to be parted from them for the blink of an eye and so he locked up his shop and followed, without realizing that 'Ajib was his son. He hurried on until he caught up with them before they had gone out of the main gate. The eunuch turned and asked what he wanted. 'When you left my shop,' replied Hasan, 'I felt that my soul had gone with you and, as I have an errand in the suburbs outside the gate, I wanted to go with you, do my errand, and then go back.' The eunuch was angry. 'This is what I was afraid of,' he told 'Ajib. 'The bite that we had to eat was unfortunate in that it has put us under an obligation, and here is that fellow following us from place to place.' 'Ajib turned, and finding Hasan walking behind him, he became angry and his face flushed red. To the eunuch he said: 'Let him walk on the public road, but if, when we come out to our tents, we find that he is still following us, then we can drive him away.'

He then lowered his head and walked on, with the eunuch behind him and Hasan trailing them, as far as the Maidan al-Hasa. When they were close to the tents, they turned and saw him still behind them. 'Ajib was afraid that the eunuch might tell his grandfather, and he became very angry for fear lest he be reported as having entered the cookshop and having been followed by the cook. So he turned and found Hasan's eyes fixed on his, while Hasan himself looked like a body without a soul. To 'Ajib it seemed as though his eyes were those of a pervert or that he was a debauchee, and so, in a fit of rage, he took a stone and hit his father with it, knocking him unconscious, with the blood running down over his face. He and the eunuch then went to the tents.

When Hasan recovered consciousness, he wiped away the blood, and after cutting off a strip of his turban, he bandaged his head. He blamed himself and said: 'I wronged the boy by shutting up my shop and following him, making him think that I was a pervert.' So he went back to the shop and went on selling his food, but he started to yearn for his mother in Basra and he recited in tears:

You wrong Time if you ask it to be fair.
Do not blame it; it was not created for fair dealing.
Take what comes easily and leave care aside.
Time must contain both trouble and happiness.

He carried on with his business, while his uncle, Shams al-Din, after spending three days in Damascus, left for Homs, which he entered, and while he was on his journey he made enquiries wherever he went. He went to Diyar Bakr, Mardin and Mosul, and he kept on travelling until he reached Basra. After entering the city and settling himself there, he went to the sultan. When they met, the sultan treated him with respect and honour and asked him the reason for his visit. Shams al-Din told him his story and that his brother was Nur al-Din 'Ali. 'May God have mercy on him,' interjected the sultan, adding: 'He was my vizier and I loved him dearly, but he died fifteen years ago. He left a son, but the son only stayed for a month after his death before going missing and we have never heard any more news of him, although his mother, the daughter of my old vizier, is still with us.'

When Shams al-Din heard that the mother of his nephew was well, he was delighted and told the sultan that he would like to meet her. Permission was immediately granted and he went to visit her in his brother's house. He let his gaze wander around it, and kissing its threshold, he thought of his brother and of how he had died in exile. So he shed tears and recited these lines:

I pass by the dwellings, the dwellings of Laila,
And I kiss first one wall and then another.
It is not love for the dwellings that wounds my heart,
But love for the one who lived in them.

He passed through the door into a large hall where there was another door, arched and vaulted with flint inset with marble of different kinds and different colours. He walked through the house, and as he looked at it and glanced around, he found the name of his brother inscribed in letters of gold. He went up to the inscription, kissed it and wept as he remembered his separation from his brother. He then recited these lines:

Every time it rises, I ask the sun for news of you,
And I question the lightning about you when it flashes.
Longing folds and unfolds me in its hands
All night, but I do not complain of pain.
Dear ones, for long, after you went,
Separation from you has left me cut to pieces.
Were you to grant my eyes a sight of you –
It would be better still if we could meet.
Do not think I am busied with another;
My heart has no room for another love.

He then walked on until he reached the room of his brother's widow, the mother of Hasan, who throughout her son's disappearance had been weeping and wailing constantly, night and day. When long years had passed, she had made a marble cenotaph for him in the middle of the hall, where she would shed tears, and it was only beside this that she would sleep. When Shams al-Din came to her room, he heard the sound of her voice, and standing behind the door, he listened to her reciting:

In God's Name, grave, are his beauties now gone,
And has that bright face changed?

Grave, you are neither a garden nor a sky,
So how do you contain both branch and moon?*

While she was reciting this, Shams al-Din came in. He greeted her and told her that he was her husband's brother, and he then explained what had happened, giving her the full story, that her son Hasan had spent a whole night with his daughter ten years earlier and had then disappeared at dawn. 'He left my daughter pregnant,' Shams al-Din added, 'and she gave birth to a son who is here with me, and he is your grandson, the son of your son by my daughter.'

When she looked at her brother-in-law and heard the news that her son was still alive, she got up and threw herself at his feet, kissing them and reciting:

How excellent is the man who brings good tidings of your coming!
He has brought with him the most delightful news.
Were he to be contented with a rag, I would give him
A heart that was torn in pieces when you said goodbye.

Shams al-Din then sent a message telling 'Ajib to come, and when he did, his grandmother got up, embraced him and wept. 'This is no time for tears,' Shams al-Din told her. 'This is the time for you to make your preparations to travel with us to Egypt, and perhaps God will allow us and you to join your son, my nephew.' She agreed to leave and instantly got up to collect what she needed, together with her treasures and her maids. As soon as she was ready, Shams al-Din went to the sultan of Basra and took leave of him, while the sultan, in his turn, sent gifts and presents with him to take to the sultan of Egypt.

Shams al-Din then left immediately and travelled to Damascus, where he halted and pitched camp at al-Qanun. He told his entourage that they would stay there for a week so that they could buy gifts for the sultan. 'Ajib went out, telling his servant, Layiq, that he wanted to look around the place, adding: 'Come with me and we shall go down to the market and pass through the city to see what has happened to that cook whose food we ate and whose head I hurt. He had been kind to me and I harmed him.' Layiq agreed and the two of them left the camp, 'Ajib being drawn to his father by the ties of kinship.

After entering the city, they went on until they came to the cookshop, where they found Hasan. It was close to the time of the afternoon prayer

*cf. p. 35.

and, as luck would have it, he had cooked a dish of pomegranate seeds. When they approached him, 'Ajib looked at him with a feeling of affection, while noting the scar on his forehead left by the blow from the stone. He greeted Hasan affectionately, while, for his part, Hasan was agitated: his heart fluttered, he hung his head towards the ground and he tried without success to move his tongue around his mouth. Then looking up at his son, with meekness and humility he recited these lines:

I wished for my beloved, but when he came in sight,
In my bewilderment I could not control tongue or eyes.
I bowed my head in reverence and respect;
I tried to hide my feelings, but in vain.
I had whole reams of blame to give to him,
But when we met I could not speak a word.

Then he said to 'Ajib: 'Mend my broken heart and eat of my food. By God, when I look at you, my heart races and it was only because I had lost my wits that I followed you.' 'You must indeed be fond of me. I took a bite to eat with you, after which you followed me, wanting to bring shame on me. I shall only eat your food on condition that you swear not to come out after me or follow me again, for otherwise I shall never come back here, although we are staying for a week so that my grandfather can buy gifts for the sultan.' Hasan agreed and 'Ajib entered with his servant. Hasan presented them with a bowl of pomegranate seeds and 'Ajib asked him to give them the pleasure of eating with him. He accepted gladly, but as his heart and body were concentrated on 'Ajib, he kept staring fixedly at his face. 'Ajib objected, saying: 'Didn't I tell you that you are an unwelcome lover, so stop staring at my face.'

When Hasan heard what his son said, he recited these lines:

You have a hidden secret in men's hearts,
Folded away, concealed and not spread out.
Your beauty puts to shame the gleaming moon
While your grace is that of the breaking dawn.
The radiance of your face holds unfulfillable desires,
Whose well-known feelings grow and multiply.
Am I to melt with heat, when your face is my paradise,
And shall I die of thirst when your saliva is Kauthar?*

*Kauthar is the water of Paradise.

Hasan kept filling 'Ajib's plate and then that of the eunuch. They ate their fill and then got up. Hasan rose himself and poured water over their hands, after which he unfastened a silk towel from his waist on which he dried their hands before sprinkling them with rosewater from a flask that he had with him. Then he left his shop and came back with a jug of sherbet mixed with musk-flavoured rosewater, which he presented to them, saying: 'Complete your kindness.' 'Ajib took it and drank, after which he passed it to the eunuch. They then drank from it in turns until their stomachs were full, as they had had more than usual.

After leaving, they hurried back to their camp, where 'Ajib went to see his grandmother. She kissed him and then, thinking of her son, she sighed, shed tears and recited:

> I hoped that we might meet, and, after losing you,
> There was nothing for me to wish for in my life.
> I swear that there is nothing in my heart except your love,
> And God, my Lord, knows every secret thing.

She then asked 'Ajib where he had been, to which he replied that he had gone into the city of Damascus. She got up and brought him a bowl of pomegranate seeds that had only been sweetened a little, and she told the eunuch to sit down with his master. 'By God,' said the eunuch to himself, 'I have no urge to eat,' but he sat down. As for 'Ajib, when he took his seat, his stomach was full of what he had already eaten and drunk, but he took a morsel, dipped it among the pomegranate seeds and ate it. Because he was full, he found it undersweetened and he exclaimed: 'Ugh, what is this nasty food?' 'My son,' said his grandmother, 'are you blaming my cooking? I cooked this myself and no one can cook as well as I can, except for your father Hasan.' 'By God, grandmother,' replied 'Ajib, 'this dish of yours is disgusting. We have just come across a cook in the city who cooked a dish of pomegranate seeds whose smell would open up your heart. His food makes one want to eat again, while, in comparison, yours is neither one thing nor another.'

On hearing this, his grandmother became very angry and, looking at the eunuch, she reproached him, telling him that he had spoiled her son by taking him into a cookshop. The apprehensive eunuch denied this, saying: 'We didn't go into the shop but merely passed by it.' 'Ajib, however, insisted that they had gone in and had eaten, adding: 'And it was better than your food.' His grandmother got up and told her brother-in-law about this, turning him against the eunuch, who was then brought before him. 'Why did you take my grandson into the cookshop?' Shams al-Din asked. In his fear, the eunuch again denied this, but 'Ajib insisted: 'We did go in and we ate pomegranate seeds until we were full, after which the cook gave us a drink with snow and sugar.' Shams al-Din became even angrier with the eunuch and asked him again. He again denied it, at which Shams al-Din said: 'If you are telling me the truth, then sit down and eat in front of me.' The eunuch came forward and tried to do this but failed and had to throw away what he had taken. 'Master,' he explained, 'I am still full from yesterday.' Shams al-Din then realized that he had indeed eaten in the cookshop. He ordered the slaves to throw him down, which they did, and he then started to beat him painfully. The eunuch called for help. 'Don't beat me, master,' he cried, 'and I'll tell you the truth.' After this, Shams al-Din stopped beating him and demanded the truth. 'We did go into the shop,' he said, 'and the cook was preparing a dish of pomegranate seeds. He gave us some of it and, by God, never in my life have I tasted anything like it, while I have never tasted anything nastier than this stuff that is before us.'

Hasan's mother was angry and told him: 'You must go to this cook and fetch us a bowl of pomegranate seeds that he has prepared. You can then show it to your master and he can then say which is better and more tasty.' The eunuch agreed and was given a bowl and half a dinar. He went to the shop and said to Hasan: 'In my master's house we have laid a bet on your cooking. They have pomegranate seeds there, so for this half dinar give me some of yours, and take care over it, for your cooking has already cost me a painful beating.' Hasan laughed and said: 'By God, this is a dish that nobody can cook properly except for my mother and me, and she is now in a distant land.' He then ladled the food into the bowl and took it to put the finishing touches on it using musk and rosewater.

The eunuch carried it back quickly to the camp, where Hasan's mother took it and tasted it. When she noted how flavoursome it was and how well it had been cooked, she realized who must have cooked it and gave a shriek before falling in a faint, to the astonishment of Shams al-Din. He sprinkled rosewater over her and after a time she recovered. 'If my son is still in this world,' she exclaimed, 'it was he and no one else who cooked these pomegranate seeds. It has to have been my son, Hasan. No one else can cook it except him, for I taught him the recipe.' When Shams al-Din heard this, he was overjoyed and exclaimed: 'How I long to see my brother's son! Will time unite me with him? But it is only from Almighty God that I may seek a meeting with him.'

He got up immediately and went to his escort, ordering twenty men to go the cookshop, demolish it, and tie up the cook with his own turban. 'Then,' he said, 'drag him here by force, but without injuring him in any way.' The men agreed to do this, and Shams al-Din himself rode immediately to the palace of the governor of Damascus, whom he met and to whom he showed the letters that he had brought with him from the sultan. The governor kissed them and then placed them on his head, before asking: 'Where is the man you are looking for?' 'He is a cook,' replied Shams al-Din, and the governor instantly ordered his chamberlains to go to his shop. They went and found the shop demolished with all its contents smashed, for when Shams al-Din had gone to the governor's palace, his men had carried out his orders. They sat there waiting for him to return, while Hasan was asking: 'What could they have seen in the dish of pomegranate seeds that led to all this?'

Shams al-Din returned with the governor's permission to carry away Hasan. When he entered his tent, he ordered the cook to be produced and he was brought in, tied up with his own turban. Hasan wept bitterly on seeing his uncle and said: 'Master, what offence do you charge me with?' 'Was it you,' asked Shams al-Din, 'who cooked these pomegranate seeds?' 'Yes,' said Hasan, 'and did you find anything in them that entitles you to cut off my head?' 'For you this would be the best and lightest punishment,' said Shams al-Din. 'Master,' said Hasan, 'are you not going to tell me what I did wrong?' 'Yes, immediately,' said Shams al-Din, but he then called to the servants to bring the camels. They took Hasan with them, put him in a box, locked it and set off, travelling until nightfall. Then they halted and ate some food. They took Hasan out of his box, gave him something to eat and then put him back in it. They followed this pattern until they reached Qamra, when Hasan was taken out of his box and was again asked whether it was he who had cooked the pomegranate seeds. When he still said yes, Shams al-Din ordered him to be fettered, which was done and he was put back in the box.

The party then travelled on to Cairo, where they halted at the Raidaniya camping ground. Shams al-Din ordered Hasan to be taken out and he ordered a carpenter to be fetched whom he told to make a wooden cross. 'What are you going to do with it?' asked Hasan. 'I will garrotte you on it and then nail you to it, before parading you around the whole city,' Shams al-Din told him. 'Why are you doing this to me?' asked Hasan. 'Because of your ill-omened cooking of the pomegranate seeds, for you cooked them without enough pepper,' replied Shams al-Din. 'Are you really doing all this to me because the dish lacked pepper?' said Hasan. 'Was it not enough for you to keep me shut up, giving me only one meal a day?' 'There was not enough pepper,' said Shams al-Din, 'and the only punishment for you is death.' Hasan was both astonished and sorry for himself. 'What are you thinking about?' asked Shams al-Din. 'About superficial minds like yours,' replied Hasan, 'for if you had any intelligence you would not treat me like this.' 'We have to punish you,' said Shams al-Din, 'so as to see that you don't do this kind of thing again.' 'The least part of what you have done to me is a punishment,' said Hasan, but Shams al-Din insisted that he must be strangled.

While all this was going on, the carpenter was preparing the wood before his eyes. This went on until nightfall when Shams al-Din took Hasan and threw him into the box, saying: 'The execution will take place tomorrow.' He then waited until he was sure that Hasan was asleep, when he got up, lifted the chest and, after mounting his horse, he placed the box in front of him. He entered the city and rode on until he came to his house. To his daughter, Sitt al-Husn, he said: 'Praise be to God, Who has reunited you with your cousin. Get up and arrange the furnishings of the house as they were on your wedding night.' The household was roused and the candles were lit, while Shams al-Din produced the paper on which he had drawn a plan showing how the furniture was to be arranged. Everything was put in its place, so that anyone looking at it would be in no doubt that this was as it had been on the actual wedding night.

Shams al-Din gave instructions that Hasan's turban should be placed where he himself had left it, as should his trousers and the purse that was beneath the mattress. He then told his daughter to wear no more than she had been wearing when left alone with her bridegroom on her wedding night. 'When your cousin comes in,' he said, 'tell him that he has been a long time in his visit to the latrine and then invite him to pass the rest of the night with you. Talk with him until daybreak, and I shall then explain the whole affair to him.' Next, he took Hasan out of the chest, having first removed the fetters from his feet. He stripped off the clothes that he was wearing, so that he was left in a thin nightshirt with no trousers.

The sleeping Hasan knew nothing about what was happening, but, as fate had decreed, he turned over and woke up to find himself in a brilliantly lit hallway. 'This is a confused dream,' he said to himself, but he then walked a short way to a second door, and, on looking, he found himself in the room in which his bride had been unveiled for him. There was the alcove and the chair and he could see his turban and his other things. He was astonished at this sight and hesitated, moving forwards and then backwards. 'Am I asleep or awake?' he asked himself, wiping his forehead and saying in amazement: 'By God, this is the room of the bride who was unveiled for me; but where am I, for I was in a box?'

While he was talking to himself, Sitt al-Husn suddenly lifted the bottom of the alcove curtain and said: 'Master, are you not going to come in? You have been a long time in the latrine.' When he heard her voice and looked at her face, he laughed and said: 'I am in a confused dream.' He went into the alcove, where he sighed, and, thinking over his experiences, he was filled with confusion, particularly at the sight of the turban, his trousers and the purse with the thousand dinars, and was at a loss to grasp what had happened. 'God knows better,' he said, 'but this is a muddled dream.' 'What are you so astonished about?' asked Sitt al-Husn. 'You weren't like that at the beginning of the night.' Hasan laughed and asked: 'How long have I been away from you?' 'Bless you,' she said, 'and may the Name of God encompass you, you left to attend to yourself and then come back. Are you out of your mind?' Hasan laughed when he heard that and said: 'You are right, but when I left you I took leave of my senses in the latrine and dreamt that I was a cook in Damascus and had been there for ten years, when a boy, a great man's son, came in with a eunuch.'

At that, he rubbed his hand over his forehead and found the scar on it. 'By God, lady,' he said, 'that almost seems to be true, because he struck me on the forehead and broke the skin, and it seemed as though I was awake at the time.' He went on: 'It was as though we had just gone to sleep in each other's arms and then I had this dream and I appeared to have arrived in Damascus with no turban and no trousers and then worked as a cook.' After remaining perplexed for a time, he said: 'By God, I seemed to see that I had cooked a dish of pomegranate seeds and had put on too little pepper, but I suppose that I must have been asleep in the latrine and I must have seen all this in a dream.' 'What else did you see?' asked Sitt al-Husn. Hasan told her, and then he said: 'By God, if I had not woken up, they would have crucified me.' 'What for?' she asked. 'Because there was too little pepper on the pomegranate seeds,' he replied. 'It seemed as though they had wrecked my shop and broken up my utensils and put me in a box. Then they brought a carpenter to make a cross for me and they were going to garrotte me. Thank God that all this happened in a dream and not in real life.' Sitt al-Husn laughed and clasped him to her breast as he clasped her to his, but then he thought for a while and said: 'By God, it seemed as though it was real, but I don't know why that should be.' He was still perplexed when he fell asleep, muttering alternately 'I was asleep' and 'I was awake'.

That went on until morning, when his uncle Shams al-Din came in and greeted him. Hasan looked at him and said: 'By God, aren't you the man who ordered me to be tied up and crucified and ordered my shop to be wrecked because there was not enough pepper on the pomegranate seeds?' 'Know, my son,' said Shams al-Din, 'that the truth is now revealed and what was hidden has been made clear. You are the son of my brother and I only did all this to make sure that it was you who slept with my daughter that night. I could only be certain of this because you recognized the room and recognized your turban and your trousers, your gold, the note that you wrote and the one that your father, my brother, wrote. For I had never seen you before and could not identify you. I have brought your mother with me from Basra.' He then threw himself on Hasan in tears. When Hasan heard what his uncle had to say, he was lost in astonishment and, embracing his uncle, he wept from excess of joy.

'The reason for all this,' Shams al-Din told him, 'was what happened between me and your father.' He then told him the story of this and of why Hasan's father, Nur al-Din, had gone to Basra. He sent for 'Ajib, and when his father saw him, he said: 'This is the one who hit me with the stone.' 'He is your son,' Shams al-Din told him. Hasan threw himself on the boy and recited these lines:

I have wept over our separation, and for long
Tears have been pouring from my eyes.
I vowed, were Time to join us once again,
My tongue would never speak the word 'parting'.
Delight has now launched its attack on me,
And my great joy has made me weep.

As soon as he had finished speaking, in came his mother, who threw herself on him and recited:

On meeting, we complained of the great suffering of which we
speak.
It is not good to send complaints by messengers.

She then told him what had happened to her after he had vanished, and he told her of his own sufferings, and they then gave thanks to God for having reunited them. Two days after his arrival, Shams al-Din went to the sultan. On entering, he kissed the ground before him and greeted him with a royal salute. The sultan, who was glad to see him, smiled at him and told him to come nearer. He then asked him what he had seen in his travels and what had happened to him. Shams al-Din told him the story from beginning to end. 'Praise be to God,' said the sultan, 'for the achievement of your desire and your safe return to your family and children. I must see your nephew, Hasan of Basra, so bring him to court tomorrow.' Shams al-Din agreed to this – 'If God Almighty wills' – and then took his leave and went out. When he got home he told his nephew that the sultan wanted to see him. 'The servant obeys the order of his master,' said Hasan, and he accompanied his uncle to the sultan's court. When he was in the sultan's presence, he greeted him with the greatest respect and courtesy, and began to recite:

The one you have ennobled now kisses the ground,
A man whose quest has been crowned with success.
You are the lord of glory; those who rest their hope on you
Obtain what will exalt them in this world.

The sultan smiled, motioning him to sit, and so he took his seat near his uncle, Shams al-Din. The sultan then asked him his name, to which he replied: 'The meanest of your servants is known as Hasan of Basra, and night and day he invokes blessings on you.' The sultan was pleased with what he said and wanted to put his apparent knowledge and good breeding to the test. 'Do you remember any poetry that describes a mole?' he asked. 'Yes,' said Hasan, and he recited:

There is a dear one at the thought of whom
My tears fall and I wail aloud.
He has a mole, in beauty and in colour
Like the pupil of the eye or the heart's core.

The sultan approved of these lines and courteously asked him to produce more. So he recited:

Many a mole has been compared to a musk grain,
But this comparison is not to be admired.
Rather, admire the face encompassing all its beauty,
So that no single part is missing from the whole.

The sultan rocked with delight and said: 'Give me more, may God fill your life with blessing.' Hasan then recited:

You, on whose cheek the mole
Is like a grain of musk set on a ruby,
Grant me your union, and do not be harsh,
You who are my heart's wish and its nourishment.

'Well done, Hasan,' said the sultan. 'You have shown great proficiency. Now explain to us how many meanings does the word *khal*, or "mole", have in Arabic.' 'Fifty-eight,' was his reply, 'although some say fifty.' 'Correct,' said the sultan, who then asked him if he knew how beauty can be particularized. 'Yes,' he replied. 'It comprises brightness of face, clear skin, a well-shaped nose, sweet eyes, a lovely mouth, a witty tongue, an elegant frame and the qualities of refinement, while its perfection is found in the hair. The poet al-Shihab al-Hijazi has combined all these in a poem written in the *rajaz* metre:

Say, brightness is in the face; the skin is clear.
Let that be what you see.
Beauty is rightly ascribed to the nose,
While sweetness is attributed to eyes.
Yes, and men talk of mouths as beautiful.
Learn this from me, and may you not lack rest.
The tongue has wittiness and the frame elegance,
Whereas refinement lies in the qualities,
And perfect loveliness, they say, is in the hair.
Listen to my verse, and hold me free from blame.'

The sultan was pleased with what Hasan had said and felt well disposed towards him. He then asked him to explain the meaning of the proverbial expression 'Shuraih is more cunning than the fox'. 'Know, your majesty,' replied Hasan, 'may God Almighty aid you, that in the plague days Shuraih went to Najaf. Whenever he was going to pray, a fox would come and stand opposite him, imitating what he was doing and distracting him from his prayer. When that had gone on for a long time, one day he took off his shirt and put it on a cane, with its sleeves spread out. He then put his turban on top of the cane, tied a belt around the middle and set it up in the place where he prayed. The fox came up as usual and stood in front of it, at which Shuraih came up from behind and seized the animal. This is the explanation of the saying.'

When the sultan heard his explanation, he said to Shams al-Din: 'This nephew of yours is a man of perfect breeding, and I do not believe that his match is to be found in all Egypt.' Hasan rose, kissed the ground before the sultan, and took his seat like a mamluk in front of his master, and the sultan, delighted at having discovered the extent of his knowledge of the liberal arts, gave him a splendid robe of honour and invested him with an office that would help him to live well.

Hasan rose and, after kissing the ground again, he prayed for the sultan's enduring glory, and then asked permission to leave with his uncle Shams al-Din. When this was granted, he left and he and his uncle returned home. Food was brought and after they had finished eating a pleasant meal, Hasan went to his wife's apartment and told her what had happened to him in the sultan's court. She said: 'He is bound to make you one of his intimate companions and shower gifts and presents on you. By God's grace, you are like a great light spreading the rays of your perfection, wherever you may be, on land or sea.' He said to her: 'I want to compose an ode in his honour, so as to increase the love that he feels for me in his heart.' 'A good idea,' she agreed. 'Produce good concepts and elegant expressions and I'm sure that he will find your poem acceptable.'

Hasan then went off by himself and wrote some well-formed and elegantly expressed lines. They ran as follows:

I have a heroic patron, soaring to the heights of greatness,
And treading on the path of generous and noble men.
His justice brings security to every land,
And for his enemies he has barred the path.
He is a lion, pious and astute;
If you call him king or angel, he is both.*
Those who ask him for favours are sent back rich.
There are no words to sum him up.
On the day of generosity, he is the shining dawn,
While on the day of battle, he is darkest night.
Our necks are fettered with his generosity,
And by his favours he masters the freeborn.
God grant us that he may enjoy long life,
Defending him from all that may bring harm.

When he had finished composing this piece, he sent it to the sultan with one of his uncle's slaves. The sultan studied it with delight and read it out to those who were in attendance on him. They were enthusiastic

* An Arabic pun on *malik* (king) and *malak* (angel).

in their praise, and the sultan summoned Hasan and told him when he came: 'From this day on, you are my intimate companion, and I have decreed for you a monthly allowance of a thousand dirhams, in addition to what I have already assigned you.' Hasan rose and thrice kissed the ground before the sultan, praying for his lasting glory and long life. From then on, he enjoyed lofty status; his fame spread throughout the lands, and he lived in the greatest comfort and ease with his uncle and his family until he was overtaken by death.

[Nights 20–24]

The Story of Taj al-Muluk and Princess Dunya

I have heard, O fortunate king, that there was once a prince, Taj al-Muluk, who became a skilled horseman, surpassing all living at that time. Because of his beauty, whenever he went out on any business, all who saw him were captivated by him, poems were composed about him and freeborn women were shamefully seduced by his love. He was as described by the poet:

I became drunk on the fragrance of scent,
Embracing a moist branch the zephyr nurtured.
The lover was drunk, but not on wine.
Rather it was the beloved's saliva that intoxicated him.
All beauty is held captive by the beloved,
And because of that he holds sway over men's hearts.
By God, I will never think of consolation for his loss
As long as I am held in the bonds of life or afterwards.
If I live, I live loving him, and if I die
Because of the passion of my love, death will be welcome.

When he reached the age of eighteen, greenish down spread over a mole on his red cheek, while a beauty spot like a speck of amber was set there as an adornment. He began to captivate minds and eyes, as the poet says:

He is a successor to Joseph in his beauty;
When he appears, lovers are filled with fear.
Turn aside with me and look at him
To see on his cheeks the black banner of the caliphate.

Another poet has said:

Your eyes have never seen a finer sight
In anything that can be seen,
Than the green mole upon the cheek,
Red as it is, beneath the dark eye.

A third has said:

I wonder at a mole that always worships your cheek's fire,
But is not burned by it, infidel though it is.
More wonderful is that a message from his glance
Should confirm God's signs, although he is a sorcerer.
How green is the crop that his cheek has produced,
Because of the many hearts it breaks.

Yet another poet has said:

I wonder at those who question where
The water of life is found to flow.
I see it on a slender gazelle's mouth
With sweet red lips, covered by a dark moustache.
How strange, when Moses found this water
Flowing there, he was not content to wait.

When Prince Taj al-Muluk, enjoying such advantages, reached manhood, he became ever more handsome. He had a number of companions and favourites, and all his close associates were hoping that he would become king after his father's death and that they would be his emirs. He became attached to hunting and the chase, spending every hour that he had in its pursuit. His father, Sulaiman Shah, tried to keep him away from it, since he was afraid of his son's exposure to the dangers of the wastelands and wild beasts, but the prince would not accept any restraint.

It happened, then, that he told his servants to take with them provisions for ten days, which they did, and he left with them on a hunting trip. For four days they travelled through the wilds until they reached a spot overlooking a green land, where they saw wild beasts grazing, trees laden with ripe fruits and gushing springs. He told them to spread out their trapping ropes in a wide ring, while they themselves were to assemble at a particular spot at the head of the ring. They followed his orders, setting up the ropes in a wide circle, within which they enclosed wild beasts of many kinds, including gazelles. This caused a disturbance among the beasts, who stampeded in the face of the horses, and the prince then released the dogs, the lynxes and the falcons at them, followed by flights of arrows which inflicted mortal wounds. Before they could reach the head of the ring, many of the beasts were taken, while the rest fled.

Taj al-Muluk then dismounted by a stream, where he collected and distributed the game, setting aside the best portion for his father, Sulaiman Shah. He sent this off to him, while he assigned other portions to his principal officers, before spending the night there. In the morning a large merchant caravan arrived, with black slaves and servants. They halted in the green meadow by the water, and when he saw them, Taj al-Muluk told one of his companions to find out about them and to ask them why they were halting there. The man went to them and said: 'Tell me who you are and answer quickly.' They told him: 'We are merchants and we have stopped here to rest, as we have a long way to go before we reach the next stage on our route. We have halted here because we have confidence in Sulaiman Shah and his son; we know that all who stay in his lands can expect safe conduct, and we have expensive materials with us which we have brought for Prince Taj al-Muluk.'

The messenger went back to the prince and told him about this, relaying what he had heard from the merchants. 'If they have something that they have brought for me,' said the prince, 'I shall not leave this spot and enter the city until I have inspected it.' He mounted his horse and rode off, with his mamluks behind him, until he reached the caravan. The merchants rose to greet him, offering prayers for victory and good fortune, as well as continued glory and honour. A tent had been pitched for him of red satin embellished with pearls and gems, in which a royal couch had been placed on a silk carpet, its front studded with emeralds.

Taj al-Muluk took his seat, with his mamluks standing in attendance on him, and he then sent word to the merchants, telling them to produce everything that they had with them. They came with their goods, all of which he inspected, choosing what pleased him and paying its full price. He then mounted, intending to set off, but on happening to glance towards the caravan, he saw a handsome young man, neatly dressed and elegant, with a radiant forehead and a face like a moon, although his beauty had altered and he showed the pallor of one who has been parted from his beloved. Moaning and sobbing, with tears pouring down from his eyes, he recited:

We have long been parted; cares and passion never cease;
Friend, the tears flow from my eyes.

I took leave of my heart on the day of parting,
And I have remained alone with no heart and no hope.
Friend, stay with me as I take leave of one
Whose words can cure all sickness and all ills.

When he had finished speaking, the young man wept for a time and then fainted, with Taj al-Muluk looking on in amazement. When he had recovered, with a wounding glance he recited:

Beware of her glance, for it works sorcery,
And no one can escape who is shot by her eyes.
For all their languor, those dark eyes
Are sharp enough to split white swords.
Do not be deceived by her soft words,
For love's fire can bemuse the mind.
She is softly formed; were silk to touch her body,
Blood would be drawn from it, as you can see.
How far it is between her anklets and her neck!
What fragrance rivals her sweet-smelling scent?

The young man then gave a groan and fainted. When Taj al-Muluk looked at him, he was baffled by his condition. He walked up to him, and when the young man had recovered consciousness, he saw Taj al-Muluk standing by his head. He rose to his feet and kissed the ground before him, after which the prince asked him why he had not shown him his merchandise. 'There is nothing among my goods that is suitable for your excellency,' the young man replied, but Taj al-Muluk insisted on being shown what he had, as well as on being told what was the matter with him, adding: 'I see that you are tearful and sad. If you have been wronged, I shall right the wrong, and if you are in debt, I shall pay it, for it has pained me to see you like this.'

He then ordered chairs to be set out, and they fetched him one made of ivory and ebony, draped with gold-embroidered silk, and they spread out a silken carpet. Taj al-Muluk sat on the chair and told the young man to be seated on the carpet, after which he said: 'Show me your goods.' 'Please don't tell me to do that, master,' said the young man. 'My goods are not fit for you.' Taj al-Muluk insisted, however, and told one of his servants to fetch them, whether or not he agreed. On seeing this, tears started from the young man's eyes. He wept, groaned, complained and sighed deeply. Then he recited:

I swear by the coquetry and the kohl of your eyes,
By the soft lissomness of your form,
By the wine and honey of your mouth,
And by the gentleness and vexation of your nature:
There came an apparition sent by you, who are my hope,
Sweeter than safety for the craven coward.

He then opened up his goods and displayed them to Taj al-Muluk, one after the other, piece by piece. Among the things that he brought out was a satin robe with gold brocade worth two thousand dinars. When he unfolded this, a piece of material fell from the middle of it, which he quickly picked up and tucked beneath his hip. Then, in a daze, he recited:

When will the tortured heart find a cure for your love?
Union with you is farther than the Pleiades.
Distance, abandonment, longing and lovesickness,
Delay, postponement – this is how life passes.
Union does not bring life nor does abandonment kill me.
Distance does not bring me near, nor are you at hand.
It is neither fairness nor mercy that you show.
You do not help me, but I cannot flee from you.
All of my roads are blocked by love for you;
I cannot make out where I am to go.

Taj al-Muluk was astonished at this recitation and wondered at the reason for it, not knowing why the young man had picked up the scrap of material and put it under his hip. So he asked what this was. 'You don't need to see it, master,' replied the young man, and when the prince insisted, he said: 'This was the reason why I refused to show you my goods, and I cannot let you see it.' 'I must see it,' insisted Taj al-Muluk, and as he was growing angry, the young man drew it out from under his hip, weeping, moaning, complaining and uttering many groans. He then recited these lines:

Do not blame him, for blame is hurtful.
I spoke the truth, but he does not listen.
I ask God to keep safe for me in the valley camping ground
A moon that rises from the sphere of buttons.
I said goodbye to him, but I would have preferred it
Had pleasant life taken its leave of me before I did.
How often did he plead with me on the morning of departure,

As both my tears and his poured down.
May God not give me the lie; parting from him
Has torn my garment of excuse, but I shall patch it.
I have no bed on which to lie, nor, since I left,
Does any place of rest remain for him.
Time did its best with its rough hand
To ban me from good fortune and to ban him too.
This was the hand that poured out unmixed grief,
Filling the cup from which he drank what I gave him.

When he had finished, Taj al-Muluk said to him: 'I see that you are in a wretched state, so tell me why it is that you weep when you look at this piece of material.' When he heard the prince mention the material, the young man sighed and said: 'Master, my story is a remarkable one and the affair that connects me with this material, its owner and the one who embroidered it with these shapes and images, is strange.' At this, he unfolded the material and there on it was the picture of a gazelle embroidered in silk picked out with red gold, while opposite it was the picture of another gazelle, picked out in silver with a collar of red gold and three pendants of chrysolite. When Taj al-Muluk looked at this and saw its fine workmanship, he exclaimed: 'Glory be to God for teaching man what he did not know.' He then became passionately interested in the young man's story and asked him to tell him how he was connected with the lady who had embroidered the gazelles.

'Know, master,' replied the young man, 'that my father was one of the great merchants and I was his only son. I had a female cousin who was brought up with me in my father's house, as her own father had died. Before his death, he had come to an agreement with my father that they should marry me to her. When we both reached puberty, she was not kept away from me and I was not kept away from her. My father then talked with my mother and said: "This year we shall draw up the marriage contract between 'Aziz and 'Aziza." My mother agreed to this and my father started to lay in provisions for a banquet. While all this was going on, my cousin and I were sleeping in the same bed, in ignorance of all this, except that she knew more than I did, being better informed and more knowledgeable.' HE WENT ON:

The Story of 'Aziz and 'Aziza

My father then completed the wedding preparations and nothing remained except for the contract to be drawn up and the marriage consummated. My father wanted the contract to be signed after the Friday prayer, and he went to his friends among the merchants and others and told them about this, while my mother went and invited her women friends and her relatives. When Friday came, they washed out the hall that was prepared for the reception, cleaning the marble and spreading carpets in the house. Everything needed was set out there; the walls were adorned with brocaded hangings, and it was agreed that the guests should come to our house after the prayer. My father went off to supervise the making of the sweetmeats and the sugared dishes, and as the only thing left was the drawing up of the marriage contract, my mother made me go off to the baths, sending after me a splendid new suit of clothes. I put these on when I came out of the baths and, as they were perfumed, a pleasant odour spread from them, scenting the air.

I had meant to go to the Friday mosque, but then I remembered a friend of mine and went back to look for him in order to invite him to the signing of the marriage contract, telling myself that this would keep me busy until close to the time of prayer. I went into a lane where I had never been before, and I was sweating because of my bath and also because of the new clothes that I had on. As the sweat ran down, the scent grew stronger and I rested on a bench at the head of the lane, spreading out an embroidered kerchief that I had with me to sit on. It grew hotter and although sweat covered my forehead and poured down my face, I could not wipe it away with the kerchief because I was sitting on it. I was about to use my gown when suddenly from above me a white kerchief fell, more delicate than the zephyr and more delightful to the eye than a sick man's cure. I caught it in my hand and looked up to see where it had come from. My gaze then fell on that of the gazelle lady, who was looking out of a window with a lattice of brass.

I had never seen anyone more beautiful; indeed, my tongue cannot describe her. When she saw me looking at her, she put one finger in her mouth, and then, joining her middle finger to her index finger, she placed them on her bosom between her breasts. She then withdrew her head from the window, closing it and disappearing from sight. Fire broke out in my heart; the flames spread; my one glance was followed by a thousand regrets, and I was bewildered. I had not been able to hear anything she said, nor had I understood her gestures. I looked at the window again, but found it closed, and although I waited until sunset, I heard no sound and saw no one. Despairing of catching sight of her again, I got up from my place, taking the kerchief with me and unfolding it. The scent of musk spread from it, so delighting me that I imagined myself to be in Paradise.

As I spread it out between my fingers, a small piece of paper fell from it. I opened this up and found that it was impregnated with the purest of scents, while on it were written these lines:

I sent him a note complaining of my love,
Written in a delicate hand – and scripts are of all kinds.
My friend said: 'Why do you write like this,
So delicately and finely that it is hardly to be seen?'
I said: 'That is because I am worn away and thin;
This is what happens to the script of lovers.'

After reading these lines, I studied the beautiful kerchief and saw the following lines on one of its borders:

Down, that excellent calligrapher,
Wrote two lines on his cheek in ornamental script.
When he appears, the sun and moon become confused,
And when he bends, branches are put to shame.

On the opposite border were these lines:

Down wrote with ambergris upon a pearl
Two lines of jet inscribed upon an apple.
There is death in the glance of languorous eyes
And drunkenness in cheeks, not in the wine.

When I saw the verses that were embroidered on the kerchief, fire spread through my heart and my longings and cares increased. I took the kerchief and the note and brought them back home, not knowing how to reach my beloved or how to particularize the generalities of love. Some of the night had already passed before I reached the house, and there I saw my cousin 'Aziza sitting weeping. When she saw me, she wiped away her tears; coming up to me, she took off my robe and asked me why I had been absent. All the emirs, she told me, together with the great men, the merchants and others, had assembled in the house. The *qadis* and the notaries had been there; they had eaten all the food and stayed sitting for a time, waiting for me to come for the signing of the contract. 'When finally they gave up hope of you,' she went on, 'they dispersed and each went his way. Your father was furious at that and swore that he would not draw up the marriage contract until next year, because of all the money that he had spent on the wedding feast.'

She then asked again what had happened to make me so late and to cause all this trouble by my absence. 'Cousin,' I said to her, 'don't ask what happened to me,' but then I told her about the kerchief and explained things from start to finish. She took the paper and the kerchief and read what was written on them, with tears running down her cheeks. She then recited these lines:

If someone says: 'Love starts with choice,' tell them:
'That is a lie; it all comes from necessity.'
Necessity is not followed by shame,
A point whose truth is shown by histories.
Sound currency cannot be falsified.
Call love sweet torture if you wish,
A throbbing in the entrails, or a blow,
A blessing, a misfortune or a goal
In which the soul finds pleasure or is lost.
Backwards or forwards – I do not know how love is to be read.
In spite of that, the days of love are feasts,
And the beloved's mouth smiles all the while.
Her spreading fragrance is a festival,
And her love cuts off all that brings disgrace,
Never alighting in the heart of a base man.

She then asked me: 'What did she say to you and what gestures did she make at you?' 'She didn't speak at all,' I replied, 'but she put her finger in her mouth, and she then put it together with her middle finger and laid both of them on her breast, pointing downwards. Then she withdrew her head and shut the window, after which I didn't see her again. She took my heart away with her and I sat until sunset, waiting for her to look out of the window a second time, but she didn't, and when I had despaired of seeing her, I got up from where I was sitting and came home. This is my story, and I wish that you would help me in my misfortune.'

My cousin lifted her head towards me and said: 'If you asked for my eye, cousin, I would pull it out from my eyelids for you, and I shall have to help you get what you want, as well as helping her, for she is as deeply in love with you as you are with her.' I asked what her gestures had meant, and my cousin told me: 'When she put her finger in her mouth, this was to show that you are like the soul in her body and that she would hold on to your union with her teeth. The kerchief is the sign of the lover's greeting to the beloved; the note signifies that her soul is attached to you; and when she put two fingers on her bosom between her breasts, she meant to tell you to come back after two days so as to relieve her distress. You must know, cousin, that she is in love with you and that she trusts you. This is the interpretation that I put on these signs, and were I able to come and go, it would not take me long to bring you together and shelter the two of you under my wing.'

When I heard what she said, I thanked her and I said to myself that I would wait for two days. So I spent the time sitting at home, neither going out nor coming in and neither eating nor drinking. I put my head in my cousin's lap and she kept consoling me and telling me to be determined, resolute and of good heart.

At the end of the two days, my cousin said to me: 'Be cheerful and joyful; strengthen your resolution; put on your clothes and set off for your rendezvous with her.' She then got up, brought me a change of clothing and perfumed me. I summoned up my strength, took heart and went out. I then walked on until I entered the lane, where I sat down on the bench for a time. Suddenly the window opened and I looked at the lady, but when I saw her I fell down in a faint. Then I recovered, summoned my resolve and took heart once more, but when I looked at her a second time, I lost consciousness again. When I came to myself, I saw that she had with her a mirror and a red kerchief. When she saw me, she uncovered her forearms, spread open her five fingers and struck her breast with the palm of her hand and her five fingers. Next, she raised her hands and put the mirror outside the window. She took the kerchief, went inside with it, and then, coming back again, she lowered it from the window in the direction of the lane. She did this three times, letting it down and raising it, after which she squeezed it and then folded it in her hand. She bowed her head and then drew it back from the window, which she shut. She went away without having said a single word to me, leaving me bemused, as I had no idea what her gestures meant.

I stayed sitting there until evening and it was almost midnight by the time I got home. There I found my cousin with her hand on her cheek and tears pouring from her eyes. She was reciting these lines:

Why should I harshly be abused for loving you?
How can I forget you, you the slender branch?
A beautiful face has ravished my heart and turned away –
I cannot escape my hopeless love for her.
With her Turkish glances she wounds my inner heart
More deeply than any polished and sharpened sword.
You have burdened me with a weight of passion,
While I am too weak to bear that of my shirt.
I shed tears of blood when those who blame me say:
'A sharp sword from your beloved's eyelids brings you fear.'
I wish my heart might be as hard as yours;
My withered body is as slender as your waist.
You lord it over me; your beauty is a steward
Treating me harshly, an unjust chamberlain.
To say all beauty was in Joseph is a lie.
How many Josephs are there in your loveliness!
I try to turn away from you, in fear
Of watching eyes. How difficult this is!

When I heard these lines, my cares and sorrows increased and multiplied, and I collapsed in a corner of the room. My cousin got up to come to me. She lifted me up, took off my robe and wiped my face with her sleeve. She then asked me what had happened and I told her everything that the lady had done. 'Cousin,' she said, 'the gesture that she made with the palm of her hand and her five fingers means: "Come again after five days." As for the mirror, the lowering and raising of the red kerchief and the fact that she put her head out of the window, this means: "Sit in the dyer's shop until my messenger comes to you."' When I heard what she said, fire blazed in my heart and I said: 'By God, cousin, your interpretation of this is right, as I saw a Jewish dyer in the lane.' Then I wept and my cousin said: 'Be resolute and firm. Others are obsessed with love for years and endure the heat of its passion with constancy, while you have only a week to wait, so why are you so impatient?'

She set about consoling me and she brought me food, but although I took a morsel and tried to eat it, I failed, and I then neither ate nor drank nor enjoyed the pleasures of sleep. My complexion turned pale and I lost my good looks, as I had never been in love before or experienced love's heat. I became weak and so did my cousin because of me. Every night until I went to sleep she would try to console me by telling me stories of lovers, and whenever I woke up, I would find her still awake thanks to me, with tears running down her cheeks. Things went on like that for me until the five days had passed. Then my cousin got up, heated water for me and bathed me, after which she dressed me in my clothes. 'Go to her,' she said, 'and may God fulfil your need and allow you to get what you want from your beloved.'

I left and walked on until I got to the head of the lane. It was a Saturday and I saw that the dyer's shop was shut. I sat by it until the call for the afternoon prayer; then the sun grew pale and the muezzins called for the evening prayer. Night fell, but I could learn nothing of my lady and I heard nothing from her or of her. I became afraid for myself as I sat there alone, and so I got up, staggering like a drunken man until I got home. When I went in, I saw my cousin 'Aziza, standing alone with one hand on a peg that had been driven into the wall and another on her breast. She was reciting, with deep sighs, the lines:

The passion of the Arab girl, whose clan have gone,
Who longs for the *ban* tree and the sweet bay of Hijaz –
When she entertains the riders, her yearning serves
For their guest fire and her tears for their water –
This passion is no more than what I feel
For my beloved, who thinks my love a fault.

When she had finished her poem, she turned and caught sight of me. She then wiped away her tears and mine with her sleeves and said, smiling at me: 'May God grant you enjoyment of His gifts, cousin. Why did you not spend the night with your beloved and get what you wanted from her?' On hearing this, I kicked her in the chest and she fell, striking her forehead on the edge of the raised floor of the room. There was a peg there and it was this that struck her forehead, and when I looked at it, I saw that the skin had been cut open and the blood was flowing. She remained silent, not saying a single word, then, getting up immediately, she burned some rags, applying the ash to the wound, which she bandaged. She wiped away the blood that had fallen on to the carpet, and it was as though all this had never happened. Then she came up to me, smiled at me and said softly: 'By God, cousin, I didn't say this to mock you or her, but I was distracted by a headache and I was thinking of having some blood let. Now my head and my forehead feel better and so tell me what happened to you today.' I told her the whole story and then burst into tears. 'There is good news for you, cousin,' she said, 'that you will succeed in your quest and achieve what you hope for, as this is a sign of acceptance. She stayed away from you because she wants to test you and to find out whether you can show patience or not, and whether you are really in love with her or not. Go to her tomorrow, to the place where you were to start with, and see what signs she makes to you, for joy is close at hand and your sorrows are nearly over.'

She started to console me for my disappointment, but my cares and sorrows increased. Then she brought me food, but I kicked out, knocking over all the bowls, and I said: 'Every lover is mad. He has no taste for food and no enjoyment of sleep.' 'Aziza said: 'By God, cousin, these are the signs of love.' She was weeping as she picked up the broken bits of the bowls and cleaned away the food. Then she sat talking to me throughout the night, while I was praying for dawn.

When morning came and the light spread, I set off to go to the lady and quickly got to the lane, where I sat down on the bench. Suddenly the window opened and she put her head out, laughing. She then disappeared but later came back with a mirror, a bag and a pot filled with green shoots. In her hand she was carrying a lamp, and the first thing she did was to take the mirror in her hand and put it in the bag, which she then tied shut and threw into the house. She let down her hair over her face and placed the lamp for a moment on top of the plants. Then, gathering up everything, she took it away and closed the window. My heart was broken by this, by the secret gestures and cryptic signs and by the fact that she had not spoken a single word to me, but as a result, the ardour of my passionate love intensified and grew stronger.

I retraced my steps, weeping and sorrowful at heart, until I got back home, where I saw my cousin seated with her face turned to the wall. Her heart was consumed by care, sorrow and jealousy, but her love kept her from telling me anything about the passion that she felt because she could see the extent of my own infatuation. When I looked at her, I saw that she was wearing two bandages, one because of the blow to her forehead and the other over her eyes because of the pain caused by the violence of her weeping. She was in the worst of states, shedding tears and reciting:

I count the nights, one night after another,
But for long I lived without counting them.
I tell you, my companions, that I do not have
What God decreed for Laila and for me.

Destiny gave her to another, afflicting me with her love.
Why did it not send me some other grief?

When she had finished these lines, she looked up and saw me through her tears. Wiping them away, she came up to me, but the extent of her emotion was such that she could not speak. After staying silent for some time, she asked me to tell her what had happened to me this time with the lady. I gave her a full account and she said: 'Show patience, for the time of your union is at hand and you will get what you are hoping for. When she gestured to you with the mirror and put it in the bag, she was telling you to wait till sunset. When she loosed her hair over her face, she was saying: "When night arrives and the fall of darkness overcomes the daylight, come." The plant pot was meant to tell you that when you do, you are to enter the garden behind the lane, and by using the lamp she was telling you that when you walk into the garden, make for the place where you see a lighted lamp, sit beneath it and wait for her, for your love is killing her.'

On hearing what my cousin had to say, I shouted out because of the vehemence of my passion and said: 'How many promises do you make me, yet when I go to her, I never get what I was hoping for? I don't think that your interpretations are right.' My cousin laughed and said: 'You only have to show patience for the rest of this day until it ends and night falls. Then you will obtain union and reach the goal of your hopes. This is true and not a lie.' Then she recited:

Allow the days to pass away;
Do not enter the house of care.
The goal of many a difficult quest
Is brought near by the hour of joy.

She then came up to me and started to console me with soft words, although she did not dare to bring me any food, for fear I might be angry with her. Hoping for my affection, all she did was to come to me and take off my robe, after which she said: 'Sit down, cousin, so that I can tell you stories to distract you until the day's end, for, if God Almighty wills it, when night falls you will be with your beloved.' I paid no attention to her but set about waiting for the coming of night, exclaiming: 'Oh my Lord, make night come soon!'

When it did come, my cousin wept bitterly. She gave me a globule of pure musk, saying 'Cousin, put this in your mouth, and when you have met your beloved and have had your way with her, after she has granted you what you wanted, recite these lines to her:

> Lovers, by God, tell me:
> What is the desperate one of you to do?'

She then kissed me and made me swear that I would not recite these lines until I was on the point of leaving the lady. I agreed to this and went out in the evening, walking on and on until I came to the garden. I found the gate open, and when I went in I could see a light in the distance. When I got there I found a large garden room vaulted over with a dome of ivory and ebony, in the middle of which hung a lamp. The room was furnished with silk carpets, embroidered with gold and silver, while in a golden candelabrum hanging beneath the lamp was a huge lighted candle. In the middle of the room was a fountain adorned with various carved figures and beside it was a table with a silken covering, flanked by a large china jug filled with wine, together with a crystal goblet ornamented with gold. Beside all this was a large silver bowl and when I removed its cover, I found that it contained fruits of all kinds – figs, pomegranates, grapes, oranges and various sorts of citrus fruit. Among these were sweet-smelling flowers, including roses, jasmine, myrtle, eglantine, narcissus and various scented herbs.

I was enchanted and overjoyed by the place, which served to dispel my cares and sorrows, except for the fact that not one of Almighty God's creatures was there. There were no slaves, male or female, to be seen, and there was no one in charge of the arrangements or guarding the contents of the room. I sat waiting for the arrival of my heart's darling until the first hour of the night had passed, and then the second and the third, but she still did not come.

I was feeling very hungry as it was a long time since I had eaten, thanks to the violence of my passion, but when I saw that place and realized that my cousin had interpreted the gestures of my beloved correctly, I relaxed and then experienced hunger pangs. My appetite had been stimulated by the aroma of the food on the table when I got there, and certain that I was going to achieve union, I felt a longing for something to eat. So I went to the table, removed the covering and found in the middle of it a china dish containing four chickens, roasted and seasoned with spices. Set around the dish were four bowls containing a mixture of sweet and sour, one with sweetmeats, another with pomegranate seeds, a third with baqlava and a fourth with honey doughnuts. I ate some of the doughnuts and a piece of the meat, and I then turned to the baqlava and ate what I could. I went on to the sweetmeats and took a spoonful, then two and three and four, which I followed with a mouthful of chicken. My stomach was full and my joints relaxed. Sleeplessness had made me sluggish and so, after washing my hands, I rested my head on a cushion and was overcome by sleep.

I don't know what happened to me after that, and I only woke up when the heat of the sun was scorching me, as it had been days since I had slept. When I did wake it was to find salt and charcoal scattered over my stomach. I stood up and shook out my clothes, looking to the right and left but seeing no one, and I found that I had been sleeping on the bare marble. Bewilderment filled me, together with great distress. Tears ran down my cheeks and I got up, feeling sorry for myself, and made for home. When I got there, I found my cousin striking her breast with her hand and shedding enough tears to rival a rain cloud. She was reciting:

The zephyr's breath flows from the guarded land,
And as it blows, it rouses love.
Come to us, breath of the east wind,
For every lover has his own allotted fate.
Could we control passion, we would embrace,
As the lover clasps the breast of his true love.
After my cousin's face, God has outlawed for me
All pleasures in this life that time can show.
I wish I knew whether his heart, like mine,
Is melting in the burning heat of love.

When she saw me, she got up quickly, wiping away her tears and approaching me with soft words. 'Cousin,' she said, 'God has shown you kindness in your love in that He has caused your beloved to love you, while I weep in sorrow for parting from you, who both blame me and excuse me, but may God not blame you for my sake.' She smiled at me, although with exasperation, spoke gently to me and removed my robe, which she spread out. 'By God,' she said, 'this is not the scent of one who has enjoyed his beloved, so tell me all that happened to you, cousin.' I told her the whole story, and again she smiled angrily, and said: 'My heart is full of pain, but may no one live who can distress you. This woman treats you with great haughtiness and, by God, cousin, she makes me afraid for you. The salt, you should know, means that you were sunk in sleep, like unpleasant food which causes disgust, and you have to be salted lest you be spat out. You claim to be a noble lover, but lovers are forbidden to sleep and so your claim is false. In the same way, her love for you is false, as she saw you sleeping and did not wake you, which she would have done had she really loved you. By the charcoal she means to say: "May God blacken your face, in that you have falsely claimed to be in love, while in fact you are a child who thinks only of eating, drinking and sleeping." This is what she meant – may God Almighty free you from her.'

When I heard what she had to say, I struck my breast with my hand and said: 'By God, it is true; I slept, although lovers do not sleep. I wronged myself and how could I have done myself more harm than by eating and falling asleep? What am I to do?' Weeping bitterly, I asked my cousin: 'Tell me what to do. Have pity on me that God may pity you, for otherwise I shall die.' My cousin, being deeply in love with me, agreed to do this, but she added: 'I have told you many times that if I could go in and out as I pleased I would quickly bring the two of you together and take you under my protection, simply in order to please you. If God Almighty wills it, I shall do my best to unite you, but listen to what I say and obey me. Go back to the same place in the evening and sit where you were before. Take care not to eat anything, for eating induces sleep and you must not sleep. She will not come until the first quarter of the night has passed – may God protect you from her evil.'

Gladdened by hearing what she had to say, I started to pray God to bring on night. When it came, I was about to go out when my cousin reminded me that after my meeting with the lady, when I was about to leave, I was to quote the lines that she had recited earlier. I agreed to this and when I went to the garden, I found the place prepared in the same way that it had been on the first occasion, with all the necessary food and drink, dried fruits, sweet-smelling flowers, and so on. I went to the room and was attracted by what I could smell of the aroma of food. I restrained myself several times, but at last I could not resist and so I got up and went to the table. I lifted the cover and found a plate of chicken, surrounded by four bowls containing four different types of food. I took a mouthful of each and then I ate what I wanted of the sweetmeats, followed by a piece of meat. I tasted a saffron sorbet which I liked, and I drank a quantity of it with a spoon until I had had enough and my stomach was full. My eyelids closed and, taking a cushion, I placed it under my head, saying: 'I will rest on it but I shall not sleep.' Then I closed my eyes and fell asleep, not waking until the sun had risen.

On my stomach I found a large dice cube, a *tab* stick,* a date stone and a carob seed. There were no furnishings in the place or indeed anything else, and it looked as though there had never been anything there the night before. I got up, brushed off what was on me and left in anger, and when I got back home, I found my cousin once again sighing deeply, and reciting these lines:

An emaciated body and a wounded heart,
With tears that flood down over cheeks,
A lover whose love is hard to harvest,
But all that beauties do is beautiful.
Cousin, you have filled my heart with passion
And my eyes' wounds are caused by tears.

I reproached her and scolded her, and she wept. Then, wiping away her tears, she came to me, kissed me and clasped me to her breast. I kept my distance from her, however, reproaching myself, and she said: 'It seems as though you went to sleep again, cousin.' 'Yes,' I replied, 'but when I woke up, I found a large dice cube, a *tab* stick, a date stone and a carob seed, and I don't know why she did this.' I then burst into tears and, going up to her, I asked her to interpret the signs for me, to tell me what I should do and to help me in my predicament. 'Willingly,' she replied. 'By the *tab* stick which she placed on your stomach she means to say that although you were present your heart was absent, and she is telling you that love is not like that and you are not to count yourself among the lovers. With the date stone she is telling you that, were you a lover, your heart would be consumed by passion and you would not enjoy the pleasure of sleep, for the pleasure of love is like a date which sets light to a coal in the heart. As for the carob seed, she is telling you that the lover's heart endures weariness, and she is saying: "Face separation from me with the patience of Job."'

When I heard this interpretation, fire spread through my heart and I became more and more sorrowful. I cried out, saying: 'God decreed that I should sleep because of my ill fortune,' and then I said: 'Cousin, by my life, I implore you to think of some scheme that will allow me to get to her.' Weeping, she said: ''Aziz, my cousin, my heart is so full of thoughts that I cannot speak, but if you go there tonight and take care not to sleep, you will get what you want. This is all the advice that I can give.' 'God

*A stick used in a children's game.

willing, I shall not sleep,' I replied, 'and I shall do as you tell me.' So 'Aziza got up and fetched food, saying: 'Eat as much as you want now, so you won't have to think of it later.' I ate my fill and when night came, 'Aziza got up and brought me a splendid robe which she made me wear, and she got me to swear that I would quote to the lady the lines that she mentioned earlier. She also cautioned me again against sleeping, and I then left her and set off for the garden.

When I got to the room, I looked out at the garden and started to prop open my eyes with my fingers, shaking my head as it grew dark. Sleeplessness, however, had made me hungry and this hunger grew worse as the aroma of food wafted over me. So I went to the table, removed the covering and ate a mouthful of every sort of food that there was, together with a piece of meat. Then I went to the wine jug, telling myself that I would drink one glass, which I did, but I followed this with a second and a third, up to a total of ten, and when a breath of wind blew over me, I collapsed on the ground like a dead man. I stayed like that until daybreak, and when I came to my senses, I found myself outside the garden with a sharp knife and an iron dirham lying on my stomach. I shuddered and, taking the things with me, I went back home.

There I found my cousin weeping and saying: 'I am wretched and unhappy in this house and my only help is in tears.' As soon as I entered, I fell down at full length in a faint, with the knife and the dirham falling from my hand. When I had recovered, I told her what had happened to me and that I had not achieved my goal. Her sorrow increased when she saw my passionate tears, and she said: 'There is nothing that I can do. I advised you not to sleep, but you didn't listen, so what I say is of no use to you at all.' 'By God,' I said to her, 'explain to me the meaning of the knife and the iron dirham.' She replied: 'By the iron dirham, she means her right eye, and she is taking an oath by it, saying: "By the Lord of creation, and by my right eye, if you come back again and fall asleep, I shall use this knife to cut your throat." Her cunning makes me afraid for you, cousin, and my heart is so full of sorrow for you that I cannot speak. If you are sure that you will not fall asleep if you go back, then go, and if you guard against sleep, you will get what you want, but if after going back you fall asleep as usual, be sure that she will cut your throat.'

'What am I to do, then, cousin?' I asked. 'For God's sake, help me in this misfortune.' 'Willingly,' she replied, 'but I will only see your affair through if you listen to what I have to say and obey me.' When I agreed that I would do this, she said: 'I shall tell you when it is time to go,' and, taking me in her arms, she placed me on the bed and continued to massage me until I was overcome by drowsiness and fell fast asleep. She took a fan and sat by my head, fanning my face until the end of the day. She then woke me up, and when I was roused, I found her sitting by my head, fan in hand, weeping. The tears had dampened her dress. When she saw that I was awake, she wiped them away and brought me some food. When I refused this, she said: 'Didn't I tell you to listen to me? Eat,' and so I ate obediently. She started to put the food in my mouth and I chewed it until I was full. Then she gave me sugared jujube juice to drink; she washed my hands and dried them with a kerchief, after which she sprinkled me with rosewater and I sat with her, feeling in perfect health. When night fell, she gave me my robe to put on and said: 'Cousin, stay awake for the whole night and don't go to sleep. She will not come until the last part of the night, and if it is God's will, you will be united with her, but don't forget my instructions.' Then she wept, and I was pained at heart by all those tears of hers and I asked what instructions they were that she meant. 'When you leave her,' she said, 'recite the lines that I quoted to you earlier.'

I then left cheerfully and went to the garden, where I went up to the room and sat down, feeling sated and staying wakeful for the first quarter of the night. I sat there for what seemed like a year, but I still stayed awake until three quarters of it had gone and the cocks had crowed. This prolonged wakefulness made me very hungry, so I got up and went to the table, where I ate my fill. My head felt heavy and I was about to fall asleep when I saw a light approaching from a distance. I got up, washed my hands and my mouth and roused myself. It was not long before the lady came, surrounded by ten slave girls, like a moon among stars. She was wearing a dress of green satin, embroidered with red gold. She was as the poet has described:

She comes walking proudly to her lovers dressed in green,
With buttons undone and her hair unloosed.
'What is your name?' I asked her and she said:
'I am she who has burned lovers' hearts on coals of fire.'
I complained to her of love's hardships I endured;
She said: 'In your ignorance you complain to rock.'
'Although your heart be rock,' I said,
'Yet God has brought pure water out of rock.'

When she saw me, she laughed and said: 'How is it that you are awake and have not been overcome by sleep? Since you have been wakeful all night, I realize that you are a lover, for it is a characteristic of lovers that they pass sleepless nights, enduring the pains of longing.' She then went up to her slave girls and gestured to them, after which they left her. She came to me, clasped me to her breast and kissed me. I kissed her and, when she sucked my upper lip, I kissed her lower lip. I stretched out my hand to her waist and squeezed it and we both came to the ground at the same time. She undid her drawers, which slipped down to her anklets. We started our love-play, with embraces, coquetry, soft words, bites, twining of legs, and a circumambulation of the House and its corners. This went on until her joints relaxed and she fainted away, losing consciousness. That night was a delight to the heart and joy to the eye, as the poet has said:

For me the pleasantest of all nights was the one
In which I did not let the wine cup slacken in its work.
I kept my eyelids from their sleep
And joined the girl's earring to her anklet.

We slept together until morning. I then wanted to leave, but she held me back and said: 'Stay, so that I can tell you something and give you instructions.' So I stopped and she undid a knotted kerchief and took out this piece of material, which she unfolded in front of me and on which I found a gazelle pictured like this. I was filled with admiration for it and I took it, arranging with her that I should come to her every night in that garden. Then I left her, being full of joy, and in my joy I forgot the lines of poetry which my cousin had told me to recite. When the lady gave me the material with the picture of the gazelle, she had told me that this was her sister's work, and when I asked her sister's name, she said 'Nur al-Huda'. She told me to keep the piece of material, after which I said goodbye to her and left joyfully.

I walked back and went in to find my cousin lying down, but when she saw me she got up, shedding tears, and coming up to me she kissed my chest. Then she asked whether I had recited the lines as she had told me, but I said: 'I forgot it, but what distracted my attention was this gazelle,' and I threw down the piece of material in front of her. She became very agitated and, being unable to control herself, she shed tears and recited these lines:

You, who seek for separation, go slowly,
And do not be deceived by an embrace.

Go slowly; Time's nature is treacherous;
The end of companionship lies in parting.

When she had finished these lines, she asked me to give her the material, which I did, and she spread it out and read what was written on it. When the time came for me to go, she said: 'Go in safety, cousin, and when you leave her, recite the lines that I told you earlier and which you forgot.' 'Repeat them,' I asked her, and so she did, after which I went to the garden, entered the room and found the girl waiting for me. When she saw me, she got up, kissed me and made me sit on her lap. We then ate, drank and satisfied our desires as before. When morning came, I recited to her the lines:

Lovers, by God, tell me:
What is the desperate one of you to do?

On hearing this, her eyes brimmed over with tears and she recited:

He must conceal his love and hide his secret,
Showing patience and humility in all he does.

I memorized this, pleased to think that I had performed the task set by my cousin. So I left and went back to her, but I found her lying down with my mother by her head, weeping over the state that she was in. When I entered, my mother reproached me for having left my cousin in poor health without asking what was wrong with her. When she saw me, my cousin raised her head, sat up and said: ''Aziz, did you recite to her the lines that I told you?' 'Yes,' I replied, 'and when she heard them, she wept and recited other lines for me, which I memorized.' My cousin asked me to tell them to her and, when I did, she wept bitterly and produced these lines:

How can the young man hide it, when love kills him,
And every day his heart is breaking?
He tried to show fair patience but could only find
A heart that love had filled up with unease.

Then my cousin said: 'When you go to her as usual, recite these lines that you have heard.' 'To hear is to obey,' I said, and, as usual, I went to the girl in the garden and no tongue could describe the pleasure that we had. When I was on the point of leaving, I recited the lines to her, and, on hearing them, her eyes brimmed over with tears and she recited:

If he finds no patience to conceal his secret,
Nothing will serve him better than to die.

I memorized the lines and set off home, but when I went in to see my cousin, I found her lying unconscious, with my mother sitting by her head. On hearing my voice, she opened her eyes and said: ''Aziz, did you recite the lines to her?' 'Yes,' I said, 'and when she heard them, she wept and recited a couplet, beginning: "If he finds no patience".' On hearing this, my cousin fainted again, and when she had recovered, she recited these lines:

I have heard, obeyed and now I die;
So greet the one who stopped this union.
May the fortunate enjoy their happiness,
While the sad lover has to drain the glass.

When night came, I went as usual to the garden, where I found the girl waiting for me. We sat down and ate and drank, made love and then slept until morning. Before leaving, I recited my cousin's lines, and when she heard them, the girl gave a loud cry of sorrow and said: 'Oh, oh, by God, the one who spoke these lines is dead!' Then, in tears, she asked me whether that person was related to me, to which I replied that she was my cousin. 'That is a lie, by God,' said the girl. 'If she had been your cousin, you would have loved her as much as she loved you. It is you who have killed her – may God kill you in the same way! By God, had you told me that you had a cousin, I would never have allowed you near me.' I said: 'She used to interpret for me the signs that you made to me; it was she who taught me how to reach you and to deal with you, and but for her I would never have got to you.' 'Did she know about us?' she asked, and when I said yes, she said: 'May God cause you to regret your youth as you have caused her to regret hers!' Then she added: 'Go and see her.'

So I left in a disturbed state and walked on until, reaching our lane, I heard cries of grief. When I asked about this, I was told: 'We found 'Aziza lying dead behind the door.' I went into the house and when my mother saw me, she said: 'It is you who are responsible for her loss and the guilt is all yours – may God not forgive you for her blood! What a bad cousin you are!' My father then came and we prepared 'Aziza for her funeral and then brought her out, accompanying her bier and burying her. We arranged for recitations of the whole Quran to be given over her grave, and we stayed there for three days before returning and going home.

I was grieving for her when my mother came to me and said: 'I want to know what you were doing to 'Aziza to break her heart. I kept on asking her about the cause of her illness but she wouldn't tell me anything. I conjure you in God's Name to let me know how it was that you led her to her death.' 'I didn't do anything,' I replied.

'May God avenge her on you,' she said, 'for she told me nothing and concealed the matter from me until the time of her death. She approved of you; I was with her when she died and she opened her eyes and said: "Aunt, may God not hold your son responsible for my death and may He not punish him for what he has done to me. God has moved me from the lower world of transience to the eternal world." "Daughter," I said, "may you enjoy your youth in well-being," and I started to ask what had caused her illness. At first she said nothing, but then she smiled and said: "Aunt, tell your son that if he wants to go to the place where he goes every day, when he leaves he is to say: 'Loyalty is good; treachery is bad.' In this I am showing pity for him, so that I may be seen to have been sympathetic to him both in my life and after my death." Then she gave me something for you and made me swear that I would not hand it over to you until I had seen you weeping for her and mourning her. I have the thing with me and when I see you doing what she said, I shall give it to you.'

I told her to show it to me, but she refused, and I then occupied myself with my own pleasures, with no thought of my cousin's death, because I was light-headed with love and wanted to spend every night and day with my beloved. As soon as I was certain that night had come, I went to the garden and found the girl sitting waiting for me, on fire with anxiety. As soon as she saw me, she embraced me, hugging me round the neck and asking me about my cousin. 'She is dead,' I replied, 'and we held a *dhikr* ceremony for her, as well as recitations of the Quran. She died four nights ago and this is the fifth.' When the girl heard this, she cried out and wept. Then she said: 'It was you who killed her and had you told me about her before her death, I would have repaid her for the good that she did me. For she did me a service by bringing you to me. Had it not been for her, the two of us would never have met and I am afraid that some disaster may strike you because of her wrongful death.' I told her: 'Before her death she absolved me from blame,' and then I repeated for her what my mother had told me. She then conjured me in God's Name to go to my mother and find out what 'the thing' was that she was holding. I said: 'My mother told me that before she died my cousin had given her instructions, saying: "When your son is about to go to the place that he is in the habit of visiting, quote these two sayings to him: 'Loyalty is good; treachery is bad.'"' When the girl heard this, she said: 'May God Almighty have mercy on her. She has saved you from me, for I had intended to harm you and now I shall not, nor shall I stir up trouble for you.'

I was surprised by this and asked what she had been intending to do to me before hearing these words, in view of the love that we had shared. She said: 'You are in love with me, but you are young and simple, and there is no deceit in your heart, so you don't know our wiles and our deceitfulness. Had your cousin lived, she would have helped you, for it is she who has saved you and preserved you from destruction. I advise you now not to speak to any woman and not to talk with any of us, young or old. Beware, beware, for in your inexperience you know nothing of the deceit of women and their wiles. The one who used to interpret signs for you is dead and I am afraid that you may meet with a disaster from which you will find no one to save you, now that your cousin is dead. Alas for her! I wish that I had known her before her death, so that I might have repaid her for the good that she did me, and visited her – may Almighty God have mercy on her. She kept her secret hidden and did not reveal her feelings. Had it not been for her, you would never have got to me.' She then said that she wanted me to do something, and when I asked what it was, she said: 'I want you to take me to her tomb, so that I may visit her in her grave and write some verses on it.' 'Tomorrow, God willing,' I replied. Then I slept with her that night, and after every hour she would say: 'I wish you had told me about your cousin before her death.' I asked her about the meaning of the two sayings: 'Loyalty is good; treachery is bad,' but she did not reply.

In the morning, she got up and, taking a purse with some dinars in it, she said: 'Get up and show me her grave so that I may visit it and inscribe these verses. I shall have a dome made over it, pray God have mercy on her, and I shall spend this money on alms for her soul.' 'To hear is to obey,' I said, and we walked off, I in front and she behind me, and as she walked she kept distributing alms, saying every time she did so: 'These are alms for the soul of 'Aziza, who kept her secret hidden, without revealing her love, until she drank the cup of death.' She kept on giving away money from her purse and saying: 'This is for the soul of 'Aziza,' until the purse was empty.

We came to the grave and when she saw it, she burst into tears and threw herself down on it. Then she produced a steel chisel and a light hammer, and with the chisel she carved on the headstone of the grave in small letters the following lines:

In a garden I passed a dilapidated grave,
On which grew seven red anemones.
'Whose is this grave?' I asked. The earth replied:
'Show respect; this is a lover's resting place.'
I said: 'God guard you, you who died of love,
And may He house you in the topmost heights of Paradise.
How sad it is for lovers, that among mankind
Their graves are covered by the soil of lowliness.
If I could, I would plant a garden around you
And water it with my flowing tears.'

She then left in tears and I went with her to the garden. 'Never leave me,' she said, 'I conjure by God.' 'To hear is to obey,' I replied, and I devoted myself to her, visiting her again and again. Whenever I spent the night with her, she would be kind to me and treat me well. She would ask me about the two sayings which my cousin 'Aziza had quoted to my mother and I would repeat them to her. Things went on like this with food and drink, embraces and hugs and changes of fine clothes, until I grew stout and fat. I had no cares or sorrows and I had forgotten my cousin.

This went on for a whole year. At the start of the new year, I went to the baths, groomed myself and put on a splendid suit of clothes. On coming out, I drank a cup of wine and sniffed at the scents coming from my clothes, impregnated as they were with various types of perfume. I was relaxed, not knowing the treachery of Time and the disasters that it brings. In the evening, I felt the urge to visit the girl, but I was drunk and didn't know where I was heading. I set off on my way to her but in my drunkenness I strayed into what was called the Naqib's Lane. While I was walking there, I suddenly saw an old woman walking with a lighted candle in one hand and, in the other, a folded letter. I went up to her and found that she was weeping and reciting these lines:

Greetings and welcome to the messenger who brings news of
consent;
How sweet and pleasant are the words you bear,
Sent as you are by one whose greeting is dear to me;
May God's peace rest on you as long as east winds blow!

When she saw me, she said: 'My son, can you read?' Inquisitiveness prompted me to reply: 'Yes, old aunt.' 'Take this letter, then,' she said, 'and read it for me.' She handed it to me and I took it from her, opened it up and read it to her. It contained greetings sent by the writer from a distant land to his loved ones. When the old woman heard this, she was happy and delighted; she blessed me and said: 'May God banish your cares as you have banished mine.' She took back the letter and walked on for a little. My bladder was overfull and I squatted down to relieve myself, after which I got up again, wiped myself, and after arranging my clothes, I was about to walk on when the old woman suddenly came back, bowed her head over my hand and kissed it. 'Master,' she said, 'may God allow you to enjoy your youth. I hope that you will walk a few steps with me to that door there. I told them what you said to me when you read the letter, but they didn't believe me. So walk a little way with me and read out the letter for them from behind the door, and accept my devout prayers.'

'What is the story behind this letter?' I asked. 'Master,' she replied, 'it comes from my son, who has been away for ten years. He went off to trade and stayed so long in foreign parts that we had abandoned hope of him and thought that he must be dead, until, some time ago, this letter came from him. He has a sister who has been weeping for him night and day. I told her that all was well with him but she didn't believe me and told me: "You must fetch someone to read the letter in my presence, so that I may be reassured and happy." You know, my son, that lovers are prone to suspicion, so do me the favour of going with me and reading her the letter. You can stand behind the curtain and I will call his sister to listen from inside the door. In this way you will free us from anxiety and fulfil our need. The Apostle of God – may God bless him and give him peace – said: "If anyone relieves an anxious man of one anxiety in this world, God will relieve him of a hundred," while another *hadith* says: "Whoever relieves his brother of one anxiety in this world, God will relieve him of seventy-two on the Day of Judgement." I have sought you out, so please don't disappoint me.'

I agreed and told her to lead the way, which she did, with me following behind. We went a little way before arriving at the door of a fine, large house, the door itself being plated with copper. I stood behind it, while the old woman called out in Persian and before I knew what was happening, a girl came out lightly and briskly, with her dress tucked up to her knees. I saw a pair of legs that bewildered thought and sight. She was as the poet described:

You gird up your dress to show lovers your legs,
So they may understand what the rest of you is like.
You hurry to fetch a glass for the lover;
It is the glass and the legs that capture them.

These legs, like twin pillars of marble, were adorned with golden anklets set with gems. Her outer robe was bunched up beneath her armpits, and her sleeves were drawn back from her forearms so that I could see her white wrists. On her arms were two bracelets, fastened with large pearls; round her neck she wore a necklace of precious gems; she had pearl earrings and on her head was a brocaded kerchief studded with precious stones. She had tucked the ends of her skirt into her waistband as though she had been busy with some task, and when I saw her, I stared in astonishment at what looked like the bright sun. In a clear, pleasant voice – I had never heard a sweeter – she asked: 'Mother, is this the man who has come to read the letter?' 'Yes,' said her mother, and so the girl stretched out her hand to me with the letter in it. She was standing some six feet or so from the door, and when I put out my hand to take the letter from her, I put my head and shoulders inside the door to get nearer her in order to read it.

As I took the letter in my hand, all of a sudden the old woman butted me in the back with her head, and before I knew what was happening, I found myself inside the hallway. Quicker than a flash of lightning, the old woman came in and the first thing she did was to lock the door. The girl, seeing me in the hallway, came up to me and clasped me to her breast. She then threw me down on the ground and straddled my chest, pressing my stomach with her hands until I almost lost my senses. She took my hand and the violence of her embrace was such that I couldn't free myself. The old woman then went ahead of us, carrying a lighted candle, as the girl took me through seven halls, bringing me at last to a large chamber with four galleries, big enough to serve as a polo ground.

She let me go and told me to open my eyes. I was still dizzy from the strength of her embraces, but I opened my eyes and I saw that the whole chamber had been built of the finest marble, and all its furnishings were of silk or brocade, as were the cushions and the coverings. There were two brass benches and a couch of red gold set with pearls and gems, together with other parlours and a princely chamber fit only for a king such as you.

The girl then said to me: "Aziz, which do you prefer – death or life?'

'Life,' I said. 'In that case,' she replied, 'marry me.' 'I don't want to marry someone like you,' I objected, but she went on: 'If you marry me, you will be safe from the daughter of Delilah the wily.' When I asked who this might be, she laughed and said: 'The girl with whom you have now been keeping company for a year and four months – may God Almighty destroy her and afflict her with someone worse than herself! By God, there is no one more cunning than she. How many people has she killed already and what deeds she has done! How is it that you have escaped after such a long time in her company without her killing you or plunging you into confusion?'

Astonished by this, I asked her how she knew the girl. 'I know her as Time knows its calamities,' she replied, and she went on to ask me to tell her everything that had happened between us so that she could find out how I had managed to escape unharmed. I told her the full story of my dealings with the girl and with my cousin 'Aziza. She invoked God's pity on 'Aziza, shedding tears and striking her hands together at the news of her death and exclaiming: 'She sacrificed her youth in the path of God, and may He compensate you well for her loss! By God, 'Aziz, she died and it was because of her that you were saved from the daughter of Delilah the wily, for had it not been for her you would have perished. I am afraid that you may still fall victim to her evil wiles, but my mouth is blocked and I am silenced.' 'Yes, by God,' I told her, 'all this happened.' She shook her head, saying: 'There is no one now to match 'Aziza.' I replied: 'On her deathbed she told me to quote these two sayings, and nothing else, to the girl: "Loyalty is good; treachery is bad."' On hearing this, the girl said: ''Aziz, these are the two sayings that saved you from being killed by her, and now I am reassured about you, for she is not going to kill you, as your cousin has saved you both in life and in death. By God, day after day I have been wanting you, but it is only now, when I played a successful trick on you, that I have been able to get you. For you are still inexperienced, and you don't know the wiles of young women and the disasters brought about by old ones.'

I agreed with this and she told me that I could be cheerful and happy, 'For the dead have found God's mercy and the living will meet with kindness. You are a handsome young man and I only want you in accordance with the law of God and His Apostle – may God bless him and give him peace. Whatever money or materials you may want will be quickly brought to you; I shall not impose any tasks on you; in my house there is always bread baking and water in the jug. All I want you to do with me is what the cock does.' 'What is it that the cock does?' I asked. She clapped her hands and laughed so much that she fell over backwards. Then she sat up, smiled and said: 'Light of my eyes, do you really not know what the cock does?' 'No, by God, I don't,' I replied. 'His business is eating, drinking and copulating,' she said. I was embarrassed by this and said: 'Is that really so?' 'Yes,' she replied, 'and I want you to gird yourself, strengthen your resolve and copulate as hard as you can.'

She then clapped her hands and said: 'Mother, bring out the people who are with you.' The old woman then came forward with four notaries, bringing with her a piece of silk. She lit four candles and the notaries greeted me and took their seats. The girl got up and veiled herself, after which she empowered one of the notaries to act for her in drawing up the marriage contract. This was written down and she testified on her own behalf that she had received her whole dowry, both the first and the second payment, and that she was holding for me the sum of ten thousand dirhams. She then paid the notaries their fees and they went back to where they had come from. After that she got up, and after taking off her outer clothes, she came forward in a delicate chemise, embroidered with gold. She then pulled off her drawers and, taking me by the hand, she got up on top of the couch with me. 'There is no shame in what is legal,' she said, as she lay there, spreading herself out on her back. Dragging me down on to her breast, she moaned and followed the moan with a coquettish wriggle. She then pulled up her chemise above her breasts and when I saw her like that I could not restrain myself. I thrust into her, after sucking her lip. She cried 'Oh!' and pretended tearful submissiveness, but without shedding tears. 'Do it, my darling,' she said, reminding me as she did so of the poet's lines:

When she lifted her dress to show her private parts,
I found what was as narrow as my patience and my livelihood.
I put it half in and she sighed.
'Why this sigh?' I asked, and she said: 'For the rest.'

'Finish off, darling,' she said. 'I am your slave. Please, give me all of it; give it to me so that I can take it in my hand and put it right into me.' She kept on uttering love cries, with tears and moans, while kissing and embracing me, until, as the noise we were making approached its climax, we achieved our happiness and fulfilment. We slept until morning, when I wanted to go out, but she came up to me laughing and said: 'Oh, oh, do you think that to enter the baths is the same as to leave them? You seem to think that I am like the daughter of Delilah the wily. Beware of any such thought. You are my lawfully wedded husband, and if you are drunk you had better sober up, for the house where you are is only open on one day in the year. Go and look at the great door.'

I went to it and found that it had been nailed shut, and when I returned and told her that, she said: ''Aziz, we have enough flour, grain, fruit, pomegranates, sugar, meat, sheep, poultry and so on to last for many years. The door will not be opened until a year from now, and up till then you will not find yourself outside this house.' I recited the formula: 'There is no might and no power except with God,' and she replied: 'What harm will this do you when you remember what I told you about of the work of the cock?' She laughed and I joined in her laughter. In obedience to her instructions, I stayed with her, acting the part of the cock – eating, drinking and copulating – until twelve months had passed. By the end of the year, she had conceived and given birth to my son.

At the start of the new year, I heard the sound of the door being opened and found men bringing in sweet cakes, flour and sugar. I was on the point of going out when my wife said to me: 'Wait until evening and go out in the same way that you came in.' So I waited and was again about to go out, despite being nervous and frightened, when she said to me: 'By God, I am not going to let you out until I have made you swear that you will come back tonight before the door is closed.' I agreed to this and swore a solemn oath by the sword, the Quran and the promise of divorce that I would come back to her. I then left her and went to the garden, which I found open as usual. I was angry and said to myself: 'I have been absent from here for a whole year and yet when I come unexpectedly I find it open as usual. I wonder if the girl is still as she was before or not. It is now evening and I must go in to see before I go to my mother.' So I entered the garden and went to the garden room, where I found the daughter of Delilah the wily seated with her head on her knees and her hand on her cheek. Her colour had changed and her eyes were sunken, but when she saw me she exclaimed: 'Praise be to God that you are safe!' She wanted to get up but in her joy she collapsed. I was ashamed and hung my head, but then I went up to her, kissed her and asked: 'How did you know that I was going to come to you tonight?' 'I didn't know,' she replied, adding: 'By God, it is a year since I enjoyed the taste of sleep, for every night I have stayed awake waiting for you. I have been like this since the day you left me. I had given you new clothes and you had promised me that you would go to the baths and then come back. I sat waiting for you on the first night, and then the second and then the third, but it is only after this time that you have come, although I have always been expecting you, in the way that lovers do. I want you to tell me why you left me all this year.'

I told her the story and when she heard that I was married, she turned pale. Then I said to her: 'I have come to you tonight but I have to go before daybreak.' 'Wasn't it enough for her,' she said, 'to have tricked you and married you, and imprisoned you with her for a year, that she made you swear by the promise of divorce to go back to her this same night before daybreak and she could not find the generosity to allow you to spend time with your mother or with me? She couldn't bear the thought of your passing the night with either of us, away from her. How about the one whom you abandoned for a whole year, although I knew you before her? May God have mercy on your cousin 'Aziza. No one else experienced what she did and she suffered what no one else could endure. She died because of the treatment to which you subjected her, and it is she who protected you from me. I thought you loved me and I let you go on your way, although I could have seen to it that you didn't leave unscathed, or I could have kept you as a prisoner or killed you.'

Then she wept bitterly, shuddering with rage, looking at me with angry eyes. When I saw the state she was in, I trembled in fear; she was like a terrifying *ghul* and I was like a bean placed on a fire. 'You are no use any more,' she told me, 'now that you are married and have a child. You are no longer suitable company for me; only bachelors are of use, while married men serve no purpose for me at all. You sold me for a bundle of filth and I am going to make that whore sorry, as you won't be here, either for me or for her.'

She gave a loud cry, and before I knew what was happening, ten slave girls had come and thrown me on the ground. While they held me down, she got up, took a knife and said: 'I am going to cut your throat as one would kill a goat, and this is the least repayment you can expect for what you did to me and to your cousin before me.' When I saw the position I was in, held down by the slave girls, with my cheeks rubbed in the dust, and the knife being sharpened, I was sure that I was going to die. I implored her to help me, but this only added to her mercilessness. She told the slave girls to pinion me, which they did, and they threw me on my back, sitting on my stomach and holding my head. Two of them sat on my shins while another two held my hands, and their mistress then came up with two more, whom she ordered to beat me. They did this until I lost consciousness and could not speak, and when I recovered I said to myself: 'It would be better for me to have my throat cut as this would be easier to bear than this beating.' I remembered that my cousin had been in the habit of saying: 'May God protect you from her evil,' and I shrieked and wept until my voice failed me and I was left without feeling or breath.

She sharpened the knife and told her girls to bare my throat. Then God inspired me to quote the two sayings that my cousin had told me and recommended to me, and so I said: 'My lady, don't you know that loyalty is good and treachery is evil?' On hearing this, she cried out and said: 'May God have mercy on you, 'Aziza, and reward you with Paradise in exchange for your youth.' Then she said to me: ''Aziza helped you both in her lifetime and after her death, and by these two sayings she has saved you from me. But I cannot let you go like this; I must leave a mark on you in order to hurt that shameless whore who has kept you away from me.'

She called out to her girls, telling them to tie my legs with rope and after that to sit on top of me, which they did. She left me and fetched a copper pan, which she put on top of a brazier. She poured in sesame oil and fried some cheese in it. I knew nothing of what was happening until she came up to me, undid my trousers and tied a rope round my testicles. She held the rope, but then gave it to two of her slave girls, telling them to pull. They both pulled and I fainted with the pain, losing all touch with this world. She then came with a steel razor and cut off my penis, so that I was left like a woman, and, while I was still unconscious, she cauterized the wound and rubbed it with powder.

When I came to my senses, the flow of blood had stopped and she told the slave girls to untie me. Then, after giving me a cup of wine to drink, she said: 'You can go now to the one whom you married and who grudged me one single night. May God have mercy on your cousin, who is the reason why you have escaped with your life. She never revealed her secret, and if you had not quoted her two sayings, I would have cut your throat. Go off now to anyone you want. There is nothing that I needed from you except what I have cut off. You have nothing more for me, and I neither want you or need you. Get up, touch your head and invoke God's mercy on your cousin.' She then kicked me and I got up, but I could not walk properly and so I moved very slowly to the door of my house, which I found open. I threw myself down there in a faint and my wife came out and carried me into the hall, where she found that I had been emasculated.

I fell into a deep sleep and when had I recovered my senses, I found that I had been thrown down by the garden gate.

I got up and walked home, moaning with grief, and when I went in I found my mother weeping for me and saying: 'My son, I wonder in what land you are.' I threw myself on her and when she looked at me and felt me, she discovered that I was unwell, with a mixture of pallor and blackness on my face. I thought of my cousin and the good that she had done me and I was certain that she had loved me. So I wept for her, as did my mother. My mother then told me that my father had died, and as my grief and anger increased, I wept until I fainted. When I had recovered, I looked at where my cousin had used to sit, and I wept again, again almost fainting because of the violence of my grief, and I continued to weep and sob until half the night had passed.

My mother told me that it was ten days since my father had died, but I said to her: 'I cannot think of anyone except my cousin. I deserve everything that has happened to me for having neglected her in spite of the fact that she loved me.' My mother then asked: 'And what did happen to you?' so I told her the story. She wept for a time and then got up and fetched me some food. I ate a little and drank and then repeated my story, telling her everything that had happened to me. 'Praise be to God,' she said, 'that it was this rather than a cut throat that you suffered.' She then tended me and treated me until I was cured and restored to full health.

'My son,' she then said, 'I shall now fetch out what your cousin left with me as a deposit, for it is yours, and she made me swear that I would not produce it for you until I saw that you remembered her, mourned her and had cut your ties with other women. Now I know that you have fulfilled the condition.' She got up, opened a chest and produced this piece of material that has on it the picture of this gazelle, and it was the daughter of Delilah who had given it to me in the first place. When I took it, I found embroidered on it the following verses:

Mistress of beauty, who prompted you to turn away,
So that you killed a pining lover through excessive love?
If after parting you have not remembered me,
God knows that I have not forgotten you.
You torture me, falsely accusing me, but your torture is sweet.
Will you be generous to me one day and allow me to see you?
Before I fell in love with you, I did not think
That love held sickliness and torment for the soul.

This was before my heart was stirred by passion
And I became a prisoner of love, ensnared by your glance.
The censurer pitied me, lamenting the state love brought me to,
But you, Hind, never have lamented one who pined for you.
By God, were I to die, I would not be consoled for you, who are my hope;
Were passion to destroy me, I would not forget.

On reading these lines, I wept bitterly, slapping my face. As I opened up the cloth, a piece of paper fell out of it, and when I opened it, I found written on it: 'Cousin, know that I do not hold you to blame for my death, and I hope that God will grant you good fortune in your dealings with your beloved. But if something happens to you at the hands of the daughter of Delilah the wily, do not go back to her or to any other woman, but endure your misfortune. Had it not been that your allotted span is an extended one, you would have died long ago. Praise be to God, Who has allowed me to die before you. I give you my greetings. Keep this piece of material with the picture of the gazelle and never part from it, for the picture used to console me when you were absent.'

The note went on: 'I implore you in God's Name that, if fate brings you together with the one who embroidered this gazelle, keep away from her. Don't let her make an approach to you and don't marry her. Even if you do not fall in with her and are not fated to meet her, and even if you can find no way of reaching her, do not make advances to any other woman. You must know that the embroiderer of the gazelle makes one every year and sends it off to the furthest lands to spread the fame of her beautiful workmanship, which no one else in the world can match. This one fell into the hands of your inamorata, the daughter of Delilah the wily, who used it to bemuse people, showing it to them and saying: "I have a sister who makes this." That was a lie – may God put her to shame! This is my advice, which I only give you because I know that, when I am dead, the world will be a difficult place for you and because of that you may go abroad and travel in foreign lands. It may be that you will hear of the lady who made this and want to make her acquaintance. You will remember me when it will do you no good and you will not recognize my value until after my death. Know that the girl who embroidered the gazelle is a noble princess, the daughter of the king of the Islands of Camphor.'

When I had read this note and grasped its meaning, I wept and my mother wept because of my tears. I went on looking at it and weeping until night came. I stayed in this state for a year. It was after this that these merchants, my companions in this caravan, made their preparations to leave my city on a journey. My mother advised me to get ready to travel with them, saying that I might find consolation and a cure for my sorrow. 'Relax,' she said, 'and abandon your grief. You may be away for one year or two or three before the caravan gets back, and it may be that you will find happiness and clear your mind of sorrow.' She kept on coaxing me until I prepared my trade goods and left with them. Throughout the length of the journey my tears have never dried and at every halting place I unfold this piece of material and look at its gazelle, weeping over the memory of my cousin, as you can see. For she loved me with an excessive love and she died of the sorrow that I inflicted on her. I did her nothing but harm and she did me nothing but good.

When the merchants return from their expedition, I shall go back with them. I shall have been away for a whole year, but my sorrow has increased, and what renewed it was the fact that I passed by the Islands of Camphor and the Crystal Castle. There are seven of these islands and their ruler is a king named Shahriman, who has a daughter called Dunya. I was told that it is she who embroiders the gazelles and that the gazelle I had with me was one of hers. On hearing this, I felt a surge of longing and sank into a sea of hurtful thoughts. I wept for myself, as I was now like a woman; there was nothing I could do and I no longer had a male organ. From the day that I left the Camphor Islands I have been tearful and sorrowful at heart. I have continued in this state for a long time, wondering whether I shall be able to go back to my own land and die in my mother's house, for I have had enough of this world.

The young man then wept, groaned and complained. Looking at the image of the gazelle, with the tears running down his cheeks, he recited these lines:

> Many a man has said to me: 'Relief must come,'
> And I have answered angrily: 'How many times?'
> 'After some time,' he said, and I replied: 'How strange!
> Who guarantees me life, O faulty arguer?'

He also recited:

God knows that, after leaving you, I wept
Until I had to borrow tears on credit.
A censurer once told me: 'Patience – you will reach your goal.'
'Censurer,' I said, 'from where will patience come?'

'This is my story, O king,' he went on. 'Have you ever heard one that is more remarkable?'

Taj al-Muluk was full of wonder, and when he heard the young man's story, fires were kindled in his heart at the mention of Princess Dunya and her beauty. Realizing that it was she who had embroidered the gazelles, the passion of his love increased. The prince said to the young man: 'By God, nothing like this adventure of yours has happened to anyone before, but you have to live out your own fate. There is something that I want to ask you.' 'Aziz asked what this was and Taj al-Muluk said: 'Tell me how you came to see the girl who embroidered this gazelle.' 'Master,' replied 'Aziz, 'I approached her by a trick. When I had entered her city with the caravan, I used to go out and wander round the orchards, which were full of trees. The orchard guard was a very elderly man and when I asked him who owned the place, he told me that it belonged to the king's daughter, Princess Dunya. "We are underneath her palace here," he said, "and when she wants to take the air, she opens the postern door and walks in the orchard, enjoying the scent of the flowers." I said: "As a favour, let me sit here until she comes past, so that perhaps I may catch a glimpse of her." "There is no harm in that," agreed the old man, at which I gave him some money, saying: "Buy some food for us." He took the money gladly, opened the gate and went in, taking me with him. We kept on walking until we came to a pleasant spot where he told me to sit, saying that he would go off and come back with some fruit. He left me and went away, coming back some time later with a roasted lamb, whose meat we ate until we had had enough. I felt a longing in my heart to see the girl, and while we were sitting there, the gate suddenly opened. "Get up and hide," the old man told me, and so I did. A black eunuch then put his head out of the wicket and asked the old man whether there was anyone with him. When he said no, the eunuch told him to lock the orchard gate, which he did. Then, through the postern appeared Princess Dunya, and when I caught sight of her I thought that the moon had risen, spreading its light from the horizon. I gazed at her for a time and was filled with longing, like a man thirsting for water.

'After a while, she shut the postern and went off, at which I left the garden and went to my lodgings. I realized that I could not get to her, nor was I man enough for her, as I had become like a woman and had no male tool. She was a king's daughter and I was a merchant, and how then could I get to one like her, or indeed to any other woman? When my companions got ready to leave, I collected my things and went with them. This was where they were making for, and when we got here, I met you. You asked me questions and I replied to you. This is the story of what happened to me and that is all.'

When Taj al-Muluk heard this, his whole mind and all his thoughts were taken up with love for Princess Dunya, and he was at a loss to know what to do. He got to his feet, mounted his horse and, taking 'Aziz with him, he went back to his father's city. Here he gave 'Aziz a house of his own and supplied him with whatever he needed in the way of food, drink and clothing. He then left him and went to his palace, with tears running down his cheeks, as instead of his seeing and meeting the princess, he had to make do with what he had heard about her. He was in this state when his father came in to see him and found that his colour had changed and that he had become thin and tearful. Realizing that something had happened to preoccupy him, he said: 'My son, tell me how you are and what has happened to make you change colour and become emaciated.'

At that, Taj al-Muluk told him all that had happened, together with what he had heard from 'Aziz, and the story of Princess Dunya, adding that he had fallen in love with her by hearsay without having seen her. 'My son,' said his father, 'she is a king's daughter; his country is far distant from us, so let this matter rest and go to your mother's palace where there are five hundred slave girls like moons. Take whichever of them you like, or otherwise we can set about trying to get for you the hand of a princess more beautiful than Dunya.' 'I shall never want anyone else, father,' Taj al-Muluk replied. 'She is the lady of the gazelle which I saw. I must have her, or else I shall wander off in the wastes and wildernesses and kill myself because of her.' 'Wait,' said his father, 'until I send word to her father, ask for her hand and get you what you want, as I did for myself in the case of your mother. It may be that God will bring you to your goal, but if her father refuses, I shall overturn his kingdom with an army whose rearguard will still be with me when the vanguard has reached him.'

He then summoned the young 'Aziz and said: 'My son, do you know the way?' When 'Aziz said that he did, the king said: 'I want you to go with my vizier.' 'To hear is to obey, king of the age,' replied 'Aziz. The king then summoned his vizier and said: 'Arrange things for me to help my son; go to the Camphor Islands and ask that he be given the hand of the princess.' When the vizier had agreed, Taj al-Muluk went back to his quarters. His lovelorn state had grown worse and he found the delay too long. In the darkness of night, he wept, moaned and complained, reciting these lines:

The night is dark; my tears flow more and more;
Passion springs out of my heart's raging fire.
Question the nights about me. They will tell
Whether I think of anything but care.
Thanks to my love, I shepherd the night stars,
While tears drop on my cheeks like hail.
I am alone; I have no one,
Like a lover without kin and with no child.

On finishing his poem, he fainted for a time and only recovered consciousness in the morning. One of his father's servants entered and stood by his head, telling him to come to his father. He went with the man and when his father saw him, he found that his son's colour had changed. Urging him to have patience, he promised that he would bring him together with his princess, and he then made preparations to send off 'Aziz and the vizier, supplying them with gifts.

These two travelled day and night until, when they were close to the Camphor Islands, they halted by a river bank, from where the vizier sent a messenger to the king to tell him of their arrival. The messenger had hardly been gone an hour when the king's chamberlains and his emirs came out to greet the visitors, and after meeting them at a *parasang*'s distance from the city, they escorted them into the king's presence. They presented their gifts to the king and were entertained by him for three days. On the fourth day, the vizier entered the king's presence, stood before him and told him of the errand on which he had come. The king was at a loss to know how to reply, as his daughter had no love for men and did not want to marry. For a time he bowed his head towards the ground and then, raising it again, he summoned one of the eunuchs and said: 'Go to your mistress, Dunya; repeat to her what you have heard and tell her of the errand on which this vizier has come.' The eunuch went off and was away for an hour, after which he came back to the king and said: 'King of the age, when I went in and told Princess Dunya what I had heard, she fell into a violent rage and attacked me with a stick, wanting to break my head. I ran away from her, but she said: "If my father forces me to marry, then I shall kill my husband."' Her father said to the vizier and 'Aziz: 'You have heard and understood. Tell this to your king. Give him my greetings but say that my daughter has no love for men and no desire for marriage.'

The unsuccessful envoys then returned and, having completed their journey, they came to the king and told him what had happened. The king ordered his commanders to proclaim to the troops that they were to march out to war, but the vizier said: 'Your majesty, don't do this. It is not the fault of King Shahriman. When she learned of the proposal, his daughter sent him a message to say that if he forced her to marry, she would first kill her husband and then herself. The refusal came from her.' When the king heard what the vizier had to say, he was afraid for Taj al-Muluk and said: 'If I go to war against the father and capture the daughter, she will kill herself and it will do me no good at all.'

He told Taj al-Muluk about this, and when he learned what had happened, Taj al-Muluk said: 'Father, I cannot bear to do without her. I shall go to her and try to reach her by some ruse, even if I die. There is no other course for me to follow.' 'How will you go to her?' asked his father, and when Taj al-Muluk said that he would disguise himself as a merchant, the king said: 'If you must do this, take the vizier and 'Aziz with you.' He then took out some money for him from his treasury and prepared trade goods to the value of a hundred thousand dinars.

Both the vizier and 'Aziz agreed to go with Taj al-Muluk, and they went to 'Aziz's house and spent the night there. Taj al-Muluk, having lost his heart, could enjoy neither food nor sleep, assaulted, as he was, by cares and shaken by longing for his beloved. He implored the Creator to grant him a meeting with her, and with tears, moans and complaints, he recited these lines:

Do you think that after parting we shall meet again?
I complain to you of my love and say:
'I remembered you, while night forgot;
You denied me sleep, while others were heedless.'

When he had finished his poem, he wept bitterly, while 'Aziz, remembering his cousin, wept too. They continued to shed tears until morning came. Taj al-Muluk then got up and went to see his mother, wearing his travelling dress. She asked him how he was, and after he had repeated his story to her, she gave him fifty thousand dinars and said goodbye to him. As he left, she wished him a safe journey and a meeting with his beloved. He then went to see his father and asked leave to go. His father granted him this and gave him another fifty thousand dinars, ordering a tent to be pitched for him outside the city. This was done and he stayed there for two days before setting off.

He had become friendly with 'Aziz and said to him: 'Brother, I cannot bear to be parted from you.' 'I feel the same,' said 'Aziz, 'and I would like to die at your feet, but, brother of my heart, I am concerned about my mother.' Taj al-Muluk reassured him: 'When we reach our goal, all will be well.' They then set off. The vizier had told Taj al-Muluk to be patient and 'Aziz would talk with him at night, reciting poetry for him and telling him histories and tales. They pressed on with their journey, travelling night and day for two full months. Taj al-Muluk found the journey long, and as the fires of his passion increased, he recited:

The way is long; cares and disquiet have increased;
The heart holds love, whose tortures worsen.
You who are my desire and the goal of my hopes, I have sworn an
  oath
By Him who created man from a clot of blood,
The sleepless passion I have borne, you who are my wish,
Is more than lofty mountains have to bear.
My lady Dunya, love has destroyed me,
Leaving me as a corpse deprived of life.
Did I not hope to gain union with you,
I would not leave on such a journey now.

When he had finished his recitation, he wept, as did 'Aziz, whose heart was wounded. The vizier felt pity for their tears, saying: 'Master, set your heart at rest and take comfort, for nothing but good will come of this.' 'This has been a long journey, vizier,' said Taj al-Muluk, 'so tell me how far we are from the city.' 'There is only a little way to go,' the vizier replied, and they went on, crossing valleys, rugged ridges and desert wastes.

One night, when Taj al-Muluk was sleeping, he dreamt that his beloved was with him and that he was embracing her and clasping her to his breast. Waking in alarm with his wits astray, he recited:

My two companions, my heart is astray and my tears fall;
I am filled with passion; infatuation clings to me.
My tearful lament is that of a woman who has lost her child;

In the darkness of night I moan as moans the dove.
If the wind blows from your land,
I find a coolness spreading over the earth.
I send you my greetings when the east wind blows,
As long as ringdoves fly and pigeons moan.

When he had finished reciting these lines, the vizier came up to him and said: 'Be glad; this is a good sign, so set your heart at rest and take comfort, for you are certain to reach your goal.' 'Aziz went up to him to urge him to have patience, entertaining him, talking to him and telling him stories. They continued to press on with their journey, travelling day and night for another two months. Then one day when the sun rose they saw in the distance something white. Taj al-Muluk asked 'Aziz what it was and he replied: 'Master, that is the White Castle and this is the city that you have been making for.' Taj al-Muluk was glad, and he and the others went on until they came close to it.

At that point the prince was transported by joy, and care and sorrow fell away from him. He and his companions entered the city disguised as traders, with Taj al-Muluk dressed as a merchant prince. They went to a large hostel known as the merchants' *khan* and Taj al-Muluk asked 'Aziz if it was where merchants stayed. 'Yes,' replied 'Aziz, 'and it is where I lodged myself.' So they halted there, making their camels kneel and unsaddling them, after which they put their goods in the storehouses and rested for four days. The vizier then advised them to rent a larger house. They agreed and hired a spacious property, well adapted for feasts, and there they took up their quarters.

The vizier and 'Aziz spent their time trying to come up with a plan for Taj al-Muluk, while he himself was at a loss, with no idea what to do except to take his wares to the silk bazaar. The vizier approached him and 'Aziz, saying: 'If we stay here like this, then you can be sure that we shall not get what we want or carry out our mission. I have thought of something which, God willing, may produce a good result.' 'Do whatever occurs to you,' said the others, 'for old men are fortunate and this is especially true of you, thanks to your experience of affairs. So tell us what you have thought of.' 'My advice,' the vizier said to Taj al-Muluk, 'is that we should take a booth for you in the silk market where you should sit, buying and selling. Everyone of whatever class, upper or lower, needs pieces of silk, and if you sit there quietly, God willing, you will succeed in your affair, especially because of your good looks. Make 'Aziz your agent, so that he can sit inside the booth to hand you the various items and materials.'

When he heard this, Taj al-Muluk agreed that it was a good and sound idea. He took out a splendid set of merchant's clothes, put them on and walked off, followed by his servants, to whom he had given a thousand dinars in order to set the new place to rights. They went on until they reached the silk market, and when the merchants saw Taj al-Muluk and noted how handsome he was, they were taken aback. 'Ridwan has opened the gates of Paradise and forgotten to close them again, and so this wonderfully handsome young man has come out,' said one. 'Perhaps he is an angel!' exclaimed another. When his party came to the merchants, they asked where the market superintendent had his booth. They were given directions and walked on until they found it. They greeted him and he and the merchants who were with him rose to meet them, invited them to sit and treated them with honour. This was because of the vizier, whom they saw to be a dignified old man. On noting that he was accompanied by the young Taj al-Muluk and by 'Aziz, they said to themselves: 'There is no doubt that this old man is the father of the two young ones.'

The vizier asked which of them was the superintendent of the market. 'This is he,' they said, and the man came forward. The vizier looked at him, studied him and found him to be a venerable and dignified old man, with eunuchs, servants and black slaves. The old man gave the visitors a friendly greeting, treating them with the greatest honour, and after making them sit beside him, he asked whether they had any need that he might be able to fulfil. 'Yes,' said the vizier. 'I am an old man, stricken in years, and I have with me these two young men with whom I have travelled to many regions and countries. I have never entered a town without staying there for a whole year so that they could see its sights and get to know its people. I have now arrived at this town of yours, and as I have chosen to stay here, I want you to provide me with a fine booth in a good situation where I can set them down to trade and to inspect the city, while adapting themselves to the manners of its people, and learning how to buy and sell, give and take.' 'There is no problem with that,' said the superintendent, as he had been glad to see the two young men, for whom he felt a surge of love, he being someone who was passionately fond of murderous glances and who preferred the love of boys to that of girls, inclining to the sour rather than the sweet. To himself he said: 'This is a fine catch – praise be to Him who created and fashioned them from vile sperm!'

He got up and stood before them as a gesture of respect like a servant, after which he made ready for them a booth in the covered market. In size and splendour it was unsurpassed, being roomy and well decorated, with shelves of ivory and ebony. The keys were handed to the vizier, dressed as he was as an elderly merchant, and the superintendent said to him: 'Take these, master, and may God bless this place for your sons.' The vizier took the keys and the three of them went to the *khan* where they had left their things and told the servants to move all their goods and materials to the booth. There was a great deal of stuff, worth huge amounts of money; all of it was shifted and they themselves went to the booth where it was stored. They spent the night there and in the morning the vizier took the two young men to the baths. They made full use of these, washing and cleaning themselves, putting on splendid clothes and applying perfume. Each of them was dazzlingly handsome and their appearance in the baths fitted the poet's lines:

Good news it was for the bath man when his hand met
A body created from a mix of water and of light.
He continued with his delicate artistry,
Plucking musk from an image made of camphor.

When they came out, the market superintendent, who had heard where they had gone, was sitting waiting for them. They moved forward like gazelles, with red cheeks, dark eyes and shining faces, like two brilliant moons or two branches laden with fruit. When the superintendent saw them, he rose to his feet and said: 'My sons, may the baths always bring you comfort.' In return, Taj al-Muluk said pleasantly: 'May God grant you grace, father. Why did you not come and bathe with us?' He and 'Aziz then bent over the man's hand and kissed it, after which they walked in front of him to the booth as a token of respect and reverence, since he was the leader of the merchants and the superintendent of the market, and he had already done them a favour by giving them the booth. When he saw their buttocks swaying, his passion increased; he snorted in his excitement and was unable to restrain himself, but staring fixedly at them, he recited these lines:

The heart studies the chapter devoted to him,
Reading nothing that covers partnership with others.
It is not surprising that weight causes him to sway;
How many movements are there in the revolving sphere?

He also recited:

My eye saw the two of them walking on the earth,
And I wished they had been walking on my eye.

When they heard what he said, they insisted that he go a second time with them to the baths. Scarcely able to believe this, he hurried back and they went in with him. The vizier had not yet left and when he heard that the superintendent was there, he came out and met him in the middle of the bath house and invited him to enter. He refused, but Taj al-Muluk took one of his hands and 'Aziz the other and they brought him to a private room. The evil old man allowed himself to be led by them and his passion increased. Taj al-Muluk swore that he and he alone should wash him, while 'Aziz swore that none but he should pour the water over him. Although this was what he wanted, he refused, but the vizier said: 'They are your sons; let them wash you and clean you.' 'May God preserve them for you,' said the superintendent. 'By God, your arrival and that of your companions has brought blessing and fortune to our city.' He then recited the lines:

You have come and our hills are clothed in green;
Whoever looks can see they bloom with flowers.
The earth and those who walk on it cry out:
'Welcome and greeting to the one who comes!'

They thanked him for that, and Taj al-Muluk continued to wash him as 'Aziz poured water over him, leading him to think that his soul was in Paradise. When they had finished attending to him, he blessed them and sat down beside the vizier to talk to him, although his eyes were fixed on the two young men. Then the servants brought towels and they all dried themselves, put on their things and left the baths. 'Sir,' said the vizier to the superintendent, 'baths are the delight of this world.' 'May God grant you and your sons health,' he replied, 'and guard you from the evil eye. Can you quote anything that eloquent men have said about baths?' 'I can quote you some lines,' said Taj al-Muluk, and he recited:

Life is at its pleasantest in the baths,
But our stay there cannot be long.
This is a paradise where we dislike to stay,
And a hell where it is pleasant to go in.

After Taj al-Muluk had finished, 'Aziz said: 'I, too, remember some lines about baths.' The superintendent asked him to recite them and he quoted:

There is many a chamber whose flowers are solid stone,
Elegant when fires are kindled round about.
To you it looks like a hell, but it is Paradise,
Most of whose contents look like suns and moons.

When he had finished, the superintendent was full of admiration for his quotation, and seeing the combination of beauty and eloquence that the two possessed, he said: 'By God, you are both eloquent and graceful, so now listen to me.' He then chanted tunefully the following lines:

Beauty of hellfire, torment of Paradise,
That gives both souls and bodies life,
A marvellous chamber filled with fresh delight,
Although beneath it there are kindled flames.
Here pleasure lives for all those who approach,
And over it the streams have poured their tears.

Then, letting his gaze roam over the gardens of their beauty, he recited:

I went into that house and saw no chamberlain
Who did not greet me with a smiling face.
I entered Paradise and visited its hell,
Thanking Ridwan and Malik the kindly.

They were filled with admiration when they heard these lines, but when the superintendent invited them home, they refused and went back to their own lodgings to rest after the intense heat of the baths. Having done this, and after eating and drinking, they spent the night there, enjoying the fortune of perfect happiness. In the morning they woke up, performed their ablutions and prayers and took their morning drink. When the sun had risen and the shops and markets were open, they walked off from the house to the market, where they opened their booth. The servants had put this in excellent order, laying down rugs and silk carpets, and in it they had placed two couches, each worth a hundred dinars and each covered with a cloth fit for a king, fringed with a border of gold, while in the middle were splendid furnishings that harmonized with the place.

Taj al-Muluk sat on one sofa and 'Aziz on the other, while the vizier took his place in the middle of the shop, with the servants standing before him. Hearing about them, the townspeople crowded around, so enabling them to sell some of their goods and their materials. The fame of Taj al-Muluk's beauty spread through the city, and after several days, on each of which more and more people had come hurrying up to them, the vizier reminded Taj al-Muluk to keep his secret hidden and, after advising him to take care of 'Aziz, he went home to concoct on his own some plan that might turn out to their advantage.

Taj al-Muluk and 'Aziz started to talk to each other, with Taj al-Muluk saying that perhaps someone might come from Princess Dunya. He kept repeating this for some days and nights, and being disturbed at heart, he was unable to sleep or rest. Love had him in its grip, and his passion and lovesickness grew worse, while the pleasure of sleep was denied him and he abstained from drinking and eating.

However, his beauty was like that of the moon on the night that it becomes full, and while he was sitting there, he was suddenly approached by an old woman, followed by two slave girls. She walked up and stood by the shop and when she saw his symmetrical physique, his beauty and elegance, she admired his gracefulness and her harem trousers became damp. 'Glory to the One who created you from vile sperm and made you a temptation for those who look at you!' she exclaimed. Then, after studying him, she added: 'This is not a mortal man but a noble angel.' She approached and greeted him; he returned the greeting and rose to his feet with a smile, being prompted in all this by gestures from 'Aziz. Asking her to sit beside him, he began to fan her until she was refreshed and rested. She then turned to him and said: 'My son, you are a pattern of all perfection: do you come from these parts?' Taj al-Muluk replied eloquently, in pleasant and agreeable tones: 'My lady, this is the first time that I have ever been here in my life and I have only stopped here in order to look at the sights.' She spoke words of welcome and then asked: 'What materials have you brought with you? Show me something beautiful, for that is the only thing that can be worn by the beautiful.'

When Taj al-Muluk heard this, his heart fluttered and he could not grasp what she meant, but 'Aziz made a sign to him and he said: 'I have here everything that you could want. I have what will suit only kings or the daughters of kings, so tell me for whom it is that you need this, in order that I can put out for you everything that might be appropriate.' By saying this he hoped to find out what she really meant. In reply she said: 'I want something suitable for Princess Dunya, the daughter of King Shahriman.'

Overjoyed to hear this reference to his beloved, Taj al-Muluk told 'Aziz to fetch him a particular package. 'Aziz brought it and opened it in front of him, after which Taj al-Muluk told the old woman: 'Choose what will suit her, for this is something that you will find nowhere else.' The old woman picked on something that was worth a thousand dinars, and asked its price, while, as she talked to him, she was rubbing the palm of her hand between her thighs. 'Am I to haggle with someone like you about this paltry price? Praise be to God who has let me come to know you,' said Taj al-Muluk. 'May God's Name guard you,' she replied. 'I ask the protection of the Lord of the dawn for your beautiful face. A beautiful face and an eloquent tongue – happy is she who sleeps in your embrace, clasps your body and enjoys your youth, especially if she is as beautiful as you!' Taj al-Muluk laughed until he fell over, exclaiming: 'You Who fulfil desires at the hands of profligate old women, it is they who satisfy needs!'

The woman asked his name and on being told that it was Taj al-Muluk, she said: 'This is a name for kings and princes, but you are dressed as a merchant.' 'Aziz said: 'It was because of the love and affection that his parents and his family had for him that they called him this.' 'That must be true,' said the old woman. 'May God protect you from the evil eye and from the evil of your enemies and the envious, even though your beauty causes hearts to break.' She then took the material and went on her way, still dazed by his beauty and symmetrical physique. She walked on until she came into the presence of Princess Dunya. 'I have brought you some fine material, lady,' she said. When the princess told her to show it to her, she said: 'Here it is, lady; turn it over and look at it.' Dunya was astonished at what she saw, saying: 'This is beautiful stuff, nurse. I have never seen its like in our city.' 'The man who sold it is more beautiful still,' said the old woman. 'It is as though Ridwan opened the gates of Paradise, and then when he forgot to close them, out came the young man who sold me this material. I wish that he could sleep with you tonight and lie between your breasts. He has brought precious stuffs to your city in order to look around it, and he is a temptation to the eyes of those who see him.'

Princess Dunya laughed at what she had to say, exclaiming: 'May God shame you, you unlucky old woman; you are talking nonsense and you have lost your wits!' Then she added: 'Bring me the material so that I can have a good look at it.' When it was given to her, she looked at it for a second time and saw that, albeit small, it was precious. She admired it, as never in her life had she seen its match, saying: 'By God, this is good material.' 'By God, lady,' said the old woman, 'if you saw its owner, you would realize that he is the most beautiful thing on the face of the earth.'

The princess enquired: 'Did you ask him to tell us whether there is any need he has that we can fulfil for him?' The old woman shook her head and said: 'May God preserve your perspicacity. By God, he does have a need, may your skill not desert you. Can anyone escape from needs and be free of them?' 'Go to him,' said the princess, 'greet him and say: "You have honoured our land and our city by coming here. Whatever needs you have we shall willingly fulfil."'

Back went the old woman immediately to Taj al-Muluk, and when he saw her, his heart leapt with happiness and joy. He got up, took her by the hand and made her sit beside him. When she had rested she told him what the princess had said to her. He was overjoyed, cheerful and relaxed; happiness entered into his heart and he said to himself: 'I have got what I wanted.' He asked the old woman: 'Would you carry a message from me and bring me the reply?' 'Willingly,' she said, and he then told 'Aziz to bring him an inkstand, paper and a brass pen. When these had been fetched, he took the pen in his hand and wrote these lines:

I have written you a letter, you who are my wish,
Telling of how I suffer from the pain of separation.
Its first line tells of the fire within my heart,
Its second of my passion and my longing.
The third tells how my life and patience waste away;
The fourth says: 'All the passion still remains.'
The fifth asks: 'When shall my eyes rest on you?'
And the sixth: 'On what day shall we meet?'

At the end of the letter he wrote: 'This letter comes from the captive of desire, held in the prison of longing, whose only chance of freedom lies in union and a meeting that follows after remoteness and separation. Parting from loved ones has left him to endure the pain and torture of passion.' With tears pouring from his eyes, he then wrote these lines:

I have written to you as my tears flood down,
Falling from my eyes in ceaseless streams.
But I am not one to despair of the grace of God;
A day may come on which we two shall meet.

He folded the letter, sealed it and gave it to the old woman, saying: 'Take this to Princess Dunya.' 'To hear is to obey,' she said, and he then handed her a thousand dinars, saying: 'Accept this as a friendly gift from me, mother.' She took the money, blessed him and left, walking back to

Princess Dunya, who, when she saw her, said: 'Nurse, what did he ask for, so that we can fulfil his request?' 'Lady,' the old woman replied, 'he sent me with this letter, but I don't know what is in it.' She handed the letter to Dunya, who took it, read it and, after having understood its meaning, exclaimed: 'What are things coming to when this trader sends me messages and writes to me?' She slapped her own face and said: 'With my position, am I to have connections with the rabble? Oh, Oh!' and she added: 'Were it not for my fear of God, I would have him killed and crucified over his shop.'

'What is in the letter that has upset and disturbed you?' asked the old woman. 'I wonder whether it is some complaint about injustice and whether he is asking payment for the material.' 'Damn you,' said Dunya, 'it is not about that. There is nothing in it but words of love. This is all thanks to you, for otherwise how could this devil have known about me?' 'Lady,' answered the old woman, 'you sit in your high palace and no one, not even the birds of the air, can reach you. May you and your youthfulness be free from blame and reproach. The dogs may bark, but this means nothing to you, who are a princess and the daughter of a king. Don't blame me for bringing you the letter, for I had no idea what was in it. My advice is that you should send him a reply, threaten him with death and tell him to give up this wild talk. That will finish the matter for him and he will not do the same thing again.' Princess Dunya said: 'I'm afraid that if I write to him, this may stir his desire for me.' 'When he hears the threats and warnings, he will draw back,' said the old woman.

The princess told her to fetch an inkstand, paper and a brass pen. When these had been brought, she wrote the following lines:

You make a pretence of love and claim sad sleeplessness,
Talking of passion and your cares;
Deluded man, do you seek union with the moon?
Has anyone got what he wanted from the moon?
I advise you to give up your quest;
Abandon it, for in it there is danger.
If you use words like these again,
You will be punished harshly at my hands.
I swear by Him Who created man from sperm
And caused the sun and the moon to spread their light,
If you should dare to talk of this again,
I shall have you crucified upon a tree.

She folded the letter, gave it to the old woman and said: 'Hand this to him and tell him to stop talking in this way.' 'To hear is to obey,' replied the old woman, who took the letter joyfully and went to her house, where she spent the night. In the morning she set off for Taj al-Muluk's shop and found him waiting for her. When he saw her, he almost flew up into the air for joy, and when she approached, he rose to meet her. He made her sit beside him, and she produced the note, handed it to him and told him to read it. 'Princess Dunya was angry when she read your letter,' she said, 'but I humoured her and joked with her until I made her laugh. Her feelings towards you softened and she wrote you a reply.' Taj al-Muluk thanked her for that and told 'Aziz to give her a thousand dinars, but when he read the note and understood what it meant, he wept bitterly. The old woman felt sympathy for him and was grieved by his tears and complaints. 'My son,' she said, 'what is in this paper that has made you weep?' 'She threatens to kill me and to crucify me,' he answered, 'and she forbids me to write to her, but if I do not, then it would be better for me to die than to live. So take the answer to her letter and let her do what she wants.' 'By your youthful life,' said the old woman, 'I must join you in risking my own life in order to get you to your goal and to help you reach what you have in mind.' 'I shall reward you for everything you do,' said Taj al-Muluk, 'and you will find it weighed out in your favour on the Day of Judgement. You are experienced in the running of affairs and you know the various types of intrigue. All difficulties are easy for you to overcome, and God has power over all things.'

He then took a piece of paper and wrote these lines on it:

She threatened me with death, alas for me,
But this would bring me rest; death is decreed for all,
And it is easier for a lover than long life
When he is kept from his beloved and oppressed.
Visit a lover who has few to help him, for God's sake;
I am your slave, and slaves are held captive.
My lady, pity me in my love for you.
All those who love the nobly born must be excused.

After writing the lines, he sighed deeply and wept until the old woman wept too. She then took the paper from him and told him to be of good cheer and to console himself, for she would bring him to his goal.

She left him on fire with anxiety and set off for the princess. Dunya had been so enraged by Taj al-Muluk's letter that the old woman found that her colour had changed, and when she was given the second note, she grew even angrier. 'Didn't I tell you that he would desire me?' she said to the old woman. 'What is this dog that he should do such a thing?' the woman replied. 'Go to him,' ordered Dunya, 'and tell him that if he sends me another letter, I shall have his head cut off.' The old woman said: 'Write this down for him in a letter and I shall take it with me, to make him even more frightened.' Dunya then took a piece of paper on which she wrote these lines:

You who are heedless of the blows of fate,
You race for union, but are bound to fail.
Do you suppose, deluded man, that you can reach a star?
The shining moon remains outside your grasp.
How is it that you set your hopes on me
Hoping for union, to embrace my slender form?
Give up this quest of yours for fear I force on you
A day of gloom to whiten the parting of the hair.

She folded the letter and handed it to the old woman, who took it off to Taj al-Muluk. When he saw her, he got to his feet and said: 'May God never deprive me of the blessing of your coming.' The old woman told him to take the reply to his letter and when he had taken it and read it, he burst into tears. 'I would like someone to kill me now so that I might find rest, for to be slain would be easier for me to bear than my present position.' He then took the inkstand, pen and paper and wrote a note with these lines:

You who are my wish, seek no harsh parting;
Visit a lover drowning in his love.
Do not think this harshness will allow me life;
The breath of life will leave with the beloved.

He folded the letter and gave it to the old woman, saying: 'Don't reproach me for putting you to trouble without reward.' Telling 'Aziz to pay her a thousand dinars, he then said to her: 'Mother, this note will lead either to complete union or to a final break.' 'My son,' she replied, 'by God, all I want is your good and I would like you to have her, for you are the radiant moon and she is the rising sun. If I fail to bring you together, then my life is of no use. I have reached the age of ninety, having spent my days in wiles and trickery, so how can I fail to unite a pair in illicit love?' She then took her leave of him and went off, having encouraged him.

When she came into the presence of Princess Dunya, she had hidden the paper in her hair. When she sat down there, she scratched her head and asked the princess to examine her head for lice, saying that it was a long time since she had been to the baths. The princess rolled back her sleeves to the elbow, let down the old woman's hair and started to search. The note fell out and when the princess saw it, she asked what it was. 'It must have stuck to me while I was sitting in the trader's shop,' the old woman said. 'Give it to me so that I can take it back to him, as there may be a bill there which he will need.' The princess opened it up and read it, and when she had seen what was in it, she said to the old woman: 'This is one of your tricks and but for the fact that you brought me up, I would strike out at you here and now. God has plagued me with this merchant, and everything that he has done to me has been thanks to you. I don't know from what land he has come; no one else has been able to take such liberties with me, and I am afraid lest this become public, especially since it concerns a man who is not of my race and is not one of my equals.' The old woman turned to her and said: 'No one will dare talk about it for fear of your power and the awe in which your father is held. There can be no harm in sending him back an answer.' 'Nurse,' the princess said, 'this man is a devil. How has he dared to talk like this? He doesn't fear the king's power, and I don't know what to do about him. If I order him to be killed, that would not be right, but if I let him be, he will grow even more daring.' 'Write him a note,' said the old woman, 'so that he may be warned off.'

The princess asked for paper, an inkstand and a pen, after which she wrote these lines:

You have long been censured, but too much folly leads you astray;
How many verses must I write to hold you back?
The more you are forbidden, the more you covet;
If you keep this secret, that is the only thing I shall approve.
Conceal your love; never let it be known;
For if you speak, I shall not listen to you,
And if you talk of this again,
The raven of parting will croak your death-knell.
Death will soon swoop down on you,
And you will rest buried beneath the earth.
Deluded man, you will leave your family to regret your loss,
Mourning that you have gone from them for ever.

She then folded the paper and gave it to the old woman, who took it and set off to Taj al-Muluk. She gave it to him and, having read it, he realized that princess was hard-hearted and that he would not be able to reach her. He took his complaint to the vizier, asking him to devise a good plan. The vizier told him that the only thing that might be of use would be for him to write her a letter calling down a curse on her. Taj al-Muluk said: ''Aziz, my brother, write for me, as you know what to say.' So 'Aziz took a piece of paper and wrote:

Lord, by the five planets I ask You, rescue me
And lead the one who torments me to taste my grief.
You know I suffer from a burning passion;
She treats me harshly and is pitiless.
How long must I be tender in my sufferings?
How long will she oppress me in my feebleness?
I stray through endless floods of misery
And find no one to help me, oh my Lord.
How often do I try to forget her love!
It has destroyed my patience; how can I forget?
You keep me from the sweet union of love;
Are you yourself safe from the miseries of Time?
Are you not happy in your life, while, thanks to you,
I am an exile from my country and my kin?

'Aziz then folded the letter and handed it to Taj al-Muluk, who read it with admiration and handed it to the old woman. She took it and went to Princess Dunya, to whom she gave the letter. When Dunya had read it and digested its contents, she was furiously angry and said: 'This ill-omened old woman is responsible for all that has happened to me.' She called to her slave girls and eunuchs and said: 'Seize this damned scheming old creature and beat her with your slippers.' They fell upon her and beat her until she fainted. When she had recovered consciousness, the princess said to her: 'By God, you wicked old woman, were it not for my fear of Almighty God I would kill you.' She then told the servants to beat her again, which they did until she fainted, after which on her orders they dragged her off face downwards and threw her outside in front of the door of the palace.

When she had recovered, she got up and moved off, walking and sitting down at intervals, until she reached her house. She waited until morning and then got up and went to Taj al-Muluk, to whom she told everything that had happened to her. Finding this hard to bear, he said: 'I am distressed by this, mother, but all things are controlled by fate and destiny.' She told him to be of good heart and to take comfort, adding: 'I shall not stop trying until I have brought the two of you together and fetched you to this harlot who has me beaten so painfully.' Taj al-Muluk then asked her what had caused the princess to hate men, and when he was told that this was because of a dream that she had had, he asked what the dream had been.

The old woman replied: 'One night when the princess was asleep she saw in a dream a hunter spreading out a net on the ground and scattering wheat around it. He sat down close by and all the birds there came to the net, among them being a pair of pigeons, male and female. While she was watching the net, the male pigeon got caught in it. It started to struggle and all the other birds took fright and flew off, but the female pigeon came back. She circled over him and then came down to the part of the net where her mate's foot was trapped, pulling at it with her beak until the foot was freed, after which the two of them flew off. The hunter, who had not noticed what was happening, came up and readjusted the net before sitting down at a distance from it. Within an hour, the birds had come down again, and this time it was the female pigeon that was trapped. All the birds took fright, including the male, who did not return for his mate, and so, when the hunter arrived, he took her and cut her throat. The princess woke from her dream in alarm and said: "All males are like this; there is no good in them, and no men are of any good to women."'

When she had finished her tale, Taj al-Muluk said: 'Mother, I want to look at her once, even if this means my death, so think of some way for me to do this.' The old woman said: 'Know that beneath her palace she has a pleasure garden to which she goes once a month from her postern door. In ten days, it will be time for her next visit, and when she is on the point of going out, I shall come and tell you so that you can go and meet her. Take care not to leave the garden, for it may be that if she sees how handsome you are, she may fall in love with you, and love is the most potent motive for union.' 'To hear is to obey,' said Taj al-Muluk, and he and 'Aziz then left the shop and, taking the old woman with them, they went back to their house, which they showed to her. Taj al-Muluk said to 'Aziz: 'Brother, I don't need the shop any more. I have got what I wanted from it and so I give it to you, with all its contents, as you have come with me to a foreign country, leaving your own land.'

'Aziz accepted the gift and the two sat talking, with Taj al-Muluk asking 'Aziz about the strange circumstances in which he had found himself and about his adventures, while 'Aziz gave him an account of everything that had happened to him. After that they went to the vizier and told him what Taj al-Muluk had determined to do, and asked him how they should set about it. 'Come with me to the garden,' said the vizier, and they each put on their most splendid clothes and went out, followed by three mamluks. They made their way to the garden, where they saw quantities of trees and many streams, with the gardener sitting by the gate. After they had exchanged greetings, the vizier handed the man a hundred dinars and said: 'Please take this money and buy us something to eat, as we are strangers here. I have with me these sons of mine and I want to show them the sights.' The gardener took the dinars and told them: 'Go in and look around, for it is all yours. Then you can sit down and wait for me to bring you food.'

He then went off to the market, and the vizier, Taj al-Muluk and 'Aziz entered the garden. After a while he brought back a roast lamb and bread as white as cotton, which he placed in front of them. They ate and drank, and he then produced sweetmeats, which they ate, and after this they washed their hands and sat talking. 'Tell me about this place,' the vizier then said to the gardener. 'Do you own or rent it?' 'It's not mine,' replied the gardener. 'It belongs to the king's daughter, Princess Dunya.' 'What is your monthly pay?' asked the vizier. 'One dinar, and no more,' replied the man. The vizier looked at the garden and saw that it contained a high pavilion, but that this was old. He then said to the gardener: '*Shaikh*, I would like to do a good deed by which you may remember me.' When the man asked him what he was thinking of, by way of reply he said: 'Accept these three hundred dinars.' When the gardener heard him talk of gold, he said: 'Master, do whatever you want.' The vizier gave him the money and said: 'If it is the will of Almighty God, we shall achieve something good here.'

The three then left the gardener and went back to their house, where they passed the night. The next day, the vizier summoned a house painter, an artist and a skilled goldsmith, and he produced for them all the tools they would need. He took them into the garden and told them to whitewash the pavilion and to decorate it with various kinds of pictures. He had gold and lapis lazuli fetched and he told the artist to produce on one side of the hall a picture of a hunter who had spread a net into which birds had fallen, with a female pigeon entangled by its beak. When the artist had painted this, the vizier told him to repeat the motif on the other side of the hall, with the pigeon alone captured by the hunter, who had put a knife to its throat. Opposite this there was to be the picture of a great hawk which had seized the male pigeon and sunk its claws into it. The artist completed the painting and when all three had finished the tasks set them by the vizier, he paid them their wages and they went off, as did the vizier and his companions. After taking leave of the gardener, they went home and sat talking.

Taj al-Muluk said to 'Aziz: 'Recite me some poetry, brother, so as to cheer me and to remove these cares of mine, cooling the raging fire in my heart.' At that, 'Aziz chanted the following lines:

All the grief of which lovers talk
Is mine alone, exhausting endurance.
If you wish to be watered by my tears,
Their seas will serve all those who come for water,
And if you wish to see what lovers suffer,
From the power of passion, then look at my body.

Shedding tears, he went on to recite:

Whoever does not love graceful necks and eyes,
But still lays claim to worldly pleasure, does not tell the truth.
Love holds a concept that cannot be grasped
By any man except for those who love.
May God not move love's burden from my heart,
Nor take away the sleeplessness from my eyes.

He next chanted the following lines:

In his *Canon*, Avicenna claims
That music is the lover's cure,
Together with union with one like his love,
As well as wine, a garden and dried fruits.
To find a cure, I chose a different girl,
Aided by fate and opportunity,
Only to find that lovesickness is fatal,
While Avicenna's 'cure' is senseless talk.

When 'Aziz had finished his poem, Taj al-Muluk was astonished at his eloquence and the excellence of his recitation and told him that he had removed some of his cares. The vizier then said: 'Among the experiences of the ancients are some that leave the hearer lost in wonder.' 'If you remember anything of this kind,' Taj al-Muluk said, 'let me hear what you can produce in the way of delicate poetry and long stories.' The vizier then chanted these lines:

I used to think that union could be bought
By prized possessions and payment of cattle.
In ignorance I thought your love too inconsiderable
A thing on which to waste a precious life.
That was before I saw you make your choice
And single out your beloved with choice gifts.
I realized there was no stratagem for me
To reach you, and I tucked my head beneath my wing,
Making my home within the nest of love,
Where endlessly I must pass all my days.

So much, then, for them, but as for the old woman, she remained isolated in her house. It happened that the princess felt a longing to take a walk in the garden. As she would not go out without the old woman, she sent a message and made her peace with her, reconciling her and telling her that she wanted to go out into the garden to look at the trees and their fruits and to enjoy herself among the flowers. The old woman agreed to go with her but said that she first wanted to return home to change her clothes before coming back. 'Go home, then,' the princess said, 'but don't be long.' The old woman left her and went to Taj al-Muluk. 'Get ready,' she said. 'Put on your most splendid clothes, go to the garden and, after you have greeted the gardener, hide yourself there.' 'To hear is to obey,' he replied, and they agreed between themselves on a signal, after which the old woman returned to Princess Dunya.

When she had left, the vizier and 'Aziz dressed Taj al-Muluk in the most splendid of royal robes, worth five thousand dinars, and around his waist they fastened a girdle of gold set with gems and precious stones. They then set off for the garden, and when they reached its gate, they found the gardener sitting there. When he saw Taj al-Muluk, he got to his feet and greeted him with reverence and honour, opening the gate for him and saying: 'Come in and look around the garden.' He did not know that the princess was going to visit it that day.

Taj al-Muluk went in, but he had been there for only an hour when he heard a noise, and before he knew what was happening, the eunuchs and the slave girls had come out of the postern gate. When the gardener saw them, he went to tell Taj al-Muluk, saying: 'Master, what are we going to do, for my lady, Princess Dunya, is here?' 'No harm will come to you,' said Taj al-Muluk, 'for I shall hide myself somewhere in the garden.' The man told him to be very careful, and then left him and went off.

The princess entered the garden with her maids and the old woman, who told herself: 'If the eunuchs come with us, we shall not get what we want.' She then said to the princess: 'Lady, I can tell you how best to relax,' and after the princess had told her to speak, she went on: 'We don't need these eunuchs now; you can't relax as long as they are with us, so send them off.' The princess agreed and sent the eunuchs away.

Soon after that, she began to walk, while, unbeknown to her, Taj al-Muluk was watching her in all her beauty. Every time he looked, he would lose his senses because of her surpassing loveliness. The old woman kept talking to her mistress in order to inveigle her into approaching the pavilion, which had been painted as the vizier had instructed. The princess entered it and looked at the paintings, where she saw the birds, the hunter and the pigeons. 'Glory be to God!' she exclaimed. 'This is exactly what I saw in my dream.' Looking with amazement at the pictures of the birds, the hunter and the net, she said: 'Nurse, I used to blame men and hate them, but look at how the hunter has cut the throat of the female pigeon. The male escaped, but he was going to come and rescue his mate when he was met by the hawk, which seized him.' The old woman, pretending to know nothing about this, kept her occupied with conversation until the two of them came close to Taj al-Muluk's hiding place.

She then gestured to get Taj al-Muluk to walk beneath the windows of the pavilion, and the princess, who was standing there, happened to turn. She caught sight of Taj al-Muluk and had the chance to study his beauty and his symmetrical form. 'Where has this handsome young man come from, nurse?' she asked. 'I know nothing about him,' the old woman told her, 'but I think that he must be the son of a great king, for he is handsome and beautiful to the furthest degree.' Princess Dunya fell in love; the ties of the spells that had bound her were undone, and she was dazzled by Taj al-Muluk's beauty and the symmetry of his form. Passion stirred in her and she said to the old woman: 'Nurse, this young man is handsome.' 'True,' replied the nurse, and she gestured to Taj al-Muluk to indicate that he should go home. He was on fire with love and his passion and ardour had increased, but he went off without stopping and, after saying goodbye to the gardener, he returned home. His longing had been aroused, but he did not disobey the old woman and he told the vizier and

'Aziz that she had signalled to him to go. They advised him to be patient, telling him that she would not have done that had she not thought that it would be useful.

So much for Taj al-Muluk, the vizier and 'Aziz, but as for the princess, she was overwhelmed by love, and her passion and ardour increased. She told the old woman: 'I don't know how I can meet this young man except with your help.' 'I take refuge in God from Satan the accursed,' said the old woman. 'You don't want men, so how have you come to be so disturbed by love for this one, although, by God, he is the only fit mate for your youth?' 'Help me, nurse,' said the princess, 'and if you can arrange for me to meet him, I shall give you a thousand dinars, while if you don't, I am sure to die.' 'Do you go back to your palace,' said the old woman, 'and I shall arrange your meeting and give my life to satisfy the two of you.'

Princess Dunya then returned to her palace, while the old woman went to Taj al-Muluk. When he saw her, he jumped to his feet and greeted her with respect and honour and sat her down beside him. 'The scheme has worked,' she said, and she told him what had happened with the princess. 'When can we meet?' he asked her, and when she said tomorrow, he gave her a thousand dinars and a robe worth another thousand. She took these and then left, going straight on until she reached the princess. 'Nurse,' the princess asked, 'what news do you have of my beloved?' 'I have found where he is,' she replied, 'and tomorrow I shall bring him to you.' In her delight at this, the princess gave her a thousand dinars and a robe worth another thousand. The old woman took these and went off to her house, where she spent the night.

In the morning, she went out and set off to meet Taj al-Muluk. She dressed him in women's clothes and told him: 'Follow behind me; sway as you walk; don't hurry and pay no attention to anyone who talks to you.' After giving him these instructions, she went out and he followed behind her in his women's clothes. All the way along she was telling him what to do and encouraging him to stop him taking fright. She continued to walk on ahead, with him at her heels, until they reached the palace door. She led him in and started to pass through doorways and halls, until she had taken him through seven doors. At the seventh, she said to him: 'Take heart, and when I shout to you: "Come in, girl," don't hang back but hurry. When you get into the hall, look left and you will see a room with several doors in it. Count five of them and go in through the sixth door, where you will find what you seek.' 'And where will you go yourself?' asked Taj al-Muluk. 'Nowhere,' she replied, 'but I may fall behind you, and if the chief eunuch detains me, I'll chat with him.'

She walked on, followed by Taj al-Muluk, until she came to the door where the chief eunuch was. He saw that she had a companion, this being Taj al-Muluk disguised as a slave girl, and he asked about 'her'. 'She is a slave girl. Princess Dunya has heard that she knows how to do various types of work and wants to buy her.' 'I know nothing about a slave girl or anyone else,' said the eunuch, 'but no one is going in until I search them, as the king has ordered.' The old woman made a show of anger and said: 'I know you as a sensible, well-mannered man, but if you have changed, I shall tell the princess and let her know that you have obstructed the arrival of her slave girl.' She then shouted to Taj al-Muluk and said: 'Come on, girl,' at which he came into the hall as she had told him, while the eunuch kept silent and said nothing.

Taj al-Muluk counted five doors and went in through the sixth, where he found Princess Dunya standing waiting for him. When she saw him, she recognized him and clasped him to her breast, as he clasped her to his. The old woman then came in, having contrived to get rid of the slave girls for fear of exposure. 'You can act as doorkeeper,' the princess told her, and she then remained alone with Taj al-Muluk. The two of them continued hugging, embracing and intertwining legs until early dawn. Then, when it was nearly morning, she left him, closing the door on him and going into another room, where she sat down in her usual place. Her slave girls came to her, and after dealing with their affairs and talking to them, she told them to leave her, saying that she wanted to relax alone. When they had gone, she went to Taj al-Muluk, and the old woman brought them some food, which they ate. She then shut the door on them, as before, and they engaged in love-play until daybreak, and things went on like this for a whole month.

So much, then, for Taj al-Muluk and Dunya, but as for the vizier and 'Aziz, after Taj al-Muluk had gone to the princess's palace and stayed there for so long, they believed that he would never come out and would undoubtedly perish. 'Aziz asked the vizier what they should do. 'My son,' said the vizier, 'this is a difficult business. If we don't go back and tell his father, he will blame us for it.' They made their preparations immediately and set off for the Green Land and the Twin Pillars, the royal seat of King Sulaiman Shah. They crossed the valleys by night and by day until they reached the king, and they told him what had happened to his son, adding that since he had entered the palace of the princess they had heard no news of him.

The king was violently agitated and bitterly regretted what had happened. He gave orders that war should be proclaimed, with the troops moving out of the city, where tents were pitched for them. The king himself sat in his pavilion until his forces had gathered from all parts of his kingdom. He was popular with his subjects because of his justice and beneficence, and so when he moved out in search of his son, Taj al-Muluk, it was with an army which spread over the horizon.

So much for them, but as for Taj al-Muluk and Princess Dunya, they continued as they had been for six months, with their love for each other growing every day. The strength of Taj al-Muluk's love and his passion and ardour increased until he told the princess what was in his heart and said: 'Know, my heart's darling, that the longer I stay with you, the more my passionate love increases, for I have not fully reached my goal.' 'And what do you want, light of my eyes and fruit of my heart?' she asked. 'For if you want more than hugs and embraces and the intertwinings of legs, then do what you want, for only God is a partner in our love.' 'That is not the kind of thing that I mean,' he said, 'but rather I would like to tell you the truth about myself. You have to know that I am not a merchant but a king and the son of a king. My father's name is Sulaiman Shah, the great king, who sent his vizier to your father to ask for your hand for me, but when you heard of this, you would not agree.' Then he told her his story from beginning to end, and there is nothing to be gained from repeating it. Taj al-Muluk went on: 'I want now to go to my father to get him to send another envoy to your father to ask him again for your hand, so that we may relax.' When she heard this, the princess was overjoyed, because it coincided with what she herself wanted, and the two of them spent the night in agreement on this.

As fate had decreed, on that particular night they were overcome by sleep and they did not wake until the sun had risen. By then, King Shahriman was seated on his royal throne with the emirs of his kingdom before him. The master of the goldsmiths came into his presence carrying a large box, and, on approaching, he opened this before the king. From it he took a finely worked case which was worth a hundred thousand dinars because of what it contained in the way of gems, rubies and emeralds, such that no king of the lands could amass. When the king saw the case, he admired its beauty and he turned to the chief eunuch, Kafur, whose meeting with the old woman has already been described, and he told him to take the case and bring it to Princess Dunya.

The eunuch took the case and went to Dunya's room, where he found the door shut and the old woman sleeping on the threshold. 'Are you still asleep as late as this?' he exclaimed. When she heard his voice, the old woman woke in alarm. 'Wait until I fetch you the key,' she said, and then she left as fast as she could and fled away. So much for her, but as for the eunuch, he realized that there was something suspicious about her and, lifting the door from its hinges, he entered the room where he found Dunya asleep in the arms of Taj al-Muluk. When he saw this, he was at a loss to know what to do and he thought of going back to the king. The princess woke up and on finding him there she changed colour, turned pale and said: 'Kafur, conceal what God has concealed.' 'I cannot hide anything from the king,' he answered, and locking the door on them, he returned to the king. 'Have you given your mistress the case?' he asked. 'Take the box,' said Kafur. 'There it is; I cannot hide anything from you, and so you have to know that I saw a handsome young man sleeping with the Lady Dunya on the same bed, and they were embracing.'

The king ordered that both of them be brought before him. 'What have you done?' he said to them, and in his rage he seized a whip and was about to strike Taj al-Muluk when the princess threw herself on him and said to her father: 'Kill me before you kill him.' The king spoke angrily to her and ordered the servants to take her to her room. He then turned to Taj al-Muluk and said: 'Where have you come from, damn you? Who is your father and how did you dare to approach my daughter?' Taj al-Muluk said: 'King, know that if you kill me, you will be destroyed and you and all the inhabitants of your kingdom will have cause for regret.' When the king asked him why this was, he went on: 'Know that I am the son of King Sulaiman Shah, and before you know it, he will bring his horse and foot against you.'

When King Shahriman heard that, he wanted to postpone the execution and to keep Taj al-Muluk in prison until he could see whether what he said was true, but the vizier said: 'My advice is that you should kill this scoundrel quickly, for he has the insolence to take liberties with the daughters of kings.' So the king told the executioner: 'Cut off his head, for he is a traitor.' The executioner seized Taj al-Muluk and bound him. He then raised his hand, by way of consulting the emirs, first once and then again. In doing so, he wanted to delay things, but the king shouted at him: 'How long are you going to consult? If you do this once more, I shall cut off your head.' So the executioner raised his arm until the hair in his armpit could be seen, and he was about to strike when suddenly there were loud screams and people shut up their shops. 'Don't be too fast,' the king said to the executioner, and he sent someone to find out what was happening. When the man came back, he reported: 'I have seen an army like a thunderous sea with tumultuous waves. The earth is trembling beneath the hooves of their galloping horses, but I don't know who they are.'

The king was dismayed, fearing that he was going to lose his kingdom. Turning to his vizier, he asked: 'Have none of our troops gone out to meet this army?' But before he had finished speaking, his chamberlains entered, escorting messengers from the newly arrived king, among them being Sulaiman Shah's vizier. The vizier was the first to greet the king, who rose to meet the envoys, told them to approach and asked them why they had come. The vizier came forward from among them and said: 'Know that a king has come to your land who is not like former kings or the sultans of earlier days.' 'Who is he?' the king asked. 'The just and faithful ruler, the fame of whose magnanimity has been spread abroad,' replied the vizier. 'He is King Sulaiman Shah, ruler of the Green Land, the Twin Pillars and the mountains of Isfahan. He loves justice and equity, hating injustice and tyranny. His message to you is that his son, who is his darling and the fruit of his heart, is with you and in your city. If the prince is safe, that is what he hopes to find, and you will be thanked and praised, but if he has disappeared from your land or if some misfortune has overtaken him, then be assured of ruin and the devastation of your country, for he will make it a wilderness in which the ravens croak. I have given you the message and so, farewell.'

When King Shahriman heard the vizier's message, he was alarmed and feared for his kingdom. He shouted a summons to his state officials, his viziers, chamberlains and deputies, and when they came, he told them to go and look for the young man. Taj al-Muluk was still in the hands of the executioner and so afraid had he been that his appearance had changed. His father's vizier happened to look around and found him lying on the execution mat. On recognizing him, he got up and threw himself on him, as did his fellow envoys. They then unloosed his bonds, kissing his hands and his feet. When Taj al-Muluk opened his eyes, he recognized the vizier and his companion 'Aziz and fainted from excess of joy.

King Shahriman was at a loss to know what to do and he was very afraid when it became clear to him that it was because of the young man that this army had come. He got up and went to Taj al-Muluk. With tears starting from his eyes, he kissed his head and said: 'My son, do not blame me; do not blame the evil-doer for what he did. Have pity on my white hairs and do not bring destruction on my kingdom.' Taj al-Muluk went up to him, kissing his hand and saying: 'No harm will come to you. You are like a father to me, but take care that nothing happens to my beloved, Princess Dunya.' 'Have no fear, sir,' said the king. 'Nothing but happiness will come to her.' He continued to excuse himself and to appease Sulaiman Shah's vizier, promising him a huge reward if he would conceal from his master what he had seen. He then ordered his principal officers to take Taj al-Muluk to the baths, give him the finest of clothes and return with him quickly. This they did, escorting him to the baths and making him put on a suit of clothes that King Shahriman had sent specially for him, before bringing him back to the audience chamber.

When he entered, the king got up for him and made all his principal officers rise to attend on the prince. Taj al-Muluk then sat down to talk to his father's vizier and to 'Aziz, telling them what had happened to him. They, in their turn, told him that during his absence they had returned to his father with the news that he had gone into the princess's apartments and not come out, leaving them unsure as to what had happened. They added: 'When he heard that, he mustered his armies and we came here, bringing great relief to you and joy to us.' 'From first to last, good continues to flow from your hands,' exclaimed Taj al-Muluk.

King Shahriman went to his daughter and found her wailing and weeping for Taj al-Muluk. She had taken a sword, fixed the hilt in the ground and placed the point between her breasts directly opposite her heart. She bent over it, saying: 'I must kill myself, for I cannot live after my beloved.' When her father came in and saw her like this, he shouted to her: 'Mistress of princesses, don't do it! Have pity on your father and your countrymen!' He then went up to her and said: 'You are not to bring down evil upon your father.' He told her that her beloved, the son of King Sulaiman Shah, wanted to marry her, adding that the betrothal and the marriage were dependent on her. She smiled and said: 'Didn't I tell you that he was a king's son? By God, I shall have to let him crucify you on a piece of timber worth two dirhams.' 'Daughter,' he said, 'have mercy on me that God may have mercy on you.' To which she replied: 'Hurry off and bring him to me quickly and without delay.'

The king then hurried away to Taj al-Muluk, to whom he whispered the news, and then the two of them went to the princess. On seeing her lover, she threw her arms around his neck in the presence of her father, embraced him and kissed him, saying: 'You left me lonely.' Then she turned to her father and said: 'Do you think that anyone could exaggerate the merits of so handsome a being? In addition, he is a king and the son of a king, one of those of noble stock who are prevented from indulging in depravity.' At that, the king went out and shut the door on them with his own hand. He then went to the vizier of Sulaiman Shah and his fellow envoys, and he told them to inform their master that his son was well and happy, living a life of the greatest pleasure with his beloved.

When they had set off to take this message to Sulaiman Shah, King Shahriman ordered that presents, forage and guest provisions should be sent out to his troops. When all this had been done, he sent out a hundred fine horses, a hundred dromedaries, a hundred mamluks, a hundred concubines, a hundred black slaves and a hundred slave girls, all of whom were led out before him as a gift, while he himself mounted and rode from the city with his chief officials and principal officers. When Sulaiman Shah learned of this, he got up and walked a few paces to meet the king. He had been delighted to hear the news brought by the vizier and 'Aziz, and he exclaimed: 'Praise be to God who has allowed my son to achieve his wish.' He then embraced King Shahriman and made him sit beside him on his couch, where they talked together happily. Food was produced and they ate their fill, after which they moved on to sweetmeats and fruit, both fresh and dried, all of which they sampled. Shortly afterwards, Taj al-Muluk arrived, dressed in his finery. His father, on seeing him, got up to embrace him and kissed him, while all those who were seated rose to their feet. The two kings made him sit between them and they sat talking for a time until Sulaiman Shah said to King Shahriman: 'I want to draw up a contract of marriage between my son and your daughter before witnesses, so that the news may spread abroad, as is the custom.' 'To hear is to obey,' said King Shahriman, and at that, he sent for the *qadi* and the notaries. When they came they drew up the contract between Taj al-Muluk and Princess Dunya, after which money and sweetmeats were distributed, incense was burned and perfume released. That was a day of happiness and delight, and all the leaders and the soldiers shared in the joy.

While King Shahriman began to prepare for his daughter's wedding, Taj al-Muluk said to his father: 'This young 'Aziz is a noble fellow who has done me a great service. He has shared my hardships, travelled with me, brought me to my goal, endured with me and encouraged me to endure until the affair was settled. For two years now he has been with me, far from his own land. I want us to equip him with merchandise from here so that he can go off joyfully, as his country is not far from here.' The king agreed that this was an excellent idea and they prepared for

'Aziz a hundred loads of the finest and most expensive materials. Taj al-Muluk then came, presented him with a huge sum of money, and said, on taking his leave of him: 'Brother and friend, take this money as a gift of friendship, and may safety attend you as you return to your own country.' 'Aziz accepted the gift and kissed the ground before him and before the king. He took his leave and Taj al-Muluk rode with him for three miles, after which 'Aziz entreated him persuasively to turn back, adding: 'Were it not for my mother, master, I would not leave you, but don't deprive me of news of you.'

Taj al-Muluk agreed to this and went back, while 'Aziz travelled on until he reached his own country. He did not stop until he had come to his mother, who, as he found, had built a tomb for him in the middle of the house, which she continually visited. When he went in, he found that she had undone her hair, which was spread over the tomb. She was weeping and reciting the lines:

I show patience in the face of each disaster,
But separation leaves me prey to care.
Who can bear to lose his friend,
And who is not brought low by the imminence of parting?

She then sighed deeply and recited:

Why is it when I pass the tombs
And greet my beloved's grave, he makes no answer?
He says: 'How can I answer you,
When I am held down here by stones and earth?
The earth has eaten my beauties; I have forgotten you,
Secluded as I am from my kin and my dear ones.'

While she was in this state, 'Aziz came in and, on seeing him, she fell fainting with joy. He sprinkled water on her face, and when she had recovered, she got up and took him in her arms, hugging him as he hugged her. They then exchanged greetings, and when she asked the reason for his absence, he told her the whole story of what had happened to him from beginning to end, including how Taj al-Muluk had given him money as well as a hundred loads of materials. His mother was delighted, and he stayed with her in his city, lamenting what had happened to him at the hands of the daughter of Delilah the wily, who had castrated him.

So much for 'Aziz, but as for Taj al-Muluk, he went in to his beloved, Princess Dunya, and deflowered her. King Shahriman then began to equip her for her journey with her husband and her father-in-law. He brought for them provisions, gifts and rarities, which were loaded on their beasts, and when they set off, he went with them for three days to say goodbye. On the prompting of King Sulaiman Shah, he then turned back, while Sulaiman Shah himself, Taj al-Muluk, his wife and their troops travelled on, night and day, until they were close to their city. News had kept coming in of their approach and the city was adorned with decorations for them. When they entered, the king took his seat on his royal throne, with Taj al-Muluk at his side. He distributed gifts and largesse, and freed all those held in his prisons. He then organized a second wedding for his son, with songs and music continuing to sound for a whole month. The dressers presented Princess Dunya in her bridal robes, and she never tired of the process and neither did the ladies tire of looking at her. Taj al-Muluk, after a meeting with his father and mother, went in to his bride and they continued to lead the most delightful and pleasant of lives until they were visited by the destroyer of delights.

[Nights 110–37]

Animal Stories

The Weasel and the Mouse

A story is told of a mouse and a weasel that once lived in the house of a poor farmer. One of the farmer's friends fell ill and the doctor prescribed for him husked sesame seeds. He asked a companion of his for sesame as a cure for his sickness and he then gave a quantity of it to the poor farmer so that he might husk this for him. The farmer brought the sesame to his wife to prepare and she, for her part, soaked it, spread it out, husked it and prepared it. When the weasel saw the sesame, she went up to it and spent the whole day carrying off seeds to her hole, until she had removed most of what was there. The farmer's wife came back and saw, to her astonishment, that there was clearly less sesame than there had been. To find out why, she sat watching to see who would come there, and the weasel, on her way back to remove more seeds, as she had been doing, saw the farmer's wife sitting there and realized that she was on the lookout. She said to herself: 'What I have done may lead to evil consequences, for I'm afraid that this woman is lying in wait for me. Whoever does not think of the consequences of what he does will find out that Time is no friend to him. I must do something good to show my innocence and wipe away all the evil that I have done.' So she started moving the sesame that was in her hole, bringing it out and taking it to put with the rest. When the woman found her doing this, she said to herself: 'It could not have been the weasel that was responsible for this. She is taking the seeds from the hole of whoever stole them and putting them back with the rest. She has done us a favour here and the reward of one who does a favour is to have a favour done to him. As it is not the weasel who has stolen the sesame, I shall go on watching until the thief falls into the trap and I find out who he is.'

The weasel, realizing what the woman was thinking, went off to the mouse. 'Sister,' she said, 'there is no good in anyone who does not respect his duty to his neighbour, maintaining friendship.' 'Yes, my friend,' said the mouse, 'and I am glad to have you as a neighbour, but why do you say this?' The weasel went on: 'The master of the house has brought sesame; he and his family have had their fill, and having no more need of it, they have left much of it uneaten. Every living creature has taken a share of it and were you to take yours, you would have a better right to it than the others.' The mouse was pleased with this; she squeaked, danced, waggled her ears and her tail and, beguiled by her greed for the sesame, she got up straight away and left her hole. She saw the sesame dried, husked and gleaming white, with the farmer's wife sitting and watching over it. The woman had armed herself with a cudgel and the mouse, taking no thought for the consequences, fell on it unrestrainedly, scattering it to and fro and starting to eat it. The woman hit her with the cudgel, splitting her skull. Greed was the cause of her death, and the fact that she ignored the consequences of what she had done.

The Crow and the Cat

I have heard that once a crow and a cat lived together as brothers. While they were together under a tree, suddenly they saw a panther coming towards them, and before they knew it, it was close at hand. The crow flew up to the top of the tree, but the cat stayed where it was, not knowing what to do. He called to the crow: 'My friend, is there anything you can do to save me? I hope you can.' The crow replied: 'In cases of need, when disaster strikes, it is one's brother who must be asked to find a way out. How well has the poet expressed it:

> The true friend is one who goes with you,
> And who hurts himself in order to help you.
> When you are shattered by the blows of fate,
> It is your friend who breaks himself in order to restore you.'

Near the tree were some herdsmen with dogs. The crow went and struck at the surface of the earth with his wing, cawing and screeching. He then went up to the men and struck one of the dogs in the face with his wing. Then he rose a little into the air and the dogs followed after him. Looking up, a herdsman saw a bird flying close to the ground and then falling to earth. He followed the crow, who only flew far enough ahead to avoid the dogs while still encouraging them to give chase. He then rose slightly higher, still pursued by the dogs, until he came to the tree beneath which was the panther. When the dogs saw it, they leapt at it and it turned in flight, giving up all thoughts of eating the cat. So the cat escaped because of the stratagem of its friend, the crow.

The Fox and the Crow

A story is told about a fox that once lived in a den on a mountain. Every time a cub of his began to gain strength, he was driven by hunger to eat it. If he had not done this and had allowed the cub to live, staying with it and guarding it, he himself would have starved to death, but it hurt him to do what he did. A crow used to come to the peak of the mountain and the fox said to himself: 'I would like to make friends with this crow and take him as a companion in my loneliness and as a helper in my search for food, since he can do things that I cannot.' So he approached the crow, going near enough for him to hear what he said. He then greeted him, saying: 'My friend, Muslim neighbours share two rights – the right of neighbourhood and the right of Islam. Know that you are my neighbour and you have a claim on me which I must satisfy, especially since this relationship of ours has gone on for so long. The affection for you that is lodged in my heart prompts me to treat you with kindness and leads me to seek to have you as a brother. What do you have to say?' The crow told the fox: 'The best things said are the most truthful. It may be that what you say with your tongue is not in your heart. I am afraid lest your talk of brotherhood may be on the surface, while concealed in your heart is enmity. You eat and I am eaten and so we cannot join together in the union of affection. What has led you to look for something that you cannot get and to want what can never be? You are a wild beast and I am a bird, and there can be no true brotherhood between us.'

The fox said: 'He who knows where great things are to be found can make a proper choice from among them, and so he may be able to find what will help his brothers. I want to be near you and choose friendship with you so that we can help each other, and our affection may lead to success. I know a number of stories about the beauty of friendship, and if you like, I shall tell them to you.' 'You have my permission to produce them,' said the crow. 'Tell me them, so that I can listen, take heed and discover their meaning.' 'Listen then, my companion,' said the fox, 'to a story told of a flea and a mouse which illustrates the point I made to you.' 'What was that?' asked the crow, AND THE FOX REPLIED:

The Flea and the Mouse

It is said that a mouse once lived in the house of a rich and important merchant. One night a flea went for shelter to that merchant's bed, where he found a soft body. As he was thirsty, he drank from the man's blood. The merchant, in pain, woke from his sleep, sat up and called to his maids and a number of his servants. They hurried up to him and set to work looking for the flea, who, in turn, realizing what was happening, fled away. He came across the mouse's hole and went in, but when the mouse saw him, she asked: 'What has made you come to me, when you are not of the same nature or the same species as I, and you cannot be sure that I will not treat you roughly, attack you or harm you?' The flea said to her: 'I have fled into your house, escaping certain death, in order to seek refuge with you. There is nothing that I covet here; you will not have to leave because of any harm that I might do you and I hope to be able to reward you with all kinds of benefits for the service that you are doing me. You will be thankful when you discover what these words of mine will bring about.' When the mouse heard what the flea had to say, she said: 'If things are as you say, then you can rest here in peace. The rain of security will fall on you; you will only experience what will bring you joy and nothing will happen to you that will not also happen to me. I offer you my friendship. Feel no regret for the opportunity you have lost to suck the merchant's blood and don't be sorry for the nourishment that you used to get from him. Content yourself with what you can find to live on, as that will be safer for you. The following lines of poetry that I once heard were written by a preacher, who said:

> I have followed the path of contentment and solitude,
> And passed my time according to circumstance,
> With a crust of bread and water to drink,
> Coarse salt and shabby clothes.
> If God grants me prosperity, well and good;
> If not, I am content with what He gives.'

When the flea heard what the mouse had to say, he said: 'Sister, I have listened to your advice; I shall do what you tell me, as I cannot disobey you, and I shall follow this virtuous course until the end of my days.' 'Good intentions are enough for true friendship,' replied the mouse. The two became firm friends and after that the flea would go to the merchant's bed at night but would only take enough blood for his needs, while by day he would shelter in the mouse's hole.

It happened that one night the merchant brought home a large number of dinars. He began to turn them over and over and, hearing the sound, the mouse put her head out of her hole and started to gaze at the dinars, until the merchant put them under a pillow and fell asleep. The mouse then said to the flea: 'Don't you see the chance that we have been given and what an enormous bit of luck this is? Can you think of a plan to allow us to get as many of these as we want?' 'It's no use trying to get hold of something unless you can do it,' said the flea. 'If you're not strong enough, then weakness will lead you into danger and, even if you use all your cunning, you will not get what you want, like the sparrow that picks up the grain but falls into the trapper's net and is caught. You don't have the strength to take the dinars and carry them out of the house, and neither have I. I couldn't even lift a single one of them. So do what you want about them yourself.'

The mouse said: 'I have made seventy ways out of this hole of mine from which I can leave if I want and I have prepared a safe place for treasures. If you can get the merchant out of the room by some means, then I'm sure that I can succeed if fate helps me.' 'I'll undertake to get him out,' said the flea, and he then went to the merchant's bed and gave him a fearful bite, such as he had never experienced before. The flea then took refuge in a place of safety and, although the merchant woke up and looked for him, he didn't find the flea and so went back to sleep on his other side. The flea then bit him even more savagely, and in his agitation the merchant left his bedroom and went out to a bench by the house door, where he slept without waking until morning. The mouse then set about moving the dinars until there were none left, and in the morning the merchant was left to suspect everyone around him.

The fox then said to the crow: 'You must know, O far-sighted, intelligent and experienced crow, that I have only told you this story so that you may get the reward for your kindness to me just as the mouse was rewarded for her kindness to the flea. You can see how he repaid her and gave her the most excellent of rewards.' The crow replied: 'The doer of good has the choice of doing good or not, as he wants, but it is not obligatory to do good to someone who tries to attach himself to you by cutting you off from others. This is what will happen to me if I befriend you, who are my enemy. You are a wily schemer, fox; creatures of your kind cannot be counted on to keep their word and no one can rely on those who are not to be trusted to do that. I heard recently that you betrayed a companion of yours, the wolf, and that you schemed against him until, thanks to your treacherous wiles, you brought about his death. You did this in spite of the fact that he was of the same species as you and you had been his companion for a long time. You did not spare him, so how can I trust in your sincerity? If this is how you act with a friend of your own race, what will you do with an enemy of a different species? Your position in regard to me is like that of the falcon with the birds of prey.' 'How was that?' asked the fox. THE CROW REPLIED:

The Falcon and the Birds of Prey

The falcon was a headstrong tyrant in the days of his youth, spreading fear among the birds and beasts of prey. None were safe from his evil-doing and there were many instances of his injustice and tyranny, it being his habit to harm all other birds. With the passing of the years, his powers weakened and his strength diminished. He grew hungry and the loss of his strength meant that he had to exert himself more. He decided to go to where the birds met, in order to eat what they left over. After having relied on strength and power, he now got his food by trickery.

'This is like you, fox: you may not have strength, but you have not lost your powers of deceit. I have no doubt that when you ask to become my companion, this is a trick on your part to get food. I am not one to put out my hand to clasp yours. God has given me strength in my wings, caution in my soul and clear sight. I know that whoever tries to be like someone stronger than himself finds himself in difficulties and may be destroyed. I am afraid that if you try to resemble someone stronger than yourself, what happened to the sparrow may happen to you.' 'What did happen to the sparrow?' asked the fox. 'By God, tell me the story.' THE CROW SAID:

The Sparrow and the Eagle

I have heard that a sparrow was flying over a field of sheep. He looked down and as he was there watching, a great eagle swooped down on one of the young lambs and, seizing it in his talons, flew off with it. When the sparrow saw this, he fluttered his wings and said proudly: 'I can do the same kind of thing,' trying to be like something greater than him. He flew off immediately and came down on a fat, woolly ram, whose coat was matted because he had been sleeping on urine and dung, as a result of which it had become sticky. When the sparrow settled on the ram's back, he clapped his wings, but his feet stuck in the wool, and although he tried to fly off, he could not get free. While all this was going on, the shepherd had been watching, seeing first what had happened with the eagle and then what had happened to the sparrow. He came up angrily to the sparrow, seized him and pulled out his wing feathers. He then tied a string round his legs and took him off and threw him to his children. 'What is this?' one of them asked. The shepherd replied: 'This is one who tried to imitate a superior and so was destroyed.'

'This is what you are like, fox, and I warn you against trying to be like one who is stronger than you, lest you perish. This is what I have to say to you, so go off in peace.' Despairing of winning the friendship of the crow, the fox went back, groaning in sorrow and gnashing his teeth in regret. When the crow heard the sound of his weeping and groaning and saw his distress and sorrow, he asked what had come over him to make him gnash his teeth. 'It is because I see that you are a greater cheat than I am,' said the fox, and he then ran off, going back to his earth.

The Hedgehog and the Doves

It is told that a hedgehog made his home by the side of a palm tree which was the haunt of a ringdove and his mate who nested there and enjoyed an easy life. The hedgehog said to himself: 'The ringdove and his mate eat the fruits of this palm tree, but I can find no way to do that and so I shall have to trick them.' He then dug out a hole for himself at the foot of the tree where he and his mate went to live. Beside it he made a chapel for prayer, where he went by himself, pretending to be a devout ascetic, who had abandoned earthly things. When the ringdove saw him at his devotions, he felt pity for him because of his extreme asceticism and he asked how many years he had spent like this. 'Thirty years,' replied the hedgehog. 'What do you eat?' asked the dove. 'Whatever falls from the tree.' 'What do you wear?' 'Spikes, whose roughness is of use to me.' 'And how did you choose this place of yours rather than somewhere else?' 'I chose it at random,' said the hedgehog, 'in order to guide those who are astray and to teach the ignorant.' 'I didn't think that you were like this,' said the dove, 'but I now feel a longing for your kind of life.' The hedgehog replied: 'I'm afraid that what you say is the opposite of what you do. You are like the farmer who at harvest time neglects to sow again, saying: "I am afraid that the days may not bring me what I want, and I shall have begun by wasting my money thanks to sowing too soon." Then, when harvest time comes round again and he sees people at work reaping, he regrets the opportunity that he lost by holding back and he dies of grief and sorrow.'

The dove asked him: 'What should I do to free myself of worldly attachments and devote myself solely to the worship of my Lord?' 'Begin to prepare yourself for the life to come,' said the hedgehog, 'and content yourself with eating only enough for your needs.' 'How am I to do that?' asked the dove. 'I am a bird and I cannot leave this tree which provides me with my food, and even if I could, I don't know where else to settle.' The hedgehog said: 'You can knock down enough fruit from the tree to last you and your mate for a year. Then you can settle in a nest underneath the tree, seeking right guidance. Afterwards, go to the fruit that you have knocked down, take it all away and store it up to eat in times of want. When you have finished the fruits and you find the waiting long, make do with bare sufficiency.' 'May God give you a good reward for the purity of your intentions,' said the dove, 'in that you have reminded me of the afterlife and given me right guidance.'

The dove and his mate then worked hard, knocking down dates until there were none left on the tree. The hedgehog was delighted to find this food; he filled his lair with the fruit and stored it up to serve as his provisions, saying to himself that if the dove and his mate needed food, they would ask him for it. 'They will covet what I have,' he said, 'relying on my godly asceticism. Then, when they hear my advice and my admonitions, they will come up close to me and I can catch them and eat them. I shall then have this place to myself and I shall get enough to eat from the fruit that falls.' After the dove and his mate had knocked down all the dates, they flew down from the tree and found that the hedgehog had removed them all to his lair. 'Virtuous hedgehog,' said the dove, 'you sincere admonisher, we have not found any trace of the dates and we don't know of any other fruit on which we can live.' 'It may be that the wind blew them away,' said the hedgehog, 'but to turn away from sustenance to the Provider of sustenance is the essence of salvation. He Who created the opening in the mouth will not leave it without food.'

On he went, giving these admonitions and making a show of piety dressed in elaborate speech, until the doves approached trustingly and tried to go in through the entrance of his lair. They were sure that he would not deceive them, but he jumped up to guard the entrance, gnashing his teeth. When the dove saw his deception unveiled, he exclaimed: 'What a difference there is between tonight and yesterday! Don't you know that the victims of injustice have a Helper? Take care not to practise trickery and deceit lest you suffer the same fate as the two tricksters who schemed against the merchant.' 'How was that?' the hedgehog asked. THE DOVE SAID:

I heard that there was a wealthy merchant from a city called Sindah. He got together goods which he packed into bales and he left on a trading trip to visit a number of cities. He was followed by two swindlers who loaded up what wealth and goods they had and then accompanied him, pretending to be merchants. When they halted at the first stage, they agreed with each other to use cunning in order to take his goods, but each man planned to deceive and betray the other, saying to himself: 'Were I to betray my companion, all would be well with me and I could take all this wealth.' With these evil intentions towards one another, each of them produced food which had been poisoned before offering it to his companion. They both ate the food and both died. They had been sitting talking with the merchant, but after they had left him and been away for some time, he went in search of them to see what had happened, only to find them dead. He then realized that they were scoundrels who had been trying to double-cross him. Their cunning recoiled on their own heads, while the merchant not only escaped but took all that they had with them.

[Nights 150–52]

The Story of Ali Baba and the Forty Thieves Killed by a Slave Girl

In a city of Persia, on the borders of your majesty's realms, there were two brothers, one called Qasim and the other Ali Baba. These two had been left very little in the way of possessions by their father, who had divided the inheritance equally between the two of them. They should have enjoyed an equal fortune, but fate was to dispose otherwise. Qasim married a woman who, shortly after their marriage, inherited a well-stocked shop and a warehouse filled with fine goods, together with properties and estates, which all of a sudden made him so well off that he became one of the wealthiest merchants in the city. By contrast, Ali Baba had married a woman as poor as himself; he lived in great poverty and the only work he could do to help provide for himself and his children was to go out as a woodcutter in a neighbouring forest. He would then load what he had cut on to his three donkeys – these being all that he possessed – and sell it in the city.

One day, while he was in the forest and had finished chopping just enough wood to load on to his donkeys, he noticed a great cloud of dust rising up in the air and advancing straight in his direction. Looking closely, he could make out a large crowd of horsemen coming swiftly towards him. Although there was no talk of thieves in the region, nonetheless it struck him that that was just what these could be. Thinking only of his own safety and not of what could happen to his donkeys, he climbed up into a large tree, where the branches a little way up were so densely intertwined as to allow very little space between them. He positioned himself right in the middle, all the more confident that he could see without being seen, as the tree stood at the foot of an isolated rock much higher than the tree and so steep that it could not be climbed from any direction.

The large and powerful-looking horsemen, well mounted and armed, came close to the rock and dismounted. Ali Baba counted forty of them and, from their equipment and appearance, he had no doubt they were thieves. He was not mistaken, for this was what they were, and although they had caused no harm in the neighbourhood, they had assembled there before going further afield to carry out their acts of brigandage. What he saw them do next confirmed his suspicions.

Each horseman unbridled his horse, tethered it and then hung over its neck a sack of barley which had been on its back. Each then carried off his own bag and most of these seemed so heavy that Ali Baba reckoned they must be full of gold and coins.

The most prominent of the thieves, who seemed to be their captain, carried his bag like the rest and approached the rock close to Ali Baba's tree. After he had made his way through some bushes, this man was clearly heard to utter the following words: 'Open, Sesame.' No sooner had he said this than a door opened, and after he had let all his men go in before him, he too went in and the door closed.

The thieves remained for a long time inside the rock. Ali Baba was afraid that if he left his tree in order to escape, one or all of them would come out, and so he was forced to stay where he was and to wait patiently. He was tempted to climb down and seize two of the horses, mounting one and leading the other by the bridle, in the hope of reaching the city driving his three donkeys in front of him. But, as he could not be sure what would happen, he took the safest course and remained where he was.

At last the door opened again and out came the forty thieves. The captain, who had gone in last, now emerged first; after he had watched the others file past him, Ali Baba heard him close the door by pronouncing these words: 'Shut, Sesame.' Each thief returned to his horse and remounted, after bridling it and fastening his bag on to it. When the captain finally saw they were all ready to depart, he took the lead and rode off with them along the way they had come.

Ali Baba did not climb down straight away, saying to himself: 'They may have forgotten something which would make them return, and were that to happen, I would be caught.' He looked after them until they went out of sight, but he still did not get down for a long time afterwards until he felt completely safe. He had remembered the words used by the captain to make the door open and shut, and he was curious to see if they would produce the same effect for him. Pushing through the shrubs, he spotted the door which was hidden behind them, and going up to it, he said: 'Open, Sesame.' Immediately, the door opened wide.

He had expected to see a place of darkness and gloom and was surprised to find a vast and spacious manmade chamber, full of light, with a high, vaulted ceiling into which daylight poured through an opening in the top of the rock. There he saw great quantities of foodstuffs and bales of rich merchandise all piled up; there were silks and brocades, priceless carpets, and, above all, gold and coins in heaps or heaped up in sacks or in large leather bags that were piled one on top of the other. Seeing all these things, it struck him that for years, even centuries, the cave must have served as a refuge for generation upon generation of thieves. He had no hesitation about what to do next: he entered the cave and immediately the door closed behind him, but that did not worry him, for he knew the secret of how to open it again. He was not interested in the rest of the money but only in the gold coins, particularly those that were in the sacks, so he removed as much as he could carry away and load on to his three donkeys. He next rounded up the donkeys, which had wandered off, and when he had brought them up to the rock he loaded them with the sacks, which he hid by arranging firewood on top of them. When he had finished, he stood in front of the door and as soon as he uttered the words 'Shut, Sesame', the door closed, for it had closed by itself each time he had gone in and had stayed open each time he had gone out.

Having done this, Ali Baba took the road back to the city, and when he got home, he brought the donkeys into a small courtyard, carefully closing the door behind him. He removed the small amount of wood which covered the sacks and these he then took into the house, putting them down and arranging them in front of his wife, who was sitting on a sofa.

She felt the sacks and, realizing they were full of money, she suspected him of having stolen it. So when he had finished bringing them all to her, she could not help saying to him: 'Ali Baba, you can't have been so wicked as to . . . ?' 'Nonsense, wife!' Ali Baba interrupted her. 'Don't be alarmed: I'm not a thief, or at least only a thief who robs thieves. You will stop thinking ill of me when I tell you about my good fortune.' He then emptied the sacks, making a great heap of gold which quite dazzled his wife, and having done this, he told her the story of his adventure from beginning to end. When he had finished, he told her to keep everything secret.

Once his wife had recovered from her fright, she rejoiced with her husband at the good fortune which had come to them and she wanted to count all the gold that was in front of her, coin by coin. 'Wife,' said Ali Baba, 'that's not very clever: what do you think you are going to do and how long will it take you to finish counting? I am going to dig a trench and bury the gold there; we have no time to lose.' 'But it would be good if we had at least a rough idea of how much there is there,' she told him. 'I'll go and borrow some small scales from the neighbours and use them to weigh the gold while you are digging the trench.' Ali Baba objected: 'There is no point in that, and, believe me, you should leave well alone. However, do as you like, but take care to keep the secret.'

To satisfy herself, however, Ali Baba's wife went out to the house of her brother-in-law, Qasim, who lived not very far away. Qasim was not at home and so, in his absence, she spoke to his wife, asking her to lend her some scales for a short while. Her sister-in-law asked her if she wanted large scales or small scales, and Ali Baba's wife said she wanted small ones. 'Yes, of course,' her sister-in-law replied. 'Wait a moment and I will bring you some.' The sister-in-law went off to look for the scales, which she found, but knowing how poor Ali Baba was and curious to discover what sort of grain his wife wanted to weigh, she thought she would carefully apply some candle grease underneath them, which she did. She then returned and gave them to her visitor, apologizing for having made her wait and saying she had had difficulty finding them.

When Ali Baba's wife got home, she placed the scales by the pile of gold, filled them and then emptied them a little further away on the sofa, until she had finished. She was very pleased to discover how much gold she had weighed out and told her husband, who had just finished digging the trench.

While Ali Baba was burying the gold, his wife, in order to show her sister-in-law how meticulous and correct she was, returned her scales to her, not noticing that a gold coin had stuck to the underside of the scales. 'Dear sister-in-law,' she said to her as she returned them to her, 'you see, I didn't keep your scales very long. I'm bringing you them back, and I'm very grateful to you.' As soon as her back was turned, Qasim's wife looked at the underside of the scales and was astonished beyond words to find a gold coin stuck there. Immediately her heart was filled with envy. 'What!' she exclaimed. 'Ali Baba has gold enough to be weighed! And where did the wretch get it from?'

As we have said, her husband, Qasim, was not at home but in his shop, from which he would only get back in the evening. So the time she had to wait for him seemed like an age, so impatient was she to tell him news which would surprise him no less than it had surprised her. When Qasim did come home, his wife said to him: 'Qasim, you may think you are rich, but you are wrong; Ali Baba has infinitely more than you; he doesn't count his money, like you – he weighs it!' Qasim demanded an explanation of this mystery and she then proceeded to enlighten him, telling him of the trick she had used to make her discovery; and she showed him the gold coin that she had found stuck to the underside of the scales – a coin so ancient that the name of the prince stamped on it was unknown to him.

Qasim, far from being pleased at his brother's good fortune, which would relieve his misery, conceived a mortal jealousy towards him and scarcely slept that night. The next morning, before even the sun had risen, he went to his brother, whom he did not treat as a real brother, having forgotten the very word since he had married the rich widow. 'Ali Baba,' he said, 'you don't say much about your affairs; you act as though you were poor, wretched and poverty-stricken but yet you have gold enough to weigh!' 'Brother,' replied Ali Baba, 'I don't know what you are talking about. Explain yourself.' 'Don't pretend to be ignorant,' said Qasim, showing him the gold coin his wife had handed to him. 'How many more coins do you have like this one, which my wife found stuck to the underside of the scales that your wife came to borrow yesterday?'

On hearing this, Ali Baba realized that, thanks to his wife's persistence, Qasim and his wife already knew what he had been so eager to keep concealed; but the damage was done and could not be repaired. Without showing the least sign of surprise or concern, he admitted everything to his brother and told him by what chance he had discovered the thieves' den and where it was, offering to give him a share in the treasure if he kept the secret. 'I will indeed claim my share,' said Qasim arrogantly, then added: 'But I also want to know precisely where this treasure is, the signs and marks of its hiding place, and how I can get in if I want to; otherwise, I shall denounce you to the authorities. If you refuse, not only will you have no hope of getting any more of it, but you will lose what you have already removed, as this will be given to me for having denounced you.' Ali Baba, more thanks to his own good nature than because he was intimidated by the insolent threats of so cruel a brother, told him everything he wanted to know, even the words to use when entering or leaving the cave.

Qasim asked no more questions but left, determined to get to the treasure before Ali Baba. Very early the next morning, before it was even light, he set out, hoping to get the treasure for himself alone. He took with him ten mules carrying large chests which he planned to fill, and he had even more chests in reserve for a second trip, depending on the number of loads he found in the cave. He took the path following Ali Baba's instructions and, drawing near to the rock, he recognized the signs and the tree in which Ali Baba had hidden. He looked for the door, found it, and said 'Open, Sesame' to make it open. When it did, he went in, and immediately it closed again. Looking around the cave, he was amazed at the sight of riches far greater than Ali Baba's account had led him to expect. The more closely he examined everything, the more his astonishment increased. Being the miser he was and fond of wealth and riches, he would have spent the whole day feasting his eyes on the sight of so much gold had he not remembered that he had come to remove it and load it on to his ten mules. He then took as many sacks as he could carry and went to open the door, but his mind was filled with thoughts far removed from what should have been of more importance to him. He found he had forgotten the necessary word and so instead of saying 'Open, Sesame', he said 'Open, Barley' and was very surprised to see that the door, rather than opening, remained shut. He went on naming various other types of grain, but not the one he needed, and still the door did not open.

Qasim had not expected this. In the great danger in which he found himself, he was so terror-stricken that, in his efforts to remember the word 'Sesame', his memory became more and more confused and soon it was as though he had never ever heard of the word. He threw down his sacks and began to stride around the cave from one side to another, no longer moved by the sight of all the riches around him. So let us now leave Qasim to bewail his fate – he does not deserve our compassion.

Towards midday, the thieves returned to their cave, and when they were a little way off, they saw Qasim's mules by the rock, laden with chests. Disturbed by this unusual sight, they advanced at full speed, scaring away the ten mules, which Qasim had neglected to tether. They had been grazing freely, and they now scattered so far into the forest that they were soon lost from sight. The thieves did not bother to run after them – it was more important for them to discover their owner. While some of them went round the rock to look for him, the captain, together with the rest, dismounted and went straight to the door, sword in hand; he pronounced the words and the door opened.

Qasim, who had heard the sound of the horses from the middle of the cave, was in no doubt that the thieves had arrived and that his last hour had come. Resolved at least to make an effort to escape from their hands and save himself, he was ready to hurl himself through the door immediately it opened. As soon as he saw it open and hearing the word 'Sesame', which he had forgotten, he rushed out headlong, flinging the captain to the ground. But he did not escape the other thieves who were standing sword in hand and who killed him on the spot.

After they had killed him, the first concern of the thieves was to enter the cave. Next to the door they found the sacks which Qasim had begun to carry off in order to load on to his mules. These they put back in their place, failing to notice what Ali Baba had previously removed. They consulted each other and discussed what had just happened, but although they could see how Qasim might have got out of the cave, what they could not imagine was how he had entered it. It struck them that he might have come down through the top of the cave, but there was nothing to show that this was what he had done, and the opening which let in the daylight was so high up and the top of the rock so inaccessible from outside that they all agreed it was incomprehensible. They could not believe that he had come in through the door, unless he knew the secret of making it open, and they were certain that no one else knew this. In this they were mistaken, unaware as they were that Ali Baba had found it out by spying on them.

They then decided that, however it was that Qasim had managed to get into the cave, it was now a question of protecting their communal riches and so they should chop his body in four and place the four pieces inside the cave near the door, two on each side, so as to terrify anyone who was bold enough to try the same thing. They themselves would only come back some time later, when the stench of the corpse had passed off. They carried out their plan, and as there was nothing else to keep them there, they left their den firmly secured, remounted their horses and went off to scour the countryside along the caravan routes, attacking and carrying out their usual highway robberies.

Qasim's wife, meanwhile, was in a state of great anxiety when she saw that night had come and her husband had not returned home. In her alarm, she went to Ali Baba and said to him: 'Brother-in-law, I believe you know well enough that your brother, Qasim, went to the forest and you know why he went there. He hasn't come back yet and as it has been dark for some time, I'm afraid that some misfortune may have befallen him.'

After the conversation that Ali Baba had had with his brother, he had suspected that he would make this trip into the forest and so he had not gone there himself that day so as not to alarm him. Without reproaching his visitor in any way which could cause offence to her or to her husband, if he was alive, he told her not to be worried yet, explaining that Qasim might well have thought fit not to come back to the city until well after dark.

Qasim's wife believed him all the more readily when she realized how important it was that her husband should act in secret. So she went home and waited patiently until midnight, but after that her fears increased and her suffering was all the more intense because she could not give vent to it nor relieve it by crying out loud, for she knew well enough that the reason for it had to remain concealed from the neighbours. The damage had been done, but she repented the foolish curiosity and blameworthy impulse which had led her to meddle in the affairs of her in-laws. She spent the night in tears, and as soon as it was light, she rushed to Ali Baba's house and told him and his wife – more through her tears than her words – what had brought her there.

For his part, Ali Baba did not wait for his sister-in-law to appeal to his kindness to find out what had happened to Qasim. Telling her to calm down, he then immediately set out with his three donkeys and made for the forest. He found no trace of his brother or of the ten mules along the way, but when he drew near the rock, he was astonished to see a pool of blood near the door. He took this for an evil omen and, standing in front of the door, he pronounced the words 'Open, Sesame'. When the door opened, he was confronted by the sorry sight of his brother's corpse, cut into four pieces. Forgetting what little fraternal love his brother had shown him, he did not hesitate in deciding to perform the last rites for his brother. He made up two bundles from the body parts that he found in the cave and these he loaded on to one of his donkeys, with firewood on top to conceal them. Then, losing no more time, he loaded the other two donkeys with sacks filled with gold, again with firewood on top, as before. As soon as he had done this and had commanded the door to shut, he set off on the path leading back to the city, but he took the precaution of stopping long enough at the edge of the forest so as to enter it only when it was dark. When he arrived home, he brought in only the two donkeys laden with the gold, leaving his wife with the job of unloading them. He told her briefly what had happened to Qasim, before leading the other donkey to his sister-in-law's house.

When he knocked at the door, it was opened by Marjana. Now this girl Ali Baba knew to be a very shrewd and clever slave who could always find a way to solve the most difficult of problems. When he had entered the courtyard, Ali Baba unloaded the firewood and the two bundles from the donkey and, taking Marjana aside, said to her: 'Marjana, the first thing I am going to ask you is an inviolable secret – you will see how necessary this is for us both, for your mistress as well as for myself. In these two bundles is the body of your master; he must be buried as though he died a natural death. Let me speak to your mistress, and listen carefully to what I say to her.'

After Marjana had told her mistress that he was there, Ali Baba, who had been following her, entered and his sister-in-law immediately cried out impatiently to him: 'Brother-in-law, what news have you of my husband? Your face tells me you have no comfort to offer me.' 'Sister-in-law,' replied Ali Baba, 'I can't tell you anything before you first promise me you will listen to me, from beginning to end, without saying a word. It is no less important to you than it is to me that what has happened should be kept a deadly secret, for your good and your peace of mind.' 'Ah!' exclaimed Qasim's wife, although without raising her voice. 'You are going to tell me that my husband is dead, but at the same time I must control myself and I understand why you are asking me to keep this a secret. So tell me; I am listening.'

Ali Baba told his sister-in-law what had happened on his trip, right up to his return with Qasim's body, adding: 'This is all very painful for you, all the more so because you so little expected it. However, although the evil cannot be remedied, if there is anything capable of comforting you, I offer to marry you and join the little God has given me to what you have. I can assure you that my wife won't be jealous and you will live happily together. If you agree, then we must think how to make it appear that my brother died of natural causes: this is something it seems to me you can entrust to Marjana, and I for my part will do everything that I can.'

What better decision could Qasim's widow take than to accept Ali Baba's proposal? With all the wealth she had inherited through the death of her first husband she had yet found someone even wealthier than herself, a husband who, thanks to the treasure he had discovered, could become richer still. So she did not refuse his offer but, on the contrary, considered the match as offering reasonable grounds for consolation. The fact that she wiped away the copious tears she had begun to shed and stifled the piercing shrieks customary to the newly widowed made it clear enough to Ali Baba that she had accepted his offer.

He left her in this frame of mind and returned home with his donkey, after having instructed Marjana to carry out her task as well as she could. She, for her part, did her best and, leaving the house at the same time as Ali Baba, she went to a nearby apothecary's shop. She knocked on the door and when it was opened she went in and asked for some kind of tablets which were very effective against the most serious illnesses. The apothecary gave her what she had paid for, asking who was ill in her master's house. 'Ah!' she sighed heavily. 'It's Qasim himself, my dear master! They don't know what's wrong with him; he won't speak and he won't eat.' So saying, she went off with the tablets – which Qasim was in no state to use.

The next morning, Marjana again went to the same apothecary and, with tears in her eyes, asked for an essence which one usually gives the sick only when they are at death's door. 'Alas!' she cried in great distress as the apothecary handed it to her. 'I am very much afraid that this remedy will have no more effect than the tablets! Ah, that I should lose such a good master!'

For their part, Ali Baba and his wife could be seen, with sorrowful faces, making frequent trips all day long to and from Qasim's house, so that it was no surprise to hear, towards evening, cries and lamentations coming from Qasim's wife, and especially from Marjana, which told of Qasim's death.

Very early the next day, when dawn was just breaking, Marjana left the house and went to seek out an elderly cobbler on the square who, as she knew, was always the first to open his shop every day, long before everyone else. She went up to him, greeted him and placed a gold coin in his hand. Baba Mustafa, as he was known to all and sundry, being of a naturally cheerful disposition and always ready with a joke, looked carefully at the coin because it was not yet quite light and, seeing it was indeed gold, exclaimed: 'That's a good start to the day! What's all this for? And how can I help you?' 'Baba Mustafa,' Marjana said to him, 'take whatever you need for sewing and come with me immediately, but I will have to blindfold you when we reach a certain place.'

When he heard this, Baba Mustafa became squeamish, saying: 'Aha! So you want me to do something that goes against my conscience and my honour?' Placing another gold coin in his hand, Marjana went on: 'God forbid that I should ask you to do anything which you couldn't do in all honour! Just come, and don't be afraid.'

The man allowed himself to be led by Marjana, who, after she had placed a handkerchief over his eyes at the place she had indicated, took him to the house of her late master, only removing the handkerchief once they were in the room where she had laid out the body, each quarter in its proper place. When she had removed the handkerchief, she said to him: 'Why I have brought you here is so that you can sew these pieces together. Don't waste any time, and when you have done this, I will give you another gold coin.'

When Baba Mustafa had finished, Marjana blindfolded him once more in the same room and then, after having given him the third gold coin that she had promised him, telling him to keep the secret, she took him back to the place where she had first blindfolded him. There she removed the handkerchief and let him return to his shop, watching him until he was out of sight in order to stop him retracing his steps out of curiosity to keep an eye on her.

She had heated some water with which to wash the body, and Ali Baba, who arrived just after she returned, washed it, perfumed it with incense and then wrapped it in a shroud with the customary ceremonies. The carpenter brought the coffin which Ali Baba had taken care to order, and Marjana stood at the door to receive it, to make sure that the carpenter would not notice anything. After she had paid him and sent him on his way, she helped Ali Baba to put the body into the coffin, and when Ali Baba had firmly nailed down the planks on top of it, she went to the mosque to give notice that everything was ready for the burial. The people at the mosque whose business it was to wash the bodies of the dead offered to come and perform their duty, but she told them it had already been done.

No sooner had Marjana returned than the imam and the other officials of the mosque arrived. Four neighbours had assembled there who then carried the bier on their shoulders to the cemetery, following the imam as he recited the prayers. Marjana, as the dead man's slave, followed bareheaded, weeping and wailing pitifully, violently beating her breast and tearing her hair. Ali Baba also followed, accompanied by neighbours who would step forward from time to time to take their turn to relieve the four who were carrying the bier, until they arrived at the cemetery.

As for Qasim's wife, she stayed at home grieving and uttering pitiful cries with the women of the neighbourhood, who, as was the custom, hurried there while the funeral was taking place, adding their lamentations to hers and filling the whole quarter and beyond with grief and sadness. In this way, Qasim's grisly death was carefully concealed and covered up by Ali Baba, his wife, Qasim's widow and Marjana, so that no one in the town knew anything about it or was in the least suspicious.

Three or four days after the funeral, Ali Baba moved the few items of furniture he had, together with the money he had taken from the thieves' treasure – which he brought in only at night – to the house of his brother's widow in order to set up house there. This was enough to show that he had now married his former sister-in-law, but no one showed any surprise, as such marriages are not unusual in our religion.

As for Qasim's shop, Ali Baba had a son who some time ago had finished his apprenticeship with another wealthy merchant who had always testified to his good conduct. Ali Baba gave him the shop, with the promise that if he continued to behave well, he would soon arrange an advantageous marriage for him, in keeping with his status.

Let us now leave Ali Baba to start enjoying his good fortune, and talk about the forty thieves. When they returned to their den in the forest at the time they had agreed on, they were astonished first at the absence of Qasim's body but even more so by the noticeable gaps among their piles of gold. 'We've been discovered, and if we don't take care we'll be lost,' said the captain. 'We must do something about this immediately, for otherwise bit by bit we shall lose all the riches which we and our fathers amassed with so much trouble and effort. What our loss teaches us is that the thief whom we surprised learned the secret of how to make the door open and that fortunately we arrived at the very moment he was going to come out. But he wasn't the only one – there must be someone else who found out about this. Quite apart from anything, the fact that the corpse was removed and some of our treasure taken is clear proof of this. There is nothing to show that more than two people knew the secret, however, and so now that we have killed one of them we shall have to kill the other as well. What do you think, my brave men? Isn't that what we should do?'

The band of thieves were in complete accord with their captain, and finding his proposal perfectly reasonable, they all agreed to abandon any other venture and to concentrate exclusively on this and not to give up until they had succeeded. 'I expected no less of your courage and bravery,' their captain told them. 'But before anything else, one of you who is bold, clever and enterprising must go to the city, unarmed and dressed as a traveller from foreign parts. He is to use all his skill to discover if there is any talk about the strange death of the wretch we so rightly slaughtered, in order to find out who he was and where he lived. That's what is most important for us to know, so that we don't do anything we might regret or show ourselves in a country where for a long time no one has known about us and where it is very important for us to stay unknown. Were our volunteer to make a mistake and bring back a false report rather than a true one, this could be disastrous for us. Don't you think, then, that he had better agree that, if he does this, he should be killed?'

Without waiting for the rest to vote on this, one of the thieves said: 'I agree and I glory in risking my life by taking on this task. If I don't succeed, remember at least that, for the common good of the band, I lacked neither the goodwill nor the courage.' He was warmly praised by the captain and his comrades, after which he then disguised himself in such a way that no one would take him for what he was. Leaving his comrades behind, he set out that night and saw to it that he entered the city as day was just breaking. He made for the square, where the one shop that he found open was that of Baba Mustafa.

Baba Mustafa was seated on his chair, his awl in his hand, ready to ply his trade. The robber went up to him to bid him good morning and, seeing him to be of great age, said to him: 'My good fellow, you start work very early, but you cannot possibly see clearly at your age, and even when it gets lighter, I doubt that your eyes are good enough for you to sew.' 'Whoever you are,' replied Baba Mustafa, 'you obviously don't know me. However old I may seem to you, I still have excellent eyes and you will realize the truth of this when I tell you that not long ago I sewed up a dead man in a place where the light was hardly any better than it is at the moment.' The thief was delighted to find that after his arrival he had come across someone who, as seemed certain, had, immediately and unprompted, given him the very information for which he had come.

'A dead man!' the thief exclaimed in astonishment, adding, in order to make him talk: 'What do you mean, "sewed up a dead man"? You must mean that you sewed the shroud in which he was wrapped?' 'No, no,' insisted Baba Mustafa, 'I know what I mean. You want to make me talk, but you're not going to get anything more out of me.'

The thief needed no further enlightenment to be persuaded that he had discovered what he had come to look for. Pulling out a gold coin, he placed it in Baba Mustafa's hand, saying: 'I don't want to enter into your secret, although I can assure you that I would not reveal it if you confided it to me. The only thing I ask is that you be kind enough to tell me or show me the house where you sewed up the dead man.' 'Even if I wanted to, I could not,' replied Baba Mustafa, ready to hand back the gold coin.

'Take my word. The reason is that I was led to a certain place where I was blindfolded and from there I let myself be taken right into the house. When I had finished what I had to do, I was brought back in the same way to the same place, and so you see that I cannot be of any help to you.' 'You ought at least to remember something of the path you took with your eyes blindfolded,' the thief went on. 'Come with me, I beg you, and I will blindfold you in that place, and we will go on together by the same path, taking the turns that you can remember. As every effort deserves a reward, here is another gold coin. Come, do me the favour I ask of you.' On saying this, he placed another gold coin in his hand.

Baba Mustafa was tempted by the two gold coins; he gazed at them in his hand for a while without uttering a word, thinking over what he should do. Finally, he pulled out a purse from his breast and put them there, saying to the thief: 'I can't guarantee I will remember the precise path I was led along, but since that's what you want, let's go. I will do what I can to remember it.'

To the thief's great satisfaction, Baba Mustafa rose and, without closing his shop – where there was nothing of consequence to lose – he led the thief to the place where Marjana had blindfolded him. When they arrived there, he said: 'Here is where I was blindfolded and I was turned like this, as you see.' The thief, who had his handkerchief ready, bound his eyes and then walked beside him, sometimes leading him and sometimes letting himself be led, until he came to a halt. 'I don't think I went any further,' said Baba Mustafa, and indeed he was standing before Qasim's house where Ali Baba was now living. Before he removed the handkerchief from his eyes, the thief quickly put a mark on the door with a piece of chalk which he had ready in his hand. He then removed it and asked Baba Mustafa if he knew to whom the house belonged. But Baba Mustafa replied that he could not tell him as he was not from that quarter. Seeing that he could not learn anything more, the thief thanked him for his trouble, and after he had left him to return to his shop, he himself took the path back to the forest, certain that he would be well received.

Shortly after the two of them had parted, Marjana came out of Ali Baba's house on some errand and when she returned, she noticed the mark the thief had made and stopped to examine it. 'What does this mark mean?' she asked herself. 'Does someone intend to harm my master, or is it just children playing? Well, whatever the reason, one must guard against every eventuality.' So she took a piece of chalk and, as the two or three doors on either side were similar, she marked them all in the same spot and then went inside, without telling her master or mistress what she had done.

The thief, meanwhile, had gone on until he had reached the forest, where he quickly rejoined his band. He told them of his success, exaggerating his good luck in finding right at the start the only man who would have been able to tell him what he had come to discover. They listened to what he said with great satisfaction and the captain, after praising him for the care that he had taken, addressed them all. 'Comrades,' he said, 'we have no time to lose; let us go, well armed but without making this too obvious. We must enter the town separately, one after the other, so as not to arouse suspicion, and meet in the main square, some of us coming from one side, some from the other. I myself will go and look for the house with our comrade who has just brought us such good news, in order to decide what we had better do.'

The thieves applauded their captain's speech and were soon ready to set out. They went off in twos and threes, and by walking at a reasonable distance from one another, they entered the town without arousing any suspicions. The captain and the thief who had gone there that morning were the last of them. The latter led the captain to the street where he had marked Ali Baba's house, and on coming to one of the doors which had been marked by Marjana, he pointed it out to him, telling him that that was the house. However, as they continued on their way without stopping so as not to look suspicious, the captain noticed that the next door had the same mark in the same spot. When he pointed this out to his companion and asked him if that was the door or the first one, the other was confused and did not know what to reply. His confusion increased when the two of them saw that the next four or five doors were marked in the same way. The scout swore to the captain that he had marked only one door, adding: 'I don't know who can have marked the others all in the same way, but I admit that I am too confused to be sure which is the one I marked.' The captain, seeing his plan had come to nothing, went to the main square and told his men through the first man he encountered that all their trouble had been wasted: their expedition had been useless and all they could do now was to return to their den in the forest. He led the way and they all followed in the same order in which they had set out.

When they had reassembled in the forest, he explained to them why he had made them come back. With one voice, they all declared that the scout deserved to be put to death; and indeed, he even condemned himself by admitting that he should have taken greater precautions, stoically offering his neck to the thief who came forward to cut off his head.

Since the preservation of the group meant that the wrong that had been done to them should not go unavenged, a second thief, who vowed he would do better, came forward and asked to be granted the favour of carrying out their revenge. They did this and he set out. Just as the first thief had done, he bribed Baba Mustafa, who, with his eyes blindfolded, showed him where Ali Baba's house was. The thief put a red mark on it in a less obvious spot, reckoning that this would surely distinguish the house from those which had been marked in white. But a little later, just as she had done on the day before, Marjana came out of the house and, when she returned, her sharp eyes did not fail to spot the red mark. For the same reasons as before, she made the same mark with red chalk in the same spot on all the other doors on either side.

The scout, on returning to his companions in the forest, made a point of stressing the precaution he had taken which, he claimed, was infallible and would ensure that Ali Baba's house could not be confused with the rest. The captain and his men agreed with him that this would succeed, and they made for the city in the same order, taking the same precautions as before, armed and ready to pull off the planned coup. When they arrived, the captain and the scout went straight to Ali Baba's street but encountered the same difficulty as before. The captain was indignant, while the scout found himself as confused as his predecessor had been. The captain was again forced to go back with his men, as little satisfied as on the previous day, and the scout, as the man responsible for the failure, suffered the same fate, to which he willingly submitted himself.

The captain, seeing how his band had lost two of its brave men, was afraid that more still would be lost and his band would diminish further if he continued to rely on others to tell him where the house really was. The example of the two made him realize that on such occasions his men were far better at using physical force rather than their heads. So he decided to take charge of the matter himself and went to the city, where Baba Mustafa helped him in the same way as he had helped the other two. He wasted no time placing a distinguishing mark on Ali Baba's house but examined the place very closely, passing back and forth in front of it several times so that he could not possibly mistake it.

Satisfied with his expedition and having learned what he wanted to find out, he went back to the forest. When he reached the cave where his band was waiting for him, he addressed them, saying: 'Comrades, nothing can now stop us from exacting full vengeance for the harm that has been done to us. I now know for sure the house of the man on whom revenge should fall, and on my way back I thought of such a clever way of making him experience it that no one will ever again be able to discover our hideaway or where our treasure is. This is what we have to aim for, as otherwise, instead of being of use to us, the treasure will be our downfall. To achieve this, here is what I thought of and if, when I finish explaining it, any one of you can think of a better way, he can tell us.' He went on to explain to them what he intended to do; and as they had all given him their approval, he then told them to disperse into the towns, surrounding villages and even the cities, where they were to buy nineteen mules and thirty-eight leather jars for transporting oil, one full of oil and the others empty.

Within two or three days, the thieves had collected all these. As the empty jars were a little too narrow at the top, the captain had them widened. Then, after he had made one of his men enter each of the jars, with such weapons as he thought they needed, he left open the sections of the jars that had been unstitched to allow each man to breathe freely. After that he closed them in such a way that they appeared to be full of oil. To disguise them further, he rubbed them on the outside with oil taken from the filled jar.

When all this had been done, the mules were loaded with the thirty-seven thieves – not including the captain – each hidden in one of the jars, together with the jar which was filled with oil. With the captain in the lead, they took the path to the city at the time he had decided upon and arrived at dusk, about one hour after the sun had set, as he had planned. He entered the city and went straight to Ali Baba's house, with the intention of knocking on the door and asking to spend the night there with his mules, if the master of the house would agree to it. He had no need to knock, for he found Ali Baba at the door, enjoying the fresh air after his supper. After he brought his mules to a halt, the captain said to Ali Baba: 'Sir, I have come from far away, bringing this oil to sell tomorrow in the market. I don't know where to stay at this late hour, so if it is not inconvenient to you, would you be so kind as to let me spend the night here? I would be very obliged to you.' Although in the forest Ali Baba had seen the man who was now speaking to him and had even heard his voice, how could he have recognized him as the captain of the forty thieves in his disguise as an oil merchant? 'You are very welcome, come in,' he replied, standing aside to let him in with his mules. When the man had entered, Ali Baba summoned one of his slaves and ordered him to put the mules under cover in the stable after they had been unloaded, and to give them hay and barley. He also took the trouble of going to the kitchen and ordering Marjana quickly to prepare some supper for the guest who had just arrived and to make up a bed for him in one of the rooms.

Ali Baba did even more to make his guest as welcome as possible: when he saw that the man had unloaded his mules, that the mules had been led off into the stable as he had ordered, and that he was looking for somewhere to spend the night in the open air, he went up to him in the hall where he received guests, telling him he would not allow him to sleep in the courtyard. The captain firmly refused his offer of a room, under the pretext of not wishing to inconvenience him, although in reality this was so as to be able to carry out what he planned in greater freedom, and he only accepted the offer of hospitality after repeated entreaties.

Not content with entertaining someone who wanted to kill him, Ali Baba went on to talk with him about things which he thought would please him, until Marjana brought him his supper, and he left his guest only when he had eaten his fill, saying: 'I will leave you as the master here; you have only to ask for anything you need: everything in my house is at your disposal.' The captain got up at the same time as Ali Baba and accompanied him to the door, and while Ali Baba went into the kitchen to speak to Marjana, he entered the courtyard under the pretext of going to the stable to see if his mules needed anything. Ali Baba once more told Marjana to take good care of his guest and to see he lacked for nothing, adding: 'I am going to the baths early tomorrow morning. See that my bath linen is ready – give it to Abdullah; and then make me a good beef stew to eat when I return.' Having given these orders, he then retired to bed.

Meanwhile, the captain came out of the stable and went to tell his men what they had to do. Beginning with the man in the first jar and carrying on until the last, he said to each one: 'As soon as I throw some pebbles from the room in which they have put me, cut open the jar from top to bottom with the knife you have been given and, when you come out, I shall be there.' The knives he meant were pointed and had been sharpened for this purpose.

He then returned and Marjana, seeing him standing by the kitchen door, took a lamp and led him to the room which she had prepared for him, leaving him there after having asked him if there was anything else he needed. Soon afterwards, so as not to arouse any suspicion, he put out the lamp and lay down fully dressed, ready to get up as soon as he had taken a short nap.

Marjana, remembering Ali Baba's orders, prepared his bath linen and gave it to the slave Abdullah, who had not yet gone to bed. She then put the pot on the fire to prepare the stew, but while she was removing the scum, her lamp went out. There was no more oil in the house nor were there any candles. What should she do? She had to see clearly to remove the scum, and when she told Abdullah of her quandary, he said to her: 'Don't be so worried: just take some oil from one of the jars here in the courtyard.'

Marjana thanked him for his advice and while he went off to sleep near Ali Baba's room so as to be ready to follow him to the baths, she took the oil jug and went into the courtyard. When she approached the first jar she came across, the thief hidden inside it asked: 'Is it time?' Although the man had spoken in a whisper, Marjana could easily hear his voice because the captain, as soon as he had unloaded his mules, had opened not only this jar but also all the others, to give some air to his men, who, though they could still breathe, had felt very uncomfortable. Any other slave but Marjana, surprised at finding a man in the jar instead of the oil she was looking for, would have caused an uproar that could have done a lot of harm. But Marjana was of superior stock, immediately realizing the importance of keeping secret the pressing danger which threatened not only Ali Baba and his family but also herself. She grasped the need to remedy the situation swiftly and quietly, and thanks to her intelligence, she saw at once how this could be done. Restraining herself and without showing any emotion, she pretended to be the captain and replied: 'Not yet, but soon.' She went up to the next jar and was asked the same question, and she went on from jar to jar until she reached the last one, which was full of oil, always giving the same reply to the same question. In this way she discovered that her master, Ali Baba, who thought he was merely offering hospitality to an oil merchant, had let in to his house thirty-eight thieves, including the bogus oil merchant, their captain. Quickly filling her jug with oil from the last jar, she returned to the kitchen where she filled the lamp with the oil and lit it. She then took a large cooking pot and returned to the courtyard where she filled it with oil from the jar and brought the pot back and put it over the fire. She put plenty of wood underneath because the sooner the pot boiled the sooner she could carry out her plan to save the household, as there was no time to spare. At last the oil boiled; taking the pot, she went and poured enough boiling oil into each jar, from the first to the last, to smother and kill the thieves – and kill them she did.

This deed, which was worthy of Marjana's courage, was quickly and silently carried out, as she had planned, after which she returned to the kitchen with the empty pot and closed the door. She put out the fire she had lit, leaving only enough heat to finish cooking Ali Baba's stew. Finally, she blew out the lamp and remained very quiet, determined not to go to bed before watching what happened next, as far as the darkness allowed, through a kitchen window which overlooked the courtyard.

She had only to wait a quarter of an hour before the captain awoke. He got up, opened the window and looked out. Seeing no light and as the house was completely quiet, he gave the signal by throwing down pebbles, several of which, to judge by the sound, fell on the jars. He listened but heard nothing to tell him that his men were stirring. This worried him and so he threw some more pebbles for a second and then a third time. They fell on the jars and yet not one thief gave the least sign of life. He could not understand why and, alarmed by this and making as little noise as possible, he went down into the courtyard. When he went up to the first jar, intending to ask the thief, whom he thought to be alive, whether he was asleep, he was met by a whiff of burning oil coming from the jar. He then realized that his plan to kill Ali Baba and pillage his house and, if possible, carry back the stolen gold had failed. He moved on to the next jar and then all the others, one after the other, only to discover that all his men had perished in the same way. Then, on seeing how the jar which he had brought full of oil had been depleted, he realized just how he had lost the help he had been expecting. In despair at the failure of his attempt, he slipped through Ali Baba's garden gate, which led from the courtyard, and made his escape by passing from garden to garden over the walls.

After she had waited a while, Marjana, hearing no further sound and seeing that the captain had not returned, was in no doubt about what he had decided to do, as he had not tried to escape by the house door, which was locked with a double bolt. She went to bed at last and fell asleep, delighted and satisfied at having so successfully ensured the safety of the whole household.

Ali Baba, meanwhile, set out before daybreak and went to the baths, followed by his slave, quite unaware of the astonishing events which had taken place in his house while he was asleep. For Marjana had not thought that she should wake him and tell him about them, as she had quite rightly realized she had no time to lose at the moment of danger and that it was pointless to disturb him after the danger had passed.

By the time Ali Baba had returned home from the baths, the sun had already risen, and when Marjana came to open the door for him, he was surprised to see that the jars of oil were still in their place and that the merchant had not gone to the market with his mules. He asked her why this was, for Marjana had left things just as they were for him to see, so that the sight of them could explain to him more effectively what she had done to save him. 'My good master,' Marjana replied, 'may God preserve you and all your household! You will understand better what you want to know when you have seen what I have to show you. Please come with me.' Ali Baba followed her and, after shutting the door, she led him to the first jar. 'Look inside,' she said, 'and see if there is any oil there.' Ali Baba looked, but seeing a man in the jar, he drew back in fright, uttering a loud cry. 'Don't be afraid,' said Marjana. 'The man you see won't do you any harm. He has done some damage but is no longer in a condition to do any more, either to you or to anyone else – he's no longer alive.' 'Marjana,' exclaimed Ali Baba, 'what is all this that you have just shown me? Explain to me.' 'I will tell you,' she replied, 'but control your astonishment and don't stir up the curiosity of your neighbours, lest they find out something that is very important for you to keep secret. But come and see the other jars first.'

Ali Baba looked into the other jars one after the other, from the first to the last one, in which he could see that the oil level was now much lower. After looking, he stood motionless, saying not a word but staring now at the jars, now at Marjana, so great was his astonishment. At last, as if he had finally recovered his speech, he asked: 'But what has become of the merchant?' 'The merchant,' replied Marjana, 'is no more a merchant than I am. I will tell you who he is and what has become of him. But you will learn the full story more comfortably in your own room, as it's time, for the sake of your health, to have some stew after your visit to the baths.'

While Ali Baba returned to his room, Marjana went to the kitchen to fetch the stew. When she brought it to him, he said to her before eating it: 'Satisfy my impatience and tell me this extraordinary story at once and in every detail.'

Obediently, Marjana began: 'Master, last night, when you had gone to bed, I prepared your linen for the bath, as you had told me, and I gave it to Abdullah. I then put the stew pot on the fire, but while I was removing the scum, the lamp suddenly went out for lack of oil. There was not a drop of oil left in the jug, and so I went to look for some candle ends but couldn't find any. Seeing me in such a fix, Abdullah reminded me of the jars in the courtyard which we both believed, as you did yourself, were full of oil. I took the jug and ran to the nearest one, but when I got to it, a voice came from inside, asking: "Is it time?" I wasn't startled, for I realized at once the bogus merchant's malicious intent, and I promptly replied: "Not yet, but soon." I went to the next jar and a second voice asked me the same question, to which I gave the same reply. I went from jar to jar, one after the other, and each time came the same question and I gave the same answer. It was only in the last jar that I found any oil and I filled my jug from it. When I considered that there were thirty-seven thieves in the middle of your courtyard, just waiting for the signal from their captain – whom you had taken for a merchant and had received so warmly – to set your house alight, I lost no time. I took the jar, lit the lamp and, taking the largest cooking pot in the kitchen, I went and filled it with oil. I put the pot over the fire and when the oil was boiling hot, I went and poured some into each of the jars where the thieves were. This was enough to stop them carrying out their plan to destroy us, and when my plan succeeded, I went back to the kitchen and put out the lamp. Then, before going to bed, I quietly went and stood by the window to see what the bogus oil merchant would do. A short time later, I heard him throw some pebbles from his window down on to the jars, as a signal. He did this twice or thrice and then, as he could neither see nor hear any movement coming from below, he came down and I saw him go from jar to jar, until after he had reached the last one, I lost sight of him because of the darkness. I kept watch for some time after that and, when he didn't return, I was sure he must have escaped through the garden, in despair at his failure. Convinced that the household was now quite safe, I went to bed.'

Having completed her account, Marjana added: 'This is the story you asked me to tell you and I am certain it all follows from something I noticed two or three days ago which I didn't think I needed to tell you. Early one morning, as I came back from the city, I saw that there was a white mark on our street door and next day there was a red mark next to it. I didn't know why this was and so on both occasions I went and marked two or three doors next to us up and down the street in the same way and in the same spot. If you add this to what has just happened, you will see that it was all a plot by the thieves of the forest who, for some reason, have lost two of their number. Be that as it may, they have now been reduced to three, at the most. This goes to show that they have sworn to do away with you and that you had better be on your guard as long as we can be sure that there is even one left alive. For my part,' she concluded, 'I will do everything I can to watch over your safety, as is my duty.'

When she had finished, Ali Baba, realizing how much he owed to her, said: 'I will not die before rewarding you as you deserve, for I owe my life to you. As a token of my gratitude, I shall start by giving you your freedom as of this moment, until I can reward you properly in the way I have in mind. I, too, am persuaded that the forty thieves set this ambush up for me, but through your hands God has saved me. May He continue to preserve me from their wickedness and, by warding off their wickedness from me, may He deliver the world from their persecution and their vile breed. What we must now do is immediately to bury the bodies of these pests of the human race, in complete secrecy, so that no one will suspect what has happened. That's what I'm going to work on with Abdullah.'

Ali Baba's garden was very long and at the end of it were some large trees. Without further delay, he went with Abdullah and together they dug a trench under the trees, long enough and wide enough for all the bodies they had to bury. The earth was easy to work, so that the job was soon completed. They then pulled the bodies out of the jars and, after removing the weapons with which the thieves were armed, they took the bodies to the bottom of the garden and laid them in the trench. After they had covered them with the soil from the trench, they scattered the rest of it around so that the ground seemed the same as before. Ali Baba carefully hid the oil jars and the weapons; while, as for the mules, for which he had no further use, he sent them at different times to the market, where he got his slave to sell them.

While Ali Baba was taking all these measures to stop people discovering how he had become so rich in such a short time, the captain of the thieves had returned to the forest in a state of unimaginable mortification. In his agitation, confused by so unexpected a disaster, he returned to the cave, having come to no decision about how or what he should or should not do to Ali Baba.

The solitude in which he found himself in this place seemed horrible to him. 'Brave lads,' he cried out, 'companions of my vigils, my struggles and adventures, where are you? What will I do without you? Have I chosen you and collected you together only to see you perish all at once by a fate so deadly and so unworthy of your courage? Had you died sword in hand like brave men, I would regret your death. When will I ever be able to get together another band of hardy men like you again? And even if I wanted to, could I do so without exposing so much gold, silver and riches to the mercy of someone who has already enriched himself with part of it? No, I could not and should not think of it before I have first got rid of him. I shall do by myself what I have not been able to do with such powerful assistance. When I have seen to it that this treasure is no longer exposed to being plundered, I will ensure that after me it will stay neither without successor nor without a master; rather, that it may be preserved and increase for all posterity.' Having made this resolution, he did not worry about how to carry it out; and so, full of hope and with a quiet mind, he went to sleep and spent a peaceful night.

The next morning, having woken up very early as he had intended, he put on new clothes of a kind suitable for his plan and went to the city, where he took up lodgings in a *khan*. Expecting that what had happened at Ali Baba's house might have caused some uproar, he asked the door-keeper in the course of his conversation what news there was in the city, to which the doorkeeper replied by telling him all sorts of things, but not what he needed to know. From that, he decided that Ali Baba must be guarding his great secret because he did not want the fact that he knew about the treasure and how to get to it to be spread abroad. Ali Baba, for his part, was well aware that it was for this reason that his life was in jeopardy.

This encouraged the captain to do everything he could to get rid of Ali Baba by the same secret means. He provided himself with a horse and used it to transport to his lodgings various kinds of rich cloths and fine fabrics which he brought from the forest in several trips, taking the necessary precautions to conceal the place from where he was taking them. When he had got what he thought enough, he looked for a shop and having found one, he hired it from the proprietor, filled it with his stock and established himself there. Now the shop opposite this one used to belong to Qasim and had recently been occupied by Ali Baba's son. The captain, who had taken the name of Khawaja Husain, soon exchanged courtesies with the neighbouring merchants, as was the custom. Since Ali Baba's son was young and handsome and did not lack intelligence, the captain frequently had occasion to speak to him, as he did to the other merchants, and soon made friends with him. He even took to cultivating him more assiduously when, three or four days after he had established himself there, he recognized Ali Baba, who had come to see his son and talk with him, as he did from time to time. He later learned from the son, after Ali Baba had left, that this was his father. So he cultivated him all the more, flattered him and gave him small gifts, entertaining him and on several occasions inviting him to eat with him.

Ali Baba's son did not want to be under so many obligations to Khawaja Husain without being able to return them. But his lodgings were cramped and he was not well off enough to entertain him as he wished. He talked about this to his father, pointing out to him that it was not proper to let Khawaja Husain's courtesies remain unrecognized for much longer.

Ali Baba was delighted to take on the task of entertaining him himself. 'My son,' he said, 'tomorrow is Friday. As it is a day when the big merchants like Khawaja Husain and yourself keep their shops closed, arrange to take a stroll with him after dinner; when you return, arrange it so that you bring him past my house and make him come in. It's better to do it this way than if you were to invite him formally. I shall go and order Marjana to prepare the supper and have it ready.'

On Friday, Ali Baba's son and Khawaja Husain met after dinner at their agreed rendezvous and went on their walk. As they returned, Ali Baba's son carefully made Khawaja Husain pass down the street where his father lived, and when they came to the house door, he stopped and said to him, as he knocked: 'This is my father's house. When I told him about the friendship with which you have honoured me, he told me to see to it that you honoured him with your acquaintance. I beg you to add this pleasure to all the others for which I am already indebted to you.' Although Khawaja Husain had got what he wanted, which was to enter Ali Baba's house and murder him without endangering his own life and without causing a stir, nevertheless he made his excuses and pretended to be about to take leave of the son. But as Ali Baba's slave had just opened the door, the son seized him by the hand and, going in first, pulled him forcibly after him, as if in spite of himself.

Ali Baba met Khawaja Husain with a smiling face and gave him all the welcome he could wish for. He thanked him for the kindness he had shown to his son, adding: 'The debt he and I owe you is all the greater, since he is a young man still inexperienced in the ways of the world and you are not above helping instruct him in these.' Khawaja Husain returned the compliment by assuring him that though some old men might have more experience than his son, the latter had enough good sense to serve in place of the experience of very many others.

After talking for a short while on unimportant matters, Khawaja Husain wanted to take his leave, but Ali Baba stopped him, saying: 'My dear sir, where do you want to go? Please do me the honour of dining with me. The meal I would like to offer you is much inferior to what you deserve but, such as it is, I hope that you will accept it in the same spirit in which I offer it to you.' 'Dear sir,' Khawaja Husain rejoined, 'I know you mean well. If I ask you not to think ill of me for leaving without accepting this kind offer of yours, I beg you to believe me that I don't do this out of disrespect or discourtesy. I have a reason which you would appreciate, if you knew it.' 'And may I ask what this can be?' said Ali Baba. 'Yes, I can tell you what it is: it is that I don't eat meat or stew which contains salt. Just think how embarrassed I would be, eating at your table.' 'If that's the only reason,' Ali Baba replied, 'it should not deprive me of the honour of having you to supper, unless you wish it. First, there's no salt in the bread which we have in my house; and as for the meat and the stews, I promise you there won't be any in what will be served you. I shall go and give the order, and so, please be good enough to stay, as I shall be back in a moment.'

Ali Baba went to the kitchen and told Marjana not to put any salt on the meat she was going to serve and immediately to prepare two or three extra stews, in addition to those he had ordered, and these were to be unsalted. Marjana, who was ready to serve the meal, could not stop herself showing annoyance at this new order and having it out with Ali Baba. 'Who is this awkward fellow, who doesn't eat salt? Your supper will no longer be fit to eat if I serve it later.' 'Don't be angry, Marjana,' Ali Baba continued. 'He's perfectly all right. Just do as I tell you.'

Marjana reluctantly obeyed, and, curious to discover who this man was who did not eat salt, when she had finished and Abdullah had set the table, she helped him to carry in the dishes. When she saw Khawaja Husain, she immediately recognized him as the captain of the thieves, in spite of his disguise. Looking at him closely, she noticed that he had a dagger hidden under his clothes. 'I am no longer surprised the wretch doesn't want to eat salt with my master,' she said to herself, 'for he is his bitterest enemy and wants to murder him, but I am going to stop him.'

When Marjana had finished serving and letting Abdullah serve, she used the time while they were eating to make the necessary preparations to carry out a most audacious scheme. She had just finished by the time Abdullah came to ask her to serve the fruit, which she then brought and served as soon as Abdullah had cleared the table. Next to Ali Baba she placed a small side table on which she put the wine together with three cups. As she went out, she took Abdullah with her as though they were going to have supper together, leaving Ali Baba, as usual, free to talk, to enjoy the company of his guest and to give him plenty to drink.

It was then that the so-called Khawaja Husain, or rather the captain of the thieves, decided that the moment had come for him to kill Ali Baba. 'I shall get both father and son drunk,' he said to himself, 'and the son, whose life I am willing to spare, won't stop me plunging the dagger into his father's heart. I will then escape through the garden, as I did earlier, before the cook and the slave have finished their supper, or it may be that they will have fallen asleep in the kitchen.'

Instead of having supper, however, Marjana, who had seen through his evil plan, gave him no time to carry out his wicked deed. She put on a dancer's costume, with the proper headdress, and around her waist she tied a belt of gilded silver to which she attached a dagger whose sheath and handle were of the same metal. Finally, she covered her face with a very beautiful mask. Disguised in this manner, she said to Abdullah: 'Abdullah, take your tambourine and let us offer our master's guest and his son's friend the entertainment we sometimes give our master.' Abdullah took the tambourine and began to play as he walked into the room in front of Marjana. Marjana, who followed him, made a deep bow with a deliberate air so as to draw attention to herself, as though asking permission to show what she could do. Seeing that Ali Baba wanted to say something, Abdullah stopped playing his tambourine. 'Come in, Marjana, come in,' said Ali Baba. 'Khawaja Husain will judge what you are capable of and will tell us his opinion. But don't think, sir,' he said, turning to his guest, 'that I have put myself to any expense in offering you this entertainment. I have it in my own home, and as you can see, it is my slave and my cook and housekeeper who provide me with it. I hope you won't find it disagreeable.'

Khawaja Husain, who had not expected Ali Baba to add this entertainment to the supper, was afraid that he would not be able to use the opportunity he thought he had found. But he consoled himself with the hope that, if that happened, another opportunity would arise later if he continued to cultivate the friendship of the father and son. So, although he would have preferred to have done without what was being offered, he still pretended to be grateful, and he courteously indicated that what pleased his host would please him too.

When Abdullah saw that Ali Baba and Khawaja Husain had stopped talking, he began to play his tambourine again and accompanied his playing by singing a dance tune. Marjana, who could dance as well as any professional, performed so admirably that she would have aroused the admiration of any company and not only her present audience, although the so-called Khawaja Husain paid very little attention. After she had danced several dances with the same charm and vigour, she finally drew out the dagger. Holding it in her hand, she then performed a dance in which she surpassed herself with different figures, light movements, astonishing leaps of marvellous energy, now holding the dagger in front, as though to strike, now pretending to plunge it into her own chest. At last, now out of breath, with her left hand she snatched the tambourine from Abdullah and, holding the dagger in her right, she went to present the tambourine to Ali Baba, its bowl uppermost in imitation of the male and female professional dancers who do this to ask for contributions from their spectators.

Ali Baba threw a gold coin into Marjana's tambourine and, following his father's example, so did his son. Khawaja Husain, seeing she was coming to him too, had already pulled out his purse from his breast to present his offering and was putting his hand out at the very moment that Marjana, with a courage worthy of the firmness and resolve she had shown up till then, plunged the dagger right into his heart and did not pull it out again until he had breathed his last. Terrified by this, Ali Baba and his son both cried out. 'Wretched girl, what have you done?' shouted Ali Baba. 'Do you want to destroy us, my family and myself?' 'I didn't do it to destroy you,' replied Marjana. 'I did it to save you.'

Opening Khawaja Husain's robe, Marjana showed Ali Baba the dagger with which he was armed. 'See what a fine enemy you've been dealing with!' she said. 'Look carefully at his face and you will recognize the bogus oil merchant and the captain of the forty thieves. Remember how he didn't want to eat salt with you – do you need anything more to convince you that he was planning evil? The moment you told me you had such a guest, before I had even seen him I became suspicious. I then set eyes on him and you can see how my suspicions were not unfounded.'

Ali Baba, recognizing the new obligation he was under to Marjana for having saved his life a second time, embraced her and said: 'When I gave you your freedom, I promised you that my gratitude would not stop there but that I would soon add the final touch to my promise. The time has now come and I will make you my daughter-in-law.' Turning to his son, he said: 'I believe you are a dutiful enough son not to find it strange that I am giving you Marjana as a wife without consulting you. You are no less obliged to her than I am. You can see that Khawaja Husain only made friends with you in order to make it easier for him to murder me treacherously. Had he succeeded, you can be sure that you also would have been sacrificed to his vengeance. Consider, too, that if you take Marjana you will be marrying someone who, as long as we both live, will be the prop and mainstay of my family and yours.' Ali Baba's son, far from showing any displeasure, gave his consent, not only because he did not want to disobey his father but because his own inclinations led in that direction.

Their next concern was to bury the body of the captain by the corpses of the thirty-seven thieves. This was done so secretly that no one knew about it until many years later, when there was no longer any interest in this memorable tale becoming known.

A few days later, Ali Baba celebrated the wedding of his son to Marjana, with a solemn ceremony and a sumptuous banquet which was accompanied by the customary dances, spectacles and entertainments. The friends and neighbours whom he had invited were not told the real reason for the marriage, but they were well acquainted with Marjana's many excellent qualities and Ali Baba had the great satisfaction of finding that they were loud in their praises for his generosity and good-heartedness.

After the wedding, Ali Baba continued to stay away from the cave in the forest. He had not been there since he had taken away the body of his brother, Qasim, together with the gold, which he had loaded on to his three donkeys. This had been out of fear that he would find the thieves there and would fall into their hands. Even after thirty-eight of them, including their captain, had died, he still did not go back, believing that the remaining two, of whose fate he was ignorant, were still alive. But when a year had gone by, seeing that nothing had occurred to cause him any disquiet, he was curious enough to make the trip, taking the necessary precautions to ensure his safety. He mounted his horse and, on approaching the cave, he took it as a good sign that he could see no trace of men or horses. He dismounted, tied up his own horse and, standing in front of the door, he uttered these words – which he had not forgotten: 'Open, Sesame.' The door opened and he entered. The state in which he found everything in the cave led him to conclude that, since around the time when the so-called Khawaja Husain had come to rent a shop in the city, no one had been there and so the band of forty thieves must all since have scattered and been wiped out. He was now certain that he was the only person in the world who knew the secret of how to open the cave and that its treasure was at his disposal. He had a bag with him which he filled with as much gold as his horse could carry, and then returned to the city.

Later he took his son to the cave and taught him the secret of how to enter it and, in time, the two of them passed this on to their descendants. They lived in great splendour, being held in honour as the leading dignitaries in the city. They had profited from their good fortune but used it with restraint.

Abu Muhammad the Sluggard

While Harun al-Rashid was seated one day on his royal throne a young eunuch came into his presence carrying a crown of red gold set with pearls and gems, sapphires and other precious stones, beyond all price. He kissed the ground before the caliph and said: 'Commander of the Faithful, the Lady Zubaida kisses the ground before you and says that you know she has had this crown made, but it needs to be topped with a great gem. She has searched through her treasures but has not found anything large enough there to suit her purpose.' Harun told his chamberlains and deputies to look for a jewel that would do, but they failed to find anything suitable. This angered Harun, who said: 'I am the caliph, king of the kings of the earth, but I cannot find one jewel. How can this be?' He told the men to ask the merchants, and when they did, the merchants said: 'Our master the caliph will only find this jewel in the possession of a man in Basra called Abu Muhammad the sluggard.'

When the caliph was told this, he ordered his vizier, Ja'far, to send a message to the emir Muhammad al-Zubaidi, the governor of Basra, telling him to make arrangements to have this man sent to the caliph. Ja'far wrote a note to this effect and gave it to Masrur, who set off with it to Basra. The emir Muhammad was delighted by his arrival and treated him with the greatest respect, after which Masrur read him the caliph's note. He obediently despatched Masrur with an escort of his servants to Abu Muhammad. When they had come to his house and had knocked on the door, a servant came out and Masrur told him to tell his master that he was wanted by the Commander of the Faithful. After the servant had gone in and told him that, Abu Muhammad came out to find Masrur, the chamberlain of the caliph, accompanied by the servants of Muhammad al-Zubaidi. He kissed the ground before Masrur and said: 'To hear the commands of the Commander of the Faithful is to obey them.'

He invited the visitors into his house and they said: 'This can only be a quick visit if we are to follow the caliph's instructions, as he is waiting for you to come.' 'Then wait a short time for me to get ready,' said Abu Muhammad. After he had done his best to persuade them, they went in with him and in the entrance hall they found hangings of blue brocade embroidered with red gold. Abu Muhammad told a number of his servants to take Masrur to the bath in his house, and when they did this Masrur discovered remarkable walls and marble slabs adorned with gold and silver, while the water was mixed with rosewater. A crowd of servants surrounded him and his companions, attending to all their needs, and when they left the bath, they were dressed in robes of brocade embroidered with gold. When they went back into the house they found Abu Muhammad seated in his upper room underneath hangings of gold brocade set with pearls and other precious stones. The room itself was furnished with couches adorned with red gold, while he himself sat on a covering laid over a throne set with gems.

When Masrur entered, Abu Muhammad came to meet him, greeted him and sat him down beside him. He ordered a table of food to be brought, and when Masrur saw it, he exclaimed: 'By God, I have never seen anything to equal this in the caliph's palace!' There was food of every kind there, all set out on gilded china. Masrur reported that they ate, drank and enjoyed themselves until the end of the day and Abu Muhammad then presented each of them with five thousand dinars, while the next day he gave them green robes embroidered with gold and showed them the greatest deference. Masrur told him that they couldn't stay any longer for fear of the caliph, but Abu Muhammad said: 'Master, let me wait until tomorrow so that I can make my preparations to go with you.'

They stayed there that day and on the following morning Abu Muhammad's servants saddled his mule with a saddle of gold studded with all kinds of pearls and jewels. 'I wonder,' said Masrur to himself, 'if, when Abu Muhammad comes before him in all this pomp, the caliph will ask how he came to be so wealthy.' They then said goodbye to al-Zubaidi and left Basra, travelling on until they reached Baghdad. When they entered the caliph's presence and stood before him, Abu Muhammad was invited to sit, and when he had done so he addressed the caliph courteously, saying: 'Commander of the Faithful, by way of presenting my services to you, I have brought you a gift, if you will allow me to fetch it.' When the caliph agreed to this, Abu Muhammad produced a chest, and after opening it he brought out presents. Among them were trees of gold with leaves of polished emeralds and fruits of rubies, topazes and gleaming pearls, which filled the caliph with astonishment. Abu Muhammad then opened another chest and took out a tent of brocade, adorned with pearls, rubies, emeralds, chrysolites and various other gems. Its supports were made from fresh Indian aloes wood; its fringes were set with emeralds; and on it were pictures, every one representing living creatures of all sorts, both birds and beasts, and these in turn were set with rubies, emeralds, chrysolites and hyacinths, as well as precious stones of all kinds.

Al-Rashid was delighted to see all this and Abu Muhammad said: 'You should not think, Commander of the Faithful, that I have brought you this because I was influenced by fear or desire. I see myself as a common man, and this treasure is suitable for no one but the caliph. If you permit me, I shall show you some of my powers.' 'Do as you wish and let us see,' said al-Rashid. 'To hear is to obey,' replied Abu Muhammad. He moved his lips and pointed towards the battlements of the palace, which bent down towards him and then after a second gesture went back to their place. At a wink from him, closets appeared with bolted doors, and when he spoke to them he was answered by birdsong.

All this astonished al-Rashid, who said: 'From where have you got all this, you who are known as Abu Muhammad the sluggard? I am told that your father was a barber surgeon working in the baths who left you nothing.' 'Listen to my story, Commander of the Faithful,' said Abu Muhammad, 'for it is so strange and wonderful that, were it written with needles on the inner corners of the eye, it would serve as a warning to those who take heed.' The caliph told him to explain and HE CONTINUED:

Commander of the Faithful, may God prolong your glory and power, when people say that I am known as 'the sluggard' and that my father left me nothing, this is true. My father, as you said, was indeed a barber surgeon, working in the baths, while I in my youth was the idlest person on the face of the earth. So ingrained was this idleness of mine that if I was sleeping on a hot day and the sun began to shine down on me, I would be too lazy to get up and move into the shade. This went on until I was fifteen years old and then my father died and was received into the mercy of Almighty God. He left me nothing, but my mother used to act as a servant and she would fetch me food and drink as I lay on my side. One day, she came to me with five silver dirhams and told me that the *shaikh* Abu'l-Muzaffar was intending to go on a journey to China, he being a good man who loved the poor. 'My son,' she said, 'take these five dirhams and come with me to ask him to use the money to buy you something from China from which, by the grace of Almighty God, you might make a profit.' I was too lazy to get up and go with her, but she swore by God that if I didn't, she would not bring me food or drink or come in to see me but would leave me to die of hunger and thirst.

When I heard that, Commander of the Faithful, I realized that she was doing this because she knew how lazy I was. So I said: 'Help me to sit up,' which she did, while I shed tears. Then I said: 'Bring me my shoes,' and when she had brought them, I asked her to put them on my feet, which she did. I told her to lift me up from the ground, and when she had done that, I told her to support me as I walked. Leaning on her and stumbling over the skirts of my robe, I walked until we got to the river bank, where we greeted the *shaikh*. 'Uncle,' I said to him, 'are you Abu'l-Muzaffar?' 'At your service,' he replied. 'Then take these dirhams,' I told him, 'and use them to buy me something from China, from which God may allow me a profit.' 'Do you recognize this young man?' he asked his companions. 'Yes,' they said. 'He is known as Abu Muhammad the sluggard, and this is the only time we have ever known him to leave his own house.' 'Hand over the dirhams, my boy,' said the *shaikh*, 'and may Almighty God add His blessing.' He took the money from me, saying: 'In the Name of God.'

After this I went back home with my mother and Abu'l-Muzaffar set off on his journey, accompanied by a number of merchants, eventually reaching China. Here he traded and then he and his companions set off for home, having finished all that they wanted to do. After he had sailed for three days, he told the others to halt, and when they asked him why, he said: 'I forgot the errand that I was supposed to run for Abu Muhammad the sluggard, so come back with me so that we can buy something for his advantage.' They said: 'For God's sake, don't make us go back. We have travelled a very long way and faced great perils and extreme hardship.' When he insisted, they offered him twice the profit that could be made on five dirhams if he would change his mind. He agreed to this and they collected a large sum of money for him.

They then sailed on until they came in sight of a populous island, where they anchored, and the merchants landed to buy up minerals, jewels, pearls and so forth. Abu'l-Muzaffar caught sight of a man sitting with a large group of monkeys in front of him, among whom was one who had had some of its hair pulled out. When their master's attention wandered, the others would lay hold of that particular monkey, strike it and throw it at their master, after which he would get up, beat them, tie them up and punish them, leading them all to become angry with the other monkey and to strike it again. When he saw it, Abu'l-Muzaffar was sorry for it and pitied it, so he asked its owner whether he would sell it to him. 'Try buying it,' the man said, and Abu'l-Muzaffar told him: 'I have five dirhams belonging to an orphan. Will you take these for it?' 'Certainly, God bless you,' the man answered, and Abu'l-Muzaffar took it and handed over the money. His servants took it to the ship and tied it up, after which they weighed anchor and sailed to another island, where they anchored.

Here there were divers who would dive for precious stones, pearls, jewels and so on. The merchants paid them a fee for this, and when the monkey saw them diving he freed himself from his bonds, jumped off the side of the ship and dived with them. 'There is no might and no power except with God, the All-Highest, the Almighty!' exclaimed Abu'l-Muzaffar. 'I've lost the monkey thanks to the ill luck of the poor fellow for whom we got it,' and he and the others despaired of ever seeing it again. At that point a number of divers broke surface and there they could see the monkey coming up with them, holding in his hands valuable jewels, which it threw down before Abu'l-Muzaffar. He was astonished and said: 'There must be some great mystery attached to this monkey.'

They again weighed anchor and sailed on to what was known as the Island of the Zanj, a race of cannibal blacks. When these people saw the ship, they sailed out to it in canoes and captured everyone on board. They tied them up and brought them to their king, who ordered that a number of the merchants be killed. Their throats were cut and their flesh was eaten, after which the remainder were left for the night tied up and in great distress. After night had fallen, however, the monkey came to Abu'l-Muzaffar and untied his bonds. When the others saw that he was free, they said: 'It may be that God will save us through Abu'l-Muzaffar.' He told them: 'Know that, by the will of Almighty God, I was freed only by this monkey, for which I shall pay him a thousand dinars.' They said: 'We too shall each pay him a thousand dinars if he rescues us.' At that, the monkey went to them and started to free them, one after the other, until he had released them all. They then went off to their ship, which they found to be intact. Nothing had been taken from it and so they weighed anchor and sailed off. It was then that Abu'l-Muzaffar told them to pay what they had promised to the monkey and, obediently, each of them handed over a thousand dinars, while Abu'l-Muzaffar produced a thousand dinars of his own. As a result, a huge sum of money was collected for the monkey.

They now sailed on until they reached the city of Basra, where their friends met them as they disembarked. 'Where is Abu Muhammad the sluggard?' asked Abu'l-Muzaffar. My mother heard of this, and she came to me while I was sleeping to tell me that Abu'l-Muzaffar had arrived back in the city. 'Get up,' she told me. 'Go and greet him and ask him what he has brought for you, as maybe Almighty God has opened up some opportunity for you.' 'Lift me up from the ground,' I told her, 'and support me, so that I can go down to the river bank.' Then I walked off, stumbling over the skirts of my robe, until I came to the *shaikh* Abu'l-Muzaffar, and when he saw me he exclaimed: 'Welcome to the man whose dirhams saved my life and the lives of these merchants, through the will of Almighty God!' He then told me: 'Take this monkey which I have bought for you. Go off with him to your house and then wait until I come to you.'

I took the monkey off with me, saying to myself: 'By God, this is a valuable piece of merchandise.' When I got home I said to my mother: 'Whenever I sleep, you tell me to get up in order to buy and sell, so look and see for yourself this piece of merchandise.' I sat down, and while I was seated Abu'l-Muzaffar's slaves came to me and asked if I was Abu Muhammad the sluggard. When I said that I was, in came Abu'l-Muzaffar himself, following behind them. I got up to meet him, and after I had kissed his hands he told me to go with him to his house. 'To hear is to obey,' I said, and I went with him until I had got to his house. Then he told his slaves to fetch the money, which they did, and he said: 'My son, God has provided you with all this money as profit on your five dirhams.' The slaves lifted it in boxes on their heads and, after giving me the keys of the boxes, Abu'l-Muzaffar told me to lead the slaves to my house, telling me that all that wealth was mine.

When I came to my mother, she was delighted and said: 'My son, as God has provided you with all this money, give up your idle ways and go and trade in the market.' So I stopped being idle and opened a shop, in which the monkey would sit with me on my seat, eating when I ate and drinking with me. Every day, however, he would go off from early morning until noon, and then he would come back with a purse containing a thousand dinars, which he would put down beside me before taking his seat. He kept on doing this for a considerable time until I had collected a large sum of money with which I bought property and estates, planted orchards and acquired mamluks, black slaves and servant girls.

One day, I happened to be sitting with the monkey when suddenly he looked to the right and left, and while I was wondering what that might mean, through God's permission he spoke with a clear voice and said: 'Abu Muhammad.' When I heard him speak I was terrified, but he told me: 'Don't be afraid and I shall tell you about myself. I am a *marid* of the *jinn*. I came to you because you were so poor, while now you don't even know how much money you have. I now need you for something which will be to your advantage.' I asked him what that might be and he said: 'I want to marry you to a girl like a full moon.' 'How?' I asked. He said: 'Tomorrow, put on your finest robes, mount your mule with the golden saddle, go to the market of the forage sellers and ask for the shop of the *sharif*. When you sit with him, tell him that you have come to ask for his daughter's hand in marriage. If he then says that you haven't any money, reputation or good family, give him a thousand dinars, and if he asks for more, give it to him and tempt him with money.' I agreed, saying that, God Almighty willing, I would do that the next day.

The next day, I put on the most splendid of my robes and mounted the mule with the golden saddle, after which I went to the market of the forage sellers and asked for the shop of the *sharif*. I found him sitting there and so I dismounted, greeted him and sat with him, having with me ten black slaves and mamluks. 'Perhaps you have some need that I may be able to fulfil,' the *sharif* said to me. 'Yes,' I said, 'I do need something,' and when he asked me what this was, I told him that I had come to ask for his daughter's hand in marriage. 'You have no money, reputation or good family,' he told me, at which I brought out a purse containing a thousand dinars of red gold and said: 'This is my reputation and my lineage. The Prophet, may God bless him and give him peace, said: "Money is an excellent reputation," and how admirable are the lines of the poet:

If someone owns two dirhams, his lips have learned
And can speak words of every kind.
His companions come to listen to him and you see
Him moving haughtily among the crowds.
Were it not for the dirhams, in which he takes such pride,
You would find him in the worst of states among the people.
If a rich man says something wrong, the people say:
"You may be right, and what you say is not impossible,"
But if a poor man speaks the truth, they say:
"You are a liar; what you say is wrong."
Money invests a man with dignity and beauty in all lands.
Money is the tongue of those who seek eloquence,
And the weapon of whoever wants to fight.'

After the *sharif* had listened to what I had to say and had understood the point of my lines, he looked down at the ground for a while and then raised his head and said: 'If this has to be, I want another three thousand dinars from you.' 'To hear is to obey,' I answered, and I then sent one of the mamluks to my house. When this man had returned with the money that the *sharif* had demanded, and he had seen it, he left his shop, telling his servants to lock it up, and after he had invited his friends from the market to come to his house he wrote a marriage contract for me and his daughter, telling me that he would bring me in to her after ten days.

I went back home in a state of delight, and when I was alone with the monkey I told him what had happened to me and he congratulated me. Then, when the time set by the *sharif* came near, the monkey said to me: 'I want you to do something for me, and if you do, then you can have whatever you want from me.' I asked him what this was and he told me: 'At the top end of the room in which you will sleep with the *sharif*'s daughter there is a cupboard whose door is fastened with a brass ring. The keys are under the ring. Take them and open the door, and you will then find an iron chest at whose four corners are four talismanic flags. In the middle of it there is a basin full of money, while beside it there are eleven snakes. In the basin a white cock is tied up and beside the chest is a knife. Take this knife and cut the cock's throat; then cut the flags in pieces and overturn the chest. After that you can come out and deflower your bride. This is what I want you to do.' 'To hear is to obey,' I replied.

I went to the *sharif*'s house, and when I entered the room I saw the cupboard that the monkey had described. When I found myself alone with my bride, I was astonished and delighted by her indescribable beauty and grace, together with the symmetry of her form. At midnight, when she was asleep, I got up and, after taking the keys, I opened the cupboard. I took the knife, killed the cock, threw down the flags and overturned the chest. My bride woke up and when she saw that the chest had been opened and the cock killed, she exclaimed: 'There is no might and no power except with God, the Most High, the Omnipotent! The *marid* has got me.' Before she had finished speaking the *marid* had swooped on the house and carried her off. In the commotion that followed the *sharif* came in, striking his own face. 'What have you done to us, Abu Muhammad,' he exclaimed, 'and is this how you repay us? I made this talisman in the cupboard as I was afraid for my daughter because of this damned *marid*, who has been trying unsuccessfully to take her for six years. There is no place left for you here so go on your way.' I left the *sharif*'s house and, after returning to my own, I looked for the monkey but failed to find him or, indeed, any trace of him, and so I realized that he was the *marid* who had taken my bride and had tricked me into destroying the talisman and the cock which had stood in his way.

In my regret I tore my clothes and struck my own face. Nowhere could I find ease, so I left immediately, making for the desert, and walked on until evening, too preoccupied to notice where I was going. Then, suddenly, two snakes came towards me, one dark and the other white. They were fighting each other and I picked up a rock from the ground and used it to kill the dark one, which had been the aggressor. The white snake went out of sight for a while, and then came back with ten other white snakes. They approached the dead snake and tore it into bits, leaving nothing but its head, after which they went away. I was so tired that I lay down where I was, and while I was lying there, thinking over what had happened to me, I heard a voice, although I could see no one there. The voice was reciting these lines:

Leave the fates to move unchecked, and pass the night free from care;
In the blink of an eye God changes one state to another.

When I heard that, Commander of the Faithful, I was very worried and concerned. Then, from behind me, I heard more lines being recited:

Muslim, guided by the Quran, be glad,
For you have reached safety.
Have no fear of the seductions of the devil;
We are a people who follow true belief.

I said: 'I conjure you, by the truth of the God whom you worship, to tell me who you are.' The disembodied voice then took human shape and said: 'Have no fear. We know about your good deed and we belong to the *jinn* who believe in the Prophet. If there is anything that you need, tell us and we will carry it out.' 'I do have a great need,' I replied, 'as I have suffered a great misfortune whose like has probably not afflicted anyone else.' 'Are you perhaps Abu Muhammad the sluggard?' the newcomer asked, and when I said that I was, he said: 'Abu Muhammad, I am the brother of the white snake whose enemy you killed. We are four full brothers, and we all owe you a debt of gratitude for the service you did us. You must know that it was a *marid* of the *jinn* who took the shape of a monkey and played this trick on you, for otherwise he would never have been able to take the girl. He had loved her for a long time and had wanted to carry her off, but the talisman prevented him, and had it remained he would not have been able to reach her. But don't distress yourself over this, for we will bring you to your bride and kill the *marid*, and the good deed you did us will not go unrewarded.' He then gave a great and terrible cry, after which he was joined by a group of *jinn*, whom he asked about the monkey. 'I know where he lives,' said one of them, and on being asked where this was, he told us: 'In the City of Brass, over which the sun never rises.'

The leader told me: 'Take one of our slaves and he will carry you on his back and teach you how to recover your bride. But you must know that he is a *marid* and so while he is carrying you don't mention the Name of God, or else he will flee from you and you will fall to your death.' 'To hear is to obey,' I said, and I picked one of the slaves of the *jinn*, who bent down and told me to mount. When I had done that, he flew up into the air with me until I had lost sight of the earth. The stars appeared as firmly rooted mountains, and I could hear the heavenly angels glorifying God. All this while, the *marid* was talking to me, distracting me and diverting me from any mention of Almighty God. Then, while I was being carried, a figure wearing green robes, with flowing locks of hair and a gleaming face, approached me, carrying a lance in his hand, from which flew sparks of fire. 'Abu Muhammad,' he ordered me, 'recite: "There is no god but God, and Muhammad is the Prophet of God," or else I shall strike you with this lance.' I was already in a state of distress from having been forced to keep silent and not pronounce the Name of Almighty God, so I recited the confession of faith. The lance carrier then struck the *marid* with his lance and he dissolved into ashes, leaving me to fall from his back down again to earth. I landed in a rough sea with clashing waves, but a ship with a five-man crew saw me, came up and carried me on board.

The sailors started to talk to me in an unknown language and I had to make signs to them to show them that I couldn't understand what they were saying. They sailed on until evening, when they cast a net and caught a fish, which they grilled and with which they fed me. The voyage continued until they reached their city, where they brought me to stand before their king. After I had kissed the ground, the king, who knew Arabic, presented me with a robe of honour and told me: 'I appoint you as one of my assistants.' I asked him the name of the city and he told me that it was a Chinese city named Hanad. He then handed me over to the vizier with instructions to show me the city. In early times its inhabitants had been unbelievers, but Almighty God had transformed them into stones. I enjoyed inspecting it and I had never seen a place with more trees and fruits.

After I had been there a month, I went to a river and sat down by the bank. While I was sitting there, a rider came up and asked if I was Abu Muhammad the sluggard. When I said that I was, he said: 'Have no fear; word of your good deed has reached us.' I asked him who he was and he said: 'I am the brother of the snake, and the girl whom you want to reach is close at hand.' He then took off his clothes and dressed me in them, repeating: 'Have no fear,' and adding: 'The *marid* who was killed while carrying you was one of our slaves.' Next he took me up behind him and rode with me to a desert, where he told me to dismount. 'Go on between these two mountains,' he said, 'until you see the City of Brass. Stop at a distance from it and don't enter until I come back to you and tell you what to do.' 'To hear is to obey,' I said.

I got down from behind the rider and walked on until I got to the city. Its wall, I could see, was of brass, and I started to walk around it in the hope of finding a gate, but I couldn't discover one. While I was circling around it, the snake's brother suddenly came up to me; he gave me a talismanic sword that would keep people from seeing me, and then went off on his way. He had not been gone long before there was a loud cry and I saw a large number of creatures whose eyes were in their chests. On catching sight of me, they asked me who I was and what had brought me there. I explained things to them and they said: 'The girl you mentioned is with the *marid* in the city here, but we don't know what he has done with her. We ourselves are brothers of the snake.' They went on: 'Go to that spring there; see where the water enters it and go into its channel, as this will bring you into the city.' I did that and the channel took me to a subterranean vault from which I came out to find myself in the centre of the city. There I discovered my bride seated on a golden throne draped with brocade, while around the throne was a garden with golden trees, whose fruits were precious stones such as sapphires, chrysolites, pearls and corals.

When she saw me, she recognized me and was the first to greet me. 'Master,' she said, 'who has brought you here?' When I told her what had happened, she said: 'You must know that this damned *marid* is so deeply in love with me that he has told me what can hurt him and what will help him. In the city is a talisman with which, if he wanted, he could kill everyone in the city and by means of which he can force the *'ifrits* to obey any order that he gives. The talisman is on a pillar.' I asked her where the pillar was and she described the spot. Then I asked her what it was and she said: 'It is a carved eagle with writing on it that I cannot read. Take it in your hands, fetch a brazier and throw in some musk. The smoke that it gives out will attract the *'ifrits*, so that when you have done that every single one of them will present himself before you. They will obey your orders and do anything at all that you tell them. So get up and do that with the blessing of Almighty God.' 'To hear is to obey,' I said.

I then went off to that pillar and carried out all her instructions, as a result of which the *'ifrits* assembled in front of me saying: 'Here we are, master; we shall do whatever you tell us.' 'Bind the *marid* who brought this girl from her home,' I told them and obediently they went to him, tied him tightly and brought him back to me. 'We have done what you told us,' they said, and then, on my instructions, they went off, while I myself went back to my bride, told her what had happened and asked her if she would come with me. 'Yes,' she said, and so I took her out through the subterranean vault by which I had found my way in, and we made our way on until we came to the creatures who had guided me to her.

I asked them to show me how to get home, which they did. They went with me to the seashore and put me on a ship, which, with favourable winds, took us to the city of Basra, and there my bride went to her father's house, where her family were overjoyed to see her. I myself burned musk as incense for the eagle talisman and the *'ifrits* came to me from all sides, saying: 'Here we are, master. What do you want us to do?' I told them to fetch all the wealth, precious stones and jewels that were in the City of Brass and to bring them to my house in Basra. When they had done that, I asked them to bring me the monkey, who was humble and dejected when they fetched him. 'Why did you deceive me, you damned creature?' I asked him, and then on my orders the *'ifrits* put him in a narrow brass bottle with a stopper of lead.

I and my wife have been living in happiness and joy and I now have treasures, wonderful jewels and quantities of wealth beyond all count or limit. If you want money or anything else, I will give my orders to the *'ifrits*, who will fetch it for you immediately. All that comes about through the grace of Almighty God.

The Commander of the Faithful was filled with wonder at this and he presented Muhammad with princely gifts and appropriate benefits in exchange for what Muhammad had brought him.

[Nights 299–305]

The Ebony Horse

A story is told that in the old days there was a king of great power and dignity who had three daughters, each like the shining full moon or like flowery meadows, and one son like the moon. One day, as the king was seated on his throne of state, three wise men came into his presence, one of whom had with him a golden peacock, the second a brazen trumpet and the third a horse made of ivory and ebony. 'What are these things,' asked the king, 'and what purpose do they serve?' The man with the peacock told him: 'The useful thing about this peacock is that at the end of every hour, night or day, it claps its wings and shrieks.' The man with the trumpet said: 'When this trumpet is placed over the city gate, it acts as the city's guardian, for when an enemy enters, it sounds a call so that the man can be recognized and arrested.' The man with the horse said: 'This horse is useful in that, when a man mounts it, it will take him to whatever land he wants.'

'I shall not reward you,' said the king, 'until I have tested the uses of these things.' First he tested the peacock and found that it did what its master said it would, and he followed this by testing the trumpet, with the same result. 'Ask me to grant you a wish,' he told the two wise men, to which they said: 'Our wish is that you should marry each of us to one of your daughters.' Accordingly the king gave them each a princess in marriage. The third of the trio, the man with the horse, then came forward, kissed the ground before the king and said: 'O sovereign of the age, grant me a favour in the same way that you have granted favours to my companions.' The king said that he must first test the horse, and at that the prince came forward and said: 'I shall mount it and try it out, father, to see how useful it is.' The king gave him permission to do this, and the prince came up and mounted it, but, however much he moved his legs, the horse would not budge from where it was. 'Where is this speed that you claimed for it, wise man?' the prince asked, but at that the man came up to him and showed him a screw that would make it rise in the air. 'Turn this,' he said, and when the prince turned it, the horse started to move and then flew up with him into the sky, going on and on until it was out of sight.

The prince was startled, and regretted having mounted it, telling himself that this was a trick that the man had played on him in order to get him killed. 'There is no might and no power except with God, the Exalted, the Omnipotent!' he exclaimed, and he then started to examine all the parts of the horse's body. While he was doing this, he noticed a protuberance like a cockscomb on its right shoulder and another on its left. As these were the only projections that he saw, he rubbed the one on the right shoulder of the horse, but as this made it go further up into the sky, he took his hand away. Then he looked at the knob on the left shoulder, and when he rubbed it, the horse's motion changed from a climb to a descent. It continued to come slowly down to earth, with the prince taking what care he could.

Now that he had seen how useful the horse could be, he was delighted and thanked Almighty God for the favour that He had shown him in saving him from death. His climb had taken him far above the earth and so the descent continued all day, with him turning the horse's head in whatever direction he wanted. Sometimes he would make it go down and at other times up, until, when he had got it to do all that he wanted, he took it down towards the ground. He started to look at the lands and cities there that he did not recognize, never having seen them before in his life.

Among the sights was that of a well-built city in the middle of a green and flourishing countryside with trees and rivers. He thought about this, wondering what the city's name might be and in what part of the world it lay. He started to circle around it and to reconnoitre it from right and left.

The day was coming to its end and, as the sun was about to set, he said to himself: 'I have found no better place in which to spend the night than this city. That is what I shall do and in the morning I shall go back to my family's capital and tell them all, including my father, what has happened and what I have seen.' He started to look for a place where he and the horse could stay safely out of sight, and while he was doing this he noticed in the centre of the city a palace soaring high into the sky, surrounded by extensive walls with tall battlements. 'This is a pleasant place,' he said to himself and he started to move the knob that controlled the horse's descent. It continued to take him downwards until all four of its legs rested on the flat roof of the palace.

When he had dismounted, the prince praised Almighty God and then walked round the horse, examining it and exclaiming: 'By God, the man who made you like this was wise and skilled indeed! If the Almighty extends my life and brings me back safely to my country and my family, reuniting me with my father, I shall give him the best of rewards and shower favours on him.' He remained sitting on the roof until he thought that everyone must be asleep. He was tormented by hunger and thirst, as he had eaten nothing since leaving his father, and he said to himself: 'There must be some provisions in a palace like this.' He left the horse where it was and walked away to see whether he could find something to eat, until he came across a staircase and went down. At the bottom he was impressed to find a beautifully laid-out courtyard paved with marble, but in the whole of the palace he could discover no sight nor sound of any human being. He stood in perplexity, looking right and left but having no idea where to go. 'The best thing I can do,' he told himself, 'is to go back to where I left the horse and spend the night with it. Then, in the morning, I can mount it and set off again.'

While he was telling himself this as he stood there, he suddenly noticed a light coming towards him. Looking at it more closely, he found that it came from a group of maids, among whom was a radiantly beautiful young girl like the light of the moon when full, with a slender body like the letter *alif*. She fitted the description of the poet:

She came unexpectedly in the twilight shadows,
Like the full moon on a dark horizon,
A slender girl with no match among humankind,
Most gloriously formed in the splendour of beauty.
When my eyes rested on her loveliness, I cried out:
'Glory to the One Who created man from a drop of sperm.'
I guard her from all envious eyes by the words:
'Say: I take refuge with the Lord of mankind and of the dawn.'*

This girl was the daughter of the king of the city, who was so fond of her that he had built the palace for her. If ever she felt depressed, she and her maids would go and stay there for one or two days or more, before returning to her own quarters. As it happened, she had come that night

*cf. Quran 113.1.

to amuse herself and relax, and so she was walking surrounded by her maids and accompanied by a eunuch with a sword. When they got to the palace, they spread out the furnishings, released incense from the censers, played and enjoyed themselves, but while they were doing this the prince suddenly attacked the eunuch, knocked him down and took the sword from his hand. He then turned on the maids, who scattered right and left.

When the princess saw how good-looking he was, she asked him: 'Are you perhaps the man who asked my father yesterday for my hand and was rejected because my father claimed that you were ugly? By God, he told a lie when he said that, for you are indeed a handsome man.' In fact, it had been the son of the king of India who had asked her father for her hand and had been rejected because of his ugliness. Thinking the prince to be this Indian, she went up to him, embraced and kissed him and then lay down with him. Her maids then told her: 'Lady, this is not the man who asked your father for your hand. He was ugly and this one is handsome. Your rejected suitor would not even be good enough to act as this man's servant and he must clearly be someone of high rank.'

They then went over to the eunuch who had been knocked out, and when they had revived him he jumped up in a panic and looked vainly for the sword that he had been holding. The maids told him that the man who had taken it and had knocked him down was sitting with the princess. It was she whom the king had employed him to guard, fearing that the disasters of time and the blows of fate might injure her, and so he came and lifted the curtain to find her sitting in conversation with the prince. After looking at them, he asked the prince: 'Master, are you mortal or *jinn*?' 'Damn you, you vilest of slaves,' answered the prince, 'how can you confuse the children of sovereign kings with infidel devils?' Then, with the sword in his hand, he went on: 'I am the king's son-in-law. He married me to his daughter and ordered me to consummate the marriage.' When he heard this, the eunuch said: 'Master, if you are a mortal, as you claim, then she is a fitting mate for none but you and you have a better right to her than anyone else.'

He then made his way to the king, shrieking, tearing his clothes and pouring dust on his head. On hearing the noise, the king said: 'You have alarmed me, so tell me quickly what has happened to you and be brief.' 'O king,' replied the eunuch, 'go to your daughter, for she is in the power of a *jinn* devil in the guise of a princely looking man. So seize him.' When the king heard this he thought of killing the eunuch and said: 'How could you have been so careless of my daughter as to allow this to happen to her?' Then he set off for the palace where she was, and when he arrived and found the slave girls standing there, he asked them what had happened to the princess. 'We were sitting with her,' they told him, 'when suddenly this young man rushed in at us. He was like a full moon, with the most beautiful face that we have ever seen and with a drawn sword in his hand. When we asked who he was, he claimed that you had married him to your daughter. This is all we know. We don't know whether he is human or a *jinni*, but he is chaste and well mannered and does not indulge in shameless actions.' This served to cool the king's anger and when he slowly raised the curtain he saw the prince and his daughter sitting and talking to each other. The prince, he could see, was a shapely man with a face like a gleaming full moon, but such was his jealousy for his daughter's honour that he could not restrain himself. He lifted the curtain and with a drawn sword in his hand he rushed in at them like a *ghul*.

'Is this your father?' the prince asked and, when she said yes, he jumped to his feet and, grasping his sword, he gave such a terrible shout that the king was astounded. The prince was about to attack, but the king, realizing that the young man was the more vigorous, sheathed his sword and stood still. When the prince came up to him, he addressed him courteously and said: 'Young man, are you human or a *jinni*?' 'Were it not for my respect for your authority and for your daughter's honour,' replied the prince, 'I would shed your blood. How can you think that I am related to devils when I am a descendant of sovereign kings who, if they wanted to seize your kingdom, would topple you from your throne of grandeur and rob you of all that is in your lands?' These words filled the king with awe and he feared for his life, but nevertheless he protested: 'If, as you claim, you are of royal blood, how is it that you have entered my palace without my leave and dishonoured me, approaching my daughter, pretending to be her husband and claiming that I gave her to you in marriage? I have killed kings and the sons of kings who have come as her suitors, and who can save you from my power? If I call to my slaves and retainers and tell them to kill you, they will do that on the spot and who will rescue you from me?'

When the prince heard this he told the king: 'Your blindness astonishes me. Do you hope to get a more handsome husband for your daughter than me, one more steadfast, more able to repay good or evil, or one with greater power and more troops and guards?' 'No, by God,' replied the king, 'but I would like you to ask me for her hand in front of witnesses so that I can marry her to you, for if I do this in secret it will bring disgrace on me.' 'Well spoken,' said the prince, 'but if you collect your slaves, your servants and your soldiers to fight me and they kill me, as you say they will, you will disgrace yourself, and your people will not know whether to believe what you tell them or not. My advice to you is that you should do what I am going to suggest.' The king asked what this was and the prince answered: 'What I have to say is this. Either you and I can fight a duel to the death between ourselves, with the victor having the better right to the kingdom, or you can leave me here tonight and in the morning fetch for me all your troops and your servants, letting me know how many they are.' 'I have forty thousand riders,' the king told him, 'as well as my black slaves, not counting their own followers whose numbers are the same again.' The prince said: 'Bring them out to me at dawn and tell them: "This man has asked me for my daughter's hand on condition that he comes out to fight you all, and he claims that he will defeat you and that you will prove to be powerless against him." Then leave me to fight them; if they kill me, that will keep your secret safe and protect your honour, while if I get the upper hand, I am the kind of son-in-law for whom you would wish.'

When the king heard this, he approved of the idea and accepted the prince's advice, impressed by his haughty words and alarmed by his determination to challenge the whole of the army, whose numbers had been described to him. He and the prince then sat talking until the king called for the eunuch and ordered him to go immediately to the vizier with instructions to muster the troops, who were to arm themselves and mount their horses. The eunuch carried these orders to the vizier, who, in his turn, summoned the army officers and the state dignitaries, telling them to mount and ride out carrying their arms.

So much for them, but as for the king, he continued talking with the prince and was impressed by his conversation, intelligence and culture. They were still talking when morning came, and at that point the king got up and went to take his seat on the throne. He ordered his men to mount and he supplied the prince with one of his finest horses, ordering it to be provided with the best of saddles and other equipment. The prince, however, refused to mount until he had seen the king's army for himself, and so the two of them went together to the *maidan*, where the prince got a view of the size of the army. The king then made a proclamation to the troops, saying: 'A young man has come to me to ask for my daughter's hand. I have never seen anyone more handsome, courageous or strong. He claims that he can defeat you single-handed and that, even if you numbered a hundred thousand, to him this would be no more than a few. When he comes out against you, meet him with the heads of your lances and the edges of your swords, for this is an enormous task that he has undertaken.'

The king then said to the prince: 'My son, do what you want with them,' but the prince said: 'This is not fair treatment. How can I go out against them on foot when they are all on horseback?' 'I told you to mount,' replied the king, 'but you refused. However, take your pick of the horses.' 'I don't like any of them,' the prince told him, 'and I shall mount only the horse on which I rode here.' When the king asked him where it was, he said: 'On top of your palace,' and when asked in what part of the palace, he said: 'On the flat roof.' 'This is the first sign that you are weak in the head,' the king told him. 'How the devil can a horse be on top of the roof? But we shall see now whether you're lying or telling the truth.' He turned to one of his officers and told him to go to the palace and fetch what he found on the roof.

The people there were amazed at what the prince had said and they asked one another: 'How can a horse come down the stairs from the roof? We have never heard anything like this,' but when the king's messenger climbed to the palace roof, he saw standing there the finest horse on which he had ever set eyes. He went up to investigate and found that it was made of ebony and ivory. Another of the king's officers had gone up there with him, and they laughed together at the sight of it and said: 'Was this the kind of horse that the young man was talking about? He must be mad, but this will soon become clear and he may be a man of importance.'

They lifted up the horse and carried it down to set in front of the king. People crowded round to look at it, admiring the beauty of its appearance together with its splendid saddle and bridle. The king was among its admirers, being full of astonishment at it. 'Is this your horse?' he asked the prince. 'Yes it is, your majesty,' the other replied, adding: 'And you will see how wonderfully it performs.' 'Take it and mount it then,' the king told him, but the prince said: 'Only when your troops keep their distance.' The king told them to retire for one bowshot and the prince then said: 'O king, I am about to mount my horse and then I shall charge your men, scattering them right and left and breaking their hearts.' 'Do what you want,' replied the king. 'You need not spare them, for they will not spare you.'

The prince went up to mount his horse, and the king's men drew up in ranks, telling each other that, when he came between them, they would meet him with lance points and sword edges. 'By God,' said one of them, 'this is an unlucky business. How can we kill this young man with his handsome face and his fine figure?' But another said: 'By God, it will be hard to get to him. He can only be doing this because he is sure of his courage and skill.'

When the prince was settled in his saddle, he turned the knob that would make the horse climb and they stared at him to see what he was going to do. The horse stirred and moved, curvetting in the most extraordinary manner. Its interior filled with air and then it took off and rose into the sky. On seeing this, the king called to his men: 'Catch him, damn you, before he gets away,' but his viziers and officers said: 'King, can anyone catch up with a bird in flight? This has to be a great sorcerer, may God preserve you from him, so give thanks to Him for having rescued you from his clutches.'

After what he had seen, the king returned to his palace, where he went to tell his daughter what had happened during his encounter with the prince in the *maidan*. He found her full of grief for her suitor and for having been parted from him, so much so that she fell gravely ill and kept to her bed. When her father saw her in this state, he clasped her to him, kissed her between the eyes and said: 'Daughter, give praise and thanks to God for having saved us from this cunning sorcerer.' He started to tell her again what he had seen the prince do and how he had flown up into the air, but she wouldn't listen to anything he said and only wept and sobbed the more, swearing to herself that she would neither eat nor drink until God had reunited her with him. This caused her father great concern, and his distress about her condition made him sad at heart, but the more tenderly he treated her, the deeper grew her love for the prince.

So much for them, but as for the prince, in his solitary flight through the air he remembered the princess's beauty and grace, and as he had asked the king's companions to tell him the name of the city as well as the names of the king and his daughter, he knew that the city was San'a'. He pressed on with his journey until he came near his father's city and, after circling around it, he made for his father's palace and landed on its flat roof, where he left the horse. When he went down and entered his father's presence, he found him sad and distressed at the loss of his son, but on seeing him come in, his father rose to greet him, embraced him and hugged him to his chest in delight.

The prince then asked his father what had happened to the wise man who had made the horse. 'May God give him no blessing,' said the king.

'That was an unlucky hour in which I saw him, as it was he who caused you to leave me, and since then he has been in prison.' The prince gave orders for him to be freed, taken from prison and brought before him. When the wise man came, the king presented him with a robe to show his favour, but although the king showered gifts on him, he refused him his daughter's hand. This made the man furiously angry and he regretted what he had done, realizing that the prince had discovered the secret of the horse and knew how to set it in motion. The king then advised his son not to go near the horse again or ever to mount it from that day on, adding: 'You don't know all its qualities and you have been tricked by it.'

The prince had told his father about what had happened to him with the princess and her father, the ruler of San'a'. 'Had the king wanted to kill you, he would have done so,' his father told him, adding: 'But you were not destined to die so soon.' The prince, however, filled with anxiety because of his love for the princess, went to the horse, mounted it and after he had turned the knob to make it climb, up it flew, high into the sky. Next morning, when the king went to look for him, he was not to be found and, full of concern, the king climbed up to the palace roof only to see his son soaring into the sky. In distress at his loss the king bitterly regretted not having hidden the horse away, and he promised himself that, if his son returned, he would put his mind at ease by destroying it, and he then started to weep and wail again, in sorrow for him.

So much for him, but as for the prince, he flew on until he came to San'a', and then landed on the roof where he had come down the first time. Taking care to keep under cover, he went to the room of the princess, but he could find neither her, her maids nor her former guard, the eunuch. In his distress he searched the palace for her until he discovered her in a different room, lying in bed and surrounded by maids and nurses. He went in and greeted them, and at the sound of his voice she got up, embraced him and started to kiss him between the eyes and to clasp him to her bosom. 'My lady,' he said, 'you have left me lonely all this time.' 'It was you who left me lonely,' she replied, 'and had you stayed away any longer, there is no doubt that I would have died.' He said: 'My lady, what do you think of my behaviour to your father and of how he acted to me? Had it not been for my love for you, who are the temptation of all mankind, I would have killed him and made an example of him for all to see, but as I love you, so I love him for your sake.' 'How could you leave me,' she asked, 'and how could there be any pleasure for me in life when you are gone?' 'Will you obey me and follow what I say?' he asked.

'Say what you want,' she replied, 'for I will agree to whatever you propose and not disobey you in anything.' 'Then come with me to my own kingdom,' he said. 'Willingly,' she told him.

The prince was overjoyed to hear this. He took her by the hand and, after getting her to swear a solemn oath that she had agreed to this, he led her to the flat roof at the top of the castle, where he mounted the horse and took her up behind him. He kept a tight grip on her, and after tying her firmly in place he moved the knob on the horse's shoulder to make it rise. When it took off with them, the maids cried out, alerting the princess's father and mother, who rushed up to the roof. Looking upwards the king saw the ebony horse flying off into the air with the eloping pair, and as he became increasingly agitated, he called out: 'Prince, for God's sake have pity on me and on my wife and do not part us from our daughter.' The prince made no reply, but, thinking to himself that the princess might regret leaving her mother and father, he asked her: 'O temptation of the age, would you like me to return you to your parents?' 'By God, my lord,' she replied, 'I don't want that, and what I do want is to be with you wherever you are, as my love for you has distracted me from everything else, even my mother and father.'

When the prince heard that, he was delighted and he made the horse travel at an easy pace so as not to alarm her. He flew on with her until he caught sight of a green meadow with a stream of running water gushing from a spring. There the two landed and after they had eaten and drunk, the prince remounted and tied the princess on behind him lest she fall. He then set off with her again and flew on until, to his great delight, he reached his father's city. He wanted to show her the seat of his father's power and to let her see that his kingdom was larger than that of her father, so he landed with her in one of the orchards where the king used to go for relaxation. He took her to a garden house that was kept ready for his father, and there at the door he left the ebony horse, telling her to look after it and saying: 'Stay here until I send a messenger to you, for I am going to my father to prepare a palace for you and to show you my kingdom.'

Hearing this, the joyful princess said: 'Do as you want,' as she realized that her entrance was to be made with the pomp and ceremony that suited one of her rank. So the prince set off, leaving her behind, and on his arrival at the city he went in to greet his father, who was delighted to see him and welcomed him warmly. The prince told him that he had brought the princess about whom he had spoken earlier. 'I have left her outside the city in an orchard,' he explained, 'and I have come to tell you so that you can prepare a procession and go out to meet her and show her your kingdom, your army and your guards.' The king willingly agreed to this and gave immediate orders for the city to be adorned with decorations. He himself, in all his pomp and splendour, rode out with all his troops, the dignitaries of his state, as well as his other officials and servants. From his own palace the prince brought out jewellery and robes and other things that are found in royal treasuries. He prepared for the princess a litter covered with green, red and yellow brocade, on which were seated Indian, Rumi and Abyssianian slave girls, together with an astonishing display of treasures. Then, leaving this with its attendants, he went on ahead to the garden house where he had deposited the princess, but although he searched through it he could not find either her or the horse. He struck himself on the face, tore his clothes and started to wander around the orchard.

At first he was bemused, but later, returning to his senses, he asked himself how she could have learned the horse's secret, when he had told her nothing at all about it. He then thought that perhaps the Persian sorcerer who had made it had come across her and had taken her in revenge for what his father had done to him. He asked the guards of the orchard whether anyone had passed them and they said: 'We have seen no one enter apart from the Persian sorcerer who went in to collect healing herbs.' When the prince heard that, he knew for certain that this was the man who had taken the girl.

As had been predestined, when the prince had left the princess in the garden house and had gone to his father's palace to make his preparations, the Persian had come to the orchard to collect healing herbs. He had detected a scent of musk and perfume filling the place and emanating from the princess. He went towards the source of the scent and when he came to the garden house he saw the horse that he had made with his own hands standing by the door. He was delighted by this, as its loss had been a great sorrow for him. He went up to it and found, after a thorough inspection, that it was undamaged. He was about to mount it and ride off when it occurred to him that he should look to see what the prince had brought and left there. So he went in and found the princess seated like the bright sun in a cloudless sky. When he saw her, he realized that here was a lady of high rank whom the prince had brought there on the horse, and that he must have left her while he went to the city in order to come back with a procession to escort her in with pomp and ceremony.

He then went in and kissed the ground before her. She looked up and found, on inspection, that here was a very ugly man of loathsome appearance. She asked him who he was and he said: 'My lady, I am a messenger from the prince. He sent me to you with orders to bring you to another orchard close to the city.' When she heard that, she asked where the prince himself was and he replied: 'He is with his father in the city and he is about to come now with a great procession.' 'Could he find no one to send me except you?' she asked, at which he laughed and said: 'My lady, don't be deceived by my ugly face and my unpleasant appearance. Were you to get from me what the prince has got, you would praise me. It was because of my ugliness and my frightening shape that he picked me as his messenger to you, both out of his jealousy for your reputation and because of his love for you. For otherwise he has vast quantities of mamluks, black slaves, pages, eunuchs and retainers.'

This convinced the princess and led her to believe him. So she got up, put her hand in his and asked: 'Father, what have you brought with you for me to ride?' 'Lady,' he replied, 'you can ride the horse on which you came.' 'I can't do that on my own,' she told him, at which he smiled, realizing that she was in his power, and he then told her that he would ride with her himself. He mounted and took her up behind him, keeping a tight grip on her and tying her securely in her place, ignorant as she was of his intentions. He moved the knob to make the horse rise, its interior filled with air, it stirred and moved and it then rose up into the air, flying on until it had left the city behind.

'Man,' said the princess, 'this is not what you told me about the prince when you claimed that he had sent you to me.' 'May God defile him,' answered the Persian, 'for he is a disgusting, sordid fellow.' 'Damn you,' she said, 'how dare you disobey an order given to you by your master?' 'He is not my master,' the Persian said, adding: 'Do you know who I am?' She told him that all she knew was what he had told her about himself, to which he replied: 'What I told you was a trick that I was playing on you and on the prince. I was about to spend the rest of my life grieving for this horse that you are riding. I made it myself, only to have the prince get hold of it, but now I have both it and you and I have burned his heart as he burned mine. He will never possess it again, but you can console yourself and be happy, for I shall be of more use to you than he would be.'

When the princess heard this, she slapped herself in the face and called out: 'O sorrow, I have lost my beloved and I did not stay with my father and mother.' While she wept bitterly over what had happened to her, the Persian flew on with her to the land of Rum and then landed in a green meadow with streams and trees. This was near the city of an important king, who, as it happened, had gone out that day to enjoy himself hunting. He was passing by the meadow when he saw the Persian standing there with the horse and the girl beside him. Before the Persian knew what was going on, the king's slaves took him by surprise and brought him before the king, together with the girl and the horse. The king looked at the Persian's ugliness and his unprepossessing appearance and then at the beauty and grace of the girl. He asked her: 'My lady, what is the relationship between this old man and you?' The Persian promptly replied: 'She is my wife and my cousin,' but, on hearing this, the princess gave him the lie and exclaimed: 'By God, your majesty, I don't know him and he is no husband of mine! He used trickery to seize me by force.' When the king heard this, he ordered the Persian to be beaten, and so severe was the beating that he almost died. On the king's orders he was carried to the city and thrown into prison. The king then took the princess and the horse with him, but he didn't know how to set it in motion.

So much for the Persian and the princess, but as for the prince, he put on travelling clothes, took what money he needed and set off on his travels in a state of great despondency. He moved quickly, trying to follow the trail of the princess from town to town and city to city, asking about the ebony horse, but everyone who heard him talk about it wondered at him, thinking that he was talking nonsense. He went on like this for some time, but in spite of his investigations and the number of questions that he asked, he could get no news of the missing pair. He then came to the city of the princess's father but, although he asked about her there, he heard no news and found her father grieving for her loss. He went back and set out for the land of Rum, still trying to track down his quarry and putting his questions.

As it happened, he stopped in a *khan* where he noticed a group of merchants sitting and talking. He took a seat near them and heard one tell his companions that he had just come across something remarkable. When they asked him what this was, he said: 'I was in a certain part of such-and-such a city' – and he gave the name of the city where the princess was – 'when I heard the people there telling an extraordinary tale of how the king had gone out hunting one day with a number of his companions and state dignitaries. When they reached open country they passed by a green meadow where they found a man standing with a girl seated beside him, and with him there was a horse made of ebony. He was an ugly-looking fellow of formidable appearance, while she was a beautiful and graceful girl, radiantly perfect with an excellent figure. The ebony horse was a wonder and no one has ever seen anything more handsome or better constructed.' 'What did the king do with them?' the other merchants asked, and their companion said: 'He took the man and asked him about the girl, whom he then claimed to be his wife and cousin, but she said that this was a lie. So the king took her from him and ordered him to be beaten and thrown into prison, but I don't know what happened to the ebony horse.'

When the prince heard this he went up to the man and started to question him courteously and politely until he was told the name of the city and of the king. When he had got this information he spent a joyful night, and in the morning he set off and continued on his way until he reached the city. He was about to go in when the gatekeepers stopped him. They wanted to take him before the king so that he might be asked about his circumstances, his reason for coming to the city and what skills he had as a craftsman, these being questions that it was the king's custom to put to strangers. The prince had arrived in the evening, and as this was a time when no one could enter the king's presence or consult with him, the gatekeepers took him to the prison, intending to leave him there. The gaolers, however, seeing how handsome he was, had no wish to imprison him, and so they made him sit with them outside the prison itself, and when food was brought for them, he ate with them until he had had enough.

After they had finished eating, they started talking and, turning to the prince, they asked him where he came from. 'From Persia, the land of the Chosroes,' he told them. They laughed and one of them said: 'I have listened to stories and accounts of many peoples, Persian, and I have seen for myself their circumstances, but I have never seen or heard a bigger liar than the Persian whom we are holding in prison here at the moment,' to which another added: 'Nor have I ever seen an uglier and more loathsome-looking man.' 'What obvious lies has he told?' asked the prince, and they told him: 'He claims to be a sorcerer. The king saw him when he was out hunting. He had with him a remarkably beautiful and graceful girl, radiantly perfect and well shaped, together with a horse made of black ebony, as fine a thing as I have ever seen. The girl is with the king, who is in love with her, but she is mad. Had the man been a sorcerer, as he claims, he would have cured her, for the king is desperately looking for some remedy for her and is trying to cure her madness. The ebony horse is in the royal treasury and the ugly man who was with the girl is here with us in prison. In the dark of night he weeps and wails in self-pity and doesn't allow us to sleep.'

It occurred to the prince that he could try to arrange things so as to reach his goal, and when the gaolers wanted to sleep, they brought him into the prison and shut the door on him. He then heard the sorcerer weeping and lamenting to himself in Persian, saying as he wailed: 'Alas for the wrong that I did to myself and to the prince, and for what I did with the girl, as I neither left her behind nor got what I wanted. It was all because of my mismanagement. I tried to get what I didn't deserve and wasn't proper for a man like me, and whoever does this meets the kind of disaster into which I have fallen.' On hearing this, the prince spoke to him in Persian and said: 'How long are you going to go on weeping and wailing? Do you think that what has happened to you has never happened to anyone else?' The sorcerer, listening to him, was glad of his company and complained to him of the miserable plight in which he found himself.

The next morning the gatekeepers took the prince to their king, explaining that he had arrived at the city the previous day too late to be presented to him. The king asked him from where he had come, his name and profession and the reason for his coming to the city, to which the prince replied: 'My name is a Persian one, Harja; my native land is Persia; and I am a man of learning, particularly in the field of medicine. I can cure the sick and the mad, and for this reason I travel through regions and cities in order to add to my knowledge, and when I see a sick person I treat him, as this is my profession.' The king was delighted to hear this and said: 'Excellent doctor, you have come to us just when you are needed.' He then went on to tell the prince about the girl, promising that if through his treatment he could cure her madness, he could have anything that he asked for. When he heard this, the prince said: 'May God ennoble you, describe the symptoms of her madness that you have seen and tell me how many days ago it was that this affected her and also how you got hold of her, together with the horse and the sorcerer.'

The king told him the whole story from beginning to end, adding that the sorcerer was in prison, and when the prince then asked him about the horse, the king said that it was in one of the palace apartments. The prince thought to himself that the prudent thing to do would be to start by inspecting the horse, for if it turned out to be sound and uninjured, then he would have all that he wanted, whereas if it no longer worked he would have to think of some other way of saving himself. He turned to the king and said: 'Your majesty, I must look at this horse you mentioned to see whether I can find anything in it that might help me cure the girl.' The king willingly gave him permission and, getting up, he took him by the hand and led him to the horse. The prince walked around inspecting it, and after checking its condition, he was delighted to discover that it was intact and undamaged. He then told the king that he would like to examine the girl, adding: 'If Almighty God wills it, I hope that I may be able to cure her by means of this horse,' and advising him to look after it carefully. The king took him to the room where the princess was, and when he went in he found her stamping and falling on the ground, as she had kept on doing, not because she was mad but to keep anyone from approaching her.

When the prince saw her in this state he said: 'O temptation of all mankind, all is well with you,' and he went on speaking to her soothingly and gently before revealing himself to her. When she recognized him, she let out a great cry before fainting from joy, while the king thought that it was through fear of him that she had collapsed. The prince then put his mouth to her ear and said: 'Temptation of all mankind, be careful not to shed my blood and your own. Wait patiently and show strength of mind, for we need patience here as well as good and subtle planning if we are to escape from this tyrant. My scheme is to go to him and tell him that what you are suffering from is something caused by an evil spirit. I shall guarantee to cure you on condition that he remove your fetters, after which the spirit will leave you. When he then comes to see you, talk to him sweetly so that he may think that I have cured you, and we can then achieve all that we want.' 'To hear is to obey,' she replied, after which he went joyfully to the king and said: 'Fortunate king, through your auspicious help I discovered what the girl's disease was and how to treat it, as a result of which I have cured her for you. Come and visit her now, but talk to her gently and treat her with kindness, promising her whatever will please her, as all that you want from her is yours.'

The king got up and went in to visit the princess, who, on seeing him, rose, kissed the ground in front of him and welcomed him. He was delighted by this and gave orders for slave girls and eunuchs to come to attend on her, take her to the baths and provide her with jewellery and robes.

They came in to greet her and she returned their greeting gracefully and eloquently. Then they dressed her in royal robes, put a jewelled necklace round her neck and took her off to the baths, where they waited on her, and when they brought her out she was like the full moon. She went to the king, greeted him and kissed the ground before him. So great was his joy that he told the prince: 'All this is thanks to the blessings you have brought; may God grant us more of your favours.' 'Your majesty,' replied the prince, 'in order to complete and perfect her cure you should go out yourself with all your guards and your troops to the place where you found her, taking the ebony horse that was with her so that I may remove the evil spirit from her by a charm, imprison it and kill it so as to keep it from ever returning to her.'

The king agreed willingly and he had the ebony horse taken out to the meadow where he had found the princess, the horse and the Persian sorcerer. He himself rode there with his troops, taking the princess with him, but they did not know what the prince intended to do. He, for his part, acting in his role as sorcerer, gave orders, when they reached the meadow, that the king and his men should stay almost out of sight of the girl and the horse. He said: 'With your permission, your majesty, I shall release incense and recite a charm so as to imprison the evil spirit and prevent it from ever coming back to her again. Then I shall mount the ebony horse and take her up behind me. When I do that, the horse will be stirred into a walk; I shall come across to you and, as the cure will then be complete, you can do whatever you want with her.' The king was delighted to hear this and he and all his men watched as the prince mounted the horse and took the girl up behind him. He held her tightly and, after tying her firmly in place, he turned the screw to make the horse take off. It climbed into the air, watched by the soldiers until it went out of sight. For half a day the king waited, expecting the prince to return, but at last, when this did not happen, he despaired and, filled with regret and sorrow for the loss of the princess, he went back with his troops to his city.

So much for him, but as for the prince, he made joyfully for his father's city, where he landed on his palace. He left the princess there, making sure of her safety, after which he went to his father and mother, greeted them and delighted them by telling them of her arrival.

So much for the prince, the horse and the princess, but as for the king of Rum, when he got back to his city he shut himself away in sorrow and dejection. His viziers visited him and started to question him, pointing out that the man who had carried off the girl was a sorcerer and that the king should thank God for having saved him from his magical wiles. They continued to comfort the king until he was consoled for her loss.

As for the prince, he gave magnificent banquets for the townspeople, who spent a whole month celebrating his wedding. The marriage was then consummated and the bride and bridegroom were happy with one another. The prince's father smashed the ebony horse, destroying its workings, while the prince wrote to the bride's father, telling him about her, that he had married her and that she was in the best of states, as well as giving his messenger precious gifts and treasures to take to him. When the messenger reached his city, San'a' in Yemen, he handed them, together with the prince's letter, to the king, who was filled with joy when he read it. He accepted the gifts, treated the messenger honourably and prepared a splendid present for his son-in-law, which he sent back with the messenger. On his return the man told the prince how pleased the king of San'a' had been to receive news of his daughter, and the prince, in his turn, was delighted to hear this.

The prince wrote every year to his father-in-law and sent him presents, and they continued in this way until the prince's father died and the prince succeeded to the throne. He treated his subjects justly, conducting himself in a way that won their approval, exercising authority and commanding obedience throughout his lands and among his people. They continued like this, enjoying the most delightful and pleasant of lives in luxury and health, until they were visited by the destroyer of delights and the parter of companions. Praise be to the living God, Who does not die and in Whose hands lie power and sovereignty.

[Nights 357–71]

'Ali, the Cairene Merchant

A story is told that there was a wealthy merchant in Cairo named Hasan al-Jauhari al-Baghdadi, a man with huge resources of money, as well as innumerable jewels, precious stones and properties. God had provided him with a handsome son, well built, rosy-cheeked, a splendid youth, the acme of beauty. His father named him 'Ali al-Misri and had him taught the Quran, scientific studies, eloquence and literature until he became outstandingly learned. It then happened that his father, under whose supervision his son had been working as a trader, fell ill and his condition worsened until he was sure that he was about to die. He summoned his son, 'Ali al-Misri, and said: 'My son, this world passes away but the next world remains. Every living creature must taste death, and as my own is near at hand, I want to give you some instructions. If you act on them, you will remain safe and happy until you meet Almighty God, while if you do not, you will accumulate troubles and have cause to regret not having followed them.' 'Ali said: 'How could I possibly not listen to you and act as you tell me, when it is an obligation and a duty for me to hear and obey you?'

Hasan then went on: 'My son, I have left you properties, estates, goods and huge quantities of money, so much so that were you to spend five hundred dinars a day, it would not make a hole in the total. In return, you must show piety towards God and follow His chosen Prophet, may God bless him and give him peace, by keeping to what tradition has recorded of his commands and prohibitions. Be assiduous in acting well, doing good and associating with the virtuous and the learned. You must look after the poor and needy and avoid stinginess, miserly conduct and associating with doubtful characters and evil men. Treat your servants and your family with kindness and do the same with your wife. She comes from a noble family and is pregnant with your child, and it may be that God will provide you, through her, with virtuous descendants.'

Hasan continued to exhort his son, weeping and saying: 'I pray to the generous God, Lord of the throne, the Omnipotent, to save you, my son, from any difficulty into which you may fall and provide you with a speedy release from troubles.' 'Ali for his part wept bitterly and said: 'What you say dissolves me with grief because you seem to be saying goodbye.' 'Yes,' said his father, 'for I know the state I am in. Do not forget my instructions.' Then he started to pronounce the confession of faith and to recite verses from the Quran, until, when he was at the point of death, he told his son to come near. When he did so, his father kissed him and gave a last sigh. Then his soul left his body and was received into the mercy of Almighty God.

'Ali was stricken with grief and the house was filled with noisy wailing. Hasan's friends gathered around him and 'Ali prepared his body for burial, rendering the last honours to him. He had the bier carried out with all pomp to where prayers were said over him, and then on to the cemetery, where the appropriate passages of the Quran were recited as he was buried. The mourners then returned to his house and paid 'Ali their condolences before going on their way. 'Ali had the Friday ceremonies of mourning and the recitations of the entire Quran performed for forty days, during which he stayed at home, only going out in order to pray. On Fridays he would visit the grave and he continued praying, reciting the Quran and performing acts of devotion until his companions from among the other young merchants came to visit him. 'How long are you going to go on mourning,' they asked, 'while you neglect your own affairs and your trade, as well as abandoning your friends? This is going on too long and doing an increasing amount of harm to your health.' When they came to him, their associate was Iblis, the damned, who was whispering to them.

They began to encourage 'Ali to go off with them to the market, and again it was Iblis who tempted him to agree so that he left the house in their company. 'Mount your mule,' they told him, 'and come with us to such-and-such an orchard, where we can enjoy ourselves and you can shed your cares and sorrows.' So 'Ali mounted his mule and, taking his slave with him, he set off with them to the orchard to which they were headed. When they arrived, one of them went to prepare a meal, which he brought there, and they ate happily and then sat talking until the end of the day, when they mounted and rode off, each to spend the night in his own house. The next morning they came back and told 'Ali to come with them. 'Where to?' he asked, and they told him that they were going to another orchard, more attractive and more pleasant than the first one. 'Ali went there with them, and on their arrival one of them went and prepared a meal, which he brought to the orchard, together with strong wine. They ate and then produced the wine, telling 'Ali: 'This is what removes care and burnishes pleasure.' They kept on encouraging him to indulge until they overcame his scruples and he joined them in drinking. They stayed talking and drinking until the end of the day and then went home. 'Ali, whose head was spinning because of what he had drunk, went to his wife's room and when she saw him in this state she asked why he was so changed. 'We were enjoying ourselves today,' he told her, 'when one of our friends brought us something to drink. I drank with the others and felt giddy.' His wife said: 'Have you forgotten your father's injunction and done what he told you not to do by associating with men of dubious reputation?' 'These aren't doubtful characters,' he told her, 'but young merchants, men with comfortable fortunes.'

He continued to go out with his friends day after day, visiting place after place, eating and drinking, until they said to him: 'We have all done our turns and now it is yours.' He agreed to this willingly and the next morning he produced the necessary food and drink in twice the quantity that the others had done and he took with him cooks, attendants and coffee-makers. They made their way to al-Rauda and the Nilometer and there they stayed for a whole month, eating, drinking, listening to music and enjoying themselves. At the end of the month 'Ali discovered that he had spent a sizeable amount of money, but Iblis, the damned, deluded him, saying: 'If you spent this much every day you would be no less wealthy.' As a result he paid no attention to his expenditure and carried on in the same way for three years in spite of the advice of his wife, who kept reminding him of what his father had said.

He paid no attention to her until he had used up all the ready cash that he had. Then he began to sell his jewels and spend what he got from them until this too was exhausted, after which he turned to his houses and property, until there was nothing of these left at all. Next came his estates and orchards, which he disposed of one after the other, and when these had gone he was left with nothing apart from the house in which he lived. He started to pull out its marble and its timbers, spending the money that these fetched until this too had gone, and then, when he was left with no source of spending money, he sold the house itself and spent what he got for it. Its purchaser told him to find somewhere else to live as he needed the house for himself. On thinking the matter over, 'Ali decided that he had no need of a house except as a place for his wife, who had presented him with a son and a daughter. He had no servants left, and as there was only himself and his family he took a large room in a courtyard, and, after having been pampered in splendour with quantities of servants and wealth, he lived there, no longer having money enough for his daily bread. 'This was what I used to warn you about,' said his wife, 'and I kept telling you to remember your father's instructions, but you wouldn't listen to me and there is no might and no power except with God, the Exalted, the Omnipotent. How are your little children going to be fed? Get up and go round your friends, the young merchants, and maybe they will give you something for today's food.'

So 'Ali got up and went to his friends, one after the other, but they refused to see him, heaping painful insults on him and refusing to give him anything. He went back and told this to his wife, who went to her neighbours to beg them to give her some food for that day. She went in to see a woman whom she had known in the old days and when she entered, the woman, seeing the state that she was in, welcomed her, shed tears and asked what had happened to her. So 'Ali's wife told her everything that her husband had done and the woman repeated her welcome and insisted that she come to her for all she needed, with no question of anything being asked in return. 'Ali's wife thanked her and was then given enough to see her and her family through an entire month. Taking this, she set off home and when 'Ali saw her he wept and asked her where she had got it. 'From So-and-So,' she told him, 'for when I let her know what had happened to us, she was generosity itself and told me to ask her for anything that we needed.' 'As you have this support,' said her husband, 'I can go off somewhere in the hope that Almighty God may grant us relief.'

He took his leave of his wife, kissed his children and left without knowing where he was going, walking on until he came to Bulaq, where he saw a ship that was going to Damietta. A man who had been a friend of his father's caught sight of him and greeted him, asking where he was off to. 'Damietta,' 'Ali replied, adding: 'I want to make enquiries about some friends of mine and visit them before coming back.' The man took him home, entertained him and provided him with provisions as well as some cash before seeing him on board the ship. When it reached Damietta, 'Ali disembarked and went off, still with no idea where he was going, but as he was walking a merchant saw him and, taking pity on him, took him to his house. 'Ali stayed with this man for some time, but at last he asked himself how long he was going to continue sitting in other people's houses. He went out and found a ship that was about to sail to Syria. His host gave him provisions and brought him on board, after which 'Ali set off and eventually reached Damascus.

As he was tramping the streets of Damascus he was seen by a virtuous man who brought him to his house, where he stayed for a time. Then, when he had gone out, he came across a caravan that was leaving for Baghdad. He went back to take his leave of the merchant with whom he had been staying and he then set off with the caravan. Almighty God, glory be to Him, inspired another merchant with pity for him, and 'Ali continued to eat and drink with this man until the caravan was only a day's journey from Baghdad. It was then attacked by highwaymen, who seized everything it was carrying, and each of the few who escaped made for some place of refuge. 'Ali himself headed for Baghdad, which he reached at sunset, arriving as the gatekeepers were about to shut the gate. He called to them to let him in, which they did, and they then asked him where he was from and where he was going. 'I've come from Cairo,' he told them, 'and I had with me merchants, laden mules, slaves and servants. I went on ahead of them to look for somewhere to store my goods, but as I did so and was riding on my mule, a band of highwaymen intercepted me. They took my mule and my goods and I was at my last gasp when I managed to escape from them.'

The gatekeepers gave him a hospitable welcome and invited him to pass the night with them, saying that in the morning they would look out somewhere suitable for him. 'Ali hunted in his pocket and found a dinar left over from the ones that he had been given by the merchant in Bulaq. He gave this to one of the gatekeepers and told him to take it and spend it on something for them to eat. The man went off to the market and used the money to buy bread and cooked meat, which they all ate together, after which 'Ali spent the night with them. The next morning one of them took him off to a merchant in the city, to whom he told the story. The man believed it and, thinking 'Ali to be a trader himself, coming with merchandise, he showed him his shop and treated him with respect. He then sent to his house for a splendid robe and took him to the baths.

'ALI SAID:

When we came out he took me back home, where he provided me with a meal, and after eating we relaxed. My host then told one of his slaves to take me off and show me two houses in such-and-such a quarter and to give me the key of whichever of them I preferred. The two of us set off and came to a street in which there were three new houses standing side by side. They were locked and the slave opened the first of them, which I looked around, and when we came out we went and inspected the second. 'Which key do you want me to give you?' the slave asked, but I said: 'Whose is this big house?' 'Ours,' he said, and so I told him to open it up for me to look at. 'You don't want to have anything to do with that one,' the slave told me, and when I asked why, he told me that *jinn* lived there, adding: 'Whoever spends the night in it is found dead next morning. We don't open the door to bring out the corpse, but we have to go up to the roof of one of the other houses and fetch it out that way. This is why my master has left it empty, saying that he is not going to give it to anyone again.' I told him to open it for me to inspect, saying to myself: 'This is what I've been looking for. I shall spend the night here and by morning I shall be dead, having found relief from my present ills.' The slave unlocked the door, and when I went in, I found that it was a place of incomparable splendour. 'This is the one I choose,' I said, 'so give me the key.' 'Not before I have consulted my master,' he replied.

Then the slave went back to his master and told him: 'The Egyptian merchant says that he will only live in the big house.'

The owner came to 'Ali and told him that he shouldn't stay there, but 'Ali insisted, saying that he wasn't worried by the gossip. The owner told him to draw up a document stating that, were anything to happen to 'Ali, the owner himself would not have any responsibility for it. 'Ali agreed, and after a court witness had been summoned a document was written and kept by the owner, who then handed over the key to 'Ali. He took it and went into the house, to which the owner sent a slave with bedding, which he spread out over a bench behind the door before going back.

When 'Ali went in, he saw a well in the courtyard of the house and over it was suspended a bucket. He lowered this into the well, filled it and used it to perform the ritual ablution, and after the obligatory prayer he sat down for a time. A slave then brought him his evening meal from the owner's house, together with a lamp, a candle and a candlestick, as well as a bowl, a ewer and a jug, before leaving him and going home. 'Ali lit the candle and ate his meal, after which he relaxed before performing the evening prayer. He then told himself: 'Come on, take the bedding upstairs and sleep up there, as that will be better than sleeping here.' So he did this, and upstairs he found a huge room with a gilded ceiling and a floor and walls of coloured marble.

He spread out his bedding and sat reading a portion of the glorious Quran when he was taken unawares by a voice that called out to him: '‘Ali, son of Hasan, shall I send you down the gold?' ‘Ali asked where this gold might be, but before he had finished, gold poured down as though shot from a mangonel, and it kept on falling until it had filled the room. When this had stopped, the voice said: 'Now set me free so that I can go on my way, as my service is done and I have given you what was left in trust for you.' 'In the Name of God, the Omnipotent,' said ‘Ali, 'I conjure you to tell me how this gold comes to be here.' 'Since ancient times,' the voice replied, 'it has been kept for you by a talismanic spell. I come to everyone who enters this house and say: "‘Ali, son of Hasan, shall I send you down the gold?" This terrifies them and they cry out, after which I come down and break their necks, and then leave. But when you came and I called out your name and that of your father, asking you whether to send down the gold, and you asked where it was, I realized that you were its rightful owner and sent it down. There is another treasure waiting for you in Yemen, and were you to go and get it before coming back here, it would be better for you. Now I want you to set me free so that I may go on my way.' 'By God,' said ‘Ali, 'I am not going to free you until you fetch me the Yemeni treasure.' 'If I do that,' said the voice, 'will you free me and free the servant of the other treasure?' ‘Ali agreed and was asked to swear to this, which he did.

The servant of the treasure was then about to set off when ‘Ali said: 'There's something else that I want you to do for me.' 'What is that?' asked the other, and ‘Ali said: 'I have a wife and children in such-and-such a place in Cairo and I want you to fetch them to me gently and without harm.' 'God willing, I shall bring them with due pomp on a litter attended by eunuchs and servants together with the treasure from Yemen,' said the servant, who asked for three days' leave, promising that by the end of this time ‘Ali would have everything delivered to him. He then left, and in the morning ‘Ali went round the room to see whether he could find a safe place in which to store the gold. The room had a dais at whose edge he saw a marble slab with a screw set in it, and when he turned this the slab slid away to reveal a door. ‘Ali opened it, and when he entered he discovered a large chamber containing sacks made from materials sewn together. He started to take these, fill them with gold and carry them to the chamber until he had transferred the whole pile of gold and put it there. Then he shut the door and turned the screw so that the slab went back to its place, after which he went down to sit on the bench behind the front door.

While he was sitting there, a knock came at the door and when he had got up and opened it he found the owner's slave. When the man saw him sitting there, he hurried back to his master to give him the good news, telling him: 'The trader who stayed in the haunted house is safe and sound and is sitting on the bench behind the front door.' His master got up joyfully and set off for the house, taking with him food for breakfast. When he saw 'Ali, he embraced him, kissed him between the eyes and asked how he had got on. 'Ali told him: 'All went well and I slept upstairs in the marble chamber.' 'Did anything approach you or did you see anything?' the man asked. 'No,' replied 'Ali. 'I recited some passages from the glorious Quran and then slept until morning, when I got up, performed the ritual ablution and prayed, after which I came down and sat on this bench.' 'Praise be to God that you are safe,' he said, after which he got up and left 'Ali, and then sent him slaves, mamluks and slave girls, together with household effects. They swept out the house from top to bottom and furnished it in lavish style, after which three of the mamluks, together with three black slaves and four slave girls, stayed to serve him while the rest went back to their master's house. When the other merchants heard about him, they sent him all kinds of valuable gifts, including food, drink and clothing, and they took him to sit with them in the market. They asked him when his merchandise would arrive, and he told them that this would be after three days. At the end of the three days, the servant of the first treasure, who had poured down the gold for him, came to him and said: 'Get up and see the treasure that I have brought you from Yemen, together with your family. Part of the treasure comes in the form of precious merchandise, but everything that accompanies it in the way of mules, horses, camels, eunuchs and mamluks consists of *jinn*.'

When the servant of the treasure reached Cairo, he had found that in 'Ali's absence his wife and children had been reduced to nakedness and ever-increasing hunger. He carried them away from their lodging and out of Cairo on a litter, and provided them with magnificent clothes from the Yemeni treasure. When he returned to tell 'Ali of that, 'Ali went to invite the Baghdadi merchants to come out of the city with him to meet the caravan that was carrying his goods, adding: 'Do me the honour of bringing your wives in order to meet mine.' 'To hear is to obey,' they said, and after sending for their wives, they sat talking in one of the orchards of the city.

While they were doing this, a dust cloud was seen rising from the heart of the desert. They got up to see what had caused it, and when it cleared, under it could be seen mules, men, baggage handlers, servants and lantern bearers. They were coming forward singing and dancing, and the leader of the baggage handlers came up to 'Ali, kissed his hand and said: 'We have been delayed on the road, sir. We had intended to enter the city yesterday, but we had to wait for four days in the same place for fear of highwaymen, until Almighty God dispersed them for us.'

The Baghdadi merchants got up, mounted their mules and accompanied the caravan, while their wives waited for 'Ali's family to mount and go with them. They entered Baghdad in a great procession, with the merchants admiring the mules loaded with chests, and their wives admiring the dress of 'Ali's wife and the clothes of her children, saying to each other: 'Not even the ruler of Baghdad or any other king, noble, or merchant has clothes like these.' The procession continued on its way, the men with 'Ali and the women with his family, until they came to his house, where they dismounted. The laden mules were led into the centre of the courtyard, where their loads were removed and placed in the storerooms. The women went with 'Ali's family to the upper room, which they found resembled a luxuriant garden, magnificently furnished, and here they sat in happy enjoyment until noon, when a meal of the most magnificent foods and sweetmeats was brought to them. They ate and tasted the most splendid of drinks, and afterwards used rosewater and incense to perfume themselves. The company then took leave of 'Ali, and both men and women went back to their own houses. When they had got home, the men began to send the kind of presents to 'Ali that matched their own wealth, while the women sent gifts of their own to his family. As a result, he and his wife collected a large number of slave girls, slaves and mamluks, as well as accumulating stores of all kinds such as grain, sugar and other goods past all number.

The owner of the house, the Baghdadi merchant, did not leave 'Ali but stayed and said: 'Let the slaves and the servants take the mules and the other animals to another house to rest,' but 'Ali told him: 'They are going to such-and-such a place tonight.' He then gave them permission to leave the city so that when night fell they could go on their way. As soon as they were sure that they had his permission, they took their leave of him. They went out of the city and then took to the air and flew back to where they came from.

'Ali sat with the owner of the house until the end of the first third of the night, when they broke off their session, the owner returning to his own house and 'Ali going to his family. He greeted them and asked what had happened to them in the period after he had left them. His wife told him of the hunger they had had to endure, their lack of clothes and their hardship. He praised God for their safety and asked how they had come to Baghdad. His wife said: 'Last night I was sleeping with the children and then before I knew where I was, someone had lifted them and me up from the ground and we were flying through the air without suffering any harm. This went on until we landed in a place that looked like a Bedouin camp. We saw a number of laden mules and a litter carried by two large mules and surrounded by eunuchs, both boys and men. "Who are you?" I asked them. "What are these loads and where are we?" They said: "We are the servants of 'Ali ibn Hasan al-Jauhari of Cairo, and he has sent us to take you to him in the city of Baghdad." "Is it a long or a short way from here to Baghdad?" I asked. "Baghdad is not far away," they said, "and we can cover the distance while it is still dark." They then set us on the litter, and by the time that it was morning we had arrived here without having suffered any harm at all.' 'And who gave you these clothes?' 'Ali asked. His wife said: 'The leader of the caravan opened one of the chests that were being carried by the mules and took the clothes out of it. He gave me this to wear and produced others for the children, after which he locked the chest and handed me the key, telling me to keep it safe until I could give it to you. I have it here.'

She brought it out for him and he asked her if she could recognize the chest. 'Yes, certainly,' she said, and 'Ali then went down with her to the storerooms and showed her the chests. When she pointed out the one from which the clothes had been taken, he took the key from her, put it in the lock and opened it. In it he discovered a great quantity of robes, together with the keys of all the other chests. He removed these and started to open the others one by one and to investigate their contents, which consisted of jewels and precious stones the like of which no king possessed. He then locked the chests, took the keys and went with his wife to the upper room. 'All this comes through the grace of Almighty God,' he told her, and he led her to the marble slab with the screw, which he turned. He opened the door of the treasure chamber and went in with his wife to show her the gold that he had deposited there.

'Where did you get all this from?' she asked, and he told her: 'This came through God's grace. When I left you in Cairo I walked off without knowing where I was going, and when I got to Bulaq, I found a ship that was going to Damietta. I boarded it and when I got to Damietta, a merchant who had known my father met me and hospitably took me in.

He asked where I was going and I told him I was on my way to Damascus, where I had friends.' He then went on to tell his wife everything that had happened to him from beginning to end. She said: 'All this has happened because of the prayers that your father offered for you before his death, when he used to say: "I pray to God that, if He ever brings you into difficulties, He may grant you speedy relief." Praise be to Him that He has done this for you and has returned to you more than you lost. So I implore you, my husband, in God's Name, not to return to your former association with notorious persons but show piety towards Almighty God, both openly and in secret.' She admonished him and he said: 'I accept what you say and I ask God to remove evil associates from me, helping me to serve Him obediently and to follow what has been sanctioned by His Prophet, may God bless him and give him peace.'

'Ali, his wife and his children now led the most prosperous of lives. 'Ali opened a shop in the merchants' market and stocked it with a quantity of jewels and precious stones, sitting there with his sons and his mamluks. He became one of the leading merchants of Baghdad and news of him reached the king, who sent for him. The king's messenger arrived to tell him to obey the summons and 'Ali replied: 'To hear is to obey.' He then prepared a gift for the king, taking four trays of red gold which he filled with jewels and precious stones such as no king possessed, and with these he went off to the king. On entering the king's presence he kissed the ground before him and prayed eloquently for the continuation of his glory and good fortune. 'Merchant,' said the king, 'your presence has delighted our land,' to which 'Ali replied: 'King of the age, your servant has brought you a gift which he hopes you will be generously pleased to accept.' He then produced the four trays. The king removed their coverings and when he looked at them, he saw jewels more splendid than any of his own, worth immense stores of money. 'Your gift is acceptable, merchant,' said the king, 'and, God willing, we shall repay you with one to match it,' after which 'Ali kissed his hands and left.

The king then summoned his principal officers of state and asked them: 'How many kings have asked for my daughter's hand?' 'Very many,' they replied. 'And did any of them give me a gift like this?' he went on. 'No,' they said in unison, 'for not one of them has ever had treasures like these.' The king then said: 'I have asked God for guidance as to whether I should marry my daughter to this merchant. What is your opinion?' 'You should do as you think fit,' they said, and he then ordered that the trays together with their contents be taken by the eunuchs to the women's quarters.

There he went to his wife and put the trays before her. When she uncovered them, she saw gems more magnificent than any single one that she owned. 'What king has sent these?' she asked, adding: 'Perhaps it is one of the suitors for your daughter's hand.' 'No,' he told her, 'this comes from an Egyptian merchant who has arrived in our city. When I heard of this, I sent a messenger to fetch him in order to enjoy his company, thinking that he might have some jewels that I could buy for our daughter's wedding. He answered the summons, bringing these four trays, which he presented as a gift. I saw that he was a handsome young man, dignified and intelligent, with a graceful appearance, who might even be a prince. I was pleased with him and attracted to him, and I would now like to marry him to my daughter.'

The king went on to tell her how he had shown the present to his officers of state and of the questions he had asked them and of their answers, as well as how he had consulted them about the princess's marriage and what they had said. 'What have you to say yourself?' he then asked. 'It is for God and for you to decide, king of the age,' she replied, 'and what God wishes will happen.' 'God willing, then,' the king said, 'we shall marry her to no one but this young man.' When he went to his court the next morning, he ordered that 'Ali be brought to him together with all the merchants of Baghdad. When they were all assembled in front of him, he ordered them to sit, and when they were seated, he sent for the *qadi* of the court. The *qadi* came and was told by the king to draw up a marriage contract between his daughter and 'Ali, the Cairene merchant. 'Forgive me, lord king,' 'Ali exclaimed, 'but it is not right that a merchant like me should become your son-in-law.' 'This is a favour that I have granted to you,' the king replied, 'together with the vizierate.' He immediately followed this by investing 'Ali as vizier, after which 'Ali took his seat on the vizier's chair.

'Ali then said: 'King of the age, you have honoured me by showing me this favour, but listen to what I have to say to you.' 'Speak on,' said the king, 'and have no fear.' 'Ali said: 'Since you have proclaimed your august intention to give your daughter in marriage, this should be to my son.' 'Have you a son?' asked the king, and when 'Ali confirmed that he had, the king told him to send for him immediately. 'To hear is to obey,' said 'Ali, and he sent one of his mamluks to fetch his son, who, when he came into the king's presence, kissed the ground before him and stood there respectfully. Looking at him, the king could see that he was better-looking than his daughter and superior to her in the symmetry of his figure and the perfection of his handsomeness. 'What is your name?' the king asked him. 'Your majesty,' the fourteen-year-old youth replied, 'my name is Hasan.' The king then told the *qadi* to draw up the marriage contract between his daughter, Husn al-Wujud, and Hasan, son of the merchant 'Ali of Cairo. The *qadi* did this, and when this stage had been successfully completed, all those who were present in the king's court went off on their way.

The merchants followed 'Ali, the new vizier, back to his house and then left, after having congratulated him on his appointment. 'Ali went to his wife, who, seeing him wearing the robe of the vizierate, asked him what had happened. He told her the whole story from beginning to end and said: 'He has given his daughter in marriage to Hasan, my son.' She was overjoyed by this, and after having spent the night at home, 'Ali returned to court the next morning, where the king greeted him warmly and seated him close to his side. 'Vizier,' he said, 'our intention is to hold the wedding feast and to bring your son to my daughter.' 'Lord king,' said 'Ali, 'whatever you consider right and proper is so.' The king then gave orders for the feast; the city was adorned with decorations and the festivities lasted for thirty days, to the enjoyment and delight of the people. At the end of the thirty days, Hasan lay with the princess, enjoying her beauty and grace.

When the king's wife saw Hasan, she became very fond of him and also of his mother. On the king's orders a large palace was quickly built for him, and when he took up residence there, his mother used to stay with him for days on end before returning home. So the queen said to her husband: 'Hasan's mother cannot stay with her son and leave her husband, the vizier, nor can she stay with her husband, leaving her son.' 'That is true,' said the king, and he gave orders for a third palace to be built next to the palace of Hasan. This was done within a few days and, on the king's instructions, 'Ali's possessions were moved to the new palace, where he took up residence. The three palaces were interconnected and when the king wanted to talk with his vizier, he could walk to his palace at night or send for him, and the same was true of Hasan and his mother and father.

They continued to lead an enjoyable and pleasant life together for some time, until the king fell ill. When his condition worsened, he summoned his principal officers of state and said: 'I am gravely ill and as this illness may prove fatal, I have brought you here in order to consult you, so advise me on what you think is the proper course.' They asked: 'On what point is it that you want advice from us, your majesty?' He said: 'I am old and ill and I am afraid that after my death my kingdom may be attacked by enemies. I want you all to agree on one man for whom I can have the oath of allegiance taken as my successor, while I am still alive, so that you may feel easy about the matter.' They replied unanimously: 'We would all be content with the husband of your daughter, Hasan, the son of the vizier 'Ali. We have seen his intelligence and perfect understanding, and he knows the position of everyone, both great and small.' 'Perhaps you are saying this in my presence out of deference, but behind my back you say something else.' 'By God,' they all said, 'what we say openly and in secret is one and the same thing, and we will accept him willingly and cheerfully.' 'If that is so,' said the king, 'order the *qadi* who decides matters of religious law, together with all the chamberlains, legates and officers of state, to present themselves before me tomorrow so that we may settle the matter in the proper fashion.' 'To hear is to obey,' they said, and they then left to brief all the religious scholars and the leading emirs.

The next morning, they arrived at court and sent a message to the king asking leave to enter. When this had been granted, they went in, greeted him and said: 'We are all here in your presence.' So the king said: 'Emirs of Baghdad, who will you be content to have as your king to succeed me, so that I can confirm him as my heir before I die in the presence of you all?' They all said: 'We are agreed on Hasan, son of the vizier 'Ali, the husband of your daughter.' The king then said: 'If that is so, then go, all of you, and bring him before me.' They all rose, and after going to Hasan's palace they told him to come with them to the king. When he asked why, they told him: 'This is for something that will be good both for us and for you.' He accompanied them to the king and kissed the ground before him. 'Sit, my son,' said the king, and when he had taken his seat, the king went on: 'All the emirs have approved of you and have agreed to appoint you as their king after my death. My intention is to nominate you as my heir while I am still alive in order to have the matter settled.'

At that, Hasan got up, kissed the ground before the king and said: 'Your majesty, some of the emirs are older and senior in rank to me, so allow me to decline.' The emirs, however, insisted that they would only be satisfied with him as their king. 'My father is older than me,' said Hasan. 'He and I are one and the same thing, and it would not be right for me to be placed ahead of him.' 'Ali, however, replied: 'I approve of nothing except what my brother emirs agree on, and as they are unanimous in their choice of you, you should not disobey the king's command or go against the choice of your brothers.' Hasan looked down at the ground out of diffidence towards the king and his father. The king then asked the emirs: 'Are you content with him?' 'We are,' they said, and they all recited the opening *sura* of the Quran seven times. '*Qadi*,' said the king, 'draw up a legal document confirming that these emirs have agreed to the transfer of power to Hasan, the husband of my daughter, and that he is to be their king.' This the *qadi* did, and he signed the document after they had all taken the oath of allegiance to Hasan as king, as had the old king himself, who then told Hasan to take his seat on the throne. Everyone rose and kissed the hands of King Hasan, son of the vizier, in a show of obedience to him. His judgements that day were exemplary and he distributed splendid robes of honour to the officers of state.

The court was then dismissed and Hasan went to his father-in-law and kissed his hands. 'Hasan,' said the old king, 'in the treatment of your subjects display piety towards God.' 'I shall achieve success through your blessing, father,' replied Hasan. He then went to his palace, where he was met by his wife and her mother, together with their servants, who all kissed his hands and congratulated him on his office, exclaiming: 'This is a blessed day!' From his own palace he then went to that of his father, where there was great rejoicing at the favour God had bestowed on him by entrusting him with the kingship. His father enjoined him to fear God and to show compassion towards his subjects, and after spending a happy and joyful night, the next morning he performed the ritual prayer, recited the specified portion of the Quran, and then went to his court. All his troops and officials were present; in delivering his judgements he ordered what was good and forbade what was evil, and he appointed some to office and deposed others. This went on until the end of the day, when the court was dismissed with due ceremony and the troops, together with everyone else, went off on their way.

Hasan then returned to the palace, where he found his father-in-law gravely ill. When Hasan wished him well, he opened his eyes and called his name. 'Here I am,' said Hasan, and the old king said: 'I am near my end. Look after your wife and her mother; fear God and be dutiful towards your parents. Live in fear and awe of God, the Judge, and know that He orders you to act with justice and charity.' 'To hear is to obey,' replied Hasan. The old king lived for three more days but was then gathered to the mercy of Almighty God. They prepared his body, covered him with a shroud, and recited the Quran, both in sections and in full, over his grave for a total of forty days. Hasan then ruled alone. His subjects were delighted with him and the days of his reign were filled with joy. His father continued to serve as principal vizier at his right hand, and he appointed a second vizier at his left. Everything was well ordered and Hasan remained as king of Baghdad for a long time. His wife, the old king's daughter, presented him with three sons, who inherited the kingdom after his death. They lived the pleasantest and happiest of lives, until they were visited by the destroyer of delights and the parter of companions – praise be to the Eternal God, Who has the power both to destroy and to establish.

[Nights 424–34]

Five Stories of Kings

The Angel of Death, the Rich King and the Pious Man

A story is told, O fortunate king, that in the old days a certain king wanted to ride out one day with a number of his courtiers and officers of state in order to show off his splendid trappings to his people. He ordered his emirs and the great men of his state to prepare themselves to accompany him. He ordered the master of his wardrobe to bring out for him the most splendid robes that would suitably adorn him, and he had the best and finest of his pure-blood horses brought out. After this had been done, he chose the clothes that he preferred and took his pick of the horses. Then he put on the clothes, mounted the horse and rode out with his cortège, wearing a collar studded with gems, pearls of all kinds and rubies. As he rode among his men, exulting in his pride and haughtiness, Iblis approached him, put his hand on his nostril and blew arrogance and conceit into his nose. He swelled with pride, telling himself that there was no one like him in the world, and he started to manifest such a measure of haughtiness and vainglory that in his arrogance he would not look at anyone.

A man wearing shabby clothes stood in front of him and greeted him, and when the king failed to return the greeting he seized his horse's rein. 'Take your hand away,' said the king, 'for you don't know whose rein it is that you are holding.' 'There is something that I need from you,' said the man. The king replied: 'Wait until I dismount and then you can tell me what it is.' 'It is a secret,' the man said, 'and I can only whisper it into your ear.' The king bent down to listen and the man said: 'I am the angel of death and I intend to take your soul.' 'Give me time to go home to say goodbye to my family, my children, my neighbours and my wife,' the king asked, but the angel said: 'You are not going to go back and you will never see them again, for the span of your life is at an end.' He then took the king's soul and he fell dead from the back of his horse.

The angel of death went from there to a pious man, with whom Almighty God was pleased. After they had exchanged greetings, the angel said: 'Pious man, there is something that I need from you and it is a secret.' 'Whisper it in my ear,' said the man, and the angel then told him: 'I am the angel of death.' 'Welcome,' said the man. 'Praise be to God that you are here, for I have often been expecting you to arrive and you have long been absent from one who has yearned for your coming.' 'If you have any business to do, finish it,' the angel told him, but the man said: 'There is nothing I have to do that is more important than meeting my Lord, the Great and Glorious God.' 'How do you want me to take your soul,' asked the angel, 'for I have been ordered to do this in whatever way you choose?' 'Wait, then,' said the man, 'until I perform the ablution and begin to pray. When I prostrate myself in prayer, then take my soul.' The angel said: 'As I have been ordered to do whatever you want in this matter, I shall do what you say.' The man got up, performed his ablution and began to pray. While he was prostrating himself, the angel of death took his soul and Almighty God brought it to the place of mercy, approval and forgiveness.

The Angel of Death and the Rich King

A story is told that a certain king had collected a vast and uncountable quantity of wealth, together with quantities of every kind of thing created in this world by Almighty God, in order to make life luxurious for himself. As he wanted to give himself the opportunity to enjoy the treasures he had collected, he built for himself a lofty palace, towering into the air, such as was suitable for kings. He gave it two strong gates and posted in it as many servants, soldiers and gatekeepers as he wanted.

One day, he ordered the cook to prepare a delicious meal and he brought together his family, his retainers, his companions and his servants to enjoy his hospitality by sharing the meal with him. He took his seat on his royal throne, reclining on a cushion, and he said to himself: 'My soul, you have collected all the good things there are in this world and now you can take your ease and taste them in the enjoyment of a long life and prosperous fortune.' But before he had finished what he was saying a man arrived from outside the palace wearing tattered clothes with a bag hung round his neck, apparently a beggar asking for food.

When he came, he knocked loudly with the door-ring, almost shaking the castle and rocking the throne.

The servants rushed to the gate in fear and shouted: 'Damn you, what is this display of bad manners? Wait until the king has eaten and we will give you some of the leftovers.' He said: 'Tell your master to come out to me, for I have business with him that is of the greatest importance.' 'Go away, you feeble-witted fellow,' they said. 'Who are you to order our master to come out to you?' 'Tell him what I said,' he insisted, and so they went to the king and told him what had happened. 'Why didn't you scare him off,' said the king, 'drawing your swords and driving him away?' There was then an even louder knock on the door, at which the servants rushed to attack the man with clubs and weapons, but he shouted to them: 'Stay where you are. I am the angel of death.' They were frightened out of their wits, and as they trembled with terror they lost control of their limbs. 'Tell him to take someone else in my place,' said the king, but the angel said: 'I shall take no substitute for you. It is for you that I have come, to part you from the treasures that you have collected and the wealth that you have acquired and stored up.'

The king then sighed deeply and, bursting into tears, he said: 'May God curse the wealth that has deceived me and harmed me by keeping me from worshipping my Lord. I used to think that it would help me, but now it is a source of grief and harm to me as I have to leave it empty-handed and it will pass to my enemies.' God then allowed his wealth to speak and it said: 'Why do you curse me? Rather, curse yourself. God created both me and you from dust, and He placed me in your hands so that through me you could make provision for your afterlife and give me as alms to the poor, the wretched and the weak, and that you could use me for the building of hospices, mosques, dykes and bridges. I would then have been a help to you in the next world, but as it is you collected me, stored me up and spent me on your own desires, showing ingratitude rather than thankfulness to me. Now you have bequeathed me to your enemies, leaving yourself remorse and regret, but what fault is it of mine and why should you abuse me?'

The angel of death then took the king's soul as he sat on his throne before he had eaten his meal, and he fell down dead. God Almighty has said: 'When they were rejoicing at what they had been given, We took them suddenly and they were in despair.'*

*Quran 6.44.

The Angel of Death and the King of the Israelites

A story is told that a powerful king of the Israelites was sitting one day on his royal throne when he saw a man coming in through the palace door with an appearance that was both unpleasing and awesome. The king shrank back in fear at this as the man approached, but then, jumping up in front of him, he said: 'Man, who are you and who gave you permission to enter my palace and come into my presence?' 'It was the master of the house who ordered me to come,' said the man. 'No chamberlain can keep me out; I need no permission to come into the presence of kings; I fear the power of no ruler or the number of his guards. I am the one from whom no tyrant can find refuge, nor can any flee from my grasp. I am the destroyer of delights and the parter of friends.' When the king heard this, he fell on his face and his whole body trembled. At first he lost consciousness, but when he recovered he said: 'Are you the angel of death?' 'Yes,' said the angel, and the king then said: 'Allow me a single day's delay so that I may ask pardon for my sins and seek forgiveness from my Lord, returning the wealth that is in my treasuries to its owners lest I have to endure the hardship of having to account for it and the pain of punishment for it.' The angel said: 'Impossible – there is no way in which you can be granted this. How can I allow you any delay when the days of your life have been counted, your breaths numbered and all your minutes set down in the book of fate?' 'Give me just one hour,' the king said, but the angel replied: 'The hour has been accounted for. It passed while you were still paying no attention and you have used up all your breaths except for one.' 'Who will be with me when I am carried to my grave?' asked the king, and the angel said: 'Nothing will be with you except for your own deeds.' 'I have no good deeds,' the king said. 'There is no doubt that your resting place will be hellfire and you will experience the anger of the Omnipotent God,' said the angel. He then took the king's soul and the king fell to the ground from his throne. There followed a great outcry among his subjects; voices were raised and there was loud wailing and weeping, but had they known what awaited the king of God's anger, their show of grief would have been even more intense and bitter.

Alexander the Great and the Poor King

A story is told that Alexander the Great passed by a people who were so poor that they owned no worldly goods at all. They used to bury their dead in graves dug at the doors of their houses, which they would constantly visit to clean and to sweep away the dust, and where they would worship Almighty God. Their only food was grass, together with plants that they got from the earth. Alexander sent them an envoy summoning their king to visit him, but he refused to answer the call, saying: 'I have no need of Alexander.' Alexander then visited him and asked about the condition of his people, saying: 'I don't see that any of you has any gold or silver or any worldly goods,' to which the king replied: 'No one is satisfied with the goods of this world.' 'Why do you dig graves by your house doors?' Alexander asked, and the king replied: 'This is so that we may have them before our eyes and remind ourselves of death as we look at them. In this way, as love for this world leaves our hearts, we shall not forget the world to come, and we shall not be distracted by it from our worship of Almighty God.' 'How is it that you eat grass?' asked Alexander. 'We do not want to make our bellies into graves for animals,' said the king, 'and the pleasure to be got from food goes no further than the throat.'

The king then reached out and produced a human skull, which he placed before Alexander. 'Alexander,' he said, 'do you know whose skull this is?' When Alexander said no, the king told him: 'This belonged to one of the kings of the world who used to treat his subjects unjustly and oppressively, wronging the weak and spending his days in amassing ephemeral goods. God took his soul and condemned him to hellfire. This is his skull.' He then reached out and put another skull before Alexander, again asking him whether he knew whose it was. When Alexander said no, the king said: 'This belonged to a ruler who treated his subjects justly and with compassion. When God took his soul, He placed him in Paradise and exalted him.' He then laid his hand on Alexander's head and said: 'Which of these two, do you think, will be yours?'

Alexander wept bitterly, clasped the king to his breast and said: 'If you would like to stay with me, I would hand over the vizierate to you and share my kingdom with you.' 'Never, never!' exclaimed the king. 'I have no desire for this.' 'Why is that?' asked Alexander. 'Because all mankind are your enemies, thanks to the wealth and the kingdom that you have been given,' replied the king, 'whereas for me they are all true friends because I am content with my poverty. I have no kingdom; there is nothing that I want or seek in the world. I have no ambition here and set store by nothing except contentment.'

Alexander clasped him to his breast, kissed him between the eyes and went on his way.

King Anushirwan the Just

A story is told that King Anushirwan the Just pretended one day that he was ill and sent out some of his trusted and reliable officers with orders to go through all the regions and quarters of his realm to look for an old brick in a ruined village, telling them that the doctors had prescribed this as a cure for his ailment. They toured every part of his empire but had to come back and tell him: 'In the whole of your realm we have found no ruined place and no old brick.' This delighted Anushirwan, who gave thanks to God and said: 'I wanted to have my lands inspected and surveyed to see whether there were still any ruins there that needed restoration, but as every single place now is flourishing, then everything that needs to be done in my kingdom has been completed; it is in good order and its prosperity has reached the stage of perfection.'

In the old days such kings used to concern themselves to do their best to bring prosperity to their realms, knowing that the more prosperous they were, the better off their subjects would be. They also knew that the wise men and philosophers were undeniably right in saying that religion depends on the king, the king on his troops, his troops on money, money on the prosperity of the land, and this prosperity on the justice with which the subjects are treated. As a result they would not allow anyone to act oppressively or unjustly, nor would they permit their retainers to commit acts of aggression, knowing, as they did, that their subjects would not endure injustice and that all the lands would be ruined if they fell into the hands of wrongdoers. If that happened, their inhabitants would disperse and escape to the lands of some other ruler. Their own kingdoms would thus be diminished, revenues would fall, treasuries would be emptied and the lives of their subjects would be made wretched. They would have no fondness for an unjust ruler and would constantly be cursing him; he would get no enjoyment from his kingdom and there would be no halting the process of his destruction.

[Nights 462–5]

Sindbad the Sailor

In the time of the caliph Harun al-Rashid, the Commander of the Faithful, there was in the city of Baghdad a man called Sindbad the porter, a poor fellow who earned his living by carrying goods on his head. On one particularly hot day he was tired, sweating and feeling the heat with a heavy load, when he passed by the door of a merchant's house. The ground in front of it had been swept and sprinkled with water and a temperate breeze was blowing. As there was a wide bench at the side of the house, he set down his bundle in order to rest there and to sniff the breeze.

From the door came a refreshing breath of air and a pleasant scent which attracted him, and as he sat he heard coming from within the house the sound of stringed instruments and lutes, together with singing and clearly chanted songs. In addition, he could hear birds twittering and praising God Almighty in all their varied tongues – turtledoves, nightingales, thrushes, bulbuls, ringdoves and curlews. He wondered at this and, filled as he was with pleasure, he moved forward and discovered within the grounds of the house a vast orchard in which he could see pages, black slaves, eunuchs, retainers and so forth, such as are only to be found in the palaces of kings and sultans. When he smelt the scent of all kinds of appetizing foods, together with fine wines, he looked up to heaven and said: 'Praise be to You, my Lord, Creator and Provider, Who sustains those whom You wish beyond all reckoning. I ask You to forgive all my sins, and I repent of my faults to You. My Lord, none can oppose Your judgement or power, or question Your acts, for You are omnipotent, praise be to You. You make one man rich and another poor, as You choose; You exalt some and humble others in accordance with Your will and there is no other god but You. How great You are! How strong is Your power and how excellent is Your governance! You show favour to those of Your servants whom You choose, for here is the owner of this house living in the greatest prosperity, enjoying pleasant scents, delicious food and all kinds of splendid wines. You have decreed what You wish with regard to your servants in accordance with Your power. Some are worn out and others live at ease; some are fortunate while others, like me, live laborious and humble lives.'

He then recited these lines:

How many an unfortunate, who has no rest,
Comes later to enjoy the pleasant shade.
But as for me, my drudgery grows worse,
And so, remarkably, my burdens now increase.
Others are fortunate, living without hardship,
And never once enduring what I must endure.
They live in comfort all their days,
With ease and honour, food and drink.
All are created from a drop of sperm;
I'm like the next man and he is like me,
But oh how different are the lives we lead!
How different is wine from vinegar.
I do not say this as a calumny;
God is All-Wise and His decrees are just.

When Sindbad the porter had finished these lines, he was about to pick up his load and carry it off when a splendidly dressed young boy, well proportioned and with a handsome face, came through the door, took his hand and said: 'Come and have a word with my master, for he invites you in.' Sindbad wanted to refuse, but finding that impossible, he left his load with the gatekeeper in the entrance hall and entered. He found an elegant house with an atmosphere of friendliness and dignity, and there he saw a large room filled with men of rank and importance. It was decked out with all kinds of flowers and scented herbs; there were fruits both dried and fresh, together with expensive foods of all kinds as well as wines of rare vintages; and there were musical instruments played by beautiful slave girls of various races. Everyone was seated in his appointed place and at their head was a large and venerable man whose facial hair was touched with grey. He was handsome and well shaped, with an imposing air of dignity, grandeur and pride. Sindbad the porter was taken aback, saying to himself: 'By God, this is one of the regions of Paradise, or perhaps the palace of a king or a sultan.' Then, remembering his manners, he greeted the company, invoking blessings on them and kissing the ground before them.

He stood there with his head bowed in an attitude of humility until the master of the house gave him permission to sit and placed him on a chair near his own, welcoming him and talking to him in a friendly way before offering him some of the splendid, delicious and expensive foods that were there. The porter, after invoking the Name of God, ate his fill and then exclaimed: 'Praise be to God in all things!' before washing his hands and thanking the company. The master of the house, after again welcoming him and wishing him good fortune, asked his name and his profession. 'My name is Sindbad the porter,' his guest replied, 'and in return for a fee I carry people's goods on my head.' The master smiled and said: 'You must know, porter, that your name is the same as mine, and I am Sindbad the sailor. I would like you to let me hear the verses which you were reciting as you stood at the door.' Sindbad the porter was embarrassed and said: 'For the sake of God, don't hold this against me, for toil and hardship together with a lack of means teach a man bad manners and stupidity.' 'Don't be ashamed,' said his host. 'You have become a brother to me, so repeat the verses that I admired when I heard you recite them at the door.' Sindbad the porter did this, moving Sindbad the sailor to delighted appreciation, after which THIS SECOND SINDBAD SAID:

The First Journey of Sindbad

I have a remarkable story to tell you covering all that happened to me before I acquired my present fortune and found myself sitting where you see me now. For it was only after great labour and hardship that I achieved this, having had to face perils upon perils and to endure difficulties and discomforts in my early days. I made seven voyages, and a surprising and astonishing story is attached to each; all this happened through the decree of fate, from whose rulings there is no escape.

Know, my noble masters, that my father was one of the leading citizens and merchants of Baghdad, a man of riches and ample means. He died when I was a small boy, leaving me money, possessions and estates. When I grew up and took all this over, I ate well, drank well, associated with other young men, wore fine clothes and went out with my friends and comrades. I was quite sure that these benefits would continue to be mine, until after a time I came to my senses and recovered from my heedlessness only to discover that the money was all gone, that my situation had changed and that all I had once owned was lost. I was frightened and bewildered, but then I thought of something I had once heard from my father about Solomon, the son of David, on both of whom be peace. Solomon is reported to have said: 'Three things are better than three other things. The day of one's death is better than the day of one's birth, a live dog is better than a dead lion and the grave is better than poverty.' So I got up and collected what I had in the way of furnishings and clothes and sold them. I went on to sell my property and everything else that I owned, all of which brought me three thousand dirhams. It then occurred to me to travel in foreign parts, as I remembered these lines of poetry:

It is through toil that eminence is won;
Whoever seeks the heights must pass nights without sleep.
The pearl fisher must brave the depth of ocean
If he is to win power and wealth.
Whoever hopes to rise without effort
Will waste his life in search of the impossible.

After I had thought all this over I made up my mind to go to sea and so I went off to buy a variety of trade goods, as well as things that I would need for the journey. I boarded a ship and sailed downriver to Basra with a number of other merchants. We then put out to sea and sailed for a number of days and nights, passing island after island and going from sea to sea and from one land to another. Whenever we passed land, we bought, sold and bartered, and we sailed on like this until we reached an island which looked like one of the meadows of Paradise. The ship's master put in there, dropping the anchors and running out the gangway. After everyone on board had disembarked they lit fires under stoves and busied themselves in various ways, some cooking, some washing and some, including me, looking around the island and exploring the various districts. Afterwards we gathered again to eat, drink, play and enjoy ourselves, but while we were doing this, the master, standing at the side of the ship, shouted out to all of us at the top of his voice: 'Save yourselves! Hurry, board the ship as fast as you can; if you want to escape destruction, leave all your things and save your lives. This island is not a real one. It is a giant fish that has stayed motionless here in the middle of the sea until it has become silted up with sand on which trees have grown over time so that it looks like an island. When you lit your fire, it felt the heat and has started to move. It is just about to dive into the sea and you will all be drowned. Save yourselves before death overtakes you, and abandon your things!' On hearing this, everyone left all their belongings, including pots and stoves. Some but not all reached the ship before the 'island' moved, plunging into the depths of the sea with everything that was on it, and the sea with its boisterous waves closed over it.

I was one of those who had been left on the 'island', and, together with the others, I found myself underwater, but Almighty God rescued me and saved me from drowning by providing me with a large wooden tub that had been used for washing. I held on to this for dear life, straddling it and using my legs like oars in order to paddle as the waves tossed me to and fro. The master had hoisted sail and he went off with those who had managed to get on board, showing no concern for the rest of us, who were drowning. I followed the ship with my eyes until it was out of sight, and I was quite sure that I was going to die. Night fell while I was still struggling in the water and my struggles lasted for a day and a night until, with the help of wind and wave, I came to rest under the high shore of an island where trees were growing out over the water. I had been on the point of drowning, but now I clutched at the branch of a lofty tree and clung on to it until I had managed to pull myself up on to the island itself. I discovered that my legs were numb and the soles of my feet showed traces of having been nibbled by fish, something I hadn't noticed earlier because of my distress and exhaustion. I was, in fact, the nearest thing to a corpse when I was thrown up there, having lost my senses and being plunged into dismay.

I stayed in this state until the sun roused me next day. My feet, I discovered, had swollen up but I moved as best I could, at times crawling and at others shuffling on my knees. There were many fruits there, which I started to eat, as well as freshwater springs, and I stayed like this for some days and nights until I had recovered my spirits and could move freely again. I started to think about my position as I walked around the island looking among the trees at what God had created there, and I made myself a crutch from the wood of the trees with which to support myself. Things went on like this for some time until one day, when I was walking along the shore, I saw in the distance something that I took to be a wild beast or some sea creature. I went towards it with my eyes fixed on it and discovered that it was a fine mare that had been tethered there on the shore. When I got near, it frightened me by giving a great scream and I was about to retrace my steps when from somewhere underground a man appeared. He shouted to me, coming after me and calling out: 'Who are you? Where have you come from and why are you here?' I told him: 'You must know, sir, that I am a stranger. I was on a ship but I and some others found ourselves washed into the sea, where God provided me with a wooden tub on which to ride. It floated off with me until the waves cast me up on this island.'

When the man heard my story, he took me by the hand and said: 'Come with me,' and when I did, he took me to an underground chamber with a large hall, at the head of which he made me sit. Then he brought me food, and, as I was hungry, I ate my fill before relaxing. He asked me about my circumstances and what had happened to me, and I told him my whole story from beginning to end, to his great astonishment. When I had finished, I implored him not to be hard on me, assuring him that what I had told him was the truth, and adding: 'I would like you to tell me who you are, why you are sitting here in this underground room and why you have tethered that mare by the shore.' He replied: 'There are a number of us scattered around the shores of this island, and we are the grooms of King Mihrjan, in charge of a number of his horses. Every month at the time of the new moon we bring thoroughbred mares that have never been covered and tether them on the island, after which we hide ourselves here underground so that no one can see us. Then a stallion, one of the sea horses, scents the mare and comes out of the sea. It looks around and when it sees nobody, it mounts her and after having covered her it gets down and wants to take her with him. Because of the tether she cannot go, and he screams at her, butting her with his head and kicking her, and when we hear the noise we know that he has got down from her, and so we come out and yell at him. This alarms him and he goes back into the sea, leaving the mare pregnant. The colt or filly to which she gives birth is worth a huge sum of money, and has no match on the face of the earth. This is the time for the stallion to come out and after it does, God willing, I shall take you with me to King Mihrjan and show you our country. You must know that, had you not met us, you would have found nobody else here and you would have died a miserable death, with no one knowing anything about you. I have saved your life and I shall see that you get back to your own country.'

I blessed the man and thanked him for having been so exceedingly good to me, and while we were talking a stallion came out of the sea and jumped on the mare with a loud snort. When it had finished its business it got off her, wanting to take her with it, and when it failed, she kicked and screamed at him. At that, the groom took sword and shield and went out of the door of the room, shouting to his companions to help him and striking his sword against his shield. A number of others arrived brandishing spears and shouting, at which the stallion took fright and made off into the sea like a water buffalo, disappearing under the surface. My man sat down briefly and was then joined by his companions, each of whom was leading a mare. When they saw me with him, they asked me about myself and I repeated what I had told him. They then came up to me, spread out a cloth, and invited me to share their meal, which I did. Then they got up and mounted, taking me with them on the back of one of the mares.

We went on until we reached the city of King Mihrjan, and when the others had gone in and told him my story, he asked for me. They took me and placed me before him, after which we exchanged greetings. He gave me a courteous welcome and then asked me about myself, at which I told him all that had happened to me and all that I had seen, from beginning to end. He was amazed by my experiences and said: 'My son, you have had a remarkable measure of good luck, and had fate not allotted you a long life, you would never have escaped from these dangers, but, thanks be to God, you are safe.' He then treated me with kindness and generosity, taking me as one of his intimates and talking to me in the friendliest of terms. He appointed me as his port agent to keep a register of all ships coming to land, and I stayed with him, carrying out his business and receiving all manner of kindnesses and benefits from him. He supplied me with the most splendid of robes and I took a principal role in presenting intercessions to him and settling the people's affairs.

I stayed with him for a long time, but whenever I found myself by the shore, I would ask the visiting merchants and the sailors where Baghdad lay in the hope that someone would be able to tell me, so that I might leave with him and go back to my own country. Not one of them, however, knew anything about Baghdad or about anyone who went there, and so I remained helpless and tired out by my long exile.

After things had gone on like that for some time, I went one day into the presence of the king and found that he had a number of Indians with him. After we had exchanged greetings they welcomed me, and when they had asked me about my country, in return I asked about theirs. They told me that their people were made up of a number of different castes, and among these were the Shakiris, the noblest of them all, who would never wrong or oppress anyone, and the so-called Brahmins, who drank no wine but lived happily, enjoying entertainment and pleasure and owning camels, horses and cattle. There were, in fact, seventy-two castes into which the Indians were divided, something that completely astonished me.

In Mihrjan's kingdom I noticed that there was an island named Kasil, from which there were to be heard the sounds of tambourines and drums being beaten all night long, although the other islanders and travellers who visited it told me that its inhabitants were serious-minded and intelligent people. In the sea there I saw a fish that was two hundred cubits in length and another with a face like that of an owl. All in all, I saw so many strange wonders on that voyage that it would take too long to tell you them all.

I continued to look around the island and note what was there until one day, as I was standing by the shore, staff, as usual, in my hand, up sailed a large ship with many merchants on board. It put in to the port and, on the orders of its master, the sails were furled, the anchors dropped and the gangways run out. The crew took a long time in unloading the cargo, while I stood there noting it all down. Then I asked the master whether there was anything left and he said: 'Yes, sir; there are some goods in the hold, but these belong to one of our company who was drowned off one of the islands on our outward voyage. We have kept them as a deposit and we intend to sell them, keep a note of the price and then pass on what they fetch to his family in Baghdad, the City of Peace.' I asked him the name of the owner and he said: 'He was Sindbad the sailor, and we lost him at sea.' When I heard what he said, I looked at him closely and recognized him. I gave a loud cry and said: 'Captain, those goods are mine and I am Sindbad the sailor. I joined the other merchants who disembarked on the "island", and when you shouted to us as the fish started to move, some got off while others, myself included, were submerged in the waves. God Almighty rescued me from drowning by providing me with a large tub which had been used on board for washing. I got on to it and paddled with my feet until the winds and waves helped me to reach this island, where I came ashore. Through God's help I met the grooms of King Mihrjan, who took me with them to this city and introduced me to him. When I told him my story he showed me favour and appointed me as clerk of this port, an office from which I have profited, and I have gained his approval. So these goods that you have are mine and they are my means of livelihood.'

The captain quoted the formula: 'There is no might and no power except with God, the Exalted, the Omnipotent,' adding: 'No one has any integrity or conscience left.' I asked him why he had said that after having listened to my story, and he said: 'You heard me say that I had with me goods whose owner had been drowned, and now you want to take them without having any right to them. This is a crime on your part, and as for the owner, we saw him sink, and of the many others with him, not one escaped. So how can you claim that the goods are yours?' 'Captain,' I told him, 'if you listen to my story and follow what I am telling you, you will see that what I say is true, for lying is a characteristic of hypocrites.' I then went over for him everything that had happened to me from the time that I left Baghdad with him until I got to the 'island', where I was plunged into the sea. When I had told him some details of what had passed between us, both he and the other merchants realized that I was telling the truth. They recognized me and congratulated me on my safety, saying: 'By God, none of us believed that you could have escaped drowning, but God has given you a new life.' Then they handed over my goods, marked with my name, from which nothing at all was missing. I opened the packages and took out something precious and expensive, which the crew helped me to carry as a gift to the king. I explained to him that this was the ship on which I had sailed and that every single one of my goods had been returned to me. It was from them, I added, that I had chosen the present.

The king was filled with amazement when he heard this, and he realized that everything I had told him was true. He showed me great affection and treated me with even greater generosity, showering me with gifts in return for mine. I then disposed of all the goods I had with me at a great profit, after which I bought more goods of all kinds in the city. When the other merchants wanted to put to sea, I loaded all that I had on to the ship and then went to the king to thank him for his goodness and kindness and then to ask him to allow me to return to my own country and my family. He said goodbye to me and presented me as I left with many goods from the city. When I had taken my leave of him, I boarded the ship and with the permission of Almighty God we sailed off. Good fortune attended us and fate helped us as we travelled night and day until we reached Basra in safety. I was delighted at my safe return, and after we had landed and stayed for a short time, I set off for Baghdad, the City of Peace, taking with me many valuable loads of all kinds of goods. When I got to my own district of the city, I went to my house and was met by all my family and friends. I bought large numbers of eunuchs, retainers, mamluks, concubines and black slaves, as well as houses, properties and estates, until I had more of these than ever before. I enjoyed the company of my friends and companions, and was more prosperous than ever, forgetting the time that I had spent abroad, together with the toils and distress that

I had suffered and the terrors of the voyage. I occupied myself with pleasures and enjoyment, good food and expensive wine, and continued to do so. This, then, is the story of my first voyage and tomorrow, God willing, I shall tell you the story of the second of my seven.

Sindbad the sailor then entertained Sindbad the landsman to supper, after which he ordered him to be presented with a hundred *mithqals* of gold, telling him: 'I have enjoyed your company today.' The other Sindbad thanked him, took the gift and went on his way, thinking with wonder about the experiences people have. He slept at home that night but the next morning he went back to the house of Sindbad the sailor, who welcomed him on his arrival and treated him with courtesy, giving him a seat in his salon. When his other companions came, he provided them with food and drink and when they were cheerful and happy he began to tell them the story of the second voyage. HE WENT ON:

The Second Journey of Sindbad

You must know, my brothers, that, as I told you yesterday, I was enjoying a life of the greatest pleasure and happiness until one day I got the idea of travelling to foreign parts, as I wanted to trade, to look at other countries and islands and to earn my living. After I had thought this over, I took out a large sum of money and bought trade goods and other things that would be useful on a voyage. I packed these up and when I went down to the coast I found a fine new ship with a good set of sails, fully manned and well equipped. A number of other merchants were there and they and I loaded our goods on board. We put to sea that day and had a pleasant voyage, moving from one sea and one island to another, and wherever we anchored we were met by the local traders and dignitaries as well as by buyers and sellers, with whom we bought, sold and bartered our goods.

Things went on like this until fate brought us to a pleasant island, full of trees with ripe fruits, scented flowers, singing birds and limpid streams, but without any houses or inhabitants. The captain anchored there and the merchants, together with the crew, disembarked to enjoy its trees and its birds, giving praise to the One Omnipotent God, and wondering at His great power. I had gone with this landing party and I sat down by a spring of clear water among the trees. I had some food with me and I sat there eating what God had provided for me; there was a pleasant breeze; I had no worries and, as I felt drowsy, I stretched out at my ease, enjoying the breeze and the delightful scents, until I fell fast asleep. When I woke up, there was no one to be found there, human or *jinn*. The ship had sailed off leaving me, as not a single one on board, merchants or crew, had remembered me. I turned right and left, and when I failed to find anyone at all, I fell into so deep a depression that my gall bladder almost exploded through the force of my cares, sorrow and distress. I had no possessions, no food and no drink; I was alone, and in my distress I despaired of life. I said to myself: 'The pitcher does not always remain unbroken. I escaped the first time by meeting someone who took me with him from the island to an inhabited part, but this time how very, very unlikely it is that I shall meet anyone to bring me to civilization!'

I started to weep and wail, blaming myself in my grief for what I had done, for the voyage on which I had embarked, and for the hardships I had inflicted on myself after I had been sitting at home in my own land at my ease, enjoying myself and taking pleasure in eating well, drinking good wine and wearing fine clothes, in no need of more money or goods. I regretted having left Baghdad to go to sea after what I had had to endure on my first voyage, which had brought me close to death. I recited the formula: 'We belong to God and to Him do we return,' and I was close to losing my reason. Then I got up and began to wander around, not being able to sit still in any one place. I climbed a high tree and from the top of it I started to look right and left, but all I could see was sky, water, trees, birds, islands and sand. Then, when I stared more closely, I caught sight of something white and huge on the island. I climbed down from my tree and set out to walk towards it. On I went until, when I reached it, I found it to be a white dome, very tall and with a large circumference. I went nearer and walked around it but I could find no door and the dome itself was so smoothly polished that I had neither the strength nor the agility to climb it. I marked my starting point and made a circuit of it to measure its circumference, which came to fifty full paces, and then I started to think of some way to get inside it.

It was coming on towards evening. I could no longer see the sun, and the sky had grown dark; I thought that the sun must have been hidden by a cloud, but since it was summer I found this surprising and I raised my head to look again. There, flying in the sky, I caught sight of an enormous bird with a huge body and broad wings. It was this that had covered the face of the sun, screening its rays from the island. I was even more amazed, but I remembered an old travellers' tale of a giant bird called the *rukh* that lived on an island and fed its chicks on elephants, and I became sure that my 'dome' was simply a *rukh*'s egg. While I was wondering at what Almighty God had created, the parent bird flew down and settled on the egg, covering it with its wings and stretching its legs behind it on the ground. It fell asleep – glory be to God, Who does not sleep – and I got up and undid my turban, which I folded and twisted until it was like a rope. I tied this tightly round my waist and attached myself as firmly as I could to the bird's legs in the hope that it might take me to a civilized region, which would be better for me than staying on the island.

I spent the night awake, fearful that if I slept, the bird might fly off before I realized what was happening. When daylight came, it rose from the egg and with a loud cry it carried me up into the sky, soaring higher and higher until I thought that it must have reached the empyrean. It then began its descent and brought me back to earth, settling on a high peak. As soon as it had landed I quickly cut myself free from its legs, as I was afraid of it, although it hadn't noticed that I was there. I was trembling as I undid my turban, freeing it from the bird's legs, and I then walked off, while, for its part, the bird took something in its talons from the surface of the ground and then flew back up into the sky. When I looked to see what it had taken, I discovered that this was a huge snake with an enormous body. I watched in wonder as it left with its prey, and I then walked on further, to find myself on a high ridge under which there was a broad and deep valley, flanked by a vast and unscalable mountain that towered so high into the sky that its summit was invisible. I blamed myself for what I had done and wished that I had stayed on the island, saying to myself: 'That was better than this barren place, as there were various kinds of fruits to eat and streams from which to drink, whereas here there are no trees, fruits or streams.' I recited the formula: 'There is no power and no might except with God, the Exalted, the Almighty,' adding: 'Every time I escape from one disaster, I fall into another that is even worse.'

I got up and, plucking up my courage, I walked down into the valley, where I discovered that its soil was composed of diamonds, the hard and compact stone that is used for boring holes in metals, gems, porcelain and onyx. Neither iron nor rock has any effect on it; no part of it can be cut off and the only way in which it can be broken is by the use of lead. The valley was full of snakes and serpents as big as palm trees, so huge that they could have swallowed any elephant that met them, but these only came out at night and hid away by day for fear of *rukhs* and eagles, lest they be carried away and torn in bits, although I don't know why that should be. I stayed there filled with regret at what I had done, saying to myself: 'By God, you have hastened your own death.' As evening drew on, I walked around looking for a place where I could spend the night, and I was so afraid of the snakes that in my concern for my safety I forgot about eating and drinking. Nearby I spotted a cave and when I approached it, I found that its entrance was narrow. I went into it and then pushed a large stone that I found nearby in order to block it behind me. 'I'm safe in here,' I told myself, 'and when day breaks I shall go out and see what fate brings me.'

At that point I looked inside my cave only to see a huge snake asleep over its eggs at the far end. All the hairs rose on my body and, raising my head, I entrusted myself to fate. I spent a wakeful night, and when dawn broke I removed the stone that I had used to block the entrance and came out, staggering like a drunken man through the effects of sleeplessness, hunger and fear. Then, as I was walking, suddenly, to my astonishment, a large carcass fell in front of me, although there was no one in sight. I thought of a travellers' tale that I had heard long ago of the dangers of the diamond mountains and of how the only way the diamond traders can reach these is to take and kill a sheep, which they skin and cut up. They then throw it down from the mountain into the valley and, as it is fresh when it falls, some of the stones there stick to it. The traders leave it until midday, at which point eagles and vultures swoop down on it and carry it up to the mountain in their talons. Then the traders come and scare them away from the flesh by shouting at them, after which they go up and remove the stones that are sticking to it. The flesh is left for the birds and beasts and the stones are taken back home by the traders. This is the only way in which they can get hold of the diamonds.

I looked at the carcass and remembered the story. So I went up to it and cleared away a large number of diamonds which I put in my purse and among my clothes, while I stored others in my pockets, my belt, my turban and elsewhere among my belongings. While I was doing this, another large carcass fell down and, lying on my back, I set it on my breast and tied myself to it with my turban, holding on to it and lifting it up from the ground. At that point an eagle came down and carried it off into the air in its talons, with me fastened to it. The eagle flew up to the mountain top where it deposited the carcass, and it was about to tear at it when there came a loud shout from behind it, together with the noise of sticks striking against rocks. The eagle took fright and flew off, and, having freed myself from the carcass, I stood there beside it, with my clothes all smeared with blood. At that point the trader who had shouted at the eagle came up, but when he saw me standing there he trembled and was too afraid of me to speak. He went to the carcass and turned it over, giving a great cry of disappointment and reciting the formula: 'There is no might and no power except with God. We take refuge with God from Satan, the accursed.' In his regret he struck the palms of his hands together, exclaiming: 'Alas, alas, what is this?'

I went up to him, and when he asked me who I was and why I had come there, I told him: 'Don't be afraid. I am a mortal man, of good stock, a former merchant. My story is very remarkable indeed, and there is a strange tale attached to my arrival at this mountain and this valley. There is no need for you to be frightened, for I have enough to make you happy – a large number of diamonds, of which I will give what will satisfy you, and each of my stones is better than anything else that you can get. So don't be unhappy or alarmed.'

The man thanked me, calling down blessings on me, and as we talked the other traders, each of whom had thrown down a carcass, heard the sound of our voices and came up to us. They congratulated me on my escape and, when they had taken me away with them, I told them my whole story, explaining the perils that I had endured on my voyage as well as the reason why I had got to the valley. After that, I presented many of the diamonds that I had with me to the man who had thrown down the carcass that I had used, and in his delight he renewed his blessings. The others exclaimed: 'By God, fate has granted you a second life, for you are the first man ever to come here and escape from the valley. God be praised that you are safe.'

I passed the night with them in a spot that was both pleasant and safe, delighted that I had escaped unhurt from the valley of the snakes and had got back to inhabited parts. At dawn we got up, and as we moved across the great mountain we could see huge numbers of snakes in the valley, but we kept on our way until we reached an orchard on a large and beautiful island, where there were camphor trees, each one of which could provide shade for a hundred people. Whoever wants to get some camphor must use a long tool to bore a hole at the top of the tree and then collect what comes out. The liquid camphor flows down and then solidifies like gum, as this is the sap of the tree, and when it dries up, it can be used for firewood. On the island is a type of wild beast known as the rhinoceros, which grazes there just as cows and buffaloes do in our own parts. It is a huge beast with a body larger than that of a camel, a herbivore with a single horn some ten cubits long in the centre of its head containing what looks like the image of a man. There is also a species of cattle there. According to seafarers and travellers who have visited the mountain and its districts there, this rhinoceros can carry a large elephant on its horn and go on pasturing in the island and on the shore without paying any attention to it. The elephant, impaled on its horn, will then die, and in the heat of the sun grease from its corpse will trickle on to the head of the rhinoceros. When this gets into its eyes, it will go blind, and as it then lies down by the coast, a *rukh* will swoop on it and carry it off in its talons in order to feed its chicks both with the beast itself and with what is on its horn. On the island I saw many buffaloes of a type unlike any that we have at home.

I exchanged a number of the stones that I had brought with me in my pocket from the diamond valley with the traders in return for a cash payment and some of the goods that they had brought with them, which they carried for me. I travelled on in their company, inspecting different lands and God's creations, from one valley and one city to another, buying and selling as we went, until we arrived at Basra. We stayed there for a few days and then I returned to Baghdad.

When Sindbad reached Baghdad, the City of Peace, he went to his own district and entered his house. He had with him a large number of diamonds, as well as cash and a splendid display of all kinds of goods. After he had met his family and his relatives, he dispensed alms and gave gifts to every one of his relations and companions. He began to enjoy good food and wine, to dress in fine clothes and to frequent the company of his friends. He forgot all his past sufferings, and he continued to enjoy a pleasant, relaxed and contented life, with entertainments of all sorts. All those who had heard of his return would come and ask him about his voyage and about the lands that he had visited. He would tell them of his experiences and amaze them by recounting the difficulties with which he had had to contend, after which they would congratulate him on his safe return.

This is the end of the story of all that happened to him on his second voyage, and when he had finished his account he said: 'Tomorrow, God willing, I shall tell you about my third voyage.' When he had told all this to Sindbad the landsman, those present were filled with astonishment.

They all dined with him that evening and he gave orders that the second Sindbad be given a hundred *mithqals* of gold. Sindbad the landsman took these and went on his way, marvelling at what his host had endured, and, filled with gratitude, when he reached his own house, he called down blessings on him.

The next morning, when it was light, he got up and, having performed the morning prayer, he went back to the house of Sindbad the sailor as he had been told to do. On his arrival he said good morning to his host, who welcomed him, and the two sat together until the rest of the company arrived. When they had eaten and drunk and were pleasantly and cheerfully relaxed, SINDBAD THE SAILOR SAID:

The Third Journey of Sindbad

Listen with attention to this tale of mine, my brothers, for it is more wonderful than what I told you before, and it is God Whose knowledge and decree regulate the unknown. When I got back from my second voyage I was happy, relaxed and glad to be safe, and, as I told you yesterday, I had made a large amount of money, since God had replaced for me all that I had lost. So I stayed in Baghdad for a time, enjoying my good fortune with happiness and contentment, but then I began to feel an urge to travel again and to see the world, as well as to make a profit by trading, for as the proverb says: 'The soul instructs us to do evil.' After thinking the matter over, I bought a large quantity of goods suitable for a trading voyage, packed them up and took them from Baghdad to Basra. I went to the shore, where I saw a large ship on which were many virtuous merchants and passengers, as well as a pious crew of devout and godly sailors. I embarked with them and we set sail with the blessing of Almighty God and His beneficent aid, confident of success and safety.

On we sailed from sea to sea, island to island and city to city, enjoying the sights that we saw, and happy with our trading, until one day, when we were in the middle of a boisterous sea with buffeting waves, the captain, who was keeping a lookout from the gunwale, gave a great cry, slapped his face, plucked at his beard and tore his clothes. He ordered the sails to be furled and the anchors dropped. 'What is it, captain?' we asked him, and he told us to pray for safety, explaining: 'The wind got the better of us, forcing us out to sea, and ill fortune has driven us to the mountain of the hairy ones, an ape-like folk. No one who has come there has ever escaped, and I feel in my heart that we shall all die.' Before he had finished speaking we were surrounded on all sides by apes who were like a flock of locusts, approaching our ship and spreading out on the shore. We were afraid to kill any of them or to strike them and drive them off, as we thought that if we did, they would be certain to kill us because of their numbers, since 'numbers defeat courage', as the proverb has it. We could only wait in fear lest they plunder our stores and our goods.

These apes are the ugliest of creatures, with hair like black felt and a horrifying appearance; no one can understand anything they say and they have an aversion to men. They have yellow eyes and black faces and are small, each being four spans in height. They climbed on to the anchor cables and gnawed through them with their teeth before proceeding to cut all the other ropes throughout the ship. As we could not keep head to wind, the ship came to rest by the mountain of the ape men and grounded there. The apes seized all the merchants and the others, bringing them to shore, after which they took the ship and everything in it, carrying off their spoils and going on their way. We were left on the island, unable to see the ship and without any idea where they had taken it.

We stayed there eating fruits and herbs and drinking from the streams until we caught sight of some form of habitation in the centre of the island. We walked towards this and found that it was a strongly built castle with high walls and an ebony gate whose twin leaves were standing open. We went through the gate and discovered a wide space like an extensive courtyard around which were a number of lofty doors, while at the top of it was a large and high stone bench. Cooking pots hung there on stoves surrounded by great quantities of bones, but there was nobody to be seen. We were astonished by all this and we sat down there for a while, after which we fell asleep and stayed sleeping from the forenoon until sunset. It was then that the earth shook beneath us, there was a thunderous sound, and from the top of the castle down came an enormous creature shaped like a man, black, tall as a lofty palm tree, with eyes like sparks of fire. He had tusks like those of a boar, a huge mouth like the top of a well, lips like those of a camel, which hung down over his chest, ears like large boats resting on his shoulders, and fingernails like the claws of a lion. When we saw what he looked like, we were so terrified that we almost lost our senses and were half-dead from fear and terror.

When he had reached the ground, he sat for a short while on the bench before getting up and coming over to us. He singled me out from among the other traders who were with me, grasping my hand and lifting me from the ground. Then he felt me and turned me over, but in his hands I was no more than a small mouthful, and when he had examined me as a butcher examines a sheep for slaughter, he found that I had been weakened by my sufferings and emaciated by the discomforts of the voyage, which had left me skinny. So he let go of me and picked another of my companions in my place. After turning him over and feeling him as he had felt me, he let him go too and he kept on doing this with us, one after the other, until he came to the captain, a powerful man, stout and thickset with broad shoulders. He was pleased with what he had found and, after laying hold of the man as a butcher holds his victim, he threw him down on the ground and set his foot on his neck, which he broke. Then he took a long spit, which he thrust up from the captain's backside to the crown of his head, after which the creature lit a large fire and over this he placed the spit on which the captain was skewered. He turned this round and round over the coals until, when the flesh was cooked, he took it off the fire, put it down in front of him and dismembered it, as a man dismembers a chicken. He started to tear the flesh with his fingernails and then to eat it. When he had finished it all, he gnawed the bones, leaving none of them untouched, before throwing away what was left of them at the side of the castle. He then sat for a while before stretching himself out on the bench and falling asleep, snorting like a sheep or a beast with its throat cut. He slept until morning and then got up and went off about his business.

When we were sure that he had gone we began to talk to one another, weeping over our plight and exclaiming: 'Would that we had been drowned or eaten by the ape men, for this would have been better than being roasted over the coals! That is a terrible death, but God's will be done, for there is no might and no power except with Him, the Exalted, the Omnipotent. We shall die miserably without anyone knowing about us, as there is no way left to us to escape from this place.' Then we went off into the island to look for a hiding place or a means of escape, as we didn't mind dying provided we were not roasted over the fire. But we found nowhere to hide and when evening came we were so afraid that we went back to the castle.

We had only been sitting there for a short while before the ground beneath us began to shake again and the black giant came up to us. He started turning us over and inspecting us one by one as he had done the first time, until he found one to his liking. He seized this man and treated him as he had treated the captain the day before, roasting and eating him.

He then went to sleep on the bench and slept the night through, snorting like a slaughtered beast. When day broke he got up and went away, leaving us, as he had done before. We gathered together to talk, telling one another: 'By God, it would be better to throw ourselves into the sea and drown rather than be roasted, for that is an abominable death.' At that point one of our number said: 'Listen to me. We must find some way of killing the giant so as to free ourselves from the distress that he has caused us, and also to free our fellow Muslims from his hostility and tyranny.' I said: 'Brothers, listen. If we have to kill him, we must move some of these timbers and this wood and make ourselves a species of ship. If we then think of a way of killing him, we can embark on it and put out to sea, going wherever God wills, or else we could stay here until a ship sails by on which we might take passage. If we fail to kill him, we can come down and put out to sea, for even if we drown we would still escape being slaughtered and roasted over the fire. If we escape, we escape, and if we drown, we die as martyrs.' 'This is sound advice,' they all agreed, and we then set to work moving timbers out of the castle and building a boat which we moored by the shore, loading it with some provisions. Afterwards we went back to the castle.

When evening came, the earth shook and the black giant arrived like a ravening dog. He turned us over and felt us one by one before picking out one of us, whom he treated as he had done the others. Having eaten him he fell asleep on the bench, with thunderous snorts. We got up and took two iron spits from those that were standing there. We put them in the fierce fire until they were red hot, like burning coals, and then, gripping them firmly, we carried them to the sleeping, snoring giant, placed them on his eyes and then bore down on them with our combined strength as firmly as we could. The spits entered his eyes and blinded him, at which he terrified us by uttering a great cry. He sprang up from the bench and began to hunt for us as we fled right and left. In his blinded state he could not see us, but we were still terrified of him, thinking that our last hour had come and despairing of escape. He felt his way to the door and went out bellowing, leaving us quaking with fear as the earth shook beneath our feet because of the violence of his cries. We followed him out as he went off in search of us, but then he came back with two others, larger and more ferocious-looking than himself. When we saw him and his even more hideous companions, we panicked, and as they caught sight of us and hurried towards us, we boarded our boat, cast off its moorings and drove it out to sea. Each of the giants had a huge rock in his hands, which they threw at us, killing most of us and leaving only me and two others.

The boat took us to another island and there we walked until nightfall, when, in our wretched state, we fell asleep for a little while, but when we woke, it was only to see that a huge snake with an enormous body and a wide belly had coiled around us. It made for one of us and swallowed his body as far as the shoulders, after which it gulped down the rest of him and we could hear his ribs cracking in its belly. Then it went off, leaving us astonished, filled with grief for our companion and fearful for our own safety. We exclaimed: 'By God, it is amazing that each death should be more hideous than the one before! We were glad to have got away from the black giant but our joy has been short-lived, and there is no might and no power except with God. By God, we managed to escape from the giant and from death by drowning, but how are we to escape from this sinister monster?'

We walked around the island until evening, eating its fruits and drinking from its streams, until we discovered a huge and lofty tree which we climbed in order to sleep there. I was up on the top-most branch, and when night fell the snake came through the darkness and, having looked right and left, it made for our tree and swarmed up until it had reached my companion. It swallowed his body as far as the shoulders, and then coiled round the tree with him until I heard his bones cracking in its belly, after which it swallowed the rest of him before my eyes. It then slid down the tree and went away. I stayed on my branch for the rest of the night and when daylight came, I climbed down again, half-dead with fear and terror. I thought of throwing myself into the sea to find rest from the troubles of the world, but I could not bring myself to commit suicide, as life is dear. So I fastened a broad wooden beam across my feet with two other similar beams on my right and my left sides, another over my stomach, and a very large one laterally over my head, to match the one beneath my feet. I was in the middle of these beams, which encased me on all sides, and after I had fastened them securely, I threw myself, with all of them, on to the ground. I lay between them as though I was in a cupboard, and when night fell and the snake arrived as usual, it saw me and made for me but could not swallow me up as I was protected on all sides by the beams and, although it circled round, it could find no way to reach me. I watched it, nearly dead with fear, as it went off and then came back, constantly trying to get to me in order to swallow me, but the beams that I had fastened all around me prevented it. This continued from sunset until dawn, and when the sun rose the snake went off, frustrated and angry, and I then stretched out my hand and freed myself from the beams, still half-dead because of the terror that it had inflicted on me.

After I had got up, I walked to the end of the island, and when I looked out from the shore, there far out at sea was a ship. I took a large branch and waved it in its direction, calling out to the sailors. They saw me and told each other: 'We must look to see what this is, as it might be a man.' When they had sailed near enough to hear my shouts, they came in and brought me on board. They asked for my story, and I told them everything that had happened to me from beginning to end, and they were amazed at the hardships I had endured. They gave me some of their own clothes to hide my nakedness and then brought me some food, allowing me to eat my fill, as well as providing me with cold, fresh water. This revived and refreshed me, and such was my relief that it was as though God had brought me back from the dead. I praised and thanked Him for His abundant grace, and although I had been sure that I was doomed, I regained my composure to such an extent that it seemed as if all my perils had been a dream.

My rescuers sailed on with a fair wind granted by Almighty God until we came in sight of an island called al-Salahita, where the captain dropped anchor. Everyone disembarked, merchants and passengers alike, unloading their wares in order to trade. The master of the ship then turned to me and said: 'Listen to me. You are a poor stranger who has gone through a terrifying ordeal, as you have told us, and so I want to do something for you that may help you get back to your own land and cause you to bless me for the rest of your life.' When I had thanked him for this he went on to say: 'We lost one of our passengers, and we don't know whether he is alive or dead, as we have heard no news of him. I propose to hand over his goods to you so that you may sell them here in return for payment that we shall give you for your trouble. Anything left over we shall keep until we get back to Baghdad, where we can make enquiries about his family, and we shall then hand over the rest of the goods to them, as well as the price of what has been sold. Are you prepared to take charge of these things, land them on the island and trade with them?' 'To hear is to obey, sir,' I said, adding my blessings and thanks for his generous conduct. So he ordered the porters and members of the crew to unload the goods on the shore and then to hand them over to me. The ship's clerk asked him whose goods these were so that he could enter the name of the merchant who owned them. 'Write on them the name of Sindbad the sailor,' the master told him, 'the man who came out with us but was lost on an island. We never heard of him again, and I want this stranger to sell them and give us what they fetch in return for a fee for his trouble in selling them. Whatever is unsold we can take back to Baghdad, and if we find Sindbad, we can give it back to him, but if not, we can hand it over to his family in the city.' 'Well said!' exclaimed the clerk. 'That is a good plan.'

When I heard the master say that the bales were to be entered under my name, I told myself: 'By God, I am Sindbad the sailor, who was one of those lost on the island,' but I waited in patience until the merchants had left the ship and were all there together talking about trade. It was then that I went up to the master and said: 'Sir, do you know anything about the owner of these bales that you have entrusted to me to sell for him?' 'I know nothing about his circumstances,' the master replied, 'only that he was a Baghdadi called Sindbad the sailor. We anchored off an island, where a large number of our people were lost in the sea, including Sindbad, and until this day we have heard nothing more about him.' At that I gave a great cry and said: 'Master, may God keep you safe. Know that I am Sindbad the sailor and that I was not drowned. When you anchored there, I landed with the other merchants and passengers and went off to a corner of the island, taking some food with me. I so enjoyed sitting there that I became drowsy and fell into the soundest of sleeps, and when I woke up I found the ship gone and no one else there with me. So these are my belongings and my goods. All the merchants who fetch diamonds saw me when I was on the diamond mountain and they will confirm that I am, in fact, Sindbad. For I told them the story of what had happened to me on your ship and how you forgot about me and left me lying asleep on the island and what happened to me after I woke up and found no one there.'

When the merchants and the passengers heard what I had to say, they gathered around me, some believing me and some convinced that I was lying. While things were still undecided, one of the merchants who heard me mention the diamond valley got up and came to me. He asked the company to listen to him and said: 'I told you of the most remarkable thing that I saw on my travels, which happened when my companions and I were throwing down carcasses into the diamond valley. I threw mine down as usual and when it was brought up by an eagle there was a man attached to it. You didn't believe me and thought that I was lying.' 'Yes,' said the others, 'you certainly told us this and we didn't believe you.' 'Here is the man who was clinging to it,' said the merchant. 'He presented me with valuable diamonds whose like is nowhere to be found, giving me more than I had ever got from a carcass, and he then stayed with me until we reached Basra, after which he went off to his own city. My companions and I said goodbye to him and went back to our own lands. This is the man. He told us that his name was Sindbad the sailor and that his ship had gone off leaving him on the island. He has come here as proof to you that I was telling the truth. All these goods are his; he told us about them when we met and what he has said has been shown to be true.'

When the master heard this he came up to me and looked carefully at me for some time. Then he asked: 'What mark is on your goods?' I told him what it was and then I mentioned some dealings that we had had together on our voyage from Basra. He was then convinced that I really was Sindbad and embraced me, saluting me and congratulating me on my safe return. 'By God, sir,' he said, 'yours is a remarkable story and a strange affair. Praise be to God, Who has reunited us and returned your goods and possessions to you.' After that I used my expertise to dispose of my goods, making a great profit on the trip. I was delighted by this, congratulating myself on my safety and on the return of my possessions.

We continued to trade among the islands until we came to Sind, where we bought and sold, and in the sea there I came across innumerable wonders. Among them was a fish that looked like a cow and another resembling a donkey, together with a bird that came out of a mollusc shell, laying its eggs and rearing its chicks on the surface of the sea and never coming out on to dry land at all. On we sailed, with the permission of Almighty God, enjoying a fair wind and a pleasant voyage until we got back to Basra. I stayed there for a few days before going to Baghdad, where I went to my own district and entered my house, greeting my family as well as my friends and companions. Feeling joyful at my safe return to my country, my family, my city and my properties, I distributed alms, made gifts, clothed widows and orphans and gathered together my companions and friends. I went on like this, eating, drinking and enjoying myself with good food, good wine and friends, having made a vast profit from my voyage and having forgotten all that had happened to me and the hardships and terrors that I had endured. I have told you the most marvellous things that I saw on it and, God willing, if you come to me tomorrow I shall tell you the story of my fourth voyage, which is even more remarkable than those of the first three.

*

Sindbad the sailor then gave orders that Sindbad the porter should be given his usual hundred *mithqals* of gold and that tables should be laid with food. The whole company ate with him, still filled with amazement at the tale of their host's experiences, and then after supper they went on their ways. As for Sindbad the porter, he took his gold and went off astonished by what he had heard. He spent the night at home and the next morning, when it was light, he got up, performed the morning prayer and walked to the house of Sindbad the sailor, greeting him as he went in. His host welcomed him with gladness and delight, making him sit with him until the rest of his companions arrived. Food was produced and they ate, drank and enjoyed themselves, until SINDBAD BEGAN TO SPEAK:

The Fourth Journey of Sindbad

Know, my brothers, that when I got back to Baghdad and met my companions, my family and my friends I enjoyed a life of the greatest happiness, contentment and relaxation, forgetting everything in my well-being, and drowning in pleasure and delight in the company of my friends and companions. It was while my life was at its most pleasant that I felt a pernicious urge to travel to foreign parts, to associate with different races and to trade and make a profit. Having thought this over, I bought more valuable goods, suitable for a voyage, than I had ever taken before, packing them into bales. When I had gone down from Baghdad to Basra I loaded them on a ship, taking with me a number of the leading Basran merchants. We put out, with the blessing of Almighty God, on to the turbulent and boisterous sea and for a number of nights and days we had a good voyage, passing from island to island and sea to sea until one day we met a contrary wind. The master used the anchors to bring us to a halt in mid-ocean lest we founder there, but while we were addressing our supplications to Almighty God a violent gale blew up, which tore our sails to shreds, plunging all on board into the sea, together with all their bales, goods and belongings.

I was with the others in the sea. I swam for half a day, but I had given up all hope when Almighty God sent me part of one of the ship's timbers on to which I climbed, together with some of the other merchants. We huddled together as we rode on it, paddling with our legs, and being helped by the waves and the wind. This went on for a day and a night, but in the forenoon of the second day the wind rose and the sea became stormy, with powerful waves. The current then cast us up on an island, half-dead through lack of sleep, fatigue and cold, hunger, thirst and fear. Later, when we walked around the place, we found many plants, some of which we ate to allay our hunger and sustain us, and we spent the night by the shore. The next day, when it was light, we got up and continued to explore the various parts of the island. In the distance we caught sight of a building and kept on walking towards it until we stood at its door. While we were there, out came a crowd of naked men, who took hold of us without a word and brought us to their king. We sat down at his command and food was brought which we did not recognize and whose like we had never seen in our lives. I could not bring myself to take it and so I ate nothing, unlike my companions, and this abstemiousness on my part was thanks to the grace of Almighty God as it was this that has allowed me to live until now.

When my companions tasted the food, their wits went wandering; they fell on it like madmen and were no longer the same men. The king's servants then fetched them coconut oil, some of which was poured out as drink and some of which was smeared over them. When my companions drank the oil their eyes swivelled in their heads and they started to eat the food in an unnatural way. I felt sorry for them, but I did not know what to do about it and I was filled with great uneasiness, fearing for my own life at the hands of the naked men. For when I looked at them closely I could see that they were Magians and that the king of their city was a *ghul*. They would bring him everyone who came to their country or whom they saw or met in their valley or its roads. The newcomer would then be given that food and anointed with that oil; his belly would swell so that he could eat more and more; he would lose his mind and his powers of thought until he became like an imbecile. The Magians would continue to stuff him with food and coconut oil drink until, when he was fat enough, they would cut his throat and feed him to the king. They themselves would eat human flesh unroasted and raw.

When I saw this I was filled with distress both for myself and for my comrades, who, in their bewildered state, did not realize what was being done to them. They were put in the charge of a man who would herd them around the island like cattle; as for me, fear and hunger made me weak and sickly, and my flesh clung to my bones. The Magians, seeing my condition, left me alone and forgot about me. Not one of them remembered me or thought about me, and so one day I contrived to move from the place where they were, and walked away, leaving it far behind me. I then saw a herdsman sitting on a high promontory, and when I looked more closely I could see that he was the man who had been given the job of pasturing not only my companions but many others as well, who were in the same state. When he saw me he realized that I was still in possession of my wits and was not suffering from what had affected the others. So he gestured to me from far off, indicating that I should turn back and then take the road to the right, which would lead to the main highway. I followed his instructions and went back, and when I saw a road on my right I followed it, at times running in terror and then walking more slowly until I was rested. I went on like this until I was out of sight of the man who had shown me the way and I could no longer see him nor could he see me.

The sun then set and as darkness fell I sat down to rest, intending to go to sleep, but I was too afraid, too hungry and too tired to sleep that night. At midnight I got up and walked further into the island, carrying on until daybreak, when the sun rose over the hilltops and the valleys. I was exhausted, hungry and thirsty and so I started to eat grass and some of the island plants, going on until I had satisfied my hunger and was satiated. Then I got up and walked on, and I continued like this for the whole of the day and the night, eating plants whenever I was hungry. This went on for seven days and seven nights until, on the morning of the eighth day, I caught sight of something in the distance and set off towards it. I got to my destination after sunset and looked carefully at it from far off, as my heart was still fluttering because of my earlier sufferings, but it turned out to be a group of men gathering peppercorns. They saw me as I approached and quickly came and surrounded me on all sides, asking me who I was and where I had come from. I told them that I was a poor unfortunate and then went on to give them my whole story, explaining my perils, hardships and sufferings.

'By God,' they exclaimed, 'this is an amazing story, but how did you escape from the blacks and get away from them on the island? There are vast numbers of them and as they are cannibals no one can pass them in safety.' So I told them what had happened to me and how they had taken my companions by feeding them on some food which I did not eat. They were astonished by my experiences and, after congratulating me on my safety, they made me sit with them until they had finished their work, after which they brought me some tasty food, which I ate because I was starving. I stayed with them for some time and then they took me with them on a ship, which brought me to the island where they lived. There they presented me to their king, whom I greeted and who welcomed me courteously and asked me about myself. I told him of my circumstances and of all my experiences from the day that I left Baghdad until I came to him. He and those with him were filled with astonishment at this tale. He told me to sit by him and he then ordered food to be brought, from which I ate my fill. Then I washed my hands and thanked, praised and extolled Almighty God for His grace.

When I left the king's court I looked around the city, which was a thriving place, populous and wealthy, well stocked with provisions and full of markets and trade goods, as well as with both buyers and sellers. I was pleased and happy to have got there, and I made friends with the people, and their king, who treated me with more honour and respect than he showed to his own leading citizens. I observed that all of them, high and low alike, rode good horses but without saddles. I was surprised at that and I asked the king why it was, pointing out that a saddle made things more comfortable for the rider and allowed him to exert more force. 'What is a saddle?' he asked, adding: 'I have never seen one or ridden on one in my life.' 'Would you allow me to make you one so that you could ride on it and see its advantages?' I asked, and when he told me to carry on, I asked him to provide me with some wood. He ordered everything I needed to be fetched, after which I looked for a clever carpenter and sat teaching him how saddles should be made. Then I got wool, carded it and made it into felt, after which I covered the saddle in leather and polished it before attaching bands and fastening the girth. Next I fetched a smith and explained to him how to make stirrups. When he had made a large pair, I filed them down and then covered them with tin, giving them fringes of silk. I fetched one of the best of the king's horses, a stallion, which I then saddled and bridled, and when I had attached the stirrups I brought him to the king. What I had done took the fancy of the king, who was filled with admiration, and, having thanked me, he mounted the horse and was delighted by the saddle. In return for my work he gave me a huge reward, and when his vizier saw what I had made, he asked for another saddle like it. I made him one and after that all the principal officers of state and the state officials began to ask me to make them saddles. I taught the carpenter how to produce them and showed the smith how to make stirrups, after which we started to manufacture them and to sell them to great men and the employers of labour. This brought me a great deal of money and I became a man of importance in the city, commanding ever greater affection and enjoying high status both with the king and with his court, and also with the leading citizens and state officials.

One day, while I was sitting with the king enjoying my dignity to the full, he said to me: 'You have become a respected and honoured companion of ours; you are one of us and we cannot bear to be parted from you or that you should leave our city. I have something to ask of you, and I want you to obey me and not to reject my request.' 'What is it that you want of me, your majesty?' I asked, adding: 'I cannot refuse you, because you have treated me with such kindness, favour and generosity, and I thank God that I have become one of your servants.' The king said: 'I want you to take a wife here, a beautiful, graceful and witty lady, as wealthy as she is lovely, so that you may become one of our citizens and I can lodge you with me in my palace. Do not disobey me or reject my proposal.' When I heard what he said, I was too embarrassed to speak and stayed silent. Then, when he asked why I did not answer, I said: 'My master, king of the age, your commands must be obeyed.' He sent at once for the *qadi* and the notaries, and he married me on the spot to a noble lady of high birth and great wealth, who combined beauty and grace with her distinguished ancestry, and who was the owner of houses, properties and estates.

After the king had married me to the great lady, he presented me with a fine, large detached house, providing me with eunuchs and retainers and assigning me pay and allowances. I lived a life of ease, happy and relaxed, forgetting all the toils, difficulties and hardships that I had experienced. I told myself that when I went back to my own country, I would take my wife with me, but there is no avoiding fate and no one knows what will happen to him. My wife and I were deeply in love; we lived in harmony, enjoying a life of pleasure and plenty over a period of time. Almighty God then widowed a neighbour of mine, and, as he was a friend of mine, I went to his house to offer my condolences on his loss. I found him in the worst of states, full of care and sick at heart. I tried to console him by saying: 'Don't grieve for your wife. Almighty God will see that you are well recompensed by providing you with another, more beautiful one, and, if it is His will, you will live a long life.' He wept bitterly and said: 'My friend, how can I marry another wife and how can God compensate me with a better one when I have only one day left to live?' 'Come back to your senses, brother,' I told him, 'and don't forecast your own death, for you are sound and healthy.' 'My friend,' he said, 'I swear by your life that tomorrow you will lose me and never see me again.' 'How can that be?' I asked him, and he told me: 'Today my wife will be buried and I shall be buried with her in the same grave. It is the custom here that, when a wife dies, her husband is buried alive with her, while if the husband dies it is the wife who suffers this fate, so that neither partner may enjoy life after the death of the other.' 'By God,' I exclaimed, 'what a dreadful custom! This is unbearable!'

While we were talking, a group comprising the bulk of the citizens of the town arrived and started to pay condolences to my friend on the loss of his wife and on his own fate. They began to lay out the corpse in their usual way, fetching a coffin in which they carried it, accompanied by the husband. They took it out of the city to a place on the side of a mountain overlooking the sea. When they got there, they lifted up a huge stone, under which could be seen a rocky cleft like the shaft of a well.

They threw the woman's body down this, into what I could see was a great underground pit. Then they brought my friend, tied a rope round his waist and lowered him into the pit, providing him with a large jug of fresh water and seven loaves by way of provisions. When he had been lowered down, he freed himself from the rope, which they pulled up before putting the stone back in its place and going away, leaving my friend with his wife in the pit.

I said to myself: 'By God, this death is even more frightful than the previous one,' and I went to the king and asked him how it was that in his country they buried the living with the dead. He said: 'This is our custom here. When the husband dies we bury his wife with him, and when the wife dies we bury her husband alive so that they may not be parted either in life or in death. This is a tradition handed down from our ancestors.' I asked him: 'O king of the age, in the case of a foreigner like me, if his wife dies here, would you treat him as you treated my friend?' 'Yes,' he replied, 'we would bury him with her just as you have seen.'

When I heard this, I was so concerned and distressed for myself that my gall bladder almost split and in my dismay I began to fear that my wife might die before me and that I would be buried alive with her. Then I tried to console myself, telling myself that it might be I who died first, for no one knows who will be first and who second. I tried to amuse myself in various ways, but within a short time my wife fell ill and a few days later she was dead. Most of the townsfolk came to pay their condolences to me and her family, and among those who came in accordance with their custom was the king. They fetched professionals who washed her corpse and dressed her in the most splendid of her clothes together with the best of her jewellery, necklaces and precious gems before placing her in her coffin. They then carried her off to the mountain, removed the stone from the mouth of the pit and threw her into it. My friends and my wife's family came up to take a last farewell of me. I was calling out: 'I'm a foreigner! I don't have to put up with your customs,' but they did not listen or pay any attention to me. Instead they seized me and used force to tie me up, attaching the seven loaves and the jug of fresh water that their custom required, before lowering me into the pit, which turned out to be a vast cavern under the mountain. 'Loose yourself from the rope!' they shouted, but I wasn't willing to do that and so they threw the rest of it down on top of me before replacing the huge stone that covered the entrance and going away.

In the pit I came across very many corpses together with a foul stink of putrefaction and I blamed myself for my own actions, telling myself that I deserved everything that had happened to me. While I was there I could not distinguish night from day and I began by putting myself on short rations, not eating until I was half-dead with hunger and drinking only when I was violently thirsty, because I was afraid of exhausting my food and my water. I recited the formula: 'There is no might and no power except with God, the Exalted, the Omnipotent,' adding: 'Why did I have the misfortune to marry in this city? Every time I say to myself that I have escaped from one disaster, I fall into another that is worse. By God, this is a terrible death. I wish that I had been drowned at sea or had died on the mountains, for that would have been better than this miserable end.'

I went on like this, blaming myself, sleeping on the bones of the dead and calling on Almighty God to aid me. I longed for death, but, in spite of my plight, death would not come and this continued until I was consumed by hunger and parched by thirst. I sat down and felt for my bread, after which I ate a little and drank a little before getting up and walking round the cavern. This was wide with some empty hollows, but the surface was covered with bodies as well as old dry bones. I made a place for myself at the side of it, far away from the recent corpses, and there I slept. I now had very little food left and I would only take one mouthful and one sip of water each day or at even longer intervals for fear of using up both food and water before my death. Things went on like this until one day, as I was sitting thinking about what I would do when my provisions were exhausted, the stone was suddenly moved and light shone down on me. While I was wondering what was happening, I saw people standing at the head of the shaft. They lowered a dead man and a live woman, who was weeping and screaming, and with her they sent down a large quantity of food and water. I watched her but she didn't see me, and when the stone had been replaced and the people had gone, I stood up with the shin bone of a dead man in my hand and, going up to her, I struck her on the middle of her head. She fell unconscious on the ground and I struck her a second and a third time, so killing her. I took her bread and what else she had, for I noticed she had with her a large quantity of ornaments, robes, necklaces, jewels and precious stones. When I had removed her food and water, I sat down to sleep in my place by the side of the cavern. Later I began to eat as little of the food as was needed to keep me alive lest it be used up too soon, leaving me to die of hunger and thirst.

I stayed down there for some time, killing all those who were buried alive with the dead and taking their food and water in order to survive. Then, one day, I woke from sleep to hear something making a noise at the side of the cavern. I asked myself what it could be, and so I got up and went towards whatever it was, carrying with me a dead man's shin bone. When the thing that was making the noise heard me, it fled away and I could see that it was an animal. I followed it to the upper part of the cave and there coming through a little hole I could see a ray of light like a star, appearing and then disappearing. At the sight of this, I made my way towards it, and the nearer I got, the broader the beam of light became, leaving me certain that there was an opening in the cave leading to the outer world. 'There must be some reason for this,' I said to myself. 'Either it is another opening, like the one through which I was lowered, or it is a crack leading out of here.' I thought the matter over for a while and then went towards the light. Here I discovered that there was a tunnel dug by wild beasts from the surface of the mountain to allow them to get in, eat their fill of the corpses and then get out again. On seeing this I calmed down, regained my composure and relaxed, being certain that, after my brush with death, I would manage to stay alive.

Like a man in a dream, I struggled through the tunnel to find myself overlooking the sea coast on a high and impassable mountain promontory that cut off the island and its city from the seas that met there. In my delight, I gave praise and thanks to God, and then, taking heart, I went back through the tunnel to the cave and removed all the food and water that I had saved. I took some clothes from the dead to put on in place of my own, and I also collected a quantity of what they were wearing in the way of necklaces, gems, strings of pearls and jewellery of silver and gold, studded with precious stones of all kinds, together with other rare items. I fastened the clothes of the dead to my own and went through the tunnel to stand by the seashore. Every day I would go back down to inspect the cave, and whenever there was a burial I would kill the survivor, whether it was a man or a woman, and take the food and the water. Then I would go out of the tunnel and sit by the shore, waiting for Almighty God to send me relief in the form of a passing ship. I started to remove all the jewellery that I could see from the cave, tying it up in dead men's clothes.

Things went on like this for some time until one day, while I was sitting by the shore, I saw a passing ship out at sea in the middle of the waves. I took something white from the clothes of the dead, fastened it to a stick and ran along with it, parallel to the shore, waving it towards the ship, until the crew turned and caught sight of me as I stood on a high point. They put in towards me until they could hear my voice, and then they sent me a boat manned by some of their crew. As they came close they said: 'Who are you and why are you sitting there? How did you get to this mountain? Never in our lives have we seen anyone who managed to reach it.' I told them: 'I'm a merchant whose ship was sunk. I got on a plank together with my belongings, and by God's aid I was able to come up on shore here, bringing them with me, but only after I had exerted myself and used all my skill in a hard struggle.'

The sailors took me with them in the boat, carrying what I had fetched from the cave tied up in clothes and shrouds. They brought me to the ship, together with all of these things, and took me to the master, who asked: 'Man, how did you get here? This is a huge mountain with a great city on the other side of it, but although I have spent my life sailing this sea and passing by it, I have never seen anything on it except beasts and birds.' 'I'm a merchant,' I told him, 'but the large ship on which I was sailing broke up and sank. All these goods of mine, and the clothes that you see, were plunged into the water, but I managed to load them on to a large beam from the ship and fate helped me to come to shore by this mountain, after which I waited for someone to pass by and take me off.' I said nothing about what had happened to me in the city or in the cave, for fear that someone on board might be from the city. Then I took a quantity of my goods to the master of the ship and said: 'Sir, it is thanks to you that I have escaped from this mountain, so please take these things in return for the kindness you have shown me.' The master did not accept, insisting: 'We take no gifts from anyone, and if we see a shipwrecked man on the coast or on an island we take him with us and give him food and water. If he is naked we clothe him, and when we reach a safe haven we give him a present from what we have with us as an act of generosity for the sake of Almighty God.' On hearing that, I prayed God to grant him a long life.

We then sailed on from island to island and from sea to sea. I was hopeful that I would escape my difficulties, but although I was full of joy that I had been saved, whenever I thought of how I had sat in the cave with my wife I would almost go out of my mind. Through the power of God we came safely to Basra, where I landed and spent a few days before going on to Baghdad. There I went to my own district and, when I had entered my house, I met my family and friends and asked them how they were. They were delighted by my safe return and congratulated me. I then stored all the goods that I had with me in my warehouses and distributed alms and gifts, providing clothes for the widows and orphans. I was filled with joy and delight and renewed old ties with friends and companions, enjoying amusements and entertainments.

These, then, were the most remarkable things that happened to me on my fourth voyage, but, my brother, dine with me this evening, take your usual present of gold, come back tomorrow and I shall tell you of my experiences on my fifth voyage, as these were stranger and more wonderful than anything that happened before.

Sindbad the sailor then ordered that Sindbad the porter be given a hundred *mithqals* of gold. Tables were set and the company dined, before dispersing in a state of astonishment, as each story was more surprising than the last. Sindbad the porter went home and spent the night filled with happiness and contentedness as well as with amazement. The next day, when dawn broke, he got up, performed the morning prayer and walked to the house of Sindbad the sailor, whom he greeted. His host welcomed him and told him to sit with him until the rest of his companions arrived, after which they ate, drank and enjoyed themselves, chatting to one another. Then Sindbad the sailor began to speak. HE SAID:

The Fifth Journey of Sindbad

Know, my friends, that when I had returned from my fourth voyage I immersed myself in pleasure, enjoyment and relaxation, forgetting all my past experiences and sufferings because I was so delighted by what I had gained in the way of profit. I then again felt the urge to travel and to see foreign lands and islands and so, after thinking things over, I bought valuable goods suitable for a voyage, packed them in bales and travelled from Baghdad, heading for Basra. When I got to the coast I saw a tall ship, large and with good lines and new fittings, which so took my fancy that I bought it. I hired a captain and a crew under the supervision of my own slaves and servants, and then loaded it with my merchandise. A number of merchants arrived and paid me to take them and their goods on board, after which we set out cheerfully and happily, looking forward to a safe and profitable voyage.

We travelled from island to island and from sea to sea, inspecting islands and lands, and disembarking to trade. Things went on like this until one day we came to a large, uninhabited island. This was a barren waste, but on it was a huge white dome which, on investigation, turned out to be a gigantic *rukh*'s egg. The merchants who came up to look at it did not recognize what it was and so they broke into it by striking at it with stones. A large amount of fluid came out and then they could see the *rukh* chick. They dragged this out of the egg, killed it and cut off large quantities of its flesh. I was on board at the time and they did not tell me what they had done until one of the passengers said to me: 'Sir, get up and look at this egg which we thought was a dome.' When I got up to look and saw the merchants striking at the egg, I shouted: 'Don't do that or the *rukh* will come, sink our ship and destroy us!' They did not listen to me, but while they were busy with the egg the sun was hidden away from us; the day was obscured and a cloud darkened the sky. We looked up to find what was between us and the sun, and there we could see the wings of a *rukh*, which were blocking the sunlight from us and shadowing the sky.

When the *rukh* found its egg cracked, it shrieked at us until it was joined by its mate, and the two of them started to circle around our ship, screaming at us with a noise louder than thunder. I cried to the captain and the crew to put out to sea for safety before we could be destroyed. The merchants came on board and the captain cast off the ship's lines as fast as he could, and we left the island heading out to sea. The *rukh* saw us and left us for a while as we sailed with all the speed we could in order to escape and win clear of its territory. Suddenly, however, we caught sight of the two of them following our course. They caught up with us, each carrying in its talons an enormous rock that it had picked up in the mountains. One of them dropped its rock on us, but as the captain hauled round the rudder, the falling rock narrowly missed us, although when it fell into the sea beneath the ship, its huge impact tossed us up and down and gave us a view of the seabed. Then its mate dropped the one that it was carrying, which was smaller than the other, but, as fate had decreed, it fell on our stern, smashing it, breaking the rudder into twenty pieces and plunging all on board into the sea. As I tried my best to save myself for dear life's sake, Almighty God sent me one of the ship's timbers and, after clinging to this, I managed to get astride it and started to use my feet as paddles, helped on my way by wind and wave.

It happened that the ship had gone down near an island in the middle of the sea and divine providence cast me ashore. I was at my last gasp when I came to land, half-dead with what I had experienced in the way of hardship, distress, hunger and thirst. For some time I lay sprawled on the shore, but when I had rested and regained my composure I penetrated into the island and discovered it to be like one of the gardens of Paradise, with flourishing trees, gushing waters and birds that chanted the praises of the Glorious and Eternal God. There were many trees and fruits, as well as flowers of all kinds, and so I ate my fill of the fruits and satisfied my thirst by drinking from the streams, giving thanks to Almighty God and praising Him.

I stayed there like that until evening came and night fell, when, thanks to the combination of hardship and fear that I experienced, I slept like the dead, having heard no sound on the island or seen anyone. I stayed asleep until morning, and then I got to my feet and was walking among the trees when I came across a stream flowing from a spring of water beside which was seated a fine-looking old man with a waist-wrapper made of leaves. I thought to myself that he might have come to the island as a survivor from a wrecked ship and so I went up to him and greeted him. He returned my greeting with a gesture but said nothing. I then asked him why he was sitting there, but he shook his head sadly and gestured with his hand as if to say: 'Carry me from here on your shoulders to the other side of the stream.' I said to myself: 'If I do him this service and carry him where he wants, God may reward me for the good deed.' So I went up to him and when I had lifted him on my shoulders I carried him to where he had been pointing before, telling him to take his time in getting down. But, far from doing that, he wrapped his legs around my neck, and when I looked at them I could see that they were black and rough as buffalo hide. I took fright and tried to throw him off, but he squeezed my neck with his legs, nearly throttling me. Everything turned black and I lost consciousness, falling to the ground in a dead faint. Then he raised his legs and beat me painfully on the back and shoulders until I got up again with him still on my shoulders. I was tired of carrying him, but he gestured to me with his hand to take him through the trees to the best fruits. When I tried to disobey him, he used his legs to strike me more violently than if he had whipped me.

He kept on pointing where he wanted to go, and I would take him there. If I faltered or was slow he would beat me, and I was like his prisoner. We went through the trees to the centre of the island with him urinating and defecating on my shoulders. This went on night and day, for when he wanted to sleep he would wind his legs around my neck, have a brief nap and then get up and beat me to make me rise in a hurry. So severe were my sufferings that I had no power to disobey him, and I blamed myself for having lifted him up in the first place out of pity. Things went on like this until I reached the point of complete exhaustion and I said to myself: 'I did him a good turn but it has turned out badly for me and, by God, I shall never do anyone else a service as long as I live.' Such were my hardships and distress that every minute and every hour I wished that Almighty God would let me die.

When this had lasted for some time, a day came when I carried my incubus to a place on the island where there were great quantities of gourds, many of which were dry. I took a large one of these, removed its top and cleaned it out, after which I took it to a vine and squeezed grapes into it until it was full. Then I closed it up again and put it out in the sun, where I left it a number of days until its contents had turned to pure wine. I started to drink some of this each day to help me fight off exhaustion in my dealings with that devil, as every sip that I took strengthened my resolution. One day, when he saw me drinking, he gestured with his hand as if to say: 'What is that?' 'Something pleasant,' I told him, 'that brings encouragement and enjoyment,' and I began to run with him, dancing between the trees, stimulated by the wine, clapping my hands and singing with joy. On seeing this, he gestured to me to hand him the gourd so that he could drink from it, and in my fear I handed it over to him. He gulped down all that was left in it, threw it on the ground and became merry and unsteady on my shoulders, until, when he had become even more sodden in his drunkenness, his whole body relaxed and he started to sway from side to side on my shoulders. When I saw that he was drunk and unconscious, I took hold of his legs and unwrapped them from my neck, after which I lowered myself to the ground with him, and sat down, throwing him off.

I could scarcely believe that I had managed to free myself and escape from my miserable state, but I then began to fear that, when he recovered from his drunkenness, he might do me some harm and so I picked up a large rock, went up to him as he slept and struck him a blow on the head that left him a lifeless mass of mixed flesh and blood, may God show him no mercy.

In my relief I walked to where I had first come ashore on the coast of the island, and there I stayed for some time, eating fruit, drinking from the streams and keeping a lookout for any passing ship. One day, I was sitting thinking over what had happened to me and the plight that I was in, wondering whether God would allow me to return safely to my own country to rejoin my family and friends, when suddenly a ship came sailing through the boisterous sea waves without a check until it anchored by the island. Those on board disembarked and I went up to them. When they caught sight of me, they hurried up and gathered around me, asking me about myself and why I had come to the island. They were astonished when I told them about my experiences, and they said: 'The man who rode on your shoulders is called the Old Man of the Sea, and you are the only one on whom he mounted who has ever escaped. God be praised that you are safe!' They fetched me food, and I ate until I had had enough, after which they gave me some clothes to wear in order to cover my nakedness and they then took me with them to their ship.

We sailed for some days and nights until fate brought us to a lofty city, all of whose houses overlooked the sea. The place is known as the City of the Apes, and at nightfall all its inhabitants leave by the sea gates and embark on skiffs and boats, spending the night at sea lest the apes come down from the mountains and attack them. I went ashore in order to look around, but before I knew it, my ship had sailed off, leaving me to regret having landed there. I remembered my companions and my first and second adventures with the apes and so I sat there weeping sorrowfully. One of the townsfolk approached me and said: 'Sir, it seems that you are a stranger here.' 'Yes,' I told him, 'I am a poor stranger. I was on board a ship that anchored here and I disembarked to look at the city, but when I got back no ship was to be seen.' 'Come with us,' he said, 'and get into this skiff, for if you stay here at night the apes will kill you.' 'To hear is to obey,' I replied, and so I got up immediately and went on board with the man and his companions. They pushed the boat out from land, sailing on until they were a mile off shore, and there I spent the night with them. The next morning they sailed back to the city, where they disembarked, and each of them went about his business. They did this every night, and any of them who stayed behind in the city at night was set upon by the apes and killed. In the day the apes would leave the city, eat fruit in the orchards and sleep in the mountains until evening, when they would come back to the city, which is in the furthest part of the lands of the Blacks.

The most remarkable thing that happened to me there was when one of the group with whom I had spent the night on the boat asked me whether I, being a stranger in those parts, had any trade that I could practise. 'No, by God, brother,' I told him. 'I am a merchant and a man of means. I owned a ship which was laden with wealth and goods, but it was wrecked at sea with the loss of everything on it and it was only by God's leave that I escaped drowning. He sent me a piece of timber on to which I clambered, and it was to this that I owed my safety.' The man then brought me a cotton bag and told me to take it and fill it with pebbles from the city. He went on: 'Go out with a group of townspeople to whom I will introduce you as a companion, telling them to look after you. Do what they do, and this may bring you something to help you get back to your own land.' He took me out of the city, where I selected a number of small pebbles to fill my bag. We then saw a group of men coming out to whom my mentor introduced me, commending me to their care and telling them: 'This man is a stranger, so take him with you and teach him the gatherers' trade so that he may be able to earn his daily bread, and God may reward you.' 'To hear is to obey,' they answered, and they welcomed me and took me with them on their expedition.

Each one of these men carried with him a bag like mine, filled with pebbles, and they walked on until they reached a broad valley with many high trees that no one could climb. In the valley were large numbers of apes who were alarmed by the sight of us and swarmed up the trees. My companions started to pelt them with the stones that they had in their bags, to which the apes replied by breaking off from the trees and throwing down what turned out to be coconuts. When I saw what the others were doing, I picked out an enormous tree with many apes on it, went up to it and started to throw stones at them. The apes tore off coconuts and when they threw them down at me, I gathered them, as the others were doing, and by the time that I had used up all the stones in my bag, I had got a large number of nuts. When everyone had finished what they were doing, they put together all they had collected and we went back to the city in what was left of the day, each of us carrying as much as he could.

I went to my friend who had introduced me to the others and gave him what I had gathered, thanking him for his kindness, but he told me to keep the nuts and sell them so as to profit from the sale price. He then gave me the key to a room in his house, telling me: 'Store the surplus coconuts here; go out with the gatherers every day just as you did today; then pick out the bad nuts and sell them, using what you get for them for your own purposes, while storing the good ones here. It may be that you can save enough to help you with your voyage home.' 'Almighty God will reward you,' I told him.

I then did what he told me, filling my bag with stones every day, going out with the gatherers and doing what they did, as they helped me with advice, showing me trees that had plenty of nuts. This went on until I had collected a large store of good coconuts and had made a lot of money from what I had sold. I started to buy whatever took my fancy and found myself enjoying life as my status increased throughout the city. Things continued like this until one day, as I was standing by the shore, I saw a ship that steered for the city and anchored off the shore. On board were merchants with their goods, and they started to trade, buying up coconuts as well as other things. I went to my friend and, after I had told him of the arrival of the ship, I said that I wanted to go back home. 'It is for you to decide,' he told me, and so I took my leave of him, having thanked him for his kindness to me. Then I went to the ship, met the captain and paid him to take me with him, after which I stowed my coconuts and what else I had on board.

The ship sailed that same day, and we went from island to island and sea to sea. Whenever we stopped at an island, I would use my coconuts for trade and barter, and God gave me in exchange more than I had had with me at the start and had lost. One island that we passed produced cinnamon and pepper, and some people told me they had seen that every bunch of pepper had a large leaf to shade it and to keep off raindrops in wet weather. When the rain stopped, the leaf would turn away and hang down at the side of the bunch. In exchange for coconuts I took away with me a large quantity of cinnamon and pepper from there. Later we passed the island of al-Asirat, which produces Qumari aloes wood, and after that another island, five days' journey in length, which has Chinese aloes wood that is superior in quality to the Qumari. The inhabitants of this latter island are more degraded and irreligious than those of the former:

they are fond of depravity, they drink wine and know nothing about the call to prayer or how to pray.

Later we came to the pearl beds, and here I gave the divers some of my coconuts and told them to go down and see what my luck would bring them. They dived there and came up with a great quantity of large and valuable pearls. 'By God, master,' they told me, 'your luck was in!' I put all that they had brought me on board and we sailed off with the blessing of Almighty God, carrying on until we reached Basra.

I landed at Basra and, having stayed there for a short time, I left for Baghdad, where I went to my own district and came to my house. When I greeted my family and my friends, they congratulated me on my safe return and, after having put all the goods that I had with me in store, I clothed widows and orphans, gave away alms and gifts and made presents to my family, my companions and my friends. God had recompensed me with four times more than I had lost, and thanks to this profit I forgot all the hardships that I had suffered and I reverted to the friendly social life that I had enjoyed before. These were my most remarkable experiences on my fifth voyage, but it is now time for supper.

When the company had finished eating, Sindbad the sailor ordered Sindbad the porter to be given a hundred *mithqals* of gold, which he took before leaving, filled with wonder at what had happened. The next morning he got up, performed the morning prayer and returned to Sindbad the sailor's house, where, on entering, he greeted his host. He was told to take a seat and the two Sindbads sat talking together until the rest of the company arrived. They chatted to one another, and when tables had been laid with food, they ate, drank and enjoyed themselves, after which SINDBAD THE SAILOR BEGAN TO SPEAK:

The Sixth Journey of Sindbad

Know, my dear friends and companions, that after my return from my fifth voyage, in my pleasures, enjoyments and happy contentment I forgot all my past hardships. I remained in this state of joy and gladness until, while I was sitting relaxed and satisfied, a number of merchants came to me having obviously just returned from a voyage. I remembered my own return and how delighted I had been to rejoin my family, my companions and my friends, together with the pleasure I had experienced at returning to my own land. I felt a longing for travel and trade and so I made up my mind to set out once again. I bought splendid and valuable goods suitable for a voyage, and, having loaded my bales, I travelled from Baghdad to Basra. There I found a large ship, on board which were traders and men of importance who had with them costly goods. I stowed my own with theirs on the ship, and we left Basra in safety.

We sailed on from place to place and city to city, trading and looking at foreign lands. Fortune was with us; our voyage went well and we made profits until one day, as we were sailing on our way, the captain suddenly gave a great cry, threw down his turban, struck his face and plucked at his beard before collapsing in the centre of the ship, overcome by distress. Merchants and passengers gathered around him to ask what was the matter. 'You must know,' he told us all, 'that we have strayed from our course. We have left the sea on which we were sailing and entered one whose ways I do not know. Unless God sends us some means of escape we are all dead, so pray to Him to save us from this.' He then got up and climbed the mast with the intention of lowering the sail, but the wind was too strong and the ship was driven back. While we were near a lofty mountain the rudder was smashed and the captain climbed down from the mast reciting the formula: 'There is no might and no power except with God, the Exalted, the Omnipotent,' and adding: 'No one can ward off fate. By God, we are in mortal peril and there is no possible escape for us.'

Everyone on the ship wept for themselves and said their farewells, convinced that their lives were at an end and there was no hope left. The ship struck the mountain and was dashed to pieces, its timbers being scattered and everything in it being submerged in the waves. The merchants fell into the sea; some were drowned while others, including me, came to land by clinging on to the mountainside. The island on which we found ourselves turned out to be a big one and was the site of a large number of wrecks; the beach was full of goods thrown up by the sea from sunken ships whose crews had been lost, the extent of this jetsam being enough to bewilder and confuse the mind.

I climbed to the highest point there, and as I walked I caught sight of a freshwater spring gushing out at the base of the mountain and flowing to a point opposite it. All the survivors from the ship who had come ashore scattered throughout the island and, dazed by the quantity of goods and effects that they saw on the beach, they started to act like madmen. For my part, I saw in the middle of the spring great numbers of gems of all sorts, precious stones, sapphires and huge pearls fit for kings. They were lying like pebbles in the bed of the stream as it flowed through the low ground, and the land surrounding the spring sparkled because of the precious stones and other such things that it contained. We also discovered there a quantity of the finest quality Chinese aloes wood together with Qumari aloes, as well as a spring that produces a type of raw ambergris which oozes out like wax over its sides, thanks to the sun's heat, and extends along the shore. Sea creatures then come out and swallow it before returning to the sea, and when it becomes heated in their bellies they vomit it out and it solidifies on the surface of the water. Both its colour and its condition change and the waves drive it on shore where travellers and traders, who can recognize it, collect it and then sell it. Pure raw ambergris that has not gone through this process overflows the side of that spring and solidifies on the ground. When the sun rises, it melts again, producing a scent which makes the whole valley smell of musk, and when the sun leaves it, it solidifies. The place where this raw ambergris is to be found is completely inaccessible, for the mountain range that rings the island is unscalable.

We continued to wander around the island looking at the resources that Almighty God had provided there, but bewildered by what we could see of our own situation and full of fear. We collected some provisions by the shore and started to ration them out, eating a mouthful every day or every second day to avoid using up our food and then dying miserably of starvation and fear. We would wash the corpses of all those who died and shroud them in what clothes and materials were washed up on the beach. Many did die, leaving only a few behind, as we had been weakened by stomach pains caused by our exposure to the sea. Within a short time every one of my friends and companions had died, one after the other, and had been buried, leaving me alone on the island. Of our large store of food, only a little was left, and I wept over my plight, saying: 'I wish that I had died before my companions so that they could have washed my body and buried me, but there is no might and no power except with God, the Exalted, the Omnipotent.'

Soon after this I got up and dug myself a deep grave beside the shore, saying to myself: 'When I sicken and know that death is at hand, I shall lie down in this grave and die there. The wind will keep blowing sand over me until it covers me and so I shall be buried.' I started to blame myself for the folly that had made me leave my country and my city in order to travel to foreign parts, in spite of what I had suffered on my first, second, third, fourth and fifth voyages. On every single one of them I had been faced with terrors and hardships that grew worse and worse each time. I did not believe that I could escape to safety and I regretted having set out to sea again, telling myself that I had been in no need of money, for I had plenty, so much, in fact, that I could not have spent it all, or even half of it, in my lifetime. That was enough and more than enough.

Then, however, I started to think the matter over and I told myself: 'The stream fed by the spring must have an end as well as a beginning, and there has to be a place where it flows into inhabited country. The right thing to do is for me to make myself a small raft, big enough for me to sit on, which I can take down and launch on the stream. I can set off on it, and if I find a way out, then God willing I shall escape, and if I don't, then it will be better to die there than here.'

Having sighed over my fate, I got up and worked hard at collecting timber from the island, both Chinese and Qumari aloes wood. What I got I lashed together on the shore with ropes from wrecked ships, and then I took matching planks from them and set them on top of the timbers. I made the raft just about as broad as the stream, or a little bit less, tying it together as firmly as I could. I took with me a store of precious stones, gems, cash and pearls as big as pebbles, together with other treasures from the island, as well as some good, pure, raw ambergris. This I loaded on to the raft together with everything else I had collected from the island, and I took all the food that was left. I then launched the raft on the stream, adding two pieces of wood, one on either side, to serve as oars, following the advice of the poet who said:

Leave a place where there is injustice;
Abandon the house to lament its builder.
You can find another land in place of that one,
But you will never find another life.
Do not let the blows of fate concern you;
Every misfortune will reach its end.
Whoever is fated to die in a certain land
Will die in no other place than that.
Send out no messenger on a grave matter;
The soul's one sincere advisor is itself.

I set out downstream on the raft, wondering what was going to happen to me. I reached the place where the stream entered an underground channel in the mountain, and as the raft came to this passage I found myself plunging into thick darkness. The raft was swept on by the current until it got to a place so narrow that its sides rubbed against the edges of the channel, while my head scraped the roof. I had no way of going back and I started to reproach myself for having put my life in danger, telling myself: 'If this is too narrow for the raft, there can be little chance that it will get out, and as I cannot go back, there can be no doubt that I will die a miserable death here.' I lay face down on the raft because of the lack of space and drifted on with no means of telling whether it was night or day because of the darkness under the mountain. I was terrified and in fear of my life the further I went along the stream, which widened at times only to narrow again. The darkness made me feel extremely tired; I couldn't resist falling into a doze and so I went to sleep, face downwards, and how far it travelled while I slept I could not tell.

When I woke, I found myself out in the light and, opening my eyes, I discovered that I was on a broad stretch of shore with the raft moored to an island. There was a crowd of Indians and Abyssinians around me, and when they saw me get up they came up to me and spoke to me in their own tongue. I couldn't understand what they were saying and I kept thinking that it was all a dream, as I was still suffering from the effects of the hardships that had overwhelmed me. Since I couldn't follow their language and could make no reply, one of them approached me and said in Arabic: 'Peace be on you, brother. What are you? Where have you come from and why are you here? How did you get into this stream and what land is there behind the mountain, as we have never known of anyone coming to us from there?' 'Who are you?' I asked in my turn, 'and what land is this?' 'Brother,' he answered, 'we are farmers and we had come to water the crops and fields that we cultivate when we discovered you asleep on this raft. We took hold of it and tied it up here so that you could get up at your leisure. But now tell us why you have come here.' 'For God's sake, sir,' I said, 'bring me some food, for I am starving, and after that ask me any questions you want.' The man hurried off to fetch food, and when I had eaten my fill, I relaxed, regained my composure and recovered my spirits. I gave thanks to Almighty God for all His mercies and was filled with joy to have emerged from the river and to have reached these people. I then told them everything that had happened to me from start to finish, including my experiences in the narrow stream.

After talking among themselves, they told me that they would have to bring me with them in order to show me to their king so that I might tell him what had happened to me. So they took me, together with the raft and all the cash, goods, gems, precious stones and jewellery that was on it, and when they brought me into the king's presence, they told him about me. He welcomed me warmly and asked me about myself and what had happened to me, after which I told him the full story of my adventures from beginning to end. The tale filled him with astonishment and he congratulated me on my escape. I then went to the raft and took a large quantity of precious stones, gems, aloes wood and raw ambergris, which I presented to him and which he accepted, showing me even greater honour and lodging me in his palace. I associated with the leading citizens, who treated me with the greatest respect, and I did not leave the palace.

Visitors to the island would ask me about my own land and in return for what I told them I would ask and receive information about theirs. One day, the king questioned me about my country and about the rule of the caliph in the lands of Baghdad, at which I told him about the justice with which he controlled his state. He was impressed by this and said: 'By God, the caliph acts in a rational and an attractive way. You have endeared him to me and I intend to prepare a present for him and to get you to take it to him.' 'To hear is to obey, master,' I said. 'I shall bring it to him and tell him that you are an affectionate friend.'

For some time I continued to stay with the king, enjoying the greatest honour and respect and leading a pleasant life, until one day, when I was sitting in the palace, I got news that a number of the townspeople had prepared a ship with the intention of sailing to the region of Basra. I told myself that I should go with them as I would never have a better opportunity than this, and so I immediately hurried off, kissed the king's hand and told him that I wanted to leave with this group on the ship that they had fitted out, as I felt a longing for my own people and my own land. 'Do what you like,' he told me, adding, 'but if you want to stay with us, you will be welcome, as we have become fond of you.' 'You have overwhelmed me with your kindness and generosity,' I replied, 'but I feel a longing for my people, my country and my family.' When he heard this, he called for the merchants who had fitted out the ship and instructed them to look after me. He made me many presents, as well as paying for my passage on the ship, and he entrusted me with a splendid gift for the caliph Harun al-Rashid in Baghdad. I took my leave of him and of all the friends whose company I had frequented, and then embarked with the merchants. We set sail, relying on God, and had a pleasant voyage with fair winds, passing from sea to sea and island to island, until, through our reliance on God, we arrived safely at Basra.

After I had disembarked, I stayed at Basra for some days and nights until I made my preparations, loaded my goods and set off for Baghdad, the City of Peace. There I had an audience with the caliph, to whom I presented the king's gift together with a full account of what had happened to me. When I had placed all my wealth and goods in store, I went to my own district, where I was met by my family and friends, and I made gifts to all my family, distributing alms and giving presents. Some time later, the caliph sent to ask me the reason behind the gift that had been given to him and details about its source. I told him: 'By God, Commander of the Faithful, I don't know the name of the city from which it came nor how to get there, but when the ship on which I was travelling was sunk, I came ashore on an island with a river in the middle of it on which I launched a raft that I had made for myself.' I went on to repeat what had happened to me on my voyage, how I had got clear of the river and reached the city, what had happened when I had got there and why I had been sent back with the gift.

The caliph was astonished by my tale, and he ordered the recorders to write it down and store the account in his treasury so as to provide a lesson for all who might read it. He then showed me the greatest favour and I stayed in Baghdad, living as well as I had done before and forgetting all my sufferings from beginning to end, while I enjoyed the pleasantest of lives in pleasure and delight. This, then, my brothers, is what happened to me on my sixth voyage and, God willing, I shall tell you of my seventh, which was even more strange and remarkable than the others.

Sindbad the sailor then ordered tables to be set with food, and when his guests had dined with him he ordered that Sindbad the porter be given a hundred *mithqals* of gold. The porter took the gift and went off as the other guests dispersed, astonished by what they had heard. He spent the night at home and then, after having performed the morning prayer, he went to the house of Sindbad the sailor, who, when all the rest of the company had assembled, began to tell them the story of the seventh voyage. HE SAID:

The Seventh Journey of Sindbad

You must know that when I returned from my sixth voyage, I resumed my former lifestyle of pleasure, relaxation and delight, and for a time I enjoyed continuous happiness and gaiety night and day, my gains and profits having been enormous. However, I then felt a longing to travel in foreign lands, to sail, to associate with merchants and to listen to their stories. When I had thought the matter over, I packed a quantity of splendid goods suitable for a voyage and transported them from Baghdad to Basra. There I found a ship ready to put to sea, on board of which were a number of leading merchants. I embarked and made friends with them, and we set out on our voyage in good health and safety and with a fair wind we reached a city called Madinat al-Sin. We were very cheerful as we talked with one another about our journey and about matters of trade, but while we were doing this, a headwind blew up into a gale. Both we and our goods were drenched by torrential rain, and we had to cover the goods with felt and canvas lest they be ruined. We addressed our prayers and supplications to Almighty God, imploring him to rescue us from the storm, and as we were doing so the captain tightened his belt, tucked up his sleeves and climbed the mast. After looking right and left, he turned to us, slapped his face and plucked at his beard. 'What is the news, captain?' we asked him. 'Ask Almighty God to rescue us from our plight,' he answered. 'Weep for yourselves and take leave of one another, for the wind has driven us to the ultimate sea in the world.'

He then climbed down from the mast and opened a box from which he took a cotton bag. He undid its fastening and took from it soil that looked like ashes, which he moistened with water. After waiting a short while, he sniffed at it and then took a little book from the box, from which he read. He then told us that it contained an astonishing revelation, the gist of which was that no one who came to this part of the world would escape from it with his life. 'This,' he told us, 'is the Region of the Kings, which contains the grave of our master Solomon, the son of David, on both of whom be peace. In it there are enormous and hideous serpents which attack and swallow every ship that comes here together with all its contents.' We were dumbfounded on hearing what he had to say, but before he had finished speaking the ship was lifted up from the sea and then crashed down again and we were terrified to hear a roar like a peal of thunder, which left us half-dead and sure that we were about to perish. Then we saw a fish as big as a huge mountain making for the ship. In our fear we wept bitterly for ourselves and prepared to die, but as we watched it coming towards us, wondering at its formidable size, suddenly another one approached that was bigger than anything we had yet seen. We had said our farewells, shedding tears for ourselves, when we caught sight of a third monster, even larger than the first two. We lost all our senses, being stunned by fear and terror as these three creatures started to circle around the ship. The third of them had just opened its mouth to swallow it and everything in it, when suddenly the ship was lifted up by a violent gust and brought down on a huge reef, where it was smashed. All its timbers were scattered and its cargo, together with the merchants and passengers, was plunged into the sea.

I stripped down to a single garment and swam for a short time before I found one of the ship's timbers, to which I clung. I managed to get astride it and, as I held on to it, the winds and waves tossed me around on the surface of the sea. One moment I would be carried up on a wave and the next hurled down again, so that in my fear I had to face the most extreme hardships as well as sufferings caused by hunger and thirst. I started to blame myself for what I had done and for abandoning a life of ease in order to court difficulty. I told myself: 'Sindbad, you have not turned away from your folly. Time after time you face these hardships and difficulties but still you go to sea, and if you say that you have given this up, you lie. So you have to endure whatever misfortune you meet, as you deserve everything that happens to you, and all this is decreed for you by Almighty God to turn you from your greed, which is the cause of your sufferings, in spite of the fact that you have riches in plenty.' Then I came to my senses and said: 'This time I make a sincere promise to Almighty God that I will renounce travelling and never again talk of it or think about it.'

I continued to address tearful supplications to Almighty God, remembering the ease, joy, pleasure and relaxation that I had enjoyed, and things went on like this through the first day and the second day, but then I came to land on a large island with many trees and streams. I began to eat the fruits of the trees and drink from the streams until I had revived. My spirits came back; my resolution strengthened and I relaxed, after which I walked through the island and found on the other side of it a large freshwater river flowing with a strong current. I remembered my earlier adventure with the raft and I said to myself that I would have to construct another one like it in the hope that I might find a way out of my predicament. If I managed to escape, I would have got all that I wanted and I would swear to Almighty God never to set out on another voyage, while if I perished, I would be at rest and no longer have to face trouble and hardship. So I started to collect wood from the trees, and this, although I did not know it, was fine sandalwood, whose like was nowhere else to be found, and when I had done that, I managed to twist boughs and creepers from the island into what could serve as ropes, with which I lashed my raft together.

'If I come off safely,' I told myself, 'it will be God's doing,' and after that I boarded the raft and launched it on the river. It took me to the end of the island but then went even further, and for three whole days I floated on. For most of the time I slept; I ate nothing at all, but when I was thirsty I drank from the river. Weariness, hunger and thirst had reduced me to little more than a sick chicken by the time the raft brought me to a high mountain, under which the river entered. When I saw that, I feared for my life, remembering the straits in which I had found myself on my last river journey. I tried to stop the raft and to get off it on to the mountain-side, but the current was too strong and it dragged the raft, with me on it, under the mountain. When I saw what was happening I was sure that I was going to die, and I recited the formula: 'There is no might and no power except with God, the Exalted, the Omnipotent.'

The raft floated on for a short distance, but then it reached a broad stretch where I could see a large valley into which the water fell with a roar like thunder and a rush like that of wind. I clutched my raft with both hands, fearful I might fall off. The waves were tossing me right and left as the current carried the raft down into the valley, and I could neither stop it nor bring it in towards the shore. This went on until it brought me alongside a large and well-built city, full of people, and when they saw the current carrying me downstream on my raft in the middle of the river, they threw me nets and ropes. They managed to bring the raft in to land and there I collapsed half-dead of hunger, sleeplessness and terror.

One of the crowd of spectators, a dignified-looking old man, welcomed me and passed me a number of fine clothes with which I covered my nakedness. He then took me with him and brought me to the baths, before providing me with revivifying drinks and fragrant perfumes. When we left the baths he took me into his house, where his family showed pleasure at meeting me. I was made to sit in an elegant room and my host prepared some splendid food for me, which I ate until I was full, and I then gave thanks to Almighty God for having rescued me. Servants brought me hot water with which I washed my hands, and slave girls fetched silk towels, which I used to dry my hands and wipe my mouth. As soon as I had finished, the old man got up and provided me with a chamber of my own, standing by itself at the side of his house, and he gave instructions to his servants and slave girls to serve me and to do anything I might want. I remained being waited on in the guest chamber for three days, eating well, with plenty to drink and surrounded by pleasant scents, until, as my fears subsided, I recovered my spirits and became calm and relaxed.

On the fourth day, the old man came to me and said: 'We have enjoyed your company, my son, and we thank God that you are safe. Would you like to come down with me to the market by the shore where you can sell your goods? With the price that you get for them you may be able to buy some things that you can use for trade.' I stayed silent for a while, saying to myself: 'Where am I to get any goods and why is he talking like this?' But he said: 'Don't be concerned or worried, my son; come with me to the market and if you find someone who will give you an acceptable price for what you have, I shall take it for you, and if not, I shall put your goods in my warehouses and keep them until a better time comes for trading.' I thought this over and decided that I had better accept his offer in order to find out what these 'goods' might be. So I said: 'To hear is to obey, uncle, for whatever you do brings blessings, and I cannot disobey you in anything.' So I went with him to the market and found that he had taken my raft to pieces, it being of sandalwood, and had told the auctioneer to call for bids.

The merchants gathered and when the bidding opened, it went up and up until it ended at a thousand dinars. The old man then turned to me and said: 'That is the price of your goods at times like these, my son. Do you want to sell at this price or would you prefer to wait? I can store the wood for you in my warehouses until the price rises and then sell it for you.' 'It is for you to decide, sir,' I told him, 'so do what you want.' 'My son,' he said, 'will you sell it to me for a hundred dinars more than the price offered by the merchants?' 'Certainly,' I told him. 'I agree to the sale and accept the price.' At that, he told his servants to remove the wood to his warehouses and I went back with him to his house. We sat down and he counted out the entire purchase price for me, after which he brought me bags in which the money was placed, and these were secured with an iron lock, whose key he handed over to me.

Some time later he said to me: 'My son, I have a proposal to make to you and I hope that you will follow my wishes in the matter.' I asked what this was, and he explained: 'I am now an old man. I have no son, but I do have a pretty young daughter, as rich as she is beautiful, whom I would like to marry to you. You could then stay with her here in this country and I would pass over to you all my wealth and my possessions. For I am old and you can take my place.' I stayed silent for a time without speaking, and he went on: 'Obey me in this, my son. I want to help you and, if you do what I ask, I will marry you to my daughter; you will be like a son to me and every single thing that I own will pass to you. If you want to go trading and to travel to your own country, no one will stop you. This wealth is at your disposal, so do what you want with it and make your own choice.' 'By God, uncle,' I told him, 'you have become like a father to me. I have experienced so many terrors that I no longer have any powers of judgement or know what to do, and as a result it is up to you to do whatever you want.' At this point the old man told his servants to fetch the *qadi* and the notaries, which they did, and he then gave his daughter to me in marriage and provided a grand feast by way of celebration. When I was taken to my bride, I found her to be very lovely indeed, well shaped and wearing ornaments, robes, valuable stones, jewellery, necklaces and precious gems which, although no one could have valued them exactly, were worth thousands upon thousands of dinars. I was filled with delight when I lay with her, and we fell in love with each other.

I stayed with my wife for some time, enjoying the greatest happiness and contentment. Her father was then gathered to the merciful presence of Almighty God. We prepared him for the funeral and then buried him, after which I took over all his possessions while all his attendants were transferred to my service. He had been the leader of the merchants, none of whom, thanks to his status, had done any dealings without his knowledge and consent, and they now put me in his place as his successor.

On further association with the townsfolk, I discovered that once a month a change came over them. They could be seen to sprout wings, with which they would fly off into the upper air, leaving no one in the city apart from children and women. I told myself that on the first of the month I would ask one of them to take me with them to wherever they were going. When the first of the month arrived, their complexions changed as their appearance altered, and so I went to one of them and begged him for God's sake to take me with him as a spectator and then bring me back. He told me that this was impossible, but I kept pressing him until he consented, and when I had got the agreement of the others, without telling any of my household, my servants or my companions, I clung on to him as he soared with me up into the sky. He flew so high with me on his shoulders that to my astonishment I heard the angels in the dome of heaven glorifying God. I said: 'Glory and praise be to God,' but before I had finished, fire came out of heaven, which almost consumed the townsfolk. They dived down and, as they were furiously angry with me, they put me down on a lofty mountain and then flew away and left me.

Alone on the mountain I blamed myself for what I had done, and I recited the formula: 'There is no might and no power except with God, the Exalted, the Omnipotent,' adding: 'Every time I escape from one disaster, I fall into another that is even worse.' I stayed on the mountain not knowing where to go when suddenly I caught sight of two young men walking there, resplendent as moons, each holding a golden staff on which he leaned. I went up to them and, after we had exchanged greetings, I conjured them in God's Name to tell me who and what they were. 'We are servants of Almighty God,' they told me, after which they gave me a staff of red gold that they had with them, before going on their way. I walked along the summit of the mountain, supporting myself on the staff and thinking about the two young men, when from beneath the mountain there emerged a snake with a man in its mouth whom it had swallowed up to his navel. He was shrieking and calling out: 'Whoever saves me will be saved by God from every calamity,' and so I advanced on the snake and struck it on the head with my golden staff, at which it spat the man out of its mouth.

He came up to me and said: 'As it was you who rescued me from that snake, I shall not leave you and you will be my companion on this mountain.' I welcomed him and we were making our way over the mountain when we were approached by a group of men. When I looked at them, I noticed that among them was the one who had flown with me on his shoulders. I went up to him and excused myself politely, adding: 'My friend, this is not the way in which friends should treat each other.' He said: 'It was you who almost had us killed by glorifying God while you were on my back.' 'Don't hold it against me,' I replied. 'I didn't know about this, but I shall not speak another word.' He agreed to take me back with him, but on condition that I would not mention the Name of God or glorify Him while he was carrying me, after which he took me up and flew off with me as he had done before, bringing me to my own house. My wife met me and greeted me, but after congratulating me on my safe return, she warned me: 'Take care not to go out with these people again and have no dealings with them. They are brothers of the devil and don't know how to call on the Name of Almighty God.' 'How did your father deal with them, then?' I asked her. 'My father was not one of them and did not do what they do. My advice, now that he is dead, is that you should sell everything that we have, use the purchase price to buy goods, and then sail back to your own country and your own family. I shall go with you as there is nothing to keep me here now that both my parents are dead.'

After that, I began to sell my father-in-law's possessions bit by bit, while waiting for someone to sail from the city whom I could accompany. I was still doing this when a group of city merchants made up their minds to embark on a voyage, and as they could not find a ship, they bought timber and built a large one for themselves. I hired myself a passage with them and, after having paid the price in full, I embarked with my wife and all that we could take with us, abandoning our properties and estates. We put out to sea and sailed on from island to island and sea to sea, enjoying fair winds, until we came safely to land at Basra. I did not stay there but hired a passage on another ship, on which I loaded everything that I had brought with me, and set off for Baghdad. There I went to my own district and, on coming to my house, I met my family, my companions and my friends, and then I stored all my goods in my warehouses. My family calculated that on this seventh voyage I had been absent for twenty-seven years and this had made them despair of ever seeing me again. When I arrived and told them of all my adventures, they were filled with astonishment and congratulated me on my safe return.

I now vowed to Almighty God that after this, my seventh and last, voyage I would never again travel either by land or sea, for I no longer felt any desire for this, and I gave thanks to Almighty God, glory be to Him, with grateful praise, for having brought me back to my family, my land and my country. So consider, Sindbad the landsman, what happened to me during my experiences and adventures.

'Don't hold against me what I said about you,' said the other Sindbad, and the two of them continued to enjoy an increasingly happy, cheerful and contented life as friends until they were visited by the destroyer of delights, the parter of companions, the wrecker of palaces and the filler of graves, the bearer of the cup of death. Praise be to the living God, Who does not die.

[Nights 536–66]

The Adventures of 'Ali al-Zaibaq

'Ali al-Zaibaq the Cairene was a trickster living in Cairo where the chief of police was a man called Salah al-Misri, who had a force of forty men. These men used to set traps for 'Ali, expecting that he would fall into one of them, but when they looked, they would find that he had slipped away like mercury and this was why he was called 'Ali al-Zaibaq.* One day, when he was sitting in his hall with his men, he felt depressed and gloomy, and when his lieutenant saw him there with a frown on his face, he asked: 'What's wrong, chief? If you're out of sorts, take a stroll through the city, as a walk in the markets will cure your cares.' So 'Ali got up to walk through Cairo, but he only became more and more depressed. He passed a wine shop and thought of going there to get drunk, but when he went in he found seven rows of people sitting there. He told the proprietor that he would only sit alone, and so the man put him in a room by himself and brought him wine. When he had drunk himself silly, he left the place and set out through the city.

He walked on and on through the streets until he reached al-Darb al-Ahmar and, thanks to the awe in which he was held, the road emptied before him. He turned to see a water carrier, with his jug, calling out on the road: 'Take and give! The only drink comes from raisins; the only union is with the beloved and only the intelligent sit at the top table.' 'Come here and pour me a drink,' 'Ali called, and the man gave him the jug, but after staring at it 'Ali upset it and poured the contents on to the ground. 'Aren't you going to drink?' the man asked, and 'Ali again said: 'Pour it for me,' but again he upset the jug and poured away the water. He went on to do this a third time, and the man said: 'If you're not going to drink, I'm off.' 'Pour me a drink,' 'Ali told him, and this time, when the man filled the jug and passed it to him, 'Ali took it from him, drank

* *Zaibaq* means 'mercury' in Arabic.

and gave him a dinar. The man looked at him contemptuously and said: 'Good luck, good luck to you, young man! Little men are great in some people's eyes.' 'Ali went up to him and seized him by his shirt, drawing a costly dagger such as the one described in the lines:

Strike the stubborn enemy with your dagger,
Fearing nothing but the Creator's power.
Avoid those who are to be blamed,
And never abandon generous qualities.

'*Shaikh*,' he said, 'talk sense. Your water skin would fetch three dirhams at the most and I only emptied out one *ratl* of water from the jug.' The water carrier agreed, and 'Ali went on: 'I gave you a gold dinar, so why do you despise me? Have you ever seen a braver or a more generous man than me?' 'Yes, I have,' the water carrier replied, 'for while women have been bearing children, there has never been a brave man in this world who was not generous.' 'Who was it whom you found to outdo me?' 'Ali asked, and THE MAN SAID:

I had a remarkable adventure. My father was the chief of the water carriers in Cairo. When he died he left me five camels, a mule, a booth and a house, but a poor man is never satisfied until he dies. I said to myself that I would go to the Hijaz, so I took my string of camels and kept on borrowing money until I had collected five hundred dinars, but I lost all this on the pilgrimage. I told myself that, were I to go back to Cairo, my creditors would imprison me for debt and so I set off with the Syrian pilgrims, and after reaching Aleppo I went on to Baghdad. There I asked for the chief of the water carriers, and after I had been directed to him I went in and recited the first *sura* of the Quran for him. He asked me about my circumstances and, when I had told him all that had happened to me, he let me have an empty booth and gave me a water skin and other equipment. The next morning I set out to walk around the city, trusting in God, but when I passed the jug to a man so that he could take a drink, he told me: 'I don't need a drink as I've not eaten. A miser invited me to his house and produced two pitchers of water. I said: "You miserable fellow, are you offering me a drink after having given me nothing at all to eat?"' So he told me to go away, adding: 'When I have had some food, then you can pour me some water.' I went up to someone else, but all he did was to say: 'May God provide for you,' and things went on like this until noon. Up till then nobody had given me anything at all and I said to myself that I wished I had never come to Baghdad.

Just then I saw a number of people running. I followed them and saw a long file of men riding two by two, with scarfs around their tarbooshes, wearing burnouses and protected with felt and steel. I asked a man who they were and he told me that this was the retinue of Captain Ahmad al-Danaf. 'What is his post?' I asked, and I was told that he was responsible for order at court and in Baghdad itself, as well as for policing the suburbs. He was paid a monthly salary of a thousand dinars by the caliph, while each of his men got a hundred and Hasan Shuman got the same pay as Ahmad. The men were now on their way from the court to their barracks. At that point, Ahmad caught sight of me and asked me for a drink. I filled the jug and passed it to him, but he upset it and poured out the water. He did this again, but the third time he took a sip, like you. Then he asked me where I came from and when I said: 'Cairo,' he exclaimed: 'God bless Cairo and the Cairenes!' before going on to ask why I had come to Baghdad. I told him my story, explaining that I owed money and had come to escape debt and poverty. He welcomed me and gave me five dinars, after which he said to his men: 'Be generous to this man for the sake of God.' They each gave me a dinar and Ahmad said: '*Shaikh*, as long as you stay in Baghdad, you can have this every time you pour water for us.' I kept on going to these people and receiving their generosity so that when, after some days, I counted up what I had got from them, I found that it came to a thousand dinars.

I said to myself that the proper thing to do would be to go back to Egypt, and so I went to Ahmad's headquarters and kissed his hands. When he asked me what I wanted, I said: 'I want to go home,' and I recited these lines for him:

Wherever a stranger stays,
It is like a castle built on winds.
A breath of air destroys what he has made,
And so this stranger has made up his mind to leave.

I added that a caravan was setting out for Cairo and that I wanted to go back to my family. He gave me a mule and a hundred dinars, before saying: '*Shaikh*, I want to entrust you with something. Do you know the people in Cairo?' 'Yes,' I said, and he told me: 'Take this letter and deliver it to 'Ali al-Zaibaq of Cairo. Tell him: "Your chief sends you his greetings, and he is now with the caliph."' So I took the letter from him and came back to Cairo, and when my creditors saw me I settled my debts. I started to work again as a water carrier, but I haven't delivered Ahmad's letter as I don't know where the man is based.'

'You can relax happily,' said 'Ali, 'for I'm the man you want and I was the first of Captain Ahmad's young men. So hand over the letter.' The water carrier gave it to him, and he opened it and read it. In it he found these lines:

Ornament of the handsome, I have written to you
On paper that will travel with the winds.
Could I fly, I would do so out of longing,
But how can a bird fly whose wings are clipped?

It went on: 'Greetings from Captain Ahmad al-Danaf to the senior of his children, 'Ali al-Zaibaq of Cairo. I have to tell you that I targeted Salah al-Din al-Misri and buried him alive with the tricks that I played on him, so that I won over his men, among them being 'Ali Kitf al-Jamal. I was then attached to the court and put in charge of policing Baghdad as well as the suburbs. If you want to keep to the agreement that we made, then come to me. You may be able to bring off some coup here that will ingratiate you with the caliph and get him to give you a salary and allowances, as well as providing you with a base, which is what I would like. Goodbye.'

When 'Ali had read the letter, he kissed it and put it on his head before handing the water carrier ten dinars as a reward for the good news. He then went back to his headquarters, where he passed this on to his followers and told them to look after each other. Next he removed the clothes that he was wearing and put on a long cloak and a tarboosh, taking a case containing a spear twenty-four cubits long made of bamboo whose sections fitted into one another. His lieutenant said: 'Are you going off when our coffers are empty?' but 'Ali said: 'When I get to Damascus, I'll send you enough to keep you going.'

He then went on his way and joined up with a caravan in which the chief of the merchants was travelling with forty of his colleagues. All their goods had been loaded except for those of their chief, which were still on the ground, and 'Ali heard the caravan leader, a Syrian, telling the muleteers to come and help him, only to be answered with insults and abuse. 'Ali told himself that the best thing for him would be to travel with this man.

He himself was a handsome, beardless boy, and so he went up and greeted the Syrian, who welcomed him and asked what he wanted. 'Uncle,' 'Ali said, 'I see that you are single-handed with forty mule-loads of goods. Why didn't you bring people to help you?' 'My son,' the Syrian replied, 'I hired two lads, provided them with clothes and put two hundred dinars in the pockets of each of them, but after they had helped me as far as al-Khanika, they ran off.' 'Where are you making for?' asked 'Ali, and when the Syrian told him: 'Aleppo,' he said: 'I shall help you.'

They loaded the goods and set out, together with the chief of the merchants on his mule. The Syrian was glad to have 'Ali with him, and fell in love with him. At nightfall the caravan halted and they ate and drank, after which, when it was time for sleep, 'Ali lay down on his side on the ground and pretended to be asleep. The Syrian slept near him, but 'Ali got up and sat down at the entrance to the chief's pavilion. The Syrian turned over, meaning to take 'Ali in his arms, and when he could not find him he said to himself: 'He may have been taken by someone else to whom he made a promise, but I have a better right to him, and another night I shall keep him with me.'

As for 'Ali, he stayed where he was by the merchant's pavilion until it was nearly dawn, after which he came and lay down near the Syrian. When the man woke up to find him there, he said to himself: 'If I ask him where he has been, he will leave me and go off.' 'Ali continued to outwit him until they came to a wood with a cave which served as a den for a fierce lion; every caravan that passed would draw lots, the loser being thrown to the lion. This time it was the chief of the merchants who drew the short straw, and the lion appeared, blocking the path and waiting for its victim. In great distress the merchant went to the caravan leader and cursed him and his journey, before telling him to give the goods that he had with him to his children after his death. The cunning 'Ali asked what this was all about, and when they told him, he said: 'Why do you run away from a desert cat? I'll undertake to kill it for you.' The caravan leader went to the merchant and told him about this, after which he promised to give 'Ali a thousand dinars if he killed the lion, while the others also promised to reward him.

'Ali then discarded his cloak, uncovering his steel coat, and then, taking a steel sword, he tightened the screw that fastened its blade to its hilt before going out alone and shouting at the lion. For its part, the lion leapt at him, but he struck it between the eyes with his sword, cutting it in half as the caravan leader and the merchants looked on. 'Have no fear, uncle,' he called to the leader, who replied: 'My son, I shall for ever be your servant,' while the chief of the merchants put his arms around him, kissed him between the eyes and presented him with a thousand dinars. Each of the other merchants gave him twenty dinars, and he deposited the whole sum with the chief.

The next morning, they started off towards Baghdad and came to the Forest of Lions and the Valley of Dogs. Here there lurked the tribe of a recalcitrant Bedouin highwayman, who came out against them, causing them to run away. The chief of the merchants exclaimed: 'My money is lost!' but just then 'Ali appeared, wearing a leather jacket hung with bells. He fitted together the sections of his spear, and mounted a horse that he had snatched from those the Bedouin had with him. He then challenged the man to a duel with spears and caused the mare he was riding to bolt as 'Ali jingled his bells. He cut through the man's spear and then struck off his head with a blow to the neck. When his followers saw this they closed in on 'Ali, but with a shout of 'God is greater!' he charged at them and put them to flight, after which he fastened the Bedouin's head on his spear point. The merchants rewarded him and the caravan went on to Baghdad. There he asked the chief of the merchants for the money that he had entrusted to him and this he gave to the caravan leader, saying: 'When you get to Cairo, ask for my headquarters and give this money to my lieutenant there.'

He entered Baghdad the next morning and went through the streets asking for the headquarters of Ahmad al-Danaf, but no one would direct him there. When he came to the square of al-Nafd he found children playing, among them a boy called Ahmad al-Laqit, and 'Ali told himself that he would only find what he wanted by asking the children. He looked round and saw a sweet seller, some of whose wares he bought. Then he called to the children, but Ahmad al-Laqit drove them away before going up to 'Ali himself and asking him what he wanted. 'Ali told him: 'I had a son who died and I saw him in a dream asking for sweetmeats, which is why I have bought some to give to every child.' He presented Ahmad al-Laqit with a piece, and when the boy looked at it he saw a dinar sticking to it. 'Go away,' he said. 'If you ask about me, you will find that I am no catamite.' 'Boy,' said 'Ali, 'a clever fellow takes the pay and a clever fellow offers it. I've been going round the town asking for the headquarters of Ahmad al-Danaf, but no one will show me the way. This dinar is for you if you direct me.' The boy said: 'Follow me as I go on ahead until I get there, and then I shall catch up a pebble with my toes and throw it against the door so that you can see which it is.' They went off, one after the other, until the boy caught up the pebble and threw it at the door, which 'Ali then marked. He now laid hold of the boy and tried unsuccessfully to get the dinar back from him, before telling him to go off, adding: 'You deserve a gift because you are sharp, intelligent and brave. If God wills that the caliph appoint me as a captain, I'll make you one of my band.'

When the boy had left, 'Ali went up to the house and knocked on the door. Ahmad al-Danaf told his lieutenant to open it, saying: 'This is the knock of 'Ali al-Zaibaq the Cairene.' When it had been opened, 'Ali went in and greeted Ahmad, who embraced him, while his forty men added their own greetings. Ahmad gave him a robe and told him: 'When the caliph appointed me captain, he gave me clothes for my followers and I kept this for you.' 'Ali was seated in the place of honour, and when food and drink had been provided they all ate and drank until they were drunk, keeping it up until morning. Ahmad then told 'Ali not to go wandering through the streets of Baghdad but to stay in the house. 'Why?' 'Ali asked, adding: 'I've not come to be shut up, but to see the sights.' 'My son,' Ahmad told him, 'don't imagine that Baghdad is like Cairo. This is the seat of the caliphate and there are vast numbers of tricksters, as roguery sprouts here like vegetables in the countryside.' For three days 'Ali stayed in the house, and Ahmad then said that he wanted to present him to the caliph so that he could be given an allowance. 'Wait for the right moment,' 'Ali told him, after which Ahmad left him alone.

Later, while 'Ali was sitting in the house and feeling depressed and ill at ease, he decided to cheer himself up by going out and walking through the city. So he went off and walked from street to street until in the middle of the market he came across a cookshop and went in to eat. When he got up to wash his hands he came across forty slaves wearing felt-padded tunics with steel swords marching two by two. Bringing up the rear and mounted on a mule was Dalila the wily, wearing a helmet covered with gold leaf and plated with iron, a mail coat and equipment to match. She was on her way back from the court to her *khan*, and, when her eye fell on 'Ali, she looked at him closely and noted that he was of the same height and breadth as Ahmad al-Danaf. He was wearing a loose robe as well as a hooded cloak and carrying a steel blade among other things, and it was quite clear that here was a man of unimpeachable courage.

On her return to the *khan*, Dalila went to her daughter, Zainab, and got out the divination table, and when she shook the sand over it she discovered that the young man was 'Ali the Cairene and that his good fortune would eclipse hers and that of her daughter. Zainab asked her: 'What did you see, mother, that made you turn to divination?' to which she answered: 'Today I saw a young man who looks like Ahmad al-Danaf, and I'm afraid that if he hears that you stripped Ahmad and his men of their clothes, he may come here in order to play a trick on us to avenge his chief and the forty men. I think he must be staying in Ahmad's headquarters.' 'What are you worried about?' Zainab asked, adding: 'I think that you have taken his measure.'

Zainab now put on her most splendid dress and went out to walk through the streets, captivating all who saw her, making promises, swearing oaths, listening to what they said and flaunting herself brazenly. She went from market to market until she saw 'Ali al-Zaibaq coming towards her. She rubbed against him with her shoulder and then turned and exclaimed: 'God preserve people of taste!' 'What a beautiful figure you have!' he told her, and asked: 'Who do you belong to?' 'To a fine fellow like you,' she said, and when he went on to ask whether she was married or single, she said that she was married. 'My place or yours?' he asked. 'I'm the daughter of a merchant,' she told him, 'and my husband is a merchant. This is the first day in my life that I have ever been outside, and that is because I had prepared food and was about to eat when I found that I had no appetite for it. Then, when I saw you, I fell in love with you. Can you bring yourself to console me and join me in a bite?' 'Whoever is invited must accept,' 'Ali replied, and as she walked on he followed her from street to street.

As he walked behind her, 'Ali said to himself: 'How can you do this in a strange city? The proverb has it that those who fornicate while abroad will have their hopes dashed by God. I shall politely put her off.' So he said: 'Take this dinar and fix another time for me,' but she swore by the Greatest Name of God: 'You must come home with me now so that I can show how I love you.' He followed her until she came to the locked door of a house with a high portal. 'Open the lock,' Zainab told him, but when he asked where the key was, she told him that it was lost. 'Whoever opens a lock without a key is a robber who should be punished by the magistrate,' he said, adding, 'and as for me, I've no idea how to do it.' She drew the veil from her face and he gave her a glance which was followed by a thousand sighs. She then let the veil hang down over the lock and recited the names of the mother of Moses over it, at which it opened without a key. She went in, and 'Ali followed and saw swords and weapons of steel.

Zainab removed her veil and sat down with him. Saying to himself:

'Finish off what God has decreed for you,' he leaned towards her to kiss her cheek, but she covered it with the palm of her hand, exclaiming: 'Pure pleasure only comes at night!' She then produced food and drink and they ate and drank, after which she got up and filled the water jug from the well and poured it over his hands, which he washed. All of a sudden, while they were doing this, she began to beat her breast and said: 'My husband had a ruby ring which was pledged for five hundred dinars. I put it on but it was too big and so I used wax to fix it more tightly, but when I let down the water bucket it must have fallen into the well. Turn to look at the door while I take my clothes off before going down there to recover it.' 'It would be a disgrace if you were to go down while I'm here,' 'Ali objected and added: 'No one is going down except me.' He stripped off his clothes and tied himself to the well rope, after which Zainab let him down into the well. The water was deep and after a time she told him: 'I haven't got enough rope left. Untie yourself and drop down.' He did this, but, far as he sank into the water, he still didn't reach the bottom. Zainab meanwhile veiled herself and, taking his clothes, she went back to her mother and told her: 'I have taken the clothes of 'Ali the Cairene and left him in the well of the house of the emir Hasan, from which he's not likely to escape.'

This emir was away at court at the time. When he came back, he found the door open and said to his groom: 'Why didn't you lock up?' 'I did, with my own hand,' the man protested, and Hasan then swore that a robber must have entered. He went in and looked around but found no one there. So he told the groom to fill the water jug so that he could wash, and the groom took the bucket and lowered it into the well. When he tried to draw it up again, he found it heavy, and when he looked down, he saw something sitting in it. He let it down again and called out: 'Master, an *'ifrit* has come out from the well.' 'Go and fetch four Quranic scholars to recite the Quran at it so it may go away,' Hasan told him. When the four had come, Hasan told them to stand around the well and recite. His servant and his groom came to let down the bucket, and this time when 'Ali took hold of it he hid himself inside it and waited until he was nearly on a level with Hasan and the others. He then jumped among the reciters, who started to hit out at each other, shouting: '*'Ifrit, 'ifrit!*' Hasan could see that this was a young man and asked: 'Are you a robber?' 'No,' said 'Ali, and Hasan went on: 'Why did you go down into the well?' 'Ali replied: 'I polluted myself in my sleep and went down to wash in the Tigris, but when I plunged into the water the current pulled me under the surface and eventually I came out in this well.' 'Tell the truth,' Hasan said, and when 'Ali had told him the whole story, Hasan sent him away dressed in some old clothes.

When he got back to Ahmad al-Danaf's base and told him what had happened, Ahmad said: 'Didn't I tell you that in Baghdad there are women who play tricks on men?', while 'Ali Kitf al-Jamal exclaimed: 'By the Greatest Name of God, tell me how you can be the leader of the Cairo youngsters and still have your clothes taken by a girl.' 'Ali found this hard to stomach and regretted what he had done, but Ahmad gave him another robe and Hasan Shuman asked if he knew the girl. When he said no, Hasan said: 'It must have been Zainab, the daughter of Dalila the wily, the gatekeeper of the caliph's *khan*. Have you fallen into her toils?' 'Yes,' said 'Ali, and Hasan went on to tell him that it was this girl who had taken the clothes of Ahmad, their chief, and of all his company. 'This is a disgrace for you!' exclaimed 'Ali, and when Hasan asked what he proposed to do, he said that he wanted to marry her. 'You'll never be able to do that, so forget about her,' Hasan told him, but when 'Ali went on to ask how to manage it, Hasan then encouraged him and said: 'If you drink out of my hand and march under my banner, I'll see that you get what you want from her.'

'Ali agreed to this, and Hasan told him to take off his clothes. When he had done that, Hasan took a cauldron and boiled up in it something that looked like pitch, which he smeared on 'Ali's body, as well as on his lips and cheeks, until he looked like a black slave. He used red kohl on his eyes and dressed him in the clothes of a servant, before giving him a tray on which were kebabs and wine. He said: 'In the *khan* there is a black cook and you now look like him. The only things that this man needs from the market are meat and vegetables, so approach him politely, address him in the argot of the blacks, greet him and say: "It has been a long time since I met you in the pub." He will tell you: "I've been busy. I've forty black slaves to look after, cooking them one meal in the morning and another in the evening, as well as feeding forty dogs and preparing food for both Dalila and her daughter, Zainab." Say to him: "Come on. Let's eat kebabs and drink some beer," after which go into the house with him and make him drunk. When you've done that, ask him how many different dishes he has to cook, what the dogs eat and where the keys of the kitchen and the pantry are kept, as a drunk man will tell you everything that he would conceal if he were sober. After that, drug him and put on his clothes, take the knives from his belt and the vegetable basket, and go to the market and buy meat and vegetables. After that you can enter both the kitchen and the pantry of the *khan* and cook the meal. Put it in a bowl and then take it to Dalila after you've added *banj* to it so as to drug the dogs, the slaves, and Dalila and Zainab as well. Go upstairs and fetch all the clothes you find, and if you want to marry Zainab, bring the forty carrier pigeons with you.'

'Ali went off, and when he saw the cook he greeted him and repeated what Hasan had told him to say. The cook told him he was busy looking after the slaves and the dogs in the *khan*, after which 'Ali took him off and made him drunk before asking how many dishes he had to cook. The man told him that he cooked five different dishes in the morning and five in the evening, adding: 'And yesterday they asked me for a sixth, rice and honey, as well as a seventh, which was cooked pomegranate seeds.' 'How do you serve this?' 'Ali asked, and the cook said: 'First I take up Zainab's tray and then that of Dalila, after which I give the slaves their evening meal. Then I feed the dogs, giving each one its fill of meat, and it takes at least one *ratl*'s weight of this to satisfy them.'

As fate would have it, 'Ali forgot to ask about the keys, but he managed to get the cook's clothes, which he put on, and he took the basket and went to the market, where he bought the meat and the vegetables. He then went back, and when he entered the door of the *khan* he saw Dalila sitting there looking at everyone who came in or went out, and he saw the forty armed slaves, but this did not daunt him. When Dalila caught sight of him, she recognized him and said: 'Go back, you robber chief. Are you thinking of playing a trick on me in this *khan*?' 'Ali, in his disguise as a black slave, turned to her and asked: 'What are you saying, doorkeeper?' 'What have you done with the cook?' she asked. 'Have you killed him or drugged him?' 'What cook are you talking about?' said 'Ali. 'I'm the only cook here.' 'You're lying,' she told him. 'You are 'Ali al-Zaibaq from Cairo.' Using the argot of the blacks, 'Ali replied: 'Doorkeeper, are Cairenes white or black? I am not going to serve here any longer.' At that, the black slaves asked: 'What's wrong, cousin?' and Dalila said: 'He's no cousin of yours. This is 'Ali al-Zaibaq from Cairo and I think that he has drugged your cousin or killed him.' They insisted that he was Saʿdullah the cook, one of theirs, but she denied it again and insisted that he was 'Ali the Cairene, who had dyed his skin. 'Who is this 'Ali?' 'Ali said. 'I am Saʿdullah.' 'I have some ointment that can test this,' Dalila said, but when she fetched it and rubbed it on his arm, the black dye didn't come off and the slaves said: 'Let him cook our meal for us.' 'If he is really one of yours,'

Dalila told them, 'he'll know what you asked for yesterday and how many dishes he cooks each day.' They asked 'Ali about this, and he said: 'I gave you lentils, rice, soup, ragout and rose sherbet, with rice and honey as a sixth dish, while a seventh was cooked pomegranate seeds, with the same in the evening.' 'True enough,' they said, and Dalila then told them: 'Go in with him, and if he knows where the kitchen and the pantry are, then he is indeed your cousin, but if not, kill him.'

As it happened the cook had brought up a cat, and whenever he came to the kitchen, this cat would stand by the door and then jump up on his shoulder as he went in. When it saw 'Ali coming, it jumped up, and when he put it down again, it walked in front of him to the kitchen. He realized that where it stopped must be the kitchen door, and so he took the keys, noticing that some feathers were still sticking to one of them. He understood that this must be the kitchen key and so he opened the door, put the vegetables inside and went out again. The cat ran on in front of him, making for another door, which he could tell must be that of the pantry, and when he took the keys he saw that one had traces of grease on it and, recognizing that this must be the right one, he used it to open the pantry door. The slaves told Dalila that, had he been a stranger, he would neither have known where the two rooms were nor have been able to pick out the right keys from the bunch. 'This is our cousin, Sa'dullah,' they insisted, but she said: 'It was the cat who showed him where the rooms were, and he picked out the keys by inference. This does not take me in.'

'Ali then went to the kitchen and cooked the meal. He took a tray up to Zainab, in whose room he saw all the clothes of his companions, and after that he went down again and prepared Dalila's tray, before feeding the slaves and giving meat to the dogs. In the evening he repeated the process. The door of the *khan* was only to be opened and shut, both morning and evening, while it was light, and so he then got up and called out to those in the *khan*: 'The slaves are on watch and the dogs have been released. Anyone who comes out has no one to blame but themselves.' He had delayed feeding the dogs and had poisoned their meat, so that when he put it down for them, they died after eating it, while he had used *banj* to drug all the slaves as well as Dalila and Zainab. He then went up and took all the clothes, together with the carrier pigeons, opened the door of the *khan* and left. When he got to Ahmad's headquarters, Hasan Shuman saw him and asked what he had done. 'Ali told him the whole story and Hasan thanked him, before getting him to strip and then restoring his natural colour by boiling up some herbs with which he washed him. 'Ali went back to the cook, returned his clothes to him and brought him back to consciousness. The cook went to the vegetable seller, collected vegetables and returned to the *khan*.

So much for 'Ali, but as for Dalila the wily, one of the merchants living in the *khan* went down at dawn from the floor on which he was living to find the door open, the slaves drugged and the dogs dead. When he came to Dalila, he discovered that she too had been drugged and that on her throat was a sheet of paper. By her head was a sponge steeped in the antidote to *banj*, and when he applied this to her nostrils she regained consciousness. 'Where am I?' she asked, and the merchant told her: 'When I came down, I found the door open; both you and the slaves were drugged and the dogs were dead.' Dalila took the note and read: ''Ali the Cairene did this.' She then applied the antidote to the slaves and to Zainab, saying: 'Didn't I tell you that this was 'Ali?' She told the slaves to keep the matter quiet and she said to Zainab: 'How many times did I tell you that 'Ali would not fail to take his revenge, and he has done this in return for what you did to him. He could have acted differently with you, but he stopped at this as a mark of goodwill in the hope of winning our affection.'

She changed her masculine clothes for those of a woman, tied a kerchief round her neck as a mark of peace and set out for the headquarters of Ahmad al-Danaf. When 'Ali had come there bringing the clothes and the carrier pigeons, Hasan Shuman had given Ahmad's lieutenant money to buy forty pigeons, which he did, before cooking them and serving them to the men. It was at this point that Dalila knocked at the door, and Ahmad, who recognized her knock, told his lieutenant to get up and open the door. When he did this, Dalila came in and Hasan Shuman said: 'What has brought you here, you ill-omened old woman? You and your brother, Zuraiq the fishmonger, are two of a kind.' 'Captain,' said Dalila, 'I was in the wrong and here am I at your mercy, but tell me which of you was it who played this trick on me.' 'He is the foremost of my company,' Ahmad told her, and she said: 'For God's sake, ask him on my behalf to do me the favour of handing back the carrier pigeons and what else belongs to them.' 'God reward you, 'Ali!' exclaimed Hasan Shuman. 'Why did you cook those pigeons?' 'I didn't know that they were carrier pigeons,' 'Ali told him, and Ahmad sent his lieutenant to fetch them. He handed the dish to Dalila, who took a piece and chewed it before saying: 'This isn't the flesh of a carrier pigeon, for I fed them on musk grains and the musk gives their flesh its own taste.' Hasan Shuman said: 'If you want to get your own pigeons back, then do what 'Ali wants.' 'What is that?'

asked Dalila, and Hasan replied: 'He wants you to marry him to your daughter, Zainab.' 'I've no power over her except through her own goodwill,' Dalila replied, and Hasan then told 'Ali to return the pigeons, which he did to her delight. 'You owe us a full reply,' Hasan said to her, and she told him: 'If 'Ali wants to marry Zainab, this trick that he has played is not a real piece of cleverness. What would be a really sharp piece of work would be for him to ask for her hand from my brother, Captain Zuraiq, who is her guardian. It is he who calls out: "A pound of fish for twopence," and who has hanging up in his shop a purse containing two thousand gold dinars.' When Ahmad and his men heard what she said, they exclaimed: 'What are you saying, you whore? You want to rob us of our brother 'Ali.'

Dalila then went back to the *khan* and told Zainab that 'Ali had asked for her hand. Zainab was delighted, as the fact that 'Ali had not raped her had made her love him, and so she asked her mother what had happened next. Dalila told her that she had made a condition that 'Ali ask her uncle Zuraiq for her hand, thus guaranteeing 'Ali's death.

'Ali himself turned to the others and asked what kind of a man Zuraiq was. They said: 'He is the leader of the gangs of Iraq. He can almost bore through mountains, grasp the stars and steal kohl from the eyes. He had no equal at this kind of thing, but he repented and opened a fish shop which brought him in two thousand dinars. He put the money in a purse to which he tied a silk thread and to this he attached brass bells of various kinds, fixing the other end of it to a peg inside the shop door. Whenever he opens up the shop, he hangs up the purse and calls out: "Where are you, knaves of Egypt, rogues of Iraq and skilled thieves of Persia? Zuraiq the fishmonger has hung up a purse in front of his shop, and whoever claims to be a subtle operator and can take it by a trick can keep it." Greedy rogues have come to try their luck, but no one has been able to take the purse, as Zuraiq keeps lumps of lead under his feet as he lights his fire and fries his fish, and whenever someone is tempted to try to surprise him and snatch the purse, he strikes him with a lump of lead, disabling or killing him. If you want to go up against him, 'Ali, you will be like a man who beats his breast in a funeral procession with no idea of who has died. You're no match for him and I'm afraid that he will harm you. There is no need for you to marry Zainab and whoever abandons something can live without it.'

'This is a disgrace, men,' 'Ali said. 'I must take the purse.' He told them to fetch him girl's clothes, and when they brought them, he put them on, dyed himself with henna and veiled his face. He killed a lamb and drained its blood, after which he removed and cleaned its intestine, tying up its rump and filling it with blood. He then fastened this between his thighs underneath his clothes and put on boots. Next he made two false breasts from the crops of birds, filling them with milk, and he put cotton over his stomach, tying cloth over it, and using a starched kerchief as a girdle. Everyone who saw him admired his buttocks.

He gave a dinar to a donkey man who happened to come up, and the man mounted him on his donkey and went off with him in the direction of Zuraiq's shop, where he could clearly see the gold in the purse that was hanging there. Zuraiq was frying fish, and when 'Ali asked the donkey man what the smell was, the man told him that it came from Zuraiq's fish. 'Ali said: 'I'm pregnant and this smell is doing me harm. Fetch me a piece of fish.' The donkey man said to Zuraiq: 'The smell of your fish this morning is affecting pregnant women. I've got with me the pregnant wife of the emir Hasan Sharr al-Tariq and she has smelt it, so give her a piece of fish, as the child is stirring in her womb. May God, the Shelterer, protect us from the evil of this day!'

Zuraiq took a slice of fish and was about to fry it when he found that his fire had gone out and so he went in to relight it. As 'Ali sat down, he leaned against the intestine, which broke open, spilling the blood out between his legs. 'Oh, my side, oh, my back,' he groaned and the donkey man turned and saw the stream of blood. 'What's wrong with you, my lady?' he asked, and 'Ali, in his character as a woman, said: 'I've miscarried.' Zuraiq looked out and then, alarmed at the sight of the blood, he ran back into the shop. 'God damn you, Zuraiq,' the donkey man said, 'the girl has had a miscarriage, and you won't be able to cope with her husband. Why did you start making smells in the morning, and when I told you to fetch a slice of fish, why wouldn't you do it?' He then took his donkey and went on his way.

When Zuraiq ran back into his shop, 'Ali reached out for the purse, but when he touched it, the gold coins in it clinked and the various bells and rings jangled. 'You scum,' cried Zuraiq, 'I can see through your swindle. Are you trying to play a trick on me dressed as a girl? Take what is coming to you,' and he threw a lump of lead at him. This missed him and hit someone else, causing consternation among the bystanders, who said to him: 'Are you a tradesman or a hooligan? If you are a tradesman, take down your purse and give the people a rest from the trouble you cause.' Zuraiq swore that he would do this.

As for 'Ali, he went back to his headquarters, and when Hasan Shuman asked what he had done, he told him the whole story. He then took off his woman's disguise and asked Hasan for the clothes of a groom. When these had been fetched, he put them on and, taking a dish and five dirhams, he went back to Zuraiq. 'What do you want, master?' Zuraiq asked him, at which 'Ali showed him the dirhams he was holding. Zuraiq was about to give him some of the fish that were on his slab, but 'Ali said that he wanted them hot. Zuraiq put them in the frying pan and was about to fry them when the fire again went out. When he went back into the shop to relight it, 'Ali reached out for the purse. He had got hold of the end of it when the bells and rings started to jingle and Zuraiq called out: 'You didn't manage to trick me, for all your disguise as a groom. I recognized you by the way you held the dirhams and the plate.' He then threw a lump of lead at 'Ali, but when 'Ali dodged, the lump fell into a pan full of hot meat. The pan broke and its gravy fell on the shoulder of the *qadi* who happened to be passing, pouring down inside his clothes to his private parts. The *qadi* cried out in pain, cursing whatever miserable fellow had done this to him. 'Master,' said the bystanders, 'it was a small boy who threw the stone that landed in the pan and but for God's help things would have been worse.' Then they turned and found the lump of lead, which made them realize that the culprit must have been Zuraiq. They went up to him and protested: 'God does not allow this, Zuraiq. You had better take down your purse.' 'So I shall, God willing,' he told them.

As for 'Ali, he went back to his comrades in their headquarters, and when they asked him where the purse was, he told them everything that had happened to him, to which they replied: 'You have made him use up two-thirds of his cunning.' He then took off the clothes he was wearing, and dressed as a merchant. When he went out, he saw a snake charmer with a sack containing snakes and a satchel in which he kept his equipment. He told the man that he wanted him to entertain his children for a fee, but when he took him to his house, he drugged his food with *banj*, dressed himself in his clothes and set off for Zuraiq's shop. When he got there he played on his flute, but Zuraiq merely said: 'Get your reward from God.' The snakes then came out of the bag and 'Ali threw them down in front of Zuraiq, who was afraid of all snakes and who ran away from them back into his shop. At this, 'Ali picked them up and put them back in their sack. He reached out for the purse, but when he touched the end of it, the rings and bells started to jangle. 'Are you still trying to play tricks on me, this time as a snake charmer?' exclaimed Zuraiq, and he threw a lump of lead at him. A soldier happened to be passing, followed by his groom, and the lead struck the groom on the head, felling him to the ground. ‘Who did that?’ demanded the soldier, but when the people there told him that a stone had fallen from a roof, he went off. They then turned and, seeing the lump of lead, they went back to Zuraiq again and said: ‘Take the purse down.’ ‘I’ll take it down this evening, God willing,’ he promised.

‘Ali went on trying trick after trick until he had made seven fruitless attempts. After he had returned the clothes and belongings to the snake charmer and made him a present, ‘Ali went back to the shop, where he heard Zuraiq saying to himself: ‘If I leave the purse here overnight, he will bore through the wall and get it, so I’ll take it home with me.’ He got up, cleared out his shop and took down the purse, which he stowed away in his cloak. ‘Ali followed him, and when Zuraiq got near his house he saw that his neighbour was giving a wedding feast and he said to himself: ‘I’ll just go home, give the purse to my wife, put on my best clothes and then come back to the feast,’ and so he walked on, still followed by ‘Ali. He had married a freed slave from the household of the vizier Ja‘far, a black girl by whom he had a son called ‘Abdallah, and he kept promising his wife that he would use the money in the purse to pay first for his son’s circumcision ceremony, and then to get his son a wife and finally to pay for the marriage feast. He now went to his wife with a frown on his face, and when she asked him why this was, he told her: ‘God has afflicted me with a sly fellow who has tried to take the purse by trickery seven times but has not succeeded.’ ‘Hand it over for me to store away for our son’s wedding,’ his wife told him, and this he did.

‘Ali had hidden in a room and was listening and looking. Zuraiq went and removed what he was wearing to put on his best clothes, after which he said: ‘Look after the purse, for I’m going to the wedding feast.’ ‘Have an hour’s sleep first,’ she told him, and after he had fallen asleep, ‘Ali got up and, walking on tiptoe, he managed to take the purse. He then went to the house where the wedding feast was being held and stopped there to look. Meanwhile Zuraiq had dreamt that a bird had taken his purse and, waking up in a panic, he told his wife to get up and take a look at it. When she tried, it was not to be found and, striking herself in the face, she exclaimed: ‘You unfortunate woman, the trickster has stolen the purse!’ ‘By God,’ Zuraiq said, ‘it can only have been ‘Ali and no one else who took it, and I’ll have to recover it.’ ‘If you don’t get it, I shall lock the door on you and leave you to spend the night in the street,’ she told him.

Zuraiq now went to the wedding feast, where he saw 'Ali looking on. 'This is the man who stole the purse,' he told himself, 'but he's staying in the house of Ahmad al-Danaf.' He got there before 'Ali, climbed the back wall and dropped down into the house, where he found everyone asleep. At that moment, 'Ali arrived and knocked on the door. 'Who's there?' Zuraiq asked, and when 'Ali gave his name he said: 'Have you brought the purse?' 'Ali, thinking that this was Hasan Shuman, said: 'Yes, I have, so open the door.' Zuraiq told him: 'I can't do that until I have seen it, as I have a bet on with your captain.' 'Stretch out your hand,' 'Ali told him and, when Zuraiq reached out through the hole by the pivot at the bottom of the door, 'Ali gave him the purse. He took it and left by the same way that he had come. He then went off to the wedding feast.

As for 'Ali, he went on standing by the door, and when nobody opened it for him he knocked so loudly that the sleepers woke up and said: 'That is the knock of 'Ali al-Zaibaq.' Ahmad's lieutenant opened the door and asked 'Ali if he had brought the purse. 'The joke has gone far enough, Shuman,' 'Ali said. 'Didn't I give it to you through the hole at the bottom of the door, after you told me that you had sworn not to open the door for me until I showed it to you?' 'By God,' said Hasan, 'I didn't take it; it must have been Zuraiq who got it from you.' 'Ali, swearing that he was going to recover it, then went back to the wedding feast. There he heard the jester saying: 'Give me a gift, Zuraiq, and you'll get the benefit of it through your son.' 'I'm in luck,' said 'Ali to himself, and he went to Zuraiq's house, where he climbed in from the back and dropped down. He found Zuraiq's wife sleeping, drugged her with *banj*, dressed himself in her clothes and took the child in his lap, after which, on looking round the house, he discovered in a basket cakes that Zuraiq had meanly saved from 'Id al-Fitr.

It was now that Zuraiq came home, and when he knocked on the door 'Ali answered him, pretending to be his wife and asking who was there. When Zuraiq gave his name, 'Ali said: 'I swore not to open the door until you brought back the purse,' and when Zuraiq said that he had it, 'Ali told him to produce it before he opened the door. 'Lower the basket,' Zuraiq instructed, 'and you can then take the purse up in it.' 'Ali did this; Zuraiq put the purse in the basket and 'Ali took it. He then drugged the child with *banj*, and after having brought the woman back to consciousness, he left by the way that he had come and returned to Ahmad's headquarters. When he went in and showed the others the purse and the child, they thanked him for what he had done and then ate the cakes that he gave them. He told Hasan Shuman that the child was Zuraiq's and asked him to keep him hidden. Hasan did this and then fetched a lamb, and after he had slaughtered it, he gave it to his lieutenant, who roasted it and then wrapped it in a shroud as though it were a dead person.

As for Zuraiq, he went on standing at the door for a while and then knocked loudly. 'Have you brought the purse?' his wife asked, and he said: 'Didn't you take it from the basket which you let down?' 'I never let down any basket,' she replied, 'and I neither saw nor took the purse.' 'By God,' he exclaimed, 'the scoundrel 'Ali has forestalled me and got it!' Then he looked in the house and found that the cakes were gone and that his son was missing. He gave a cry of grief and his wife beat her breast. 'You and I must go to the vizier,' she told him, 'as he can only have been killed by the scoundrel who played those tricks on you, and you're responsible for this.' 'I guarantee to get the child back,' Zuraiq told her, and he tied a kerchief round his neck as a mark of peace and set off for the headquarters of Ahmad al-Danaf. When he knocked on the door, it was opened for him by Ahmad's lieutenant, and when he went in, Hasan Shuman asked him why he had come. 'I want you to intercede for me with 'Ali the Cairene so that he gives me my son back, and in exchange I'll let him have my purse of gold,' Zuraiq told him. 'May God pay you back for this, 'Ali!' Hasan exclaimed. 'Why didn't you tell me that this was Zuraiq's son?' 'What has happened to him?' Zuraiq asked. 'We gave him some raisins to eat, but he had a choking fit and died,' Hasan said, adding, 'and this is his body.'

Zuraiq called out in grief, saying: 'What am I going to tell his mother?' Then he got up and undid the shroud only to find the roasted lamb. 'You have been trying to get a rise from me, 'Ali,' he said, and Ahmad's men then handed over the child. Ahmad said: 'You hung up the purse for any clever thief to take, saying it would then be his by right. So it now belongs to 'Ali the Cairene.' 'I make him a present of it,' Zuraiq told him, but 'Ali said: 'Take it back for the sake of your niece Zainab.' 'I accept it,' said Zuraiq. 'Ali's companions then went on: 'We ask that she be given in marriage to 'Ali,' to which Zuraiq pointed out: 'My only authority over her is a matter of goodwill.' He took his son and the purse, but Hasan asked him: 'Have you accepted this offer of marriage?' 'I shall accept an offer from someone who can pay her bride price,' Zuraiq replied, and when Hasan asked what this was, Zuraiq explained: 'She has sworn not to give herself to anyone unless he can bring her the robe of Qamar, the daughter of 'Adhra the Jew, together with the rest of her finery.'

'If I don't bring the robe tonight, I shall have no right to ask for her hand,' 'Ali agreed, but Zuraiq warned him: 'If you play any of your tricks on Qamar, you are a dead man.' 'Ali asked why and was told: 'The Jew is a wily and treacherous sorcerer who has *jinn* under his command. He has a castle outside the city whose walls are made of alternate bricks of gold and silver. While he is there it is visible, but when he leaves it disappears. He has a daughter named Qamar for whom he brought this robe from a talismanic hoard, and every day he places it on a gold tray, opens the castle windows and calls out: 'Where are you, knaves of Egypt, rogues of Iraq and skilled thieves of Persia? Whoever takes this robe may keep it.' Every young hopeful has tried his tricks, but no one has succeeded and they have then been transformed by magic into apes and donkeys.' 'I have to take the robe,' said 'Ali, 'so that Zainab may wear it at her wedding.'

He went to the Jew's shop, and found him to be a coarse, rough man, with a pair of scales, brass weights, gold, silver and a number of boxes. He also saw that the Jew had a mule there, and when he got up to shut his shop, he put the gold and silver in two purses, which he placed in a pair of saddlebags and loaded them on the mule. He then rode out of the city, followed without his knowledge by 'Ali, until he took some earth from a purse that he had in his pocket, recited a spell over it and scattered it into the air. At that, a castle of unrivalled splendour appeared in front of 'Ali, and the mule carried the Jew up its steps, it being a *jinni* in his service. When the saddlebags had been taken off, it went away and disappeared.

As for the Jew himself, 'Ali watched as he took his seat in the castle. He brought out a rod of gold to which he attached a golden tray by means of golden chains, and in the tray he put the robe. As 'Ali looked from behind the door, he made his proclamation to the knaves, rogues and thieves that whoever was clever enough to take the robe could keep it. He then recited a spell, and a table laden with food appeared in front of him, and after he had finished eating, it removed itself, while a second spell produced wine, which he drank. 'Ali said to himself that the only way in which he could take the robe was if the Jew became drunk.

He crept up behind the Jew and drew his steel sword, but the Jew turned round and uttered a spell that paralysed 'Ali's sword hand, leaving it holding the sword in mid-air. He tried with his left hand, but it too was paralysed, as was his right foot, leaving him balanced on one leg. The spell was then removed and 'Ali returned to normal while the Jew used geomancy to discover his name. He turned to him and said: 'Come here. Who are you and what are you doing?' 'Ali gave him his name and added that he was one of Ahmad al-Danaf's band. 'I have asked for the hand of Zainab, the daughter of Dalila the wily, and by way of bride price they have asked me for the robe of your daughter. If you want to live in safety, let me have it and accept Islam.' 'Not until you are dead,' the Jew told him. 'Many people have tried to trick me out of this, but no one has been able to take it away from me. If you are willing to accept advice, save your own life. The only reason that they asked you for the robe was to get you killed, and had I not seen that your good fortune was greater than mine, I would have cut off your head.' 'Ali was glad to hear what the Jew told him about his good fortune, and insisted: 'I must have the robe and you must accept Islam.' 'This is what you want and what you think you have to have?' asked the Jew, and when 'Ali said yes, he took a cup, filled it with water, recited a spell over it and said: 'Quit your human shape and become a donkey.' He sprinkled some of the water on 'Ali, who was promptly transformed into a donkey, with hooves and long ears. He started to bray and the Jew traced a circle around him, which became a wall keeping him in, and after that the Jew went on drinking until morning.

The next day he told 'Ali: 'I shall give the mule a rest and ride you,' after which he put the robe, the tray, the rod and the chains away in a cupboard. He summoned 'Ali with a spell, put the saddlebags on his back and mounted. The castle vanished from sight as 'Ali moved off with his rider and they got to the shop. Here the Jew dismounted and emptied out the two purses, one containing gold and the other silver, into the box that he kept in front of him. 'Ali, in his donkey shape, was left tethered and, while he could hear and understand, he was unable to speak. Just then, up came the son of a merchant who had fallen on hard times and, in the absence of any other available occupation, had become a water carrier. He had taken his wife's bracelets and had brought them to sell to the Jew so that he could use the money to buy a donkey. 'What are you going to carry on it?' the Jew asked, and the man told him that he proposed to load it with water from the river and make a living by selling this. 'Take this donkey of mine,' said the Jew, and so the man exchanged the bracelets for the donkey and the Jew paid over the difference in price.

The man took 'Ali, still under the spell, back to his house and 'Ali told himself: 'If this fellow puts a wooden pack saddle and a water skin on me, it will only take ten trips to ruin my health and kill me.' So when the man's wife came out to put down his fodder, he butted her with his head, knocking her over on to her back. He then jumped on her and stuck his mouth into her face while lowering his private parts. She shrieked to the neighbours for help and they came and beat 'Ali off her. When her husband, the would-be water carrier, came home, she said: 'Either divorce me or take this donkey back to its owner.' 'What's happened?' he asked, and she told him: 'This is a devil in the shape of a donkey. It jumped on me, and if the neighbours hadn't removed it from on top of me it would have defiled me.' Her husband took 'Ali back to the Jew, who asked why he was bringing back his purchase. 'It did something disgusting to my wife,' the man said, and so the Jew gave him the money and the man went off.

As for the Jew, he turned to 'Ali and said: 'Are you trying to play tricks, you miserable creature, to make him return you to me? But since you are happy to be a donkey, I shall let you be a spectacle for old and young alike.' He took 'Ali the donkey, mounted him and rode out of the city, before taking some ashes, reciting a spell over them and then scattering them in the air, at which the castle reappeared. When he had gone up into it, he unloaded the saddlebags and took away the purses of gold and silver. He then fetched out the rod and, after attaching it to the tray with the robe, he made his proclamation to the rogues of every district, challenging them to take the robe. As before, he proceeded to conjure up a meal, and after he had finished eating, another spell produced wine, from which he drank his fill.

At this point he brought out a cup of water and, when he had recited a spell over it, he sprinkled it on the donkey and said: 'Change back from this to your original shape.' When 'Ali had returned to his human form, the Jew said to him: 'Take my advice, lest I do something worse to you. There is no need for you to marry Zainab and to take my daughter's robe, for this is not going to be easy for you. It will be better for you not to be greedy, or else I shall turn you into a bear or an ape or hand you over to one of the *jinn*, who will throw you behind Mount Qaf.' ''Adhra,' replied 'Ali, 'I have undertaken to get the robe and get it I must, and, unless you accept Islam, I shall kill you.' 'You are like a nut which cannot be eaten until it has been cracked,' the Jew told him, and then he took a cup of water, recited a spell over it and sprinkled it over 'Ali, saying: 'Take the shape of a bear.' 'Ali was immediately turned into a bear, and the Jew put a collar round his neck, muzzled him and tethered him to an iron stake. As he ate, he would throw 'Ali some scraps and pour out some of the leftover water.

The next morning he got up and, after removing the tray and the robe, he forced the bear by means of a spell to follow him to his shop, where he emptied out the gold and silver into his box and took his seat. He fastened the chain round the bear's neck inside the shop and, as a bear, 'Ali could hear and understand but was unable to speak. While he was there, a merchant came to visit the Jew in his shop to ask if he would sell him 'the bear', explaining that doctors had advised his wife, who was his cousin, to eat bear meat and to rub herself with bear fat. The delighted Jew said to himself: 'I shall sell him so that this man may kill him and I shall be rid of him,' while 'Ali told himself: 'He wants to kill me, and it is only God who can save me.' 'I shall give you the bear as a present,' the Jew told the merchant, who then took 'Ali and brought him to a butcher, telling the man to fetch his tools and go with him. The butcher followed with his knives, tied up 'Ali and started to sharpen a knife in order to slaughter him. When 'Ali saw the man coming towards him, he found himself free and he then started to fly through the air, not stopping until he came down in front of the Jew in his castle.

The reason for this was that when the Jew had gone home after having given 'the bear' to the merchant, in answer to a question from his daughter he had told her all that had happened. She advised him to summon a *jinni* and ask him whether this really was 'Ali al-Zaibaq or someone else who was trying to play a trick. He used a spell to conjure up a *jinni*, and when he put the question to him the *jinni* snatched up 'Ali and brought him there. 'This is 'Ali the Cairene and no one else,' the *jinni* said. 'The butcher had tied him up, sharpened his knife and was just about to cut his throat when I snatched him away and brought him to you.'

The Jew took a cup of water, recited a spell over it and then sprinkled some of it on 'Ali, saying: 'Return to your human form.' When this happened, the Jew's daughter, Qamar, saw a handsome young man and fell in love with him. 'Unfortunate young man,' she said, 'why do you try to take my robe when my father does this kind of thing to you?' 'I have undertaken to get it for Zainab the trickster, so as to marry her,' 'Ali said. 'Others have tried to trick my father out of it but have failed, so stop coveting it,' she told him, to which he replied: 'I must get it, and if your father does not accept Islam, I shall kill him.' 'See how this wretched fellow does his best to get himself killed,' her father said. 'I shall turn him into a dog.' He took an inscribed cup with water in it, recited a spell and sprinkled some of the water over 'Ali, saying: 'Take the shape of a dog,' and a dog he became.

The Jew caroused with his daughter until morning and then, after taking away the robe and the tray, he mounted the mule and recited a spell over the 'dog', which followed him with all the other dogs barking at it. He passed the shop of a second-hand dealer who got up and drove the other dogs away, after which 'Ali fell asleep in front of him. When the Jew looked round, 'Ali was not to be seen, and when the dealer closed his shop and went home, 'Ali followed him. When the man went into his house and his daughter caught sight of the dog, she covered her face and said: 'Father, are you bringing a strange man in to see me?' 'This is a dog, daughter,' her father said, but she insisted: 'This is 'Ali the Cairene, whom the Jew has bewitched.' Then she turned to the 'dog' and said: 'Are you 'Ali the Cairene?' at which it nodded its head. 'Why did the Jew put a spell on him?' her father asked, and she said: 'Because of the robe of his daughter, Qamar, but I can set him free.' 'This is the time for a good deed,' he told her, and she said: 'I shall free him if he will marry me.' The 'dog' nodded and she took a cup with writing on it, but as she was reciting a spell over it, there was a loud cry and it fell from her hand. She turned and saw that it was her father's slave girl who had cried out, and this girl now said: 'Mistress, is this the arrangement we made? I was the only one who taught you this art, and you agreed to do nothing without my advice, and also that whoever married you should marry me as well and that he should come to us on alternate nights.' Her mistress confirmed that this was so, and when her father asked her who had taught this girl magic, she said: 'It was she who taught me, but you have to ask her yourself who taught her.'

When he did this, the girl told him: 'You must know, master, that I was in service with 'Adhra the Jew, and I used to creep in while he was reciting his spells. Then, when he went off to his shop, I would open his books and read them until I had mastered the art of magic. One day, when he was drunk, he asked me to sleep with him, but I refused and told him: "That cannot be until you become a Muslim." He refused and I insisted that he take me to the sultan's market, which is where he sold me to you. When I came to your house, I taught my mistress on condition that she should do nothing without my advice and that any man who married her should marry me as well, and that we would have him on alternate nights.'

The slave girl then took the cup of water, recited a spell over it and sprinkled some of it over the 'dog', after which 'Ali regained his original human shape. The second-hand dealer greeted him and asked why he had been enchanted, at which 'Ali told him everything that had happened to him. The man then said: 'Will my daughter and the slave girl not be enough for you?' but 'Ali insisted: 'I must have Zainab as well.' At that moment there was a knock on the door, and when the slave girl asked who was there, a voice answered: 'Qamar, the daughter of the Jew. Is 'Ali the Cairene with you?' The dealer's daughter said: 'If he is, Jew's daughter, what do you want with him?' She then told the slave girl to open the door for her, and when Qamar came in and saw 'Ali and he saw her, he said: 'What has brought you here, daughter of a dog?' She recited the confession of faith, saying: 'I bear witness that there is no god but God and that Muhammad is the Prophet of God,' so becoming a Muslim. Then she asked: 'In Islam do women receive the bride price or do they bring a dowry to their husbands?' 'It is the men who provide the bride price,' 'Ali told her, but she went on: 'I have brought my own bride price, the robe, the rod, the chains and the head of my father, your enemy and the enemy of God,' and, with these words, she threw the head down in front of him.

The reason why she had killed him was that, when he had turned 'Ali into a dog, she saw in a dream a figure who had told her to accept Islam, which she had done. When she woke, she offered conversion to her father, who refused, and she had then drugged him with *banj* and killed him. 'Ali now took what she had brought and said to the dealer: 'We shall meet tomorrow at the caliph's court when I shall marry your daughter and the slave girl.'

'Ali then left full of happiness, but on his way to Ahmad's headquarters with what he had been given he came across a sweet seller who was clapping his hands together and exclaiming: 'There is no might and no power except with God, the Exalted, the Almighty. Hard work has become forbidden and nothing prospers except fraud. I ask you in God's Name to taste this sweet.' 'Ali ate a piece of it and was promptly drugged by the *banj* that it contained. The man took the robe, the rod and the chains and put them inside his sweetmeat box, which he then carried away together with the tray of sweets. As he went, however, a *qadi* shouted at him: 'Come here!' He stopped and put down the box, with the tray on top of it, and asked the *qadi* what he wanted. 'Sweetmeats and sugared nuts,' the *qadi* told him, but when he took some of each of these in his hand the *qadi* said: 'These are adulterated,' after which he himself brought out a sweet from his pocket and said to the man: 'See how well made this is. Taste it, and then try to make another like it.' The sweet seller took it and ate, only to be drugged by the *banj* that was in it. The *qadi* took his paraphernalia, together with the robe and the other things, put the man in a sack and carried everything back to Ahmad's headquarters.

The '*qadi*' was, in fact, Hasan Shuman and this had happened because, when 'Ali had undertaken to fetch the robe and had gone to get it, Ahmad al-Danaf and his band had heard no news of him and as a result he had told them to go and search for him. They looked for him throughout the city and it was then that Hasan Shuman, disguised as a *qadi*, met the sweet seller and recognized him as Ahmad al-Laqit. Having drugged him, he took him off to his quarters, taking the robe with him. Meanwhile, as the forty men of his band were searching the streets, 'Ali Kitf al-Jamal had caught sight of a crowd of people and had gone off to join them. He found that they were standing round the drugged 'Ali al-Zaibaq, who was lying unconscious. He revived him and told him to pull himself together, at which 'Ali, finding himself in the middle of a crowd, said: 'Where am I?' 'Ali Kitf al-Jamal and his companions told him: 'We saw you lying here drugged, but we didn't know who had done this to you.' 'It was a sweet seller who did it,' 'Ali said, 'and he has gone off with my things, but where to?' 'We haven't seen anyone,' the others told him, 'but come back home with us.'

They set off to their base and when they went in they found Ahmad al-Danaf, who greeted them before asking 'Ali the Cairene whether he had brought the robe. 'I got it,' 'Ali said, 'and the other things too, as well as the Jew's head, but I then came across a sweet seller who drugged me and took them from me.' He told Ahmad everything that had happened to him, adding: 'Were I to see that sweet seller again, I'd pay him back for this.' At that point, Hasan Shuman came out of a side room and he too asked 'Ali about the robe and was given the same answer: 'I brought it together with the Jew's head, but a sweet seller whom I met drugged me and took both it and the other things as well. I don't know where he went, but if I could find where he is I would do him an injury.' He then asked Hasan: 'Do you know where he went?' and Hasan said: 'I know where he is now.' He then opened the door of the side room and there 'Ali saw the sweet seller lying drugged. He revived him and when the man opened his eyes he found himself in the presence of 'Ali the Cairene and Ahmad al-Danaf, together with his forty followers. The man jumped up, saying: 'Where am I and who has laid hands on me?' 'I did that,' said Hasan, and 'Ali exclaimed: 'You sly fellow, is this what you get up to?' He was about to cut the man's throat when Hasan stopped him, saying: 'This is a relative of yours by marriage.' 'How is that?' 'Ali asked, and Hasan told him: 'He is Ahmad al-Laqit, the son of Zainab's sister.'

'Ali now asked Ahmad why he had drugged him, and he said: 'My grandmother, Dalila the wily, told me to do it because Zuraiq the fishmonger had met her and told her that 'Ali the Cairene was so skilled a trickster that he was certain to kill the Jew and get the robe. So she got hold of me and asked me whether I could recognize 'Ali. I said that I could as I had directed him to Ahmad al-Danaf's headquarters, and she then told me to prepare a trap for him, so that if he came with the goods I could play a trick on him and take them from him. I went round the streets until I came across a sweet seller, and for ten dinars I got his clothes, his sweets and his equipment, after which you know what happened.'

'Ali told him: 'Go to your grandmother and to Zuraiq the fishmonger and tell them that I have brought the goods, together with the Jew's head, and tell them to meet me tomorrow at the caliph's court where I shall pay over Zainab's bride price.' Ahmad al-Danaf was delighted and exclaimed: 'Your training was not wasted, 'Ali!' The next morning, 'Ali took the robe, the tray, the rod and the golden chains, with the Jew's head mounted on a spear. When he arrived at court with his mentor and his young men, they kissed the ground in front of the caliph, who turned to see a young man of unsurpassed bravery. In reply to the caliph's question, Ahmad told him: 'Commander of the Faithful, this is 'Ali al-Zaibaq of Cairo, leader of the young men there, and the first of my pupils.' When the caliph looked at him he felt affection for him, as the signs of courage on 'Ali's face testified in his favour rather than against him. At this point 'Ali threw down the Jew's head in front of him, saying: 'May all your enemies end like this, Commander of the Faithful.' 'Whose head is it?' the caliph asked, and 'Ali told him: 'It is the head of 'Adhra the Jew.' 'Who killed him?' the caliph asked, after which 'Ali told him the whole story from beginning to end. 'I did not think that you could kill him, as he was a sorcerer,' the caliph said, and 'Ali replied: 'It was my Lord Who enabled me to do this, Commander of the Faithful.'

The caliph now sent the *wali* to the castle, where he discovered the Jew's headless body, which he brought in a coffin to the caliph. On the caliph's orders it was burned, and it was then that Qamar arrived and kissed the ground before him. She told him who she was and that she had accepted Islam, after which she renewed her conversion in his presence and asked him to arrange her marriage to 'Ali, nominating him as her guardian. The caliph granted him 'Adhra's castle, with its contents, and allowed him to make a wish. 'I would like to stand on your carpet and eat from your table,' 'Ali told him. 'Have you any followers?' the caliph then asked, and when 'Ali told him that he had forty lads, but that they were in Cairo, the caliph said: 'Send and fetch them.' He went on to ask whether 'Ali had a base, and when he said no, Hasan Shuman said: 'I shall give him mine, Commander of the Faithful.' 'Keep it for yourself,' the caliph told him, and he ordered his treasurer to give ten thousand dinars to his architect to build 'Ali a house with four halls and forty rooms for his followers.

'Do you have any other need that I can satisfy for you?' the caliph asked, and 'Ali replied: 'King of the age, would you approach Dalila the wily on my behalf to ask her to let me marry her daughter Zainab, accepting as a bride price the robe and the other trappings of Qamar, the daughter of the Jew?' Dalila accepted the caliph's approach and took the tray, the robe, the rod and the golden chains. The marriage contract was drawn up, and this was also done for the daughter of the second-hand dealer, her slave girl and for Qamar. The caliph assigned 'Ali a salary, a free meal every morning and evening, allowances, fodder and other favours.

After a thirty-day feast, 'Ali sent a message to his followers in Cairo to tell them of the honours that the caliph had showered on him. He added: 'You must come to celebrate with me as I have married four girls.' It was not long before they had all arrived to attend the wedding feast. 'Ali lodged them in his new house and treated them with the greatest liberality, as well as presenting them to the caliph, who gave them robes of honour. Zainab's attendants displayed her to 'Ali in Qamar's robe, after which he lay with her and discovered her to be an unpierced pearl and a filly whom no one else had mounted. Later he lay with the other three girls, finding them to be perfect in all points of beauty.

As he was talking with the caliph one night, the caliph asked him to tell him the full story of his adventures from start to finish, and when he had detailed all that had happened to him with Dalila, Zainab and Zuraiq, the caliph ordered that the story be written down and stored in his treasury. A full account was written and it became one of the epics of the followers of Muhammad, the best of men. They all then remained enjoying the easiest and pleasantest of lives until they were visited by the destroyer of delights and the parter of companions. The Blessed and Exalted God knows better.

[Nights 708–19]

The Story of Aladdin, or The Magic Lamp

In the capital city of a rich and vast kingdom in China whose name I cannot at the moment recall, there lived a tailor called Mustafa, whose only distinguishing feature was his profession. This Mustafa was very poor, his work hardly producing enough to live on for him, his wife and a son whom God had given him.

The son, who was called Aladdin, had received a very neglected upbringing, which had led him to acquire many depraved tendencies. He was wicked, stubborn and disobedient towards his father and mother, who, once he became little older, could no longer keep him in the house. He would set out first thing in the morning and spend the day playing in the streets and public places with small vagabonds even younger than himself.

As soon as he was of an age to learn a trade, his father, who was not in a position to make him learn any trade other than his own, took him into his shop and began to show him how to handle a needle. But he remained unable to hold his son's fickle attention, neither by fear of punishment nor by gentle means, and could not get him to sit down and apply himself to his work, as he had hoped. No sooner was Mustafa's back turned than Aladdin would escape and not return for the rest of the day. His father would punish him, but Aladdin was incorrigible, and so, much to his regret, Mustafa was forced to leave him to his dissolute ways. All this caused Mustafa much distress, and his grief at not being able to make his son mend his ways resulted in a persistent illness of which, a few months later, he died.

Aladdin's mother, seeing how her son was not going to follow in his father's footsteps and learn tailoring, closed the shop so that the proceeds from the sale of all the tools of its trade, together with the little she could earn by spinning cotton, would help provide for herself and her son.

Aladdin, however, no longer restrained by the fear of a father, paid so little attention to his mother that he had the effrontery to threaten her when she so much as remonstrated with him, and now abandoned himself completely to his dissolute ways. He associated increasingly with children of his own age, playing with them with even greater enthusiasm. He continued this way of life until he was fifteen, with his mind totally closed to anything else and with no thought of what he might one day become. Such was his situation when one day, while he was playing in the middle of a square with a band of vagabonds, as was his wont, a stranger who was passing by stopped to look at him.

This stranger was a famous magician who, so the authors of this story tell us, was an African, and this is what we will call him, as he was indeed from Africa, having arrived from that country only two days before.

Now it may be that it was because this African magician, who was an expert in the art of reading faces, had looked at Aladdin and had seen all that was essential for the execution of his journey's purpose, or there might have been some other reason. Whatever the case, he artfully made enquiries about Aladdin's family and about what sort of fellow he was. When he had learned all that he wanted to know, he went up to the young man and, drawing him a little aside from his companions, asked him: 'My son, isn't your father called Mustafa, the tailor?' 'Yes, sir,' replied Aladdin, 'but he has been dead a long time.'

At these words, the magician's eyes filled with tears and, uttering deep sighs, he threw his arms round Aladdin's neck, embracing and kissing him several times. Aladdin, seeing his tears, asked him why he was weeping. 'Ah, my son,' exclaimed the magician, 'how could I stop myself? I am your uncle and your father was my dear brother. I have been travelling for several years and now, just when I arrive here in the hope of seeing him again and having him rejoice at my return, you say that he is dead! I tell you it's very painful for me to find I am not going to receive the comfort and consolation I was expecting. But what consoles me a little in my grief is that, as far as I can remember them, I can recognize his features in your face, and that I was not wrong in speaking to you.' Putting his hand on his purse, he asked Aladdin where his mother lived. Aladdin answered him straight away, at which the magician gave him a handful of small change, saying: 'My son, go and find your mother, give her my greetings and tell her that, if I have time, I will go and see her tomorrow, so that I may have the consolation of seeing where my brother lived and where he ended his days.'

As soon as the magician had left, his newly invented nephew, delighted with the money his uncle had just given him, ran to his mother. 'Mother,' he said to her, 'tell me, please, have I got an uncle?' 'No, my son,' she replied, 'you have no uncle, neither on your late father's side nor on mine.' 'But I have just seen a man who says he is my uncle on my father's side,' insisted Aladdin. 'He was his brother, he assured me. He even began to weep and embrace me when I told him my father was dead. And to prove I am telling the truth,' he added, showing her the money he had been given, 'here is what he gave me. He also charged me to give you his greetings and to tell you that tomorrow, if he has the time, he will come and greet you himself and at the same time see the house where my father lived and where he died.' 'My son,' said his mother, 'it's true your father once had a brother, but he's been dead a long time and I never heard him say he had another brother.' They spoke no more about the African magician.

The next day, the magician approached Aladdin a second time as he was playing with some other children in another part of the city, embraced him as he had done on the previous day and, placing two gold coins in his hand, said to him: 'My son, take this to your mother; tell her I am coming to see her this evening and say she should buy some food so we can dine together. But first, tell me where I can find your house.' Aladdin told him where it was and the magician then let him go.

Aladdin took the two gold coins to his mother, who, as soon as she heard of his uncle's plans, went out to put the money to use, returning with abundant provisions; but, finding herself with not enough dishes, she went to borrow some from her neighbours. She spent all day preparing the meal, and towards evening, when everything was ready, she said to Aladdin: 'My son, perhaps your uncle doesn't know where our house is. Go and find him and, when you see him, bring him here.'

Although Aladdin had told the magician where to find the house, he was nonetheless prepared to go out to meet him, when there was a knock on the door. Opening it, Aladdin discovered the magician, who entered, laden with bottles of wine and all kinds of fruit which he had brought for supper and which he handed over to Aladdin. He then greeted his mother and asked her to show him the place on the sofa where his brother used to sit. She showed him and immediately he bent down and kissed the spot several times, exclaiming with tears in his eyes: 'My poor brother! How sad I am not to have arrived in time to embrace you once more before your death!' And although Aladdin's mother begged him to sit in the same place, he firmly refused. 'Never will I sit there,' he said, 'but allow me to sit facing it, so that though I may be deprived of the satisfaction of seeing him there in person as the head of a family which is so dear to me, I can at least look at where he sat as though he were present.' Aladdin's mother pressed him no further, leaving him to sit where he pleased.

Once the magician had sat down in the place he had chosen, he began to talk to Aladdin's mother. 'My dear sister,' he began, 'don't be surprised that you never saw me all the time you were married to my brother Mustafa, of happy memory; forty years ago I left this country, which is mine as well as that of my late brother. Since then, I have travelled in India, Arabia, Persia, Syria and Egypt, and have stayed in the finest cities, and then I went to Africa, where I stayed much longer. Eventually, as is natural – for a man, however far he is from the place of his birth, never forgets it any more than he forgets his parents and those with whom he was brought up – I was overcome by a strong desire to see my own family again and to come and embrace my brother. I felt I still had enough strength and courage to undertake such a long journey and so I delayed no longer and made my preparations to set out. I won't tell you how long it has taken me, nor how many obstacles I have met with and the discomfort I suffered to get here. I will only tell you that in all my travels nothing has caused me more sorrow and suffering than hearing of the death of one whom I have always loved with a true brotherly love. I observed some of his features in the face of my nephew, your son, which is what made me single him out from among all the children with whom he was playing. He will have told you how I received the sad news that my brother was no longer alive; but one must praise God for all things and I find comfort in seeing him again in a son who retains his most distinctive features.'

When he saw how the memory of her husband affected Aladdin's mother, bringing tears to her eyes, the magician changed the subject and, turning to Aladdin, asked him his name. 'I am called Aladdin,' he replied. 'Well, then, Aladdin,' the magician continued, 'what do you do? Do you have a trade?'

At this question, Aladdin lowered his eyes, embarrassed. His mother, however, answered in his place. 'Aladdin is an idle fellow,' she said. 'While he was alive, his father did his best to make him learn his trade but never succeeded. Since his death, despite everything I have tried to tell him, again and again, day after day, the only trade he knows is acting the vagabond and spending all his time playing with children, as you saw for yourself, mindless of the fact that he is no longer a child. And if you can't make him feel ashamed and realize how pointless his behaviour is, I despair of him ever amounting to anything. He knows his father left nothing, and he can himself see that despite spinning cotton all day as I do, I have great difficulty in earning enough to buy us bread. In fact, I have decided that one of these days I am going to shut the door on him and send him off to fend for himself.'

After she had spoken, Aladdin's mother burst into tears, whereupon the magician said to Aladdin: 'This is no good, my nephew. You must think now about helping yourself and earning your own living. There are all sorts of trades; see if there isn't one for which you have a particular inclination. Perhaps that of your father doesn't appeal to you and you would be more suited to another: be quite open about this, I am just trying to help you.' Seeing Aladdin remain silent, he went on: 'If you want to be an honest man yet dislike the idea of learning a trade, I will provide you with a shop filled with rich cloths and fine fabrics. You can set about selling them, purchasing more goods with the money that you make, and in this manner you will live honourably. Think about it and then tell me frankly your opinion. You will find that I always keep my word.'

This offer greatly flattered Aladdin, who did not like manual work, all the more so since he had enough sense to know that shops with these kinds of goods were esteemed and frequented and that the merchants were well dressed and well regarded. So he told the magician, whom he thought of as his uncle, that his inclination was more in that direction than any other and that he would be indebted to him for the rest of his life for the help he was offering. 'Since this occupation pleases you,' the magician continued, 'I will take you with me tomorrow and will have you dressed in rich garments appropriate for one of the wealthiest merchants of this city. The following day we will consider setting up a shop, as I think it should be done.'

Aladdin's mother, who up until then had not believed the magician was her husband's brother, now no longer doubted it after hearing all the favours he promised her son. She thanked him for his good intentions and, after exhorting Aladdin to make himself worthy of all the wealth his uncle had promised him, served supper. Throughout the meal, the talk ran upon the same subject until the magician, seeing the night was well advanced, took leave of the mother and the son and retired.

The next morning, he returned as he had promised to the widow of Mustafa the tailor and took Aladdin off with him to a wealthy merchant who sold only ready-made garments in all sorts of fine materials and for all ages and ranks. He made the merchant bring out clothes that would fit Aladdin and, after putting to one side those which pleased him best and rejecting the others that did not seem to him handsome enough, said to Aladdin: 'My nephew, choose from among all these garments the one you like best.' Aladdin, delighted with his new uncle's generosity, picked one out which the magician then bought, together with all the necessary accessories, and paid for everything without bargaining.

When Aladdin saw himself so magnificently clothed from top to toe, he thanked his uncle profusely with all the thanks imaginable, and the magician repeated his promise never to abandon him and to keep him always with him. Indeed, he then took him to the most frequented parts of the city and in particular to those where the shops of the rich merchants were to be found. When he reached the street which had the shops with the richest cloths and finest fabrics, he said to Aladdin: 'As you will soon be a merchant like these, it is a good idea for you to seek out their company so that they get to know you.' The magician also showed him the largest and most beautiful mosques and took him to the *khans* where the foreign merchants lodged and to all the places in the sultan's palace which he was free to enter. Finally, after they had wandered together through all the fairest places in the city, they came to the *khan* where the magician had taken lodgings. There they found several merchants whom the magician had got to know since his arrival and whom he had gathered together for the express purpose of entertaining them and at the same time introducing them to his so-called nephew.

The party did not finish until towards evening. Aladdin wanted to take leave of his uncle to return home, but the magician would not let him go back alone and himself accompanied him back to his mother. When his mother saw Aladdin in his fine new clothes, she was carried away in her delight and kept pouring a thousand blessings on the magician who had spent so much money on her child. 'My dear relative,' she exclaimed, 'I don't know how to thank you for your generosity. I know my son does not deserve all you have done for him and he would be quite unworthy of it if he was not grateful to you or failed to respond to your kind intention of giving him such a fine establishment. As for myself, once again I thank you with all my heart; I hope that you will live long enough to witness his gratitude, which he can best show by conducting himself in accordance with your good advice.'

'Aladdin is a good boy,' the magician replied. 'He listens to me well enough and I believe he will turn out well. But one thing worries me – that I can't carry out what I promised him tomorrow. Tomorrow is Friday, when the shops are closed, and there is no way we can think of renting one and stocking it at a time when the merchants are only thinking of entertaining themselves. So we will have to postpone our business until Saturday, but I will come and fetch him tomorrow and I will take him for a walk in the gardens where all the best people are usually to be found. Perhaps he has never seen the amusements that are to be had there. Up until now he has only been with children, but now he must see men.' The magician took his leave of mother and son and departed. Aladdin, however, was so delighted at being so smartly turned out that he already began to anticipate the pleasure of walking in the gardens that lay around the city. In fact, he had never been outside the city gates and had never seen the surroundings of the city, which he knew to be pleasant and beautiful.

The next day, Aladdin got up and dressed himself very early so as to be ready to leave when his uncle came to fetch him. After waiting for what seemed to him a very long time, in his impatience he opened the door and stood on the doorstep to see if he could see the magician. As soon as he spotted him, Aladdin told his mother and said goodbye to her, before shutting the door and running to meet him.

The magician embraced Aladdin warmly when he saw him. 'Come, my child,' he said to him, smiling, 'today I want to show you some wonderful things.' He took him through a gate which led to some fine, large houses, or rather, magnificent palaces, which all had very beautiful gardens that people were free to enter. At each palace that they came to, he asked Aladdin whether he thought it beautiful, but Aladdin would forestall him as soon as another palace presented itself, saying: 'Uncle, here's another even more beautiful than those we have just seen.' All the while, they were advancing ever deeper into the countryside and the wily magician, who wanted to go further still in order to carry out the plan he had in mind, took the opportunity of entering one of these gardens. Seating himself near a large pool into which a beautiful jet of water poured from the nostrils of a bronze lion, he pretended to be tired in order to get Aladdin to take a rest. 'Dear nephew,' he said to him, 'you, too, must be tired. Let's sit here and recover ourselves. We shall then have more strength to continue our walk.'

When they had sat down, the magician took out from a cloth attached to his belt some cakes and several kinds of fruit which he had brought with him as provisions, and spread them out on the edge of the pool. He shared a cake with Aladdin but let him choose for himself what fruits he fancied. As they partook of this light meal, he talked to his so-called nephew, giving him numerous pieces of advice, the gist of which was to exhort Aladdin to give up associating with children, telling him rather to approach men of prudence and wisdom, to listen to them and to profit from their conversation. 'Soon you will be a man like them,' he said, 'and you can't get into the habit too soon of following their example and speaking with good sense.' When they had finished eating, they got up and resumed their walk through the gardens, which were separated from each other only by small ditches which defined their limits without impeding access – such was the mutual trust the inhabitants of the city enjoyed that there was no need for any other boundaries to guard against them harming each other's interests. Gradually and without Aladdin being aware of it, the magician led him far beyond the gardens, making him pass through open country which took them very close to the mountains.

Aladdin had never before travelled so far and felt very weary from such a long walk. 'Uncle,' he asked the magician, 'where are we going? We have left the gardens far behind and I can see nothing but mountains. If we go any further, I don't know if I'll have enough strength to return to the city.' 'Take heart, my nephew,' replied the bogus uncle. 'I want to show you another garden which beats all those you have just seen. It's not far from here, just a step away, and when we get there you yourself will tell me how cross you would have been not to have seen it after having got so close to it.' Aladdin let himself be persuaded and the magician led him even further on, all the while entertaining him with many amusing stories in order to make the journey less tedious for him and his fatigue more bearable.

At last they came to two mountains of a moderate height and size, separated by a narrow valley. This was the very spot to which the magician had wanted to take Aladdin so that he could carry out the grand plan which had brought him all the way from the furthest part of Africa to China. 'We are not going any further,' he told Aladdin. 'I want to show you some extraordinary things, unknown to any other man, and when you have seen them, you will thank me for having witnessed so many marvels that no one else in all the world will have seen but you. While I am making a fire, you go and gather the driest bushes you can find for kindling.'

There was such a quantity of brushwood that Aladdin had soon amassed more than enough in the time that the magician was still starting up the fire. He set light to the pile and the moment the twigs caught fire, the magician threw on to them some incense that he had ready at hand. A dense smoke arose, which he made to disperse right and left by pronouncing some words of magic, none of which Aladdin could understand.

At the same moment, the earth gave a slight tremor and opened up in front of Aladdin and the magician, revealing a stone about one and a half feet square and about one foot deep, lying horizontally on the ground; fixed in the middle was a ring of bronze with which to lift it up. Aladdin, terrified at what was happening before his very eyes, would have fled if the magician had not held him back, for he was necessary for this mysterious business. He scolded him soundly and gave him such a blow that he was flung to the ground with such force that his front teeth were very nearly pushed back into his mouth, judging from the blood which poured out. Poor Aladdin, trembling all over and in tears, asked his uncle: 'What have I done for you to hit me so roughly?' 'I have my reasons for doing this,' replied the magician. 'I am your uncle and at present take the place of your father. You shouldn't answer me back.' Softening his tone a little, he went on: 'But, my child, don't be afraid. All I ask is that you obey me exactly if you want to benefit from and be worthy of the great advantages I propose to give you.' These fine promises somewhat calmed Aladdin's fear and resentment, and when the magician saw he was completely reassured, he went on: 'You have seen what I have done by virtue of my incense and by the words that I pronounced. Know now that beneath the stone that you see is hidden a treasure which is destined for you and which will one day make you richer than the greatest kings in all the world. It's true, you are the only person in the world who is allowed to touch this stone and to lift it to go inside. Even I am not allowed to touch it and to set foot in the treasure house when it is opened. Consequently, you must carry out step by step everything I am going to tell you, not omitting anything. The matter is of the utmost importance, both for you and for me.'

Aladdin, still in a state of astonishment at all he saw and at what he had just heard the magician say about this treasure, which was to make him happy for evermore, got up, forgetting what had just happened to him, and asked: 'Tell me then, uncle, what do I have to do? Command me, I am ready to obey you.' 'I am delighted, my child, that you have made this decision,' replied the magician, embracing him. 'Come here, take hold of this ring and lift up the stone.' 'But uncle, I am not strong enough – you must help me,' Aladdin cried, to which his uncle replied: 'No, you don't need my help and we would achieve nothing, you and I, if I were to help you. You must lift it up all by yourself. Just say the names of your father and your grandfather as you hold the ring, and lift. You will find that it will come without any difficulty.' Aladdin did as the magician told him. He lifted the stone with ease and laid it aside.

When the stone was removed, there appeared a cavity about three to four feet deep, with a small door and steps for descending further. 'My son,' said the magician to Aladdin, 'follow carefully what I am going to tell you to do. Go down into this cave and when you get to the foot of the steps which you see, you will find an open door that will lead you into a vast vaulted chamber divided into three large rooms adjacent to each other. In each room, you will see, on the right and the left, four very large bronze jars, full of gold and silver – but take care not to touch them. Before you go into the first room, pull up your gown and wrap it tightly around you. Then when you have entered, go straight to the second room and the third room, without stopping. Above all, take great care not to go near the walls, let alone touch them with your gown, for if you do, you will immediately die; that's why I told you to keep it tightly wrapped around you. At the end of the third room there is a gate which leads into a garden planted with beautiful trees laden with fruit. Walk straight ahead and cross this garden by a path which will take you to a staircase with fifty steps leading up to a terrace. When you are on the terrace, you will see in front of you a niche in which there is a lighted lamp. Take the lamp and put it out and when you have thrown away the wick and poured off the liquid, hold it close to your chest and bring it to me. Don't worry about spoiling your clothes – the liquid is not oil and the lamp will be dry as soon as there is no more liquid in it. If you fancy any of the fruits in the garden, pick as many as you want – you are allowed to do so.'

When he had finished speaking, the magician pulled a ring from his finger and put it on one of Aladdin's fingers, telling him it would protect him from any harm that might come to him if he followed all his instructions. 'Be bold, my child,' he then said. 'Go down; you and I are both going to be rich for the rest of our lives.'

Lightly jumping into the cave, Aladdin went right down to the bottom of the steps. He found the three rooms which the magician had described to him, passing through them with the greatest of care for fear he would die if he failed scrupulously to carry out all he had been told. He crossed the garden without stopping, climbed up to the terrace, took the lamp alight in its niche, threw away the wick and the liquid, and as soon as this had dried up as the magician had told him, he held it to his chest. He went down from the terrace and stopped in the garden to look more closely at the fruits which he had seen only in passing. The trees were all laden with the most extraordinary fruit: each tree bore fruits of different colours – some were white; some shining and transparent like crystals; some pale or dark red; some green; some blue or violet; some light yellow; and there were many other colours. The white fruits were pearls; the shining, transparent ones diamonds; the dark red were rubies, while the lighter red were spinel rubies; the green were emeralds; the blue turquoises; the violet amethysts; the light yellow were pale sapphires; and there were many others, too. All of them were of a size and a perfection the like of which had never before been seen in the world. Aladdin, however, not recognizing either their quality or their worth, was unmoved by the sight of these fruits, which were not to his taste – he would have preferred real figs or grapes, or any of the other excellent fruit common in China. Besides, he was not yet of an age to appreciate their worth, believing them to be but coloured glass and therefore of little value. But the many wonderful shades and the extraordinary size and beauty of each fruit made him want to pick one of every colour. In fact, he picked several of each, filling both pockets as well as two new purses which the magician had bought him at the same time as the new clothes he had given him so that everything he had should be new. And as the two purses would not fit in his pockets, which were already full, he attached them to either side of his belt. Some fruits he even wrapped in the folds of his belt, which was made of a wide strip of silk wound several times around his waist, arranging them so that they could not fall out. Nor did he forget to cram some around his chest, between his gown and his shirt.

Thus weighed down with such, to him, unknown wealth, Aladdin hurriedly retraced his steps through the three rooms so as not to keep the magician waiting too long. After crossing them as cautiously as he had before, he ascended the stairs he had come down and arrived at the entrance of the cave, where the magician was impatiently awaiting him. As soon as he saw him, Aladdin cried out: 'Uncle, give me your hand, I beg of you, to help me climb out.' 'Son,' the magician replied, 'first, give me the lamp, as it could get in your way.' 'Forgive me, uncle,' Aladdin rejoined, 'but it's not in my way; I will give it you as soon as I get out.' But the magician persisted in wanting Aladdin to hand him the lamp before pulling him out of the cave, while Aladdin, weighed down by this lamp and by the fruits he had stowed about his person, stubbornly refused to give it to him until he was out of the cave. Then the magician, in despair at the young man's resistance, fell into a terrible fury: throwing a little of the incense over the fire, which he had carefully kept alight, he uttered two magic words and immediately the stone which served to block the entrance to the cave moved back in its place, with the earth above it, just as it had been when the magician and Aladdin had first arrived there.

Now this magician was certainly not the brother of Mustafa the tailor, as he had proudly claimed, nor, consequently, was he Aladdin's uncle. But he did indeed come from Africa, where he was born, and as Africa is a country where more than anywhere else the influence of magic persists, he had applied himself to it from his youth, and after forty years or so of practising magic and geomancy and burning incense and of reading books on the subject, he had finally discovered that there was somewhere in the world a magic lamp, the possession of which, could he lay hands on it, would make him more powerful than any king in the world. In a recent geomantic experiment, he had discovered that this lamp was in an underground cave in the middle of China, in the spot and with all the circumstances we have just seen. Convinced of the truth of his discovery, he set out from the furthest part of Africa, as we have related. After a long and painful journey, he had come to the city that was closest to the treasure, but although the lamp was certainly in the spot which he had read about, he was not allowed to remove it himself, he had ascertained, nor could he himself enter the underground cave where it was to be found. Someone else would have to go down into it, take the lamp and then deliver it into his hands. That is why he had turned to Aladdin, who seemed to him to be a young boy of no consequence, just right to carry out for him the task which he wanted him to do. He had resolved, once he had the lamp in his hands, to perform the final burning of incense that we have mentioned and to utter the two magic words that would produce the effect which we have seen, sacrificing poor Aladdin to his avarice and wickedness so as to have no witness. The blow he gave Aladdin and the authority he had assumed over him were only meant to accustom him to fear him and to obey him precisely so that, when he asked him for the famed lamp, Aladdin would immediately give it to him, but what happened was the exact opposite of what he had intended. In his haste, the magician had resorted to such wickedness in order to get rid of poor Aladdin because he was afraid that if he argued any longer with him, someone would hear them and would make public what he wanted to keep secret.

When he saw his wonderful hopes and plans for ever wrecked, the magician had no other choice but to return to Africa, which is what he did the very same day, taking a roundabout route so as to avoid going back into the city he had left with Aladdin. For what he feared was being seen by people who might have noticed him walking out with this boy and now returning without him.

To all appearances, that should be the end of the story and we should hear no more about Aladdin, but the very person who had thought he had got rid of Aladdin for ever had forgotten that he had placed on his finger a ring which could help to save him. In fact it was this ring, of whose properties Aladdin was totally unaware, that was the cause of his salvation, and it is astonishing that the loss of it together with that of the lamp did not throw the magician into a state of complete despair. But magicians are so used to disasters and to events turning out contrary to their desires that all their lives they forever feed their minds on smoke, fancies and phantoms.

After all the endearments and the favours his false uncle had shown him, Aladdin little expected such wickedness and was left in a state of bewilderment that can be more easily imagined than described in words. Finding himself buried alive, he called upon his uncle a thousand times, crying out that he was ready to give him the lamp, but his cries were in vain and could not possibly be heard by anyone. And so he remained in the darkness and gloom. At last, when his tears had abated somewhat, he descended to the bottom of the stairs in the cave to look for light in the garden through which he had passed earlier; but the wall which had been opened by a spell had closed and sealed up by another spell. Aladdin groped around several times, to the left and to the right, but could find no door. With renewed cries and tears, he sat down on the steps in the cave, all hope gone of ever seeing light again and, moreover, in the sad certainty that he would pass from the darkness where he was into the darkness of approaching death.

For two days, Aladdin remained in this state, eating and drinking nothing. At last, on the third day, believing death to be inevitable, he raised his hands in prayer and, resigning himself completely to God's will, he cried out: 'There is no strength nor power save in Great and Almighty God!'

However, just as he joined his hands in prayer, Aladdin unknowingly rubbed the ring which the magician had placed on his finger and of whose power he was as yet unaware. Immediately, from the ground beneath him, there rose up before him a *jinni* of enormous size and with a terrifying expression, who continued to grow until his head touched the roof of the chamber and who addressed these words to Aladdin: 'What do you want? Here am I, ready to obey you, your slave and the slave of all those who wear the ring on their finger, a slave like all the other slaves of the ring.'

At any other time and on any other occasion, Aladdin, who was not used to such visions, would perhaps have been overcome with terror and struck dumb at the sight of such an extraordinary apparition, but now, preoccupied solely with the danger of the present situation, he replied without hesitation: 'Whoever you are, get me out of this place, if you have the power to do so.' No sooner had he uttered these words than the earth opened up and he found himself outside the cave at the very spot to which the magician had led him.

Not surprisingly, Aladdin, after so long spent in pitch darkness, had difficulty at first in adjusting to broad daylight, but his eyes gradually became accustomed to it. When he looked around, he was very surprised not to find any opening in the ground; he could not understand how all of a sudden he should find himself transported from the depths of the earth. Only the spot where the kindling had been lit allowed him to tell roughly where the cave had been. Then, turning in the direction of the city, he spotted it in the middle of the gardens which surrounded it. He also recognized the path along which the magician had brought him and which he proceeded to follow, giving thanks to God at finding himself once again back in the world to which he had so despaired of ever returning.

When he reached the city, it was with some difficulty that he dragged himself home. He went in to his mother, but the joy of seeing her again, together with the weak state he was in from not having eaten for nearly three days, caused him to fall into a faint that lasted for some time. Seeing him in this state, his mother, who had already mourned him as lost, if not dead, did all she could to revive him. At last Aladdin recovered consciousness and the first words he addressed to her were to ask her to bring him something to eat, for it was three days since he had had anything at all. His mother brought him what she had, and, placing it before him, said: 'Don't hurry, now, because that's dangerous. Take it easy and eat a little at a time; eke it out, however much you need it. I don't want you even to speak to me; you will have enough time to tell me everything that happened to you when you have quite recovered. I am so comforted at seeing you again after the terrible state I have been in since Friday and after all the trouble I went to to discover what had happened to you as soon as I saw it was night and you hadn't come home.'

Aladdin followed his mother's advice and ate and drank slowly, a little at a time. When he had finished, he said to his mother: 'I would have been very cross with you for so readily abandoning me to the mercy of a man who planned to kill me and who, at this very moment, is quite certain either that I am no longer alive or that I will die at first light. But you believed him to be my uncle and so did I. How could we have thought otherwise of a man who overwhelmed me with both affection and gifts and who made me so many other fair promises? Now, mother, you must see he is nothing but a traitor, a wretch and a cheat. In all the gifts he gave me and the promises he made he had but one single aim – to kill me, as I said, without either of us guessing the reason why. For my part, I can assure you that I didn't do anything to deserve the slightest ill treatment. You will understand this yourself when you hear my faithful account of all that happened since I left you, right up to the time he came to execute his deadly plan.'

Aladdin then began to tell his mother all that had happened to him since the previous Friday, when the magician had come to take him with him to see the palaces and gardens outside the city, and what had happened along the way until they came to the spot by the two mountains where the magician's great miracle was to take place. He told her how, with some incense cast into the fire and a few words of magic, the earth had opened up, straight away, revealing the entrance to a cave which led to a priceless treasure. He did not leave out the blow he had received from the magician, nor how, once the magician had calmed down a little, he had placed his ring on Aladdin's finger and, making him countless promises, had got him to go down into the cave. He left out nothing of all that he had seen as he passed through the three rooms, in the garden and on the terrace from where he had taken the magic lamp. At this, he pulled the lamp from his clothes to show to his mother, together with the transparent fruits and those of different colours which he had gathered in the garden on his return and with which he had filled the two purses that he now gave her, though she did not make much of them. For these fruits were really precious stones; in the light of the lamp which lit up the room they shone like the sun and glittered and sparkled in such a way as to testify to their great worth, but Aladdin's mother was no more aware of this than he was. She had been brought up in very humble circumstances and her husband had never been wealthy enough to give her jewels and stones of this kind. Nor had she ever seen such things worn by any of her female relatives or neighbours. Consequently, it is not surprising that she should regard them as things of little value – a pleasure to the eye, at the very most, due to all their different colours – and so Aladdin put them behind one of the cushions of the sofa on which he was seated. He finished the account of his adventures by telling her how, when he returned to the entrance to the cave, ready to come out, he had refused to hand over to the magician the lamp that he wanted to have, at which the cave's entrance had immediately closed up, thanks to the incense which the magician had scattered over the fire that he had kept lit and to the words he had pronounced. Aladdin could not go on without tears coming to his eyes as he described to her the wretched state in which he found himself after being buried alive in that fatal cave, right up to when he emerged and returned to the world, so to speak, as the result of having touched the ring (of whose powers he was still unaware). When he had come to the end of his story, he said to his mother: 'I don't need to tell you any more; you know the rest. That was my adventure and the danger I was in since you last saw me.'

Aladdin's mother listened patiently and without interrupting to this wonderful and amazing story which at the same time was so painful for a mother who loved her son so tenderly despite all his faults. However, at the most disturbing points when the magician's treachery was further revealed, she could not prevent herself from showing, with signs of indignation, how much she hated him. As soon as Aladdin had finished, she broke out into a thousand reproaches against the impostor, calling him a traitor, trickster, murderer, barbarian – a magician, an enemy and a destroyer of mankind. 'Yes, my son,' she added, 'he's a magician and magicians are public menaces; they have dealings with demons through their spells and their sorcery. Praise the Lord, Who wished to preserve you from everything that his great wickedness might have done to you! You should indeed give thanks to Him for having so favoured you. You would have surely died had you not remembered Him and implored Him for His help.' She said much more besides, all the while execrating the magician's treachery towards her son. But as she spoke, she noticed that Aladdin, who had not slept for three days, needed some rest. She made him go to bed and went to bed herself shortly afterwards.

That night Aladdin, having had no rest in the underground cave where he had been buried and left to die, fell into a deep sleep from which he did not awake until late the following day. He arose and the first thing he said to his mother was that he needed to eat and that she could not give him a greater pleasure than to offer him breakfast. 'Alas, my son,' she sighed, 'I haven't got so much as a piece of bread to give you –

yesterday evening you ate the few provisions there were in the house. But be patient for a little longer and I will soon bring you some food. I have some cotton yarn I have spun. I will sell it to buy you some bread and something else for our dinner.' 'Mother,' said Aladdin, 'leave your cotton yarn for some other occasion and give me the lamp I brought yesterday. I will go and sell it and the money I get will help provide us with enough for both breakfast and lunch, and perhaps also for our supper.'

Taking the lamp from where she had put it, Aladdin's mother said to her son: 'Here it is, but it's very dirty. With a little cleaning I think it would be worth a little more.' So she took some water and some fine sand in order to clean it, but no sooner had she begun to rub it than all of a sudden there rose up in front of them a hideous *jinni* of enormous size who, in a ringing voice, addressed her thus: 'What do you want? Here am I, ready to obey you, your slave and the slave of all those who hold the lamp in their hands, I and the other slaves of the lamp.'

But Aladdin's mother was in no state to reply; so great was her terror at the sight of the *jinni*'s hideous and frightening countenance that at the first words he uttered she fell down in a faint. Aladdin, on the other hand, had already witnessed a similar apparition while in the cave, and so, wasting no time and not stopping to think, he promptly seized the lamp. Replying in place of his mother, in a firm voice he said to the *jinni*: 'I am hungry, bring me something to eat.' The *jinni* disappeared and a moment later returned, bearing on his head a large silver bowl, together with twelve dishes also of silver, piled high with delicious foods and six large loaves as white as snow, and in his hands were two bottles of exquisite wine and two silver cups. He set everything down on the sofa and then disappeared.

This all happened so quickly that Aladdin's mother had not yet recovered from her swoon when the *jinni* disappeared for the second time. Aladdin, who had already begun to throw water on her face, without effect, renewed his efforts to revive her, and whether it was that her wits which had left her had already been restored or that the smell of the dishes which the *jinni* had brought had contributed in some measure, she immediately recovered consciousness. 'Mother,' said Aladdin, 'don't worry. Get up and come and eat, for here is something to give you heart again and which at the same time will satisfy my great hunger. We mustn't let such good food grow cold, so come and eat.'

Aladdin's mother was extremely surprised when she saw the large bowl, the twelve dishes, the six loaves, the two bottles and the two cups, and when she smelt the delicious aromas which came from all these dishes. 'My son,' she asked Aladdin, 'where does all this abundance come from and to whom do we owe thanks for such great generosity? Can the sultan have learned of our poverty and had compassion on us?' 'Mother,' Aladdin replied, 'let us sit down and eat; you need it as much as I do. When we have eaten, I will tell you.' They sat down and ate with all the more appetite in that neither had ever sat down before to such a well-laden table.

During the meal, Aladdin's mother never tired of looking at and admiring the large bowl and the dishes, although she did not know for sure whether they were of silver or some other metal, so unaccustomed was she to seeing things of that kind, and, to tell the truth, as she could not appreciate their value, which was unknown to her, it was the novelty of it all that held her admiration. Nor did her son Aladdin know any more about them than she did.

Aladdin and his mother, thinking to have but a simple breakfast, were still at table at dinner time; such excellent dishes had given them an appetite and while the food was still warm, they thought they might just as well put the two meals together so as not to have to eat twice. When this double meal was over, there remained enough not only for supper but for two equally large meals the next day.

After she had cleared away and had put aside those dishes they had not touched, Aladdin's mother came and seated herself beside her son on the sofa. 'Aladdin,' she said to him, 'I am expecting you to satisfy my impatience to hear the account you promised me.' Aladdin then proceeded to tell her exactly what had happened between the *jinni* and himself while she was in a swoon, right up to the moment she regained consciousness.

Aladdin's mother was greatly astonished by what her son told her and by the appearance of the *jinni*. 'But, Aladdin, what do you mean by these *jinn* of yours?' she said. 'Never in all my life have I heard of anyone I know ever having seen one. By what chance did that evil *jinni* come and show itself to me? Why did it come to me and not to you, when it had already appeared to you in the treasure cave?'

'Mother,' replied Aladdin, 'the *jinni* who has just appeared to you is not the same as the one that appeared to me; they look like each other to a certain extent, being both as large as giants, but they are completely different in appearance and dress. Also, they have different masters. If you remember, the one I saw called himself the slave of the ring which I have on my finger, while the one you have just seen called himself the slave of the lamp which you had in your hands. But I don't believe you can have heard him; in fact, I think you fainted as soon as he began to speak.'

'What?' cried his mother. 'It's your lamp, then, that made this evil *jinni* speak to me rather than to you? Take it out of my sight and put it wherever you like; I don't want ever to touch it again. I would rather have it thrown out or sold than run the risk of dying of fright touching it. If you were to listen to me, you would also get rid of the ring. One should not have anything to do with *jinn*; they are demons and our Prophet has said so.'

Aladdin, however, replied: 'Mother, with your permission, for the moment I am not going to sell – as I was ready to do – a lamp which is going to be so useful to both you and me. Don't you see what it has just brought us? We must let it go on bringing us things to eat and to support us. You should see, as I have seen, that it was not for nothing that my wicked and bogus uncle went to such lengths and undertook such a long and painful journey, since it was to gain possession of this magic lamp, preferring it above all the gold and silver which he knew to be in the rooms as he told me and which I myself saw. For he knew only too well the worth and value of this lamp than to ask for anything other than such a rich treasure. Since chance has revealed to us its merits, let's use it to our advantage, but quietly and in a way that will not draw attention to ourselves nor attract the envy and jealousy of our neighbours. I will take it away, since the *jinn* terrify you so much, and put it somewhere where I can find it when we need it. As for the ring, I can't bring myself to throw it away either; without the ring, you would never have seen me again. I may be alive now but without it I might not have lasted for very long. So please let me keep it carefully, always wearing it on my finger. Who knows whether some other danger may happen to me that neither of us can foresee and from which it will rescue me?' Aladdin's reasoning seemed sound enough to his mother, who could find nothing to add. 'My son,' she said, 'you can do as you like. As for myself, I wouldn't have anything to do with *jinn*. I tell you, I wash my hands of them and won't speak to you about them again.'

The next evening, there was nothing left after supper of the splendid provisions brought by the *jinni*. So, early the following day, Aladdin, who did not want to be overtaken by hunger, slipped one of the silver dishes under his clothes and went out to try to sell it. As he went on his way, he met a Jew whom he drew aside and, showing him the dish, asked him if he wanted to buy it. The Jew, a shrewd and cunning man, took the dish, examined it and, discovering it to be good silver, asked Aladdin how much he thought it was worth. Aladdin, who did not know its value, never having dealt in this kind of merchandise, happily told him that he was well aware what it was worth and that he trusted in his good faith. The Jew found himself confused by Aladdin's ingeniousness. Uncertain as to whether Aladdin knew what the dish was made of and its value, he took out of his purse a piece of gold, which at the very most was equal to no more than a seventy-second of the dish's true value, and gave it to him. Aladdin seized the coin with such eagerness and, as soon as he had it in his grasp, took himself off so swiftly that the Jew, not content with the exorbitant profit he had made with this purchase, was very cross at not having realized that Aladdin was unaware of the value of what he had sold him and that he could have given him far less for it. He was about to go after the young man to try to recover some change from his gold, but Aladdin had run off and was already so far away that he would have had difficulty in catching up with him.

On his way home, Aladdin stopped off at a baker's shop where he bought some bread for his mother and himself, paying for it with the gold coin, for which the baker gave him some change. When he came to his mother, he gave it her and she then went off to the market to buy the necessary provisions for the two of them to live on for the next few days.

They continued to live thriftily in this way; that is, whenever money ran out in the house, Aladdin sold off all the dishes to the Jew – just as he had sold the first one to him – one after the other, up to the twelfth and last dish. The Jew, having offered a piece of gold for the first dish, did not dare give him any less for the rest, for fear of losing such a good windfall, and so he paid the same for them all. When the money for the remaining dish was completely spent, Aladdin finally had recourse to the large bowl, which alone weighed ten times as much as each dish. He would have taken it to his usual merchant but was prevented from doing so by its enormous weight. So he was obliged to seek out the Jew, whom he brought to his mother. The Jew, after examining the weight of the bowl, there and then counted out for him ten gold pieces, with which Aladdin was satisfied.

As long as they lasted, these ten gold coins were used for the daily expenses of the household. Aladdin, who had been accustomed to an idle life, had stopped playing with his young friends ever since his adventure with the magician and spent his days walking around or chatting with the people with whom he had become acquainted. Sometimes he would call in at the shops of the great merchants, where he would listen to the conversation of the important people who stopped there or who used the shops as a kind of rendezvous, and these conversations gradually gave him a smattering of worldly knowledge.

When all ten coins had been spent, Aladdin had recourse to the lamp once again. Taking it in his hand, he looked for the same spot his mother had touched and, recognizing it by the mark left on it by the sand, he rubbed it as she had done. Immediately the selfsame *jinni* appeared in front of him, but as he had rubbed it more lightly than his mother had done, the *jinni* consequently spoke to him more softly. 'What do you want?' he asked in the same words as before. 'Here am I, ready to obey you, your slave and the slave of all those who hold the lamp in their hands, I and the other slaves of the lamp.'

'I'm hungry,' answered Aladdin. 'Bring me something to eat.' The *jinni* disappeared and a little later he reappeared, laden with the same bowls and dishes as before, which he placed on the sofa and promptly disappeared again.

Aladdin's mother, warned of her son's plan, had deliberately gone out on some errand in order not to be in the house when the *jinni* put in his appearance. When she returned a little later and saw the table and the many dishes on it, she was almost as surprised by the miraculous effect of the lamp as she had been on the first occasion. They both sat down to eat and after the meal there was still plenty of food for them to live on for the next two days.

When Aladdin saw there was no longer any bread or other provisions in the house to live on nor money with which to buy any, he took a silver dish and went to look for the Jew he knew in order to sell it to him. On his way there, he passed in front of the shop of a goldsmith, a man respected for his age, an honest man of great probity. Noticing him, the goldsmith called out to him and made him come in. 'My son,' he said, 'I have frequently seen you pass by, laden, just like now, on your way to a certain Jew, and then shortly after coming back, empty-handed. I imagine that you sell him something that you are carrying. But perhaps you don't know that this Jew is a cheat, even more of a cheat than other Jews, and that no one who knows him wants anything to do with him. I only tell you this as a favour; if you would like to show me what you are carrying now and if it is something I can sell, I will faithfully pay you its true price. Otherwise, I will direct you to other merchants who will not cheat you.'

The hope of getting more money for the dish made Aladdin draw it out from among his clothes and show it to the goldsmith. The old man, who at once recognized the dish to be of fine silver, asked him whether he had sold similar dishes to the Jew and how much the latter had paid him for them. Aladdin naively told him he had sold the Jew twelve dishes, for each of which he had received only one gold coin from him. 'The robber!' exclaimed the goldsmith, before adding: 'My son, what is done is done. Forget it. But when I show you the true value of your dish, which is made of the finest silver we use in our shops, you will realize how much the Jew has cheated you.'

The goldsmith took his scales, weighed the dish and, after explaining to Aladdin how much an ounce of silver was worth and how many parts there were in an ounce, he remarked that, according to the weight of the dish, it was worth seventy-two pieces of gold, which he promptly counted out to him in cash. 'There, here is the true value of your dish,' he told Aladdin. 'If you don't believe it, you can go to any of our goldsmiths you please and if he tells you it is worth more, I promise to pay you double that. Our only profit comes from the workmanship of the silver we buy, and that's something even the most fair-minded Jews don't do.'

Aladdin thanked the goldsmith profusely for the friendly advice he had just given him which was so much to his advantage. From then on, he only went to him to sell the other dishes and the bowl, and the true price was always paid him according to the weight of each dish. However, although Aladdin and his mother had an inexhaustible source of money from their lamp from which to obtain as much as they wanted as soon as supplies began to run out, nonetheless they continued to live as frugally as before, except that Aladdin would put something aside in order to maintain himself in an honest manner and to provide himself with all that was needed for their small household. His mother, for her part, spent on her clothes only what she earned from spinning cotton. Consequently, with them both living so modestly, it is easy to work out how long the money from the twelve dishes and the bowl would have lasted, according to the price Aladdin sold them for to the goldsmith. And so they lived in this manner for several years, aided, from time to time, by the good use Aladdin made of the lamp.

During this time, Aladdin assiduously sought out people of importance who met in the shops of the biggest merchants of gold and silver cloth, of silks, of the finest linens and of jewellery, and sometimes joined in their discussions. In this way, he completed his education and insensibly adopted the manners of high society. It was at the jewellers', in particular, that he discovered his error in thinking that the transparent fruits he had gathered in the garden where he had found the lamp were only coloured glass, learning that they were stones of great price. By observing the buying and selling of all kinds of gems in their shops, he got to know about them and about their value. But he did not see any there similar to his in size and beauty, and so he realized that instead of pieces of glass which he had considered as mere trifles, he was in possession of a treasure of inestimable value. He was prudent enough not to speak about this to anyone, not even to his mother; and there is no doubt that it was by keeping silent that he rose to the heights of good fortune, as we shall see in due course.

One day, when he was walking around in a part of the city, Aladdin heard a proclamation from the sultan ordering people to shut all their shops and houses and stay indoors until Princess Badr al-Budur, the daughter of the sultan, had passed on her way to the baths and had returned from them.

This public announcement stirred Aladdin's curiosity; he wanted to see the princess's face but he could only do so by placing himself in the house of some acquaintance and looking through a lattice screen, which would not suffice, because the princess, according to custom, would be wearing a veil over her face when going to the baths. So he thought up a successful ruse: he went and hid himself behind the door to the baths, which was so placed that he could not help seeing her pass straight in front of him.

Aladdin did not have to wait long: the princess appeared and he watched her through a crack that was large enough for him to see without being seen. She was accompanied by a large crowd of her attendants, women and eunuchs, who walked on both sides of her and in her train. When she was three or four steps from the door to the baths, she lifted the veil which covered her face and which greatly inconvenienced her, and in this way she allowed Aladdin to see her all the more easily as she came towards him.

Until that moment, the only other woman Aladdin had seen with her face uncovered was his mother, who was aged and who never had such beautiful features as to make him believe that other women existed who were beautiful. He may well have heard that there were women of surpassing beauty, but for all the words one uses to extol the merits of a beautiful woman, they never make the same impression as a beautiful woman herself.

When Aladdin set eyes on Badr al-Budur, any idea that all women more or less resembled his mother flew from his mind; he found his feelings were now quite different and his heart could not resist the inclinations aroused in him by such an enchanting vision. Indeed, the princess was the most captivating dark-haired beauty to be found in all the world; her large, sparkling eyes were set on a level and full of life; her look was gentle and modest, her faultless nose perfectly proportioned, her mouth small, with its ruby lips charming in their pleasing symmetry; in a word, the regularity of all her facial features was nothing short of perfection. Consequently, one should not be surprised that Aladdin was so dazzled and almost beside himself at the sight of so many wonders hitherto unknown to him united in one face. Added to all these perfections, the princess also had a magnificent figure and bore herself with a regal air which, at the mere sight of her, would draw to her the respect that was her due.

After the princess had entered the baths, Aladdin remained for a while confused and in a kind of trance, recalling and imprinting deeply on his mind the image of the vision which had so captivated him and which had penetrated the very depths of his heart. He eventually came to and, after reflecting that the princess had now gone past and that it would be pointless for him to stay there in order to see her when she came out of the baths, for she would be veiled and have her back to him, he decided to abandon his post and go away.

When he returned home, Aladdin could not conceal his worry and confusion from his mother, who, noticing his state and surprised to see him so unusually sad and dazed, asked him whether something had happened to him or whether he felt ill. Aladdin made no reply but slumped down on the sofa, where he remained in the same position, still occupied in conjuring up the charming vision of the princess. His mother, who was preparing the supper, did not press him further. When it was ready, she served it up near to him on the sofa, and sat down to eat. However, noticing he was not paying any attention, she told him to come to the table and eat and it was only with great difficulty that he agreed. He ate much less than usual, keeping his eyes lowered and in such profound silence that his mother was unable to draw a single word out of him in reply to all the questions she asked him in an attempt to discover the reason for such an extraordinary change in his behaviour. After supper, she tried to ask him once again the reason for his great gloom but was unable to learn a thing and Aladdin decided to go to bed rather than give his mother the slightest satisfaction in the matter.

We will not go into how Aladdin, smitten with the beauty and charms of Princess Badr, spent the night, but will only observe that the following day, as he was seated on the sofa facing his mother – who was spinning cotton, as was her custom – he spoke to her as follows: 'Mother,' he said, 'I am breaking the silence I have kept since my return from the city yesterday because I realize it has been worrying you. I wasn't ill, as you seemed to think, and I am not ill now, but I can't tell you what I was feeling then, and what I am still feeling is something worse than any illness. I don't really know what this is, but I'm sure that what you are going to hear will tell you what it is.' He went on: 'No one in this quarter knew, and so you, too, cannot have known, that yesterday evening the daughter of the sultan, Princess Badr, was to go to the baths. I learned this bit of news while walking around the city. An order was proclaimed to shut up the shops and everyone was to stay indoors, so as to pay due respect to the princess and to allow her free passage in the streets through which she was to pass. As I was not far from the baths, I was curious to see her with her face uncovered, and so the idea came to me to go and stand behind the door to the baths, thinking that she might remove her veil when she was ready to go in. You know how the door is placed, so you can guess how I could see her quite easily if what I imagined were to happen. And indeed, as she entered she lifted her veil and I had the good fortune and the greatest satisfaction in the world to see this lovely princess. That, then, mother, is the real reason for the state you saw me in yesterday when I came home and the cause for my silence up till now. I love the princess with a passion I can't describe to you; and as this burning passion grows all the time, I feel it cannot be assuaged by anything other than the possession of the lovely Badr; which is why I have decided to ask the sultan for her hand in marriage.'

Aladdin's mother listened fairly carefully to what her son told her, up to the last few words. When she heard his plan to ask for the princess's hand, she could not help interrupting him by bursting out laughing. Aladdin was about to go on but, interrupting him again, she exclaimed: 'What are you thinking of, my son? You must have gone out of your mind to talk to me about such a thing!'

'Mother,' replied Aladdin, 'I can assure you I have not lost my senses but am quite in my right mind. I expected you would reproach me with madness and extravagance – and you did – but that will not stop me telling you once again that I have made up my mind to ask the sultan for the princess's hand in marriage.'

'My son,' his mother continued, addressing him very seriously, 'I can't indeed help telling you that you quite forget yourself; and even if you are still resolved to carry out this plan, I don't see through whom you would dare to make this request to the sultan.' 'Through you yourself,' Aladdin replied without hesitating. 'Through me!' exclaimed his mother, in surprise and astonishment. 'I go to the sultan? Ah, I would take very great care to avoid such an undertaking! And who are you, my son,' she continued, 'to be so bold as to think of the daughter of your sultan? Have you forgotten that you are the son of a tailor, among the least of his capital's citizens, and of a mother whose forebears were no more exalted? Don't you know that sultans don't deign to give away their daughters in marriage even to the sons of sultans, unless they are expected to reign one day themselves?' 'Mother,' replied Aladdin, 'I have already told you that I had foreseen all that you have said or would say, so despite all your remonstrances, nothing will make me change my mind. I have told you that through your mediation I would ask for Princess Badr's hand in marriage: this is a favour I ask of you, with all the respect I owe you, and I beg you not to refuse, unless you prefer to see me die rather than give me life a second time.'

Aladdin's mother felt very embarrassed when she saw how stubbornly he persisted in such a foolhardy plan. 'My son,' she said, 'I am your mother and, as a good mother who brought you into the world, there is nothing right and proper and in keeping with our circumstances that I would not be prepared to do out of my love for you. If it's a matter of speaking about marriage to the daughter of one of our neighbours, whose circumstances are equal or similar to ours, then I would gladly do everything in my power; but again, to succeed, you would need to have some assets or income, or you should know some trade. When poor people like us want to get married, the first thing they need to think about is their livelihood. But you, not reflecting on your humble status, the little you have to commend you and your lack of money, you aspire to the highest degree of fortune and are so presumptuous as to demand no less than the hand in marriage of the daughter of your sovereign – who with a single word can crush you and bring about your downfall. I won't speak of what concerns you; it is you who should think what you should do, if you have any sense. I come to what concerns me. How could such an extraordinary idea as that of wanting me to go to the sultan and propose that he give you the princess's, his daughter's, hand in marriage ever have come into your head? Supposing I had the – I won't say courage – effrontery to present myself to his majesty to put such an extravagant request to him, to whom would I go to for an introduction? Don't you think that the first person to whom I spoke about it would treat me as a mad woman and throw me out indignantly, as I deserved? And what about seeking an audience with the sultan? I know there is no difficulty when one goes to him to seek justice and that he readily grants it to his subjects when they ask him for it. I also know that when one goes to ask him a favour, he grants it gladly, when he sees that one has deserved it and is worthy of it. But is that the position you are in and do you think you merit the favour that you want me to ask for you? Are you worthy of it? What have you done for your sultan or for your country? How have you distinguished yourself? If you haven't done anything to deserve so great a favour – of which, anyhow, you are not worthy – how could I have the audacity to ask him for it? How could I so much as open my mouth to propose it to the sultan? His majestic presence alone and the brilliance of his court would make me dry up immediately – I, who used to tremble before my late husband, your father, when I had to ask him for the slightest thing. There is something else you haven't thought about, my son, and that is that one does not go to ask a favour of the sultan without bearing a present. A present has at least this advantage that, if, for whatever reason, he refuses the favour, he at least listens to the request and to whoever makes it. But what present do you have to offer? And if you had something worthy of the slightest attention from so great a ruler, would your gift adequately represent the scale of the favour you want to ask him? Think about this and reflect that you are aspiring to something which you cannot possibly obtain.'

Aladdin listened quietly to everything his mother had to say in her attempt to make him give up his plan. Finally, after reflecting on all the points she had made in remonstrating with him, he replied to her, saying: 'Mother, I admit it's great rashness on my part to carry my pretensions as far as I am doing, and that it's very inconsiderate of me to insist with such heat and urgency on your going and putting my proposal of marriage to the sultan without first taking the appropriate measures for you to obtain a favourable and successful audience with him. Please forgive me, but don't be surprised if, in the strength of the passion which possesses me, I did not at first envisage all that could help me procure the happiness I seek. I love Princess Badr beyond anything you can imagine, or rather, I adore her and will continue to persevere in my plan to marry her – my mind is quite made up and fixed in this matter. I am grateful to you for the opening you have just given me; I see it as the first step which will help me obtain the happy outcome I promise myself. You tell me that it is not customary to go before the sultan without bearing him a present, and that I have nothing which is worthy of him. I agree with you about the present, and I admit I hadn't thought about it. As for your telling me that I have nothing I can possibly offer him, don't you think, mother, that what I brought back with me the day I was saved from almost inevitable death could not make a very nice gift for the sultan? I am talking about what I brought back in the two purses and in my belt, which you and I both took to be pieces of coloured glass. I have since learned better and I can tell you, mother, that these are jewels of inestimable value, fit only for great kings. I discovered their worth by frequenting jewellers' shops, and you can take my word for it. None of all those I have seen in the shops of our jewellers can compare in size or in beauty to those we possess, and yet they sell them for exorbitant prices. The fact is that neither you nor I know what ours are worth, but however much that is, as far as I can judge from the little experience I have gained, I am convinced that the present will please the sultan very much. You have a porcelain dish large enough and of the right shape to contain the jewels; fetch it and let's see the effect they make when we arrange them according to their different colours.'

Aladdin's mother fetched the porcelain dish and Aladdin took out the stones from the two purses and arranged them in it. The effect they made in full daylight, by the variety of their colours, their brilliance and sparkle, was such as to almost dazzle them both and they were greatly astonished, for neither of them had seen the stones except in the light of a lamp. It is true that Aladdin had seen them hanging on the trees like fruit, which must have made an enchanting sight; but as he was still a boy, he had only thought of these stones as trinkets to be played with, and that is the only way he had thought of them, knowing no better.

After admiring for some time the beauty of the jewels, Aladdin spoke once more. 'Mother,' he said, 'you can no longer get out of going and presenting yourself to the sultan on the pretext of not having a present to offer him; here is one, it seems to me, which will ensure you are received with the most favourable of welcomes.'

For all the beauty and splendour of the present, Aladdin's mother did not think it was worth as much as Aladdin believed it to be. Nonetheless she thought it would be acceptable and she knew she had nothing to say to the contrary; but she kept thinking of the request Aladdin wanted her to make to the sultan with the help of this gift and this worried her greatly. 'My son,' she said to him, 'I don't find it difficult to imagine that the present will have its effect and that the sultan will look upon me favourably; but when it comes to my putting the request to him that you want me to make, I feel I won't have the strength and I will remain silent. My journey will have been wasted as I will have lost what you claim is a gift of extraordinary value. I will come home completely embarrassed at having to tell you that you are disappointed in your hopes. I have already explained this to you and you should realize that this is what will happen. However,' she added, 'even if it hurts me, I will give in to your wish and I will force myself to have the strength and courage to dare to make the request you want me to make. The sultan will most probably either laugh at me and send me away as a madwoman or he will quite rightly fly into a great rage of which you and I will inevitably be the victims.'

Aladdin's mother gave her son several other reasons in an attempt to make him change his mind; but the charms of Princess Badr had made too deep an impression on his heart for anyone to be able to dissuade him from carrying out his plan. Aladdin continued to insist his mother go through with it; and so, as much out of her love for him as out of fear that he might resort to some extreme measure, she overcame her aversion and bowed to her son's will.

As it was too late and the time to go to the palace for an audience with the sultan that day had passed, the matter was put off until the following day. For the rest of the day, mother and son spoke of nothing else, Aladdin taking great care to tell his mother everything he could think of to strengthen her in the decision which she had finally made, to go and present herself to the sultan. Yet, despite all his arguments, his mother could not be persuaded that she would ever succeed in the matter, and, indeed, one must admit she had good reason to doubt. 'My son,' she said to Aladdin, 'assuming the sultan receives me as favourably as I wish for your sake, and assuming he listens calmly to the proposal you want me to put to him, what if, after this friendly reception, he should then ask about your possessions, your riches and your estates? For that's what he will ask about before anything else, rather than about you yourself. If he asks me about that, what do you want me to reply?'

'Mother,' said Aladdin, 'let's not worry in advance about something which may never happen. Let's first see what sort of reception the sultan gives you and what reply he gives you. If he happens to want to know all you have just suggested, I will think of an answer to give him, for I am confident that the lamp, which has been the means of our subsistence for the past few years, will not fail me in time of need.'

Aladdin's mother could think of nothing to say to this. She agreed that the lamp might well be capable of greater miracles than simply providing them with enough to live on. This thought satisfied her and at the same time removed all the difficulties which could have stopped her carrying out the mission she had promised her son. Aladdin, who guessed what she was thinking, said to her: 'Mother, above all remember to keep the secret; on it depends all the success you and I expect from this affair.' They then left each other to have some rest; but Aladdin's mind was so filled with his violent passion and his grand plans for an immense fortune that he was unable to pass the night as peacefully as he would have wished. Before daybreak, he rose and immediately went to wake his mother. He urged her to get dressed as quickly as possible in order to go to the palace gate and to pass through it as soon as it was opened, when the grand vizier, the other viziers and all the court officials entered the council chamber where the sultan always presided in person.

Aladdin's mother did everything her son wanted. She took the porcelain dish containing the jewels, wrapped it in two layers of cloth, one finer and cleaner than the other, which she tied by all four corners in order to carry it more easily. She then set out, to Aladdin's great satisfaction, and took the street which led to the sultan's palace. When she arrived at the gate, the grand vizier, accompanied by the other viziers and the highest-ranking court officials, had already entered. There was an enormous crowd of all those who had business at the council. The gate opened and she walked with them right up into the council chamber, which was a very handsome room, wide and spacious, with a grand and magnificent entrance. She stopped and placed herself in such a way as to be opposite the sultan, with the grand vizier and the nobles who had a seat at the council to the right and left of him. One after the other, people were called according to the order of the requests that had been presented, and their affairs were produced, pleaded and judged until the time the session usually adjourned, when the sultan rose, dismissed the council and withdrew to his apartments where he was followed by the grand vizier. The other viziers and the court officials withdrew, as did all who were there on some particular business, some happy to have won their case, others less satisfied as judgement had been made against them, and still others left in the hope of their case being heard at the next session.

Aladdin's mother, seeing that the sultan had risen and withdrawn and that everyone was leaving, concluded rightly that he would not reappear that day and so she decided to return home. When Aladdin saw her coming in with the present destined for the sultan, he did not know at first what to think. Afraid that she had some bad news for him, he did not have the strength to ask her about her trip. The good woman, who had never before set foot in the sultan's palace and who had not the slightest acquaintance with what normally happened there, helped him out of his difficulty by saying to him with great naivety: 'My son, I saw the sultan and I am quite sure he, too, saw me. I was right in front of him and nobody could prevent him seeing me, but he was so occupied with all those talking to the right and left of him, that I was filled with pity to see the trouble he took to listen patiently to them. That went on for such a long time that I think he finally became weary; for he arose all of a sudden and withdrew quite brusquely, without wishing to listen to the many other people who were lined up to speak to him. I was, in fact, very pleased because I was beginning to lose patience and was very tired from standing up for so long. However, all is not lost and I intend to return there tomorrow; perhaps the sultan will be less busy.'

However great his passion, Aladdin had to be content with this excuse and remain patient. But he at least had the satisfaction of seeing that his mother had taken the most difficult step, which was to stand before the sultan; he hoped that she would follow the example of those whom she saw speaking to him, and not hesitate to carry out the task with which she was charged when she found an opportunity to speak to him.

The next day, arriving early, as she had done the previous day, Aladdin's mother again went to the sultan's palace with the present of gems; but her journey once again proved futile. She found the door of the council chamber closed, council sessions being held only every other day, and realized that she would have to return the following day. This news she reported back to Aladdin, who had to remain patient. She returned six more times to the council chamber, on the appropriate days, always placing herself in front of the sultan, but with the same lack of success as on the first occasion. She would perhaps have returned a hundred more times, all to no avail, had not the sultan, who had seen her standing in front of him at each session, finally paid attention to her. Her lack of success is hardly surprising in that only those who had petitions to present approached the sultan, one by one, to plead their cause, whereas Aladdin's mother was not among those lined up before him.

At last, one day, after the council had risen and he had returned to his apartments, the sultan said to his vizier: 'For some time now I have noticed a certain woman who comes regularly every day that I hold my council session. She carries something wrapped up in a cloth and remains standing from the beginning of the audience to the end, always deliberately placed in front of me. Do you know what she wants?'

The grand vizier, who knew no more about her than the sultan but did not wish to appear to be stuck for an answer, replied: 'Sire, your majesty knows well how women often raise complaints about matters of no importance: this one, apparently, has come to complain to you about having been sold bad flour, or about some other, equally trivial, wrong.' But the sultan was not satisfied with this reply and said: 'On the next council day, if this woman comes again, be sure to have her summoned so that I can hear what she has to say.' To this the grand vizier replied by kissing the sultan's hand and raising it above his head to indicate that he was prepared to die if he failed to carry out the sultan's command.

Aladdin's mother had by now become so accustomed to going to the council and standing before the sultan that she did not think it any trouble, as long as she made her son understand that she was doing everything she could to comply with his wishes. So she returned to the palace on the day of the next session and took up her customary position at the entrance of the chamber, opposite the sultan.

The grand vizier had not yet begun to bring up any case when the sultan noticed Aladdin's mother. Feeling compassion for her, having seen her wait so long and so patiently, the sultan said to him: 'First of all, in case you forget, here is the woman I was telling you about; make her come up and let us begin by hearing her and getting her business out of the way.' Immediately, the grand vizier pointed the woman out to the chief usher, who was standing ready to receive his orders, and commanded him to fetch her and bring her forward. The chief usher went up to her and made a sign to follow him to the foot of the sultan's throne, where he left her, before taking his place next to the grand vizier.

Aladdin's mother, having learned from the example of the many others she had seen approach the sultan, prostrated herself, with her forehead touching the carpet that covered the steps to the throne, and remained thus until the sultan ordered her to rise. When she rose, the sultan asked her: 'My good woman, for some time now I have seen you come to my council chamber and remain at the entrance from the beginning to the very end of the session – so what brings you here?'

Hearing these words, Aladdin's mother prostrated herself a second time; standing up again, she said: 'King of all kings, before I reveal to your majesty the extraordinary and almost unbelievable business which brings me before your exalted throne, I beg you to pardon me for the audacity, not to say the impudence, of the request I am going to make to you – a request so unusual that I tremble and am ashamed to put it to my sultan.'

The sultan, to allow her to explain herself in complete freedom, ordered everyone to go out of the council chamber, except the grand vizier. He then told her she could speak and explain herself without fear. But Aladdin's mother, not content with the sultan's kindness in sparing her the distress she would have endured in speaking in front of so many people, wished to protect herself from what she feared would be his indignation at the unexpected proposal which she was going to put to him, and continued: 'Sire, I dare to entreat you that if you find the request I am going to put to your majesty in any way offensive or insulting, you will first assure me of your forgiveness and grant me your pardon.' 'Whatever it is,' replied the sultan, 'I now forgive you and assure you that no harm will come to you. So speak out.'

Having taken all these precautions because of her fear of arousing the sultan's anger at receiving a proposal of so delicate a nature, Aladdin's mother then went on to relate faithfully how Aladdin had first seen Princess Badr, the violent passion which the sight of her had inspired in him, what he had said to her; and how she had done everything she could to talk him out of a passion so harmful not only to his majesty but also to the princess, his daughter, herself. 'But my son,' she continued, 'far from profiting from my advice and admitting his audacity, has obstinately persisted in his purpose. He even threatened that he would be driven to do something desperate if I refused to come and ask your majesty for the hand of the princess in marriage. And it was only with extreme reluctance that I finally found myself forced to do him this favour, for which I beseech your majesty once more to pardon not only me but also my son, Aladdin, for having deigned to aspire to so elevated a union.'

The sultan listened to this speech very gently and kindly, showing no sign of anger or indignation, nor making fun of her request. But before giving her an answer, he asked her what it was she had brought wrapped in a cloth, whereupon she immediately took the porcelain dish, which she had set down at the foot of the throne before prostrating herself, unwrapped it and presented it to him.

One can hardly describe the sultan's surprise and astonishment when he saw such a quantity of precious gems, so perfect, so brilliant and of a size the like of which he had never seen before, crammed into this dish. For a while he remained quite motionless, lost in admiration. When he had recovered, he received the present from the hands of Aladdin's mother, exclaiming ecstatically: 'Ah! How beautiful! What a splendid present!' When he had admired and handled virtually all the jewels, one by one, examining each gem to assess its distinctive quality, he turned towards his grand vizier and, showing him the dish, said to him: 'Look, don't you agree you won't find anything more splendid or more perfect in the whole world?' The grand vizier was dazzled. 'So, what do you think of such a present?' the sultan asked him. 'Isn't it worthy of the princess, my daughter, and can't I then give her, at a price like that, to the man who asks me for her hand in marriage?'

These words roused the grand vizier into a state of strange agitation. Some time ago, the sultan had given him to understand that it was his intention to bestow the princess in marriage to one of his sons, and so he feared, and with some justification, that the sultan, dazzled by such a sumptuous and extraordinary gift, would now change his mind. He went up to the sultan and whispered into his ear: 'Sire, one can't disagree that the present is worthy of the princess; but I beg your majesty to grant me three months before you come to a decision. Before that time, I hope that my son, on whom you have been so kind as to indicate you look favourably, will be able to present her with a much more valuable gift than that offered by Aladdin, who is a stranger to your majesty.'

The sultan, although he was quite sure that his grand vizier could not possibly come up with enough for his son to produce a gift of similar value to offer the princess, nonetheless listened to him and granted him this favour. Turning, then, to Aladdin's mother, he said: 'Go home, good woman, and tell your son that I agree to the proposal you have made on his behalf; but I can't marry the princess, my daughter, to him before I have furnishings provided for her, and these won't be ready for three months. At the end of that time, come back.'

Aladdin's mother returned home, her joy being all the greater because she had first thought that, in view of her lowly state, access to the sultan would be impossible, whereas she had in fact obtained a very favourable reply instead of the rebuffs and resulting confusion she had expected. When Aladdin saw his mother come in, two things made him think that she was bringing good news: one was that she was returning earlier than usual, and the other was that her face was all lit up and she was smiling. 'So, Mother,' he said to her, 'is there any cause for hope, or must I die of despair?' Having removed her veil and sat down beside him on the sofa, she replied: 'My son, I'm not going to keep you in a state of uncertainty and so will begin at once by telling you that far from thinking of dying you have every reason to be happy.' She went on to tell him how she had received an audience, before everyone else, and that was the reason she had returned so early. She also told him what precautions she had taken not to offend the sultan in putting the proposal of marriage to Princess Badr, and of the very favourable response she had received from the sultan's own mouth. She added that, as far as she could judge from indications given by the sultan, it was above all the powerful effect of the present which had determined that favourable reply. 'I least expected this,' she said, 'because the grand vizier had whispered in his ear before he gave his reply and I was afraid he would deflect any goodwill the sultan might have towards you.'

When he heard this, Aladdin thought himself the happiest of men. He thanked his mother for all the trouble she had gone to in pursuit of this affair, whose happy outcome was so important for his peace of mind. And although three months seemed an extremely long time such was his impatience to enjoy the object of his passion, he nonetheless prepared himself to wait patiently, trusting in the sultan's word, which he considered irrevocable.

One evening, when two months or so had passed, with him counting not only the hours, days and the weeks, but even every moment as he waited for the period to come to an end, his mother, wanting to light the lamp, noticed that there was no more oil in the house. So she went out to buy some. As she approached the centre of the city, everywhere she saw signs of festivity: the shops, instead of being shut, were all open and were being decorated with greenery, and illuminations were being prepared – in their enthusiasm, every shop owner was vying with each other in their efforts to display the most pomp and magnificence. Everywhere were demonstrations of happiness and rejoicing. The streets themselves were blocked by officials in ceremonial dress, mounted on richly harnessed horses, and surrounded by a milling throng of attendants on foot. Aladdin's mother asked the merchant from whom she was buying her oil what this all meant. 'My good woman, where are you from?' he replied. 'Don't you know that the son of the grand vizier is to marry Princess Badr, daughter of the sultan, this evening? She is about to come out of the baths and the officials you see here are gathering to accompany her procession to the palace, where the ceremony is to take place.'

Aladdin's mother did not wish to hear any more. She returned home in such haste that she arrived almost breathless. She found Aladdin, who little expected the grievous news she was bringing, and exclaimed: 'My son, you have lost everything! You were counting on the sultan's fine promises – nothing will come of them now.' Alarmed at these words, Aladdin said to her: 'But, mother, in what way will the sultan not keep his promise to me? And how do you know?' 'This evening,' she replied, 'the son of the grand vizier is to marry Princess Badr, in the palace.' She went on to explain how she had learned this, telling him all the circumstances so as to leave him in no doubt.

At this news, Aladdin remained motionless, as though he had been struck by a bolt of lightning. Anyone else would have been quite overcome, but a deep jealousy prevented him from staying like this for long. He instantly remembered the lamp which had until then been so useful to him: without breaking out in a pointless outburst against the sultan, the grand vizier or his son, he merely said to his mother: 'Maybe the son of the grand vizier will not be as happy tonight as he thinks he will be. While I go to my room for a moment, prepare us some supper.'

Aladdin's mother guessed her son was going to make use of the lamp to prevent, if possible, the consummation of the marriage, and she was not deceived. Indeed, when Aladdin entered his room, he took the magic lamp – which he had removed from his mother's sight and taken there after the appearance of the *jinni* had given her such a fright – and rubbed it in the same spot as before. Immediately, the *jinni* appeared before him and asked: 'What is your wish? Here am I, ready to obey you, your slave and the slave of all those who hold the lamp, I and the other slaves of the lamp.'

'Listen,' Aladdin said to him, 'up until now, you have brought me food when I was in need of it, but now I have business of the utmost importance. I have asked the sultan for the hand of the princess, his daughter; he promised her to me but asked for a delay of three months. However, instead of keeping his promise, he is marrying her tonight to the son of the grand vizier, before the time is up: I have just learned of this and it's a fact. What I demand of you is that, as soon as the bride and bridegroom are in bed, you carry them off and bring them both here, in their bed.' 'Master,' replied the *jinni*, 'I will obey you. Do you have any other command?' 'Nothing more at present,' said Aladdin, and the *jinni* immediately disappeared.

Aladdin returned to his mother and had supper with her, calmly and peacefully as usual. After supper, he talked to her for a while about the marriage of the princess as if it were something which no longer worried him. Then he returned to his room, leaving his mother to go to bed. He himself did not go to sleep, however, but waited for the *jinni*'s return and for the order he had given him to be carried out.

All this while, everything had been prepared with much splendour in the sultan's palace to celebrate the marriage of the princess, and the evening passed in ceremonies and entertainments which went on well into the night. When it was all over, the son of the grand vizier, after a signal given him by the princess's chief eunuch, slipped out and was then brought in by him to the princess's apartments, right to the room where the marriage bed had been prepared. He went to bed first. A little while after, the sultana, accompanied by her ladies and by those of the princess, her daughter, led in the bride, who, as is the custom of brides, put up a great resistance. The sultana helped to undress her and put her into bed as though by force; and, after having embraced her and saying goodnight, she withdrew, together with all the women, the last to leave shutting the door behind her.

No sooner had the door been shut than the *jinni* – as faithful servant of the lamp and punctual in carrying out the commands of those who had it in their hands – without giving the bridegroom time to so much as caress his wife, to the great astonishment of them both, lifted up the bed, complete with bride and groom, and transported them in an instant to Aladdin's room, where he set it down.

Aladdin, who had been waiting impatiently for this moment, did not allow the son of the grand vizier to remain lying with the princess but said to the *jinni*: 'Take this bridegroom, lock him up in the privy and come back tomorrow morning, a little after daybreak.' The *jinni* immediately carried off the son of the grand vizier from the bed, in his nightshirt, and transported him to the place Aladdin had told him to take him, where he left the bridegroom, after breathing over him a breath which he felt from head to toe and which prevented him from stirring from where he was.

However great the passion Aladdin felt for Princess Badr, once he found himself alone with her, he did not address her at length, but declared passionately: 'Don't be afraid, adorable princess, you are quite safe here, and however violent the love I feel for your beauty and your charms, it will never go beyond the bounds of the profound respect I have for you. If I have been forced to adopt such extreme measures, this was not to offend you but to prevent an unjust rival from possessing you, contrary to the word in my favour given me by your father, the sultan.'

The princess, who knew nothing of the circumstances surrounding all this, paid little attention to what Aladdin had to say and was in no state to reply to him. Her terror and astonishment at so surprising and unexpected an adventure had put her into such a state that Aladdin could not get a word out of her. He did not leave it at that but decided to undress and then lie down in the place of the son of the grand vizier, his back turned to the princess, after having taken the precaution of putting a sword between them, to show that he deserved to be punished if he made an attempt on her honour.

Happy at having thus deprived his rival of the pleasure which he had flattered himself he would enjoy that night, Aladdin slept quite peacefully. This was not true of the princess, however: never in all her life had she spent so trying and disagreeable a night; and as for the son of the vizier, if one considers the place and the state in which the *jinni* had left him, one can guess that her new husband spent it in a much more distressing manner.

The next morning, Aladdin did not need to rub the lamp to summon the *jinni*, who came by himself at the appointed hour, just when Aladdin had finished dressing. 'Here am I,' he said to Aladdin. 'What is your command?' 'Go and bring back the son of the grand vizier from the place where you put him,' said Aladdin. 'Place him in this bed again and carry it back to the sultan's palace, from where you took it.' The *jinni* went to fetch the son of the grand vizier, and when he reappeared, Aladdin took up his sword from the bed. The *jinni* placed the bridegroom next to the princess and, in an instant, he returned the marriage bed to the same room in the sultan's palace from where he had taken it.

It should be pointed out that, all the while, the *jinni* could not be seen by either the princess or the son of the grand vizier – his hideous shape would have been enough to make them die of fright. Nor did they hear any of the conversation between Aladdin and him. All they noticed was how their bed shook and how they were transported from one place to another; which was quite enough, as one can easily imagine, to give them a considerable fright.

The *jinni* had just restored the nuptial bed to its place when the sultan, curious to discover how his daughter, the princess, had spent the first night of her marriage, entered her room to wish her good morning. No sooner did he hear the door open than the son of the grand vizier, chilled to the bone from the cold he had endured all night long and not yet having had time to warm up again, got up and went to the closet where he had undressed the previous evening.

The sultan approached the princess's bed, kissed her between the eyes, as was the custom, and asked her, as he greeted her with a smile, what sort of night she had had; but raising his head again and looking at her more closely, he was extremely surprised to see that she was in a state of great dejection and neither by a blush spreading over her face nor by any other sign could she satisfy his curiosity. She only gave him a most sorrowful look, which indicated either great sadness or great discontent. He said a few more words to her but, seeing that he could get nothing more from her, he decided she was keeping silent out of modesty and so retired. Nevertheless, still suspicious that there was something unusual about her silence, he went straight away to the apartments of the sultana and told her in what a state he had found the princess and how she had received him. 'Sire,' the sultana said to him, 'this should not surprise your majesty; there's no bride who does not display the same reserve the morning after her wedding night. It won't be the same in two or three days: she will then receive her father, the sultan, as she ought. I am going to see her myself,' she added, 'and I will be very surprised if she receives me in the same way.'

When the sultana had dressed, she went to the princess's room. Badr had not yet risen, and when the sultana approached her bed, greeting and embracing her, great was her surprise not only to receive no reply but also to see the princess in a state of deep dejection, which made her conclude that something she could not understand had happened to her daughter. 'My daughter,' she said to her, 'how is it that you don't respond to my caresses? How can you behave like this to your mother? Don't you think I don't know what can happen in circumstances like yours? I would really like to think that that's not what's in your mind and something else must have happened. Tell me quite frankly; don't leave me weighed down by anxiety for a moment longer.'

At last, the princess broke her silence and gave a deep sigh. 'Ah! My dear and esteemed mother,' she exclaimed, 'forgive me if I have failed to show you the respect I owe you. My mind is so preoccupied with the extraordinary things that happened to me last night that I have not yet recovered from my astonishment and terror and I hardly know myself.' She then proceeded to tell her, in the most colourful detail, how shortly after she and her husband had gone to bed, the bed had been lifted up and transported in a moment to a dark and squalid room where she found herself all alone and separated from her husband, without knowing what had happened to him; how she had seen a young man who had addressed a few words to her which her terror had prevented her understanding, who had lain beside her in her husband's place, after placing a sword between them; and how her husband had been restored to her and the bed returned to its place, all in a very short space of time. 'All this,' she added, 'had just taken place when the sultan, my father, came into the room; I was so overcome by grief that I had not the strength to reply even with a single word, and so I have no doubt he was angry at the manner in which I received the honour he did me by coming to see me. But I hope he will forgive me when he knows of my sad adventure and sees the pitiful state I'm still in.'

The sultana listened calmly to everything the princess had to say, but she did not believe it. 'My daughter,' she said, 'you were quite right not to talk about this to the sultan, your father. Take care not to talk about it to anyone – they will think you mad if they hear you talk like this.' 'Mother,' she rejoined, 'I can assure you that I am in my right mind. Ask my husband and he will tell you the same thing.' 'I will ask him,' replied the sultana, 'but even if his account is the same as yours, I won't be any more convinced than I am now. Now get up and clear your mind of such fantasies; a fine thing it would be if you were to let such a dream upset the celebrations arranged for your wedding, which are set to last several days, not only in this palace but throughout the kingdom! Can't you already hear the fanfares and the sounds of trumpets, drums and tambourines? All this should fill you with pleasure and joy and make you forget the fantastic stories you've been telling me.' The sultana then summoned the princess's maids and, after she had made her get up and seen her set about getting dressed, she went to the sultan's apartments and told him that some fancy had, indeed, entered the head of his daughter, but that it was nothing. She sent for the son of the vizier to discover from him a little about what the princess had told her; but he, knowing himself to be greatly honoured by his alliance with the sultan, decided it would be best to conceal the adventure. 'Tell me, son-in-law,' the sultana said to him, 'are you being as stubborn as your wife?' 'My lady,' he replied, 'may I enquire why you ask me this?' 'That will do,' retorted the sultana. 'I don't need to hear anything more. You are wiser than she is.'

The rejoicings continued in the palace all day, and the sultana, who never left the princess, did all she could to cheer her up and make her take part in the entertainments and amusements prepared for her. But the princess was so struck down by the visions of what had happened to her the previous night that it was easy to see she was totally preoccupied by them. The son of the vizier was just as shattered by the bad night he had spent but, fired by ambition, he concealed it and, seeing him, no one would have thought he was anything else but the happiest of bridegrooms.

Aladdin, knowing all about what had happened in the palace and never doubting that the newly-weds would sleep together, despite the misadventure of the previous night, had no desire to leave them in peace. So, after nightfall, he had recourse once again to the lamp. Immediately, the *jinni* appeared and greeted him in the same way as on the other occasions, offering him his services. 'The son of the grand vizier and Princess Badr are going to sleep together again tonight,' explained Aladdin. 'Go, and as soon as they are in bed, bring them here, as you did yesterday.'

The *jinni* served Aladdin as faithfully and as punctually as on the previous day; the son of the grand vizier spent as disagreeable a night as the one he had already endured and the princess was as mortified as before to have Aladdin as her bedfellow, with the sword placed between them. The next day, the *jinni*, following Aladdin's orders, returned and restored the husband to his wife's side; he then lifted up the bed with the newly-weds and transported it back to the room in the palace from where he had taken it.

Early the next morning, the sultan, anxious to discover how the princess had spent the second night, and wondering if she would receive him in the same way as on the previous day, went to her room to find out. But no sooner did the son of the grand vizier, more ashamed and mortified by his bad luck on the second night, hear the sultan come in than he hastily arose and hurled himself into the closet.

The sultan approached the princess's bed and greeted her, and after embracing her in the same way as he had the day before, asked her: 'Well, my dear, are you in as bad a mood this morning as you were yesterday? Tell me what sort of night you had.' But the princess again remained silent, and the sultan saw that her mind was even more disturbed and she was more dejected than the first time. He had no doubt now that something extraordinary had happened to her. So, irritated by the mystery she was making of it and clutching his sword, he angrily said to her: 'My daughter, either you tell me what you are hiding from me or I will cut off your head this very instant.'

At last, the princess, more frightened by the tone of her aggrieved father and his threat than by the sight of the unsheathed sword, broke her silence, and, with tears in her eyes, burst out: 'My dear father and sultan, I beg pardon of your majesty if I have offended you and I hope that in your goodness and mercy anger will give way to compassion when I give you a faithful account of the sad and pitiful state in which I spent all last night and the night before.' After this preamble, which somewhat calmed and softened the sultan, she faithfully recounted to him all that had happened to her during those two unfortunate nights. Her account was so moving that, in the love and tenderness he felt for her, he was filled with deep sorrow. When she had finished her account, she said to him: 'If your majesty has the slightest doubt about the account I have just given, you can ask the husband you have given me. I am convinced your majesty will be persuaded of the truth when he bears the same witness to it as I have done.'

The sultan now truly felt the extreme distress that such an astonishing adventure must have caused the princess and said to her: 'My daughter, you were very wrong not to have told me yesterday about such a strange affair, which concerns me as much as yourself. I did not marry you with the intention of making you miserable but rather with a view to making you happy and content, and to let you enjoy the happiness you deserve and can expect with a husband who seemed suited to you. Forget now all the worrying images you have just told me about. I will see to it that you endure no more nights as disagreeable and as unbearable as those you have just spent.'

As soon as the sultan had returned to his own apartments, he called for his grand vizier and asked him: 'Vizier, have you seen your son and has he not said anything to you?' When the vizier replied that he had not seen him, the sultan related to him everything Princess Badr had just told him, adding: 'I do not doubt my daughter was telling the truth, but I would be very glad to have it confirmed by what your son says. Go and ask him about it.'

The grand vizier made haste to join his son and to tell him what the sultan had said. He charged him to not conceal the truth but to tell him whether all this was true, to which his son replied: 'Father, I will conceal nothing from you. All that the princess told the sultan is true, but she couldn't tell him about the ill treatment I myself received, which is this: since my wedding I have spent the two most cruel nights imaginable and I do not have the words to describe to you exactly and in every detail the ills I have suffered. I won't tell you what I felt when I found myself lifted up four times in my bed and transported from one place to another, unable to see who was lifting the bed or to imagine how that could have been done. You can judge for yourself the wretched state I found myself in when I tell you that I spent two nights standing, naked but for my nightshirt, in a kind of narrow privy, not free to move from where I stood nor able to make any movement, although I could see no obstacle to prevent me from moving. I don't need to go into further detail about all my sufferings. I will not conceal from you that all this has not stopped me from feeling towards the princess, my wife, all the love, respect and gratitude that she deserves; but I confess in all sincerity that despite all the honour and glory that comes to me from having married the daughter of the sultan, I would rather die than live any longer in such an elevated alliance if I have to endure any further such disagreeable treatment as I have done. I am sure the princess feels the same as I do and will readily agree that our separation is as necessary for her peace of mind as it is for mine. And so, father, I beseech you, by the same love which led you to procure for me such a great honour, to make the sultan agree to our marriage being declared null and void.'

However great the grand vizier's ambition was for his son to become the son-in-law of the sultan, seeing how firmly resolved he was to separate from the princess, he did not think it right to suggest he be patient and wait a few more days to see if this problem might not be solved. He left his son and went to give his reply to the sultan, to whom he admitted frankly that it was only too true after what he had just learned from his son. Without waiting even for the sultan to speak to him about ending the marriage, which he could see he was all too much in favour of doing, he begged him to allow his son to leave the palace and to return home to him, using as a pretext that it was not right for the princess to be exposed a moment longer to such terrible persecution for the sake of his son.

The grand vizier had no difficulty in obtaining what he asked for. Immediately, the sultan, who had already made up his mind, gave orders to stop the festivities in his palace, the city and throughout the length and breadth of his kingdom, countering those originally given. In a very short while, all signs of joy and public rejoicing in the city and in the kingdom had ceased.

This sudden and unexpected change gave rise to many different interpretations: people asked each other what had caused this upset, but all that they could say was that the grand vizier had been seen leaving the palace and going home, accompanied by his son, both of them looking very dejected. Only Aladdin knew the secret and inwardly rejoiced at the good fortune which the lamp had procured him. Once he had learned for certain that his rival had abandoned the palace and that the marriage between him and the princess was over, he needed no longer to rub the lamp nor to summon the *jinni* to stop it being consummated. What is strange is that neither the sultan nor the grand vizier, who had forgotten Aladdin and his request, had the slightest idea that he had any part in the enchantment which had just caused the break-up of the princess's marriage.

Meanwhile, Aladdin let the three months go by that the sultan had stipulated before the marriage between him and Princess Badr could take place. He counted the days very carefully, and when they were up, the very next morning he hastened to send his mother to the palace to remind the sultan of his word.

Aladdin's mother went to the palace as her son had asked her and stood at the entrance to the council chamber, in the same spot as before. As soon as the sultan caught sight of her, he recognized her and immediately remembered the request she had made him and the date to which he had put off fulfilling it. The vizier was at that moment reporting to him on some matter, but the sultan interrupted him, saying: 'Vizier, I see the good woman who gave us such a fine gift a few months ago; bring her up – you can resume your report when I have heard what she has to say.' The grand vizier turned towards the entrance of the council chamber, saw Aladdin's mother and immediately summoned the chief usher, to whom he pointed her out, ordering him to bring her forward.

Aladdin's mother advanced right to the foot of the throne, where she prostrated herself as was customary. When she rose up again, the sultan asked her what her request was, to which she replied: 'Sire, I come before your majesty once more to inform you, in the name of my son Aladdin, that the three months' postponement of the request I had the honour to put to your majesty has come to an end and I entreat you to be so good as to remember your word.'

When he had first seen her, so meanly dressed, standing before him in all her poverty and lowliness, the sultan had thought that by making a delay of three months to reply to her request he would hear no more talk of a marriage which he regarded as not at all suitable for his daughter, the princess. He was, however, embarrassed at being called upon to keep his word to her but he did not think it advisable to give her an immediate reply, so he consulted his grand vizier, expressing to him his repugnance at the idea of marrying the princess to a stranger whose fortune he presumed was less than the most modest.

The grand vizier lost no time in telling the sultan what he thought about this. 'Sire,' he said, 'it seems to me there is a sure way of avoiding such an unequal marriage which would not give Aladdin, even were he better known to your majesty, grounds for complaint: this is to put such a high price on the princess that, however great his riches, he could not meet this. This would be a way of making him abandon such a bold, not to say foolhardy, pursuit, about which no doubt he did not think carefully before embarking on it.'

The sultan approved of the advice of the grand vizier and, turning towards Aladdin's mother, he said to her, after a moment's reflection: 'My good woman, sultans should keep their word; I am ready to keep mine and to make your son happy by marrying my daughter, the princess, to him. However, as I can't marry her before I know what advantage there is in it for her, tell your son that I will carry out my word as soon as he sends me forty large bowls of solid gold, full to the brim with the same things you have already presented to me on his behalf, and carried by a similar number of black slaves who, in their turn, are to be led by forty more white slaves – young, well built, handsome and all magnificently clothed. These are the conditions on which I am prepared to give him my daughter. Go, good woman, and I will wait for you to bring me his reply.'

Aladdin's mother prostrated herself in front of the sultan's throne and withdrew. As she went on her way, she laughed at the thought of her son's foolish ambition. 'Really,' she said to herself, 'where is he going to find so many golden bowls and such a large quantity of those coloured bits of glass to fill them? Will he go back to that underground cave with the entry blocked and pick them off the trees there? And all those slaves turned out as the sultan demanded, where is he going to get them from? He hasn't the remotest chance and I don't think he's going to be happy with the outcome of my mission.' When she got home, her mind was filled with all these thoughts, which made her believe Aladdin had nothing more to hope for, so she said to him: 'My son, I advise you to give up any thought of marrying the princess. The sultan did, indeed, receive me very kindly and I believe he was full of goodwill towards you; but the grand vizier, I am almost sure, made him change his mind, and I think you will think the same after you have heard what I have to say. After I reminded his majesty that the three months had expired and had begged him, on your behalf, to remember his promise, I noticed that he only gave the reply I am about to relate after a whispered conversation with his grand vizier.' Aladdin's mother then proceeded to give her son a faithful account of all that the sultan had said to her and the conditions on which he said he would consent to the marriage between him and the princess, his daughter. 'My son,' she said in conclusion, 'he is waiting for your reply, but, between ourselves,' she added with a smile, 'I believe he will have to wait for a long time.'

'Not so long as you would like to think, mother,' said Aladdin, 'and the sultan is mistaken if he thinks that by such exorbitant demands he is going to prevent me from desiring his daughter. I was expecting other insurmountable difficulties or that he would set a far higher price on my incomparable princess. But for the moment, I am quite content and what he is demanding is a mere trifle in comparison with what I would be in a position to offer him to obtain possession of her. You go and buy some food for dinner while I go and think about satisfying his demands – just leave it to me.'

As soon as Aladdin's mother had gone out to do the shopping, Aladdin took the lamp and rubbed it; immediately the *jinni* rose up before him and, in the same terms as before, asked Aladdin what was his command, saying that he was ready to serve him. Aladdin said to him: 'The sultan is giving me the hand of the princess his daughter in marriage, but first he demands of me forty large, heavy bowls of solid gold, filled to the brim with the fruits from the garden from where I took the lamp whose slave you are. He is also demanding from me that these forty bowls be carried by a similar number of black slaves, preceded by forty white slaves – young, well built, handsome and magnificently clothed. Go and bring me this present as fast as possible so that I can send it to the sultan before he gets up from his session at the council.' The *jinni* told him his command would be carried out without delay, and disappeared.

Shortly afterwards, the *jinni* reappeared, accompanied by the forty black slaves, each one bearing on his head a heavy bowl of solid gold, filled with pearls, diamonds, rubies and emeralds, all chosen for their beauty and their size so as to be better than those which had already been given to the sultan. Each bowl was covered with a silver cloth embroidered with flowers of gold. All these slaves, both black and white, together with all the golden dishes, occupied almost the whole of the very modest house, together with its small courtyard in front and the little garden at the back. The *jinni* asked Aladdin if he was satisfied and whether he had any other command to put to him, and when Aladdin said he had nothing more to ask him, he immediately disappeared.

When Aladdin's mother returned from the market and entered the house, she was very astonished to see so many people and so many riches. She put down the provisions she had bought and was about to remove the veil covering her face when she was prevented by Aladdin, who said to her: 'Mother, we have no time to lose; before the sultan finishes his session, it is very important you return to the palace and immediately bring him this present, Princess Badr's dowry, which he asked me for, so that he can judge, by my diligence and punctuality, the sincerity of my ardent desire to procure the honour of entering into an alliance with him.'

Without waiting for his mother to reply, Aladdin opened the door to the street and made all the slaves file out in succession, a white slave always followed by a black slave, bearing a golden bowl on his head, and so on, to the last one. After his mother had come out, following the last black slave, he closed the door and sat calmly in his room, in the hope that the sultan, after receiving the present he had demanded, would at last consent to receive him as his son-in-law.

The first white slave who came out of Aladdin's house made all the passers-by who saw him stop, and by the time eighty black and white slaves had finished emerging, the street was crowded with people rushing up from all parts of the city to see this magnificent and extraordinary sight. Each slave was dressed in such rich fabrics and wore such splendid jewels that those who knew anything about such matters would have reckoned each costume must have cost more than a million dinars: the neatness and perfect fit of each dress; the proud and graceful bearing of each slave; their uniform and symmetrical build; the solemn way they processed – all this, together with the glittering jewels of exorbitant size, encrusted and beautifully arranged in their belts of solid gold, and the insignias of jewels set in their headdresses, which were of a quite special type, roused the admiration of this crowd of spectators to such a state that they could not leave off staring at them and following them with their eyes as far as they could. The streets were so crowded with people that no one could move but each had to stay where he happened to be.

As the procession had to pass through several streets to get to the palace, a good number of the city's inhabitants, of all kinds and classes, were able to witness this marvellous display of pomp. When the first of the eighty slaves arrived at the gate of the first courtyard of the palace, the doorkeepers, who had drawn up in a line as soon as they spotted this wonderful procession approaching, took him for a king, thanks to the richness and splendour of his dress and they went up to him to kiss the hem of his garment. But the slave, as instructed by the *jinni*, stopped them and solemnly told them: 'We are but slaves; our master will appear in due course.'

Then this first slave, followed by the rest, advanced to the second courtyard, which was very spacious and was where the sultan's household stood during the sessions of the council. The palace officials who headed each rank looked very magnificent, but they were eclipsed in splendour by the appearance of the eighty slaves who bore Aladdin's present. There was nothing more beautiful, more brilliant in the whole of the sultan's court; however splendid his courtiers who surrounded him, none of them could compare with what now presented itself to his sight.

The sultan, who had been informed of the procession and arrival of the slaves, had given orders to let them in, and so, as soon as they appeared, they found the entrance to the council chamber open. They entered in orderly fashion, one half filing to the right, one half to the left. After they had all entered and had formed a large semicircle around the sultan's throne, each of the black slaves placed the bowl he was carrying on to the carpet in front of the sultan. All then prostrated themselves, touching the carpet with their foreheads. At the same time, the white slaves did the same. Then they all got up and the black slaves, as they rose, skilfully uncovered the bowls in front of them and stood with their hands crossed on their chests in great reverence.

Aladdin's mother, who had, meanwhile, advanced to the foot of the throne, prostrated herself before the sultan and addressed him, saying: 'Sire, my son, Aladdin, knows well that this gift he sends to your majesty is far less than Princess Badr deserves, but he hopes nonetheless that your majesty will be pleased to accept it and consider it acceptable for the princess; he offers it all the more confidently because he has endeavoured to conform to the condition which your majesty was pleased to impose on him.'

The sultan was in no state to pay attention to her compliments: one look at the forty golden bowls, filled to the brim with the most brilliant, dazzling and most precious jewels ever to be seen in the world, and at the eighty slaves who, as much by their handsome appearance as by the richness and amazing magnificence of their dress, looked like so many kings, and he was so overwhelmed that he could not get over his astonishment. Instead of replying to Aladdin's mother, he addressed the grand vizier, who likewise could not understand where such a great profusion of riches could have come from. 'Well now, vizier,' he publicly addressed him, 'what do you think about a person, whoever he may be, who sends me such a valuable and extraordinary present, someone whom neither of us knows? Don't you think he is fit to marry my daughter, Princess Badr?'

For all his jealousy and pain at seeing a stranger preferred before his son to become the son-in-law of the sultan, the vizier nonetheless managed to conceal his feelings. It was quite obvious that Aladdin's present was more than enough for him to be admitted to such a high alliance. So the vizier agreed with the sultan, saying: 'Sire, far from believing that someone who gives you a present so worthy of your majesty should be unworthy of the honour you wish to do him, I would be so bold as to say that he deserves it all the more, were I not persuaded that there is no treasure in the world precious enough to be put in balance with your majesty's daughter, the princess.' At this, all the courtiers present at the session applauded, showing that they were of the same opinion as the grand vizier.

The sultan did not delay; he did not even think to enquire whether Aladdin had the other qualities appropriate for one who aspired to become his son-in-law. The mere sight of such immense riches and the diligence with which Aladdin had fulfilled his demand without making the slightest difficulty over conditions as exorbitant as those he had imposed on him, easily persuaded the sultan that Aladdin lacked nothing to render him as accomplished as the sultan wished. So, to send Aladdin's mother back with all the satisfaction she could desire, he said to her: 'Go, my good woman, and tell your son that I am waiting to receive him with open arms and to embrace him, and that the quicker he comes to receive from me the gift I have bestowed on him of the princess, my daughter, the greater the pleasure he will give me.'

Aladdin's mother left with all the delight a woman of her status is capable of on seeing her son, contrary to all expectations, attain such a high position. The sultan then immediately concluded the day's audience and, rising from his throne, ordered the eunuchs attached to the princess's service to come and remove the bowls and carry them off to their mistress's chamber, where he himself went to examine them with her at his leisure. This order was carried out at once, under supervision of the head eunuch.

The eighty black and white slaves were not forgotten; they were taken inside the palace and, a little later, the sultan, who had been telling the princess about their magnificence, ordered them to be brought to the entrance of her chamber so that she could look at them through the screens and realize that, far from exaggerating anything in his account, he had not told her even half the story.

Meanwhile, Aladdin's mother arrived home with an expression which told in advance of the good news she was bringing. 'My son,' she said to him, 'you have every reason to be happy: contrary to my expectations – and you will recall what I told you – you have attained the accomplishment of your desires. In order not to keep you in suspense any longer, the sultan, with the approval of his entire court, has declared that you are worthy to possess Princess Badr. He is waiting to embrace you and to bring about your marriage. You must now think about how to prepare for this meeting so that you may come up to the high opinion the sultan has formed of you. After all the miracles I have seen you perform, I am sure nothing will be lacking. I must not forget to tell you also that the sultan is waiting impatiently for you, and so waste no time in going to him.'

Aladdin was delighted at this news and, his mind full of the enchanting creature who had so bewitched him, after saying a few words to his mother, withdrew to his room. Once there, he took the lamp which had hitherto been so useful to him in fulfilling all his needs and wishes, and no sooner had he rubbed it than the *jinni* appeared before him and immediately proceeded to offer him his services as before. 'O *jinni*,' said Aladdin, 'I have summoned you to help me take a bath and when I have finished, I want you to have ready for me the most sumptuous and magnificent costume ever worn by a king.' No sooner had he finished speaking than the *jinni*, making them both invisible, lifted him up and transported him to a bath made of the finest marble of every shade of the most beautiful colours. Without seeing who was waiting on him, he was undressed in a spacious and very well-arranged room. From this room he was made to go into the bath, which was moderately hot, and there he was rubbed and washed with several kinds of perfumed waters. After he had been taken into various rooms of different degrees of heat, he came out again transformed, his complexion fresh, all pink and white, and feeling lighter and more refreshed. He returned to the first room, but the clothing he had left there had gone; in its place the *jinni* had carefully set out the costume he had asked for. When he saw the magnificence of the garments which had been substituted for his own, Aladdin was astonished. With the help of the *jinni*, he got dressed, admiring as he did so each item of clothing as he put it on, for everything was beyond anything he could have imagined.

When he had finished, the *jinni* took him back to his house, to the same room from where he had transported him. He then asked Aladdin whether he had any other demands. 'Yes,' replied Aladdin, 'I want you to bring me as quickly as possible a horse which is finer and more beautiful than the most highly valued horse in the sultan's stables; its trappings, its harness, its saddle, its bridle – all must be worth more than a million dinars. I also ask you to bring me at the same time twenty slaves as richly and smartly attired as those who delivered the sultan's present, who are to walk beside me and behind me in a group, and twenty more like them to precede me in two files. Bring my mother, too, with six slave girls to wait on her, each dressed at least as richly as the princess's slave girls, and each bearing a complete set of women's clothes as magnificent and sumptuous as those of a sultana. Finally, I need ten thousand pieces of gold in ten purses. There,' he ended, 'that's what I command you to do. Go, and make haste.'

As soon as Aladdin had finished giving him his orders, the *jinni* disappeared; shortly afterwards, he reappeared with the horse, the forty slaves – ten of whom were each carrying a purse containing a thousand pieces of gold, and the six slave girls – each one bearing on her head a different costume for Aladdin's mother, wrapped up in a silver cloth, and all this he presented to Aladdin. Of the ten purses Aladdin took four, which he gave to his mother, telling her she should use them for her needs. The remaining six he left in the hands of the slaves who were carrying them, charging them to keep them and throw out handfuls of gold from them to the people as they passed through the streets on their way to the sultan's palace. He also ordered these six slaves to walk in front of him with the others, three on the right and three on the left. Finally, he presented the six slave girls to his mother, telling her that they were hers to use as her slaves and that the clothes they brought were for her.

When Aladdin had settled all these matters, he told the *jinni* as he dismissed him that he would call him when he needed his services and the *jinni* instantly disappeared. Aladdin's one thought now was to reply as quickly as possible to the desire the sultan had expressed to see him. So he despatched to the palace one of the forty slaves – I will not say the most handsome, for they were all equally handsome – with the order to address himself to the chief usher and ask him when Aladdin might have the honour of prostrating himself at the feet of the sultan. The slave was not long in carrying out his task, returning with the reply that the sultan was awaiting him with impatience.

Aladdin made haste to set off on horseback and process in the order already described. Although this was the first time he had ever mounted a horse, he appeared to ride with such ease that not even the most experienced horseman would have taken him for a novice. In less than a moment, the streets he passed through filled with an innumerable crowd of people, whose cheers and blessings and cries of admiration rang out, particularly when the six slaves with the purses threw handfuls of gold coins into the air to the left and right. These cheers of approval did not, however, come from the rabble, who were busy picking up the gold, but from a higher rank of people who could not refrain from publicly praising Aladdin for his generosity. Anyone who could remember seeing him playing in the street, the perpetual vagabond, no longer recognized Aladdin, and even those who had seen him not long ago had difficulty making him out, so different were his features. This is because one of the properties of the lamp was that it could gradually procure for those who possessed it the perfections which went with the status they attained by making good use of it. Consequently, people paid more attention to Aladdin himself than to the pomp which accompanied him and which most of them had already seen that same day when the eighty slaves marched in procession, bearing the present. The horse was also much admired for its beauty alone by the experts, who did not let themselves be dazzled by the wealth or brilliance of the diamonds and other jewels with which it was covered. As the news spread that the sultan was giving the hand of his daughter, Princess Badr, in marriage to Aladdin, without regard to his humble birth, no one envied him his good fortune nor his rise in status, as they seemed well deserved.

Aladdin arrived at the palace, where all was set to receive him. When he reached the second gate, he was about to dismount, following the custom observed by the grand vizier, the generals of the armies and the governors of the provinces of the first rank; but the chief usher, who was waiting for him by order of the sultan, prevented him and accompanied him to the council chamber, where he helped him to dismount, despite Aladdin's strong opposition, but whose protests were in vain for he had no say in the matter. The ushers then formed two lines at the entrance to the chamber and their chief, placing Aladdin on his right, led him through the middle right up to the sultan's throne.

As soon as the sultan set eyes on Aladdin, he was no less astonished to see him clothed more richly and magnificently than he himself had ever been, than surprised at his fine appearance, his handsome figure and a certain air of grandeur, which were in complete contrast to the lowly state in which his mother had appeared before him. His astonishment and surprise did not, however, prevent him from rising from his throne and descending two or three steps in time to stop Aladdin from prostrating himself at his feet and to embrace him in a warm show of friendship. After such a greeting Aladdin still wanted to throw himself at the sultan's feet, but the sultan held him back with his hand and forced him to mount the steps and sit between the vizier and himself.

Aladdin now addressed the sultan. 'Sire,' he said, 'I accept the honours your majesty is so gracious as to bestow on me; but permit me to tell you that I have not forgotten I was born your slave, that I know the greatness of your power and I am well aware how much my birth and upbringing are below the splendour and the brilliance of the exalted rank to which I am being raised. If there is any way I can have deserved so favourable a reception, it is maybe due to the boldness that pure chance inspired in me to raise my eyes, my thoughts and my aspirations to the divine princess who is the object of my desires. I beg pardon of your majesty for my rashness but I cannot hide from you that I would die of grief if I were to lose hope of seeing these desires accomplished.'

'My son,' replied the sultan, embracing him a second time, 'you do me wrong to doubt for a single instant the sincerity of my word. From now on, your life is too dear to me for me not to preserve it, by presenting you with the remedy which is at my disposal. I prefer the pleasure of seeing you and hearing you to all my treasures and yours together.'

When he had finished speaking, the sultan gave a signal and immediately the air echoed with the sound of trumpets, oboes and drums. At the same time, the sultan led Aladdin into a magnificent room where a splendid feast was prepared. The sultan ate alone with Aladdin, while the grand vizier and the court dignitaries stood by during the meal, each according to their dignity and rank. The sultan, who took such great pleasure in looking at Aladdin that he never took his eyes off him, led the conversation on several different topics and throughout the meal, in the conversation they held together and on whatever matter the sultan brought up, Aladdin spoke with such knowledge and wisdom that he ended by confirming the sultan in the good opinion he had formed of him from the beginning.

Once the meal was over, the sultan summoned the grand *qadi* and ordered him immediately to draw up a contract of marriage between Princess Badr, his daughter, and Aladdin. While this was happening, the sultan talked to Aladdin about several different things in the presence of the grand vizier and his courtiers, who all admired Aladdin's soundness and the great ease with which he spoke and expressed himself and the refined and subtle comments with which he enlivened his conversation.

When the *qadi* had completed drawing up the contract in all the required forms, the sultan asked Aladdin if he wished to stay in the palace to complete the marriage ceremonies that same day, but Aladdin replied: 'Sire, however impatient I am fully to enjoy your majesty's kindnesses, I beg you will be so good as to allow me to put them off until I have had a palace built to receive the princess in, according to her dignity and merit. For this purpose, I ask you to grant me a suitable spot in the palace grounds so that I may be closer at hand to pay you my respects. I will do everything to see that it is accomplished with all possible speed.' 'My son,' said the sultan, 'take all the land you think you need; there is a large space in front of my palace and I myself had already thought of filling it. But remember, I can't see you united to my daughter soon enough to complete my happiness.' After he had said this, the sultan embraced Aladdin, who took his leave of the sultan with the same courtesy as if he had been brought up and always lived at court.

Aladdin remounted his horse and returned home the same way he had come, passing through the same applauding crowds, who wished him happiness and prosperity. As soon as he got back and had dismounted, he went off to his own room, took the lamp and summoned the *jinni* in the usual way. The *jinni* immediately appeared and offered him his services. 'O *jinni*,' said Aladdin, 'I have every reason to congratulate myself on how precisely and promptly you have carried out everything I have asked of you so far, through the power of this lamp, your mistress. But now, for the sake of the lamp, you must, if possible, show even more zeal and more diligence than before. I am now asking you to build me, as quickly as you can, at an appropriate distance opposite the sultan's residence, a palace worthy of receiving Princess Badr, my wife-to-be. I leave you free to choose the materials – porphyry, jasper, agate, lapis lazuli and the finest marble of every colour – and the rest of the building. But at the very top of this palace, I want you to build a great room, surmounted by a dome and with four equal sides, made up of alternating layers of solid gold and silver. There should be twenty-four windows, six on each side, with the latticed screens of all but one – which I want left unfinished

– embellished, skilfully and symmetrically, with diamonds, rubies and emeralds, so that nothing like this will have ever been seen in the world. I also want the palace to have a forecourt, a main court and a garden. But above all, there must be, in a spot you will decide, a treasure house, full of gold and silver coins. And I also want this palace to have kitchens, pantries, storehouses, furniture stores for precious furniture for all seasons and in keeping with the magnificence of the palace, and stables filled with the most beautiful horses complete with their riders and grooms, not to forget hunting equipment. There must also be kitchen staff and officials and female slaves for the service of the princess. You understand what I mean? Go and come back when it's done.'

It was sunset when Aladdin finished instructing the *jinni* in the construction of his imagined palace. The next day, at daybreak, Aladdin, who could not sleep peacefully because of his love for the princess, had barely risen when the *jinni* appeared before him. 'Master,' he said, 'your palace is finished. Come and see if you like it.' No sooner had Aladdin said he wanted to see it than in an instant the *jinni* had transported him there. Aladdin found it so beyond all his expectations that he could not admire it enough. The *jinni* led him through every part; everywhere Aladdin found nothing but riches, splendour and perfection, with the officials and slaves all dressed according to their rank and the services they had to perform. Nor did he forget to show him, as one of the main features, the treasure house, the door to which was opened by the treasurer. There Aladdin saw purses of different sizes, depending on the sums they contained, piled up in a pleasing arrangement which reached up to the vault. As they left, the *jinni* assured him of the treasurer's trustworthiness. He then led him to the stables where he showed him the most beautiful horses in the world and the grooms who were grooming them. Finally, he took him through storerooms filled with all the supplies necessary for both the horses' adornment and their food.

When Aladdin had examined the whole palace from top to bottom, floor by floor, room by room, and in particular the chamber with the twenty-four windows, and had found it so rich and magnificent and well furnished, beyond anything he had promised himself, he said to the *jinni*: 'O *jinni*, nobody could be happier than I am and it would be wrong for me to complain. But there's one thing which I didn't tell you because I hadn't thought about it, which is to spread, from the gate of the sultan's palace to the door of the room intended for the princess, a carpet of the finest velvet for her to walk on when she comes from the sultan's palace.'

'I will be back in a moment,' said the *jinni*. A little after his disappearance, Aladdin was astonished to see that what he wanted had been carried out without knowing how it had been done. The *jinni* reappeared and carried Aladdin back home, just as the gate of the sultan's palace was being opened.

The palace doorkeepers, who had just opened the gate and who had always had an unimpeded view in the direction where Aladdin's palace now stood, were astounded to find it obstructed and to see a velvet carpet stretching from that direction right up to the gate of the sultan's palace. At first they could not make out what it was, but their astonishment increased when they saw clearly Aladdin's superb palace. News of the marvel quickly spread throughout the whole palace. The grand vizier, who had arrived almost the moment the gate was opened, was as astonished as the rest at the extraordinary sight and was the first to tell the sultan. He wanted to put it down to magic but the sultan rebuffed him, saying: 'Why do you want it to be magic? You know as well as I do that it's the palace Aladdin has had built for my daughter, the princess; I gave him permission to do so in your presence. After the sample of his wealth which we saw, is it so strange that he has built this palace in such a short time? He wanted to surprise us and to show us what miracles one can perform from one day to the next. Be honest, don't you agree that when you talk of magic you are perhaps being a little jealous?' He was prevented from saying anything more, as the hour to enter the council chamber had arrived.

After Aladdin had been carried home and had dismissed the *jinni*, he found his mother had got up and was beginning to put on the clothes that had been brought to her. At about the time that the sultan had just left the council, Aladdin made his mother go to the palace, together with the slave girls who had been brought her by the *jinni*'s services. He asked her that if she saw the sultan she was to tell him that she had come in order to have the honour of accompanying the princess when she was ready to go to her palace towards evening. She left and although she and the slave girls who followed her were dressed like sultanas, the crowds watching them pass were not so large, as the women were veiled and wore appropriate overgarments to cover the richness and magnificence of their clothing. As for Aladdin, he mounted his horse and, leaving his home for the last time, without forgetting the magic lamp whose help had been so helpful to him in attaining the height of happiness, he publicly left for his palace, with the same pomp as on the previous day when he had gone to present himself to the sultan.

As soon as the doorkeepers of the sultan's palace saw Aladdin's mother, they told the sultan. Immediately the order was given to the bands of trumpets, cymbals, drums, fifes and oboes who had been stationed in different spots on the palace terraces, and all at once the air resounded to fanfares and music which announced the rejoicings to the whole city. The merchants began to deck out their shops with fine carpets, cushions and green boughs, and to prepare illuminations for the night. The artisans left their work, and the people hastened to the great square between the sultan's palace and that of Aladdin. But it was Aladdin's palace that first attracted their admiration, not so much because they were accustomed to see that of the sultan but because it could not enter into comparison with Aladdin's. The sight of such a magnificent palace in a place that, the previous day, had neither materials nor foundations, astonished them most and they could not understand by what unheard-of miracle this had come about.

Aladdin's mother was received in the sultan's palace with honour and admitted to the princess's apartments by the chief eunuch. When the princess saw her, she immediately went to embrace her and made her be seated on her sofa; and while her maidservants were finishing dressing her and adorning her with the most precious jewels, which Aladdin had given her, the princess entertained her to a delicious supper. The sultan, who came to spend as much time as he could with his daughter before she left him to go to Aladdin's palace, also paid great honour to Aladdin's mother. He had never seen her before without a veil, although she had spoken several times to him in public, but now without her veil, though she was no longer young, one could still see from her features that she must have been reckoned among the beautiful women of her day when she was young. The sultan, who had always seen her dressed very simply, not to say shabbily, was filled with admiration at seeing her clothed as richly and as magnificently as the princess, his daughter, which made him reflect that Aladdin was equally capable, prudent and wise in everything he did.

When night fell, the princess took leave of her father, the sultan. Their parting was tender and tearful; they embraced several times in silence, and finally the princess left her apartments and set out, with Aladdin's mother on her left, followed by a hundred slave girls, all wonderfully and magnificently dressed. All the bands of musicians, which had never stopped playing since the arrival of Aladdin's mother, now joined up and began the procession; they were followed by a hundred sergeants and a similar number of black eunuchs, in two columns, led by their officers. Four hundred of the sultan's young pages walked on each side of the procession, holding torches in their hands which, together with the light from illuminations coming from both the sultan's palace and Aladdin's, wonderfully took the place of daylight.

Accompanied in this fashion, the princess stepped on to the carpet which stretched from the sultan's palace to Aladdin's; as she advanced, the bands of musicians who led the procession approached and joined with those which could be heard on the terraces of Aladdin's palace. This extraordinary confusion of sounds nonetheless formed a concert which increased the rejoicing not only of the great crowd in the main square but also of those who were in the two palaces and indeed in the whole city and far beyond.

At last the princess arrived at the new palace and Aladdin rushed with all imaginable joy to receive her at the entrance to the apartments destined for him. Aladdin's mother had taken care to point out her son to the princess amid the officials who surrounded him, and the princess, when she saw him, found him so handsome that she was quite charmed. 'Lovely princess,' Aladdin addressed her, going up to her and greeting her very respectfully, 'if I have been so unlucky as to have displeased you by my rashness in aspiring to possess so fair a lady, the daughter of the sultan, then, if I may say so, you must blame your beautiful eyes and your charms, not me.' 'O prince – I can rightly call you this now – I bow to my father, the sultan's wishes; but it is enough for me to have seen you to tell you that I am happy to obey him.'

Overjoyed by such a satisfying reply, Aladdin did not keep the princess standing any longer after this unaccustomed walk. In his delight, he took her hand and kissed it, and then led her into a large room lit by innumerable candles where, thanks to the *jinni*, a magnificent banquet was laid out on a table. The plates were of solid gold and filled with the most delicious food. The vases, bowls and goblets, with which the side tables were well provided, were also of gold and of exquisite craftsmanship. All the other ornaments and decorations of the room were in perfect keeping with all this sumptuousness. Delighted to see so many riches gathered together in one place, the princess said to Aladdin: 'O prince, I thought that there was nothing in the world more beautiful than my father's palace; but seeing this room alone I realize how wrong I was.' 'Princess,' said Aladdin, seating her at the place specially set for her at the table, 'I accept such a great compliment as I ought; but I know what I should think.'

The princess, Aladdin and his mother sat down at table, and immediately a band of the most melodious instruments, played and accompanied by women, all of whom were very beautiful, started up and the music was accompanied by their equally beautiful voices; this continued uninterrupted until the end of the meal. The princess was so charmed that she said she had never heard anything like it in the palace of the sultan, her father. She did not know, of course, that these musicians were creatures chosen by the *jinni* of the lamp.

When the supper was over and the dishes had been swiftly cleared away, the musicians gave way to a troupe of male and female dancers who danced several kinds of dances, according to the custom of the land. They ended with two solo dances by a male and female dancer who, each in their turn, danced with surprising lightness and showed all the grace and skill they were capable of. It was nearly midnight when, according to the custom in China at that time, Aladdin rose and offered his hand to Princess Badr to dance with her and so conclude the wedding ceremony. They danced so well together that the whole company was lost in admiration. When the dance was over, Aladdin, still holding her by the hand, took the princess and together they passed through to the nuptial chamber where the marriage bed had been prepared. The princess's maidservants helped undress her and put her to bed, and Aladdin's servants did the same, then all withdrew. And so ended the ceremonies and festivities of the wedding of Aladdin and Princess Badr al-Budur.

The following morning, when Aladdin awoke, his servants came to dress him. They put on him a different costume from the one he had worn the day of the wedding, but one that was equally rich and magnificent. Next, he had brought to him one of the horses specially selected for him, which he mounted and then went to the sultan's palace, surrounded by a large troupe of slaves walking in front of him and behind him and on either side. The sultan received him with the same honours as on the first occasion, embraced him and, after seating him near him on the throne, ordered breakfast to be served. 'Sire,' said Aladdin, 'I ask your majesty to excuse me this honour today. I came to ask you to do me the honour of partaking of a meal in the princess's palace, together with your grand vizier and your courtiers.' The sultan was pleased to grant him this favour. He rose forthwith and, as it was not very far, wished to go there on foot, and so he set out, with Aladdin on his right, the grand vizier on his left and the courtiers following, preceded by the sergeants and principal court officials.

The nearer he drew to Aladdin's palace, the more the sultan was struck by its beauty. But he was much more amazed when he entered it and never stopped praising each and every room he saw. But when, at Aladdin's invitation, they went up to the chamber with the twenty-four windows, and the sultan saw the decorations, and above all when he caught sight of the screens studded with diamonds, rubies and emeralds – jewels all so large and so perfectly proportioned – and when Aladdin remarked that it was just as opulent on the outside, he was so astonished that he remained rooted to the spot.

After remaining motionless for a while, the sultan turned to the grand vizier standing near him and said: 'Vizier, can there possibly be such a superb palace in my kingdom, so near to my own palace, without my having been aware of it till now?' 'Your majesty may recall,' replied the grand vizier, 'that the day before yesterday you granted Aladdin, whom you accepted as your son-in-law, permission to build a palace opposite your own; that same day, at sunset, there was as yet no palace on that spot. Yesterday I had the honour to be the first to announce to you that the palace had been built and was finished.' 'Yes, I remember,' said the sultan, 'but I would never have thought this palace would be one of the wonders of the age. Where in the whole wide world can one find a palace built of layers of solid gold and silver rather than of stone or marble, where the windows have screens set with diamonds, rubies and emeralds? Never has anything like this been heard of before!'

The sultan wished to see and admire the beauty of the twenty-four screens. When he counted them, he found that only twenty-three of the twenty-four were each equally richly decorated but that the twenty-fourth, he was very surprised to discover, had been left unfinished. Turning to the vizier, who had made it his duty always to stay at his side, he said: 'I am surprised that a room of such magnificence should have been left unfinished.' 'Sire,' the grand vizier replied, 'Aladdin apparently was in a hurry and didn't have time to make this window like the rest; but I imagine he has the necessary jewels and that he will have the work done at the first opportunity.'

While this was going on, Aladdin had left the sultan to give some orders and when he came back to join him again, the sultan said to him: 'My son, of all the rooms in the world this one is the most worthy to be admired. But one thing surprises me – that is, to see this one screen left unfinished. Was it forgotten through carelessness or because the workmen didn't have time to put the finishing touches to so fine a piece of architecture?' 'Sire,' replied Aladdin, 'it's for neither of these reasons that the screen has remained in the state in which your majesty sees it. It was done deliberately and it was at my order that the workmen left it untouched: I wanted your majesty to have the glory of finishing this room and the palace at the same time. I beg that you will accept my good intentions so that I will be able to remember your kindness and your favours.' 'If that's how you intended it, I am grateful to you and shall immediately give the orders for it to be done.' And indeed he then summoned the jewellers with the greatest stock of jewels, together with the most skilled goldsmiths in the capital.

The sultan then went down from this chamber and Aladdin led him into the room where he had entertained the princess on the day of the wedding. The princess arrived a moment later and received her father in a manner which showed him how happy she was with her marriage. Two tables were laid with the most delicious dishes, all served in golden vessels. The sultan sat down at the first table and ate with his daughter, Aladdin and the grand vizier, while all the courtiers were served at the second table, which was very long. The sultan found the dishes very tasty and declared he had never eaten anything more exquisite. He said the same of the wine, which was, indeed, delicious. What he admired still more were four large side tables filled and laden with an abundance of flagons, bowls and goblets of solid gold, all encrusted with jewels. He was also delighted with the bands of musicians scattered around the room, while the fanfares of trumpets accompanied by drums and tambourines resounding at a suitable distance outside the room gave a most pleasing effect.

When the meal was over, the sultan was told that the jewellers and goldsmiths who had been summoned by his order had arrived. He went up again to the room with the twenty-four screens and, once there, showed the jewellers and goldsmiths who had followed him the window which had been left unfinished. 'I have brought you here,' he said, 'so that you will bring this window to the same state of perfection as the others; examine them well and waste no time in making it exactly the same as the rest.'

The jewellers and goldsmiths examined the twenty-three other screens very closely, and after they had consulted together and were agreed on what each of them would for his part contribute, they returned to the sultan. The palace jeweller, acting as spokesman, then said to the sultan: 'Sire, we are ready to employ all our skills and industry to obey your majesty, but many as we are, not one of our profession has such precious jewels and in sufficient quantities for such a great project.' 'But I have enough and more than enough,' said the sultan. 'Come to my palace; I can supply you with them and you can choose those you want.'

After the sultan had returned to the palace, he had all his jewels brought in to him and the jewellers took a great quantity of them, particularly from among those which Aladdin had given him as a present. They used all these jewels but the work did not seem to progress very much. They returned several times to fetch still more, but after a whole month they had not finished half of the work. They used all the sultan's jewels as well as some borrowed from the grand vizier; yet, despite all these, all they managed to do was at most to complete half of the window.

Aladdin, who knew that all the sultan's efforts to make this screen like the rest were in vain and that he would never come out of it with any credit, summoned the goldsmiths and told them not only to cease their work but even to undo everything they had done and to return to the sultan all his jewels together with those he had borrowed from the grand vizier.

In a matter of hours, the work that the jewellers and goldsmiths had taken more than six weeks to do was destroyed. They then departed and left Aladdin alone in the room. Taking out the lamp, which he had with him, he rubbed it and immediately the *jinni* stood before him. 'O *jinni*,' said Aladdin, 'I ordered you to leave one of the twenty-four screens in this room unfinished and you carried out my order; I have now summoned you here to tell you that I want you to make this window just like the rest.' The *jinni* disappeared and Aladdin went out of the room. When he went back in again a few moments later, he found the screen exactly as he wanted it and just like the others.

Meanwhile, the jewellers and goldsmiths had arrived at the palace and had been introduced and presented to the sultan in his apartments. The first jeweller, on behalf of all of them, presented the sultan with the jewels which they were returning and said: 'Sire, your majesty knows how long and how hard we have been working in order to finish the commission that you charged us with. The work was far advanced when Aladdin forced us not only to stop but even to undo all we had done and to return to your majesty all these jewels of yours and those of the grand vizier.' The sultan asked them whether Aladdin had told them why they were to do this, to which they replied no. Immediately, the sultan gave the order for a horse to be brought and when it came, he mounted and left with only a few of his men, who accompanied him on foot. On arriving at Aladdin's palace, he dismounted at the bottom of the staircase that led to the room with the twenty-four windows. Without giving Aladdin any advance notice, he climbed the stairs where Aladdin had arrived in the nick of time to receive him at the door.

The sultan, giving Aladdin no time to complain politely that his majesty had not forewarned him of his arrival and that he had thus obliged him to fail in his duty, said to him: 'My son, I have come myself to ask the reason why you wish to leave unfinished so magnificent and remarkable a room in your palace as this one.'

The real reason Aladdin concealed from him, which was that the sultan was not rich enough in jewels to afford such an enormous expense. However, in order to let the sultan know how far his palace surpassed not only his own, such as it was, but any other palace in the world, since the sultan had been unable to complete the smallest part of it, he said to him: 'Sire, it is true your majesty has seen this room, unfinished; but I beg you will come now and see if there is anything lacking.'

The sultan went straight to the window where he had seen the unfinished screen and when he saw that it was like the rest, he thought he must have made a mistake. He next examined not only one or two windows but all the windows, one by one. When he was convinced that the screen on which so much time had been spent and which had cost so many days' work had been finished in what he knew to be a very short time, he embraced Aladdin and kissed him between the eyes, exclaiming in astonishment: 'My son, what a man you are to do such amazing things and all, almost, in the twinkling of an eye! There is no one like you in the whole wide world! The more I know you, the more I admire you.' Aladdin received the sultan's praises with great modesty, replying: 'Sire, I am very honoured to merit your majesty's kindness and approval, and I can assure you I will do all I can to deserve them both more and more.'

The sultan returned to his palace in the same manner as he had come, not allowing Aladdin to accompany him. There he found the grand vizier waiting for him and the sultan, still filled with admiration at the wonders he had just seen, proceeded to tell him all about them in terms that left the vizier in no doubt that everything was indeed as he had described it. But it also confirmed him in his belief that Aladdin's palace was the effect of an enchantment – a belief that he had already conveyed to the sultan almost as soon as the palace appeared. The vizier started to repeat what he thought, but the sultan interrupted him: 'Vizier, you have already told me that, but I can see that you are still thinking of my daughter's marriage to your son.'

The grand vizier could see that the sultan was prejudiced against him and so, not wishing to enter into a dispute with him, made no attempt to disabuse him. Meanwhile, the sultan every day, as soon as he had arisen, regularly went to a small room from which he could see the whole of Aladdin's palace and he would come here several times a day to contemplate and admire it.

As for Aladdin, he did not remain shut up in his palace but took care to let himself be seen in the city several times a week, whether to go and pray at one mosque or another or, at regular intervals, to visit the grand vizier, who affected to pay court to him on certain days, or to do honour to the leading courtiers, whom he often entertained in his palace, by going to see them in their own houses. Every time he went out, he would instruct two of his slaves, who surrounded him as he rode, to throw handfuls of gold coins into the streets and squares through which he passed and to which a great crowd of people always flocked. Furthermore, no pauper came to the gate of his palace without going away pleased with the liberality dispensed there on his orders.

Aladdin passed his time in such a way that not a week went by without him going out hunting, whether just outside the city or further afield, when he dispensed the same liberality as he rode around or passed through villages. This generous tendency caused everyone to shower blessings on him and it became the custom to swear by his head. In short, without it giving any offence to the sultan to whom he regularly paid court, one may say that Aladdin, thanks to his affable manner and generosity, won the affection of all the people and that, in general, he was more beloved than the sultan himself. Added to all these fine qualities, he showed such valour and zeal for the good of the kingdom that he could not be too highly praised. He showed this on the occasion of a revolt which took place on the kingdom's borders: no sooner had he heard that the sultan was raising an army to put the revolt down than he begged the sultan to put him in command of it, a request which he had no difficulty in obtaining. Once at the head of the army, he marched against the rebels, and throughout this expedition he conducted himself so industriously that the sultan learned that the rebels had been defeated, punished and dispersed before he learned of Aladdin's arrival in the army. This action, which made his name famous throughout the kingdom, did not change his good nature, for he remained as amiable after as before his victory.

Several years went by in this manner for Aladdin, when the magician, who unwittingly had given him the means of rising to such heights of fortune, was reminded of him in Africa, to where he had returned. Although he was till then convinced that Aladdin had died a wretched death in the underground cave where he had left him, the thought nonetheless came to him to find out exactly how he had died. Being a great geomancer, he took out of a cupboard a covered square box which he used to make his observations. Sitting down on his sofa, he placed the box in front of him and uncovered it. After he had prepared and levelled the sand with the intention of discovering if Aladdin had died in the cave, he made his throw, interpreted the figures and drew up the horoscope. When he examined it to ascertain its meaning, instead of discovering that Aladdin had died in the cave, he found that he had got out of it and that he was living in great splendour, being immensely rich; he had married a princess and was generally honoured and respected.

As soon as the magician had learned through the means of his diabolic art that Aladdin lived in such a state of elevation, he became red with rage. In his fury, he exclaimed to himself: 'That wretched son of a tailor has discovered the secret and power of the lamp! I took his death for a certainty and here he is enjoying the fruit of my labours and vigils. But I will stop him enjoying them much longer, or die in the attempt.' He did not take long in deciding what to do. The next morning, he mounted a barbary horse which he had in his stable and set off, travelling from city to city and from province to province, stopping no longer than was necessary so as not to tire his horse, until he reached China and was soon in the capital of the sultan whose daughter Aladdin had married. There he dismounted in a *khan* or public hostelry, where he rented a room and where he remained for the rest of the day and the night to recover from his tiring journey.

The next day, the first thing the magician wanted to find out was what people said about Aladdin. Walking around the city, he entered the best-known and most frequented place, where the most distinguished people met to drink a certain hot drink* which was known to him from his first journey. As soon as he sat down, a cup of this drink was poured and presented to him. As he took it, he listened to the conversation going on around him and heard people talking about Aladdin's palace. When he had finished his drink, he approached one of them, singling him out to ask him: 'What's this palace everybody speaks so well of?' To which the man replied: 'Where are you from? You must be a newcomer not to have

*i.e. tea.

seen or heard talk of the palace of Prince Aladdin' – that is how he was now called since he had married Princess Badr – 'I am not saying it is one of the wonders of the world, I say it is the only wonder of the world, for nothing so grand, so rich, so magnificent has ever been seen before or since. You must have come from very far away not to have heard talk of it. Indeed, the whole world must have been talking about it ever since it was built. Go and look at it and see if I'm not speaking the truth.' 'Excuse my ignorance,' said the magician. 'I only arrived yesterday and I have indeed come from very far away – in fact the furthest part of Africa, which its fame had not yet reached when I left. For in view of the urgent business which brings me here, my sole concern in travelling was to get here as soon as possible, without stopping and making any acquaintances. I knew nothing about it until you told me. But I will indeed go and see it; and so great is my impatience that I am ready to satisfy my curiosity this very instant, if you would be so kind as to show me the way.'

The man the magician had spoken to was only too happy to tell him the way he must take to have a view of Aladdin's palace, and the magician rose and immediately set off. When he reached the palace and had examined it closely and from all sides, he was left in no doubt that Aladdin had made use of the lamp to build it. Without dwelling on Aladdin's powerlessness as the son of a simple tailor, he was well aware that only *jinn*, the slaves of the lamp which he had failed to get hold of, were capable of performing miracles of this kind. Stung to the quick by Aladdin's good fortune and importance, which seemed to him little different from the sultan's own, the magician returned to the *khan* where he had taken up lodging.

He needed to find out where the lamp was and whether Aladdin carried it around with him, or whether he kept it in some secret spot, and this he could only discover through an act of geomancy. As soon as he reached his lodgings, he took his square box and his sand which he carried with him on all his travels. When he had completed the operation, he found that the lamp was in Aladdin's palace and he was so delighted at this discovery that he was beside himself. 'I am going to have this lamp,' he said, 'and I defy Aladdin to stop me from taking it from him and from making him sink to the depths from which he has risen to such heights!'

Unfortunately for Aladdin, it so happened that he had set off on a hunting expedition for eight days and was still away, having been gone for only three days. This is how the magician learned about it. Having performed the act of geomancy which had given him so much joy, he went to see the doorkeeper of the *khan* under the pretext of having a chat with him. The latter, who was of a garrulous nature, needed little encouragement, telling him that he had himself just been to see Aladdin's palace. After listening to him describe with great exaggeration all the things he had seen which had most amazed and struck him and everyone in general, the magician said: 'My curiosity does not stop there and I won't be satisfied until I have seen the master to whom such a wonderful building belongs.' 'That will not be difficult,' replied the doorkeeper. 'When he is in town hardly a day goes by on which there isn't an opportunity to see him; but three days ago, he went out on a great hunting expedition which was to last for eight days.'

The magician needed to hear no more. He took leave of the doorkeeper, saying to himself as he went back to his room: 'Now is the time to act; I must not let the opportunity escape me.' He went to a lamp maker's shop which also sold lamps. 'Master,' he said, 'I need a dozen copper lamps – can you supply me with them?' The lamp maker told him he did not have a dozen but, if he would be patient and wait until the following day, he could let him have the whole lot whenever he wanted. The magician agreed to this and asked that the lamps be clean and well polished, and after promising him to pay him well, he returned to the *khan*.

The next day, the twelve lamps were delivered to the magician, who gave the lamp maker the price he had asked for, without bargaining. He put them in a basket which he had specially acquired and, with this on his arm, he went to Aladdin's palace. When he drew near, he began to cry out: 'Old lamps for new!'

As he approached, the children playing in the square heard him from a distance and rushed up and gathered around him, loudly jeering at him, for they took him for a madman. The passers-by, too, laughed at what they thought was his stupidity. 'He must have lost his mind,' they said, 'to offer to exchange old lamps for new ones.' But the magician was not surprised by the children's jeers nor by what people were saying about him, and he continued to cry out to sell his wares: 'Old lamps for new!'

He repeated this cry so often as he went to and fro in front of and around the palace that Princess Badr, who was at that point in the room with the twenty-four windows, hearing a man's voice crying out something but unable to make out what he was saying because of the jeers of the children who followed him and who kept increasing in number, sent down one of her slave girls to go up to him and see what he was shouting.

The slave girl was not long in returning and entered the room in fits of laughter. Her mirth was so infectious that the princess, looking at her, could not stop herself from laughing too. 'Well, you crazy girl,' she said, 'tell me why you are laughing.' Still laughing, the slave replied: 'O princess, who couldn't stop himself laughing at the sight of a madman with a basket on his arm full of brand new lamps wanting not to sell them but to change them for old ones? It's the children, crowding around him so that he can hardly move and jeering at him, who are making all the noise.'

Hearing this, another slave girl interrupted: 'Speaking of old lamps, I don't know if the princess has observed that there is an old lamp on the cornice. Whoever owns it won't be cross to find a new one in its place. If the princess would like, she can have the pleasure of finding out whether this madman is really mad enough to exchange a new lamp for an old one without asking anything for it in return.'

The lamp the slave girl was talking about was the magic lamp Aladdin had used to raise himself to his present high state; he himself had put it on the cornice before going out to hunt, for fear of losing it, a precaution he had taken on all previous occasions. Up until now, neither the slave girls, nor the eunuchs, nor even the princess herself had paid any attention to it during his absence, for apart from when he went out hunting, Aladdin always carried it on him. One may say that Aladdin was right to take this precaution, but he ought at least to have locked up the lamp. Mistakes like this, it is true, are always being made and always will be.

The princess, unaware how precious the lamp was and that it was in Aladdin's great interest, not to mention her own, that no one should ever touch it and that it should be kept safe, entered into the joke. She ordered a eunuch to take the lamp and go and exchange it. The eunuch obeyed and went down from the room, and no sooner had he emerged from the palace gate when he saw the magician. He called out to him and, when he came up, he showed him the old lamp, saying: 'Give me a new lamp for this one here.'

The magician was in no doubt that this was the lamp he was looking for – there could be no other lamp like it in Aladdin's palace, where all the plates and dishes were either of gold or silver. He promptly took it from the eunuch's hand and, after he had stowed it safely away in his cloak, he showed him his basket and told him to choose whichever lamp he fancied. The eunuch picked one, left the magician and took the new lamp to the princess. As soon as the exchange had taken place, the square rang out again with the shouts and jeers of the children, who laughed even more loudly than before at what they took to be the magician's stupidity.

The magician let the children jeer at him, but not wanting to stay any longer in the vicinity of Aladdin's palace, he gradually and quietly moved away. He stopped crying out about changing new lamps for old, for the only lamp he wanted was the one now in his possession. Seeing his silence, the children lost interest and left him to go on his way.

As soon as he was out of the square between the two palaces, the magician escaped through the less frequented streets and, when he saw there was nobody about, he set the basket down in the middle of one, since he no longer had a use for either the lamps or the basket. He then slipped down another street and hastened on until he came to one of the city gates. As he made his way through the suburbs, which were extensive, he bought some provisions before leaving them. Once in the countryside, he left the road and went to a spot out of sight of passers-by, where he stayed a while until he judged the moment was right for him to carry out the plan which had brought him there. He did not regret the barbary horse he had left behind at the *khan* where he had taken lodgings, for he reckoned that the treasure he had acquired was fair compensation for its loss.

The magician spent the rest of the day in this spot until night was at its darkest. He then pulled out the lamp from under his cloak and rubbed it. Thus summoned, the *jinni* appeared. 'What is your wish?' it asked him. 'Here am I, ready to obey you, your slave and the slave of all those who hold the lamp, I and the other slaves.' 'I command you,' replied the magician, 'this very instant to remove the palace that the other slaves of the lamp have built in this city, just as it is, with all the people in it, and transport it and at the same time myself to such-and-such a place in Africa.' Without answering him, the *jinni*, with the assistance of other *jinn*, like him slaves of the lamp, transported the magician and the entire palace in a very short time to the place in Africa he had designated, where we will leave him, the palace and Princess Badr, and describe, instead, the sultan's surprise.

As soon as the sultan had arisen, as was his custom he went to his closet window in order to have the pleasure of gazing on and admiring Aladdin's palace. But when he looked in the direction of where he had been accustomed to see this palace, all he could see was an empty space, such as had been before the palace had been built. Believing himself mistaken, he rubbed his eyes, but still saw nothing, although the weather was fine, the sky clear and the dawn, which was just breaking, had made everything sharp and distinct. He looked through the two windows on the right and on the left but could only see what he had been used to seeing out of them. So great was his astonishment that he remained for a long time in the same spot, his eyes turned towards where the palace had stood but was now no longer to be seen. He could not understand how so large and striking a palace as Aladdin's, which he had seen as recently as the previous day and almost every day since he had given permission to build it, had vanished so completely that no trace was left behind. 'I am not wrong,' he said to himself. 'It was there. If it had tumbled down, the materials would be there in heaps, and if the earth had swallowed it up, then there would be some trace to show that had happened.' Although he was convinced that the palace was no more, he nonetheless waited a little longer to see if, in fact, he was mistaken. At last he withdrew and, after taking one final look before leaving, he returned to his room. There he commanded the grand vizier to be summoned in all haste and sat down, his mind so disturbed with conflicting thoughts that he did not know what he should do.

The vizier did not keep the sultan waiting long; in fact, he came in such great haste that neither he nor his officials noticed as they came that Aladdin's palace was no longer there, nor had the doorkeepers, when they opened the palace gates, noticed its disappearance. When he came up to the sultan, the vizier addressed him: 'Sire, the urgency with which your majesty has summoned me makes me think that something most extraordinary has happened, since you are well aware that today is the day the council meets and that I must shortly go and carry out my duties.' 'What has happened is indeed truly extraordinary, as you will agree. Tell me, where is Aladdin's palace?' asked the sultan. 'Aladdin's palace?' replied the vizier in astonishment. 'I have just passed in front of it – I thought it was there. Buildings as solid as that don't disappear so easily.' 'Go and look through my closet window,' said the sultan, 'and then come and tell me if you can see it.'

The grand vizier went to the closet, and the same thing happened to him as had happened to the sultan. When he had quite convinced himself that Aladdin's palace no longer stood where it had been and that there did not appear to be any trace of it, he returned to the sultan. 'Well, did you see Aladdin's palace?' the sultan asked him. 'Sire,' he replied, 'your majesty may remember that I had the honour to tell you that this palace, which was the subject of your admiration, with all its immense riches, was the result of magic, the work of a magician, but your majesty would not listen to this.'

The sultan, unable to disagree with what the vizier had said, flew into a great rage which was all the greater because he could not deny his incredulity. 'Where is this wretch, this impostor?' he cried. 'Bring him at once so that I can have his head chopped off.' 'Sire,' replied the vizier, 'he took leave of your majesty a few days ago; we must send for him and ask him about his palace – he must know where it is.' 'That would be to treat him too leniently; go and order thirty of my horsemen to bring him to me bound in chains,' commanded the sultan. The vizier went off to give the sultan's order to the horsemen, instructing their officer in what manner to take Aladdin so that he did not escape. They set out and met Aladdin five or six miles outside the city, hunting on his return. The officer went up to him and told him that the sultan, in his impatience to see him, had sent them to inform him and to accompany him back.

Aladdin, who had not the slightest suspicion of the real reason which brought this detachment of the sultan's guard, continued to hunt but, when he was only half a league from the city, this detachment surrounded him and the officer addressed him: 'Prince Aladdin, it is with the greatest regret that we have to inform you of the order of the sultan to arrest you and bring you to him as a criminal of the state. We beg you not to think ill of us for carrying out our duty and we hope you will forgive us.'

Aladdin, who believed himself innocent, was very much surprised at this announcement and asked the officer if he knew of what crime he was accused, to which the officer answered that neither he nor his men knew anything about it. When he saw how few his own men were compared to the horsemen in the detachment and how they were now moving away from him, he dismounted. 'Here I am,' he said. 'Carry out your order. I have to say, though, that I don't believe I am guilty of any crime, either against the sultan himself or against the state.' A very long, thick chain was immediately passed around his neck and tied around his body in such a manner as to bind his arms. Then the officer went ahead to lead the detachment, while a horseman took the end of the chain and, following the officer, led Aladdin, who was forced to follow him on foot. In this manner, Aladdin was led towards the city.

When the horsemen entered the outskirts, the first people who saw Aladdin being led as a criminal were convinced he was going to have his head chopped off. As he was held in general affection, some took hold of their swords or other weapons, while those who had no weapons armed themselves with stones, and they followed the detachment. Some horsemen in the rear turned round to face the people as though to disperse them; but the crowd quickly grew to such an extent that the horsemen decided on a stratagem, being concerned to get as far as the sultan's palace without Aladdin being snatched from them. To succeed in this, they took great care to take up the entire street as they passed, now spreading out, now closing up again, according to whether the street was broad or narrow. In this way, they reached the palace square, where they all drew themselves up in a line facing the armed populace, until their officer and the horseman who led Aladdin had entered the palace and the doorkeepers had shut the gate to stop the people entering.

Aladdin was led before the sultan, who was waiting for him on the balcony, accompanied by the grand vizier. As soon as he saw him, the sultan immediately commanded the executioner, whom he had ordered to be present, to chop off his head, without wanting to listen to Aladdin or receive an explanation from him. The executioner seized Aladdin and removed the chain which he had around his neck and body. On the ground he spread a leather mat stained with the blood of the countless criminals he had executed and made him kneel on it before tying a bandage over his eyes. He then drew his sword, sized him up before administering the blow and, after flourishing the sword in the air three times, sat down, waiting for the sultan to give the signal to cut off Aladdin's head.

At that moment, the grand vizier noticed that the crowd, who had broken through the horsemen and filled the square, were scaling the palace walls in several places and were beginning to demolish them in an attempt to breach them. Before the sultan could give the signal to the executioner, the vizier said to him: 'Sire, I beseech your majesty to reflect carefully on what you are about to do. You will run the risk of seeing your palace stormed, and should such a disaster occur, the outcome could be fatal.' 'My palace stormed!' exclaimed the sultan. 'Who would be so bold?' 'Sire,' replied the vizier, 'if your majesty were to cast a glance towards the walls of your palace and towards the square, you would discover the truth of what I say.'

On seeing the excited and animated mob, the sultan was so terror-stricken that he instantly commanded the executioner to put away his sword in its sheath and to remove the bandage from Aladdin's eyes and let him go free. He also ordered the guards to proclaim that the sultan was pardoning him and that everyone should go away. As a result, all the men who had already climbed on top of the palace walls, seeing what had happened, now abandoned their plan. They very quickly climbed down and, filled with joy at having saved the life of a man they truly loved, they spread the news to everyone around them and from there it soon spread to all the crowd assembled in the palace square. And when the guards proclaimed the same thing from the top of the terraces to which they had climbed, it became known to all. The justice the sultan had done Aladdin by pardoning him pacified the mob; the tumult died down and gradually everyone went home.

Finding himself free, Aladdin looked up at the balcony and, seeing the sultan, cried out in an affecting manner to him: 'Sire, I beseech your majesty to add one more favour to the one you have already granted me and to let me know what crime I have committed.' 'Crime! You don't know your crime?' exclaimed the sultan. 'Come up here and I'll show you.'

Aladdin went up on to the balcony, where the sultan told him to follow him, and without looking back, led him to his closet. When he reached the door, the sultan turned to him, saying: 'Enter. You ought to know where your palace stood; look all around and then tell me what has happened to it.' Aladdin looked and saw nothing. He could see the whole area which his palace had occupied but, having no idea how the palace could have disappeared, this extraordinary event put him into such a state of confusion that in his astonishment he could not utter a single word in reply.

'Go on, tell me where your palace is and where my daughter is,' the sultan repeated impatiently. Aladdin broke his silence, saying: 'Sire, I see very well and have to admit that the palace I built is no longer where it was. I see that it has disappeared but I cannot tell your majesty where it can be. I can assure you, however, that I had no part in this.' 'I am not so concerned about what happened to your palace,' the sultan continued. 'My daughter is a million times more valuable to me and I want you to find her for me, otherwise I will cut off your head and nothing will stop me.'

'Sire,' replied Aladdin, 'I beg your majesty to grant me forty days' grace to do all I can, and if in that time I don't succeed in finding her, I give you my word that I will offer my head at the foot of your throne so you can dispose of it as you please.' 'I grant you the forty days you ask for,' answered the sultan, 'but don't think to abuse this favour by believing you can escape my anger, for I will know how to find you, in whatever corner of the earth you may be.'

Aladdin left the sultan, deeply humiliated and in a truly pitiful state: with head bowed, he passed through the palace courtyards without daring to raise his eyes in his confusion. Of the chief court officials, whom he had treated graciously and who had been his friends, not one for all their friendship went up to him to console him or to offer to take him in, but they turned their backs on him as much to avoid seeing him as to avoid being recognized by him. But even had they gone up to Aladdin to say something consoling to him or to offer to help him, they would not have known him, for he no longer knew himself, being no longer in his right mind. This was evident when he came out of the palace, as, without thinking what he was doing, he went from door to door and asked passers-by, enquiring of them whether they had seen his palace or could give him any news of it. Consequently, everyone became convinced that Aladdin had gone out of his mind. Some only laughed, but the more reasonable, and in particular those linked to him either by friendship or business, were filled with compassion. He stayed three days in the city – walking hither and thither and only eating what people offered him out of charity – unable to decide what to do.

Finally, in the wretched state he was in and feeling he could no longer stay in a city where he had once cut such a fine figure, he left and went out into the countryside. Avoiding the main roads and after crossing several fields in a state of great uncertainty, eventually, at nightfall, he came to the bank of a river. There, greatly despondent, he said to himself: 'Where shall I go to look for my palace? In which province, which country or part of the world shall I find it and recover my dear princess, as the sultan demands of me? I will never succeed. It's best if I don't go to all of this wearisome effort, which will in any case come to nothing, but free myself of all this bitter grief that torments me.' Having made this resolution, he was on the point of throwing himself into the river but, being a good and faithful Muslim, he thought he ought not to do this before first performing his prayers. Wishing to prepare himself, he approached the river in order to wash his hands and face according to custom, but as the bank sloped at that point and was damp from the water lapping against it, he slipped and would have fallen into the river had he not been stopped by a small rock which protruded about two feet above the ground. Fortunately for him, he was still wearing the ring which the magician had put on his finger before he had gone down into the cave to remove the precious lamp that had now been taken away from him. As he caught hold of the rock, he rubbed the ring quite hard against it and immediately the same *jinni* who had first appeared to him in the cave in which the magician had shut him up appeared once again, saying: 'What is your wish? Here am I, ready to obey you, your slave and the slave of all those who wear the ring on their finger, I and the other slaves of the ring.'

Delighted at this apparition, which he had so little expected in his despair, Aladdin replied: 'Save me a second time, *jinni*, and either tell me where the palace I built is or bring it back immediately to where it was.' 'What you ask of me,' replied the *jinni*, 'is not within my power to bring back; I am only the slave of the ring. You must address yourself to the slave of the lamp.' 'If that's the case,' said Aladdin, 'I command you, by the power of the ring, to transport me to the place where my palace is, wherever it is in the world, and set me down underneath the windows of Princess Badr.' Hardly had he finished speaking than the *jinni* transported him to Africa, to the middle of a meadow where the palace stood, not far from a large town, and set him down right underneath the windows of the princess's apartments, where he left him. All this happened in a moment. Despite the darkness of the night, Aladdin easily recognized his palace and the princess's apartments; but as the night was already advanced and all was quiet in the palace, he moved off a little way and sat down at the foot of a tree. There, filled with hope as he reflected on the pure chance to which he owed his good fortune, he found himself in a much more peaceful state than he had been in since the time when he had been arrested and brought before the sultan and had been delivered from the recent danger of losing his life. For a while he entertained himself with these agreeable thoughts but eventually, not having slept at all for five or six days, he could not stop himself being overwhelmed by sleep and fell asleep at the foot of the tree where he was sitting.

The next morning, as dawn was breaking, Aladdin was pleasantly awoken by the singing of the birds, not only those that roosted on the tree beneath which he had spent the night but all those on the luxuriant trees in the very garden of his palace. When he cast his eyes on that wonderful building, he felt a joy beyond words at the thought that he would soon be its master once more and possess once again his dear princess. He got up and, approaching the princess's apartments, walked for a while underneath her windows until it was light and he could see her. As he waited, he searched his mind for a possible cause for his misfortune, and after much thought he became convinced that it all came from his having left the lamp out of his sight. He blamed himself for his negligence and his carelessness in letting it leave his possession for a single moment. What worried him still more was that he could not imagine who could be so jealous as to envy him his good fortune. He would have soon guessed had he known that such a man and his palace were both in Africa, but the slave of the ring had not mentioned this, while he himself had not even asked about it. The name of Africa alone should have reminded him of the magician, his avowed enemy.

That morning, Princess Badr arose earlier than she had done ever since the wily magician – now the master of the palace, the sight of whom she had been forced to endure once a day but whom she treated so harshly that he had not yet been so bold as to take up residence there – had by his cunning kidnapped her and carried her off to Africa. When she was dressed, one of her slave girls, looking through the lattice screen, spotted Aladdin and ran to tell her mistress. The princess, who could not believe the news, rushed to the window and saw her husband. She opened the screen and, hearing the sound, Aladdin raised his head. Recognizing her, he greeted her with great delight. 'So as to waste no time, someone has gone to open the secret door for you; enter and come up,' said the princess and closed the screen.

The secret door was beneath the princess's apartments. Finding it open, Aladdin entered and went up. It is impossible to describe the intensity of their joy at their reunion after believing themselves parted for ever. They embraced several times and showed all the signs of love and affection one can imagine after such a sad and unexpected separation. After many an embrace mingled with tears of joy, they sat down. Aladdin was the first to speak: 'Before we talk about anything else, dear princess, I beg you, in the Name of God, in your own interest and that of your worthy father, the sultan, and no less of mine, to tell me what has happened to the old lamp that I put on the cornice in the room of the twenty-four windows before I went off to hunt.' 'Ah, my dear husband!' sighed the princess. 'I did indeed suspect that all our troubles came from the loss of that lamp and what distresses me is that I myself am the cause of it.' 'Dear princess,' said Aladdin, 'don't blame yourself; it's all my fault and I should have taken greater care in looking after it. Let's now think only about how to repair the damage, and so please be so good as to tell me how it happened and into whose hands the lamp fell.'

The princess then proceeded to tell Aladdin how the old lamp had been exchanged for a new one, which she ordered to be brought in for him to see; and how the following night she had found the palace had been transported and, the next morning, she woke to find herself in an unknown country, where she was now talking to him, and that this was Africa, a fact she had learned from the very mouth of the traitor who had transported her there by his magic arts.

'Dear princess,' Aladdin interrupted her, 'you have already told me who the traitor is by explaining that I am with you in Africa. He is the most perfidious of all men. But now is not the time nor the place to give you a fuller picture of his evil deeds. I only ask you to tell me what he has done with the lamp and where he has put it.' 'He carries it with him carefully wrapped up close to his chest,' the princess answered, 'and I can bear witness to that since he pulled it out and unwrapped it in my presence in order to show it off.'

'Princess, please don't be annoyed with me for wearying you with all these questions,' said Aladdin, 'for they are as important to you as they are to me. But to come to what most particularly concerns me, tell me, I beg you, how you yourself have been treated by this wicked and treacherous man.' 'Since I have been here,' replied the princess, 'he only visits me once a day, and I am sure that he does not bother me more often because these visits offer him so little satisfaction. Every time he comes, the aim of all his conversation is to persuade me to break the vows I gave you and to make me take him for my husband, by trying to make me believe that I should not hope ever to see you again; that you are no longer alive and that the sultan, my father, has had your head chopped off. He adds, to justify himself, that you are ungrateful and that you owed your good fortune only to him, and there are a thousand other things I will leave him to tell you. And as all he gets from me in reply are tears and moans, he is forced to depart as little satisfied as when he came. However, I have no doubt that his intention is to let the worst of my grief and pain pass, in the hope that I will change my mind, and, finally, if I persist in resisting him, to use violence. But, dear husband, your presence has already dispelled my worries.'

'Princess,' said Aladdin, 'I am confident that it is not in vain and your worries are over, for I believe I have found a way to deliver you from your enemy and mine. But to do that, I have to go into the town. I will return towards noon and will then tell you what my plan is and what you will need to do to help make it succeed. I must warn you not to be astonished if you see me return dressed in different clothes, but give the order not to have me kept waiting at the secret door after my first knock.' The princess promised him that someone would be waiting for him at the door, which would be opened promptly.

When Aladdin had gone down from the princess's apartments, leaving by the same door, he looked around and saw a peasant who was setting off on the road which led into the country. The peasant had already gone past the palace and was a little way off, so Aladdin hastened his steps; when he had caught up with him, he offered to change clothes with him, pressing him until the peasant finally agreed. The exchange was done behind a nearby bush; and when they had parted company, Aladdin took the road back to the town. Once there, he went along the road leading from the city gate and then passed into the most frequented streets. On coming to the place where all the merchants and artisans had their own particular street, he entered that of the apothecaries where he sought out the largest and best-supplied store and asked the merchant if he had a certain powder which he named.

The merchant, who, from his clothes, imagined Aladdin to be poor and that he had not enough money to pay him, said he had but that it was expensive. Aladdin, guessing what was on the merchant's mind, pulled out his purse and, showing him gold coins, asked for half a drachm of the powder. The merchant weighed it out, wrapped it up and, as he gave it to Aladdin, asked him for a gold coin. Aladdin handed it to him and, stopping only long enough in the town to eat something, he returned to his palace. He did not have to wait at the secret door, which was immediately opened to him, and he went up to the princess's apartments.

'Princess,' he said, 'the aversion you have shown me you feel for your kidnapper will perhaps make it difficult for you to follow the advice I'm going to give you. But allow me to tell you that it is advisable that you should conceal this and even go against your own feelings if you wish to deliver yourself from his persecution and give the sultan, your father and my lord, the satisfaction of seeing you again. If you want to follow my advice,' continued Aladdin, 'you must begin right now by putting on one of your most beautiful dresses, and when the magician comes, you must be prepared to welcome him as warmly as possible, without affectation or strain, and with a happy smile, in such a way that, should there still remain a hint of sadness, he will think it will go away with time. In your conversation, give him to understand that you are doing your best to forget me; and so that he should be all the more persuaded of your sincerity, invite him to have supper with you and indicate to him that you would be very pleased to taste some of the best wine his country has to offer. He will then have to leave you to go and find some. Then, while waiting for him to return, when the food is laid out, pour this powder into one of the goblets out of which you usually drink. Put it aside and tell the slave girl who serves you your drink to bring it to you filled with wine after you have given her a pre-arranged signal. Warn her to take care and not to make a mistake. When the magician returns and you are seated at table and when you have eaten and drunk what you think is sufficient, ask for the goblet containing the powder to be brought to you and exchange it for his. He will think you will be doing him such a favour that he won't be able to refuse you, but no sooner will he have emptied it than you will see him fall down backwards. If you don't like drinking from his goblet, just pretend to drink; you can do so without fear, for the effect of the powder will be so swift that he won't have time to notice whether you are drinking or not.'

When Aladdin had finished speaking, the princess said: 'I must admit I find it very distasteful to have to agree to make advances towards the magician, even though I know I must; but what can one not resolve to do when faced with a cruel enemy! I will do as you advise me, for on it depends my peace of mind no less than yours.' Having made these arrangements with the princess, Aladdin took his leave and went to spend the rest of the day near the palace, waiting for night to fall before returning to the secret door.

From the moment of her painful separation, Princess Badr – inconsolable not only at seeing herself separated from her beloved husband, Aladdin, whom she had loved and whom she continued to love more out of inclination than out of duty, but also from the sultan, her father, whom she cherished and who loved her tenderly – had remained very neglectful of her person. She had even, one may say, forgotten the neatness which so becomes persons of her sex, particularly after the first time the magician had come to her and she discovered through her slave girls, who recognized him, that it was he who had taken the old lamp in exchange for a new one. Following her discovery of this outrageous swindle, he had become an object of horror to her, and the opportunity to take the revenge on him that he deserved, and sooner than she had dared hope for, made her content to fall in with Aladdin's plans. Thus, as soon as he had gone, she sat down at her dressing table; her slave girls dressed her hair in the most becoming fashion and she took out her most glamorous dress, searching for the one which would best serve her purpose. She then put on a belt of gold mounted with the largest of diamonds, all beautifully matched; to go with it she chose a necklace all of pearls, of which the six on both sides of the central pearl – which was the largest and the most precious

– were so proportioned that the greatest queens and the wives of the grandest sultans would have thought themselves happy to have a string of pearls the size of the two smallest pearls in the princess's necklace. The bracelets of diamonds interspersed with rubies wonderfully complemented the richness of the belt and the necklace.

When the princess was fully dressed, she looked in her mirror and consulted her maids for their opinion on her dress. Then, having checked that she lacked none of the charms which might arouse the magician's mad passion, she sat down on the sofa to await his arrival.

The magician came at his usual hour. As soon as she saw him come into the room of the twenty-four windows where she awaited him, she arose apparelled in all her beauty and charm, and showed him to the place of honour where she wanted him to take his seat so as to sit down at the same time as he did, a mark of courtesy she had not shown him before. The magician, more dazzled by the beauty of the princess's sparkling eyes than by the brilliance of the jewellery with which she was adorned, was very surprised. Her stately air and a certain grace with which she welcomed him were so different from the rebuffs he had up till then received from her. In his confusion, he would have sat down on the edge of the sofa but, seeing the princess did not want to take her seat until he had sat down where she wished him to, he obeyed.

Once the magician was seated where she had indicated, the princess, to help him out of the embarrassment she could see he was in, was the first to speak. Looking at him in such a manner as to make him believe that he was no longer odious to her, as she had previously made him out to be, she said: 'No doubt you are astonished to see me appear so different today compared to what you have seen of me up till now. But you will no longer be surprised when I tell you that sadness and melancholy, griefs and worries, are not part of my nature, and that I try to dispel such things as quickly as possible when I discover there is no longer a reason for them. Now, I have been thinking about what you told me of Aladdin's fate and, knowing my father's temper, I am convinced as you are that Aladdin cannot have avoided the terrible effects of his wrath. And I can see that if I persist in weeping for him all my life, all my tears would not bring him back. That is why, after I have performed for him the final rites and duties that my love dictates, now that he is in his grave it seems to me that I should look for ways of consoling myself. This is the reason for the change you see in me. As a start, to remove any cause for sadness, I have resolved to banish it completely; and, believing you very much wish to keep me company, I have given orders for supper to be prepared for us. However, as I only have wine from China and I am now in Africa, I fancied trying some that is produced here and I thought that, if there is any, you would be able to procure some of the best.'

The magician, who had thought it would be impossible for him to be so fortunate as to find favour so quickly and so easily with the princess, told her he could not find words sufficient to express how much he appreciated her kindness. But to finish a conversation which he would otherwise have found difficult to bring to an end, once he had embarked on it, he seized upon the subject of African wine that she had mentioned. He told her that one of the main advantages of which Africa could boast was that it produced excellent wines, particularly in the region where she now found herself; he had a seven-year-old cask which had not yet been opened, whose excellence, not to set too high a value on it, surpassed the most exquisite wines in the whole of the world. 'If my princess will give me leave, I will go and fetch two bottles and I will be back immediately,' he added. 'I would be sorry to put you to such trouble,' the princess replied. 'It might be better if you sent someone else.' 'But I shall have to go myself,' said the magician, 'as only I know where the key of the storeroom is, and only I know the secret of how to open it.' 'If that is the case,' said the princess, 'then go, but come back quickly. The longer you take, the more impatient I will be to see you again, and bear in mind that we will sit down to eat as soon as you return.'

Filled with hope at his imagined good fortune, the magician did not so much run as fly to fetch his seven-year-old wine, and returned very quickly. The princess, well aware that he would make haste, had herself put the powder that Aladdin had brought her into a goblet which she had set aside and had then started to serve the dishes. They sat down opposite each other to eat, the magician so placed that his back was turned to the refreshments. The princess presented him with all the best dishes, saying to him: 'If you wish, I will entertain you with singing and music, but as there are only the two of us, it seems to me that conversation would give us more pleasure.' The magician regarded this as one more favour granted him by the princess.

After they had eaten a few mouthfuls, the princess asked for wine to be brought. She then drank to the health of the magician, after which she said to him: 'You were right to sing the praises of your wine. I have never drunk anything so delicious.' 'Charming princess,' replied the magician, holding the goblet he had just been given, 'my wine acquires an extra virtue by your approval.' 'Then drink to my health,' said the princess, 'and you will see for yourself what an expert I am.' The magician drank to the princess's health, saying to her as he handed back the goblet: 'Princess, I consider myself fortunate for having kept this wine for such a happy occasion, and I, too, must admit that I have never before drunk any so excellent in so many ways.'

At last, when they had finished eating and had drunk three more times of the wine, the princess, who had succeeded in charming the magician with her gracious and attentive ways, beckoned to the slave girl who served the wine and told her to fill her goblet with wine and at the same time fill that of the magician and give it to him. When they both had their goblets in their hands, the princess said to the magician: 'I don't know what one does here when one is in love and drinks together, as we are doing. Back home, in China, lovers exchange goblets and drink each other's health.' As she was speaking, she gave him the goblet she had, in one hand, while holding out the other to receive his. The magician hastened to make this exchange, which he did all the more gladly as he regarded this favour the surest sign that he had completely won over the heart of the princess. His happiness was complete. Before he drank to her, holding his goblet in his hand, he said: 'Princess, we Africans are by no means as skilled in the refinements of the art and pleasures of love as the Chinese. I learned from you something I did not know and at the same time I have learned how much I should appreciate the favour you grant me. Dear princess, I will never forget this: by drinking out of your goblet, I rediscovered a life I would have despaired of, had your cruelty towards me continued.'

Princess Badr, bored by the magician's endless ramblings, interrupted him, saying: 'Let us drink first; you can then say what you wish later.' At the same time, she raised the goblet to her mouth but only touched it with her lips, while the magician, who was in a hurry to drink first, drained his goblet without leaving a drop behind. In his haste to empty the goblet, when he finished, he leaned backwards a little and remained a while in this pose until the princess, her goblet still only touching her lips, saw his eyes begin to roll as he fell, lifeless, on his back.

She had no need to order the secret door to be opened for Aladdin: as soon as the word was given that the magician had fallen upon his back, her slave girls, who were standing several paces from each other outside the room and all the way down to the foot of the staircase, immediately opened the door. Aladdin went up and entered the room. When he saw the magician stretched out on the sofa, the princess got up and was coming towards him to express her joy and embrace him, but he stopped her, saying: 'Princess, now is not yet the time. Please would you go back to your apartments and see that I am left alone while I try to arrange to have you transported back to China as quickly as you were brought from there.'

As soon as the princess and her slave girls and eunuchs were out of the room, Aladdin closed the door and, going up to the magician's lifeless corpse, opened up his shirt and drew out the lamp which was wrapped up as the princess had described to him. He unwrapped it and as soon as he rubbed it, the *jinni* appeared with his usual greeting. '*Jinni*,' said Aladdin, 'I have summoned you to command you, on behalf of the lamp in whose service you are, to have this palace transported immediately back to China, to the same part and to the same spot from where it was brought here.' The *jinni* nodded to show he was willing to obey and then disappeared. Immediately, the palace was transported to China, with only two slight shocks to indicate the removal had taken place – one when the palace was lifted up from where it was in Africa and the other when it was set down again in China, opposite the sultan's palace. All this happened in a very short space of time.

Aladdin went down to the princess's apartments. He embraced her, saying: 'Princess, I can assure you that tomorrow morning, your joy and mine will be complete.' Then, as the princess had not yet finished eating and Aladdin was hungry, she had the dishes – which had hardly been touched – brought from the room of the twenty-four windows. She and Aladdin ate together and drank of the magician's fine old wine, after which, having no doubt enjoyed conversation which must have been very satisfying, they withdrew to her apartments.

Meanwhile, the sultan, since the disappearance of Aladdin's palace and of Princess Badr, had been inconsolable at having lost her, or so he thought. Unable to sleep by night or day, instead of avoiding everything that could keep him in his sorrow, he, on the contrary, sought it out all the more. Whereas previously he would only go in the morning to his closet to enjoy gazing at the palace – of which he could never have his fill – now he would go there several times a day to renew his tears and plunge himself into ever deeper suffering by the thought that he would never again see what had given him so much pleasure and that he had lost what he held dearest in the world. Dawn was just breaking when the sultan came to this room the morning that Aladdin's palace had just been restored to its place. He was lost in thought as he entered it and filled with grief as he glanced sadly at the spot, not noticing the palace at first, as he was expecting to see only an empty space. When he saw that the space was no longer empty, he thought at first that this must be the effect of the mist. But when he looked more closely, he realized that it must be, without doubt, Aladdin's palace. Sadness and sorrow immediately gave way to joy and delight. He hastened to return to his apartments where he gave orders for a horse to be saddled and brought to him, and as soon as it was brought, he mounted and set off, thinking he could not arrive fast enough at Aladdin's palace.

Aladdin, expecting this to happen, had got up at first light and had taken out of his wardrobe one of his most magnificent costumes, put it on and gone up to the room of the twenty-four windows, from where he could see the sultan approaching. He went down and was just in time to welcome him at the foot of the staircase and to help him dismount. 'Aladdin,' the sultan said to him, 'I can't speak to you before I have seen and embraced my daughter.' Aladdin then led the sultan to the princess's apartments, where she had just finished dressing. He had already told her to remember that she was no longer in Africa but in China, in the capital of her father, the sultan, and next to his palace once again. The sultan, his face bathed in tears of joy, embraced her several times, while the princess, for her part, showed him how overjoyed she was at seeing him again.

For a while the sultan was unable to speak, so moved was he at having found his beloved daughter again after having so bitterly wept for her loss, sincerely believing she must be dead. The princess, too, was in tears, in her joy at seeing her father again. Finally, the sultan said to her: 'My daughter, I would like to think that it's the joy of seeing me again which makes you seem so little changed, as though no misfortune had happened to you. But I am convinced you have suffered a great deal, for one is not carried off with an entire palace as suddenly as you were without great alarm and terrible anguish. I want you to tell me all about it and to hide nothing from me.'

The princess was only too happy to tell him what he wanted to know. 'Sire,' she said, 'if I appear to be so little changed, I beg your majesty to bear in mind that I received a new life early yesterday morning thanks to Aladdin, my beloved husband and deliverer whom I had looked on and mourned as lost to me and whom the joy of seeing and embracing again has all but restored me. Yet my greatest distress was to see myself snatched both from your majesty and from my dear husband, not only because of my love for my husband but also because of my worry that he, innocent though he was, should feel the painful consequences of your majesty's anger, to which I had no doubt he would be exposed. I suffered only a little from the insolence of my kidnapper – whose conversation I found disagreeable, but which I could put an end to, because I knew how to gain the upper hand. Besides, I was as little constrained as I am now. As for my abduction, Aladdin had no part in it: I alone – though totally innocent – am to blame for it.'

In order to persuade the sultan of the truth of what she said, she told him in detail all about the African magician, how he had disguised himself as a seller of lamps who exchanged new lamps for old ones, and how she had amused herself by exchanging Aladdin's lamp, not knowing its secret and importance; how, after this exchange, she and the palace had been lifted up and both transported to Africa together with the magician; how the latter had been recognized by two of her slave girls and by the eunuch who had exchanged the lamp for her, when the magician first had the effrontery to come and present himself to her after the success of his audacious enterprise, and to propose marriage to her; how she had suffered at his hands until the arrival of Aladdin; and what measures the two of them had taken to remove the lamp which the magician carried on him and how they had succeeded, particularly by her dissimulation in inviting him to have supper with her; and, finally, she told him of the poisoned goblet she had offered to the magician. 'As for the rest,' she concluded, 'I leave it to Aladdin to tell you about it.'

Aladdin had little more to tell the sultan. 'When the secret door was opened and I went up to the room of the twenty-four windows,' he said, 'I saw the traitor stretched out dead on the sofa, thanks to the virulence of the poison powder. As it was not proper for the princess to remain there any longer, I begged her to go down to her apartments with her slave girls and eunuchs. As soon as I was there alone, I extracted the lamp from the magician's clothing and made use of the same secret password he used to remove the palace and kidnap the princess. By that means the palace was restored to where it had formerly stood and I had the happiness of bringing the princess back to your majesty, as you had commanded me. I don't want to impose upon your majesty but if you would take the trouble to go up to the room, you would see the magician punished as he deserves.'

The sultan, to convince himself that this was really true, got up and went to the room and when he saw the magician lying dead, his face already turned livid thanks to the virulent effect of the poison, he embraced Aladdin very warmly, saying: 'My son, don't think ill of me for my conduct towards you – I was forced to it out of paternal love and you must forgive me for being overzealous.' 'Sire,' replied Aladdin, 'I have not the slightest cause for complaint against your majesty, since you did only what you had to do. This magician, this wretch, this vilest of men, he is the sole cause of my fall from favour. When your majesty has the time, I will tell you about another wicked deed he did me, no less foul than this, from which it is only by a particular favour of God that I was saved.' 'I will indeed make time for this and soon, but let us think only of rejoicing and have this odious object removed.'

Aladdin had the magician's corpse taken away and gave orders that it be thrown on to a dunghill for the birds and beasts to feed on. The sultan, meanwhile, after having commanded that tambourines, drums, trumpets and other musical instruments be played to announce the public rejoicing, proclaimed a festival of ten days to celebrate the return of Princess Badr and Aladdin with his palace. Thus was Aladdin faced for a second time with almost inevitable death, yet managed to escape with his life. But it was not the last time – there was to be a third occasion, the circumstances of which we will now tell.

The magician had a younger brother who was no less skilled in the magic arts; one may even say that he surpassed him in wickedness and in the perniciousness of his schemes. They did not always live together nor even stay in the same city, and often one was to be found in the east and the other in the west. But every year they did not fail to inform each other, by geomancy, in what part of the world and in what condition they were, and whether one of them needed the assistance of the other.

Some time after the magician had failed in his attempt to destroy Aladdin's good fortune, his younger brother, who had not heard from him for a year and who was not in Africa but in some far-off land, wanted to know in what part of the world his brother resided, how he was and what he was doing. Wherever he went this brother always carried with him his geomancy box, as had his elder brother. Taking the box, he arranged the sand, made his throw, interpreted the figures and finally made his divination. On examining each figure, he found that his brother was no longer alive, that he had been poisoned and had died a sudden death, and that this had happened in the capital city of a kingdom in China, situated in such-and-such a place. He also learned that the man who had poisoned him was someone of good descent who had married a princess, a sultan's daughter.

Having learned in this way of his brother's sad fate, the magician wasted no time in useless regret, which could not restore his brother to life, but immediately resolving to avenge his death, he mounted a horse and set off for China. He crossed plains, rivers, mountains and deserts, and after a long and arduous journey, without stopping, he finally reached China and shortly afterwards the capital city whose location he had discovered by geomancy. Certain that this was the place and that he had not mistaken one kingdom for another, he stopped and took up lodgings there.

The day after his arrival, this magician went out into the city, not so much to see its fine sights – to which he was quite indifferent – as to begin to take the necessary steps to carry out his evil plan, and so he entered the most frequented districts and listened to what people were saying. There, in a place where people went to spend the time playing different kinds of games, some playing while others stood around chatting, exchanging news and discussing the affairs of the day or their own, he heard people talking of a woman recluse called Fatima, about her virtue and piety and of the miracles she performed. Believing this woman could be of some use to him for what he had in mind, he took one of the men aside and asked him to tell him particularly who this holy woman was and what sort of miracles she performed.

'What!' the man exclaimed. 'Have you never seen or even heard of her? She is the admiration of the whole city for her fasting, her austerity and her exemplary conduct. Except for Mondays and Fridays, she never leaves her little cell, and on the days she shows herself in the city she does countless good deeds, and there is not a person with a headache who is not cured by a touch of her hands.'

The magician wished to know no more on the subject, but only asked the man where in the city the cell of this holy woman was to be found. The man told him, whereupon – after having conceived and drawn up the detestable plan which we will shortly reveal and after having made this enquiry – so as to make quite sure, he observed this woman's every step as she went about the city, never leaving her out of his sight until evening when he saw her return to her cell. When he had made a careful note of the spot, he went back to one of the places we have mentioned where a certain hot drink is drunk and where one can spend the whole night should one so wish, especially during the days of great heat when the people in such countries prefer to sleep on a mat rather than in a bed.

Towards midnight, the magician, after he had settled his small bill with the owner of the place, left and went straight to the cell of this holy woman, Fatima – the name by which she was known throughout the city. He had no difficulty in opening the door, which was fastened only with a latch, and entered, without making a sound, and closed it again. Spotting Fatima in the moonlight, lying asleep on a sofa with only a squalid mat on it, her head leaning against the wall of her cell, he went up to her and, drawing out a dagger he wore at his side, woke her up. When poor Fatima opened her eyes, she was very astonished to see a man about to stab her. Pressing the dagger to her heart, ready to plunge it in, he said to her: 'If you cry out or make the slightest sound, I will kill you. Get up and do as I say.'

Fatima, who had been sleeping fully dressed, got up trembling with fear. 'Don't be afraid,' said the magician. 'All I want is your clothes. Give them to me and take mine instead.' They exchanged clothes and after the magician had put hers on, he said to her: 'Paint my face like yours so that I look like you and so that the colour doesn't come off.' Seeing that she was still trembling, he said to her, in order to reassure her and so that she might be readier to do what he wanted: 'Don't be afraid, I say. I swear by God that I will spare your life.' Fatima let him into her cell and lit her lamp. Dipping a brush into a liquid in a certain jar, she brushed his face with it, assuring him that the colour would not change and that his face was now the same colour as hers. Then she put her own headdress on his head and a veil, showing him how to conceal his face with it when he went through the city. Finally, after she put around his neck a large string of beads which hung down to the waist, she placed in his hand the same stick she used to walk with. 'Look,' she said to him, handing him a mirror, 'you will see you couldn't look more like me.' The magician looked just as he wanted to look, but he did not keep the oath he had so solemnly sworn to the saintly woman. In order to leave no trace of blood, he did not stab her but strangled her and when he saw that she had given up the ghost, he dragged her corpse by the feet to a cistern outside her cell and threw her into it.

Having committed this foul murder, the magician, disguised as Fatima, spent the rest of the night in her cell. The next day, an hour or two after sunrise, he left the cell, even though it was not a day when the holy woman would go out, quite sure that no one would stop and question him about it but ready with an answer if they did. One of the first things he had done on his arrival in the city was to go and look for Aladdin's palace, and as it was there he intended to put his plan into action, he went directly to it.

As soon as people saw what they thought to be the holy woman, a large crowd gathered around the magician, some asking for his prayers, some kissing his hands – the more reserved among them kissing the edge of his garment – and others, whether they had a headache or merely wanted to be protected from one, bowing their heads for him to lay his hands on them, all of which he did, mumbling a few words in the guise of a prayer. In fact, he imitated the holy woman so well that everyone believed it was really her. After frequent stops to satisfy such requests – for while this sort of laying-on of hands did them no harm, nor did it do them any good – he finally arrived in the square before Aladdin's palace where, the crowd being even greater, people were ever more eager to get close to him. The strongest and most zealous forced their way through to get to him and this caused such quarrels that they could be heard from the palace, right from the room with the twenty-four windows where Princess Badr was sitting.

The princess asked what all the noise was about and as no one could tell her anything about it, she gave orders for someone to go and see and report back to her. Without leaving the room, one of her slave girls looked out through a screen and came back to tell her that the noise came from the crowd of people who gathered around the saintly lady, to be cured of headaches by the laying-on of her hands. Now the princess, who had heard a lot about the holy woman and the good she did but had never yet seen her, was curious to talk to her. When she expressed something of her desire to the chief eunuch, who was present, he told her that if she wished, he could easily have the woman brought in – she had only to give the command. The princess agreed, and he immediately chose four eunuchs and ordered them to fetch the so-called holy woman.

As soon as the crowd saw the eunuchs come out of the gates of Aladdin's palace and make for the disguised magician, they dispersed and the magician, finding himself once more alone and seeing the eunuchs coming for him, stepped towards them, delighted to see his deceit was working so well. One of the eunuchs then said to him: 'Holy lady, the princess wants to see you; come, follow us,' to which the pseudo-Fatima replied: 'The princess does me a great honour; I am ready to obey her,' and followed the eunuchs, who had already set out back to the palace.

The magician, whose saintly dress concealed a wicked heart, was then led into the room of the twenty-four windows. When he saw the princess, he said to her: 'May all your hopes and desires be fulfilled,' and he began to launch into a long string of wishes and prayers for her health and prosperity. Under the cloak of great piety, he used all the rhetorical skills of the impostor and hypocrite he was to ingratiate himself into the princess's favour, which was all the more easy to achieve because the princess, in her natural goodness of heart, believed everyone was as good as she was, especially those who retreated from the world in order to serve God.

When 'Fatima' had finished her long harangue, the princess thanked her, saying: 'Lady Fatima, I thank you for your prayers and good wishes; I have great confidence in them and hope that God will fulfil them. Come, sit yourself beside me.' 'Fatima' took her seat with affected modesty. 'Holy lady,' the princess went on, 'there is something I ask you to grant me – please don't refuse it me – which is that you stay with me and tell me about your life, so that I can learn by your good example how I should serve God.' 'Princess,' replied 'Fatima', 'I beg you not to ask me something I can't consent to, without being distracted from and neglecting my prayers and devotions.' 'Don't worry about that,' the princess reassured her. 'I have several rooms which are not occupied. Choose the one you like and you shall perform all your devotions there as freely as if you were in your cell.'

Now the magician's only aim had been to enter Aladdin's palace, for he could more easily carry out there his pernicious plan under the auspices and protection of the princess than if he had been forced to go back and forth between the palace and the holy woman's cell. Consequently, he did not put up much resistance in accepting the princess's kind offer. 'Princess,' he said to her, 'however much a poor wretched woman like myself has resolved to renounce the pomp and grandeur of this world, I dare not presume to resist the wishes and commands of so pious and charitable a princess.' In reply, Badr rose from her seat and said to the magician: 'Get up and come with me, and I will show you the empty rooms I have, so that you may choose.' The magician followed the princess, and from among all the neat and well-furnished apartments she showed him he chose the one which he thought looked the humblest, saying hypocritically that it was too good for him and that he only chose it to please her.

The princess wanted to take the villain back to the room with the twenty-four windows to have him dine with her. The magician realized, however, that to eat he would have to uncover his face, which he had kept veiled until then, and he was afraid that the princess would then recognize that he was not the holy woman Fatima she believed him to be, and so he begged her earnestly to excuse him, telling her he only ate bread and some dried fruit, and to allow him to eat his modest meal in his room. She granted him his request, replying: 'Holy lady, you are free to do as you would do in your own cell. I will have some food brought you, but remember I expect you as soon as you have finished your meal.'

After the princess had dined, 'Fatima' was informed of it by one of her eunuchs and she went to rejoin her. 'Holy lady,' the princess said, 'I am delighted to have with me a holy lady like you, who will bring blessings to this place. Incidentally, how do like this palace? But before I show you round it, room by room, tell me first what you think of this room in particular.'

At this request, 'Fatima', who, in order better to perform her part, had affected to keep her head lowered, looking to neither right nor left, at last raised it and surveyed the room, from one end to the other; and when she had reflected for a while, she said: 'Princess, this room is truly wonderful and so beautiful. Yet, as far as a recluse such as myself can judge who does not know what the world thinks is beautiful, it seems to me that there is something lacking.' 'What is that, holy lady?' asked the princess. 'Tell me, I beseech you. I myself thought, and I have heard other people say the same, that it lacked nothing, but if there is anything it does lack, I shall have that put right.'

'Princess,' the magician replied, with great guile, 'forgive me for taking the liberty but my advice, if it is of any importance, would be that if a *rukh*'s egg were to be suspended from the middle of the dome, there would be no other room like this in the four quarters of the world and your palace would be the wonder of the universe.' 'Holy lady, what sort of bird is this *rukh* and where can one find a *rukh*'s egg?' Badr asked. 'Princess,' replied 'Fatima', 'this is a bird of prodigious size which lives on the summit of Mount Qaf. The architect of your palace will be able to find you one.'

After she had thanked the so-called holy woman for what she believed to be her good advice, the princess conversed with her on other things, but she did not forget the *rukh*'s egg, which she intended to mention to Aladdin as soon as he returned from hunting. He had been gone for six days and the magician, who was well aware of this, had wanted to take advantage of his absence, but Aladdin returned that same day, towards evening, just after 'Fatima' had taken her leave of the princess to retire to her room. As soon as he arrived, he went up to the princess's apartments, which she had just entered, and greeted and embraced her, but she seemed a little cold in her welcome, so he said to her: 'Dear princess, you don't seem to be as cheerful as usual. Has something happened during my absence to displease you and cause you worry and dissatisfaction? For God's sake, don't hide it from me; there's nothing that were it in my power I would not do to make it go away.' 'It's nothing, really,' replied Badr, 'and I am so little bothered by it that I didn't think it would show on my face enough for you to notice. However, since, contrary to my intentions, you have noticed a change in me, I won't hide from you the cause, which is of very little importance. Like you,' she continued, 'I thought that our palace was the most superb, the most magnificent, the most perfect in all the world. But I will tell you now about something that occurred to me when I was looking carefully around the room of the twenty-four windows. Don't you agree that it would leave nothing to be desired if a *rukh*'s egg were to be suspended from the middle of the dome?' 'Princess,' replied Aladdin, 'it is enough that you should find it lacks a *rukh*'s egg for me to agree with you. You shall see by the speed with which I put this right how there is nothing I would not do out of my love for you.'

Aladdin left the princess at once and went up to the room of the twenty-four windows; there he pulled out the lamp, which he always carried with him wherever he went, ever since the danger he had run into through neglecting to take this precaution, and rubbed it. Immediately the *jinni* stood before him and Aladdin addressed him, saying: '*Jinni*, what this dome lacks is a *rukh*'s egg suspended from the middle of its dome; so I command you, in the name of the lamp I am holding, to repair this deficiency.'

No sooner had Aladdin uttered these words than the *jinni* uttered such a terrible cry that the room shook and Aladdin staggered and nearly fell down the stairs. 'What, you miserable wretch!' cried the *jinni* in a voice which would have made the most confident of men tremble. 'Isn't it enough that I and my companions have done everything for you, but you ask me, with an ingratitude that beggars belief, to bring you my master and hang him from the middle of this dome? For this outrage you, your wife and your palace, deserve to be reduced to cinders on the spot. But it's lucky you are not the author of the request and that it does not come directly from you. The man really behind it all, let me tell you, is the brother of your enemy, the African magician, whom you destroyed as he deserved. This man is in your palace, disguised in the clothes of the holy woman Fatima, whom he has killed. It's he who suggested to your wife to make the pernicious demand you have made of me. His plan is to kill you – you must be on your guard.' And with these words, he disappeared.

Aladdin did not miss a single of the *jinni*'s final words; he had heard about the holy woman Fatima and he knew all about how she supposedly cured headaches. He returned to the princess's apartments, saying nothing about what had just happened to him, and sat down, telling her that he had been seized all of a sudden with a severe headache, upon which he put his hand up to his forehead. The princess immediately gave orders for the holy woman to be summoned and, while she was being fetched, she told Aladdin how she had come to be in the palace where she had given her a room.

'Fatima' arrived, and as soon as she appeared, Aladdin said to her: 'Come in, holy lady, I am very glad to see you and very fortunate to find you here. I've got a terrible headache which has just seized me and I ask for your help, as I have faith in your prayers. I do hope you will not refuse me the favour you grant to so many who suffer from this affliction.' On saying this, he stood up and bowed his head, and 'Fatima' went up to him, but with her hand clasping the dagger she had on her belt underneath her dress. Aladdin, observing her, seized her hand before she could draw it out and, stabbing her in the heart with his own dagger, he threw her down on the floor, dead.

'My dear husband, what have you done?' shrieked the astonished princess. 'You have killed the holy woman!' 'No, my dear,' replied Aladdin calmly, 'I have not killed Fatima but a scoundrel who would have killed me if I hadn't forestalled him. This evil fellow you see,' he said as he removed his veil, 'is the one who strangled the real Fatima – this is the person whom you thought you were mourning when you accused me of killing her and who disguised himself in her clothes in order to murder me. And for your further information, he was the brother of the African magician, your kidnapper.' Aladdin went on to tell her how he had discovered all this, before having the corpse removed.

Thus was Aladdin delivered from the persecution of the two brothers who were both magicians. A few years later, the sultan died of old age. As he had left no male children, Princess Badr al-Budur, as the legitimate heir, succeeded him and transferred to Aladdin the supreme power. They reigned together for many years and were succeeded by their illustrious progeny.

'Sire,' said Shahrazad when she had finished the story of the adventures which had happened through the medium of the wonderful lamp, 'your majesty will no doubt have seen in the person of the African magician a man abandoned to an immoderate passion, desirous to possess great treasures by wicked means, a man who discovered vast quantities of them which he could not enjoy because he made himself unworthy of them. In Aladdin, by contrast, your majesty sees a man of humble birth rising to royalty itself by making use of those same treasures, which came to him without him seeking them, but who used them only in so far as he needed them for some purpose he had in mind. In the sultan he will have learned how a good, just and fair-minded monarch faces many a danger and runs the risk even of losing his throne when, by a gross injustice and against all the laws of fairness, he dares, with unreasonable haste, to condemn an innocent man without wanting to hear his pleas. And finally, your majesty will hold in horror the abominations of those two scoundrel magicians, one of whom sacrifices his life to gain treasure and the other his life and his religion in order to avenge a scoundrel like himself, both of whom receive due punishment for their wickedness.'

Conclusion

During this period Shahrazad had had three sons by the king and when she finished her last story, she got to her feet before kissing the ground in front of the king. 'King of the age and unique ruler of this time,' she said, 'I am your servant and for a thousand and one nights I have been telling you stories of past generations and moral tales of our predecessors. May I hope to ask you to grant me a request?' 'Ask and your wish will be granted,' he told her, and she then called to the nurses and the eunuchs, telling them to fetch her children, which they quickly did. Of the three boys one could walk, another was at the stage of crawling and the third was still a suckling. When they were brought in, she took them and placed them before the king. Then she kissed the ground again and said: 'King of the age, these are your children and my wish is that as an act of generosity towards them you free me from sentence of death, for if you kill me, these babies will have no mother and you will find no other woman to bring them up so well.' At that, the king shed tears and, gathering his sons to his breast, he said to her: 'Even before the arrival of these children, I had intended to pardon you, as I have seen that you are a chaste and pure woman, freeborn and God-fearing. May God bless you, your father and mother, and your whole family, root and branch. I call God to witness that I have decided that no harm is to come to you.' At this, she kissed his hands and feet in her delight, exclaiming: 'May God prolong your life and increase your dignity and the awe that you inspire!'

Joy spread through the palace and from it to the city and this was a night that stood outside the ordinary span of life, whiter than the face of day. In the morning, the happy king, overwhelmed by his good fortune, summoned his troops and when they came he presented a splendid and magnificent robe of honour to his vizier, Shahrazad's father. 'May God shelter you,' he said, 'because you gave me your noble daughter as a wife, and it is thanks to her that I have turned in repentance from killing the daughters of my subjects. I have found her noble, pure, chaste and without sin; God has provided me with three sons by her and I give thanks to Him for this great good fortune.'

He then presented robes of honour to all the viziers, emirs and ministers of state. On his instructions, the city was adorned with decorations for thirty days and he did not ask any of the citizens for contributions from their own funds, as all the costs and expenses were borne by the royal treasury. The splendour of the decorations had never been matched before; drums were beaten; pipes sounded and every entertainer displayed his skill. The king showered gifts and presents on them; he gave alms to the poor and needy and his bounty extended to all his subjects living in his realm. He and his kingdom continued to enjoy prosperity, happiness, pleasure and joy, until they were visited by the destroyer of delights and the parter of companions. Praise be to God, Whom the passage of time does not wear away. He is not subject to change; His attention cannot be distracted and He alone possesses the qualities of perfection. Blessing and peace be on the leader of His choice, the best of His creation, Muhammad, the lord of mankind. It is through him that we pray to God to bring us to a good end.

Glossary

Many of the Arabic terms used in the translation are to be found in *The Oxford English Dictionary*, including 'dinar', 'ghazi' and 'jinn'. Of these the commonest – 'emir' and 'vizier', for instance – are not entered in italics in the text and, in general, are not glossed here. Equivalents are not given for coins or units of measure as these have varied throughout the Muslim world in accordance with time and place. The prefix 'al-' (equivalent to 'the') is discounted in the alphabetical listing; hence 'al-Mansur' is entered under 'M'. Please note that only the most significant terms and figures, or ones mentioned repeatedly, are covered here.

al-'Abbas *see* 'Abbasids.

'Abbasids the dynasty of Sunni Muslim caliphs who reigned in Baghdad, and for a while in Samarra, over the heartlands of Islam, from 750 until 1258. They took their name from al-'Abbas (d. 653), uncle of the Prophet. From the late ninth century onwards, 'Abbasid rule was nominal as the caliphs were dominated by military protectors.

Abu Ja'far al-Mansur *see* al-Mansur.

Abu Nuwas Abu Nuwas al-Hasan ibn Hani (*c.*755–*c.*813), a famous, or notorious, poet of the 'Abbasid period, best known for his poems devoted to love, wine and hunting.

'Ad the race of 'Ad were a pre-Islamic tribe who rejected the prophet Hud and who consequently were punished by God for their impiety and arrogance.

alif the first letter of the Arabic alphabet. It takes the shape of a slender vertical line.

Allahu akbar! 'God is the greatest!' A frequently used exclamation of astonishment or pleasure.

aloe aloe was imported from the Orient and the juice of its leaves was used for making a bitter purgative drug.

aloes wood the heartwood of a South-east Asian tree, it is one of the most precious woods, being chiefly prized for its pleasant scent.

al-Amin Muhammad al-Amin ibn Zubaida (d. 813), the son of Harun al-Rashid, succeeding him as caliph and reigning 809–13. He had a reputation as an indolent pleasure lover.

Atiya *see* Jarir ibn 'Atiya.

Avicenna the Western version of the Arab name Ibn Sina (980–1037), a Persian physician and philosopher, the most eminent of his time, whose most famous works include *The Book of Healing* and *The Canon of Medicine.*

***ban* tree** Oriental willow.

banj frequently used as a generic term referring to a narcotic or knock-out drug, but sometimes the word specifically refers to henbane.

banu literally, 'sons of', a term used to identify tribes or clans, e.g. the Banu Quraish.

Barmecides *see* Harun al-Rashid, Ja'far.

bulbul Eastern song thrush.

Chosroe in Persian 'Khusraw', in Arabic 'Kisra' – the name of several pre-Islamic Sasanian kings of Persia, including Chosroe Anurshirwan – 'the blessed' (r. 531–79).

dhikr a religious recitation, particularly a Sufi practice.

dinar a gold coin. It can also be a measure of weight.

dirham a silver coin, approximately a twentieth of a dinar.

faqih a jurisprudent, an expert in Islamic law.

faqir literally, 'a poor man', the term also is used to refer to a Sufi or Muslim ascetic.

ghul a cannibalistic monster. A *ghula* is a female *ghul.*

hadith a saying concerning the words or deeds of the Prophet or his companions.

Harun al-Rashid (766–809) the fifth of the 'Abbasid caliphs, reigning from 786. In Baghdad, he presided over an efflorescence of literature and science and his court became a magnet for poets, musicians and scholars. Until 803, the administration was largely in the hands of a Persian clan, the Barmecides, but in that year, for reasons that are mysterious, he had them purged. After his death, civil war broke out between his two sons, al-Amin and al-Ma'mun. In retrospect, Harun's caliphate came to be looked upon as a golden age and in the centuries that followed numerous stories were attached to his name.

houri a nymph of the Muslim Paradise. Also a great beauty.

Iblis the devil.

'Id al-Fitr the Feast of Fast Breaking, marking the end of Ramadan.

'ifrit a kind of *jinni*, usually evil; an *'ifrita* is a female *jinni.*

imam the person who leads the prayers in a mosque.

Ja'far the Barmecide a member of a great Iranian clan which served the 'Abbasid caliphs as viziers and other functionaries. In the stories, he features as Harun's vizier, though in reality it was his father, Yahya, who held this post. For reasons that are mysterious, Ja'far and other members of his clan were executed in 803.

Jarir ibn 'Atiya (d. 729) a leading poet of the Umaiyad period, famous for his panegyric and invective verse.

jinni a (male) spirit in Muslim folklore and theology; *jinniya* is a female spirit. *Jinn* (the collective term) assumed various forms: some were servants of Satan, while others were good Muslims and therefore benign.

Joseph features in the Quran as well as the Bible. In the Quran, he is celebrated for his beauty.

kaffiyeh a headdress of cloth folded and held by a cord around the head.

khan an inn, caravanserai or market.

Magian a Zoroastrian, a fire worshipper. In the *Nights*, the Magians invariably feature as sinister figures.

al-Mahdi (b. *c.*743) the 'Abbasid caliph who reigned from 775 to 785.

maidan an exercise yard or parade ground; an open space near or in a town.

Malik the angel who is the guardian of hell.

mamluk slave soldier. Most mamluks were of Turkish origin.

al-Ma'mun (786–833) son of Harun al-Rashid and the 'Abbasid caliph from 813 until his death. He was famous for his patronage of learning and his sponsorship of the translation of Greek and Syriac texts into Arabic.

al-Mansur (r. 754–75) 'Abbasid caliph.

marid a type of *jinni.*

Masrur the eunuch who was sword-bearer and executioner to Harun al-Rashid.

mithqal a measure of weight.

months of the Muslim year from the first to the twelfth month, these are: (1) al-Muharram, (2) Safar, (3) Rabi' al-awwal, (4) Rabi' al-akhir, (5) Jumada al-ula, (6) Jumada al-akhira, (7) Rajab, (8) Sha'ban, (9) Ramadan, (10) Shawwal, (11) Dhu'l-Qa'da, (12) Dhu'l-Hijja.

muezzin the man who gives the call to prayer, usually from the minaret or roof of the mosque.

parasang an old Persian measure of length, somewhere between three and four miles.

qadi a Muslim judge.

Qaf Mount Qaf was a legendary mountain located at the end of the world, or in some versions one that encircles the earth.

Quraish the dominant Arab clan in Mecca at the time of the Prophet.

rak'a in the Muslim prayer ritual, a bowing of the body followed by two prostrations.

Ramadan the ninth month of the Muslim year, in which fasting is observed from sunrise to sunset. *See also* months of the Muslim year.

ratl a measure of weight, varying from region to region.

Ridwan the angel who is the guardian of the gates of Paradise.

rukh a legendary bird of enormous size, strong enough to carry an elephant (in English 'roc').

Rum/Ruman theoretically designates Constantinople and the Byzantine lands more generally, but in some stories the name is merely intended to designate a strange and usually Christian foreign land.

Rumi of Byzantine Greek origin.

Sakhr an evil *jinni* whose story is related by commentators on the Quran.

Sasanian the Sasanians were the Persian dynasty who ruled in Persia and Iraq from 224 until 637, when Muslim armies overran their empire.

Sha'ban *see* months of the Muslim year.

shaikh a tribal leader, the term also commonly used to refer to an old man or a master of one of the traditional religious sciences or a leader of a dervish order. Similarly, a *shaikha* is an old woman or a woman in authority.

sharif meaning 'noble', often used with specific reference to a descendant of the Prophet.

Sufi a Muslim mystic or ascetic.

sura a chapter of the Quran.

wali a local governor.

Yahya ibn Khalid the Barmecide a Persian who was a senior government official under the 'Abbasid caliphs al-Mansur and Harun. He was disgraced and executed in 805 for reasons that remain mysterious.

Zubaida (762–831) the granddaughter of the 'Abbasid caliph al-Mansur and famous for her wealth. She became chief wife of the caliph Harun al-Rashid and was mother to al-Amin and al-Ma'mun, both later caliphs.

Further Reading

Ballaster, Ros, *Fabulous Orients: Fictions of the East in England 1622–1785* (Oxford University Press, Oxford, 2005). Ballaster's book explores the impact of *The Arabian Nights* and other Oriental fictions on British and, to a lesser extent, French literature.

Burton, Richard F. (tr.), *A Plain and Literal Translation of the Arabian Nights' Entertainments*, 10 vols. (Karma Shastra Society, London, 1885). A full translation of the Calcutta II Arabic text of *The Arabian Nights*, this work was impressive for its time, but there are many errors in it and Burton's contorted literary style makes it heavy going for the modern reader.

Byatt, A. S., *The Djinn in the Nightingale's Eye: Five Fairy Stories* (Chatto, London, 1994). Despite its fictional status, Byatt's title story in this collection contains some serious and penetrating observations about the characteristics of storytelling in the *Nights*.

Caracciolo, Peter L. (ed.), *The Arabian Nights in English Literature: Studies in the Reception of* The Thousand and One Nights *into British Culture* (Macmillan, London, 1988). A collection of essays by various hands. Caracciolo's lengthy introductory survey is a masterpiece of intelligently directed erudition.

Clute, John, and Grant, John (eds.), *The Encyclopedia of Fantasy* (Orbit, London, 1997). This mighty work of reference is 1,049 double-columned pages long. Apart from the article 'Arabian Fantasy', it contains many entries on authors and works influenced by the *Nights*. It also has serious analytical articles about the literary tropes and devices of fantastic and magical fiction.

El-Shamy, Hasan M., *A Motif Index of* The Thousand and One Nights (Indiana University Press, Bloomington, Indiana, 2006). Weighing in at 680 pages, this classification of thousands of motifs in the *Nights* serves as an index to themes, people, animals, objects and social practices in the stories. The motifs are cross-referenced to the Burton translation and to Victor Chauvin's *Bibliographie des ouvrages arabes ou relatifs aux arabes; publiés dans l'Europe chrétienne de 1810 à 1885*, 12 vols. (Bibliothèque de la Faculté de Philosophie et Lettres de l'Université de Liège, Liège, 1892–1922). They include such topics as 'series of living corpses to serve as phantom guards', 'compulsion to steal', 'severed head speaks', 'taste of food eaten in a dream still in the mouth next day', 'fool recognized by his long beard', 'wish for exalted husband realized' and 'woman thinking lover dead erects cenotaph and mourns before it'.

Haddawy, Husain (tr.), *The Arabian Nights* (Everyman's Library Classics, London, 1992). This is a (good) translation of Muhsin Mahdi's scrupulously edited text of a Syrian manuscript dating from the fourteenth or fifteenth century. The manuscript in question was used by Antoine Galland for his eighteenth-century French translation. However, it contains only thirty-five stories.

Irwin, Robert, *The Arabian Nights: A Companion*, 2nd edition (I. B. Tauris, London and New York, 2004). A survey of the composition, collection and translation of the stories, the leading themes of the tales (including sex and magic), structuralist classifications of the tales, medieval storytelling techniques, the influence of the *Nights* on European and American literature, and much else besides.

—, *The Penguin Anthology of Classical Arabic Literature* (Penguin, London, 2006). The *Nights* are placed in the broader context of medieval Arabic prose and poetry.

Marzolph, Ulrich (ed.), *The Arabian Nights Reader* (Wayne State University Press, Detroit, Michigan, 2006). A collection of key twentieth-century essays by various academic hands, on such matters as the dating, structure and contents of the *Nights*.

—, and van Leeuwen, Richard (eds.), *The Arabian Nights Encyclopedia*, 2 vols. (ABC Clio, Santa Barbara, California, 2004). The essential reference work for *Nights* scholars and fanatics. Volume 1 contains fourteen essays by experts on such matters as literary style, oral features, illustrations, manuscripts and cinema. It also has individual articles on every story found in the Calcutta II text, Galland and other versions of the *Nights*. Volume 2 has articles on a wide range of *Nights*-related topics, such as George Eliot, Richard Burton, Harun al-Rashid, Shahrazad, camels, slaves and music. It also has tables of concordances, international tale types and narrative motifs.

Yamanaka, Yuriko, and Nishio, Tetsuo (eds.), *The Arabian Nights and Orientalism: Perspectives from East and West* (I. B. Tauris, London and New York, 2006). Essays by various scholars, the majority of them Japanese, on such subjects as the reception and translation of *The Arabian Nights* in Japan, Alexander the Great in the *Nights*, and the *Nights* in folklore research and in illustration.

Zipes, Jack (ed.), *The Oxford Companion to the Fairy Tale* (Oxford University Press, Oxford, 2000). Apart from an article on *The Arabian Nights*, there are also entries on 'Aladdin', 'Ali Baba', 'The Thief of Baghdad', Shahrazad, Galland, Edmund Dulac and Salman Rushdie.

Maps

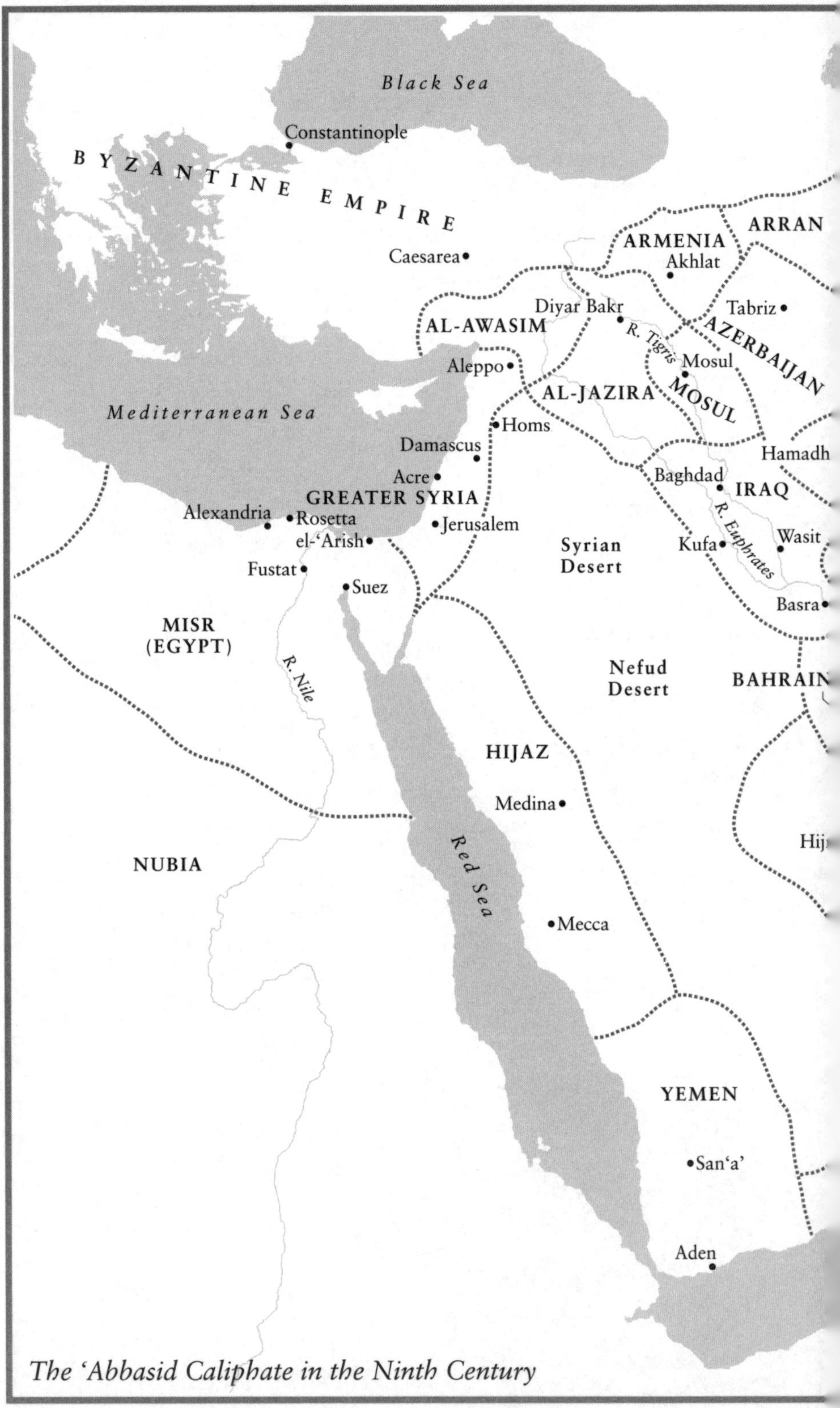

The 'Abbasid Caliphate in the Ninth Century

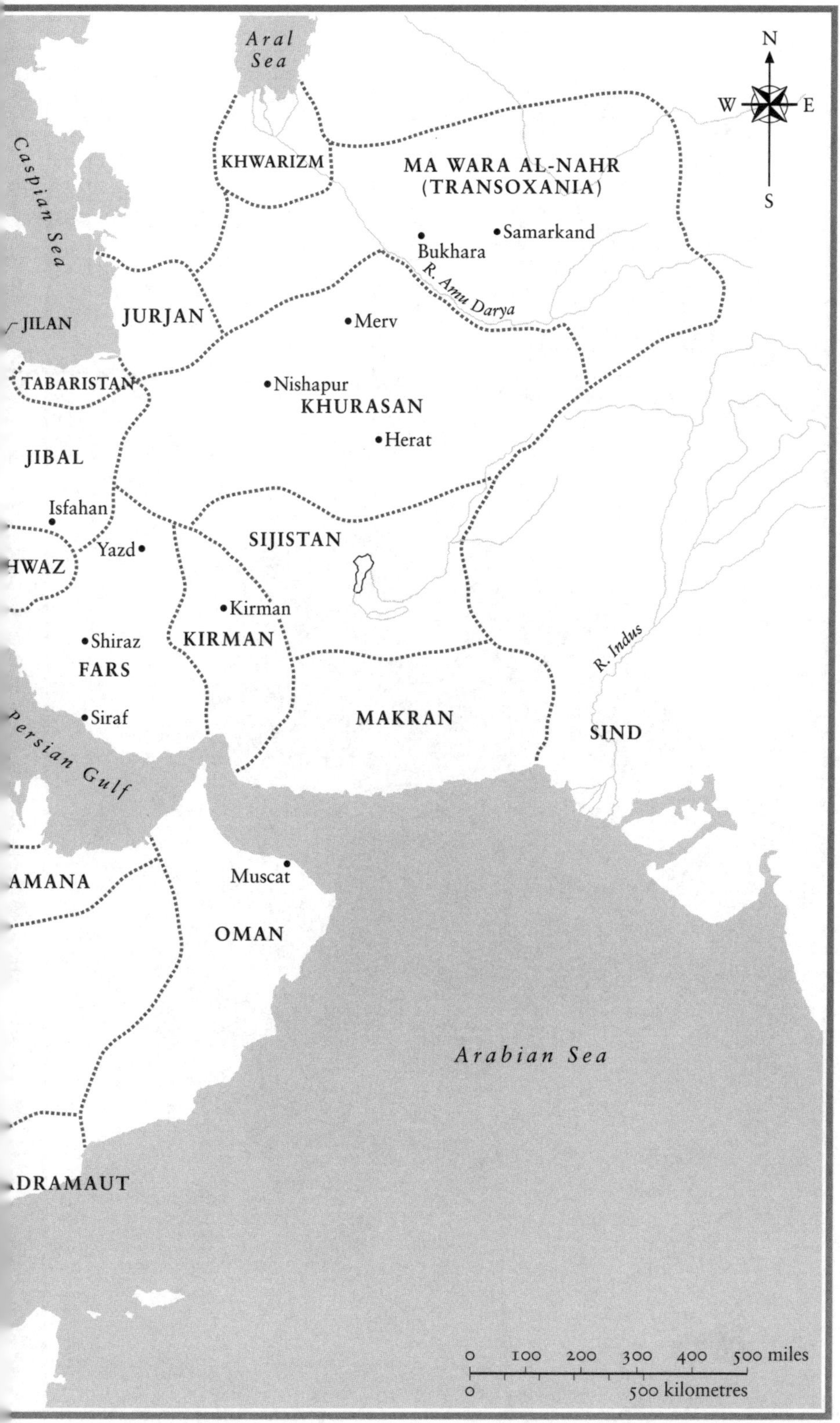

Aral Sea
Caspian Sea
KHWARIZM
MA WARA AL-NAHR (TRANSOXANIA)
Samarkand
Bukhara
R. Amu Darya
JURJAN
JILAN
Merv
TABARISTAN
Nishapur
KHURASAN
Herat
JIBAL
Isfahan
SIJISTAN
Yazd
HWAZ
Kirman
Shiraz
KIRMAN
FARS
R. Indus
Siraf
MAKRAN
SIND
Persian Gulf
Muscat
AMANA
OMAN
Arabian Sea
DRAMAUT
N
W
E
S
0 100 200 300 400 500 miles
0 500 kilometres

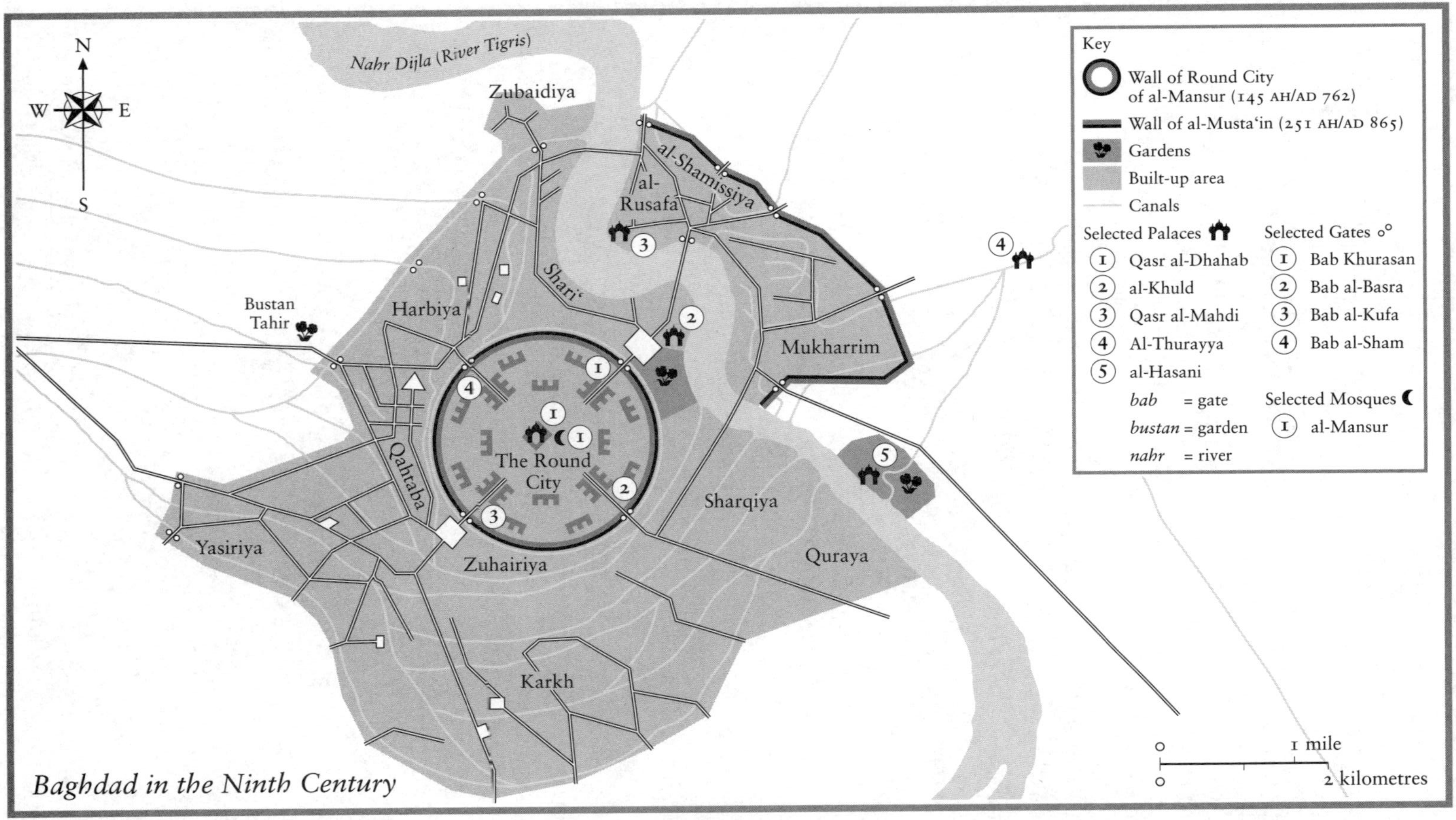

Baghdad in the Ninth Century

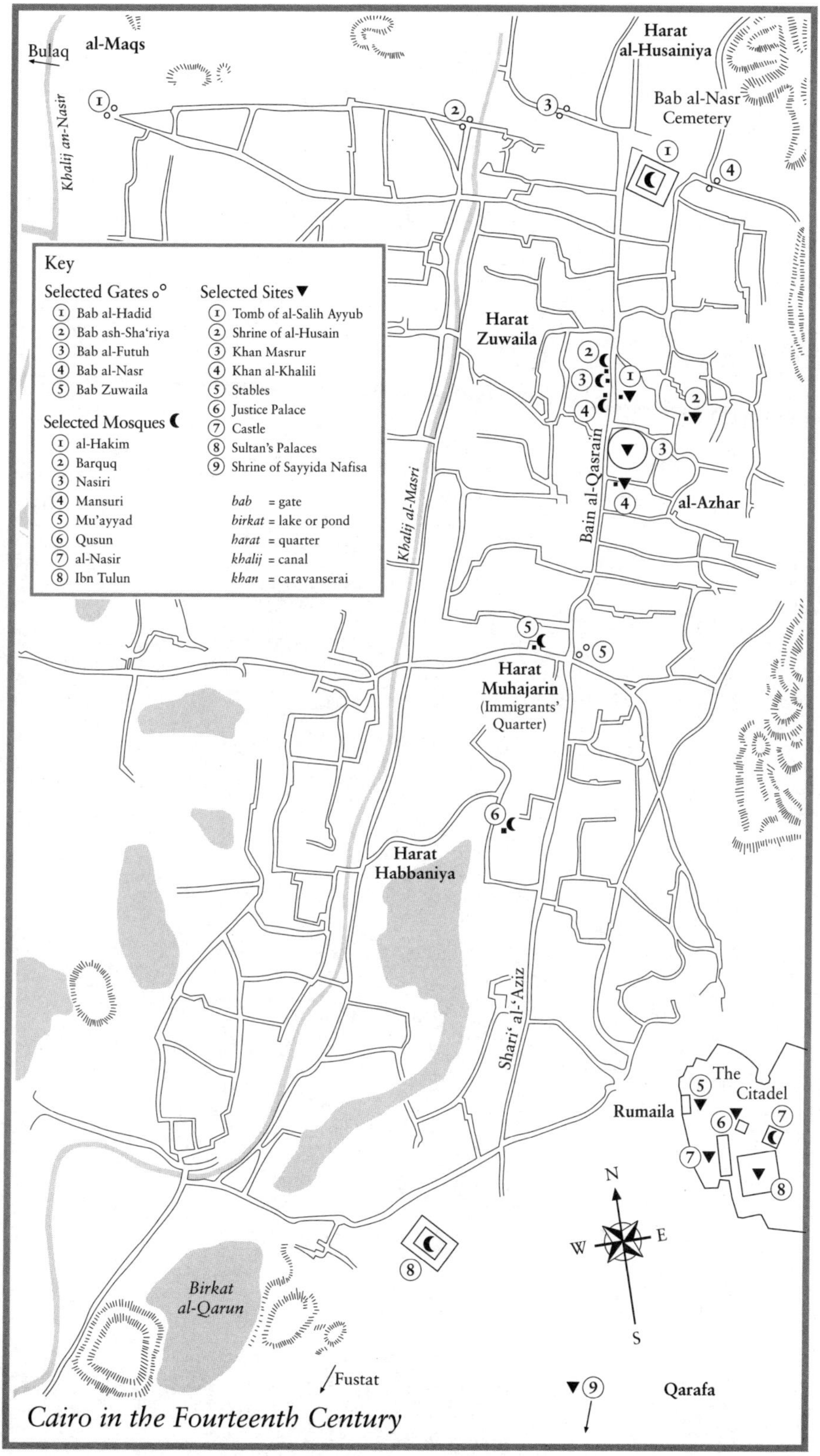

Key
Selected Gates
1 Bab al-Hadid
2 Bab ash-Sha'riya
3 Bab al-Futuh
4 Bab al-Nasr
5 Bab Zuwaila
Selected Mosques
1 al-Hakim
2 Barquq
3 Nasiri
4 Mansuri
5 Mu'ayyad
6 Qusun
7 al-Nasir
8 Ibn Tulun
Selected Sites
1 Tomb of al-Salih Ayyub
2 Shrine of al-Husain
3 Khan Masrur
4 Khan al-Khalili
5 Stables
6 Justice Palace
7 Castle
8 Sultan's Palaces
9 Shrine of Sayyida Nafisa
bab = gate
birkat = lake or pond
harat = quarter
khalij = canal
khan = caravanserai
Bulaq
al-Maqs
Khalij an-Nasir
Harat al-Husainiya
Bab al-Nasr Cemetery
Harat Zuwaila
Bain al-Qasrain
al-Azhar
Khalij al-Masri
Harat Muhajarin (Immigrants' Quarter)
Harat Habbaniya
Shari' al-'Aziz
The Citadel
Rumaila
N
E
W
S
Birkat al-Qarun
Fustat
Qarafa

Cairo in the Fourteenth Century